Cry of the Newborn

THE ASCENDANTS OF ESTOREA
BOOK 1

Cry of the Newborn

THE ASCENDANTS OF ESTOREA
BOOK 1

James Barclay

Copyright © James Barclay 2005
All rights reserved

The right of James Barclay to be identified as the author
of this work has been asserted by him in accordance with
the Copyright, Designs and Patents Act of 1988.

First published in Great Britain in 2005
by Gollancz
An imprint of the Orion Publishing Group
Orion House, 5 Upper St Martin's Lane
London WC2H 9EA

This edition published in Great Britain in 2006
by Gollancz

3 5 7 9 10 8 6 4

A CIP catalogue record for this book
is available from the British Library

ISBN-13: 9 780 57507 812 3

Printed in Great Britain by
Clays Ltd, St Ives plc

The Orion Publishing Group's policy is to use papers that
are natural, renewable and recyclable products and made
from wood grown in sustainable forests. The logging and
manufacturing processes are expected to conform to the
environmental regulations of the country of origin.

www.orionbooks.co.uk

For Clare, who is the centre of my life

This book is the result of a huge effort by many. From art-worker to copy editor, I have a lot of people to thank. Particularly though, Simon Spanton who gave me such unstinting support and advice during the whole of the writing process; Gillian Redfearn, a blessing in the guise of an editorial assistant; and to Graham Diss who came and saw me every month and who doesn't get the credit he deserves.

I also want to thank David Gemmell who is a constant source of inspiration; Howard Morhaim who brought me lasting confidence in the future; to Robert Kirby for always being there; to Ariel, ace webmaster; and to Pete, George, Dave and Dick . . . same old, same old but I couldn't do it without you.

And finally, to Dan Westfallen, who has lent his name to the heart of the book; to William Montanero who has worked so hard to help my website forum be a success; and to all the forumites – you've brought a smile to my face on the worst of days. Thank you.

www.jamesbarclay.com

Cast List

THE CITIZENS OF WESTFALLEN	*Ardol Kessian* FATHER OF THE ASCENDANCY, WIND HARKER
	Willem Geste ASCENDANCY ECHELON, FIREWALKER
	Genna Kessian ASCENDANCY ECHELON, PAIN TELLER
	Andreas Koll ASCENDANCY ECHELON, LAND WARDEN
	Hesther Naravny ASCENDANCY ECHELON, LAND WARDEN
	Gwythen Terol ASCENDANCY ECHELON, HERD MASTER
	Meera Naravny ASCENDANCY ECHELON, FIREWALKER
	Jen Shalke ASCENDANCY ECHELON, WATERBORN
	Arducius ASCENDANT
	Gorian ASCENDANT
	Mirron ASCENDANT
	Ossacer ASCENDANT
	Elsa Gueran READER OF WESTFALLEN
	Bryn Marr A BLACKSMITH
OFFICERS OF THE ESTOREAN CONQUORD	*Herine Del Aglios* ADVOCATE OF THE ESTOREAN CONQUORD
	Paul Jhered EXCHEQUER OF THE GATHERERS
	Felice Koroyan CHANCELLOR, ORDER OF THE OMNISCIENT
	Arvan Vasselis MARSHAL DEFENDER OF CARADUK
	Thomal Yuran MARSHAL DEFENDER OF ATRESKA
	Katrin Mardov MARSHAL DEFENDER OF GESTERN
	Orin D'Allinnius CHIEF SCIENTIST TO THE ADVOCATE

Harkov CAPTAIN OF THE PALACE GUARD
Erith Menas A GATHERER
Harin A GATHERER

NORTHERN FRONT LEGIONS

Roberto Del Aglios GENERAL OF THE ARMY
Davarov MASTER OF SWORD, 21ST ALA
Elise Kastenas MASTER OF HORSE, 8TH LEGION
Goran Shakarov MASTER OF SWORD, 15TH ALA
Dahnishev MASTER SURGEON
Rovan Neristus MASTER ENGINEER
Ellas Lennart ORDER SPEAKER

EASTERN FRONT LEGIONS

Gesteris GENERAL OF THE ARMY
Pavel Nunan MASTER OF SWORD, 2ND LEGION
Dina Kell MASTER OF HORSE, 2ND LEGION

SOUTHERN FRONT LEGIONS

Jorganesh GENERAL OF THE ARMY
Parnforst MASTER OF SWORD, 34TH ALA

SAILORS OF THE CONQUORD

Gaius Kortonius PRIME SEA LORD OF THE OCETANAS
Karl Iliev SQUADRON LEADER, OCENII SQUADRON
Patonius CAPTAIN OF *CIRANDON'S PRIDE*
Anthus RIGGER, *CIRANDON'S PRIDE*
Gorres SURGEON, *CIRANDON'S PRIDE*

CITIZENS AND OTHERS

Lena Pretal PRAETOR OF GULL'S FORD, ATRESKA
Han Jesson A POTTER FROM GULL'S FORD
Harban Qvist KARKU GUIDE
Icenga Qvist GOR-CAMAS OF THE KARKU
Rensaark SENTOR, TSARDON FORCES
Kreysun PROSENTOR, TSARDON FORCES

Chapter 1

834th cycle of God, 1st day of Genasrise
1st year of the true Ascendancy

And there they were, lying asleep and at peace. Newborn and helpless. Beautiful and fragile. And in that, no different from any other infants born to this world blessed by God.

Never though, had a quartet of newborns undergone such lengthy and mute observation; been examined with such anxiety, hope and wonder. The atmosphere was so deeply charged it should have made them fretful enough to wake and cry. They did not.

Crowded around the line of cribs and looking down on the tiny faces were those for whom these three boys and one girl, scant hours into life, represented the culmination of generations of dedication. Yet for all the accumulated wisdom brought to bear and the endless paper records of all that had gone before, they still did not know if these four would achieve their birthrights.

However long they stared there would be no sign. The infants would give no hint if they possessed everything, or anything, that the exhaustive calculations suggested they would. But still they stared, reverent. The Ascendancy's Echelon had gathered around the cribs in complete accord. They could all sense something. After countless disappointments and false dawns, this time it was different. It had to be.

Shela Hasi stood behind the cribs with seven of the Echelon's nine members in front of her. There would be the inevitable, interminable wait for signs of true talent. But until the frustration of those years set in, they would hope and dream for the realisation of a destiny whose genesis was lost in the mists of ancient religion and belief. She felt awed by their presence. The entire community of Westfallen was close for many good reasons, of centuries longstanding, yet the Echelon had an aura that set them apart. In them rested lingering ability, extraordinary dedication and an all-consuming determination.

Shela couldn't deny the occasional spark of envy. She'd been a Waterborn herself until she was ten. Wonderful times that would live with her forever. The day the talent had deserted her she'd nearly drowned.

That had been almost forty years ago now and there were still times she felt the loss as she had at that first moment. A violation of her body. The robbery of something she had come to assume was hers by right. So she envied the Echelon their continued link with the Ascendancy, their taste of the potential that they all prayed these infants possessed.

Yet she also pitied them the daily anxiety. While those whose talents faded usually suffered their loss early in life, it was not unknown for one in more advanced years to be shorn of their link. That pain would be terribly hard to bear. Every night she, like every strand member, prayed that the Echelon remained undamaged. So far, God had answered their prayers.

She smiled at them. These most revered of Westfallen's people were held rapt by the new arrivals. From Ardol Kessian, one of only three survivors of the first strand, to Jen Shalke, barely into her teens and only just coming to terms with her destiny. Such a sweet man, Ardol Kessian. One hundred and thirty-two years old now, completely hairless and stooped but still robust. His smile took the chill from a cold day and his voice, deep and sonorous, had been a comfort to the Echelon across the generations. He was a peerless Wind Harker and indeed had told them all how warm it would be during the births and in the days after. His was a keen talent and one they would inevitably miss when he returned to the earth and God's embrace.

'They are beautiful, aren't they?' said Shela, her whisper carrying loud across the silence of the cosy, sun-bathed nursery. A light breeze blew fresh sea air through the open windows. Shela could hear the hot air channelling through the hypocaust beneath the flagstones under their feet, adding further gentle warmth for the delicate newborns.

Kessian's deep green eyes twinkled beneath his bald brows. 'Glorious. Treasured. Carrying all our hopes and desires, though they cannot know it.' He nodded. 'And I approve of the names, too. Fine choices all.'

He reached out a minutely trembling hand to smooth the brow of each child in turn, speaking quietly as he did so.

'Mirron, much will rest on your shoulders. You will bear the pressure of motherhood in addition to all else that will fall on you. Your strand-brothers lying beside you this day will support you always as you will them. Ossacer and Arducius, you carry the names of great warrior heroes but never should you be moved to strike another down. Your destiny is in peace. And Gorian. Blessed indeed by the name of our father. Keep it well. Be true to his memory. Fulfil your destiny and, with your brothers and sister, achieve that which we cannot. Use it for the benefit of us all under God the Omniscient.'

He turned to his friend of a hundred years, Willem Geste of the second strand. 'Willem, a prayer.'

The Echelon came together and each knelt on one knee. One hand touched the ground, the other held palm up and open to the sky. Shela rested her hands on the outer cribs, embracing them all.

'The Ascendancy stands before you, our God, to commend these newborn children to your care. Newborn who we pray will become your most powerful servants on this earth. We promise to nurture and train them, that they in turn will do your work while they are blessed by you with life; preserving the land and the sea and all those who depend upon them. We ask that you protect them, watch over them and love them as you do all your children. We ask this in the name of the true faith of the Omniscient. We of the pure strands of the Ascendancy beseech you, our God. So it will be.'

'As it always was,' they intoned as one.

'Thank you, Willem,' said Kessian, standing. 'Now, before Shela throws us all out of here, I think we should take our leave and let these little ones rest.'

'Can't I stay longer with them?' Jen Shalke's voice carried a whine. Kessian put a finger to his lips. Shela smiled to herself.

'In a moment, young Jen,' he said. 'First of all, Gwythen, Meera, back to bed. I have no idea what possessed you to stand with us so soon after giving birth. You must be exhausted.'

'We are of the Ascendancy Echelon,' said Gwythen Terol, mother of Ossacer. 'It is our duty.' Her voice was proud but her face was drawn.

'Nevertheless, please rest now,' he said gently, the warmth never leaving his voice despite his chiding words. 'Willem, Genna, we have work to do and texts to study. There are answers we still need though I suspect much of our evidence lies sleeping in these cribs. Everything else will have to wait until we see what they become.

'And as for you, young Jen, I'm sure Shela will be happy to have your company in the days and seasons to come. However, today our nursemaid must introduce and accustom herself to her charges alone. Meanwhile, there are fish to be caught and fishers wanting to know where to cast their nets. It's a beautiful day and the sea is warm. Perhaps you could find us a shoal, eh? Or the feast tonight will be lessened, will it not?'

Jen's smile was adoring and Shela felt again that familiar moment of envy at the young Waterborn's ability. She had known the free-dom of the world beneath the waves until it had been wrenched from her. She dreamed often of what she had seen and the places she had gone. She relived her past through Jen's tales and, for her part, was the only one who really understood the young woman. It had brought them very close. Shela dropped her gaze. For all that they respected her as a strand member and for her skills as nursemaid, she could never be one of them and feel that bond the Ascendancy shared so effortlessly.

The door to the nursery opened. Hesther Naravny entered, closing it behind her. A Land Warden of the fifth strand, she was a passionate, fiery woman in her mid-sixties. Hesther looked around the Ascend-ancy, her expression darkening as her eyes travelled over them.

'Meera, what do you think you're doing here? You too, Gwythen, for that matter. You should not be out of bed.'

'The Echelon gathered to bless the newborns,' said Meera. 'So perhaps I should be asking you why you *weren't* here?'

'Always the petulant child,' muttered Hesther. 'Will I have to look out for you into your dotage, Meera?'

'If I've told you once, I've told you a thousand times. You are not my mother.'

Hesther's face softened and she stepped close to Meera, cupping the woman's cheeks in her hands. 'No, but I am your sister and I love you more than any living thing under God's sky. You are a mother of the ninth strand, the strand we all pray is the one to take us to ascendancy, and I would not see you risk yourself. Please Meera, the labour was difficult. You must rest.'

Meera sagged and nodded. 'I know. But this is just so . . . and look at my beautiful child.'

Hesther's face lit up. 'I am a proud aunt and a proud sister before I am part of the Echelon. You have a beautiful son, an important son. But come now. Gwythen, you as well. Help each other back to bed.'

The Echelon gave them room, Willem opening the door.

'Bless you both,' he said. 'Sleep well.'

'Right,' said Hesther when the door had closed once again. 'Ardol, the forum has been packed since first light. They are patient but surely it's time to give them some news.'

Kessian inclined his head. 'No sense in keeping them in suspense any longer. There is plenty to prepare.'

'So there is,' said Hesther. 'Shela, how are they?'

'Peaceful. But they can always have more peace.'

Hesther winked at her and walked to the door. 'I'll address the town. The rest of you, out.'

The nursery opened directly on to the marble-floored colonnade that enclosed the central courtyard gardens of the Ascendancy villa. Hesther walked quickly between two columns and out into the sun which warmed the flagstones under her sandaled feet and sparkled on the water trickling from the four fountains, each set in the centre of a quadrant of the courtyard. All around her, the scents and colours of flowers, grasses and small trees created a powerful sense of burgeoning life. Hesther breathed it in, feeling energised.

Behind her, she had left the best and brightest hopes of the Ascendancy. It filled her with a childlike excitement that hurried her to a trot across the beautiful gardens, down the long entrance vestibule, through the cool reception hall and out into the streets of Westfallen.

Westfallen nestled at the head of a steep-sided inlet which opened out, a hundred miles south, into the vastness of the ocean. Half a mile beyond the harbour walls the spectacular Genastro Falls cascaded over a thousand feet into the inlet, taking with them the run-off from Willows Lake, away to the east, two miles from the town.

The villa sat on a rise above the bulk of the town, overlooking the glorious golden bay with its stone- and concrete-built harbour. Scattered about the gentle slopes of the town sat larger villas surrounded by their farmland. Crops were ripening in the fields and animals grazed or basked in the tranquillity of the day. Down towards the forum, the narrower, tightly packed, streets were lined with low houses and a few tenements under which shops opened onto pavement or square.

The town was deserted. The fleet of thirty fishing boats was dragged up onto the beach. No one stirred beneath the lazily flapping shop awnings. Everyone was at the forum. Hesther could hear the hubbub of voices and see the crowd gathered in front of the oratory. Hundreds of people waiting for news. Approaching as quickly as she dared without getting out of breath, Hesther heard a ripple of laughter through the crowd. Someone was entertaining them at least.

She entered the forum at the rear of the oratory and climbed the few steps onto the stage. Surrounding the paved space, shops and stalls were empty. The sun reflected from polished columns, white painted walls and warm red-tiled roofs. Every voice quietened the moment Hesther was seen. The young tumblers and jugglers scattered away from her and back into the crowd.

She breathed deep to calm herself, smoothing the front of her simple sleeveless blue dress and adjusting the cinch at her waist. She arranged the long auburn curls on her head and surveyed the townsfolk, all of whom had waited all day just to hear her words. She felt the weight of her sixty-five years then, the expectations that she carried on everyone's behalf and what success would bring.

All anyone here wanted was a life free of change and the pressure for change. Yet what she was about to announce would signal change of a most fundamental nature. In all their faces she saw expectation. In those not touched by the strands, she saw excitement and naivety too. A craving for the news she brought and no notion that it would affect their lives so deeply should the newborn grow into their potential.

She felt no guilt, only exhilaration. Because every face told of a spirit that would stand with them forever. The hush was unbearable. She was compelled to speak.

'My friends. They are born and they are well.'

The roar all but knocked her from her feet.

Ardol Kessian rested his elbows on the table and his chin in his hands. He shifted his backside against the hard bench, grunting at the discomfort. Someone really should have fetched him a cushion by now. Night was full. The stars spread to the horizon in every direction. The air was clear and still warm. There would be no rain for seven days though the scattered cloud in a couple of days would keep them a little cooler.

In front of him, the floor of the forum was awash with people, faces bright in the fire and lantern light. On the oratory, the band roused weary dancers again with another old favourite. Hand drum and tympani beat the rhythm, kithara and pipes provided the melody and a strong voice guided the moves.

It was a long time since he had dared take to the centre of the forum to dance. He missed it. The energy and the joy, the close touch of a woman, and the scent of her in the spin. Her eyes on him as they stepped and turned. Now he contented himself with watching the younger generations make all the same mistakes he had made in his youth. A long time ago now. He glanced to his right and laid his hand on Genna's.

'Remember how we met on the floor?'

'Yes, Ardol,' said Genna, resignation in her tone. 'You ask me every time we watch a dance.'

'Do I?' Kessian's mouth turned up at the corners. 'I forget.'

'When it suits you.'

He squeezed Genna's hand. He would go first. Genna was thirty years his junior. They'd been tilling the earth together this last eighty years. He wondered how she would bear up without him. She'd probably be glad of the peace and quiet.

'Jen did well today,' he said, refusing to slip into melancholy on a night of celebration like this.

'That she did,' agreed Genna.

The fresh smells of grilling fish mixed with woodsmoke, roasting meats and the yeasty odour of spilt ale. Jen had found seabass and sardines. The nets had bulged and there would be plenty on the market when the hangovers had cleared the next morning.

'Do you mind if I interrupt you?'

Kessian looked up and across the table. There stood Arvan Vasselis, Marshal Defender of Caraduk. He had ridden in with his wife and young son late in the afternoon, having received the message five days previously that the births were imminent. His flag, deep blue, trimmed with gold and displaying rearing twin bears, flew above his residence which commanded peerless views of bay and harbour.

'Impeccable timing as always,' said Kessian, making to rise. Vasselis gestured him not to.

'Never known to miss a Westfallen party. I even brought some wine with me.' Vasselis placed two ornately carved ceramic jugs of something no doubt old and expensive on the table. 'Mind if I sit down?'

'You hardly have to ask,' said Kessian.

'Rank is no excuse for rudeness,' Vasselis said, dragging the opposite bench back a little. He leaned over and kissed Genna's cheeks before he sat. 'Pour away.'

Genna poured the dregs out of their two goblets and snared another that someone had abandoned on their table. She wiped them all out with a cloth from her waist before filling them with Vasselis's wine.

'And where is our country's first lady?' she asked.

'Netta? Oh, settling Kovan, I expect. This would all be a little much for him. Best he sleeps through it.'

'Don't you have a retinue for that sort of thing?'

'I think you'll find we can cope as parents,' said Vasselis. 'Besides, we hardly need to worry, do we? Not here.'

'You're never quite going to get used to the trappings of your position, are you?'

Vasselis chuckled. 'Step out of line, Kessian and you'll find I understand certain of my trappings very well indeed.'

He raised his goblet and the three of them chinked and drank.

'Very good,' said Kessian, feeling the full red wine soothe its way down his throat, leaving the aftertaste of rich, ripe plums.

'You doubted it?' asked Vasselis.

The friends fell silent. Kessian studied Vasselis as he watched the dancing and celebration all around him. He felt proud, observing this man sitting among his citizens. So much at ease, feeling neither superior nor under any threat to his authority.

Kessian had seen him grow from a young lad fascinated with the sea to become the ruler of Caraduk. He was the Ascendancy's most powerful ally and fiercest protector of its secrets. Even with him on their side, maintaining the secrecy beyond Westfallen's borders was a constant battle and a dreadful anxiety. If what they hoped turned out to be true, they would need him more than ever in the years to come.

Abruptly, Vasselis stopped tapping his fingers on the table in time to the drums and turned his large brown eyes on Kessian. Vasselis had short dark hair and a soft, friendly face which an unfortunate few would always mistake for a sign of weakness.

'So,' he said. 'Is it them?'

Kessian shrugged. 'It depends how much you believe in omen and how much in science. Even for me, the coincidence is exciting. Mathematically though, we set no store by it.' His face cracked into a smile and he shook his head, trying in vain to dislodge the thrill that strained at every nerve the moment he thought about them. 'They were all born in the same hour to mothers from within and without the Echelon and after almost identical difficult labours. An hour where the rain passed, the clouds broke and the sun burst through. And if you believe people like Andreas Koll and Hesther Naravny, an hour where the birds fell silent and every cow, sheep and pig, every dog and cat, turned its head to the villa.'

'And do you believe it?' asked Vasselis.

Kessian's smile broadened and he drained his goblet. 'I believe there is something in the atmosphere that affected this whole community around the time of the births. I also believe in the theory of mass empathetic outpouring of an emotion like hope or love. I don't believe in omens and portents. At least, I try not to.'

'Ardol, my old friend, you are avoiding my question. Is it them?'

Kessian chewed his lip. He looked out across the forum and the dancing, the crowds of animated talkers and drinkers. The noise of the music and laughter, the strong cooking smells and the harsh light of flame and lantern clamoured around his head. It was a clamour the wine amplified uncomfortably. He wondered when he had started feeling like this.

'I'm old, Marshal Vasselis. I cannot afford for it not to be them.'

Chapter 2

'Advance in line.'

Captain Elise Kastenas, 2nd legion cavalry, the Bear Claws of Estorr, urged her company to the walk. On the opposite side of the forum, Captain Dina Kell mirrored her and between them, the hastati legionaries marched with shields up in well-spaced ranks, five deep. Rioters fell back ahead of them, all the way across the rubble-strewn space.

Hoofbeats rang out on stone cobbles. Elise looked over her small round shield. Beneath her, her horse was steady. Its armour blinkered it, keeping its focus ahead. The mob was densely packed and determined. Their shouts, threats and taunts echoed from the surrounding buildings. At their backs was the basilica which they had occupied two days before, stoked by the anger of Dornosian rebels. They had refused to give the Gatherers access to the accounts and the revenue chests, triggering the appearance of the legion. And she had been informed by Roberto Del Aglios, son of the Advocate and Master of Sword for the Bear Claws, that there were Gatherers captive inside.

She shook her head. Tax riots. That they should occur here in Cabrius, the usually peaceful capital city of the northern state of Dornos, was symptomatic of problems occurring all too frequently throughout the Estorean Conquord. The Bear Claws were here fresh from the flood harvest massacre in Tundarra. She prayed that this situation would not descend into slaughter.

The front edge of the crowd backed away, compressing the whole. Ripples of anger spread out.

'Step up,' said Kastenas. She held out her sword arm

The company increased pace on its far right, curving out into a crescent formation designed to corral the rioters. On the left, Kell kept her line straight, giving the crowd a single exit in to the central gardens of the city where it could be better contained. In the centre, Del Aglios shouted for the crowd to drop any weapons and kneel with hands behind heads. No one did. There were several hundred rioters and they hooted and spat derision at the Conquord force.

The detachment from the 2nd legion moved on. Discipline was impeccable. Every piece of armour shone with fresh polish. Every gladius and spear tip had been honed in the hours before dawn. Elise had known armies break merely on seeing a Conquord advance. This mob of ordinary citizens backed off but refused to disintegrate. They didn't believe the Conquord would attack and they were right. Up to a point.

The stones started to fly when they were within twenty yards. The mood turned uglier. The plaintive shouts of citizens who believed their protest to be just, mingled with the anti-Conquord taunts of those hoping to incite more than just rhetoric.

'Shell!' roared Del Aglios.

Behind the front rank, his hastati raised their long, gold and green rectangular shields over their heads. Stone rattled on metal. There was the clash of ceramics shattering as brightly coloured pottery joined the rain of missiles.

'Steady,' came the powerful voice of the Master of Sword. 'Push in right.'

Horses stamped and snorted. Legionaries rattled swords and spears on the backs of their shields. The pace increased on the left flank. Kastenas ordered her company to the trot. In front of her, the crowd began to bunch towards the exit but it was a reluctant move. Unwilling to give up their blockade of the basilica, the ringleaders shouted for courage and strength. Still the missiles came, primarily from the head of the stairs where Kastenas could see piles of stones. She saw too, the flash of metal and the curve of a bow. She hoped for their sakes that no one in the crowd chose to use those weapons.

The noise in the forum was deafening now. She could see faces in the crowd. Uncertain and fearful. Beginning to waver. Most of these were just innocent citizens whipped into a frenzy by ringleaders who stood at the back and out of immediate danger. She glanced across at Del Aglios. He turned his head, feeling her gaze. He nodded. Time to end this. She drew her sword and raised her arm. Tension flashed through the forum.

'Claws! Move in.' Her arm swept down and the cavalry drove forwards. The infantry took the lead. 'Keep secure. Keep close.'

The front of the crowd began to break and move left. People fled along the line, looking for the way out that Kell and her company were only too pleased to show them. But still the hardcore centre was unmoved. They stood defiant in front of the Conquord flags hanging high from the grand marble columns at the entrance to the basilica. The stones kept coming, more pottery shattered on shields and sprayed shards across the forum.

Contact was made on the bottom step. Kastenas held her cavalry while the infantry shields thumped into those brave enough to continue resistance. The taste of violence was in the air. A knot of men and women stood in front of the barred wooden doors of the basilica. It was a close-sided building, unusual for a Conquord basilica but necessary because of the hurricanes that periodically struck the region.

The crowd surged down the stairs, pushed from behind. Kastenas watched citizens flattened against the implacable shield wall. The legionaries reacted, punching forwards hard, bloodying noses and breaking bones. A spear flew out from the back of the crowd. Kastenas cursed. It fell into the midst of the infantry.

'Break them!' ordered Del Aglios.

Kastenas led her company up the steps. Citizens fell back ahead of her.

'Push, Claws, push.'

Using the butts of spears and the pommels of swords, they moved into the midst of the mob, striking down on those not fast enough to clear the way. The infantry stepped up hard with their shields, still keeping their weapons tucked away. Angry shouts turned to screams of pain and panic. The crowd's cohesion fragmented. People turned tail and ran left. Out in the gardens, the rest of the Bear Claws were waiting for them. Legionaries lashed out, keeping the momentum in their favour. Chanting, driving.

Kastenas rode behind them, seeing them away. Among the stones that still fell, an arrow thudded into her shield. It came from the columns surrounding the doors. She moved her shield to defend her and called her company to do the same. She turned to the tall man striding in the wake of the cavalry. He wore a green-plumed helmet above a heavy-featured face, his cloak streaming out behind him as he walked.

'Exchequer Jhered, arrows at the entrance.'

Paul Jhered nodded his understanding.

'Levium,' he barked. 'Shields high. Move.'

He drew his gladius, held his shield in front of his body and led his thirty levium, elite Gatherer warriors, up the steps in the wake of the horses. Here and there, citizens lay on the ground, clutching their faces and bodies where they had been struck. He had no time or sympathy for them and stepped around or over them, not breaking his stride.

He trotted up the dozen marble steps and past the first line of columns decorating the entrance to the basilica. A group of over fifty people stood in front of the doors. The legion had cleared the mass of the crowd exactly as planned, leaving him the ringleaders too stubborn or stupid to run with those they had goaded to action.

Jhered saw spears, blades and bows. But none were armoured. Jhered and his levium had moulded breastplates, greaves and shields over their deep green tunics. Any contest would be uneven. Arrows flew. Three of them. One missed high and wide, two struck the shields of the men either side of him. Jhered moved faster, pausing no more than two yards from the tip of the nearest blade.

'I'll give you those because you're scared. Any further action and I will attack you,' he said.

'We will not yield, Gatherer. Not even to you,' said a man to the fore. He was tall, bearded and powerful.

'Be assured that you will,' said Jhered quietly.

He motioned the levium to the left to hem them in. He saw anxious faces tracking the movement and hoped this could be resolved peacefully. Further left, the cavalry and infantry had moved out of the forum. Soldiers guarded its perimeter.

'The levy is too steep,' said the man. 'I cannot afford to buy seed, I have too little livestock to trade for breeding stock. You take the food from our children's mouths and the citizens from our fields to fight for you. What tax will you collect next time? I already have nothing and no means to make more.'

Jhered stood his shield down. 'My citizens. The levy is set and agreed by your legislature and posted at the beginning of every collection period. Your avenue of complaint about your personal contribution is via your quaestors or your magistrates. But consider first if you are paying too much for feed, for your workers or whether perhaps you indulge too often in your luxuries. We are the Gatherers. We collect.'

'Tax man.' The man spat on the floor. 'You know nothing of our struggle.'

'I understand your concerns. But I will not react to threats. You must talk to your legislators.' He paused to take in the whole crowd. 'You are all law-abiding, hard-working citizens. Any man can see that. Don't let that change. Stand aside.'

The farmer shook his head. 'You leave us no choice.' The group tensed for action.

Jhered nodded his head sharply. Levium to his left and right ran at them, shields battering protesters back. Jhered stepped forward very quickly. His shield struck the farmer's sword arm, stalling his fledgling strike. His own gladius point touched the farmer's neck. The man stared at him, undone by the speed of movement and aware of his sudden isolation.

'One day,' said Jhered quietly, 'you will be glad I did not push my blade home. Who would feed your family then? The Conquord provides all that you see around you. And it takes what it must. Yield now and you will walk home from here.'

The farmer frowned and stared him in the eye. 'You will let us go without further action?'

Jhered removed his sword. 'I could add to your ill-feeling by seeing you in a cell for a year but what will that serve? Criminals sit in cells, honest men have no place there. I need you working for, and loyal to, the Conquord. Put up your sword, go back to your family and your farm. What is your name?'

'Jorge Kyinta, sir.'

'And I am Exchequer Paul Jhered. The Conquord will provide. I will come back and speak with you again. And should I find the struggle to meet your levy is genuine, I will pay it for you.'

Jhered watched the fight drain out of the big farmer. He motioned his levium aside and Kyinta led his people from the forum. Jhered smiled before turning his attention to the basilica. The doors were daubed in slogans demanding tax cuts, the end of the Conquord and the death of the Gatherers. It was not the first time.

'Inside,' he ordered the levium. 'Let's clear whoever's in there, get my people and the chests and get out of here. I expect when we're gone the Bear Claws will have an easier ride.'

'Did you mean what you said, sir? About paying the farmer's levy?'

Jhered stared at the young man. At the rank of Addos, he was fresh to the Advocate's prestigious force.

'You will discover, Addos Harin, that I mean everything I say.'

Jhered trotted down the steps of the basilica, handing his shield to an attendant and sheathing his sword. A man destined for greatness was walking in his direction, that destiny not merely a function of the family crest he carried.

'Roberto!' he called. He took off his helmet and tucked it under one arm.

The young Del Aglios waved a hand and came over. 'A satisfactory outcome, Paul?'

'Barely,' said Jhered. He gestured at the rubble covering the forum. 'I worry about these events. Too many of them to ignore.'

'It's an inevitable consequence of expansion.'

Jhered raised his eyebrows. 'It's an inevitable consequence of excessive taxation. You listen to your mother too closely, Roberto and she is starting to embarrass me. My Gatherers suffer resistance and refusal everywhere they travel. We are draining the lifeblood from the Conquord. One day we must pause for breath.'

'She's the Advocate.' Roberto shrugged. 'You know how she views the Advocacy and the future of the Conquord.'

'It is a mantra I repeat in my sleep,' grumbled Jhered. 'Security and wealth through conquest and expansion. The latest revenue chests are not for improvements in the sewers and water courses, I take it?'

Roberto chuckled. 'No, my Lord Exchequer.' The smile was brief. 'Much is happening back in Estorr. The revenue is only part of it. We are recruiting more legions from across the Conquord. My mother is planning on opening a front into Omari.'

Jhered gaped and felt a flash of irritation. 'Dornos is not secure enough to seat a campaign. And she will not risk opening the front from Gosland, will she? Not with the Tsardon border so difficult.' Jhered paused and frowned. 'Are you being groomed for command of this venture?'

Roberto shook his head. 'No, indeed not, though you are closer than you realise. This was my last action for the Bear Claws. And the last action for the 2nd legion in the north.'

A thrill warmed Jhered's heart. 'You *are* being given your own command.'

'Two legions, two alae. From raw recruit to trained legion. I won't see action for two years at least, but still.'

Jhered could see the delight and he gripped Roberto's shoulder hard. 'Congratulations. If I may say, it's about time.'

'Thank you. I'm sure my mother will be happy not to have to hear you go on about it any more. I am indebted to your support.'

'I wouldn't have spoken up if I didn't believe you capable. General.' Both men laughed. 'Sounds good, doesn't it? We'll drink to it tonight. She has plans for you, I am sure.'

'Oh, yes,' said Roberto. 'She certainly does. It's the big one. She plans to open a triple front in Tsard in four years.'

Jhered stopped, stunned. He grabbed Roberto's arm and moved him to a quieter spot, away from prying eyes and cocked ears. Jhered felt his heart thumping and knew he had to speak.

'She must not do this,' he hissed. 'This is foolhardy. Gosland might be a jewel of Conquord stability but Atreska is too new. There will be civil war there, I stake my life upon it. Four years is too short a time. We do not have the strength to take on the kingdom for a decade at least. She will rip the heart from the citizenry. Roberto . . . you know I am right.'

'Then you must speak to her yourself, Paul,' said Del Aglios sharply. 'I have only so much influence over my mother and you are too often in the field. She will listen to you like no one else.'

Jhered blew out his cheeks and shook his head. 'Tsard. She thinks us greater than we are. She might as well attack Sirrane . . .' He paused, feeling suddenly hot. 'God-embrace-us-all. Sirrane will not stand silent if we go to war in Omari and Tsard simultaneously. She has diplomats speaking to them already, I trust?'

'Marshal Defender Vasselis is leading the team,' confirmed Roberto.

'Good,' said Jhered. 'At least we have the best chance of success. We cannot afford to lose the little we have gained from them.'

'I know,' said Roberto. 'Talk to my mother. There are other territories more vulnerable, smaller, that we should tackle first.'

'I will, young Del Aglios, I will. As soon as I can.'

Jhered turned to check on his levium at the basilica, feeling the sands already running short.

Chapter 3

838th cycle of God, 40th day of Dusasrise
5th year of the true Ascendancy

A thick layer of frost carpeted the garden path of the Solastro Palace. An inappropriate name since the season of harvest and sun had given way to the freezing depths of a particularly bitter dusas. Built on the tripartite border between the countries of Estorea, Phaskar and Neratharn, the palace was the seat of the Conquord outside Estorr and a symbol of its scale and strength.

Herine Del Aglios, Advocate of the Estorean Conquord, walked as easily as she dared across the treacherous ground. Beside her, Paul Jhered and Arvan Vasselis were welcome support. And where her fur trimmed knee-highs slithered, their heavy metal-shod boots rendered the frost to crumbs. All three were wrapped in heavy woollen cloaks of Conquord green, edged with the white and gold fur of Tundarran mountain lions.

Above, the sky was slate grey and coming on to snow. It would be a heavy and prolonged fall. Herine shivered. The short walk back to the palace cloisters from the Prima Chamber in the dark of evening would be singularly unpleasant. Jhered seemed to be entertained by her discomfort. She looked up into his looming features. His ice-blue eyes sparkled with ill-suppressed humour. There was frost in the hairs of his prominent nose and thick eyebrows.

'You are about to tell me that back in Tundarra you would still be wearing sleeveless shirts beneath your togas,' she said, gripping his arm tight with her mittened hand.

Jhered laughed. 'Not quite,' he said. 'Just comment on the fragility of the average Estorean constitution. Or Caraducian, for that matter.'

On her other side, Vasselis snorted. 'I'd survive bare-chested in the ice longer than you, Jhered. The south of my country is as bleak as any mountain top in yours when dusas calls.'

'Listen to you two,' said Herine, shaking her head. 'Posturing like schoolboys. Don't do that inside the Prima. I don't need your appointments questioned along with everything else.'

'You will listen to them, won't you, Herine?' said Jhered. 'Their pleas for caution and time are not mere bleatings.'

Herine blew twin clouds from her nostrils. 'Yes, and like the sheep in the fields we hear them every day and the sound never changes.' She relented. 'But yes, I will listen and of course I will do what I can. But I will not change my plans. The Conquord's future must be secured.'

'It is what we all desire,' said Vasselis. 'Well, almost all of us.'

Another chuckle from Jhered. 'Do I detect a barb aimed at our esteemed Order Chancellor?'

'You really shouldn't keep on upsetting her, you know, Arvan,' said Herine, feeling the warmth of mischief within her.

Vasselis sighed. 'With all due respect to your position as figurehead of the Order of Omniscience, my Advocate, Chancellor Koroyan is a sharp pain where I sit. And for you too, I have no doubt. Her desire for powers separate from the laws of state worries me. And we all know what her beloved Armour of God are capable of when our backs are turned.'

'Oh dear,' said Jhered. 'I had heard she'd been worrying about certain parts of Caraduk again. What heresy is it she thinks you are hiding from her?'

'I only wish I knew,' said Vasselis, missing the humour in Jhered's question. 'She has her Readers and Speakers over me like a bad nettle rash. They ask questions about ancient history while they should be tending to those many citizens who need the guidance of their ministry. I do not like her constant suspicion.'

'Oh, Arvan, stop being so stuffy. You are so exemplary in heading her off,' said Herine smiling up at him and seeing his face relax a little. 'And since you have nothing to hide, and my unswerving backing, please don't deny us our entertainment by making me stop her. She goes such a wonderful colour when she is embarrassed by her own actions in public.'

Advocacy guards on the steps of the Prima Chamber snapped to attention. The three of them climbed the swept marble steps to the colonnaded entrance and walked through the entrance hall in which stood busts of every Advocate since the First Cycle of God and the establishment of the Estorean Conquord.

It was a bright hall, lit by enormous vaulted windows along both sides and warmed by huge fires in six grates. Nonetheless, Herine found it depressing rather than glorious.

'Don't let me end up here too soon,' she muttered.

Aides swarmed around them, taking cloaks, furs, gloves and hats and straightening their togas. They paused and sat to change into more formal sandals and each of them attended to their hair while mirrors were held in front of them.

'Would you like me to enter ahead of you?' asked Vasselis.

Herine shrugged. 'It really doesn't matter. The assembly believes I favour Caraduk, whatever you and I do. Come on. But let's not make a song and dance. Just keep on talking to me.'

Ahead of them, the doors to the Prima Chamber stood closed. They towered forty feet to the vaulted ceiling, their white-painted wooden panels carved with the crest of the Estorean Conquord. The doors were pulled open on their approach, giving them their first view of the chamber. Modelled on the senate building in Estorr, four stepped marble benches ran down its length, left and right of a carpeted path that led to the Advocate's seat. Behind her seat were six of her senior advisers, waiting with every scrap of information she might need and to record every word spoken. The chamber itself was beautifully warm from the hypocaust running beneath it. The bright painted walls and ranks of delegates in white and green togas made it feel as comfortable as a solastro afternoon.

There were upwards of three hundred delegates in the chamber awaiting the Advocate's arrival. Marshal Defenders of each territory were present, along with their delegations of aediles and propraetors. Further up the chamber, the Chancellor of the Order of Omniscience, Felice Koroyan, sat on the left with her inner circle of four High Speakers. On the right, the praetors and consuls of the Conquord were arranged in order of seniority. Jhered's twelve-strong Gatherer council was on the bottom bench below them.

Ranks of faces turned towards her. Herine Del Aglios strode along the deep green carpet with her head high, nodding left and right at the assembly. Once a year, they met like this, the leaders of the territories all in one place to set the agenda for the next cycle to be administered centrally from Estorr. And every year, the agenda was much the same. Herine suppressed a smile at the thought of sheep bleating.

Every voice had stilled by the time she reached her seat and sat down to look back at the assembly. Jhered and Vasselis took their places and she noted the envious looks cast by more than a few in their direction. Honour and service meant favour. So it had always been.

'My friends, welcome,' she said, her voice carrying clear across the chamber. 'It is a cold day outside but the glory of the Conquord warms us in here. And I would take such warmth beyond the Conquord's present borders.' She waited while the rumble of conversation died. 'First, I will hear reports from you all concerning the state of your armies and navies, both standing and marching. I will then outline any increases necessary in those forces and finally will take questions before we get on to mundane matters of administration.

'Marshal Defender Katrin Mardov, please, the state of the Gesternan armed forces. The floor is yours.'

Herine leaned back and watched Katrin rise. A great woman. She settled in her cushions and prepared to listen.

Hesther Naravny blew on her hands and rested them on the tree trunk. The orchard's owner, Lucius Endrade, stood nearby, wrapped in furs against the wind that howled across the open plateau from the sea.

'I wish you'd told me sooner,' said Hesther.

'I didn't think it serious,' he said. 'Just frost burn.'

Hesther turned and looked around the orange and lemon grove. Every single tree was encased in a lumber box tied with burlap against the onset of the short chill season Westfallen always experienced around this time of the year. Three of them had been partially unboxed for Hesther to examine. Lucius said that thirty more were afflicted. All in the same area of the orchard.

'It was never likely to be that, was it?' she said rather tartly.

Snow began to fall and her mood cooled with every flake. She glanced at the young Ascendants grouped near her. She had brought them up here at the insistence of Ardol Kessian, who had thought it a good opportunity to see if any of them evidenced Land Warden abilities. All she wanted right now was to load them back on the cart and get them back to the villa. They'd begun by running around screeching and throwing snowballs but the cold had got into them quickly. Now, the four of them stood in a huddle, with hands in gloves and bodies covered in scarves, fur-lined leather coats and woollen hats. Blue noses protruded.

'So what is it?' asked Lucius. He had been a Land Warden himself in his early years, much to the delight of his father. The ability had gone before he was eight.

'In a moment.' She smiled at the Ascendants. They were getting on for five years old now and their core abilities were developing well. No sign of a crossover yet, though. 'Gorian, you're the most likely. Want to try?'

Gorian beamed at her, dropped a sneering look to his companions that Hesther didn't much like and walked over.

'It doesn't make you better than them,' said Hesther. 'But this is more like when you put your hands on a sick animal. Do you understand?'

Gorian nodded.

'Good. So I don't want to see that look again, do you understand?'

'Yes,' said Gorian, almost inaudibly.

It would have to do. 'All right. Now, put your hands on the tree trunk. You'll have to take your gloves off. Here, I'll hold them for you. Don't drop them in the snow. Tell me what you feel.'

'It's cold and rough, Hesther,' said Gorian.

There was a snorted giggle from behind. Gorian looked round.

'Shush, Ossacer or you'll be next.'

'He can't do it if I can't,' said Gorian.

Hesther raised her eyebrows. 'He might, you know. He is a Pain Teller and if he can sense where people hurt he might be able to find where the trees are hurt.'

'He can't.' Gorian was dismissive.

Hesther frowned. 'Concentrate. Try and feel below the bark. Like you would if a dog was hurt and you wanted to find out where so the surgeon could help it.'

Gorian was silent for a moment. His little hands, white with the cold, searched the bark. She saw him squeeze his eyes shut as they had been taught, to help their concentration. She smiled, love for her sister's child warming her. He, like all of them, was exhibiting a great deal of early promise. And even at such tender years, they understood so much. There was something special about them, everyone could feel it. How special was yet to be determined.

Eventually, Gorian turned back to her and took his hands from the bark. 'It must be dead. I can't feel it inside.'

Hesther kissed him on top of the head and handed him his gloves. 'Never mind, darling. But it's not dead, just sick.'

'It's dead,' Gorian was quite adamant.

Hesther stroked his cheek to turn his face to hers and knelt in front of him. 'You tried your hardest and that's all anyone can ask of you. Next time, I'm sure you'll feel what I feel.' He stared at her, furious. 'Don't be angry. It's all right. You did nothing wrong.'

She stood and looked at the other Ascendants. She could feel Gorian's anger and it made her decision for her. 'All right. It's too cold up here. Get yourselves back to the cart and we'll join you in a moment. Go on, Gorian. Find the mule an apple in the sack, why don't you?'

He brightened and trotted off towards the cart. The others went quickly in his wake, no doubt to argue about who would feed the animal and be first to burrow beneath the blankets for some warmth.

'Right,' she said and put her own frozen hands on the tree to make sure of her diagnosis.

It was never good to feel a sick plant or tree. She felt nausea through her own body but she had learned to accept it over the years. A healthy trunk would imbue her with a vibrancy. This one, though, was dull and the bleakness of its energy was shocking. Up in the branches there was still health but it was being poisoned from deep inside. She'd seen it before once or twice. She took her hands away and slid on her gloves gratefully. Lucius looked at her.

'Hopefully we aren't too late though the problem is embedded deep in this one. The soil must be too acidic in this area. You have to balance it out. Today.'

'You're sure? It's not a fungal infection?' He gestured at the bole of the tree where a cluster of tenacious mushrooms had managed to grow inside the box.

'That's why you brought me up here. It's acid, not fungus. Trust me.'

'You know I do,' said Lucius.

'You'll save them,' she said. 'And even if you don't, you need to balance the soil to stop it leaching elsewhere.'

Lucius made to reply but a loud and angry child's voice cut across the orchard. Hesther raised her eyebrows.

'Come on,' she said. 'Time to go before the children freeze to death.'

Hesther hurried back towards the cart. All the Ascendants were gathered near the mule's head. The animal looked on mournfully while they argued. But it wasn't about the apple. She heard snatches of accusation and taunt. Quite without warning, Gorian's hand, ungloved, whipped out. She heard the slap like a whip crack in the crisp air. Ossacer screamed and fell to the ground.

'Gorian!' she bellowed. 'Come here.'

'But—'

'Right now!'

He dragged himself over reluctantly, she speeding her pace to meet him. She grabbed the errant hand.

'He said I couldn't ever do it,' said Gorian, almost beside himself with infantile rage.

'Do what, exactly?'

'Feel the tree.'

'And what had you said to him already?'

'Nothing.'

'I don't believe you,' she said, exasperated and irritable with cold. 'He never starts it, does he? Now you listen to me, Gorian. You never, never hit your brothers or sister. You never, never hit anyone. And if I ever see or hear of you hitting someone again, I will stop you learning.'

He tried to retreat, his eyes suddenly frightened, his face crumbling towards tears. She held his hand firm.

'Do you understand me?' He nodded, his eyes welling up. 'Then learn to behave yourself. Now go and say sorry to Ossacer and get on the cart. I don't want to hear you until we get back to the villa.'

She let him go and stood, sighing.

'Little boy temper,' said Lucius. 'He's just cold.'

Hesther shook her head. 'I'm sure you're right.'

Herine had to keep her expression deliberately neutral and her body outwardly relaxed. From either side of the Prima Chamber, shouts were exchanged and papers waved. Men and women stood to point and accuse. Their ire was directed at Marshal Defender Thomal Yuran of Atreska. The Conquord's latest member was already a controversial figure with his country simmering on the edge of civil strife. And Herine's announcement of planning for future campaigns had brought him angrily to his feet.

She waited and watched while he shouted back at his abusers or looked to her for an order for silence. Something he should already have learned she would not give. It was his words that had provoked this brief outrage and it was he who was riding the tiger. Eventually, the din subsided enough for Herine to raise a languid hand. All bar Yuran took their seats. He stood proud, his large brown eyes blazing from beneath his greying hair. He looked uncomfortable in a formal toga, clothing not indigenous to Atreska.

'Marshal Yuran, it was lax of me not to welcome you officially to the Prima Chamber of the Estorean Conquord. My apologies. Welcome.'

Ironic cheers and applause. The atmosphere relaxed and a brief smile crossed the Marshal's face. Next to him, his Estorean consul spoke some encouraging words.

'Thank you, my Advocate,' he said.

'It was also perhaps lax of me not to brief you earlier of our intentions although I must say that the same information has not brought my esteemed Marshals of Gestern and Gosland to their feet in protest.'

'With all due respect, my Advocate, the positions of Gestern and Gosland are not as ours. We have just gained accession to the Conquord, following a bitter campaign against it. A campaign in which legions from all our former neighbours were sent against us. There are those in my country whose memories will be long and whose loyalty will be hard to gain.'

He paused as another ripple of chatter ran around the chamber.

'My honoured members of the Prima Chamber,' he continued. 'I apologise for the nature of my earlier outburst but not for its subject. Atreska and its citizens are only just beginning to accept the sight of the Conquord crest and its legions in every corner of their once independent kingdom. They are only just accepting me as a Marshal Defender of the Conquord in place of their king. Many are still loyal to him and would have gladly followed him into death.

'Our internal problems are unique in Conquord history. And putting aside my personal view on the sense of an invasion of Tsard, you must understand Atreska's close links to that kingdom.'

'Actually,' said Herine. 'I would be very much interested in your views on the invasion. From Exchequer Jhered's and Marshal Vasselis's words, it would seem you are not alone in your objections. Please, since you are on your feet, speak.'

Yuran bowed. 'Thank you, my Advocate.' He drew himself up a little taller and embraced the chamber with an open-armed gesture. 'Honoured delegates, there are none here with more knowledge of the Tsardon mind than myself. Tsardon warriors and the steppe cavalry fought with us against the Conquord. We share beliefs, faiths, familial histories and trade. We are friends. And they are naturally desperately concerned at the expansion of the Conquord to encompass Atreska.

'You are all aware of the constant strife along the Gosland border and it will inevitably filter south to ours. Currently, our assurances of peace and continued trade are accepted but when word reaches them of the recruiting and movement of Conquord forces then we will become the enemy. The border forts being erected are creating suspicion and limiting trade in their wake. It feeds tension in my country and affects our profits though not, I notice, our levy demands.

'The Kingdom of Tsard is huge and sprawling and shares borders with Kark and Sirrane, just as the Conquord does. But every empire has a finite size. They know they have reached theirs. I believe we have reached ours. Invading Tsard, or even threatening invasion would prove disastrous. The country is too big, the people too numerous and the terrain too difficult. They are proud and they are fierce and we in Atreska will be the first to fall victim. Because there is nothing more they hate than a friend who they feel has turned against them.

'Please, listen to me. Be satisfied. If you must expand, do so north where the primitive countries would benefit from the rule of the Conquord. Tsard will not, and neither will we prosper by attacking the kingdom. Indeed, developing trade with them is an infinitely more profitable way forward. I need help from you to stabilise my country. I do not need an invasion force marching across my land to a campaign that will inevitably end in defeat.'

The volume of comment had been growing steadily through his speech and as he sat the hoots of derision and the claims of his dishonour of Conquord strength grew to a clamorous level.

'Enough!' Herine stood. Silence fell quickly. 'I will not sit while you bandy insults. Take it outside into the snow. There is not complete accord about the Advocacy plans to invade Tsard as there is for our campaign into Omari. You have heard the arguments. I am the Advocate of this Conquord. I speak for you but I do not dictate to you. We will vote as the law allows when a clear split is evident.' She waved one of her propraetors forward to conduct the vote and sat down.

There was a curious, almost childish excitement that accompanied a free vote. That hint of risk that the will of the Advocacy would not be carried. It was rare but not unheard of to experience defeat, though rarely over matters of expansion. Herine felt the vote would be close yet carry in her favour.

But the shows of hands and the quiet in the chamber turned her confidence to ash. She shifted in her seat and regarded the propraetor closely as the hands were shown again and recounted. She was presented with the results and her heart began to beat hard in her chest. Gosland, Atreska, Dornos, Gestern. All had come out against her. But so had Tundarra and Phaskar. She had to be grateful that Marshal Vasselis had eventually sided with her and brought his Caraduk delegation with him. It had saved her from embarrassment but had given her no certainty. And now she would have to rely on that most capricious of minds.

'We are split,' she said to a flurry of voices. 'Under God the Omniscient we are split. The majority in favour of Tsardon expansion is too small on which to proceed. And so as the law allows, there will be a decision made under God by those appointed by me to divine the word and rule of God. Felice, the floor is yours.'

She gestured at Chancellor Felice Koroyan, who rose gracefully to her feet. The Order did not vote on matters of state, holding an advisory brief until a split occurred. It was a position the Senate had always respected.

'My Advocate, I am surprised at the equality of this vote and really have no decision to make. The Order spreads through education of its wisdom throughout the Conquord and beyond. But it spreads more quickly through conquest. We do not demand others follow our faith—' Vasselis coughed loudly '—we do not demand that others follow our faith blindly but merely seek the opportunity to open the eyes of all peoples to the glory and mercy of the Omniscient god. The quickest way to ensure stability in Atreska is to accelerate the spread of the Omniscient through a people clinging on to allegiances with Tsardon faiths that are little more than false idol worship.

'And the quickest way to break them from their Tsardon past is to make Tsard a member of the Conquord and bring them all under the embrace of God. Expansion is not just a desire of the Conquord. Surely it is our duty. We move in favour of the Advocacy.'

As the cheers and boos rose to a crescendo, Herine saw Yuran place his head in his hands. He would see the path soon enough. She turned to nod her thanks to Chancellor Koroyan, expecting to see her waiting for this acknowledgement. She was not. Instead she was glaring with undisguised disgust at Marshal Defender Vasselis.

Herine shook her head. One day. One day, when she could pause for breath, she resolved to find out what on God's earth was going on. Until then, she had new armies to build and a war to plan.

And Tsard would be a most challenging enemy.

Chapter 4

842nd cycle of God, 10th day of Solasrise
9th year of the true Ascendancy

Master Dina Kell's cavalry company were riding hard through sparse woodland to the eastern end of the valley while Pavel Nunan led three hundred of the 2nd legion light infantry at a dead run to the nearer west end. Triarii were moving to scale the steep southern slope to block off any agile escapees.

Atreskan rebels were attacking a small fort just ten miles from the Tsardon border. The fort was a messenger post, security barracks and dormitory for the road gangs building the Conquord highway to the border. It was also isolated, tucked into the head of a densely wooded valley. The 2nd legion, the Bear Claws of Estorr, had been marching to join the muster, prior to the launch of the Tsardon campaign the following genasrise. There they were to secure the borders, train for the campaign and oversee the building of the army's artillery through the cold dusas season. Around them, the army would build to its initial fighting strength of almost thirty thousand.

General Gesteris had warned them all about the rise in rebel activity in this region as civil war spread through Atreska. The legions themselves were hardly vulnerable but their supply lines were. And when they had seen the smoke rise from two miles away, the General had given vent to his fury. His decisions had been made without hesitation.

'These are not citizens loyal to the Conquord.' Nunan reminded them as they ran. 'These are traitors to Estorea and to God. Their smiles are false, their words are traps. They will cower when they see us, and it is right they should be afraid. We are the Bear Claws. And we will crush them.'

Nunan breasted the wide valley mouth. Woodland hemmed them in on both sides as they descended the sharp gradient. His leading hundred had bows, his remaining two hundred, javelins. Each had a gladius and a light round shield in addition to their scale armour. Ahead, the valley floor was wide and rock-strewn. At the bottom, the river rose from its underground course and it was along this river that the road was being built. The fort lay a mile away towards the valley's eastern end, on a natural plateau. It was burning, the black smoke spiralling high into a cloudy sky.

Down by the fort, he could see a mass of people moving. Hundreds. On the apron that ran down to the road, bodies littered the ground. Here and there, pockets of Conquord troops fought in the burning buildings, but they wouldn't last long. Wagons and materials lay scattered across the valley. The river was stained red and carried the bodies of men, oxen and horses. This had been a devastating attack by a large rebel force.

'Advance!' yelled Nunan.

He ran down the road, hoping he had timed it right for Kell and her cavalry to pen them in from the other end of the valley. Before too long, the thunder of his infantry at his heels was heard, the flash of their armour in the sunlight seen. Shouts echoed up into the sky. Soldiers, archers and riders gathered back on the road, streaming away from their attacks on the fort.

A rugged fighting line emerged from the smoke and dust. Riders formed up against Nunan's left flank. At a rough estimate, he faced around four hundred. Not ideal odds but around him were battle-hardened citizens. Ahead of him were disorganised irregulars, tired at the end of a long, hard action they had thought won. But the Conquord would prevail.

'Fighting spread,' called Nunan as they closed to a quarter of a mile. 'Archers, target the riders.'

His orders were relayed across the infantry. Soon, the archers had overtaken him and were working up to slightly higher ground. Around him, his infantry formed a running line over thirty yards wide, spanning the road and the rough ground either side. At two hundred yards he saw enemy archers preparing to stretch their bows. At a hundred and fifty, a little too early, they began to fire. At a hundred, the enemy riders moved to their attack.

'Keep pace.'

Nunan held his shield in front of his face and hefted a javelin in his hand. Arrows whipped by overhead. He heard them thump into wood and flesh. To his left, the enemy cavalry were riding hard. His archers stopped. They fired. The volley crossed the gap and fell among the enemy horsemen. Man and beast fell in their midst but they did not break. Another volley fell. And another. The charge faltered and reformed. On they came again, closing.

Nunan was forty yards from the standing line of rebels. He saw stolen Conquord armour, Atreskan crests and a mess of weapons and helmets. He saw fear in their eyes.

'Javelins.'

Nunan opened his stance and threw. Short spears thronged the air. In front of him, shields moved above heads. The missiles fell, bouncing, piercing, the sound like hail on an iron roof. Men and women screamed. Arrows flew in reply. Nunan closed his shield, a shaft thumping hard into the Conquord crest in front of him. The tip came through, grazing his forearm. He took his second javelin from behind his shield.

'Javelins.'

Again the short powerful weapons crashed into the enemy ranks. And this time, the 2nd legion crashed in right after them. The noise was extraordinary, the pressure suddenly immense. Nunan leaned all his weight into his shield and ran straight through his first man, trampling his body. The protruding shaft snapped away. Left and right, his infantry were with him, roaring the Conquord on.

Slowed now, he found himself deep in the heart of the enemy ranks. He battered his shield ahead and left, feeling it slap against his enemy's. In front, an open flank. He buried his gladius in it to the hilt and kicked out at the falling body even as he dragged his shield back to the guard. He stood for a heartbeat. Right, he lost a man to a downward strike that drove hard into the citizen's neck. It was the rebel's last blow. Nunan's blade struck over his shield and took the defenceless man through the throat.

'Claws, drive on!'

His cry was taken up along the short line. He heard the neigh of horses and the stamp of hooves. There was another surge of noise and the multiple thud of sword on shield. Nunan glanced left. The remnants of the rebel cavalry had hit the side of the Conquord line.

Infantry was streaming in from the back to attack. Archers were charging down the slope, bows discarded, blades ready.

A sword came at him, high and carving down. He took the blow on his shield. The impact sent pins and needles along his arm. He stepped back a pace. Nunan wasn't a small man but the rebel was huge. His blade was an ancient longsword held in two hands. He was crisscrossed with scars, heavily bearded and wore a rusting hauberk, broken in a dozen places. Others clustered around him.

'To me,' ordered Nunan.

The man struck again. He was quick. It was a battering blow on to the top of his shield, trying to drive his guard down. Nunan had to trust he'd been heard. That second blow had badly jolted his shoulder. The rebel raised his sword over his head a third time. Nunan thrust his shield forward hard and fast, catching the man in his chest. He hardly moved but had no room to strike down, sweeping his sword around instead to block Nunan's blade, stabbing through waist-high.

He was a careless fighter and his blade gouged a rent in another rebel's side but his power kept it moving fast enough to stop his enemy. Nunan angled his gladius to deflect and jabbed his shield in again. Higher this time, bloodying the rebel's nose. The man stepped back, winding his sword up behind him, missing another rebel by a breath. Nunan brought gladius and shield together, catching the blade and forcing it down and left.

Nunan stepped up, cracking his shield into the rebel's ribs, keeping him off balance. The man leant briefly on his sword to avoid stumbling. Nunan saw the gap and punched his gladius up under the man's ribcage and into his heart. The rebel gasped and swayed backward, a tree falling on saplings.

'Come on!' roared Nunan. A horn blared across the valley. Kell. Right on time. 'Push, Bear Claws, push.'

Nunan drove on, heedless of the pain in his shoulder and the numbness spreading down his arm. In a few blows he could barely lift his shield but the infantry around him kept him safe. The rebels were wavering. Already he could hear the shouts of alarm, and through the tangle of limb and steel he could see a few breaking away from the back.

The chaos slowly resolved. Captains dragged their citizens into line and the shield wall formed. Men stepped in front of him and pushed him gently back. The 2nd legion closed ranks and moved relentlessly forward in close formation, opening their shields to stab out, closing again to punch ahead. The survivors among the rebel horsemen had already put heel to flank and were racing away behind him. His archers returned to their bows and the thunder of Kell's cavalry was loud in his ears. He looked over the heads of his people.

'Hold!' he bellowed.

They stopped. The rebels paused, uncertain and trapped, hoping for the chance to surrender. But for them there would be no mercy. His infantry paced backwards in perfect order. He heard Dina Kell's voice loud and a hundred lances were levelled. Realisation ran through the remaining rebels like disease. They panicked. Ahead an implacable shield formation. Behind, galloping cavalry.

Nunan spat on the ground and turned away, finding he had no desire to look.

Praetor Lena Gorsal wiped her hands down her tunic and walked to the open west face of the basilica. It was a glorious day in Gull's Ford, a small Atreskan town a hundred miles west of the Tsardon border. The air was filled with endeavour. Tucked away from the new highway being built to the south, it was sometimes difficult to believe that her country of Atreska had descended into civil conflict or that the Conquord was mustering for war. They had healthy trade from east and west and found the whole idea of a new campaign simply bad for business.

Neither she nor any citizen in Gull's Ford wanted any part in it. Whoever held sway in Haroq City was of complete indifference to most of them, people who had not even seen the realities of battle during Atreska's fall to the Conquord five years back. They had welcomed the Reader of the Order of Omniscience easily enough and for his part he had proved a sound counsellor and a fine teacher. Many had converted. Those that didn't found their differences respected.

The calls that had brought her to the forum had an edge of urgency. There were riders, about twenty of them at first count. Tsardon from the Tarit Plain, where the steppe cavalry kept up a strong presence in the face of the Conquord's fortifications along the Atreskan and Goslander borders. They all dismounted at her approach and she smiled as she recognised their leader.

'Sentor Rensaark,' she said in an Atreskan dialect they both spoke fluently. 'It's a long way for a ride on a hot solas day.'

'We are camping not far from here,' said the sentor, a gruff man with cold eyes.

He and all his men were garbed in light wools. Scale armour was bound to their saddles. Swords were strapped to their sides.

'Trading?' she asked.

Rensaark shook his head. 'Speaking,' he said.

'I understood the border to be closed to those not trading,' she said. 'How did you get past?'

'A little money can make men blind,' he said.

'So speak,' she said. 'May I offer you a drink? Or at least shelter from the heat for your men and horses while we talk.'

'Thank you. Very gracious.'

'It is the only way to treat friends,' she said.

'Yes,' said the sentor stiffly.

They moved back into the relative cool of the basilica. Gorsal showed him to her office and had watered wine brought in, along with oranges and rare beef. Rensaark was uncomfortable. He licked his lips often and a frown was stamped on his face as if he was remembering something unpleasant. Gorsal didn't know what to expect but found herself a little nervous as she invited him to say what he had come to say.

'These are difficult times,' said Rensaark. 'We have seen old allies turn against us and the Conquord reach out its fist to swat others. But even in the midst of conquest, Atreska has remained our friend. Marshal Yuran is a great man, keen to maintain his allegiance with our king but his eye is drawn by the promise of Conquord riches.'

'There are many in Atreska who share his view but take more direct action than mere verbal protest,' said Gorsal.

'I know. And we are grateful. For five years we have hoped for rebellion. We have helped where we can but have had to look to our own security and armies. Gosland is like a stranger to us now. Their rulers may as well have been born in togas, sitting on columns, so lost are they to the Conquord. But Atreska, we thought, was not. Now we are not so sure.'

'The civil war still thrives,' said Gorsal. 'We do not want war with Tsard. We've had peace for too long.'

Rensaark nodded. 'But you do not wish to dismiss the Conquord either.'

'Trade is good,' admitted Gorsal.

'The time has come to make a choice.' Rensaark's tone was as cold as his eyes. 'Estorea is building armies along the Gosland and Atreskan borders, the like of which they have never assembled before. Their best generals are in command. Their finest legions lead the muster. Not thirty miles from here, the Bear Claws have slaughtered true Atreskans who got in their way. You cannot have failed to see the smoke on your horizon. In the face of their own faith they are burning the bodies of those who oppose them.

'They are coming to war with Tsard, and Atreska must chose its allegiance and its loyalty. There can be no split. Not any more.'

Gorsal swallowed, feeling prickly with anxiety. 'What do you mean? We deny you nothing. We are your friends and always will be. But Haroq City is where our rulers make their laws. I am a loyal Atreskan. I will abide by them.'

'It is a respectful position and one I understand,' said Rensaark. He rose. 'It is in friendship that I give you this warning, praetor. The moment any Conquord soldier places his foot on our soil, we are at war. And that war will include Atreska. None of you will be safe, despite their promises. All will suffer in this pointless conflict. And I will do what I am ordered.'

'I don't understand,' said Gorsal.

Rensaark was at the door. 'It is not too late. Atreska must rise up against the folly marching across its lands. You must turn from the Conquord. They have not the strength to beat us. Stop them from trying. We cannot talk to Yuran; we cannot gain access to him. You can. You are his subjects and he must hear you. Please, Lena, make him see. Before war makes evil out of us all.'

Gorsal stared at the door for an age after he was gone, trying to calm her heart and the shaking in her hands.

Ardol Kessian sat on a grassy slope with Arducius, the vista of Westfallen laid out below them. It was impossible to feel old on a day like today. Golden corn swaying in a light sea-breeze. The orchards packed with ripe citrus and rich colour. The herds of sheep and cattle grazing contentedly or pigs slumbering in the shade. And the vibrant sounds of children's laughter mingled with the distant wash of waves on the shore, the clank of hammer on steel and nail, the sawing of blade on wood.

The young Ascendant was sitting with Kessian under a parasol which shielded them from the worst of the sun's blanket heat. A pitcher of water was at their feet and a half-eaten plate of fruit lay between them. School was over for the day, but for the Ascendants learning was not.

'What do you feel when you test the sky, Arducius?' asked Kessian.

Arducius was a supreme Wind Harker already and not yet nine. Almost as accurate as Kessian himself, he had shown the aptitude from a very early age. Kessian would always remember the first moments fondly. Arducius had not known how to communicate what he felt in the weather and the climate as it modulated around him. It caused him to react in absurdly practical ways. Walking out in his rain leathers on a hot solas day. That was before he worked out the difference in time between his sensing of a weather front and its arrival. Kessian chuckled.

'What's funny?' asked Arducius.

'I was just thinking about you strolling the streets, sweating in your leather cape and staring at the sky, wondering why it was blue.'

Arducius laughed too, a peal that made heads rise to see. 'They used to say to me, "rain tomorrow, is it?" '

'And you'd get angry and claim it would be today. At five you could look so furious.'

'And you all laughed at me,' said Arducius.

Kessian ruffled his hair. 'Still, they don't laugh now, do they?'

'No,' agreed Arducius. 'Most of them look at me, at all of us, like they are expecting something.'

'Well, they are. We all are.'

And there it was. Eight years old and brilliant in their individual talents. But of the rest . . . the multiple abilities, the elemental manipulation. Not a sign. The Echelon had studied and dissected every one of the elder Gorian's writings, looking for cracks in his theories. They could find none. But the weight was growing in his mind that they were just theories. No concrete evidence existed anywhere.

The questions were beginning to be asked. Whether these four of the ninth strand of the Ascendancy were really the first. Whether the waiting was set to go on. Every day, Kessian prayed to be allowed to live to see it happen and every day he could feel God tugging him harder towards a return to the earth. He had no belief that the recent births into the potential tenth strand would amount to anything. Others were carrying children now. He would not live to see any of them grow to maturity. He was one hundred and forty now and he felt it with every creak of his bones and every missed beat of his heart.

'Are you all right, Father Kessian?' asked Arducius.

Kessian forced a smile. 'Yes, of course. Now, back to your lesson. What do you feel? Tell me.'

'I feel the wind as if it is passing through my head and body,' said Arducius. 'I can smell a drop of rain that has fallen three hundred miles away, carried here on the breeze. I can feel high into the air to see when the temperature will fall or rise. I can feel the thickness of cloud and tell you how much rain will fall from it. I can look at the surface of the sea and know a storm is coming.' Arducius shrugged. 'Like always. Just like you.'

There was a note of despondency in Arducius's voice and Kessian couldn't blame him. The weight of expectation was growing on their young shoulders. And it would be nothing when compared to the wave of disappointment that would sweep over them if they did not meet those expectations.

'I'm sorry, Arducius,' said Kessian.

'What for?'

'That this has proved to be your fate.'

Arducius frowned. 'Yes but loads of us in Westfallen have had abilities.'

'But none so well attuned from such an early age. And none on whom have been pinned such hopes.' Kessian sighed. 'It was unfair of us to expect and assume. Though of course, there is still time. Much time.'

Arducius stared at him, his expression revealing his uncertainty before he spoke. 'But we are better than all the others at our age. Even you, right?'

Kessian nodded. 'Oh yes, yes, you are.'

A child will always give you hope and Kessian clung gratefully to this tendril. Down below them, Gorian was sitting with Gwythen Terol, two Herd Masters together. Gorian was learning the biology of a cow in minute detail. As ever, the animal calmed when he approached. And like always with him, and only him, the rest of the herd were gathered like an audience, chewing and staring. The animals knew.

But what did they know and why on God's earth was it that he couldn't make his charges take the next step? It had to be soon. It had to be.

Chapter 5

843rd cycle of God, 35th day of Solasrise
10th year of the true Ascendancy

The pall of smoke was thickening over Gull's Ford. Flames from two dozen fires intensified the heat of the day. A heat haze shimmered across the south of the town and through it more raiders were riding in hard, their figures silhouetted against burning crops.

In the centre of the main street, the garrison commander was trying to organise terrified volunteer militia into some semblance of order. They were hopelessly outnumbered, poorly equipped and barely trained. But still they formed into a four-deep defensive rank with their few pikes bristling to the front. Behind them, a handful of archers stood with hunting bows ready.

Han Jesson shook his head. Pitiful. Almost pointless. He had half a mind to urge them to run and hide, save themselves if they could. But they represented just a little more time for others to spare themselves and his urge for self-preservation overcame his pity.

The north side of the town was lost. Houses were burning all the way down to the river. He could still hear the sounds of fighting but the raiders were cleaning up there, driving farm animals back to the north-east. Now they were turning their attentions to the centre of the settlement. He had two choices. He could either stay hidden in his house and risk it being burned around him or run south with his family, hoping to be ignored until he reached the stables where they kept their cart and horses.

He stepped from the window and looked into the gloom of his house and shop. His heart was thrashing in his chest. He couldn't focus his mind beyond his fears. He didn't know what to do for the best.

In the corner of the shop, his wife comforted their young son. The attack had come without warning, the raiders bursting from the woods a half mile distant as the sun reached its zenith. The noise of the screaming and panic had chilled his heart and sent his boy into a shivering fit. Poor Hanson was only five. He shouldn't have to face this terror.

He stared into his wife's eyes. Kari was imploring him to do something. Stacked all around him were the trappings of his business. Amphorae, pots, plates, vases, goblets, artworks. All designed, fired and hand-painted on the premises. To abandon it was the ruin of a life's work. To stay was to risk being burned alive.

There was more noise out in the street. He could hear the sound of approaching horses. People were running blindly away towards the south. How could this be? They were over three days from the border with Tsard. He assumed that was where the raiders were coming from. He rubbed his fingers in his eyes and pressed himself against the cracked open shutter to get a view of the end of the street. He'd waited too long. It was too late to run now.

'We'll be all right here,' he said. 'We'll be fine. Just stay back there and keep your heads down.'

'Han, what is happening?' Kari's voice was pleading.

'The militia can't stop them. People are running. We'll be safe here, I promise.'

His words sounded hollow in his head. He felt a dry, bitter feeling in the pit of his stomach and his eyes kept on misting over with tears.

The raiders attacked the fragile line of pikes. He saw them wheel broadside on. There had to be over fifty of them. Arrows thudded into the defending line. Men fell. Some writhed and screamed. A few arrows answered. Maybe two horsemen were hit on the move. The enemy horse archers turned again and fired another volley. This time, the pike line broke at its left-hand edge. Other riders drove into the fracture, swords carving downwards. Blood misted into the air. The defending archers turned and ran.

The sound of hoofs on the cobbles rang out loud against the buildings either side of the street. Jesson ducked away as the first of the riders clattered past. Right in front of his house, a man he knew was cut down, body thudding into the wall. Blood sprayed onto the cobbles and sightless eyes bored into his.

He staggered back, a hand across his mouth. Nausea swept through him. He gagged, breathing in huge gasps.

'Oh dear God the Omniscient, preserve us your servants,' he muttered. 'We throw ourselves on your mercy.'

'He has turned away from us,' hissed Kari. 'Don't waste your time talking to God. Bend your mind to saving your family.'

Jesson felt the shame cascade through him. He moved towards them, mind starting to clear. Outside, the sound of horses was diminished for the moment though he could still hear running feet, shouts of fear and alarm and the shattering of thin timber further up the street to the north.

'We're in the right place,' he said, crouching in front of them and stroking his son's hair. 'If they pass by, we are safe from prying eyes. If they set a fire, we can escape back or front from here, out through the stock room and studio if we have to. We have our valuables with us. God will watch over us.' This last said staring into Kari's eyes, needing her to believe him.

'So all we can do is wait, is that it?'

'I am no fighter,' said Han. 'This is where we belong.'

There was a heavy thud from the adjoining shop. Through the wall, they could hear foreign voices and a dragging as of wood on stone. And unmistakeably, there was the crackle of flame.

'We will burn in here,' said Kari, desperate. 'Why didn't we run when the first attack came?'

He couldn't face her gaze. He straightened and backed away. 'We have to defend what is ours.'

'What with? You didn't take us out because you were too scared to move. And now we are trapped. Will your God save us from flame and blade?'

The shutters burst inwards, showering wood into the shop. The face of a raider was framed in the light, ringed by smoke and flame from across the street. He nodded in satisfaction, called behind him and hauled himself up and through the opening. Another two raiders beat down the wide front doors. Kari screamed and hugged Hanson to her. Han stepped in front of her. It was all he had left to do.

He raised his hands to fend them off.

'Leave them alone,' he said, voice trembling.

They didn't even pause. Dressed in light armour and riding cloaks they tramped across the short distance. One backhanded him across the side of the head and he fell into another's grip. He felt faint, the stench of sweat and oiled leather in his nostrils. He struggled but he was caught solid. The point of a blade in his side stilled him.

A raider leant down and barked an order into Kari's face. She was still screaming. He shouted the same words again and when she made no move, dragged the boy from her grasp and into the waiting arms of another.

'It'll be all right,' managed Han. 'Keep calm.' He felt tears on his cheeks. 'Please don't hurt my family,' he said. 'Please.'

The raider only dug the swordpoint in a little harder. His comrade slapped Kari once across the cheek to stop her screaming for her son. He took her face in one gauntleted hand and turned it left and right, grunting appreciatively.

'Let her go,' said Han, struggling anew. 'Take your hands off her, Tsardon bastard.'

The swordpoint broke his skin and edged in just a little way. The pain was extraordinary. Hot blood coursed down his side.

The raider grabbed Kari's dress at the neck, surely meaning to tear it away but instead he stood up, dragging her with him. He pushed her in front of him.

'Han help me!' she began to scream again. 'Help us!'

But Han couldn't move against the sword point. He watched helpless as his son and wife were herded from the shop and out into the street. Abruptly, the sword point was gone from his side. He spun in the raider's grasp, the Tsardon pushing him back. He glared into the trail-hardened face, bunched his fists and charged, yelling for his family.

The raider laughed and the pommel of his sword collided with Han's temple.

It was a full day's ride to Gull's Ford from Haroq City, the capital of Atreska. He had left his team poring over Atreska's books in fine detail before confirming the tax levy for the half-year. He should be with them. Atreska had been a member of the Estorean Conquord for less than six years and remained a difficult province.

The tax reporting system was inefficient and in the remote north and along the Gosland and Tsardon borders, significant resistance remained. The Atreskan collectors were happy to hinder where they could and as a result, Jhered had over five hundred Gatherers setting up and enforcing the admittedly complex system amidst the simmering civil war.

Incursions and raids from Tsard made his job all the more difficult and so he understood why he was being taken to Gull's Ford. But he'd seen it all before and he expected to neither hear nor see anything new this time around.

Jhered was riding with six of his people and fifty of Atreska's soldiers. The cavalry detachment was heavily armed and armoured and surely uncomfortable in the heat of the day. Lances were held upright with pennants fluttering from their tips. Bows were across backs and swords in scabbards. Polished greaves, vambraces, helms and cuirasses shone in the sun. Wagons were with them, bringing emergency supplies, a mobile forge and tent canvas for those rendered homeless. It was a show of support, strength and intent for any that cared to see. Thomal Yuran, Marshal Defender of Atreska, was a proud national and Jhered would have expected nothing less from him.

The two men rode at the head of the column, along the main highway from Haroq City to Tsard. Built for the armies of the Conquord, it ran close to Gull's Ford. Parched dense shrub land rolled away on both sides and the land rose gently ahead of them towards a shimmering horizon that was smudged with smoke to the left of the road. They were close to the small settlement now.

'It's a very peaceful place,' said Yuran abruptly, following a long period of silence. His voice, gruff and deep, was a little muffled by his helmet, which was tied too tightly under his chin, restricting his jaw movement.

Jhered looked across at him, riding bolt upright, brown eyes fixed ahead, and with sweat running down from underneath his plumed helmet. He respected Yuran for his loyalty to his people but was endlessly frustrated by his refusal to understand the effects Atreska's civil disturbance had on the wider Conquord. He had questioned Yuran's appointment exactly because of this introspection, this desire to remain apart from the empire. His fears had been overruled by the senate in Estorea, though he was certain the Advocate herself had her doubts. Shame.

'I am sure it is,' responded Jhered evenly. 'I still doubt the wisdom of bringing me here, Marshal Yuran. My visit is for three days only, during which time you have my ear for all your concerns. We will be spending two days on the road and throughout this one, you have barely spoken with me. Am I to understand this unfortunate township is your sole concern?'

Yuran turned to him, eyes narrowed.

'As always, I fear your puffed-up image of your own importance will stop you listening to the problems Atreska faces.'

Jhered kept his face impassive, letting Yuran give vent to his anxiety.

'I am bringing you to Gull's Ford because I believe that seeing how the Conquord is failing us will open your mind. Words you can ignore. Images you cannot.'

'I have seen the effects of raids and bandits more times than I care to, Thomal. I have fought more battles than you have seen years on God's earth. Like me, you must learn to accept such events as unfortunate steps on the difficult road to peace and stability.'

Yuran barked a short, bitter laugh. 'I would respect you if you were in any way an individual. Let your heart feel what we feel. Let your mouth respond with honesty, not with trite statements scratched by the quills of Advocacy clerks and politicians. Those people have never seen destruction. They have never seen war. They cannot understand our troubles. You have the capacity to help. It pains me that in the years I have known you, you have never exercised it.'

'Everything I say, I believe,' replied Jhered. 'And I work for what I believe. I am an agent of the Estorean Conquord and its Advocate. My work is unpopular with everyone but I have to live with that.' He shrugged. 'I'm a tax collector and so no one likes me. But it is nevertheless to the benefit of everyone that I do my work. Even those citizens of Gull's Ford. Even at a time like this.'

'You ask why I chose not to speak to you today? Perhaps you have your answer.'

'In that case, Marshal, I shall respect your desire for silence.'

Gull's Ford straddled the flat bottom and gentle slopes of a valley through which the River Gull ran north to south. It rose in the lakes region in the south of Gosland and emptied into the Tirronean Sea. The ford around which the township grew up was at the southern end of the settlement and had taken the principal trading route across the Gull east and west. With the arrival of the Estorean Conquord and the campaigns in Tsard, the river had been bridged with stone further downstream, providing surer and more direct access to the base of operations in enemy territory.

Gull's Ford had still managed to prosper in recent years, as Conquord armies bought supplies wholesale and traded booty from Tsard on a regular basis. Gull's Ford traders were linked to the markets in Haroq and were able to provide competitive pricing or trade goods that sold at a premium in the capital. But its good name had surely led to its targeting by the Tsardon.

Two days after the raid, responding to a messenger who had ridden an exhausted horse into Yuran's castle courtyard, the Atreskans and Jhered's people looked down on a ruined township. The destruction in Gull's Ford was widespread. Across the valley sides and beyond, cropland was blackened and destroyed. Villas stood in smouldering ruins, smoke rising into the clear blue sky. In the town itself, the path of the raiders was picked out by burned buildings, dark stains on the cobbles and a scattering of broken possessions: clothing, pottery, furniture. Some houses and streets had been completely ignored, the raiders concentrating on the main thoroughfares and the farmland. Barely an animal grazed. The air stank of ash and damp.

The town was quiet. Jhered could see people moving about the settlement, engaged in clearing up where they could. Any bodies had already been removed and presumably buried. There were a host of new flags outside the House of Masks, testament to the death that had visited so recently and so violently. He made a mental note to pray and turn earth at the House before he left.

Jhered rode into the township, acutely aware of his appearance. In contrast to the sparkling armour of the Atreskan cavalry, he and his people rode in clothes fitting for long periods on the road. His light chainmail shirt was worn over a leather undershirt, his trousers were in-sewn with leather and his cloak designed only to keep out the chill of clear nights. In his saddle bags he carried his seal and orders of office. At his waist was strapped a scabbarded Estorean gladius.

None of that would necessarily identify him but embroidered on the back of his cloak, on the sash he wore across his torso, and embossed on the round shields of his people was the sign of the Gatherers; arms encircling the crest of the Estorean Conquord and the family Del Aglios. The crest on its own was enough to engender mistrust in Atreska. For it to be encircled turned that mistrust to hostility in places like this.

Clear-up work was ceasing as the sight and sound of the column deflected attention from grim tasks. People started to gather. Yuran led them into the town's forum, dismounting and ordering his men do the same. Jhered and his charges followed suit. The Gatherers were cautious, grouping around their commander to protect him should that prove necessary. Jhered watched the citizens gather. There was no aggressive intent behind the move. They wanted to hear news. They wanted help and Marshal Defender Yuran was there to offer it. But there were no smiles of greeting and no gratitude on any of the grimy, exhausted faces. All they displayed with any clarity were loss, confusion and shock.

A middle-aged woman came forward. She rubbed ash-stained hands on a dress that had once been a deep green but which was now streaked and stained black. Her grey hair was tied back with a red and white headscarf. The lines on her face were mired with soot and her eyes were red-rimmed and bloodshot. She took Yuran's outstretched hand and linked fingers in the traditional Atreskan greeting.

'Marshal Defender Yuran, your presence is welcome.' She spared a disgusted glance for Jhered.

'Yet two days late. I salute your dead, Praetor Gorsal and will pray with your Reader at the House of Masks later. For now, tell me what you need of me.'

Gorsal's shoulders slumped. 'Where do I begin? We have had our houses, crops and businesses burned. We have had our people taken and our livestock driven off. We had no capacity to defend ourselves against the Tsardon. We were overwhelmed. Grown men and women were forced to turn and run from their homes. Our bravest have been slaughtered. Marshal, some of them have been burned to ashes and their cycles are finished. No more will they walk God's earth. There is such anger here. These were not murderers. They were innocents under the supposed protection of the Conquord.'

A murmur ran around the crowd. Jhered estimated over a hundred people had gathered. He made a small hand gesture, encouraging his people to relax. The mood was bitter and angry. It was a display Yuran seemed happy to encourage.

'I understand your frustrations, Lena,' said Yuran. 'I too was assured our borders were secure. All the forces I can spare are in our border forts. I am doing absolutely everything in my power to ensure the safety of all Atreskan people. But you understand the pressures I am under financially. Most of our standing legions are gone. You know how many Atreskans are even now on campaign deep inside Tsard. We debated it at council just ten days ago.'

'So what am I supposed to tell my people? That we must rise every day and hope the raiders don't return because if they do we are helpless to stop them? That the Conquord will not protect us? That our own rulers in Haroq City sit by, unable to provide us with the means to defend ourselves?'

The praetor's voice was rising and cracking, her desperation showing through. Behind her, the crowd shifted, muttering unhappily. Jhered caught the odd shouted insult. He cleared his throat. Yuran turned briefly.

'Are you certain you are achieving what you wish?' asked Jhered quietly. He clasped his hands across his chest.

'I am hearing my people,' said Yuran. 'Have respect.'

Jhered moved closer to Yuran pitching his voice to ensure the crowd could not hear him 'I mean no disrespect but to stir up anger is counterproductive. Better to inspect the damage with the praetor. Assess what must be done and then hear the town governors in the basilica. In accordance with protocol. Night will soon fall and I will not answer questions in front of a mob.'

'It is your ruinous taxation that has left us open to this attack,' hissed Gorsal. 'You are directly responsible for the deaths here.'

Jhered raised his chin, aware he loomed over both Yuran and the praetor. He raised one black-gloved finger and ticked it once at Gorsal.

'Such allegations will require substantiation. Fortunately, I have here experts to examine your books and point out errors and inefficiencies in your local economy. You may have had more opportunity for profit than you thought. But first things first, I am on a tour of your town and would see the damage firsthand and the effects it will have on the level of taxation we expect from you next half year.

'Should you wish to accuse me and the wider Conquord of any impropriety, do so within the confines of the basilica. We are at war. All must provide for its success. Now, I suggest we set our respective workforces to tasks more constructive than listening to our tiresome voices.'

He knew they would not defy him. You could only push the Gatherers so far, particularly their leader. Somewhere within their anger, they were impressed by his presence. Few enough people got to see Paul Jhered in the flesh, much less speak to him one to one. He had been the leader of the Gatherers for seventeen years now and at forty-seven was still a young man in the job. He had heard all the rumours about him and the one he played to most, his towering height, was also the one most given to outrageous exaggeration. One thing he wasn't was taller than a house. Sometimes, he wished he were.

He turned to his people, four men and two women. Five at the junior rank of addos, one recently promoted to appros. All relatively new to journeying to outlying settlements and suitably nervous.

'I will walk the town alone,' he said. 'All of you, begin examining the accounts and books. Undoubtedly you will hear tales of woe and hardship. Keep yourselves to the facts. Maintain vigilance and look for embellishment in the ledgers. Note down anything you suspect. What I want from you is an honest assessment of the level of taxation levied here and whether it really left them without the means to purchase defence.

'I will bring back my thoughts on the cost of rebuilding Gull's Ford, replanting and restocking. We can at least leave them with some supportive news about their levy for this half year, can we not?

'Any questions?' Heads shook. 'Good. Appros Harin, you know where my seal and orders are. Make sure you present them before asking for information. Do not bear arms. Go.'

'Sir.'

He watched them for a moment. Decent students, all of them. Harin was a man with the potential for high office should he last the exhausting pace of the Gatherer's life. Swinging away, Jhered took in the town from the viewpoint of the forum. He would need to tour the two central streets, both of which led into the forum. A visit to a villa on the valley side and the House of Masks would also be necessary. The work of two hours, no more. Then a long night listening to the wailings of people with no idea how the Conquord operated.

Jhered set off across the forum, gesturing people from his path and assuming Yuran and Gorsal would fall into step with him. Never a bad thing to have the local leaders trot to catch up. The good people of Gull's Ford might respect them but it was right they understood who was the real voice of authority. Atreska was a proud and powerful nation but it was foremost a servant of the Estorean Conquord.

He walked down the centre of a once neat cobbled street. Pavements and gutter were choked with debris, drains were clogged and the stains where blood had dried were cloaked by flies. Left and right, dark holes where windows had been were framed by smoke-blackened walls. Roofing tiles had cracked and tumbled in the heat of the fires that had ravaged building upon building along the terrace of shops and businesses.

The smells were as acrid and bitter as the mood of the citizenry. Pacing deliberately along the street, his metal-shod boots ringing on the cobbles, Jhered could call to mind the terror that had blown through Gull's Ford. These people were not soldiers. A most unfortunate event. By no means the first that had afflicted Atreska during the Tsardon campaign and certainly not the last.

'We are almost a hundred miles from the Tsardon border,' said Gorsal, reading his thoughts. 'We are only a day from Haroq. Yet they attacked us in broad daylight. The Tsardon were our friends. Your war has made them unnecessary enemies. I had people killed by those with whom they used to trade and drink. You know why they do it, don't you? And you know why they have said they will return.'

'Because they are desperate. It is a common enough tactic among those losing a war. Atreska employed it too. You are relatively new members of the Conquord. The scars of the wars that led to your annexation by Estorea are fresh in the minds of many. And they feel that they can undermine your faith in the Conquord by such actions.'

'With some success,' said Gorsal shortly, glancing up at Jhered and meeting his firm gaze. 'You felt the mood. What are we supposed to think? What are we supposed to do? Your hawks will find that the tax levied on us left us with no proper funds to maintain our militia. We relied on volunteers and rusting weapons. The results are all around you.'

Jhered was silent for a short time. 'I expect you to agree that you have never been more prosperous. That the Conquord has given you economic stability and a better potential to improve yourselves should that be your desire. And I expect you to believe that the Conquord will bring you peace and security.'

'When? I see no prosperity. And what good is it anyway to those burned to ashes?' Gorsal gestured at the ruins of the street. 'How many more times will we be chased from our homes, helpless to defend ourselves?'

Jhered stopped walking and faced her.

'I was brought up in a border state. I lived in a village that suffered raids. And like you, nobody asked me or my people whether we wanted to be a member of the Conquord. We were defeated in war, just as you and all the provinces of Atreska have been. Like me, you have to live with the reality and know that your futures are assured under the Conquord in a way they would never be with your haphazard trade and treaties with Tsard.

'The Conquord will provide. Until then, I regret your losses and those you may still suffer. Staffing border forts is not the only way to ensure safety. Mind that your ruler is genuinely giving you all the protection he can. That is his responsibility.'

Yuran choked, or sounded like it. Jhered gazed down at him, unwavering.

'You have something to say, Marshal?'

'Exchequer Jhered, I find your implication offensive.' Yuran's face was red in sunlight that was beginning to fade towards evening. 'My people know I do everything I can. I grieve for every one of them that dies on behalf of the Conquord while those that would defend them are pressed into campaign service in Tsard. Your attempts to sow suspicion are beneath contempt.'

Jhered smiled, a bleak expression. 'I merely want to ensure everyone receives that to which they are entitled. The Exchequer is an easy target for blame. I have simply asked that all angles be considered.'

They walked on, Jhered's experienced eye assessing damage and cost, his mind calculating, storing information. Perhaps this visit wasn't such a waste after all. This town had been hit hard, very hard for one so far from the border. It would suffer in the short term.

Yuran stalked just behind him, the waves of outrage washing from him. Praetor Gorsal walked to his left, a distance between them. She was tight-lipped, clearly not trusting herself to speak further.

A few yards ahead of them, a man shambled out into the street from a broken doorway. He was unshaven, filthy. His hair was lank and his face held a despair that touched Jhered's heart. He saw them, took them all in. His eyes settled on Jhered. His expression changed, darkened. He grabbed a piece of broken pottery and rushed at the Gatherer.

Gorsal froze, a cry stifled on her lips. Jhered swayed inside the intended blow and blocked hard with his left arm. The pottery shard flew away to shatter against the far wall. Jhered grabbed the man by his upper arms, holding him away. Phlegm sprayed into Jhered's face with every wailing word.

'She's gone because of you, you bastard. They're both gone. We only wanted to live in peace and because of you they've taken everything. All I loved is gone.' He relaxed just a little, the cords in his neck fading. 'Back. I just want them back. Where are they? They've taken my wife and son. You have to help me. You have to.'

The man sagged. Jhered hooked an arm around his neck and pulled him close. He was sobbing uncontrollably now, his body heavy with his pain. Jhered felt each shudder and clutched him tighter.

'Tsard will fall,' he said, his breath ruffling the man's hair. 'The Conquord will bring it to order and everything that has been taken will be returned. God will protect your loved ones. Believe in what I say. Trust the Advocate. Trust the Conquord.

'What is your name?'

'Jesson.' His voice was muffled in Jhered's chest. 'Han Jesson.'

'Be strong, Han Jesson. I am Paul Jhered. I am the Exchequer of the Gatherers and I speak for the Conquord. We will return your wife and son.'

He released Jesson into the arms of Praetor Gorsal. She was regarding him with an expression bordering on disbelief.

'This man should not be alone,' said Jhered. 'Listen to me. The only way to stop the raids is to conquer Tsard. That is where your taxes go, it is where your citizens are drafted. There will be peace and Atreska will bloom, its people taken to the heart of the Conquord. We are all in this battle. And we will prevail.

'Now, to the House of Masks. I must pray for the continuing cycles of those who have fallen.'

Chapter 6

'Settle down now, come on,' said Shela Hasi, clapping her hands.

Three of them had dissolved into laughter again and a smile even tugged at the corner of Gorian's mouth. Rare and welcome. Ten years old and so serious. It seemed he was coming to terms perhaps too early with what he was. Kessian didn't want the moment to end. But end it must and nerves were already picking away at his mind, though he would never let the children see them. Soon. It had to be soon. Today, God, please.

The four of them had walked with Shela and Kessian up the long slope to the orchard plateau above the harbour. It was, without doubt, the most glorious day of the year so far. The sun radiated down from an unbroken blue sky, a breeze off the bay keeping the temperature bearable.

From their peerless vantage point, they could see the sunlight dancing on the water between the fishing boats in the bay and reflecting from the bright painted sides of the clutch of merchantmen anchored a little way off shore. Up on the slopes behind Westfallen, sheep and cattle grazed or idled in the heat. On the terraces, crops swayed, lazy and almost ripe. It would be a fine harvest, just as Hesther had said it would be way back in the chill of early genasrise.

Kessian leaned back against the orange tree under which he sat, its shade welcome, its leaves rustling against ripening fruit. They were all sat out of the glare of the sun for the moment; even tanned skins could burn on a day like today. He looked at the young Ascendants while they gathered themselves under Shela's gentle chiding. All were dressed in light pastel-shaded tunics slashed with the red of the Ascendancy. They wore open sandals and wide-brimmed straw hats.

Gorian had stopped smiling now and a frown was deepening on his handsome young face. His pale blue eyes speared into his peers from beneath his mass of curled fair hair and his arms were crossed tight. Next to him, Mirron noticed his change of mood and sobered herself in impersonation. Kessian smiled.

'See that?' he said to Shela.

'I see it,' she said. 'Sweet, isn't it?'

'Very,' agreed Kessian. 'Come on now, you two. Arducius, Ossacer. Come on. Much to learn and I am an old man.'

The two boys tried to pay attention but the giggles were right behind their first words.

'Gorian. Our Father . . .' mimicked Ossacer in as deep a voice as he could muster. They two of them looked across at Gorian and submitted to another fit.

'They shouldn't laugh at me,' said Gorian.

'Oh, they aren't,' said Shela soothingly. 'It's just a silly joke about fathers, isn't it?'

'They are laughing at my name,' said Gorian, his voice suddenly chill. 'They are laughing at our history.'

Kessian looked hard at Gorian, searching for any sign he was mocking them.

'Well, perhaps they are, though they do not realise it,' said Kessian gently. He spared them a sharp glance which quelled their mirth. 'And perhaps they should have more regard for your feelings. But they mean no harm, do they?'

Gorian didn't react to the question. 'Gorian died a hero, and made us all possible. Arducius and Ossacer were both mere warriors. Both died in their sleep. Hardly heroic. Shall we laugh at them?'

'You do not have to die a hero's death to be a hero,' said Kessian. 'Your deeds throughout life determine the regard in which you are held.'

'Two old men,' said Gorian. 'Wetting the bed like newborns. Dying helpless like babies. That is worthy of laughter.'

And he did, clutching himself in imitation of Arducius and Ossacer earlier but stopping abruptly. Not because he knew he'd gone too far but to gauge their reactions. Kessian felt a cold anger settle on him. His hand tensed on the stick at his side.

Mirron's support had given way to confusion and the two boys looked to Kessian for justice. Any others would surely have pounced on Gorian. Not these two. Both so peaceable. Ossacer so frail and sickly and Arducius brittle, delicate of bone. And both woefully weak in comparison to their taunter's bold physique.

Kessian turned to Gorian. The boy gazed back, defiant. Too much. 'You do not insult the memories of the Ascendancy's heroes,' he allowed his voice, always powerful, to ring out across the orchard. The quartet in front of him flinched.

'But—' began Gorian, pointing to his right.

'Their poor joke was spoken with warmth and love. Your jibes sought to hurt and lessened the memories of our finest defenders. Learn the difference before you speak again.'

'I—'

'Do you think me such a feeble old man that you can talk back at will?' Kessian's eyes blazed. He could feel his limbs quivering. His voice boomed out. Echoes would be heard down in Genastro Bay. 'Do you consider yourself learned enough to challenge me? You are but ten and a sapling. I am one hundred and forty. I am the Father of the Echelon. The only member of the first strand still alive.' His voice dropped low. 'And I can assure you I have full control of my bladder.'

Mirron had a hand over her mouth. Gorian was swallowing tears, desperate to uphold his image.

'Now,' said Kessian, once more the gentle tutor. 'Let us never be unclear again. All of your names resound with glory through the history of the Ascendancy. Without all of your namesakes, none of us would be here. Instead our ancestors would be ashes, scattered by the Order of Omniscience to deny the continuance of their cycles under God.

'You are right, Gorian, that your ancestor was the Father of all the Ascendants. He was the one man who understood the pattern and committed everything he saw, heard and learned to parchment so that those who came after him could continue his work. He placed himself knowingly in the way of great threat. He effectively ranged himself against the Order, believing the Ascendancy to be the rightful evolution of people.

'But he was not a man alone. Mirron laid more false trails for those seeking to capture Gorian than you have had hot suppers. She loved and supported Gorian. She was his strength, the rock to which he tied his life. She drew the charts and diagrams that we use today. She took the huge risk of hiding all they had learned from prying, thieving eyes when Gorian was forced to flee and, ultimately, caught and murdered. If Gorian was the Father of the Ascendancy, Mirron was our Mother.'

He had their attention so utterly that it drew a smile to his lips. All of them, crosslegged and leaning forwards, sucking in all the information he gave to them. Once again, they were just children. In a moment, they would be something far, far more. He recognised the difficulty of the balance they had to strike every day. It would get no easier.

'But it is equally clear through all our writings, and the stories passed down through the generations, that none of the work would have been possible had it not been for the tireless efforts of Arducius and Ossacer. It was they who built the network of loyal men and women who reported on the movements of the Order. They who rode to the assistance of fledgling strand members under threat. They who stood side by side with Gorian in the Battle of Carao and they who facilitated his escape from the dungeons of Cirandon on the day before a supposed execution. And that at a time long before he came upon the most crucial knowledge that we now possess.

'Yes, Arducius and Ossacer died old men. But they died tended by those who loved them and in the knowledge that their lives had been spent making possible everything that has since come to pass. Most recently, the four of you. Though as you have seen, more have been born and five strand mothers are pregnant. We have high hopes.

'Heroes all. And you sit here because of their combined efforts. Do not forget that, and I will hear no more jibes, and no more jokes, however innocent you think them to be.' His smile broadened. 'You do understand me, don't you?'

'Yes, Father Kessian,' they chimed.

'Good. Now, to work.'

He saw the eagerness in their expressions and nodded his pleasure. They, like all strand members, had accepted their abilities without question. The problem had been explaining that not everyone had such talents and that they were valuable beyond measure. In generations to come, all should have some talent by right of birth. Surely, this was what God intended for His people on His earth. Until then . . .

'Today, I want you to try and think beyond that which comes

naturally to you.' Groans rang around the orchard. He held up his hands. 'I know, I know, it is as we have tried a hundred times, as you are so fond of telling me, but I felt we were close last time. Now, I know this tries your patience but remember, we are new at it too.' He threw up his hands. 'Who knows, in a few generations, this teaching should be as second nature to those who come to practise it. People like you, perhaps.'

Mirron raised her hand.

'Yes, my little one.'

'We don't understand. You won't tell us. Why must we seek other talents?'

'It is part of the learning for all of us. Mirron, you are a Firewalker the like of whom has never been seen before in the Ascendancy. Likewise, your brothers display their talents better than any.' He winked at Arducius. 'And we need another great Wind Harker, young man. The present one is getting very tired. But the teachings of Gorian say that a true Ascendant will display more. And that when they do, they will be able to manipulate their talents and the world around them. That will be the start.'

Kessian wasn't sure they understood but it seemed to placate them anyway.

'So, Mirron, why don't you begin. You needn't move. Here we are in the orange grove for a reason. These trees burst with life as does the grass around them. You can smell it, can't you? But can you really *feel* it? Place your hands on the ground. Lose yourself in what you feel beneath your fingertips. Tell me everything. But be honest. Guesswork will get us nowhere.'

'Why isn't Hesther here?' asked Ossacer. 'She could tell us what we are supposed to be searching for.'

'For precisely that reason, my young warrior,' said Kessian. 'If you have no clue you cannot be led. Everything you sense will be from your heart. Mirron, continue, please.'

Mirron looked quickly at Gorian before dropping her head, feeling herself blush under his intense gaze. She could sense them all as she placed her hands on the grass, its warmth pleasant on her fingertips. Father Kessian was speaking softly to her, encouraging her. As she had been taught, she cleared her mind of cluttering thoughts and tried to focus on the space immediately around her.

It was easy with fire. It had always been so. She felt a natural closeness to it and with her eyes closed saw images of flames wrapping around her, caressing her, keeping her safe. She could see pathways through fire and could sense where fire was causing critical damage just as she could see cool spots in a fire or in new forged steel. The blacksmith loved her.

So it should be with the earth beneath her feet and fingers. Mirron calmed herself, slowed and deepened her breathing. She spread her fingers across the grass, focusing on them, trying to feel the earth below them and the individual blades beneath her skin.

'Now,' said Kessian. 'Seek downwards to the energy that lies under the surface of the earth. That which binds everything and gives life to every plant that waves in the wind and grows under the guiding hand of the sun. What can you feel, Mirron, my child? Speak to us.'

Mirron tried. She wanted to know a worm was burrowing through the dirt. She wanted to feel the minute movement of roots as they sought new purchase, thickened and grew. She wanted to detect the tiniest drops of water feeding life into the soil. She wanted to know it was healthy, or that it was not.

She opened herself as she would to a fire, to let the energies flow through her. She poured herself into the land beneath her fingers. Nothing. Not a murmur, not a flicker. Her brow creased.

'I can't feel anything. Just the grass. It isn't working. I don't know what I should be feeling.'

It was pointless. She must look stupid. How could she be expected to sense what was going on down there. She was a Firewalker, not a Land Warden. She opened her eyes.

'Perhaps we aren't what you think we are,' said Arducius, the one always able to put her thoughts into words.

'You're just doing it wrong,' said Gorian, his tone dismissive.

'Then you try it,' snapped Mirron, feeling his words like a scratch on her heart.

'Patience, patience,' said Kessian, his voice soothing. 'Arducius, please, don't let a small setback upset you. Remember that you are all already the best in your fields and at such a tender age. You are special. But to learn more will take time. I'm afraid Gorian, the first Gorian, didn't say how long it would take for true Ascendancy to display itself.' His eyes settled on Gorian. 'There is no wrong way because we do not know the right way. But if you can show us, we would all be very, very happy. Please.'

Gorian smiled that smile attended by a sneer and began. But he could not do it either. Neither could Arducius, nor Ossacer. And though Father Kessian cajoled and encouraged them, told them again that they would succeed, today was not that day. So Mirron led them from the plateau, dispirited as the sun dipped below the cliff tops and the heat fell from the day.

That evening, Kessian ate with Genna, Hesther, Willem Geste and Andreas Koll. It was a sombre gathering, not helped by the constant bickering of the children in the courtyard gardens beyond the dining room windows.

Kessian looked out through the open frames, past the colonnades, and felt real doubt creep through him for the first time since they had been born. On a bench by one of the fountains, Shela sat and watched her charges. They had begun with a bragging match based on whose talent was of the greatest use. Harmless enough and debated for the thousandth time. Indeed, some of the reasons and statements they made had lightened the mood, such was their ludicrous nature.

'At least they demonstrate imaginations far beyond those of non-strand ten-year-olds,' said Genna.

'I particularly enjoyed the early warning of a tidal wave as counter-point to the saving of Westfallen from cattle plague,' agreed Willem Geste.

'Yes, catastrophes indeed,' said Kessian. 'And one to rival the hurricanes we also never see here. Still, Arducius is confident he can detect their development. We should all sleep more soundly as a result.'

The chuckles that had followed rang hollow now, cooling to memory with the night air, while the candles fluttered in a breeze that blew in the bickering voices ever louder. Kessian knew what they were thinking. It was inevitable.

'Is there any progress at all?' asked Andreas.

'On the face of it, I'd have to say not but we do not know what is truly developing in their minds and bodies,' said Kessian. 'Do any of you see signs of advancement?'

'We are of one mind,' said Hesther. 'We know their obvious talents but in terms of their ability to manipulate, not really.' She shrugged. 'How can we know but by demonstration?'

Kessian sagged. 'I work with them so hard, so carefully. But tell me, any of you. How on God's earth do we teach that which we do not know?'

There was a silence. Deep. Contemplative. Broken by a shout from Gorian, harsh and resonant. Kessian boiled.

'For God's sake, Shela, still those babbling children,' he bellowed, instantly regretting his words and volume. 'Please, a little peace.'

A hiatus. Silence for a moment followed by Shela's strong words. No complaint from the children. Kessian calmed himself before continuing.

'I'm sorry,' he said. 'Old man, little patience.'

Their words of comfort fell unheard.

'The question is, how long do we continue to try?' Willem sounded weary. Kessian knew how he felt.

'We have no choice but to continue trying until the Omniscient calls us back to the earth,' said Kessian. 'There is no written time limit after which Ascendancy cannot be reached. We have no precedent. What else can we do?'

Hesther rubbed her chin. 'Then we have to ask ourselves if our teaching methods are to blame?'

Willem laughed and spread his hands. 'How can we possibly know?' He refilled his wine goblet and passed the jug to his right. Hesther accepted it gratefully. 'I'd rather question whether we have missed something in Gorian's writings. Or indeed, whether he has made mistakes in his conclusions.'

'We must question everything we think we know,' said Kessian. 'And we must continue to adapt our teaching methods. But I have to give voice to that which we are all thinking. Are we simply wasting our time here? We are honour-bound to continue, but is it folly? Is there a future for the Ascendancy?'

This time the silence signified a shattering of illusion. A rude intrusion of reality. Kessian moved his hand to his wine goblet but it was shaking too much and he withdrew it. The mutton on his plate looked tainted, the sauce covering it sickly, the vegetable leaves curled and bitter. He looked into Genna's age-lined face. She tried to smile but it crumbled. She placed a hand on his forearm and squeezed.

'They are but young,' she said. 'Their minds are not formed. They are just children, Ardol. Give them time.'

'Every piece of evidence we have points to them being able to display genuine multiple talents by this time,' he said, his tired mind flashing with a thousand thoughts and none of them positive. 'We have been trying to tease them into it for three years now, ever since their primary talents matured.' He smiled. 'Remember the joy we felt then? How their understanding of their talents was so complete, so natural that we knew without any shadow of doubt that they were the first true Ascendants? Wonderful days.'

'And that's why you are right and we must not give up,' said Willem. 'Not ever. Ardol, your energy has sustained us all for decades and has burned so bright these last ten years it puts to shame people forty years your junior. I'm glad you have voiced your doubts and fears here tonight. And there is not one among us who hasn't felt as you feel now. But it must stop here, my very old friend. We cannot afford to let our doubts infect what we do. We have lived and worked too long to be beaten now. I speak for us all, Ardol. We stand behind you. We will bring these children to their destiny.

'And I know what you are thinking, and yes, we will do it before you return to the earth.'

Kessian felt his eyes fill with tears. He nodded his gratitude, unable to speak the words of thanks Willem deserved. These people, this Echelon, were stronger than he had ever imagined. He let their spirits lift his.

The sharp cry of a child cut through his thoughts and brought him back to himself. Kessian turned to the window. He could still see them in the courtyard, lit by candles floating in traps at the edges of the fountain pools. They were silhouettes against the light.

'Let go of him!' shouted Mirron, her voice high and trembling.

Arducius yelped in sudden pain. 'Please,' he said.

'You'll break his arm, you know you will,' said Mirron.

'Gorian, let him go right now,' ordered Shela.

'Make him say sorry,' said Gorian. 'Make him.'

'I will not,' said Arducius through tight lips, pain in his every word. 'I have nothing to be sorry for.'

'Then I will squeeze harder until you do.' Gorian's voice carried awful promise.

'Put him down right now.' Shela's tone was low and angry.

Kessian dragged himself to his feet. Willem thrust his stick into his hand. Andreas was leading them out into the courtyard.

'You're breaking it, you're breaking it!' yelled Mirron. 'Stop, Gorian, stop.'

Arducius howled in agony but still Gorian clung on.

'Gorian!' thundered Kessian, standing at the window.

There was a flash, a sudden tongue of flame leaping from the candles in the fountain behind Shela. Every one was extinguished. Gorian screamed and fell backwards, clutching at his hand. Arducius ran to Shela, his right arm held across his chest, broken no doubt. Ossacer was pointing at Mirron, mumbling something incoherent. Mirron was slumped on the lawn, shivering.

Kessian stepped over the sill and hurried into the garden. Hesther had run to Mirron, Willem and Andreas to Gorian.

'What happened,' demanded Kessian. 'What happened here?' He bent and placed a hand on Ossacer's shoulder.

'Ossacer,' he said. 'What happened. Did you see?'

The boy looked up at him, face blank with his shock, his eyes huge in the half-light, blinking rapidly. His lips were quivering.

'Dear God,' he whispered. 'Genna, come and see to Ossacer. Warm blankets, hot drink. Quickly. Try and get him to talk.'

Kessian turned. Gorian was sitting up in Andreas's arms, breathing hard and staring at Mirron who was crying in Hesther's embrace. Willem was examining Gorian's hand.

'It's burned,' he said, his voice carrying a mixture of wonder and disbelief.

'She did it,' said Gorian, sniffing. 'Mirron did it. She burned me.'

He was badly frightened and when Mirron moved her head to look at him, he tried to back away into Andreas's body.

'You wouldn't let go,' sobbed Mirron. 'I only wanted you to stop. I'm sorry, Gorian.'

'You burned me,' said Gorian. 'How can that be?'

Kessian caught Willem's gaze and had to fight hard to keep the smile from his face. This was a most unfortunate incident but what it represented could not be understated. Decisions. Decisions.

'Shela, take Ossacer. Genna, take Arducius to the physician. His arm will need setting and splinting. You can direct him to the centre of the pain. Try and speak to him, find out what he saw or felt. Andreas, let's get a dressing on Gorian's wound. I have some burn salve in the cabinet by my wash bowl. All these children sleep apart from each other tonight.'

He knelt by Mirron and Hesther, feeling his old bones creaking and protesting. Someone would have to help him up.

'Now, Mirron, do you know what happened? Try and tell me what you did.'

Mirron turned her tearstained face to his. It was very pale, very scared. He smoothed her hair and she snuggled a little tighter to Hesther.

'It's all right, my little one,' he whispered. 'No one is angry with you.'

'Gorian is,' she said in a tiny cracked whisper.

Kessian smiled. 'Yes, perhaps he is. But he will forgive you. Now, can you tell me what happened?'

She sniffed and dragged a hand across her nose and mouth. 'He wouldn't let Arducius go. He knew he was hurting him but he wouldn't stop. All I wanted him to do was stop.'

'I know, Mirron, and you should always protect your brothers. Can you tell me what happened in your mind?'

She was silent for a while, trying to unravel her thoughts. Kessian felt his heart burgeoning with hope.

'The flames spoke to me,' she said eventually. 'I could feel them warm me.'

Kessian glanced back to the fountain and its smoking dead candles. It was a good ten feet away. 'And what happened next?'

She frowned. 'It was bad.'

'What was?'

'I knew the flame would hurt Gorian. He isn't a Firewalker yet. But the candles were too far away and Arducius was crying. Gorian was breaking his arm.' She began to sob again and Hesther hugged her close.

'Shhh,' she said. 'Shhh. It's all right.'

'You had to stop him, didn't you?' said Kessian. Mirron managed a nod. 'And you thought that if he felt a flame, he would let go?' Another nod. 'Well, what could you do, eh?' He smiled down at her and she looked at him as if he was stupid, her face clear now, certainty in her eyes.

'I gathered all the candle flames up and threw them at him,' she said.

Kessian leaned back. It had begun.

Chapter 7

844th cycle of God, 41st day of Solasrise
11th year of the true Ascendancy

Mirron awoke from a sleep plagued by nightmares to a bitter feeling deep in the pit of her stomach. Beyond her shutters she could hear the sounds of gulls. Strong, hot sunlight forced its way through the gaps in the slats. Westfallen was alive and perfect once again.

Yesterday, she would have sprung from her bed, pausing only to belt on her tunic before rushing out to glory in the day. But that was yesterday. Today her head pounded, her stomach writhed with sickness and in her mind she replayed the events of last night over and over again.

She felt as if something had been taken from her and that today she was different. She felt altered somehow and it confused her. She fought to be who she had been but it would not come. Instead, she saw the lance of flame spring from the fountain candles and burn into Gorian's wrist. She saw it all, the wreathing of the fire and the damage it had done, in the most minute detail. She could still smell the stink of burned hair and skin and she was horribly aware of the damage the flame had done. Gorian would be scarred forever. He would never forgive her and she would never forgive herself.

There were tears on her cheeks again. They had all lied to her. Father Kessian, Willem, Hesther. Even her own mother. They had told her that the Ascendancy was something wonderful, that it was the future of everyone and would bring all closer to God. But it was not. She knew what she had done was to do with her birthright but it had not been beautiful or peaceful. It had caused harm.

The first time anyone had been able to use their talent in the way she had and someone had got hurt. And not just anyone. Gorian. The last person in the whole world she would see hurt, and she had done it. And at the time, she had meant it too. What she had done scared her. What would happen the next time?

There shouldn't ever be a next time. She turned her head into her pillow and began to cry. There was a soft knock on her door.

'Go away!' she wailed.

She heard the handle turn and the door open. Fresh air flooded in. She turned.

'I told you to go a—' It was Father Kessian. 'I thought you were my mother.'

'And is that how you speak to your mother, my child? She loves you and only wants the very best for you. You know that, don't you?'

She shook her head. 'Why did she lie to me? Why did all of you lie?'

Kessian frowned and came into the room, pulling up her bedside chair and sitting on it. He looked very old in the half-light, his skin all folded and wrinkled. But his eyes were warm and he melted her with his smile as he always had done.

'Why do you think we lied?' he asked. He placed a hand over his heart. 'I would be hurt if I thought that was what I had done.'

'You told me I would be a person who was good because I am a true Ascendant. But I have burned Gorian and made him hate me forever. I don't want to be an Ascendant any more.'

Kessian leaned forward and smoothed away her tears with his thumb. 'Oh, my child, I know you must be feeling very upset this morning. None of us wish harm on those we love but sometimes our frustration leads us to hurt them anyway, through words or actions.

'You must try to think that you acted with the best thoughts in your heart. You wanted to stop Gorian hurting Arducius and you did that. But in doing so you did something you wish you hadn't. You can't change that but you must not hate yourself because it happened.'

'It won't happen again, I promise. I will never touch the fire again.'

Kessian leaned back. 'And that would sadden me more than anything else. Mirron, you are a treasured daughter of the Ascendancy. And in your action last night, something truly momentous and wonderful happened.'

'I hurt him!' Mirron shouted. Gorian's blistered, red wrist was large in her mind's eye again.

'And he will heal. He is strong. But you cannot turn your back on what you are. It's difficult, I know. You are so young, so innocent. But you must help us to understand how you did what you did so that we can help you control it and help your brothers make it happen. Do you not see?'

'No one should have it,' she said, confused by his tone and the sense of what he was saying. Her heart was beating fast. He couldn't really want her to try again, could he? Not after what she had done. 'It's dangerous.'

'Yes, it is,' said Kessian. 'Unless it is controlled. And when we all understand it, you and your brothers can make it work to help and to heal. To do all those things people want and need. And then you will be happy with what you are. It will happen, I promise.'

She shook her head again. 'I can't, Father Kessian. I'm scared.' She felt tears welling up again.

'I know, little one. And if I'm honest, we are all a bit scared. You gave us quite a fright.' He smiled. 'Tell you what, I've brought someone who wants to see you. Perhaps he can help you. Come in, Gorian.'

And in he came. Tall and handsome though he looked very tired. A smile was on his lips, his bright blue tunic was clean and freshly pressed, and his hair clean and shining. She wished she had hair like that. Curls were lovely. Her eyes fell to his arm and she felt herself crumple. A bandage ran from the centre of his palm all the way up to his elbow. She realised she had still been clinging to the hope that it hadn't been as bad as she remembered in her nightmares. But it was.

'Hello, Mirron, how are you feeling?'

She burst into tears. Gorian looked at Kessian who ushered him forward. He moved to the bed and put his hand on her arm. She felt the bandage against her skin. She looked at him.

'I'm sorry, Gorian,' she managed, through her sobs.

Kessian had found a handkerchief and passed it to Gorian who handed it on to her. 'Thank you,' she said.

'I know you're sorry,' said Gorian. 'I know you didn't really mean to hurt me. I know you just wanted to help Arducius. I've said sorry to him.' He dropped his gaze. 'His arm is broken.'

'You shouldn't have done that,' said Mirron, wiping at her eyes.

Gorian's head snapped back up. 'And you . . . We were both wrong last night. Arducius says he forgives me. I forgive you.'

Relief cascaded through Mirron then, as if she were standing under a fall of pure water. She felt refreshed where she had felt dirty.

'I prayed you would say that.'

'We all want to be able to do what you did . . . no, I don't mean that. I mean, to be able to use our talents. Perhaps it might help us to discover new ones. I can help you to understand. We all can. Please, Mirron. Come out and play. Father Kessian says we don't have to learn today.'

Mirron smiled and this time her tears were of happiness. He really did forgive her. She breathed deeply, the fresh air making her feel alive.

'Yes, all right. Let me get dressed. I'm hungry too.'

Gorian stood and she caught the look in his eye. It was strange, not warm and happy. Relieved, perhaps. 'I'm glad. I'll see you in the courtyard. Perhaps we can go swimming.'

'If Jen comes with us.'

'I'll go and ask her.'

He ran out of her bedroom and Mirron heard his footsteps echoing away on the marble floor of the villa. Kessian pushed himself to his feet and bent to kiss her forehead.

'Thank you, Mirron. You know you're very grown up for one so young.'

She giggled and squirmed.

'And remember, we will always be with you to help you and support you. You and your brothers are such treasures. We won't let anything happen to you.'

Mirron beamed at him. Perhaps today would be like yesterday after all.

Over the next few days, while Westfallen worked and traded under a beautiful, cloudless sky, Kessian and the Echelon began to understand the workings of the true Ascendant mind. Kessian had sent a message to Marshal Defender Vasselis the morning after the incident in the courtyard and their ruler was on his way from Cirandon even now, to see the progress for himself. He was bringing his wife and son with him, having decided to take a short holiday in the tranquillity of the village.

It added an element of pressure as Kessian had no real certainty that Mirron would be able to communicate her experience effectively or indeed repeat it. But, having consulted Gorian's papers extensively throughout that first night, he was convinced that once a breakthrough was made, as Gorian had written; "There can be no denial of the awakening ability by practitioner or witnesses. It will become as natural as the act of breathing. All that is needed is time for expression."

As it happened, not a great deal of time was needed. After the day's rest, where they had witnessed something of a transformation in Gorian's attitude to his siblings, Kessian had taken them all to the main forge just to the north of the forum. There was a little risk involved, given the numbers of traders in for the solastro high festival, but they could close themselves off effectively enough for it to be no real problem. Only Ossacer had stayed at home. His shock at what he had seen had run deeper than that of his peers and his deeply flawed constitution had let him down again. Subsequently, he was running a worrying fever.

Bryn Marr, Westfallen's blacksmith, was a burly, powerful man, moving into his middle years, with a habitual scowl. A Firewalker himself in his early years, he had fathered children of the seventh and eighth strands and was to be a father again in the eleventh.

His family roots lay deep in the Ascendancy. He was a trusted and dedicated servant but embittered that his seed had yielded nothing but fleeting talent. Even so, he and Willem had schooled Mirron as her talent had burgeoned. At ten years old, she was far beyond him. Kessian wondered what he would make of her now.

Bryn was ready for them, the Echelon and the three young Ascendants. He had cleared as much space as he could from around the stone-clad forge fire. Tools were stacked in boxes. Pieces of iron and steel work were gathered in the fenced yard. Despite its open sides, the forge was extremely hot and choked with the heady scents of charcoal and peat. Kessian was forced to admit he would need a chair, Willem and Genna likewise.

'We'd better get this done,' said Bryn testily, wiping his filthy hands on an equally filthy cloth. 'We'll be drawing a crowd before long.'

Kessian leaned forwards in his chair, hands on the pommel of the stick held under his chin. 'Mirron, are you ready to try?'

Mirron was standing next to Gorian and Arducius, both boys bandaged around their damaged arms. She looked nervous, pale around the eyes. Although she had agreed she would try to help them understand how she had performed her manipulation of the candle flames, she had shied from it. Her normally bubbly personality had been submerged beneath anxiety and a growing sense of shock. Kessian understood she felt out of control of her own actions and it had taken a full day for him to persuade her to come here; that what she had done was a natural progression. He was not at all sure she really believed them.

She looked at him and her nod of assent was tiny and frightened.

'Step forward, then, come close to the fire. After all, you know it won't hurt you.' His comment was rewarded with a brief small smile.

She stepped up to the forge. The charcoals glowed orange. Occasional flame licked over them, their smoke funnelled out of the forge and into the clear sky. Bryn held out a huge hand and she took it.

'So, my pretty student, what is it you've come to show me?' he asked, voice soft but still gruff.

She glanced again at Kessian. 'What should I do, Father?'

'Try to tease flame from the charcoals. Hold it in your hands if you can. Direct it if you feel strong enough. But do nothing that makes you feel you can't control it.'

'It all feels like that,' she said.

'You know what I mean.'

Bryn had raised his eyebrows, sceptical. His expression was shared by those of the Echelon who had not been present in the courtyard gardens.

'I'll try,' said Mirron.

'Good girl,' said Kessian. 'Take your time.'

He found his heart beating fast as Mirron faced the forge. She stood on a stool to allow her to look down on the fire, Bryn standing close behind her, protective though he needn't be. She was standing side-on to Kessian, wearing a sleeveless dress and with her hair tied back out of her eyes. She moved her hands towards the fire. Kessian lost sight of them at the lip of the forge, just as they entered the charcoals.

A calm expression settled on Mirron's face while she prepared. Genna clutched Kessian's hands on top of his stick. Hesther was behind him, her hands on his shoulders. He ignored the sweat forming on his face and body, praying Mirron could repeat her display.

'I am one with the fire,' she said. 'I understand its strength. The charcoals are of high standard, Bryn, but your peat is spread a little thick left centre of the forge. There is a cool spot there. Let me just . . .' She moved her hands. Kessian heard the grate of charcoals. 'There. Fit for steel.'

'Thank you,' said Bryn. He smiled, a little embarrassed.

'The heat map is even,' continued Mirron.

She withdrew her hands and the mask of calm slipped. She was thinking about what she must next attempt. She scratched at her upper lip with her teeth and breathed deep. Kessian saw the shudder through her body. She swayed slightly. Bryn placed a hand on her back to steady her.

Mirron closed her eyes, snapping them open almost immediately. The fire glowed hotter, reflecting bright across the roof of the forge. Everyone took an unconscious pace away and Kessian leaned back in his chair. He watched Mirron's face intently. He saw fear flash across it followed by a curious serenity. Her eyes widened and her body relaxed.

Mirron drew her hands slowly away from the charcoals, palms downwards. The temperature rose in the forge. Tongues of flame followed her hands, wreathing them, caressing them it seemed, bathing them in a warm orange light. Kessian leaned forward again, breath stopped on his lips. The heat in him now had little to do with the forge and everything to do with the sense of wonder that swept through him. The swiftest of glances revealed a breadth of emotions among the Echelon and sheer joy on the faces of Gorian and Arducius.

The flame licked up Mirron's forearms, tracing the pathways of her nerves or veins perhaps. She appeared completely in control. She turned her palms to face each other. Flame spanned the gap of perhaps two feet between them. It steadied, thickened into a tubular shape, fed by the fire beneath it. Mirron moved her hands delicately, causing the tube to distend then curve upwards. The young Ascendant licked her lips.

'Can you tell us how you are feeling and what you can see?' asked Kessian.

Mirron rocked on the stool. The flame guttered and fell away. She sagged back into Bryn's arms.

'Oh, my child, I am sorry,' said Kessian. 'I disturbed your concentration.'

Mirron gazed at him, her expression a little detached but intensely satisfied.

'I tried to talk but the flame wouldn't stay,' she said. 'It was beautiful.'

'It was indeed,' said Kessian.

'No,' she said. 'Inside.'

'What do you mean?'

'In my body and in my head. I could see paths in the air and through the ground.'

Kessian's throat dried. It was a direct quote from Gorian's writings. His theory about what an Ascendant would see. Hesther's hands tightened on his shoulders.

'Are you sure?' he whispered, voice almost lost in the roar of the forge.

Mirron nodded. 'Am I all right?' she asked, voice trembling.

Kessian chuckled. 'Oh, my dear I think you are very much more than that.'

Bryn placed Mirron back on the floor and pushed her gently but firmly towards Kessian. The blacksmith cupped his hands together at his chest in the traditional Order of Omniscience encompassing sign. The Father frowned. 'Bryn, that's a little . . .'

He stopped when he saw Bryn's face. He'd seen that expression on Ossacer's face just a couple of nights before.

Dread fear.

Chapter 8

844th cycle of God, 42nd day of Solasrise
11th year of the true Ascendancy

Every day for Han Jesson had been dark. The chill of loneliness engulfing him every time he awoke and taunting him every time he tried to close his eyes. The memories of that hideous day in Gull's Ford a year ago would not go away. The terror in his wife's eyes, her mute shock and screaming helplessness. The wails of his son. The blood across his street, and the bodies of people he had known for thirty years. The choking smell of burning. It was everywhere he walked, in every face he saw and in the dark scars on buildings that would never be repainted.

Those first days were vague. A despair so deep he barely registered living. He could recall but two things from them. The word 'gone' thundering through his muddled mind; and the tall man. The Gatherer.

The man who had promised him he would return his family to him. And though Jhered wrote to him at each levy time, he had no real news. Gave him no particular hope to cling onto. The letters were like reading reports on the war. They were disassociated from his pain.

Every day, Han walked to the east of the village and up to the crest of the valley where he would sit. Through the blistering heat of solastro, the shocking cold of dusas and the freshness of genastro, he made his short pilgrimage. And while he sat, the world passed him by.

Crops grew, were harvested and stored. New livestock was driven into the settlement. The sound of hammer and saw echoed up the valley, mixed with the shouts of men and the excitable chatter of children. Traders came and went. The legion wagons rattled through the streets, buying supplies on their way to the Tsardon front and selling spoils on the way back. The Gatherers came back too. Not the tall man this time but others. Assessing their progress, demanding a rise in the levy based on what they saw. And the civil war came ever closer to them.

But no sign of his family. No news but that the campaigns progressed and one day the Tsardon ruling dynasty would fall and reparations would begin. 'One day' was no good to Han Jesson. It was meaningless. And for every day that it did not come, his hope leached away.

It was late evening and the day had been searing hot with barely a puff of breeze to move the air. Han had been sitting in the shade of rock and tree for the larger part of the day, watching the hills to the east, the shimmer over the road to the south and the scattered river traffic. He'd seen riders moving in the distance in the late morning, impossible to say how many. Almost certainly Conquord cavalry though whenever he saw and heard bands of riders now, he shivered, his memories surfacing sharp and painful.

When the sunlight was gone, Han made his way back down the well-trodden path. In the early days he had lit fires for beacons and sat by them all night. But he had to live and maintain his business if his family were to have anything to return home to enjoy. So he lit the lanterns outside his repaired shop front and walked inside. Those lights would burn until dawn, just in case.

He shuffled about his workshop, lighting candles and more lanterns. He'd kept the shutters closed all day and the shop was relatively cool though the heat of solas had permeated his tiles and whitewashed walls. It was a small house with the workspaces dominating the ground floor while up the single flight of stairs were living and sleeping areas and a roof terrace. But it felt cavernous and his every movement echoed sadly from the stained walls.

He rubbed his hands over his face, the action reminding him he needed to shave. Just one more thing, like enjoying food, that seemed so unimportant. Most days he had to remind himself to keep going, to try to live as normal a life as he was able so that he was ready when they came home. Though when even bathing and washing his clothes were chores all but beyond him, it was a difficult reminder to fulfil.

Out in his back yard he could feel the heat from the kiln that he fired every night. Scattered about its base was the wreckage of too many cracked pots and vases. He unhooked the kiln door and opened it, feeling the wash of hot air over his face and arms.

He picked the two sets of tongs up from their rack and dragged the stone tray towards him, hooking its iron handles and laying it on the ground to cool. He cast his eyes briefly over the assortment of plates and mugs he had been asked to make, sighing at the breakages that told of the lack of attention to his clay mix and the variation in the thickness of the work he was trying to fire. He could see bubbles in the clay too. Nothing seemed to work any more, not how it should.

Han worked the same routine into the early hours of every morning, knowing he had to be exhausted to stop the voices keeping him from sleep. Take out last night's work; refire the kiln; sit at the wheel to make new orders; and decorate the fired work, what was left of it.

It was that last that drew tears from him more often than not. Kari had been the artist, he the potter. Without her, the vases, plates, jugs and mugs that were his stock in trade were plain and clumsy-looking. He couldn't be proud of anything he made now and he was dimly aware that the orders he was getting had more to do with the desire of Gull's Ford to look after its own than for any thought of selling on for profit in Haroq.

But as God-around-them-all was his witness, he could do nothing else. He hoped they understood that. He fell asleep at the paints and glaze that night. He'd eaten nothing all day, drunk a little too much wine and the heat eventually took its toll.

He awoke with a start, unsure what had awakened him. The night was warm and humid. He looked up at the stars, guessing it was a couple of hours before dawn. He had a slight headache and a thirst but neither of these was sufficient to have brought him round. It had been a dead, deep sleep, sprawled across the table. His paint brush was still in his hands, its tip red in the bright light from the lanterns set at the back corners.

He sat up and stretched his back. There was a glow in the sky to the north, a fire of some sort. Then the screams repeated and he knew why he had woken and the reason for the fire. He had heard that sort of fear before and remembered it like it was yesterday.

Dread crushed his gut and chest, left him fighting for breath. He was frozen to his chair while the sound of feet and hoofs gained in volume, matching that of the panicked voices and the wails of terror.

It couldn't be happening again. They'd already taken everything in Gull's Ford once. Not again, he whispered, God have mercy, please not again.

Han fought himself to a standing position. His body was shaking and his mind was blank, numb. His breathing shallow and very quick. He tried to calm himself, leaning hard on the back of the chair. He swallowed on a dry throat and blinked away the tears that had welled up. He had no idea what to do. Nothing suggested itself.

From out in the road, he heard the clatter of horses and the harsh shouts of the Tsardon. The yells and cries of the citizens of Gull's Ford grew louder still, more and more of them on the streets outside. The glow in the northern sky grew brighter and in a moment's lull, he heard the crackle of flames and a ragged cheer.

Han turned from the painting table. There was quiet in the street outside his front door and he moved towards it gingerly. There was something very different in the tenor of this raid. Before, in the glare of daylight, the Tsardon had attacked at random. Whole areas of the town had been totally ignored that time, while some houses in other streets had been destroyed, others passed by and others, like his own, damaged only enough to take the prize of his wife and son before attention went elsewhere.

He stopped and pressed his ear to the shutters, confused at what he was hearing. There was still a hubbub but it was passing away towards the north, leaving something surrounding him that he couldn't place. He cracked the shutters as quietly as he could to see out. He looked first to his left and his breath caught in the back of his throat. He switched sides and looked right and south. The same. He closed and hooked the shutters, backing away.

Tsardon. Approaching from both directions and riding down the centre of the street with swordsmen to either side, kicking in every door. Jesson shrank away, vision blurring. His lanterns were a welcome for his enemies. His door would burst in like it had before and they'd drag him away like they had his wife and child. He couldn't let that happen. He had to be here when she returned.

The thought cleared his head of the fog which had encased it. There was no time to grab anything. He was dressed and that would have to do. He ran back through the shop, out into the yard, past the kiln and to the wooden shelving attached to the back wall. It used to be filled with works awaiting decoration. Now it stood empty but it might just save his life.

Han scrambled up the racks, feeling the timbers give under his weight, hearing them protest their treatment, the sound awfully loud in his ears. Reaching the top shelf, he jumped with hands outstretched to grasp the lip of the roof terrace above him. Praetor Gorsal's house. She wouldn't begrudge him this chance to escape.

Behind him, his door was beaten in. Shouts ran through his shop and the noise from the street was much louder. Using it as a spur, he pulled and scrabbled, dragging his body onto Gorsal's terrace. He rolled once, gathered his breath and ran to the stairs underneath the sun porch. The quickest of glances behind him told him they had not seen him; there was no one in the yard.

Gorsal's house was dark and empty. His sandals whispered on the stone and his hand brushed the wall to give him balance. Below, a wan light washed the small hallway. He knew he shouldn't but he felt relief that the Tsardon had already been here and taken any they had found inside.

The door had been forced and Gorsal's collection of amphorae and vases from across the Conquord was smashed and scattered across the floor, clubbed from the alcove stands where they had stood so proudly. One of his own was among the debris, the fragments crushing under his feet on his way to the door.

His heart was hammering loud enough for the Tsardon to hear; it was painful in his chest. The quake in his limbs was back. He stopped. Surely he should hide here. The house had been cleared, there was no reason to risk running outside. He'd be safe. New hope flooded through his body.

He backed up a pace. He could hear the drone of noise that indicated where the citizens had been taken. Away north towards the fire and the House of Masks. He turned, thinking to hide up the stairs, perhaps under a bed. Two Tsardon stood at the head of the short stairway, hard eyes boring through him. Han closed his eyes and sagged to the floor. There was no escape.

They didn't kill him. Instead they pushed him into the street and herded him to the north of the town with others who had so nearly slipped the net. The fire resolved itself as the Reader's house, adjacent to the House of Masks. The two-storey building was engulfed. Stone glowed red, the last of the timbers were cracking in the intense heat and the roof tiles had long since collapsed into the body of the house.

In front of the blaze, the Reader stared mute at the destruction. He was flanked by Tsardon who held his arms at his sides though he made no attempt to resist. And assembled on the prayer grass in front of the House of Masks was the entire citizenry of Gull's Ford.

Jesson was pushed into the silent mass. He could feel the anxiety deepening as it swept through them. He caught sight of frightened eyes, wringing hands and quivering lips, ghastly in the light of the fire. People clung to each other for support and searched each other's faces for comfort and comprehension. Quiet sobbing surrounded him. He was sweating; the fire and the night unbearably hot. His mouth was dry and his throat tight. He didn't think he could have spoken even if he had found words. Whatever was going to happen to them, he just wanted it to be over quickly.

Tsardon horsemen with torches surrounded them on three sides. Ahead, the view of the blaze and those before it were unobstructed. The Reader had been moved and now stood adjacent to the offerings table where so recently, gifts of fruit, fish and meat had decorated its surface for the solasrise festival. Now it was cleared, its polished white marble surface, black-veined, reflecting the firelight, garish and mesmerising.

Three Tsardon moved to stand in front of the table. All were tall men, shaven-headed and bearded. Their leather jerkins were studded with steel and each wore a long, curved sword on the right hip. They studied the citizens of Gull's Ford dispassionately.

'You were warned,' said the man in the centre, his voice heavily accented. 'You were told to renounce the Conquord and its false God. You were told to take our words to your Marshal. Either you did not speak or he did not listen and now you must accept the consequences of the choice you have made.'

A shifting in the crowd.

'The Conquord is a blight on our world and its peoples are our enemies. Its faith is weak. It has prosecuted an unjust war against Tsard and we will not fall before its legions. Look at where we stand now. Estorea cannot protect you. Its God cannot protect you.'

He turned and spat on the table.

'Tell your Marshal Yuran what you see and hear in Gull's Ford tonight. Make him understand that you will not remain in the

Conquord, that you want your independence back. We are the power here. We are your neighbours and we were your friends. Ask yourselves, did we raid and kill before the Conquord came? Yet you betrayed us and your Gods to join them.'

He shook his head.

'And where are your protectors now? They sit in their great palaces counting the money they have taken from you and make themselves blind to your vulnerability. What the eye does not see does not weigh on the conscience. They promise you everything and they give you nothing. I do not understand why you remain faithful to them. Why you don't resist them like more and more of your countrymen are doing. It would save you from this.'

'Please.' Lena Gorsal raised her voice above the fear. 'I know you. We have taken bread and wine together, Sentor Rensaark. You are not an evil man. Don't do this. You mustn't.'

'It's too late, Lena,' said Rensaark. 'I warned you. I have begged you in years gone by. But you have proved deaf to my words. Now, I do what I must.'

'The Conquord will provide!' shouted the Reader, voice clear and unwavering. 'God will protect you all. His—'

A Tsardon fist thumped into his gut and he doubled over. He was forced to his knees, his head pushed forward to face the ground.

'You cannot silence me.' The Reader's voice was choked with pain and dust. 'Join me in prayer: Under the skies and above the soil; across the waves and on the mountain's peak, we bask in the glory of your creation . . .'

A few muttered voices joined the prayer. Rensaark strode to the kneeling man and lashed a kick into his face. A spray of blood flew and the prayer was halted. At a nod the Reader was hauled back to his feet. The Tsardon grabbed his bloodied mouth in one gloved hand.

'Let your God save you. If he is able.'

Another nod. Four raiders carrying torches ran into the House of Masks. Han froze. Quickly, the flames sprang up, feasting on the drapes, tapestries and wooden racks that held the masks of the recent dead. The raiders retreated. Fire spread upwards into the rafters. Smoke began to billow from the top of the doorway. Han saw the Reader mouthing a silent prayer against the desecration.

A third nod. The Reader was bundled towards the gathering

inferno. He made no attempt to struggle and his words once again rang out across the prayer grass.

'Forgive those who destroy because they are blind to your light and mercy. Save those who stand in your presence. Though I go to the devils in the wind, my ashes denying me the warmth of your return-ing embrace, I go knowing your strength will guide those who yet live.'

He was shoved inside and the door pulled shut. A spear was pushed through the handle and braced against the door frame. People were screaming and shouting in the crowd. Gorsal led a movement forward but the riders pressed in from the sides, forcing the citizens back hard.

The roar of the flames was muted within the windowless building. Han could hear the Reader shouting his prayers through the coughs that racked his body. There was no attempt to escape. The door didn't thud in its frame, there was no beating on the walls.

Han joined with other citizens, praying for the Reader who was being stolen from God, never to return to the earth. With their tears staining their cheeks, they prayed until the Reader's shouts became choking screams torn from his lips and, mercifully soon, stopped altogether.

There was silence among the citizenry, against the backdrop of crackling flames and the shifting of horses.

'That was unforgivable, Sentor,' said Gorsal when the Tsardon faced them once more. 'That man was not your enemy. We are not your enemies.' Her voice was thick with emotion.

Jesson nodded his agreement, helpless anger boiling through him.

'Any who live by choice under the banner of the Estorean Con-quord are our enemies,' said Rensaark. 'All of your lives are forfeit. It is fortunate that we are more merciful than your own rulers who even now are butchering their way through settlements just like this. Settlements full of my people who want nothing but peace and the freedom to live in the Kingdom of Tsard.'

Rensaark turned and made a circling movement with his finger. A dozen Tsardon ran into the citizens, curved swords drawn and held before them. The crowd fell back. The raiders moved through, pushing them into rough ranks, daring them to move further than demanded.

'Your Reader has discovered the price of worshipping a false God.

Now you will discover the price of bowing to Estorea. The price you pay for not heeding my words, Lena.'

It happened so quickly. From back and front they came, Tsardon walking among the ranks, counting. At every tenth they touched a citizen on the forehead and he or she was dragged from the crowd to stand in a ring of swordsmen. A sick sensation gripped Jesson. The counting neared him. The woman next to him was the tenth, dragged screaming from her husband, who begged to be taken in her place. He took a sword pommel on the back of the neck and fell to the ground, unmoving.

Jesson felt no relief. His head was full of the shouting of those taken from their loved ones, the exhortations for mercy and the pressure of the raiders in their midst, dealing out violent order. Twenty-nine citizens were corralled, fate in the hands of God, obscured by horseflesh, leather and steel.

'And though we hate the Conquord, that doesn't mean we cannot learn anything from it,' said Rensaark. He laughed, a chill sound that cut straight through Jesson to his heart.

Realisation was swift. Decimation. Jesson wanted to close his eyes but found he could not. One of those corralled was picked up bodily by six Tsardon. She bucked and screamed in their arms, her terror echoed by those that remained and those helpless but to witness.

They pinned her face down to the table, muscled arms clamped on her limbs, hips and back. Her head and neck protruded from the end of the table. Rensaark drew his sword, measured quickly and swung. The woman's head was cut clean away, her screams silenced, the blood sluicing. Her head rolled to lie in the grass, eyes open in the moment of death, staring at them, disbelieving.

Again the horses pressed in, denying the citizens space. The twenty-eight captured citizens pleaded and pushed but there were so many Tsardon, all armed and strong. More than a hundred must have been in the raiding party.

Jesson dropped his head and stared at his sandals while his body trembled and shook to the sound of every scream. The awful sounds of those knowing they were going to die. Calling on God, calling on their families, begging to be spared, cursing the Tsardon, cursing the Conquord, howling out words of love. He clenched his fists at the whisper of the sword, the sick whip of the cut and the dead thud of head on dry earth and grass.

He counted each one. Praying for them to find peace in the embrace of God and a return to a life spared of fear and blessed with peace and light. The count was tortuously slow. He found he was rocking back and forth on his feet, breathing in short gasps. All that kept him upright were the words he sent to God while the shivers ran the length of his body.

By the time it was done, he could barely think at all and the words of the Tsardon only just registered.

'You have had two warnings,' Rensaark said. 'There will not be a third.'

And with scarcely a sound, his men melted back into the night beyond the fires, leaving the survivors of Gull's Ford with nothing but the bodies that defiled their place of prayer; and the gruesome task of gathering and honouring the slaughtered.

Jesson dropped to his knees and found his hope had deserted him.

Chapter 9

844th cycle of God, 43rd day of Solasrise
11th year of the true Ascendancy

Kessian had organised a discreet watch kept on Bryn Marr since his reaction in the forge two days before and had decided to visit him to try and right his mind. Bryn had closed the forge after the Ascendants and the Echelon had left and hadn't opened it since. Instead, he'd spent the time in solitary, drunken introspection, either inside his house or, more worryingly, in one of the bars that bordered the forum. He hadn't said anything injudicious so far but a slip was inevitable. And there were too many merchants in town.

With Kessian came a woman destined to fulfil a pivotal role in the years to come if the Ascendants were to develop unhindered. Elsa Gueran was a Reader of the Order of Omniscience. She was its sole representative in Westfallen and the Echelon was eternally grateful for her posting and the influence of her predecessor in that posting.

Kessian had called for her at her simple, single-storey house next to the House of Masks at the western end of the bay. He was feeling the heat today. Solastro was in full glorious cry, and the wind was still. Without the mitigating breeze off the sea the temperature was high and stifling. In the town, business was sluggish, with people sitting under shades to discuss deals or working bare-backed in the open. On the slopes above the town, animals sought tree and shrub cover where they could and farmers moved slowly across the shimmering landscape.

Elsa provided a shoulder on which to lean while Kessian's stick took the rest of his weight. He had worn his loosest tunic and sported a huge straw hat to guard his scalp and neck but was immediately damp with sweat.

'I am feeling very old this morning,' he said as they walked through the forum, acknowledging the many greetings that came their way.

'That's because you are, Ardol,' replied Elsa, smiling at him. 'It's God's way of telling you that time's almost up.'

Elsa was forty-seven and beautiful. Like many of those dedicated to the service of the Order she had chosen celibacy, believing that she was already mother to every one of Westfallen's citizens through God. Black hair cascaded down her back, decorated with the occasional beaded braid. Her athletic figure was the envy of women half her age and her face, smiling and welcoming, held features sculpted almost to perfection by nature.

She was also deeply irreverent which, in her very difficult position, was a blessing and an enormous strength.

'There are some would have you burned for that stating of unpalatable reality,' Kessian said, chuckling.

'There are many things many would have me burned for if they knew what was going on here, Ardol. Telling you that you're not far from death is the least of my concerns, believe me.'

Her expression had sobered. Kessian patted the shoulder on which he leant.

'Not in your lifetime, eh?' he said.

Elsa shrugged. 'What's hard to take in is the reality. I've seen Mirron and now Arducius and I'm still not sure I really believe it.'

'I suspect that's what lies at the heart of Bryn's problem,' said Kessian.

'Undoubtedly. It's hard to express for those of us who had no lasting talent. Or in my case, no talent at all.' She fell silent, trying to organise her thoughts.

Kessian noticed some particularly fine Tundarran weave on a nearby stall. Deep green and threaded in red and gold. Genna would love a yard or two of it.

'Special price for a poor old man?' suggested Kessian, pointing at the material.

'You have been using that line on me for a decade, Ardol,' said the stallholder, a tall, thin man approaching old age.

'And it becomes more true every time I speak it.'

'As do the threats of my contacts wondering why a cloth that comes so far is sold on for so little. For you as for everyone, it's a denarius a yard. Discount if you buy ten.'

Kessian blew out his cheeks, catching Elsa's mildly anxious gaze at the same time. 'I'll think about it. Maybe come back later when you're feeling more generous.'

'Will your good lady ever forgive you if she finds I sold out before you decided to treat her?'

'Will I ever forgive you if she finds I was even enquiring?' Kessian winked. He turned and rested his hand back on Elsa's shoulder. The two moved off slowly. 'I'm sorry, Elsa, you were about to say.'

'I believe in the true path of the Order. That's why I'm here. Because I can help keep the Chancellor's inquisitors clear of Westfallen. But like our belief in the cycle of life, the true Ascendant's path is just that, a belief. Or it was. There was no proof, not really. And now I'm confronted with it. It's like being in the presence of God. It scares me. I'm sure it scared Bryn too.'

'Don't let the Ascendants hear you say that. At least one of them already has enough delusions of his own impending greatness.' Kessian was only half-joking.

'Yes, it's something you'll have to watch,' agreed Elsa, not raising a smile. 'Look, Ardol, we're sitting on the best-kept secret in the Conquord, probably on the whole of God's earth. The Order still think they put an end to it all when they killed Gorian. You know better than all of us how hard it's been to keep it that way.

'What I've seen . . . dear God-of-the-world, there are others pregnant even now, with the same potential. It cannot remain a secret forever.'

'I know,' said Kessian. 'It's the main reason Marshal Vasselis is here.'

'I mean, these people are what we believe we should *all* be in generations to come.' Elsa paused, stared at him as they exited the forum on a quiet street heading towards the blacksmith's. 'Can you imagine what this is going to do to the Order? To the Conquord, for that matter?

'There will be no flags to herald their arrival. No ready acceptance. Dear Ardol, these people you've created, their fight has only just begun. You can't contain them here. What they are, real or imagined, will out. I am preparing for that. I suggest the Echelon does the same.'

'We are, Elsa. That's why I'm going to talk to Bryn now,' he said, though he felt his words woefully inadequate. 'But at the back of all our minds is the knowledge that we have been rather naïve. All of us. You included. It's only now that we've truly started to appreciate the potential consequences of what we've done. Everything has been geared towards creation, precious little towards education. The Conquord is big and the Order is powerful and paranoid. It isn't going to be easy.'

'Ardol Kessian, your gift for understatement is undimmed by age.'

The forge was cold, the house quiet and shuttered. Disgruntled customers had tacked notes to his door and there was evidence that pieces had been removed from the yard. Theft or recovery of property, it was impossible to say.

Kessian rapped sharply on the heavy door with his stick, not expecting nor getting a response. The streets in this part of Westfallen were quiet but narrow, the forge being on a crossroads. Terraced houses, most atop businesses of one kind or another, meandered away in curving cobbled streets. In the heat of the morning, most of those doing business were inside but in a small town it was easy to draw attention.

He looked at Elsa who shrugged. 'What choice do we really have? The whole town knows he's involved in the Ascendancy programme. We were bound to come. But remember why we're here, Ardol. We have to stop him making a mistake while the festival is on or news will reach the Conquord uncontrolled.'

Kessian nodded. 'You know we're going to have to tell the town very soon, don't you? They must suspect already that there's been a breakthrough.'

'Yes but in the way we always said we would. One thing at a time, Ardol.'

Elsa thumped her fist on the door, Kessian with his stick again.

'Bryn!' shouted Kessian. 'Open the door. We're here to help you. It's Ardol and Elsa. Come on now.'

He glanced around him. Faces were already appearing at doorways. He waved them away and struck the door again.

'Bryn, come on out. We don't want to have to call the militia to break in to check you're still alive.'

'You're sure he's in there?' asked Elsa.

'Unless he dug a tunnel last night,' said Kessian.

'Or his own grave,' said Elsa.

'That isn't funny.'

'It wasn't meant to be.'

Kessian put his stick to the door once more. 'Bryn! Last chance.' He waited, and eventually shook his head. 'I don't think . . .'

The sound of a bolt being slid back stopped his words. The door opened a crack.

'Can't a man have a little solitude if he wants?' growled Bryn.

They heard him walk away back into his house. Kessian pushed open the door into the gloom. Every shutter was closed. Stale air drifted out along with a sour smell. He shrugged and walked in and up the short hallway that led to Bryn's reception and dining room. Empty wine jugs, goblets and plates were scattered about the floor, side tables and couches.

Beyond the dining room, the kitchen was off a short passageway to the right. To the left, stairs led up to a bedroom. The forge and yard were through the kitchen but they didn't have to go that far. Bryn was sitting at the work table, his back to his cold stove, staring into space. He was carrying the dirt of three days. He was unwashed, unshaven and his hair was lank on his head. His eyes were red from alcohol and lack of sleep and his hands were shaking the goblet he held in front of him. More jugs stood or lay in a rough arc in front of him. Bryn had always enjoyed his wine. It looked like he had consumed the better part of his cellar.

'Do you mind if I sit down?' asked Kessian already pulling back a chair.

Bryn made a small gesture of acquiescence. Kessian sat hard and puffed out his cheeks, leaning his stick against the edge of the table. Elsa stood at his side, a hand resting on his shoulder. Close to, Bryn stank of sweat, vomit and stale alcohol.

'We just want to talk to you,' said Elsa. 'See if you're all right.'

'Well, now you've seen me you can go,' said Bryn. 'Don't worry, I won't give away your precious secret.'

He didn't look at them but had fixed his gaze instead on the goblet that he rolled between his filthy fingers.

'It's your secret too, Bryn. It's all of ours. Everyone in Westfallen,' said Kessian.

'Look, we know you're scared,' said Elsa.

'Scared?' Now he faced them, red eyes wide and wild in his deeply tanned, weathered face. 'No, I'm not scared. I have too much regret and despair to be scared. No point in being frightened now we've produced this unconscionable evil.'

Kessian felt sadness tumble through him like a fall of ice. He shook his head, his heart reaching out to his troubled friend.

'Bryn, no. Can it be evil to bring new life into the world that is more closely bonded to all God's creations than any before it?'

'It cannot be right,' said Bryn, his voice a hoarse whisper. 'What have we done?'

'We have brought new understanding to the world,' said Kessian. 'We have taken human beings to the next plane. Closer to God. Better able to do the Omniscient's work. It is a natural progression.'

Bryn snorted. '*Natural*. That girl held flame in her hands. It did her bidding.'

'There would be those who say all strand talents, innate or otherwise, are unnatural. You were a Firewalker in your youth, after all. Are you unnatural?'

'God bestows such talents,' said Bryn icily. 'And God removes them too. They are the natural order of things. But this? We have bred for this. It is not nature's course. It is against God.'

'You are confused, Bryn,' said Kessian sharply. 'All of our talents, brief or otherwise, are bred for. Yours included.'

Elsa squeezed Kessian's shoulder and straightened. 'I stand here before you, a Reader for the Order of Omniscience. I spend my life in the service of God. What we have achieved here is wonderful. A miracle. God put us here to develop his world during the cycles of life. That is what we have done. We have developed. Progressed.'

Bryn barked a short laugh and turned his growing ire on her. 'And, esteemed Reader, is that the belief of your peers and superiors? Is that what the Chancellor believes? Do you think me so stupid I would swallow your pronouncements as gospel? When they caught Gorian, the Order denounced him as heretic. And if they had any inkling his work was being continued here, the armies would come. You do not represent either the Order or the Conquord, Elsa Gueran. You are the puppet of the Echelon.'

Kessian could feel Elsa tense. She took a long, considered breath, then sat on the edge of the table.

'I understand your point of view, Bryn, and I understand your fears. But you are wrong to think me a puppet. I am a believer in the true path of the Order. Today's Order is strong and all-pervasive but here in Westfallen and in pockets across the Conquord, we hold beliefs on which the Order was founded. That the people shall move ever closer to God. Should ascend to be one with God.'

Kessian could see Bryn wasn't listening. Rational statements falling mute on an irrational mind.

'It is now we need your strength, my friend,' said Kessian. 'You have worked so hard, given so much. Now we must stand together. There are testing times to come, dangerous times. We need you.'

Bryn dropped his head. 'The Order will sweep you aside. I have been complicit for too long. All I can do is throw myself upon the mercy of the Omniscient.'

Kessian looked at Elsa. She was shaking her head. The two of them rose to leave.

'Get some rest, Bryn,' said Kessian. 'We'll send someone in. Prepare you some food to go with that fine wine of yours. Maybe clean up a little.'

Bryn didn't raise his head. 'I am already sullied enough. I will see no one that you send, Father Kessian.'

Andreas Koll was outside waiting for them. He smiled a little sadly.

'Not good?' he asked.

'Not at all,' said Kessian. 'I want him watched. Day and night. He is not to speak of what he saw to anyone save Elsa and the Echelon. We need trusted people on this, Andreas. Talk to his friends. See he is kept away from outsiders.'

'Aren't you overreacting?' asked Elsa. 'He is not a danger. Just confused and scared.'

Kessian frowned. 'You contradict yourself. He wants God's mercy. Who do you think he will ask for it. Not you, Elsa. One careless word now and everything we have striven for could be lost. I will not let him risk that. Anyway, it has to be done. He will be kept silent.'

And Kessian knew with a calm certainty that he meant every word he said. No weakness. They could not afford it. Not now.

'When does the solastro festival end?' he asked.

'Five days,' said Andreas.

'A critical time. When the festival is over and outsiders gone, we will address the town. We must know the scale of what we face within our own compass before we decide what must be done in the wider world.' Kessian passed a hand over his face. Bryn had shaken him to the core. His fear was palpable. And this in a man dedicated to the cause until so recently.

'Elsa, I need you to consult your scriptures. Anything that supports us. Think of anything you can say that will calm people.'

'We're going to have to show them what our Ascendants can do, aren't we?' she said.

'I can see no way around it. Bryn's reaction has started the questions and we have no credible answers now. We have kept the Ascendants away from the people for long enough. We have to trust our own. If we cannot, we are lost.'

'Then perhaps Bryn is a blessing for us,' said Andreas.

Kessian smiled at the fourth strand Land Warden. Such a strong man. 'Your optimism is a lesson to us all.'

'He's right, though,' said Elsa. 'Here we are in danger of wallowing in self pity and all that has happened is that one man has been badly frightened. Let's not lose sight of the miracle that Mirron and Arducius have shown us. Everything we prayed for has come to pass.'

Kessian nodded. 'But can you not feel the passing of innocence?' He turned to walk back towards the docks. 'I should go to the lake, see the Marshal. We need to accelerate our security plans.'

Chapter 10

844th cycle of God, 43rd day of Solasrise
11th year of the true Ascendancy

Willows Lake was two miles to the south-east of Westfallen and provided the town with all its fresh water, piped downhill to the town fountains and directly into the houses of the wealthy. It was over three miles long, had several fine shingle beaches and was bordered on three sides by its namesake trees, which offered shade at the water's edge. Fed by underground streams and rivers running in from the north and west, its surplus ran off to Genastro Falls via Garret's River, which could be dammed in times of drought.

The lake was popular with Westfallen's people for fishing and for sail and oar training; and it was where the Ascendants had gone for the day to try and build on Mirron's progress. It was a place of peace to rival the plateau orchard. Marshal Vasselis, his wife and son had gone with them to learn what they could while Father Kessian went to talk to Bryn Marr.

Gorian had watched Mirron and now Arducius make the first true link to the earth and they had both begun to blossom. Just two days and they were new people. Mirron was still afraid because she did not fully understand what it was she did. Arducius likewise though he had a more analytical mind. What fascinated Gorian was that both of them now had other talents at their fingertips.

Arducius had developed a gentle breeze from a still sky when he broke through yesterday. Today, he had caused a small column of water to stand on the lake surface. Mirron could water-breathe now and had also brought worms to the surface, merely by placing her hands on the land. Small victories but it was as if doors had been opened in their minds.

Gorian knew he was not far behind them. At least he was further advanced than the sickly Ossacer. Pathetic. Even Arducius was strong in mind despite his brittle bones. Ossacer was weak in mind and body and still in bed, shivering and moaning.

Gorian had never had a day's sickness in his life. He might be behind now but he could feel his breakthrough coming. Today would be the perfect day. Marshal Vasselis was here and had stared speechless at the small tricks the other two had performed. And his son, Kovan, had been hanging around Mirron all day, overexuberant in his congratulations. A demonstration from Gorian better than the others put together would only be right. It would show who was destined to be the best of them.

It was early afternoon and a perfect day, still and hot with the lake so calm your reflection hardly wavered in it. And so clear that the fish that had chased Mirron and Jen Shalke through the water were ribbons of flashing silver beneath the surface. It was an amazing sight and Gorian wanted a part of it.

He had been sitting alone under the shade of a willow tree, watching the other two intently. Both were tired from their exertions now but talking to Willem, Genna and Hesther, who logged everything they said. Shela, Jen and his mother served a salad lunch at the tables permanently set up on the lakeside. Marshal Vasselis and his wife were holding court while Kovan sported in the water near the jetty, showing off for Mirron.

Gorian pushed himself to his feet, feeling suddenly hungry. He wandered the short distance around the lakeside and crunched across the beach to the tables. From behind the big boathouse, he could hear the sound of an approaching horse and cart. Father Kessian was being driven to the lake by one of his servants. Now everyone was here. Perfect.

The carriage rolled to a stop and the servant helped Father Kessian down. He walked slowly over to the lunch tables, relying heavily on his walking stick. Marshal Vasselis jumped up from his bench seat to embrace the Father. Mirron and Arducius broke from their mentors to do the same. Gorian didn't hurry, content to hear the Father's deep-voiced laughter carry over the water's surface.

'Go steady on an old man,' he said. 'One at a time, one at a time.'

Mirron and Arducius were babbling loud, recounting their triumphs. Gorian left them to it, standing by the jetty. He saw Kovan had stopped his swimming and diving now he was ignored. He was hanging on to a jetty stay, looking unhappy. Gorian smiled.

'You'll never be one of us, will you? However hard you try. And that makes you unimportant. She knows that. You are wasting your time.'

'You should watch what you say,' said Kovan. 'When my father dies, I will be Marshal Defender of Caraduk. I will be the one who rules you. All of you.'

Gorian stared at him, wanting to laugh at his stupidity. 'No one will rule me.'

'Gorian?' Kessian's voice beckoned him.

He trotted over to the Father, who was taking a seat by Marshal Vasselis for lunch.

'Yes, Father?'

'Come and sit down. Tell me what you've done this morning.'

'I've been waiting for you,' he replied, realising it was the absolute truth.

'Oh? And why is that?'

'I have something to show you. All of you. But I wanted to wait until you were here.'

Kessian frowned and glanced aside to Genna who shrugged. 'I see. I heard you had been quiet, working by yourself over there. Have you discovered something?'

'No.'

'So what can you have to show me?'

Gorian felt a stab of anger at his doubt. Vasselis saw it and laid a hand on Kessian's arm.

'Come on, Ardol, just let the lad show you want he wants. You never know, he might surprise and delight you.'

Kessian smiled, but the doubt remained. 'Go on, Gorian.'

Gorian walked away a couple of paces to make sure they could all see him. Around him, on the edge of the beech, the grass was a healthy deep green, fed by the water and warmed by the sun. He checked to make sure they were all looking at him. Father Kessian, the Echelon, the Ascendants, and Marshal Vasselis. Then he knelt down.

With his hands almost lost in the grass, he could feel what his eyes had already told him. The vegetation here was strong and vibrant, the conditions ideal for growth. The grass was thick, the stems tough.

Beneath the grass he could sense tree roots seeking fertile ground and moisture from the lake. The tiny movements of mites, insects, spiders and worms filtered up through his fingers, taking a place in the organisation of his mind. He was a Herd Master of extraordinary skill and had already played his part in the saving of many an animal on Westfallen's farms. Yet that had been his only ability so far.

But today, the world of the Land Warden was his, too. Strange. He had never doubted that this would be the moment. Not since they had walked up here this morning, laughing and joking, playing and swimming together. He had felt a lightness of spirit, a closeness to Mirron in particular, but to Arducius too. It was not something he was used to but he found he liked it. It was something he could use to gain advantage. And what he felt today made all those years of endless learning and effort worthwhile.

Around him, all voices were silent. Perhaps his face was giving away that he could truly feel the land. But he wasn't finished yet. He focused hard on the grass that surrounded him. While he gazed at the green on which he knelt, he delved deep into the structure of the stems themselves. He applied the understandings of his Herd-Mastership. The methods of looking past that which the naked eye can see, sensing the trails of energy that bound cells together and promoted growth and life.

In a cow or a horse, if there was damage or disease, it appeared as a break in the trails with the centre of the problem an indistinct area. If it had a colour, it would be grey, vaguely shifting and formless. That's how it appeared to Gorian's mind's eye.

No such damage here, though. He traced the trails that surged through the earth. He could tell where they branched to feed into each individual strand. It was like a map laid out in intricate detail, all available through his touch and decoded by his mind.

It was truly wonderful. He felt a surge of joy, of power potential. And of greatness. So he searched for the way to change what he could sense. The area was small; little more than that cast by his shadow before the trails and sensations began to fade.

He tried to remember what Mirron had said. About letting your muscles relax and directing the free energy all around into the trails you wanted. She had said it was like making your mind a net and then just pointing your finger to make the trails swell with energy and life.

But it was vague. She couldn't put her feelings and senses into words. And she was talking about directing fire and water. His task was to alter living matter. Looking deep into the structure of the grass, he could see what he had to do. In the heart of the stalk, down at the base where the root thickened to burst above ground, there was a pulsing. It was different in every strand. There bright and dominant, there faint and weak, with the energy trails leading to each and every one. He sought deeper, tried to channel his focus on the pulsing.

He paused, his heart suddenly beating hard. How was it that it felt this natural . . . this intuitive? These feelings, these extraordinary sensations, had been concealed for so long. Always at the edge of his comprehension but never close enough for him to savour. Until now. Exhilaration flooded him. It could have broken his concentration. Instead, he channelled it into the pulsing of the stems. He diverted his excitement into forcing energy hard and fast into the life-force of hundreds of blades of grass surrounding him. It had to be the right course of action for the result he desired.

And in the moment he did so, every pulse flared in his mind's eye. Some quickly guttered like dying candle flames and snuffed out. Others roared with health, growth and energy. Immediately, he felt his concentration begin to wane. Like he was standing holding two ends of ropes, each pulling him hard in opposite directions. And he desperate to cling on to both, fearing what might happen if he let go of either. Yet the more he tried, the more he was unable to maintain his focus.

It was over abruptly. No longer could he force the lines of energy into the flaring and fading pulses. He withdrew into himself, knowing he was spent. In his mind, both ends of the rope were let go. He felt himself falling sideways but there, in his sudden fatigue, was the thrill of triumph.

Kessian watched Gorian emerge in awed silence. They all did. He was ashamed that he had mistaken the boy's bearing for arrogance and bravado like so often before. Fortunately, Vasselis had seen it for what it was.

He knew he shouldn't have been as impressed with the display as with the understanding of the processes behind it but he couldn't help it. None of the first Gorian's writings had prepared them for the sights they had seen these past few days. Of course, he had only been able to theorise, having witnessed nothing like it himself. Yet in the midst of his amazement, Kessian found the time to marvel at Gorian's vision.

So to his namesake. A boy surely destined for similar mythical status. But at this moment hidden inside a thick curtain of grass stems three feet tall and more. Kessian had watched them grow from a tenth of that height in less time than he could count thirty. And all the while, Gorian's face had begun to wrinkle. Not much, and it could have been with the effort but Kessian didn't think so. The boy had developed tiny crow's feet around his eyes before the grass had obscured him.

Now he lay still and his mother, Meera Naravny, was running to his side. The rest of them were not far behind. Mirron and Arducius were first to jump on him and hug him, Mirron fiercely, Arducius gently, both delirious at his achievement. And the others trailing their hands through the lustrous long grass, all smiles and satisfaction.

It was as the Echelon had planned. Kessian felt that warmth within him again that had nothing to do with the heat from above. His walk was more stately, more knowing than before. He could not deny the joy in his heart that suffused his aching, aged, tired body.

Like the others, he let his hand brush the tall new-grown grass. He looked down at it and frowned, curious. In amongst the vibrant green thicket of stems were scattered the brown and brittle of the long dead and dried out. Perhaps Gorian could explain it later. An oddity, though.

Meera had Gorian cradled in her arms now, kneeling by the exhausted Ascendant, having shooed away his friends. She was stroking his hair and speaking soothing, proud words. He clung to her, needing her closeness and warmth.

'Well, will you look at that,' she said. 'Ardol, over here.'

Kessian moved to her. Meera pointed to Gorian's temple. He didn't see what bothered her for a moment but soon it became very obvious. His hair. Among all the richness of youth there was grey.

Kessian shrugged at Vasselis's question. The two men were dining alone in a small private room in the villa. In the main dining room, Netta and Kovan Vasselis hosted the rest of the Echelon.

It had been a true day of contrasts. From his despair at Bryn's condition to the joy of Gorian's emergence and now the flat weight of reality that was becoming twined about them as a consequence.

'There are undoubtedly many effects of ascendancy that we are yet to witness. We'll watch young Gorian, though I am sure he'll recover very quickly.'

The boy had been supported to the wagon with no strength in his legs. As well as the grey in his hair there had been the tiny wrinkles around his eyes that Kessian had seen form. These had remained even when Gorian's broad smile had faded. There was a great deal to document. Genna and Meera had begun before dinner was served.

Kessian breathed out and sat up from his reclining position on his couch. Between him and Vasselis, a low table held the remains of their food and drink. Bread, mutton and roasted vegetables. Rich sauces still steamed gently in beautifully crafted and decorated jugs from the potteries of Atreska. A half-full jug of spiced, heated red wine was at Vasselis's right hand. Kessian waved his empty goblet at the Marshal while examining the food and concluding he had eaten enough.

Vasselis filled the proffered goblet and his own. He allowed himself an indulgent smile, Kessian seeing the care in his early middle-aged face.

'And are you pleased you lived to see it?' he asked.

'Damn fool question,' replied Kessian. 'Remember how I didn't ever ask if you were happy to see the birth of your son?'

'You know precisely what I am talking about, Ardol. You are hardly beside yourself with delight as we sit here. The same is true of the entire Echelon.'

'I can't help thinking ahead,' said Kessian.

'And your blacksmith's reaction has worried you.'

'It has shaken me deeply,' admitted Kessian, finding comfort in Vasselis's understanding. 'It's why we're sitting here and not in there with everyone else, after all. Funny. Although we'd always known we would have to face this, that we couldn't keep them hidden forever – didn't want to – I didn't think it would be beginning now. They are so young.' He sighed and shook his head, an uncomfortable feeling in his gut.

Vasselis put down his wine glass and sat up himself, leaning across the table to touch Kessian's hands, which had begun to shake.

'Ardol, the first thing is not to panic. Not to let the tasks ahead appear so large they are impossible to achieve. That's why I'm here.' He smiled in that self-deprecating way that Kessian had grown to love. 'Hey, I run this country. I'm good at this sort of thing.'

Kessian felt the tightness in his throat ease. He kneaded his forehead with his thumb and forefinger.

'Sorry,' he said. 'Silly old man.'

'Not at all,' said Vasselis softly. 'As God-stands-by-me you are the only one of the Echelon who truly understands the scale of what we face now the Ascendants have started to emerge. We cannot underestimate the problems that are to come. We have to be realistic. We have to ignore nothing, however small, and we have to be single-minded in our efforts. Bryn has merely brought our task into sharper focus.'

Kessian nodded, his relief palpable. Thank God for delivering Arvan Vasselis to the world. Thank God for the Vasselis family of the last four generations, come to that. Taking the then new Marshal Defender dynasty into their confidence had proved a masterstroke.

A family with centuries-old roots in Caraduk and a history of open-minded religious attitudes, the Echelon had been persuaded to speak to them at a time when the Order was becoming suspicious about the rumours surrounding Westfallen. The incumbent Marshal had revealed herself to be a believer in the ascendant strand of the Order of Omniscience and so the partnership was sealed.

Soon, her choice of Reader was installed in Westfallen, information was being passed to the Echelon concerning military, religious and merchant traffic that might pose a threat, and the ascendancy experiments, research and developments could continue free of the suffocating veil of secrecy within the town.

Three generations later, every citizen of Westfallen knew what was being attempted and all played their part in ensuring secrecy was maintained. To this day, Caraducian ships patrolled beyond the inlet, soldiers manned guard posts on every route from the town, and Vasselis and the Echelon used the Advocacy messenger service to keep up the vital flow of communications.

No one who presented any potential threat got out and, indeed, the various Marshal Defenders Vasselis had made some hard choices. Innocent people were dead, their only crime having been to see or hear something they should not. Unpalatable though it was, Kessian found his guilt did not interfere with his sleep. His belief in the greater good they served was unshakeable.

He looked at his benefactor, a man who provided money, security and above everything else, friendship undimmed.

'So,' said Kessian. 'Where do we begin?'

'Right,' said Vasselis, adjusting his formal toga, deep blue and gold trim on cream. 'Your timetable for talking to Westfallen's citizens is sound. Usual practice will surround those merchants leaving at the end of the festival. What we must do though is seal off the town in the aftermath of your announcement, in whatever form that takes. I'll organise that. You'll see nothing here, don't worry. No point in scaring people. As far as my soldiers are concerned it'll be an exercise. I'll dream up some plausible pretext.'

'I'm intrigued to know what.'

'How about quarantine for containment of a bovine flu outbreak? It'll allow us to keep any of your citizens in, should there be any, well, sudden desire for departure. And of course, we can stop anyone getting in by land or sea.'

Kessian chuckled. 'Too easy, isn't it?'

'Like I say, I'm good at this.' Vasselis's expression hardened. 'Unfortunately, that is the easy part. I cannot keep my soldiers on exercise indefinitely and you cannot survive without trade. Where we must get to, and quickly, is a state where we have your borders as secure as they can be without arousing suspicion. I will review my plans for that and confirm them with you at the earliest opportunity.

'It's only at that point when we can begin to consider moves to introduce the Ascendants to anyone, and I mean anyone, on the outside. It's very difficult to assess what the reaction of others will be but we would be naïve to assume mass acceptance, I am sure you will agree. Fear and misunderstanding are likely to dominate, I suspect.'

'But if only people knew what it could mean for us all,' said Kessian, before he could stop himself.

'You can't afford to think like that,' said Vasselis sharply. 'And you know it as well as I do. We have to put a cap on information getting into the public arena for as long as we can. But one thing is certain. This will leak out. As the Ascendants get older and more come through, people will see things and they will talk. Before that happens, we have to have the backing of other, powerful individuals. I have to think when to talk to the Advocate and the Gatherers. She and they would be particularly useful allies. Other Marshal Defender dynasties too and those we know in the Order who believe as we do.'

Vasselis paused and sipped his wine. Kessian could see worry in the set of his mouth and eyes.

'What is it, Arvan?' he asked gently.

The Marshal smiled as he spoke.

'I've known this town for forty years. Since I was a small boy, playing at Willows Lake and swimming in the sea under Genastro Falls. I love every street, every tenement and villa. I love the smell of the fishing nets on the harbour walkways and the sound of ships bumping against the deep water docks when the tide is on the turn. I count you and Genna among my dearest and closest friends, never mind you are ninety years my senior. I used to badger my father to move here and I haven't changed at all. By God-who-walks-beside-us, if I was not Marshal Defender I would settle here permanently, such is the love I have for Westfallen and its people. It is the most beautiful, warm place in the entire Conquord, and you know I have seen a good deal of our beloved empire.'

'There is a major "but" coming, isn't there?' said Kessian, feeling his pride in the town swell as Vasselis enunciated so succinctly why so many who came here fell in love with the place and why those born here were so reluctant ever to leave.

'I am terrified of all that being destroyed,' Vasselis said. 'You have to know this, Ardol, and rightly you will be scared too. You, the Echelon, Westfallen, you have been of necessity cocooned from the real face of the Order of Omniscience for generations. And of necessity, I have not. They are powerful and they are as determined as they are zealous. The Chancellor is a woman blinded by her own faith, unable to see beyond the sanctity of that over which she presides.

'I know you have heard about them through Elsa Gueran but she does not tell you everything. If one of the Chancellor's people, just one, gets wind of what we have done here before we are ready, the armies of the Order will descend. After all, they are not interested in anyone coming closer to God except through their own good offices, are they? And their justice will see Westfallen burned to its last timber and the ashes of its people dispersed into the air to be tormented at the hands of the wind demons.

'If we do not have our allies around us, they will instead stand behind the Chancellor, ignorant of the crime they commit against all the people of this world.'

Kessian stared at Vasselis, unable to take his eyes from the Marshal's face as the words poured out. He could all but smell the timbers burning in his villa, see the citizens run but with nowhere to hide while the flames from their houses reared at their backs. He felt a surge of hopelessness and a despair at what they had done to so many innocents. Abruptly, he could understand where the path of Bryn's thoughts had taken him.

'Tell me what we must do,' Kessian said, keeping his voice firm and calm.

Vasselis nodded. 'You are a strong man, Ardol. And the good news is that our plans are sound. But don't ever forget that your friends are in constant danger from this day on, Elsa first among them. Have faith in the security I can bring you. Remain vigilant as the import of what has happened dawns on your citizens. Relearn again and again, all your plans for escape.

'Remember this and pass it down to those who will shepherd the Echelon after you are returned to the earth: the Ascendancy and its Echelon are the single critical link to our future. Should the worst come, never look back, never feel the guilt for those left in your wake who fall to obstruct those who would kill you. We have all chosen our paths and will live or die as a result.

'You must never, never hesitate to sacrifice any of us if it means you save yourselves.'

'Pray God it never comes to that,' said Kessian.

'Every day,' said Vasselis. 'Yet be prepared lest it does.'

Next morning, the preparations began. And Kessian had been right; Gorian was fully recovered and none the worse for his exertions. His grey had gone as had the wrinkles on his face. Looking at Gorian, it was difficult to believe the age he had displayed the day before. Indeed, Kessian would have doubted his memory but for the weight of witnesses. His ability to renew himself was one more wonder at a most extraordinary time.

A time tempered by a terribly sad reminder of why they had to be so careful how word of the Ascendancy came into the public domain. That same morning, they found Bryn hanging above his forge.

Chapter 11

Jen Shalke was out in the deeps, seeking shoals of white fish for the fleet bobbing on the surface. She'd brought the Ascendants to the safe haven where they loved to play above and below the waves, and had then left them, trailing her drift line and flag behind her to alert the skiffs to her position.

Mirron had watched her go through the clear calm waters, her arms by her sides, her strong legs propelling her away. They'd all learned the underwater techniques from Jen these last two years. From the first moments of drawing water into the lungs, when the fear was terrible and the reflex to choke unstoppable, to the understanding of pressure effects on the body and how to breathe and rise slowly to combat them, to the sheer joy of swimming beneath the surface, spotting fish and discovering the wonders and dangers of the sea floor.

She turned away, glancing up quickly to see the brightness of the sun on the surface about forty feet above her and swam towards the others who were already nearing their favourite place, cavorting under the waters of Genastro Falls where they plunged into the sea. It was a great place for underwater hide and seek. She worked her legs harder to catch them up, feeling a pang of isolation as she did so. Ever more, these three whom she considered her brothers were the only real friends she had.

Jen tried her best but she was too old and it just felt awkward. Mirron had friends from the school but less and less often did their parents want her in their homes, or their daughters in hers. Mirron didn't really understand. She knew she was different because her abilities were active. But most of her friends used to have one ability or another in their early years. Perhaps they were jealous, though if they were they didn't show it.

The others were already into a game by the time she arrived. Gorian was hovering in the water, almost lost in the air bubbles that stormed around the plunge pool. They felt soft on the skin and the roar of the falls in their ears was like muted thunder. It sent tingles through Mirron's body every time. He saw her and beckoned her towards him. She felt a small thrill and did as he asked, aware they were alone for the moment.

Gorian was beautiful. So moody but so alive. His hair eddied around his head and his eyes shone in the water, the muscles in his arms, chest and legs stood proud. She swam up close to him and hung there while the bubbles coursed in front of their faces. She had the powerful urge to kiss him then and it frightened her a little because she saw the same thing in his eyes as well. There was peace for them here. She didn't want the moment to end and fought to resist the desire to touch him lest that should spoil it. Gorian opened his mouth, sucked in bubbles and blew them out towards her. She laughed, the sound alien in her ears.

Who seeks? she asked, using the signs of upraised palms and a hand on her brow, hooding her eyes.

Ossacer, he replied, holding up four fingers to indicate his sign. She was two, Arducius three. Gorian of course, was one. It was hardly fair but it was the reason why Gorian was hiding in the water and air bubble streams. Ossacer's sight was fading rapidly. The illness he'd contracted following the shock of Mirron's emergence two years before had begun the process and nothing the doctors did would halt or reverse the problem. He would be blind before the coming dusas reached its height. But until then, he enjoyed what little sight he had, making his work and play ferocious and determined.

Where Arducius? She used the seek and three signs.

Gorian shrugged then pointed downwards.

Ossacer?

Gorian smiled and pointed down again repeatedly, indicating a long distance. He moved a hand towards her and let it drift through her hair, some of which had escaped its band to wisp about her eyes in the swirling warm water. She had no desire to pull away. There was a hot lump low in her stomach. She trembled. A shoal of tiny silver grey fish flowed past them, enveloping them for a few moments before moving on across the bay. Gorian leant in, his face coming closer to hers. She imagined feeling his breath on her face, his lips large in her vision.

A dull clang echoed through the water. Once, twice, three times. It was Hesther or Shela, summoning them back to the shore. Mirron backed away from Gorian who frowned and beckoned her. She shook her head and pointed up and away towards the beach, raising her eyebrows in the 'now' sign. Gorian nodded. The moment was gone. He held out his hand. She took it and the two of them led the way back to Westfallen, the others swimming to join them from below.

'When can we start developing our Waterborn ability?' asked Gorian. 'Jen says we're already as good as her. We should be trying to be better.'

'Fancy controlling the fish, do you?' asked Mirron, head emerging from her towel to see Gorian's skin glistening in the sunlight.

'Dolphins and sharks, more like,' said Gorian.

'All in good time,' said Hesther. 'I don't think we've worked out a method just yet. I think you'd be better trying that sort of trick on sheep.'

Ossacer chuckled. 'You can see it, can't you? Gorian controlling the mind of a sheep and ordering it to attack.'

They all laughed at the joke. All but Gorian.

'Well you won't be able to because you'll be blind,' he said.

'Gorian, you will apologise for that right now,' ordered Shela.

'Well, he will be.'

'And he does not need reminding by that nasty mouth of yours, does he?' Shela said. 'Apologise.'

Gorian gazed defiance at Shela for a moment. 'Sorry,' he muttered.

Mirron had been trying to see Ossacer's reaction. He'd been staring at the ground and fiddling with the sand at his feet. Now he looked up.

'Anyway, I won't need my eyes,' he said. 'One day, the animals will see for me.'

Hesther was frowning at that, eyes locked on Ossacer. After a moment, her expression cleared and she clapped her hands together.

'Right. If you're all rested and mostly dry, grab your things because it's time for something to eat and a surprise.'

Mirron and the others got to their feet and followed Hesther and Shela away from the beach towards the slopes leading up to the orchard. They passed the Marshal Defender's house on the way. Mirron looked at its shuttered windows and wondered when the family would be back. It was more fun when Kovan came to stay. He always joined in whenever he could and didn't seem worried by them like some of the others in the town. He never strayed far from her side either, unless they were playing Waterborn of course, and that was a comforting feeling. Pity he and Gorian didn't get on very well.

The Marshal's villa boasted a beautiful private garden that stretched for fifty yards on each side. Its walls were whitewashed and high, capped with red slate. At each corner and in the middle of each wall, statues of previous Marshals stood in heroic or philosophical poses. The wooden side door into the gardens stood open and Hesther ushered them inside.

Mirron loved these gardens with their marble paths crisscrossing the lawns; the fruit trees offering them apples, oranges and lemons; and the ornamental fish pond and fountains in which great golden carp swam lazily. The centrepiece was a raised marble plinth, opensided and with a domed roof held up by four columns. It had a ring of benches and on one of them sat Father Kessian. She yelped in delight and ran forward, leading the Ascendants in an excited babble.

They were taught by Hesther more and more these days. Father Kessian was old and always seemed to have a cold or an ache or something. But when he did come to teach them, it swelled her heart and not just because it would be something important. She loved him. They all did. There was silence when he spoke and warmth when he smiled. And every word he spoke struck to their hearts and showed them things they had not understood. Made them better.

'Hello, my young Ascendants,' he said, his voice soft and soothing. 'I trust the water was warm and the fish friendly.'

'It was lovely,' gushed Mirron, planting a kiss on his cheek and hugging him around the neck. She was joined by the others.

'Steady, steady,' said Kessian, chuckling and struggling to keep upright under the weight of them all. 'Give an old man the space to breathe.'

They let him go.

'Gorian wants to control the sharks,' said Arducius.

'Does he indeed?' Kessian raised his eyebrows. 'Ambitious, aren't you? Well nothing wrong with that. Now then, sit down. Shela will bring you food and I will take your teaching this afternoon.'

Mirron clapped her hands together and sat down right next to the Father. She gazed up into his knowing eyes, half-hooded by the folds of skin on his old face. One day he wouldn't be here to teach them or encourage them. He was reaching the end of his cycle and would be embraced by God. She didn't want that day ever to come.

'Are you feeling better?' she asked.

Kessian smiled. 'Yes, my child, and thank you for asking. My chest is clear and Genna says I no longer snore.'

'I'm glad,' she said.

'Right then. All comfortable? Then let's learn something new,' said Kessian.

Mirron felt her heart beat faster. She shared a smile with Gorian. Nothing was better than new skills. It meant the Echelon thought they were improving.

'Now, during all that I am about to say and the experiment I want you all to do, bear in mind the heart of your learning since your emergence. Almost two years ago now . . . time passes so quickly doesn't it? What can you tell me about elemental energy cores? Arducius?'

'They are the most concentrated sources of life energy that we can use.'

'Good,' Father Kessian stretched the word. 'But what more is there than mere use that you have found so surprising?'

'We can make more energy with it,' said Ossacer.

'Yes, you can amplify it. But I know you've all found it difficult even when the source is steady and strong. We've all seen the temporary ageing effects you suffer when you have used your abilities. And we have noted also that there is only so much work you can do with your abilities before you are both exhausted and grey, do you agree? Yes, Gorian.'

'But we are much better than we were even a year ago,' he said. 'We can already do so much more than we could then.'

Kessian nodded enthusiastically. 'Oh indeed, and I'm delighted you are all developing so well. That will undoubtedly continue. But I want you all to bear in mind that there will always be limits and that you must make yourselves aware of how far your bodies and minds can go. Particularly when you are causing growth in living things. Yes? Good.

'Now, the reason I've reminded you about that is that I want to begin your understanding of other ways to use the energies that you have all proved so adept at finding and directing into your work.' Father Kessian picked up a sheet of paper that was on the seat to his left. 'Gorian wrote that—'

'The first Gorian?' asked Arducius.

Kessian looked at him with a slight frown. 'Well, obviously.'

The three boys dissolved into laughter, clutching at each other helplessly, trying to speak and doing little more than spitting half words.

'All right, all right,' said Kessian with a broad smile on his face.

Mirron shook her head, happy that she had a little more control. She looked up at the Father and shrugged.

'Boys,' she said, echoing her mother's tone.

Kessian chuckled. 'Indeed. All right boys,' he said. 'I think it's time you told us why my words are so funny to you.'

They looked to each other, threatened to lose control again but sobered enough to explain themselves. Gorian was the spokesman.

'Sorry, Father, but it's what you always say. You and all the Echelon.'

'What, exactly?' asked Kessian.

'You always say, "well, obviously", Father. All the time.'

'Do we,' said Kessian. 'Well, the way to stop us is to stop asking dim questions, isn't it? Eh?' He smiled and reached forward to ruffle Gorian's hair. 'Now, if I may be allowed to continue?'

'Well, obviously,' managed Ossacer before roaring with laughter and taking the other two with him.

Even Mirron couldn't quite contain herself. They were right as well, now it had been pointed out. Father Kessian waited for it all to subside, taking the chance to lean back and let Shela serve them some lunch before calling for order once more.

'Gorian – the original Gorian – wrote this: "We accept the existence of energies within all things, living and silent, and that shapes and densities of energies are moulded to particular tasks. For instance, the specific signature of energy trails typical in an orange tree versus that in a farm animal. This is as much learned from ancient scriptures discussing the veins and blood of God through his earth as it is from my own observations and those of the Ascendancy with the vision to see.

' "We also believe and accept that when the first true Ascendant is born, he or she will be able, once emerged, to divert and determine uses for these energies other than that which is their current purpose; though that determination will likely be kin to the current purpose." ' Kessian paused and smiled. 'He was at times rather long-winded. All he means is, fire for fire work, earth for root and branch. And I can see what you are about to say, young Gorian, so don't. The joke will quickly wear thin.

'Gorian said this last too, which is important as well as brief: "There is no reason, however, that energies moulded for one purpose by God should not be adjusted by an Ascendant for an entirely different purpose. After all, all energy is essentially the same at its core and guides the overall cycle of life that is the glory of God and to which we all of us are bound." '

Kessian put down the parchment and looked around the Ascendants. Mirron felt excitement growing. If she'd guessed right what they were going to try today, it was a big step forward. A difficult one, too.

'Now, I'm not going to push any of you into this but let me say this first. You have all mastered, and mastered quickly, the basic rules of adapting the life energies to produce the effect you want. It means you understand how the lifelines work and how you can augment them with your bodies to amplify your effect. You are all capable of doing what I am about to ask.

'Now, what I want you to consider this afternoon is this. By example . . . Mirron, you are a peerless Firewalker. We have seen you manufacture a blaze from smouldering kindling that could heat a forge. Your challenge is to use the life energies of any tree in this garden and use them to create fire. Can you remember the signature of energy that is present in fire? Can you mould that of a lemon tree and bring flame where there was none? And, if you can do that, do you have the strength within yourself to fuel that fire, to amplify what you have built?'

Father Kessian placed a hand on her knee. He favoured her with a warm smile, seeing the anxiety that must have crossed her face as it passed through her mind. This was a bigger step than she had imagined. She looked to Gorian. Even he seemed a little worried, while the other two appeared lost in thought.

'Do not worry, Mirron Westfallen. This is a difficult lesson and you may not solve it today. It is why we brought you all here to the peace of Marshal Vasselis's garden. And it is why you will find that the whole Echelon are here to help you. I will move among you and there will be two of the Echelon watching over you always. You have the whole of the afternoon to think, to ask questions and to experiment. Expect frustration and enjoy every small success. Will you try for me?'

Mirron almost burst into tears. She managed to hold them back and nod instead, unable to find words.

'Good,' said Father Kessian. 'Then eat and take yourself away to wherever you need. Willem and Meera will be with you shortly.'

Mirron found that her hands were trembling. It was a mixture of excitement and fear of the unknown. Quietly, the whole of the Ascendancy Echelon had come into the garden and were gathered near the gate. She looked down at her plate of cold meat and sweetly spiced bread and tried to focus on it while she half-listened to Kessian outlining her brothers' tasks. She ate only because she knew she had to, not through any desire.

She put her plate down, got up and brushed crumbs from her simple blue tunic dress. She made to move off. There was a lone orange tree sitting in a patch of sunlight in the corner furthest from the gate. It would do perfectly.

'Hold on,' said Arducius. 'Before we split up.' He beckoned them all towards him. 'Link arms.'

He'd done this before when they'd been asked to do something difficult. It was so comforting.

'Remember who we are,' said Arducius. 'We are all here for each other and will support each other. None of us is ever alone.'

They split up and Mirron trotted over to her place. The sun was warm on her body and the garden walls sheltered her from the slight breeze. She sat on the grass outside the shade of the tree's branches. Footsteps behind her belonged to Willem Geste and Meera Naravny, the Echelon's Firewalkers. She glanced over her shoulder and smiled at them. Meera smoothed her hair and Willem crouched carefully in front of her, wincing at some pain in his joints. Perhaps Ossacer would be able to identify it for him.

'Now remember, we are here to watch over you, to guide you and to support you. Father Kessian will be walking around slowly. All you need to do is take your time,' said Willem. 'Are you feeling all right?'

'Fine,' said Mirron. 'But a little nervous.'

'Of course you are, dear,' said Meera. 'It's nothing to worry about. It's a good thing.'

'Where do I start?' asked Mirron, aware quite suddenly that she had no idea.

'Well,' said Willem, 'what you might want to try is first look closely at the signature of this tree. And remember, we cannot help you with that. What we will do is bring you a small fire so you can compare signatures. And then, if you are comfortable, create one from the other and amplify it with yourself. We will be able to see the fire signature as it forms.'

Mirron nodded. 'I'll do my best.'

'You always do,' said Meera. 'Come on, Willem, leave her for a moment.'

Mirron placed her hands on the ground and reached out with her mind, her eyes open. Immediately, trails of energy were revealed to her. In the early days, even that had taken great effort but now she could do it indefinitely. She concentrated on the tree roots which pulsed with bright life all through the earth beneath her feet. This was a young and healthy tree and the trails ran bright green and yellow up into its trunk and through into its branches, only fading to grey at leaves that were beginning to pale with the imminent onset of dusas.

She frowned. The signature of lifelines in the tree was, well, tree-shaped. Was that what Father Kessian wanted her to see? She broke concentration and looked round. As if knowing she'd be confused, the Father was walking towards her, leaning hard on his sticks and taking each step gingerly. Shela was at his side, ready in case he stumbled.

'You look perplexed, my little one,' he said, wheezing slightly.

'I don't know what I'm looking for. The energy trails are just the same shape as the tree. What else can they be?'

'Nothing,' said Kessian. 'Not without help. But I see your confusion. What I want you to consider are the differences between a living signature like this tree, and that of fire which is a destructive, powerful but short lived energy. The density of energies at the heart of the structure is the biggest clue to the differences. In a tree, the heart is spread throughout the roots. In a fire, there is a very dense and violent core. If I read Gorian correctly, this is what you should be trying to make. Examine the fire Willem is bringing to you.'

He brought a small iron cauldron over, carrying it by its handles with no covering. He didn't need it. One hundred and twenty-two years old and still impervious to heat. He set it down on the stone Meera was carrying. Inside, coal and wood was burning hot. Mirron took off her charm bracelet and pushed her hand into the fire, feeling its beautiful warmth spread along her arm. She focused on the energy within. She gasped.

'I can see it,' she said, wondering why it had not occurred to her before.

'Describe it for me,' said Father Kessian.

'It is bound, though it appears random. All the energy trails start in the same place. Where the coal and wood are hottest, the heart of the fire is the darkest red, like blood almost. The trails make other coals hot as they pass by and those coals in turn feed back some of their energy as well as passing the heat outwards.'

She turned to the Father. 'So there is a complete circuit. Even in a fire and even if the energy is always eventually wasted into the air.'

'So if you think about it, a fire grows even as it consumes its fuel, eventually dying and becoming cold and dead. That is not much different than a tree which grows even as the life energies in its roots are slowly consumed. And roots, branches, leaves and eventually whole trees die, becoming cold and dead. The cycle of a fire, without renewed fuel for energy, is faster than that of a tree. Does that help you in moulding earth energy into that of fire?'

Mirron considered for a moment. 'I suppose I should . . . isn't it about compressing the energies I draw from the tree?'

'Yes, but don't forget you need a target on which to place those energies. A fire cycle must have fuel mustn't it?'

Mirron bit her tongue before saying, "well, obviously". She suppressed a smile. 'I cannot even mould the energies without a source for them, can I?'

Father Kessian raised his eyebrows. 'Are you sure? If Gorian is correct, you can perhaps maintain the energy signature within you and then project it on to target fuel such that the signature can survive. Do you see?'

Mirron scratched her head and thought hard. It was not that much different from adapting fire energies from one work to another, she supposed. But there was never a break in the circuit of the energy. Father Kessian was saying she could hold fire within her body without there being the fuel for fire present.

'I'm not sure.'

'Well, try for me. And don't worry if nothing happens. We have all the time in the world.'

With Father Kessian there, Mirron felt she could achieve anything. She smiled up at him, saw the encouragement in his lovely, old wrinkled face and determined to try her very best. She moved her hands back to the ground and brought the energy signature of the tree back to her mind. Surrounding it in the earth, trails that signified other roots, worms and insects fled away in every direction, all identifiable to her if she looked hard enough.

She opened herself to the orange tree, feeling its lifelines link with hers. She knew its grace, the deliberation of its growth and the gentle pulsating of its life that were all so much at odds with the racing of her own body.

Mirron paused, letting the lifelines settle following her delicate interruption of them, before considering how to tap the strength of the tree to make fire. She felt a sense of disquiet. The violence of fire was directly at odds with the peaceful life of the tree and using the latter to create the former seemed wrong. But this was just experiment after all.

The solution was not too difficult to see. If Mirron wanted to force growth into the tree, all she would do was focus her bright, quick energies into the roots of the tree's lifelines, forcing the pools of latent growth potential at the base of the roots up through the structure. Her life force would amplify that growth. Tiring but efficient. And if she wanted to divert the tree's energy to give growth to a linked elemental life like a flower, she used herself as conduit and amplifier but the work was essentially the same.

For fire, then, it was akin to diverting energy but without a destination until the energy map of fire was drawn in her mind and held in her body. It seemed clear to Mirron that she had to compress the tree's gentle lifelines into the harsher, quicker model of fire using her own body as a temporary home. It wouldn't hurt her, after all, and she couldn't create it in the clear air or it would be whipped away by the devils in the wind, lost to God forever.

She held out her left hand, seeing her pink, smooth palm overlaid with bright lifelines, while her right stayed in contact with the cycle of the orange tree. Compared to her, the energy in the roots, branches and leaves was infinite. She picked at individual energy strands, seeing the deep green and brown diverting into her body where its relatively ancient power made her gasp as it always did.

Concentrating harder than she ever had before, aware that Father Kessian was watching her, she used the trails of her body to bind around the tree's energy, squeezing it hard, feeling it begin to race. In her mind's eye, the energy map of the fire grew in her palm. Dark thudding reds and sparkling yellows, released to the sky at their very tips but feeding back into her body at their base, keeping the circle complete.

Now she could consider where the fire should be directed. Willem had already thought of that. She saw him place a triangle of dead branches on a stone slab, their grey and black signatures clear. She reached out her hand towards the fuel, meaning to touch the wood to transfer the energy.

But the lifelines of the tree flowing through her were far more powerful than she was ready to accept. Without an instant destination, she was having trouble regulating their volume now she had teased a break in the cycle. The tree pulsed too strong and the fire energy map she was building sought purchase. Her hand was not close enough to the dead wood and there was other fuel far closer.

Mirron shrieked and flew to her feet, stumbling backwards. Her clothes and hair were ablaze, the smoke and crackling covering her. She could see flame reaching past her eyes and the stink clogged her nose. Dimly, she could hear shouting around her. The fire was hot. Hotter than the forge. It was pure at its centre, corrupted only when it reached the fuel of her clothes and hair.

The shock wore off quickly and she breathed the power in. That was a mistake. Smoke from her clothes made her cough. But she felt invigorated, clean. And when the water was poured over her head she felt a short sensation of loss. She stood for a moment, looking down at her feet, unashamed by her nakedness. The Echelon and the Ascendants were standing in a loose circle around her.

She raised her head, and scratched at her skull. Her hair was gone. She smiled, almost laughed. She knew she should be upset but she felt so alive. She understood what had happened. She knew that she should have closed the circle of the tree's energy before attempting to direct the fire energy map she had made to its ultimate destination. How, she didn't know. She had made a small, pure fire map but the drain on the tree was disproportionately large. So much had been wasted by her inability to keep it all within her. There had to be a better way.

Mirron sighed and nodded reassuringly at them all, seeing the anxiety leaving their faces and the eagerness to know building in its place.

'So,' she said, voice a little rough from the smoke. 'It can be done.'

'Well, obviously,' said Father Kessian.

Laughter rang around the walled garden.

Chapter 12

847th cycle of God, 10th day of Dusasrise
14th year of the true Ascendancy

Estorr. Capital of the Estorean Conquord. A magnificent city of white and red splendour, sparkling in the dawn sun. It dominated the horizon for the last hours of a voyage to Estorea across the Tirronean Sea. A sight to lift the heart and swell the body with pride.

Paul Jhered stood in the prow of the *Hark's Arrow*, his cloak wrapped about him, hood over his head against the freezing temperatures. Above him, the main sail was full in the strong wind, driving them across their last miles, the Gatherers' crest proud at its centre.

The massive fortified harbour of concrete and stone speared half a mile into the sea, its dual walls shaped like a crab's claws with a fortress at the pincer of each. Trebuchets adorned their flat roofs and stone-projecting ballistae occupied positions on three levels towards the sea and the harbour, presenting a withering fire for any enemy and a warning to those seeking to flee the harbour carrying contraband or fugitives. The harbour walls provided deep water berths for large merchant and naval vessels while in the shallows and at the shoreline, fishing smacks clustered in the mill-pond calm.

From the harbour, the great walled city spread out north and south along the coast and up a series of slopes to a hilltop, its peak flattened centuries before to build the first of the Conquord palaces. Jhered had often said that every citizen should be afforded the opportunity to see the city from the sea. There really was no sight like it in the entire Conquord, and he was uniquely placed to make such a judgement.

Estorr was laid out before him in almost map-like order. He could see the wide main avenues, tree-lined and hung with flags, angling up towards the hills and palace like the spokes of a cartwheel. In between them, houses and businesses were packed in a maze of tight streets and alleys. Concrete and stone were whitewashed and decorated in a kaleidoscope of colour for individual identity and advertisement.

As the city rose to its peaks, so the wealth and space increased. Parkland studded the cityscape. Villas rose from behind manicured gardens and curtains of tall, shaped evergreens. To the south, the principal arena towered five storeys into the sky, its processional road to the palace complex wide and bannered along its length. The Gardens of the Advocates stood by the arena, beautiful and reverent. Marble statues of Advocates going back to the earliest days of the Conquord stood on proud fluted columns lining the paths of the park or grouped around stone seats and fountains.

Jhered could see the central forum, thick with activity, set in the centre of the city. Colonnaded on all four sides, it was the single largest open space in Estorr, with an amphitheatre to its north, an oratory to its south and a flood of stalls and people teeming at its centre. City life pulsed here like nowhere else.

And if the forum was the heart of the city, then the three aqueducts were its arteries. Staggering structures of double arches carrying water to the fountains and pipes, city ponds and small lakes, they dominated the higher reaches behind the city. But his eye as ever was inevitably drawn to the palace complex itself, gazing down on all it possessed. He could already imagine the sights that would greet him when he entered it a few hours from now.

Passing through the ceremonial gates the visitor was awed by the grandeur before his eyes. Inside the walls, at the centre of the grand courtyard was the Victory Fountain; four cavalrymen raising the flag of the Conquord, with horses rearing triumphant to the points of the compass. South and east lay the senate administrative buildings and the military and Gatherer headquarters. They presented a blank, colonnaded façade, their imposing doors leading into vaulted chambers and a myriad rooms from where the Conquord was organised, taxed, secured and expanded.

West, the basilica. Delicately carved columns, over a hundred feet tall, standing in eight rows of twelve facing the courtyard, supported a stone roof adorned with carvings of the great battles of the early Conquord as it expanded through Gestern, Avarn, Caraduk and

Easthale. Inside, laws were passed, justice dispensed and pleas heard by the Advocate and her inner circle of propraetors, praetors, aediles and magistrates.

And north, the palace itself. Forty steps, each two hundred feet wide, led up to a dramatic colonnaded entrance. A flag was draped from the ceremonial balcony, shading the huge, gilt inlaid and steel bound doors that led into the grand hallway. This in turn opened into the mighty atrium, at a fountain its centre cascading water over lilies and goldfish.

The atrium was bordered by columns on all four sides and from it the throne room, dining halls, private chambers and gardens were reached. Tapestries and works of art hung from every wall. Statues stood proudly in every alcove and the weight of glory and history pressed on even the strongest man, rendering him weak and humble.

Jhered drew in a deep breath, feeling the cold air sear his lungs and fill him with vitality. The palace, too, should be a place all citizens saw. It was an edifice that spoke so eloquently of the majesty and power of the Conquord. A reminder of what the Conquord had brought the world. It was its absolute shining centre but some of those who walked its corridors were becoming its rotten, decadent core.

It was why Jhered felt compelled to journey back from his current duties in Gestern, leaving the bulk of the Gatherers in the field and bringing only his honour guard with him. Too many problems, too many rumours and too many raids in this peaceful country with the misfortune of sharing a border with Atreska. Generally speaking, Jhered felt uncomfortable when he had sympathy for the ruler of a province where tax concerns were raised. But the Marshal Defender of Gestern was a woman for whom he had enormous respect. And following his meetings with Katrin Mardov, he had taken the decision to travel home with the revenue chests and approved accounts.

With the pale sun at its zenith, the *Hark's Arrow* moved serenely between the guardian fortresses. Her three banks of oars were in the water now and her sail furled. The arrival of the Gatherers' flagship was announced by a sounding of the quadruple horns in their flag towers. The sound split the day, echoing across the water and rolling up the hills on which Estorr stood. Activity ceased on the dockside for a moment, people turning to stare at the vessel rowing in close control towards her permanent berth at the portside wall. From the harbour garrison, whistles were sounded and a detachment of riders came to meet the ship, flying the flag of the Advocate and shadowing an armoured carriage.

The master of the *Hark* barked out a series of orders as the ship manoeuvred towards the berth. Crewmen ran forward and aft to ready the hawsers. Twelve spread along the port rail with poles to fend the ship off the dock wall as it came to rest. The ship angled in, port oars shipped, starboard oars driving the vessel slowly round. With the slightest grating, the *Hark* nudged the dock wall. A wide gangplank slapped into place.

'Exchequer Jhered, welcome back to Estorr,' said the master.

Jhered turned and nodded his acknowledgement, striding down the deck to the gangplank, where the master was standing.

'Thank you. It was a fine voyage. Tell me, how long are you due to stay in port?'

'Ten days, my Lord. We have some minor repairs, stores to take on and my crew will rest. Then we head north to Neratharn.'

'Ah yes, you'll be taking Appros Derizan and team. A challenging brief for them. South-western Atreska is not an easy place.'

'Indeed, my Lord. We have been requested to stand offshore until their investigation is complete.'

Jhered nodded. 'Do so. I may be travelling back with you. I'll send word. Have my bags sent to my quarters on the hill.'

Jhered thumped down the gangplank, his honour guard of eight soldiers at his back. Approaching the cavalry and wagon that were halted waiting for the chests, he smiled at the surprise on the captain's face. The man dismounted in a hurry and slapped his left hand to his right shoulder.

'We had not expected you, Exchequer Jhered.'

'Then you must be glad you had your guards polish their greaves this morning, Captain Harkov,' said Jhered, smiling. He nodded at the cavalry, a ripple of laughter running through them. But it was true. Not just greaves but breastplates, scabbards, plumed helmets, bits and bridles. All gleaming and beautifully prepared. Jhered was impressed.

'It would not do for the Advocate's cavalry to appear anything less than perfect, my Lord.'

'You do her credit.'

'Where are you headed? Our horses are at your disposal.'

'Straight to the hill for an audience with the Advocate,' replied Jhered. 'And thank you for your offer but your duty is to the revenue chests. It is a bracing day. We will walk the harbour wall to your offices. I expect you have horses enough there.'

'Naturally, my Lord. I'll see sufficient are readied for you.' He pointed at a cavalrywoman who wheeled and galloped away. 'It's a popular destination at the moment.'

'Oh, really?' Jhered smoothed his cloak over his breastplate and skirts. The wind whipped inside, chilling his legs.

'I escorted the Marshal Defender of Atreska there myself two days ago, my Lord. And I understand delegations from Gosland and Dornos have been in residence for seven days. I should also tell you that the Chancellor's banner flies above the Principal House too.'

'Hasn't she got heretics to burn elsewhere?' muttered Jhered for Harkov's ears only.

'Apparently there are problems in some farflung areas,' said Harkov. He raised his eyebrows under his helmet. 'She is suing for more enforcement strength, I understand.'

'It is a common theme,' said Jhered, irked by the competition he would have for the Advocate's ear. 'I'm grateful for the information.' He nodded. 'Good to see you, Captain Harkov. You really should reconsider my offer.'

'Perhaps when my children are a little older, my Lord.' He saluted again.

'Your family are more fortunate than they know.' He turned to his guard. 'Let's go. Two by four behind me, eyes front. March.'

From the palace guard barracks, Jhered took horses through the city to the palace on the hill. Once there, Jhered led his honour guard on foot to the Gatherer barracks where he dismissed them for the day before walking in under the Victory Gates. The gates had been built to celebrate the life of the first Advocate of the Conquord, Jennin Havessel. They were a dominating and towering monument, the highest ramparts reaching three hundred feet into the sky.

Nevertheless, it was easy to walk through the grand arch, eyes fixed on the glories inside the courtyard and ignore the intricate carvings that covered every face of the marble and sandstone structure, depicting Havessel's battles and the return of spoils to Estorr. On a dull day, the gold inlay did not sparkle. Nor did the sentinels, statues of four warrior heroes, each a hundred and fifty feet high, seem to intimidate so much, drawing instead into the shadows. But Jhered always paused to run his hands over the centuries-old stonework to remind himself of the legacy he had sworn to protect and to develop.

Jhered emerged from the lantern-light inside the arch, took the salute of the palace guard and swept across the marble courtyard, with its mosaic depictions of battles won and glories long consigned to myth and legend. He ignored the temptation to freshen up in his private offices, instead making directly for the basilica. He could see the multiple colours of togas and the flash of polished armour inside the matrix of columns. The Advocate's banner was hanging down in front of the main entrance to the open structure, marking it as an official day of petition, debate and statement.

A drift of voices carried on the breeze, one dominating the others on his approach: Felice Koroyan, Chancellor of the Order of Omniscience. Nominally, the second most powerful person in the Conquord and a woman whom Jhered would die to protect but with whom he would not choose to share the same air. Still, he enjoyed the sparring that inevitably accompanied an open meeting between her and the Advocate. Today, the heat appeared to be high.

Jhered took the dozen polished marble steps two at a time and marched quickly through the entrance hallway, past banners flying from every column and guards snapping spears to attention as he passed. The sound of his steel-shod road boots echoed from the cavernous ceiling, sounding through the basilica. He was aware of voices falling silent.

He swung left into the audience chamber. It was crowded with the great, the good and the degenerate of the Advocate's sanctum. The Advocate herself sat on a throne placed on a stage two steps above her subjects. It was a wide seat, made for a far larger body, and boasted carved and gilded wood upholstered in the deep green of the Conquord.

She was dressed in flowing robes of state. Finest Tundarran spun wool, dazzling white and edged in green and gold with a sash of office from right shoulder to left hip. Her short dark and greying hair was threaded with gold and fronted by a tiara. She had been half-slouched on her throne, elbow on one plush arm and hand supporting her chin but she was sitting upright now, a smile creeping across her face.

Every eye was on him. He strode through the benches filled with courtiers and petitioners and into the space between the stage and the two arcs of five, high-backed chairs closest to the throne. He stopped on coming level with the Chancellor who was standing by her chair, to his right, and glaring at him. All conversation had long since ceased.

He bowed, the last ricochets of his steps fading in the timber rafters.

'My apologies, my Advocate, for my unannounced arrival.' He turned fractionally towards the Chancellor. 'Please, don't let me interrupt you.'

In front of him, the Advocate stifled a laugh, putting a hand quickly across her mouth. The Chancellor was silent for a moment.

'Then sit, Exchequer Jhered,' she said. 'I have the floor and your appearance is not further prioritised by its volume.'

'Nevertheless, it is a welcome surprise,' said the Advocate, her smooth authoritative voice a stark counterpoint to the Chancellor's heavy south-eastern accent. Jhered bowed again and took his seat to the left. He reached out a hand and squeezed that of Marshal Defender Vasselis of Caraduk whom he had not realised would be present. Finally, he nodded curtly at Marshal Defender Yuran of Atreska whom he was far less pleased to see. The man had become a serial complainer concerning a civil war he had done little to quell but which affected all the legions marching to Tsard.

However, his presence on this occasion might just be beneficial. At least he had a separate perspective on the campaigns in Tsard and might, just might if he could be persuaded to look beyond his own petty troubles for a moment, add useful insight into the problems facing Gosland and Gestern.

Chancellor Koroyan had resumed speaking. She took a rolled parchment from one of her advisers. Jhered craned his neck and saw it was the Speaker of the Earth. A heady delegation indeed.

'The fact is that in all seven of our newest outlying territories, we do not have enough strength to carry the message of the Order. Native religions flourish while my Readers, Pastors and Speakers are at best ignored, or driven from their Houses of Masks. Some have been even less fortunate and I will leave you this list for the Conquordian records of those murdered for their beliefs.'

She snapped her fingers and was handed another parchment which she unrolled.

'A few more details for you—'

The Advocate glanced briefly at Jhered who rolled his eyes.

'— Gosland's bemusing animal icon religion has resurfaced throughout the territory; Atreska's well-known allegiance to the multifarious and heretical faiths of Tsard shows no sign of diminishing; and in north-eastern Gestern, the mountain idols, statues and carvings favoured by the Kark are gathering worshippers and pilgrims by the thousand.

'Now, before all those here present protest that our Tsardon borders are bound to foster discontent and drive the misguided to seek solace in their old faiths, let me tell you that I understand that. I also understand that it strengthens my petition. And if these territories were my only challenges, I would not be standing here. Rather, I would be diverting my missionaries and few legions to the Tsardon border states myself.

'However, it seems this insurgency of bewilderingly loose and groundless faiths is growing in strength rather closer to home.' She spared Vasselis a meaningful look, which he returned unflinching. 'Among your closest allies, my Readers are ignored and obstructed in their God-given duties. And in the heartlands of the Conquord, in Avarn, Neratharn, Phaskar . . . countries steeped in centuries of Conquord glory, still there are significant numbers of citizens openly flouting the teachings of the Order.

'Only in Estorea, it seems, is God truly worshipped and respected. That is undoubtedly why here we are spared retribution and the citizens enjoy long, peaceful and productive lives before returning to the bosom of the Omniscient in triumph.'

Koroyan paused, letting her words hang in the light air of the basilica.

'My Advocate, the Conquord population expands at a rate that none of us could have foreseen even fifteen years ago. The accessions of Gosland and Atreska have stretched Order resources beyond our capacity to control as we must. And that was before the border and insurgency troubles began taking their combined tolls.

'The Conquord needs its religion to be a dominant force or all the good work of our legions will ultimately come to nothing, a result none of us desire. You are the Prime Speaker of the Order, you know this to be true. I must have more funding because I must have more people to carry the word and to bear arms against those who would strike against God and everything we hold close to our hearts.

'My papers and calculations are at your disposal for scrutiny.'

The Chancellor bowed slightly and took a single pace backwards. A ripple of conversation broke out in the public benches behind while the Advocate considered her response. Jhered frowned, concerned at what he had heard despite the Chancellor's tendency for exaggeration. Unfortunate echoes were sounding in his mind.

'Are you in Estorr for a long stay?' It was Vasselis.

Jhered turned. Vasselis regarded him with those deep, intelligent eyes, a smile welcoming his friend.

'Ten days, no more. I had not thought to see you.'

'Nor I you. You're a rare visitor these last few years.'

'There's a great deal of work to do in the east.'

Vasselis's smile broadened. 'The work of the Exchequer is ever distant and lonely.'

Jhered chuckled. 'It was me said that to you, wasn't it?'

Vasselis nodded. 'Indeed. And I would welcome the chance to hear more pearls over dinner before we both leave.'

'I wouldn't miss it.'

'Chancellor Koroyan.' The Advocate leaned forward in her throne, one hand rubbing her chin. Immediately, conversation ceased. Jhered relaxed into his chair to listen. 'I'll keep this short because I will of course study your papers at length. But I find making a judgement in your favour very difficult, your writings notwithstanding. The reasons are these.

'As the Prime Speaker of the Order, I of course want to see the word of God the Omniscient spread to the furthest corners of the Conquord. We worship the one true God and all other faiths, with their false idols and false Gods, promote false promises. So we all believe. But, as I grow rather tired of explaining, the path to enlightenment of those following rogue religions is one of education and demonstration, not of force and control.

'Surely, if you find you have to force a populace to follow the Omniscient then you have lost the argument on theological grounds, no?'

She held up a hand to cut off the Chancellor's protests.

'I have no doubt in the desire of all of the Order to preach and convert every heathen they encounter. But resistance is natural. You cannot hope to over throw centuries of faith with a few ancient words backed by sword and bow. It takes time and in the outlying territories, wounds are still fresh. They will come round. Faster when Tsard comes under the rule of the Conquord. But even then, some will never convert and we have to respect them. Chancellor Koroyan, we *have* to respect them. They are simply non-believers and theirs will be a short, single cycle on God's earth where we renew to deliver more glories.

'Seek to understand them, not suppress them or you will create those you hate with your own hand. I find it almost impossible to see that I will release funds from the treasury to help you build your already considerable armies. Surely they are enough to police the word of God among those who swear by it and to protect those missionaries beyond our borders.

'If, and I say if, I was to agree to more funding, it could only be to recruit and educate more Readers, Pastors and Speakers. For the building of more Houses of Masks. There is where your true strength should lie. Perhaps you should consider how your budget is currently allocated. Or perhaps you would like an independent audit, to see what, if anything, is being wasted in your name.'

She gestured at Jhered then, and the Gatherer's Exchequer could not hide his smile. The Chancellor's face was stone while the Advocate's remained deliberately neutral.

'I believe that the word of God must come from the mouths of believers, not the weapons of its defenders. I will read your entreaty and my final decision will be with you tomorrow by nightfall.'

The Chancellor shook her head, bowed and spun to leave the basilica, her cohort at her back. The Advocate watched her go, worry in her expression and the chewing of her teeth at her top lip.

'Now, on to other matters,' she said. 'There is a petition list as long as my daughter's hair and evening approaches.'

Chapter 13

847th cycle of God, 10th day of Dusasrise
14th year of the true Ascendancy

Herine Del Aglios, Advocate, Prime Speaker and mother of four, linked her arm through Paul Jhered's once the palace doors had closed behind them. At sixty-seven she was moving gracefully into middle age and presided over a Conquord she was determined to settle before handing the reins to Roberto, her eldest.

She slowed the pace of the tall soldier to little more than an amble, determining to enjoy a private stroll with him through her gardens and courtyards, columns and statues. Her guards, advisers and current consort had all been dismissed.

'If we go any slower we'll grind to a halt,' grumbled Jhered.

'You would march me to an early return to the earth,' said Herine. 'Relax. Enjoy my house. Look.'

She stopped him and gestured with her free hand. The garden might have been cold and lacking in the glorious colours of a late genasfall day, but even in its stark dusas livery it was stunning amid the hundreds of lantern-lights that pushed away the night. They nestled in the crooks of the arms of statues, shone through glass panes set into the bases of fountains, littered the flower beds and swung gently from poles set at head height.

It gave the colonnaded open space a dreamlike quality, turned it into a sanctuary from the noise and confusion of state. A day in the basilica left Herine shattered, however much she enjoyed the cut and thrust of debate, and despite the value she gained from hearing both the ordinary citizen and the senior statesperson.

Jhered's arrival that afternoon had been a genuine blessing, offering her intelligent company and conversation in addition to first-hand, unbiased news from the outer territories. Sometimes she felt as if she existed in a cocoon. Jhered was a breath of fresh air.

'It is one of my favourite places in the entirety of the Conquord, my Advocate,' conceded Jhered.

'Oh, listen to you, Paul,' said Herine. 'Ever the formal soldier. We're on our own here.'

Jhered smiled. 'Authority and respect are cornerstones of our government, Herine. Sorry. Sometimes I find it difficult to revert even when I'm with friends.'

'And am I your friend?' asked Herine.

Jhered looked down at her, frowning. He really was a tall man, very imposing. Striking rather than handsome. But at a full sixteen inches taller than her, he quite literally towered above her.

'Never doubt it,' he said. 'You are one of the few I would term such. So few really have the Conquord scored into their hearts, even some of those you hold dear.'

Herine felt the gentle stab and whistled breath in over her teeth. 'Do I detect a rebuke?'

'You know how I view those who close around you, day by day, and in that, if in nothing else, I am in agreement with the Chancellor. They do not see what we see, merely the riches that your position brings. If I were one of them, I would not seek to ripple the water either.'

Herine tugged at his arm. 'You'd have been unafraid. I still say you should have agreed to be a consort. Father a child of mine.'

'I value my balls far too much for that.'

They both laughed aloud.

'You think it would have affected your career in later years?' she asked mischievously.

'The perfect physical specimen you see before you would be a slothful, overweight buffoon wearing gay coloured clothes and trapped in the backwater palace in Phaskar, as you well know. It is as well none of your children will ever know their fathers.'

'I might have taken you as my husband. I have always preferred younger men.' She knew she shouldn't feel a thrill at the flirting but she couldn't help it. How wonderful to shed the shackles of state and be a woman for a moment.

'You know why you can never do that,' said Jhered, not catching her mood.

'It does no harm to dream,' she said.

'Is it something you wish for?' asked Jhered.

'Would it be a sign of weakness if I said yes?' she countered, a well of loneliness threatening to open up.

'It is never weakness to yearn for love and companionship. It is human to desire one person to share your life.'

'But we have both chosen paths that deny us fulfilment of that desire.'

'Until we retire at least. And all we can do until then is protect the right for every citizen of the Conquord.'

She tugged his arm again. 'You should be at the oratory, saying things like that. Come on. It may be beautiful out here but it's also cold and you haven't come here merely to swap pleasantries and explain the value of avoiding castration. Take wine with me.'

They strolled through the colonnades, Herine glancing up to see the fine ionic scrollwork lit by lantern as they passed. She often wondered who had taken the chisel and hammer to these great pieces of stone. She loved the artistry and the imagination that had resulted in these columns, so often taken for granted, merely seen as the masonry that supported the roof above their heads.

It was a short walk to a warm private dining room, luxuriously furnished, hung with tapestries and with rugs covering the mosaic floor under which the hot air thrummed gently through the foundations. Herine pointed Jhered to a long leather recliner, studded in bronze and with green and gold feather cushions scattered along it. She took one at right angles to him such that their heads were close together. When the servant had poured the first glasses of warm, spiced wine, she indicated that the girl withdraw. The door closed behind her. Herine wafted a hand at the table.

'Meats, breads and a particularly good honey and herb sauce. My eldest brought back the recipe from campaign ten years ago. Such a young boy then in so many ways, my Roberto.'

'And a very capable general now,' said Jhered. 'I hear fine reports of him from Tsard.'

'A difficult campaign,' said Herine.

'It was always going to be so,' said Jhered. 'A large and proud country. Very fierce, very independent.'

'And they will make a fine addition to the Conquord in the years to come. Fantastic wealth there. Extraordinary resources and a hard-working citizenry. Just think. Taking Tsard will open up the entire east to us by land and sea. What an opportunity.'

'Have you given thought to your consuls for the area?' asked Jhered. 'It will be a challenge unlike any other.'

'And one where the Tsardon must know our respect for them. I had thought members of the family would be the right candidates.'

'Wise as always, as long as you can keep the jealousies of your more senior generals under control. And the Order.'

Herine bridled a little. 'That's my job, Paul. Now, tell me about yours. What's taxing you, if you'll pardon the expression.'

Jhered took a long sip of his wine and raised his eyebrows, pleased at the taste.

'Do you mind if I ask one question before I begin?'

'Of course not.' Herine settled back, cradling her warm glass and letting the scent float into her nostrils.

'What is the detail of the reports you receive from the Tsardon campaigns?'

Herine blew out her cheeks and tried quickly to recall some figures. 'I have twenty legions and sixteen alae in Tsard, operating on three separate fronts. Almost a hundred and twenty thousand men and women fighting for the Conquord over two thousand miles away. With the campaigns suspended for the cold season, and I understand dusas to be harsh in Tsard this year, I am getting the reports I need to assess requirements for more forces and equipment. I seldom feel the need to ask for more and the distance makes that difficult anyway. During the campaign season reports can be a little more fragmentary.'

She frowned suddenly, a frission of anxiety across her body. 'Why do you ask?'

'And what about from behind the forward legions. From the supply chain and the border fortifications?' Jhered was pressing her for information and she didn't like the way it felt.

'Is there something I'm not hearing? I take a dim view of being kept in the dark.'

Herine saw Jhered regarding her carefully, weighing up her mood. He knew her quick and dangerous temper. It was a testament to him that he was unafraid. Nor should he be. She needed a hundred Jhereds. A thousand. God-embrace-her but she had missed him.

'My Advocate, Herine. I hear things and I see things. Indeed, people are very keen for me to see anything that might reduce their tax burden. But of late I've been feeling uneasy. Not everything I see and hear can be ignored as the bleatings of the greedy wishing to keep their wealth from being used for the good of the Conquord.'

'I hear these things too, Paul. I've been hearing them for forty-two years, ever since I achieved the Advocacy. Why are you uneasy now? We are wealthier and more successful than we have ever been. The Conquord remains a triumph.'

'Now who should be at the oratory?' Jhered smiled.

Herine felt some of the heat leave her face. She drank her wine, feeling a slight shake in her hands.

'I believe in what we achieve.'

'It is why you are Advocate and I love you and serve you. Please, Herine, if I didn't share your determination and belief I could not do the job you have asked me to do.'

'I am not questioning you.'

Jhered raised a hand. 'I know, I know. And I know you hear pleas and hard-luck stories every day you are in the basilica. I appreciate you're sick to the stomach of it all. But if I may, I think perhaps you never hear an account that might link apparently independent incidents together.'

'You mean yours.' Jhered inclined his head. 'You know I'll listen to you, Paul. But please, let's eat first and talk about something a little lighter. I'm famished and that sauce is cooling. It would be a shame to let it spoil.'

'So it would. And Herine, what I have to say does include some conjecture of course but it is honestly given – and more important, we do not face a crisis. Not yet. So long as we act soon.'

They ate largely in silence as it happened. Jhered admitted the sauce was excellent. It was only towards the end of the meal, when again the servants had been told to withdraw, that Jhered opened up just a little. He was holding the same goblet of wine when the briefest of smiles touched his lips.

'Oh, I have a new candidate for most ridiculous attempt to avoid tax levy. This is a good one, I promise.'

'You know I need new stories for banquets,' she said, gesturing for him to continue and relaxing back into her recliner.

'As you know I've just returned with the revenue chests from Gosland via Atreska and Gestern. One of my people got suspicious about the reasons for a very low returned levy from a farming community on the south-eastern border with Tsard. Menas, her name is. Very capable. She'll end up in Atreska or some other trouble spot, I expect. I sent her and a team of six out there, it was only a two-day ride and good experience. It goes like this.' He sat up, swinging his feet on to the floor so he could use both arms for emphasis.

'It's a settlement called Ruthirin. Small place, about two hundred people. All farmers, mostly goat and cattle. The team arrive there, the snow is six inches deep and there's an icy gale blowing through the valley. They are shown damage to properties, some smashed pottery and largely empty fields. The story is, they've suffered a Tsardon raid for livestock. But it just doesn't feel right. They see a few half-hearted bandages but no one looks hurt. No one looks shocked. But the fact is that the livestock is gone and we know from connecting settlements that there has been no sudden surge in trade. So . . .'

'They've hidden them of course. Forest or next-door valley, right?' Herine was warming to the tale. Jhered never embellished these stories but he painted a vivid enough picture nonetheless. Herine could see the citizens shifting uncomfortably and looking at their feet under questioning.

'Almost,' said Jhered, holding up a finger. 'But it's far more stupid than that. Beggars belief.' He paused to shake his head, apparently having to remind himself that what he said was true. 'The team rode out to any likely holding place. They found caves, valleys and forest land but no sign at all – and there would have been. There should have been a mess of hoof prints in the snow but there was nothing.'

'And of course, that was their downfall.'

'Absolutely. They said it proved the livestock had been taken but when the team asked to see the exit trails, it all started falling apart. They'd made some small effort but a one-day trained tracker could have seen through it.' He smiled. 'Want to know what they'd done?'

'Immediately.'

'They've slaughtered the bloody lot, barring breeding stock of course. Then jointed it and buried it in the snow to preserve it before selling it on after we'd gone, tax-free.'

Herine spat wine back into her glass to allow herself to laugh, coughing as she sucked a little into her lungs.

'Oh Paul, no. How did they think it would be worth it?'

'I don't know,' said Jhered, shoulders shaking. 'We did some calculations and reckon that given that butchered meat will fetch a lower price on an open market, given no guarantee of freshness, they might have saved themselves in total perhaps twenty-five denarii, no more.'

'So what did you do?'

Jhered sobered. 'Had this been a protest I would have been far more sympathetic as I will explain later. But for these criminals I did exactly what I had to. We are the justice and I will not have anyone defrauding the Conquord and attempting to cheat the Gatherers. We have a reputation hard earned. So, the ringleaders were executed and every other able-bodied man and woman is now serving with the fourth ala, the Gosland Spear, in Tsard. Anyone else has been shipped back to the capital for resettlement and the village itself has been destroyed.'

Herine composed herself. Correct punishment undoubtedly but shocking to hear it related so dispassionately in the heart of the Conquord.

'We should place all these in a book and make sure every citizen reads it,' she said. 'Pointless for those people. Misguided, you think?'

'I have ordered the sentence be nailed to every announcement board in every basilica in Gosland. Misguided? No I don't think so. I think they felt beyond the reach of the Gatherers out there near the border. Now everyone in Gosland knows different. What worries me is why they felt that way. That's what we need to talk about before you retire for the night.'

'I've diverted you for long enough, eh?'

'Yes, my Advocate.'

Herine sighed and refilled her glass. Jhered refused any more, pouring water into a goblet instead. She felt she'd heard enough problems today and no doubt Jhered's would be the most pressing.

'So, why should I be worried?'

'Because a great deal I have seen or heard through solas and into this dusas tells me that the Conquord is struggling to maintain cohesion at its outer markers.'

Herine jerked back, feeling as if she'd been slapped. She felt a flush across her face and a familiar anger began to grow in the pit of her stomach.

'You're serious, aren't you?'

'I wouldn't have travelled here otherwise. There are challenges out in the wilds that I should be overseeing.'

'I don't understand this. The campaigns are progressing well.'

'Well enough but you aren't getting complete information from the borders. Problems are growing that, if the Chancellor is right, are beginning to spread deeper into the Conquord. Your reports shouldn't be so erratic during the campaigning season. We have an Advocacy messenger service after all and the roads and seaways to Tsard are well-trodden and of good quality, even through Atreska.'

'Paul, you are in danger of patronising me. I do see more than these four walls.' Herine cleared her throat and sighed. 'Just tell me. Stop prevaricating.'

Jhered's eyes went a little cold and Herine caught a glimpse of why he was so feared. An enemy would not want to face that expression.

'Four years ago, very early in the Tsardon campaigns, you'll recall that the report I sent back from Atreska with the revenue chests mentioned Tsardon raids deep into Atreskan territory. I witnessed the aftermath of one myself. At the time, I concluded that these were the price of expansion and that they would cease as the Tsardon campaign gathered momentum. This has not happened.

'Raids into Atreska have continued and by the accounts of my teams there, backed up by anecdotal evidence, are increasing in ferocity and probe ever deeper. The result is that vulnerable settlements are abandoned as more and more people seek the security of larger settlements. There is an inevitable knock-on effect for revenue and trade. And, more seriously, as border settlements are destroyed, our supply lines to the legions in Tsard are put under increasing pressure. I have no doubt that Marshal Yuran is here to tell you exactly the same things, and to ask for a reduction in levy and a reduction in the number of citizens taken to the alae in Tsard so he can defend his own lands.'

Herine thought to speak but a small hand gesture from Jhered stopped her. Her ire blossomed. Undermining of her conquest of Tsard was not an option.

'Now, we both know that Yuran is given to gross exaggeration and that many of his people still resent their accession to the Conquord. But I am getting the same stories from Gosland and, more significantly, from Gestern.

'You know I opposed the Tsardon campaign at the Prima

Chamber when it was proposed. This is why we are struggling. We don't have the back-up, we don't have the men in the fields and we don't have the militias we should have. And Gestern's problems are not to be shrugged off.'

Herine didn't like this at all. Gestern. Governing the trade with Kark without whose metals and minerals, the Conquord would suffer catastrophically. Jhered continued.

'I spent several days with Marshal Mardov before returning here. She has had to raise a new Gesternan legion to defend her northern borders. Tsardon raiders are travelling Atreska's border with Kark to attack them. Amazing I know but I also know better than to question Katrin Mardov.'

Herine shook her head. 'This is very difficult to take in. Is Gestern actually under threat?'

'Let's not get too far ahead. The raids have been repulsed and so far they are sporadic but the fact they are happening at all is a significant concern.'

'That is an understatement, Paul. This is very serious.'

'Only should we ignore it.'

'And is there more?'

'Yes, but this is where I start to use conjecture so please bear with me. Something is wrong in our organisation of the Tsardon campaigns that allows them to undertake what I believe to be organised raids. There's a pattern emerging here. It began with Gosland and Atreska and it is clearly designed to unsettle citizenries relatively recently taken into the Conquord. Remember that both those countries were Tsardon trading partners, if not allies, less than fifteen years ago.

'But it isn't just the trade that is being disrupted. The Tsardon are targeting settlements that have embraced Omniscience. When they attack, their first raid will normally be one of abduction, livestock theft and cursory damage. A second raid will destroy the House of Masks and involve the execution of citizens, often mimicking Conquord decimation. A third will see the settlement destroyed if it has not already been abandoned or fortified.

'Think of the effect this has on ordinary Atreskans or Goslanders. Survivors take tales of raids back to towns and cities. There is fear and anxiety. People stop believing that the Conquord has the capability or the will to protect them. They return to their old religions because they see that the Order cannot save them - so the Chancellor is right, but as usual she doesn't see the whole picture.

'They begin to lose faith in their Marshal Defenders, who in turn seek to prop up their support by refusing to send citizens to Tsard and instead use them for defence. Territories begin to lose cohesion. I don't have to explain further. We are stretched to the east and also to the north. Dornos is still an uneasy partner in the Conquord and its Marshal has close ties with Atreska. The Omari campaign is a desperate slog. Should someone like Yuran take matters into his own hands, we will struggle to find the strength to force him back to the Conquord or replace him.

'And now the Tsardon are making a statement by raiding Gestern. They are strong, mobile and determined.'

Herine dragged her tiara from her head and rubbed a hand through her hair, removing some of the gold thread as she did so. Jhered's words had pierced deep into her heart, sending her pulse high and clouding her thoughts temporarily.

'You are talking of outright rebellion,' she whispered, not wanting to hear the words herself. 'Not just civil disobedience.'

'Eventually, yes. But it is eminently avoidable, Herine. So I'm urging you to listen to Yuran when he has his audience with you. Hear the messages beneath his whines. I think he is feeling under immense pressure from his citizens and he feels trapped by the level of taxation we have to impose. He doesn't know where to turn and he is a weak man, unable to force his authority on his citizens. Gosland will be the next knocking on your door asking for help.

'I am sorry to have to present you with this but it is something we cannot afford to dismiss as transitory. Our supply lines to the legions will be under real threat in the near future, and in the last two years, the Gatherers have seen revenues decrease for genuine reasons, all Tsardon-induced. The treasury has the deficit reports. Yuran won't want me involved in his talks with you. I'm afraid we don't see eye to eye. But I'm here to help you with your response if you want me.'

Herine nodded, organising herself. She felt calm return to her body and poise to her thoughts. There were solutions. She'd been finding them for forty years.

'The Conquord is a powerful entity,' she said. 'It is inconceivable that we can't nip this in the bud. Whether it's more legions, more

Readers, new Marshals, reinstatement of prefects and consuls from Estorr, we will find a way.'

'In that I have every confidence,' said Jhered.

'I'll listen and I'll consult. When do you leave?'

'Ten days or so.'

'Excellent.' Herine refilled her glass and now Jhered consented to a second glass himself. 'You'll be taking messages and plans back with you for the Advocacy messenger service. Some you'll deliver personally.'

'Whatever you need me to do.'

'Thank you, Paul.'

Jhered rose to take his leave. 'You should sleep on this. I'm not trying to panic you but the situation is more dangerous out there than most in the palace appreciate.'

'I know.' She smiled though it didn't relax her body. 'Well, I do now.'

'What brings Arvan Vasselis here, by the way?' he asked at the door to the dining room.

Herine shrugged. 'I don't know. He wants to talk to me on some matter or other but it's largely a social call, I think. And he upsets Felice, which is always fun.'

'Good night, my Advocate,' said Jhered, bowing his head.

'Good night, Paul.'

Herine kissed his cheeks and closed the door behind him, his footsteps fading like the last echoes of a comforting dream, leaving her awake and alone.

Chapter 14

847th cycle of God, 14th day of Dusasrise
14th year of the true Ascendancy

It was four days since her troubling dinner with Paul Jhered and Herine had not been slow to act. She had ordered a report from the Treasury on inconsistencies and reductions in tax levies from the Tsardon border states as well as trade figures from Sirrane and Kark. She had ordered volumes of minerals and metals to be assessed and a report drawn up on shortages should Kark be cut off as a trading partner. Timber they could source from countries other than Sirrane but it would be of lesser quality.

She had sent messengers to every country in the Conquord on her seal, requesting information. Some asked merely for projected revenues against levy target and explanations of any shortfalls. Some required additional information on citizenry available for cavalry and foot duty, supply and transport. But of the legions in Tsard and of the Marshal Defenders of Gosland and Gestern, she demanded complete information on incursions, security of borders, state of the armies and morale of the citizens. She had advised that she would consider all requests for reinforcement but reminded people that the Treasury was not bottomless and the landed citizenry could not supply endless horses with the men and women to ride them to battle.

Herine had time right now. Dusas had only just begun and in the north-east it was a harsh, freezing season. Campaigns were halted until the genastro sun warmed the earth. The Tsardon had withdrawn to strongholds and fastnesses to repair and resupply. But dusas would last only around ninety days and then the campaigns would begin again. She couldn't afford to delay and she couldn't afford tardy responses to her demands for information. It was a point on which she had been particularly forceful.

Marshal Defender Thomal Yuran of Atreska sat before her. The welcome had been warm enough and he had been happy to talk about more mundane matters for a time. But he had never relaxed, despite her best efforts. She couldn't blame him. He felt he had severe problems and it was beginning to appear that not everything he complained about was fabrication or even exaggeration.

Herine had done as Jhered had, easing back on the wine to keep a clear head. She had chosen a setting not too sumptuous, a private reception chamber in the administrative offices of the basilica, and had worn a formal toga. The pair of them sat facing each other opposite a grand open fire, the heavy stone floor of the basilica unsuited to a hypocaust. She wore a woollen shawl around her shoulders against the embedded chill in the high-ceilinged room. Yuran wore a toga slashed with the yellow and green of Atreska and Estorea and his shoulders were draped in furs.

'It is a trade I am keen to encourage,' continued Herine. 'Your ceramic artistry is the finest in the Conquord, as your gift this visit so amply demonstrates. I'm sure there are ways I can help facilitate better distribution to the north-west and south-west. Tundarra and Bahkir have no idea what their dining tables are missing.'

'And we regularly lose our potters and artists to Tsardon raids,' said Yuran bluntly.

Herine sensed the atmosphere that settled over the room. He had been waiting his opportunity and Herine felt ready to let him exploit it.

'I am aware of your concerns, Thomal.'

'Yet, my Advocate, you determine to discuss trade with countries who struggle to afford what we must charge because we and they are so heavily taxed at the behest of your Treasury. And to what end? The Tsardon appear to have free run of my borders and my citizens are clamouring for more security that I literally cannot afford to give them. I am compelled to ask what the legions are actually achieving in Tsard that so many raiders, apparently not needed in the front line against the Conquord, are able to circumvent them.'

'You will recall the agreement you and I signed on Atreska's accession to the Conquord.'

'It was a time I will never forget, my Advocate,' said Yuran, his voice thickly accented, his words sometimes difficult to understand.

'As I will not forget my apparently misplaced belief in the security and sanctity of the Conquord.'

Herine chose to ignore the slight against all that she ruled.

'Then you will recall that levies would be assessed twice in each year and that Atreska would at all times be responsible for her own domestic defence.'

'It is a defence we cannot afford to train, let alone arm and maintain.'

'Come, come,' said Herine indulgently, allowing herself a smile. 'Surely it is not beyond you or your citizens to organise individual citizen militia to protect their own properties.'

Yuran gaped, a reaction that took Herine a little by surprise. 'I am not the Marshal Defender of Phaskar or Caraduk. Law officers and trusted citizens bearing arms are completely inadequate. I am dealing with trained Tsardon horse archers, steppe cavalry and veteran foot soldiers. I have to fight fire with fire and I do not have the funds to do so. You must reduce the burdens placed upon Atreska in terms of both men and tax. Just temporarily, until the burden of training and deployment is over.'

'Let me assure you, Marshal Defender Yuran, that there is nothing that I *must* do. I will, as always, listen to your petitions but I must satisfy myself that you have already done everything in your power to solve your problems before you approach me. That, after all, is the price of local autonomy, is it not?'

Yuran's face reddened. 'I do not deserve to be patronised, my Advocate. I deserve to be treated seriously and with sympathy and objectivity. During my tenure as Marshal Defender I have struggled with endless civil strife and rebel action. And I have suffered constant raids from Tsard as a direct result of the Conquord's ill-judged desire for further conquest in a kingdom too strong to take on. The border fortresses are clearly inadequate as a first line of defence, not least because so many of them stand empty as to make a mockery of their construction.

'The alae attached to the legions in Tsard are full of my men and women, robbing me of people to plant and harvest and to fire and paint the ceramics you value so highly. I can barely match your treasury's assessment as it is. If I remove more to train as domestic defence, they will not produce revenue, hence squeezing my finances still further and your treasury will lose out. And then of course, Exchequer Jhered will be knocking on my door, demanding reasons.

'Tell me, my Advocate, where I am going to find the men and the money to do what my citizens demand? I am asking you to reduce the burden on my country at the least, and preferably to provide me with more troops. Bahkir, Neratharn, your own country of Estorea, they do not suffer the raids and plunder of Atreska, Gosland and now Gestern. Give each border state the means to protect itself. Admit you have underestimated the strength of the Tsardon.

'The Conquord must act as one if it is to be as glorious as it deserves to be. Now, in Atreska's hour of need, do not turn your back and pretend nothing is wrong. Even your man Jhered knows I speak the truth, as does your Chancellor.'

Herine didn't reply at once. She pushed her tongue into her cheek and replayed Yuran's words. Brief. Briefer than his usual meandering entreaties and for that she was grateful. She felt tired today, weighed down by her responsibilities, and for the first time a little anxious about the security of the Conquord. Hard to believe there could be any discontent from her position on the hill. And that was exactly what Jhered always worried about. The whispered words in her ears from her advisers clashed with what she was hearing now.

But she had to be sure. It was natural to feel jealous about the luxuries of the palace when travelling from the outlying provinces. What people like Yuran failed to understand was that she wanted them all to have such riches as of right. But it had to be earned. Pain was inevitable before gain.

'Marshal Yuran,' she said, excited about the reaction she was likely to provoke. 'I am sorry you feel your tax burden is too high. So it's fortunate that I have the Exchequer visiting. I will ask him to organise a complete review of Atreska's accounts for the last five years and the proposed levy his Gatherers are planning to collect when genastro warms the earth. Perhaps they will find an error in your favour. Perhaps not.'

'My Advocate, that isn't—'

Herine raised a hand, irritation flooding her. 'You are now listening to me,' she said. 'Remember your place. You have asked me to reduce your levy. I shall investigate whether there is any justification for that. And I support your thought to employ soldiers from Conquord countries. It is exactly what our structure allows, although I don't know why you've come to me first. It isn't necessary.'

Yuran was shaking his head delicately as if he wasn't sure he was hearing correctly. 'Because I cannot afford to pay Conquord soldiers just as I cannot afford to train my own.' He spoke quietly, as if to someone slow to learn.

'Then you must make economies to free funds. Gestern has raised a defensive legion by doing just that.'

Yuran slapped his hands on the table and stood up. A glass wobbled, fell and shattered on the marble top.

'Damn you but you tie both hands behind my back and order me to climb mountains! Will you not listen, woman? I have no money, I have no defence and your legions leave me exposed. I am trying to maintain the cohesion of the Conquord against Tsard and at every turn you place obstacles in my path. It is as if you want me to fail and Atreska to be overrun.' Then, as if remembering where he was and to whom he was speaking, he breathed deep, made the Omniscience encompassing symbol and sat back down, face red, eyes down.

Behind Herine, the door to the chamber had been thrust open and two guards were already halfway across the room. She waved them back without looking round, waiting until the door closed. She looked across at Yuran, whose embarrassment forbade him to look up at her. She felt a short stab of guilt at provoking his outburst now it had happened and decided against a formal rebuke, though she was disappointed at his lack of self-control. His desperation was more acute than she had anticipated. She supposed that was what she had been trying to ascertain.

She spoke quietly and deliberately, seeing his head come up at her first words. 'I will do everything I can,' she said. 'And believe me when I say I worry about every citizen who dies on a Tsardon sword. But over this dusas, you have to learn to help yourself. Work with the legions in Tsard. Put faces on the battlements of the border forts, trained or not. Encourage your citizens to prepare their own defences if they are all you have. Deterrents are powerful, even in the face of Tsardon raiders.

'Before you go, and you will go without saying another word, let me remind you of three facts. First, the Conquord works because its member states provide their own backbone to aid the cause of the whole. All have gone through what you experience now. All succeeded because they believed and were prepared to stand up when faced with enemies they once thought of as partners in trade, if not friends.

'Second, short-term austerity is often the price of long-term prosperity. I note that you wear enough wealth on your fingers and around your neck to fund much of the trained defence you so crave. Perhaps you should consider personal sacrifice above that of your citizens.

'Third, I am not a woman. I am Marshal Defender of Estorea, Prime Speaker of the Order of Omniscience and Advocate of the Estorean Conquord. You should take care who it is you choose to damn.

'The breeze is harsh. Be sure to close the door firmly on your way out.'

Exchequer Paul Jhered strode along the magnificent colonnaded road that led away from the palace complex, feeling the deep chill of a dusas night slice into his body despite his leggings, the wool he wore beneath his moulded leather breastplate and the fur-lined cloak wrapped close about him.

It was a walk he had so often enjoyed. The cold invigorated him. The lanterns suspended from columns and trees shed pools of light on cobbles that rang beneath his steel toecaps and heels. Taverna Alcarin, where he was meeting Vasselis, was easily the finest in Estorr and that was up against significant competition. Glorious cuts of meat, the freshest catches from the Tirronean Sea and rich sauces, the mere thought of which caused him to salivate in anticipation.

Yet on this quiet mid-evening, with stars scattered thickly across the skies and barely another citizen on the street, Jhered felt at odds with himself. It had all stemmed from his summoning to an audience with the Advocate. It had been a particularly one-sided conversation. Herine had meandered through a series of requests, from opening new investigations into Atreskan levies, through an assessment of the troop levels in Tsard and on the conflict borders, and to an unusual demand on him to seek the detailed views of the Chancellor of the Order with regard to Conquord-wide loyalty, morale and religious education.

None of these, unwelcome though at least one of them was, had led to his mood tonight. It was the fact that Herine had been distracted throughout the meeting; and it wasn't that her mind was wandering to the new lover that awaited her. Another pretty young man destined for castration and guarded banishment to the Advocate palace in Phaskar, should he prove fertile enough within her womb.

Something she had learned from her meeting with Vasselis had disturbed her deeply. Indeed, Jhered had never seen her so unfocused on the matters in hand. Matters of great importance to the Conquord. One of the many reasons Jhered had such respect for the Advocate was the sharpness of her mind and her determination that the Conquord should prosper above all personal goals.

She would not be drawn on what Vasselis had revealed to her but the trouble it had caused had been inscribed in her every word and movement. Herine had locked eyes with him just once to say:

'You are his friend are you not? You respect and love him like a brother, don't you?'

And it had seemed almost an accusation. And his reply, that indeed he was meeting Vasselis for dinner that night drew tears to her eyes.

'He trusts so completely and he might have need of those he trusts. You are one. I am another. Why do I wonder if he is mistaken in that trust?'

She would say nothing more on the subject and had left Jhered confused and ill-at-ease. When he had taken his leave, her enigmatic words had hastened his steps to his rooms and thence to the taverna, the door handle of which was now in his gloved grip. He opened the door on to a wash of heat, light, noise and beautiful cooking scents.

The taverna was crowded. Packed tables lit by candles sat amongst narrow black marble columns that supported a low wooden roof. There was another equally busy room on the floor above. Jhered was well used to the reaction of the appearance of his imposing frame and famous face in a place such as this. Stooping under the lintel, he was seen by one diner and, quick as a brushfire, conversation dipped and faces turned to and away from him, nervous for no reason he cared to consider.

It alerted the taverna's owner who hurried over, his delicate-looking hands outstretched and his face bearing a wide smile below his bald pate. He crushed Jhered's left hand in his surprisingly strong grip.

'Exchequer Jhered, it is too long since you graced our modest tables. Welcome. Welcome.'

Jhered forced a smile on to his face while the conversation picked up once more. 'And I have missed the God-blessed taste of your dishes, Master Alcarin.'

'There are new ideas for you to sample,' said Alcarin, letting go his hand and beginning to weave through the tables. 'I'll bring some to you. Marshal Defender Vasselis is this way.'

He clucked happily as he led Jhered through the taverna. Jhered was acutely aware of how he dominated the room. How chairs moved automatically for him, how heads nodded respect and recognition and how all eyes followed his progress. The taverna had two private rooms and it was to one of these that Jhered was happy to be taken.

The door opened on a richly decorated room. Timbered walls were painted in deep red. Two green and gold recliners were at right-angles to each other with a table inside them covered in food and wine. A fire roared in a grate surrounded by a sculpted marble mantle. Vasselis was standing by the fire in a cream and yellow toga, looking out of the single window on to the cold street beyond, hands clenched behind him.

Alcarin withdrew and Jhered ducked his head and walked in. The atmosphere was anxious and nervous, leaving him unable to smile as Vasselis turned. Instead he frowned, unsure. Vasselis looked more than nervous, scared even. His eyes were pinched and the corners of his mouth tugged up unconvincingly. He wasn't much older than Jhered but tonight, he looked haggard. What had happened in that meeting with the Advocate?

'I hope you don't mind, I ordered for both of us and Alcarin says he has some treats for us to try.'

Vasselis gestured to a recliner and took the other himself. He sat upright, too fidgety to lie back. Jhered felt like a stranger and he had little appetite though the food on the table looked sumptuous. He poured himself a goblet of wine, mimicked Vasselis's position and drank deeply.

'I'm sure you've chosen wisely as always,' he said.

'I'm not sure I am always wise,' said Vasselis, his voice barely above a whisper.

'Right,' said Jhered, pushing both hands through his hair. 'I am not about to play cat and mouse with you like I tried to with the Advocate. What has gone on today? And if you refuse to tell me, I am leaving now and I am taking this meal with me.'

Vasselis stared at him, Jhered seeing him weigh up whether he should trust his old friend with whatever it was he had to say. Jhered found it hard to believe it could be so serious that the question was being posed. The Marshal Defender took a sip of wine. His hand was shaking.

'Paul, I have either taken the bravest decision of my life, or have made the biggest mistake of it. And on it rest the lives of almost everyone I hold dear.'

'That is some statement,' said Jhered, finally, after a chasm of a pause. 'Care to elucidate?'

'It's curious,' said Vasselis after a moment's contemplation. 'I travelled from Caraduk knowing I was doing the right thing, absolutely the right thing. But equally, I knew that I might never leave Estorr. It made "goodbye" a hard word to speak to Netta and Kovan.

'I had courage though, and pride in the virtue of my mission. I had rehearsed speeches and the answers to every question. And I was happy that I was pursuing the best interests of my citizens and – God-take-me-to-rest-in-his-embrace – I was and am prepared to burn for them.

'But the day I breasted Gorn's Rise and I saw the pennants flying from the Hill, I felt my courage begin to ebb. And now I sit before you little more than a child forced to confess a guilty secret.'

Jhered blew out his cheeks, completely intrigued to discover the source of Vasselis's troubles. But he was never above empathy with this man.

'It is easy to be courageous five miles from the fog of battle,' he said. 'Less so to hurl yourself at the pikes ranged against you when you can see the fervour in the eyes of your enemy. Surely the fact that you are here speaks all that needs be spoken about your bravery.'

'You say that without knowing what it is I have to tell you.'

'I have faced enemies across the lines of a battlefield that I respect for their bravery,' said Jhered. 'Now, enough prevarication. Remember, I am your friend. Tell me what you must.'

Vasselis nodded and rubbed a hand across his chin. Jhered could see him struggling with how to begin. Eventually, he nodded again and clapped his hands lightly on his thighs. His voice remained so quiet that Jhered had to lean in to hear him. The smells of the food assaulted his nostrils.

'Paul, what I'm going to tell you goes to the very heart of who we are and who we want to be. It goes against teachings thought inviolate by most but demonstrates that there is so much more that people can be. All we need do is open our eyes, accept evolution and not be afraid.

'Fourteen years ago, four children were born in a small fishing town in Caraduk. They are special, very special. They are the future of man and the Conquord. And they are proof that those persecuted by the Order over the centuries were right all along. We are more than farmers and guardians of God's earth. God has given us the ability to bring ourselves closer to him. To heal the earth and all his creatures, to purify the water and engender growth. To bring rain where there was drought and banish cloud so the sun can warm the crops. All using the power of their bodies and minds. To make us one with the world God has created for us so we can better do his work.

'Others have been born since but we know nothing of their potential as yet. These four have the talents I describe and so much more. They are a glory to see and a joy to entertain. But they are a danger as well. I am not naïve. I understand what they represent to the eyes of the Order as I understand the reactions of those who fear change and the unknown thrust into their midst.

'It is why I have to come to the Advocate and to you. I trust you. And the Conquord must trust me now and protect them from those who would have them killed. You must believe me, Paul, they are the Conquord's greatest triumph. Incalculable treasures. The Ascendancy lives.'

Jhered sank back into his recliner, his hands covering his nose and mouth. All thoughts of food were banished by a roiling nausea that reached up into his throat. Vasselis's words sank into his mind, the import of them causing palpitations in his chest. For sometime, he was unable to respond, only able to consider that the reason for the Advocate's distraction was all too clear.

He forced himself to focus on his friend, seeing the anxious, earnest face and those honest brown eyes searching his for a sign of support or comfort. Jhered fought the desire to ridicule Vasselis for his claims. There was no doubting he believed utterly in what he was saying. But how to react to such blasphemy? He opened his mouth to speak three times before finding the words he knew were as much for his benefit as for Vasselis.

'Even to claim such notions is a crime against the core of our faith,' he said, mimicking Vasselis's whisper. 'But for them to be true and for you to be complicit goes beyond even that.'

'But only if you hold up discredited thinking, assumptions and dogma as evidence against me. I have living proof.'

Jhered found it almost impossible to take in. 'I have to ask you as a friend if you understand the consequences of what you are saying. As an official of the Estorean Conquord and an upholder of the scriptures of the Order of Omniscience, I have to ask whether you are prepared to set seal on your statements.'

Vasselis chuckled. 'You will do as you must. And yes, I know what I am saying and I would set my seal. I have seen and you have not. I trust you to do the right thing. You know me. You know I am no heretic, nor am I a traitor.'

Jhered threw up his hands and battled to keep his voice quiet.

'The right thing? And what is that? Loyalty to a friend or to the faith I have followed since a child and in which I have unflinching belief? God-speak-for-me, Vasselis, what you have told me flies in the face of all reason and of God. It is the propagation of evil on this earth. It is the placing of man above God. How are you not heretic?'

'And yet you sit there and wonder why you do not strike me down, don't you, Paul?' Vasselis was quite calm now.

Jhered paused. He was right. And the gladius would stay scabbarded at his side.

'Because it's you, damn you,' he growled. 'Because of what I believe you to be . . . who I *know* you to be.'

Vasselis nodded his thanks. 'I know this is difficult for you. As-God-warms-the-earth it is difficult enough for me and I have known of this potential all my life. Caraduk is steeped in the lore of the Ascendancy and was the centre of protest and demonstration against the rule of the Order when the Ascendancy belief was outlawed.'

'I have read my history,' said Jhered. 'And it's all ancient. It has no bearing.'

'Of course it does,' said Vasselis a little sharply. 'It leaves a mark in the heart of everyone born in Caraduk. We respect and revere the Order if not all of its officers and methods. We believe in the sanctity of God and the holiness of the Advocate. But ancient or not, faith never dies merely because it is repressed.'

Jhered shook his head. 'I had no idea you harboured such ideologies.'

'Oh, Paul, so many times I have wanted to take you into my confidence. You and the Advocate. The people who should stand behind us. But all the time, just one slip and . . .'

'The Order,' said Jhered. Vasselis nodded and spread his hands. 'So why now?'

'Because before, even these four only exhibited potential. Now they are emerged, they are true Ascendants. They can manipulate the elements. Word will get out one day and when it does, I need all the power I can muster on my side against what the Order will try to do.'

Jhered sighed. Vasselis had appeared so reasonable. 'And you went to Herine, the living embodiment of God on earth to ask for that power? Come on, Arvan, what do you expect me, or Herine, to do with this?'

'Just try to view it with an open mind. Trust me that this is good and not evil.'

'It goes against every teaching I have ever learned,' snapped Jhered and he couldn't help but raise his voice a notch.

Vasselis held out his hands in a calming gesture. 'I know. I know. Sleep on it, talk about it with the Advocate. Whatever you decide, of course I will abide by, and will give myself up to you if you so demand it. But don't make a snap decision based on fears propagated through the Order's doctrine.'

'You mean, don't tell the Chancellor what you have told me.'

'That rather goes without saying, Paul, don't you think? One hint and we are lost before we have begun.'

'We?' Jhered raised a finger. 'I am not with you, Marshal Vasselis.'

Jhered growled in his throat. He felt utterly at a loss. His faith screamed at him to denounce Vasselis but the soldier in him knew that the Marshal deserved more respect than the justice that would undoubtedly be meted out by the Chancellor's court.

'Come to Caraduk,' urged Vasselis. 'You are long overdue a visit anyway. See for yourself before you decide whether I am on the side of the future or of destruction.'

'I cannot, Arvan,' replied Jhered. 'In case it has escaped your attention these past few days, we have significant problems on our borders with Tsard and my presence is required there by the

Advocate for the remainder of dusas. Meantime, you expect me to carry this knowledge with me in secret, I suppose?'

Vasselis spread his hands. 'It'll give you time to think.'

Jhered shook his head, feeling an anger growing. 'You have placed me in an invidious position. Merely by not reporting you to the Order, I am committing an offence that would see me burn next to you.' He paused, noting that Vasselis was clearly all too aware what he had done. 'Yet I know you believed you had no choice and I respect what you felt you had to do.

'Any other man, I would arrest here and now as my duty dictates . . . damn but this is not what I, the Advocate nor the Conquord needs. Internal strife among the closest of allies would be so dangerous and we cannot allow the Chancellor reason to enact her more repressive plans. Reason that you, you fool, have given her, should she discover what you have done.'

He sighed again. 'Here's what I will do. I will talk with the Advocate before I take ship back to Gestern. We will decide on a course of action and notify you of it, so I suggest you don't leave Estorr before you are summoned back to the palace. That is all I can do and if you experience sleepless nights in the interim, good. Consider it a fraction of the price you are asking us to pay on your behalf.'

Vasselis breathed deep and relaxed, leaning back again on the recliner.

'It is all I could ask of you, Paul. Thank you.'

'You are lucky it is you,' said Jhered, feeling the edges of a smile on his face. He leaned forward to grip Vasselis's arm briefly. 'Meanwhile, be sure your people are defended. You must be prepared for everything.' He clapped his hands once, feeling a desperate need to change the mood and calm his thumping heart.

'Now, let's try and eat. You can tell me how that son of yours is getting on. I heard great reports of his swordsmanship from the academy masters. And still so young. You must be very proud.'

He thought for a moment that Vasselis was going to burst into tears.

Chapter 15

847th cycle of God, 34th day of Dusasfall
14th year of the true Ascendancy

'Duck!'

The snowball caught Arducius full in the face. He cried out at the shock of the impact and the sudden cold across his already chilled and red face. Remembering himself, he pirouetted and collapsed dramatically to the ground, feeling the fresh soft snow puff around him.

'Yes!' Mirron's voice was loud in triumph. 'I told you we'd win. I told you you'd do it.'

Arducius pushed himself up on his elbows. He could see around the snow barricades he and Gorian had built in the walled gardens behind the Ascendancy villa. Mirron was laughing, her arms around Ossacer's neck. A rare smile split his face too. Ossacer had said he'd worked something out but this was amazing. Arducius caught the mood and began to laugh himself.

He loved dusas. Most particularly, he loved the fall of fresh snow. It was like spreading feathers across the land for him and he could run and fall and play like all of them with hardly a fear of bruising or breaking his brittle bones. He felt strong when dusas came and the land became cold. Like Gorian did all year round. In dusas, he could compete just like all the others.

'Why didn't you duck?' Gorian's voice was sulky and unhappy.

Arducius looked round and a familiar vague fear settled on him. He stopped laughing. Gorian was staring down at him, snowball still in his gloved hand, ready to throw at the others. No point now; the game was lost. But Gorian hated to lose. Even a snowball fight was treated with all the seriousness of his Ascendancy studies.

Arducius didn't know whether to feel contempt or admiration for

Gorian sometimes. Mostly, he just wished the boy he so wanted to be his friend would learn to enjoy himself once in a while, not treat everything like it was a struggle to save the world. But Gorian was so often aloof. Only Mirron seemed to be able to get through to him. It was obvious why that was. She had always liked him, wanted to be with him. He responded to that. Arducius guessed he was flattered by the attention.

'I didn't believe he could get it anywhere near me, let alone hit me, did you?'

'I told you to duck.' Gorian shrugged. 'I could see it coming and you weren't even looking.'

Arducius got up and brushed snow from his cloak. Mirron and Ossacer were walking towards them.

'Still, never mind,' he said. 'It was only a game.'

'We lost,' said Gorian. 'And we shouldn't have.'

'What do you think Ossacer has worked out, then?' asked Arducius, keen to change the subject. Gorian had an angry look in his eye but the moment he mentioned the other boy that expression changed.

'I wonder,' he said.

The defeat forgotten, he turned his attention to Ossacer, whose arm rested gently on Mirron's while the two of them walked slowly across the white carpet. Above, the sky was dark grey and the wind was picking up beneath the clouds. There would be more snow soon. A fall that would go on through the night before the clouds broke in the late morning. It was probably just as well the game had ended when it did. Gorian trotted quietly around to Ossacer's left-hand side.

'Gorian,' whispered Arducius. 'Don't.'

'Hey Ossacer,' said Gorian, voice loud just by the boy's ear.

Ossacer jumped and stopped, turning his head towards the sound, frowning. His eyes searched in vain as they always did. He could tell the difference between light and dark and he said that sometimes vague shapes would be there, but that was all. The infection that had robbed him of his sight had robbed him of his joy too for a long time. His bitterness at his misfortune was fading but it would never truly be gone.

'Why do you have to do that?' snapped Mirron.

'It's all right,' said Ossacer, his voice deep, broken early. 'It's a pity I didn't hit you, Gorian.'

'I'm too clever for you,' said Gorian. He was smiling at Mirron, happy at her infuriated reaction. 'Don't treat him like a baby. You'll make him weaker than he is already.'

'I am not weak,' said Ossacer. 'Only blind.'

'But how long is it until you catch something else? And what will go wrong then? Your ears, your mouth?'

'Stop it, stop it!' shouted Mirron. 'Leave him alone.'

'I can look after myself,' said Ossacer.

He let go of Mirron's arm and turned to face Gorian full on. Gorian laughed and danced around him.

'You'll never be able to catch me, blind man.'

He stopped on Ossacer's left and reached out an arm slowly, meaning to push. Ossacer frowned deeply and then, quite deliberately, moved his hand to grab Gorian's palm.

'I am blind but it does not mean I cannot see,' he said quietly.

Gorian's expression cleared of mischief and returned to one of fascination. 'How did you do that?'

'Why would you want to know?' asked Ossacer, releasing his hand. 'After all, you aren't blind.'

'Just tell me.' Gorian's tone was immediately threatening.

'Not quite so weak now, am I?' Ossacer was taunting Gorian now and Arducius felt his heart rate increase. 'Don't know it all, do you? And you don't like it.'

'Don't tease him,' warned Mirron.

'You know what happens when you do,' said Gorian. 'Make it easy on yourself, Ossacer . . . Ossicker—' He chuckled at his own poor joke '—tell me.'

'No,' said Ossacer, and he stood straight and defiant, his eyes fixed on nowhere, his body turned to face Gorian. 'I won't.'

'Oh, big man are we now?' Gorian advanced the pace and pushed Ossacer in the chest. He staggered back, barely keeping his balance, his hands flailing.'

'Leave him,' said Arducius.

'And what will you do? Punch me and you'll break your own hand. You are weaker than he is.' Gorian turned his attention back to Ossacer. 'No one to save you, blind man and you won't even know where I'm coming from next. Tell me what you have learned.'

'No,' said Ossacer, though there was a quiver in his voice.

'Stop it, Gorian,' said Mirron, taking a pace towards him.

'Make me,' he replied. He stepped forwards again and slapped Ossacer very lightly on the cheek. 'Harder next time.'

Ossacer took a pace back and stumbled. Gorian's hand shot out and grabbed his arm, holding him upright.

'Only me here to save you, Ossacer.' He held his grip firmly, strong hand biting into the flesh of Ossacer's upper arm. He looked round at Arducius and Mirron. Arducius felt his heart hammering and a sick feeling in his stomach. He was powerless to do anything. 'I'm better than you. I'm better than all of you put together.'

Gorian stilled and almost immediately, the air froze around them. Arducius saw the skin on his bare forearm paling and frost form on his glove. Ossacer cried out and tried to fall back. He thrashed his arm in Gorian's grip of ice but couldn't break it. Arducius made a move towards them, knowing he had to do something but fearing he would get badly hurt. He could see Mirron standing stock still, her mouth moving soundlessly.

'Tell me,' grated Gorian, voice full of menace.

Arducius had to do something. Gritting his teeth against the pain he knew would come, he ran headlong at Gorian. His ears were full of the screams of Ossacer, his eyes of Gorian's expression, one almost of glee at the pain he was causing.

'Leave him alone!' yelled Arducius.

Gorian looked round, his face registering his surprise at what was coming at him. He had precious little time to react. And as Arducius collided with him, trying to fend off the bigger boy with his hands to keep him from his rib-cage, he heard Mirron's voice once more and at the last, Father Kessian bellowing Gorian's name.

Kessian put his head in trembling hands. This would get round like every tiny aberration had. And the citizens of Westfallen would have one more reason to keep their sons and daughters from the Ascendants. Deny them the interaction that was so vital to their development as young people. The isolation was affecting them in subtle ways at the moment but eventually would drag its nails through every aspect of their lives.

It was precisely the opposite of the reaction Kessian wanted and represented a serious blow to the integration of Ascendants into the wider world. If they couldn't be accepted into the community that understood them the most there was surely little hope.

It was a paradox for them all. To stop behaviour like Gorian's required more integration with normal young people. It would give him and the other Ascendants more boundaries based on experience and an understanding of the huge responsibility on them to control themselves and the power they harboured. And yet Kessian could not blame any parent in Westfallen for their actions. They were scared and so were their children.

Two years since their announcement to the citizens of Westfallen had been greeted with triumphant celebration, the mood of the town had reversed almost completely. And while the Ascendancy Echelon was still respected and citizens still participated in the programme, volunteering for fatherhood or motherhood, there was a growing anxiety about the apparent results.

Kessian shook his head. The abilities were exactly as had always been predicted. It was an unfortunate fact that reality was far harder to accept than theory. He felt a hand on his shoulder. Genna, recently recovered from an illness which had almost claimed her life. She was still weak but had it not been for Ossacer's identification of the infection sites, she would not have survived at all. It was the glory of the Ascendants.

Kessian removed his hands and smiled at her.

'You're going to tell me to stop seeing things so bleakly aren't you?'

'I'm still here because of them, aren't I?' she said.

The Echelon was gathered in the central reception room of the villa. Behind Kessian's chair, a hypocaust flue roared. It gave him a measure of comfort. Simple normality. And there seemed very little of that these days. He found every day such a struggle. Not just because it was dusas. His legs were so painful and his breath was cruelly short. And he could barely write because of the shake in his hands. He was old and he was dying. He should have felt reassured by his imminent return to the embrace of God but he wasn't. He couldn't leave the Echelon and Westfallen without solutions to their current problems.

'Ardol?' It was Genna.

Kessian started. 'Eh? Oh, sorry. Old mind meandering I'm afraid.'

'We don't have to do this tonight,' said Hesther Naravny. 'It's been a long day.'

'There's no purpose in us going to our beds, only to lie awake,' said Meera, sitting next to her sister. She was pregnant and looked far more tired and strained than Kessian felt. Hopes were high that she, Jen Shalke and Gwythen Terol were all carrying one of the twelfth strand. But there was a question mark over whether West-fallen would welcome the new arrivals. 'He's my son. I need your help with how to deal with him.'

'Absolutely,' said Kessian, noting the nods from around the room. 'So how is he now?'

'How are all of them,' said Willem Geste dryly.

'Indeed. But one at a time. Meera?'

'Oh, Ardol, I just don't understand it,' she replied, suddenly on the verge of tears. Hesther laid a hand on her arm. 'I've spent hours with him, when I haven't been apologising to Ossacer's mother, poor woman. He's impenetrable.'

'What do you mean?' asked Andreas Koll.

'He doesn't think he's done anything wrong,' whispered Meera.

There was a hush in the room. All that could be heard were the hypocaust and the rasp of Kessian's breathing. They waited for Meera to continue. Kessian watched while she gathered her thoughts under their sympathetic gaze.

'He believes that he had the right to know immediately what Ossacer had learned and when Ossacer wouldn't tell him, he had to make him speak. He's not showing any guilt or remorse. If anything, he thinks Ossacer is to blame.'

'And what about Arducius? Surely Gorian saw in what he did that he must have been doing wrong?' said Genna into the deepening shock.

Meera shook her head. 'He has no sense of it at all. He said that in life, the strong succeed because they take what they want when they need it. The weak might fight bravely but they will always fail. Arducius is broken by his own hand.'

'He said all that?' Willem gaped.

'Almost word for word.'

'He's not even fourteen,' hissed Willem. 'How can he be saying such things.'

'He's always had a temper,' said Jen.

'This isn't temper,' said Hesther. 'This is cold calculation. Willem's right. He's too young to be like this. Isn't he?'

Every time the Echelon was unsure, it turned as one to Kessian.

This time was no exception. What would they do when he had returned to the earth? He had been listening to the exchange with a growing sense of gloom. They wanted him to explain Gorian's behaviour, make it seem not so deplorable. Kessian was not about to mitigate the indefensible.

'Let us make no mistake. The timing of this incident could hardly have been worse. Arvan Vasselis is in Estorr telling the Advocate what we have here. No doubt he is explaining to her the glories we can achieve for the whole of the Conquord if the programme is allowed to flourish now it has achieved its first emergences. And today, we have demonstrated to any that cared to see that for all the good we want to do, the Ascendants' abilities can be used to perpetrate harm and evil.

'We are certain to come under scrutiny from the Advocacy. There will be pressure from the Order too once the knowledge that something is happening here is known. And if the murmur in the town is that what we have bred are dangerous and violent freaks then inevitably, someone in Westfallen will ask the Order to investigate. Let us not forget that so far as the Order is concerned, we are heretic and face the flames when found guilty. And while the town remains with us at present, people are nervous about our four Ascendants. I don't blame them. It will not take much more for some to start to turn against us. Generations of trust stand for nothing when individuals feel threatened by those they are asked to believe in.

'We have always known we would be at risk from the world outside our borders. We now have to accept that we are at risk from those closest to us as well unless we can change Gorian's behaviour.'

He stopped to look around the Echelon. None of the faces gazing back at him registered any surprise at what he had said. He nodded and forced himself to smile.

'We are pioneers,' he said, tone gentle and encouraging. 'And we face problems that those who come after us will not. It is up to us to find solutions and to keep the belief in the Ascendancy strong and unwavering. I know it's hard. God-embrace-me but I have had black moments this day as I'm sure you all have. I doubt any of us will sleep too well, will we? So let's do what we can. We are practical, resourceful and determined.

'So. First things first. Genna, how are Ossacer and Arducius faring?'

The Echelon's Pain Teller blew out her cheeks and pushed her hands back through her hair. 'Shela is sitting with them. We've moved them into one room to be together. Ossacer is silent. He won't talk. We've bathed and bandaged his arm. Fortunately the burns weren't too deep. Frostbite takes fingers and toes. Had Arducius not intervened, it might have taken Ossacer's arm.

'He's fortunate he has a protector but that protector is in a sorry state. He has fractured both wrists. One shoulder has dislocated again and his left elbow has blown up like a diseased bladder. I've splinted the breaks and reset the shoulder. The elbow is in ice every hour. But I worry about his dexterity long-term. He's so fragile.'

'But this time they will recover from their physical wounds,' said Hesther. 'Which means we can turn to their emotional and mental ones. Far more difficult to gauge and treat.'

'You took the words right out of my mouth,' said Kessian. 'I will speak with Gorian in the morning. We have to get to the bottom of his thinking and I flatter myself that he is still in awe of me if not a little scared at times which is no bad thing, I'm sure you'll agree. He has exhibited such tendencies before. Remember when he was growing up? How serious he has always been and how easy to provoke? And remember when Mirron emerged, it was a violent episode. The difference here is premeditated use of his ability to do harm. Something we have expressly forbidden.

'I will get through to him. I have to. In the meantime, Gwythen, please continue talking with your daughter. You know how she'll react, I feel sure.'

Gwythen shrugged. 'She's done what she always has when Gorian has caused trouble. She starts by expressing her disgust and ends up defending his actions. We all know why that is.' A dry chuckle ran around the room. 'I don't think that will ever change.'

'No, indeed,' said Willem. 'But it is something we might use. Gorian will listen to her, won't he? After all, the feelings are not merely one way.'

'I'm not so sure,' said Meera. 'I don't like to say this but he is manipulative. He'll be lovely with her when it suits him. Don't be surprised to find him the soul of charm in a couple of days when he believes his shame has lifted. We've seen it before.'

'And the other two?' asked Kessian.

'Give them the night to rest, see how they wake up,' said Genna.

'Ossacer has shown no signs of ailing as a result of this incident which is a blessing. And from what Arducius said to me, he was standing proud against Gorian which is something new. Arducius . . . well, Arducius is Arducius.' Another chuckle. 'He'll be privately furious with Gorian for the rest of dusas, I expect, but he's a born diplomat. He'll bring them back together pretty soon. He sees the strength of the four of them learning as one. I think most of his anger will be frustration at Gorian's attitude rather than his physical pain and why it was inflicted.'

Kessian felt lifted by what he was hearing. The Echelon was closing ranks and moving forwards.

'Good,' he said. 'One last thing. Hesther, I know I always turn to you but assuming word, if not detail, of this trouble leaks out through the servants, we need to have a response. You and Elsa Gueran should work together. We need the Order to stand with us, even if it is through a Reader we all know believes as we do and needs to fear the Chancellor as we do.'

'Of course, Ardol,' said Hesther.

'Only when we have the Ascendants settled will we talk to Ossacer about his learning. I have the distinct feeling it will be quite a breakthrough but we need the right atmosphere. Agreed?'

Nods all around. Kessian pushed himself painfully up on his sticks. 'Then let us all get to bed. God keep you all in bliss until he wakes you with the light of dawn.'

It was night and it was very quiet but for the breathing of Shela Hasi and Arducius. Ossacer listened to the patterns they made while the lids on his eyes blinked away the phantom shapes that swam across his blindness. Shela's breath was deep and regular, her body was still. Arducius snuffled and sighed. Ossacer smiled in the dark, his gratitude for his friend swelling again in his chest.

'You are awake, Arducius,' he said softly.

'I am,' he replied. 'I can't sleep. It hurts. How is your arm?'

'It's all right,' said Ossacer, scratching at his bandages absently, the throbbing ache not dimmed by the cooling balm Genna had spread on the wound. 'Shela is asleep, isn't she?'

'Until Genna comes in to do the ice thing again in the morning. Ugh, it's horrible.'

'Doesn't it help?' asked Ossacer, imagining Arducius's shudder.

'It just makes it numb. It still aches and everything. And my fingers tingle all the time.'

'Do you trust me?'

Arducius was silent for a while. 'I. Well, yes, of course. What sort of question is that in the middle of the night?'

'I can help you,' said Ossacer. His heart tapped quickly in his chest. 'If you'll let me.'

'Help me with what?'

'I think I can fix you.' Ossacer shifted and pushed himself up on his good elbow so he was looking in Arducius's direction. 'If you'll let me try.'

There was another silence. Ossacer could feel Arducius weighing it all up. He'd survived so many breaks from his brittle bones because Genna Kessian was so expert at locating the exact fracture point and Westfallen's doctors and surgeons could set the limb or digit under her instruction. Yet now here was an Ascendant, not two years emerged, offering him something untried and absolutely new. And they all knew the risks of trying out new abilities from embarrassing and painful experience.

'Is this what you wouldn't tell Gorian about?'

'It's the reason you're lying there,' agreed Ossacer.

'Will it hurt me? Will it hurt you?'

'I don't think so,' said Ossacer. 'Not if I get it right.'

Arducius managed a chuckle at that and the slight tension broke. 'Well, obviously.'

Ossacer smiled as well. He moved nearer his friend, shifting across his bed. They were separated by a gap of a couple of feet. Shela was by the door, sleeping in a chair with her feet up on a padded stool.

'Well?'

'Are you sure you can do this?'

'I'll let you know,' said Ossacer.

'Very funny,' said Arducius. 'Just take the pain away, that's enough. And tell me what you're doing.'

Ossacer felt a wash of pride. Trust in him. It was a wonderful feeling.

'I won't let you down.'

Ossacer closed his eyes and concentrated hard. He breathed deeply and carefully. He held his hands out from his body, his fingers spread and moving gently as if playing an invisible kithara. His ears pricked, listening for the creaking of timbers in the roof above him, in the marble supports and the beds on which they lay.

Slowly, colour and light swam into his mind, warming his whole body, reminders of a time when all he had to do to experience colour was open his eyes. But this was far more breathtaking than memories; this was his window on the world and no one would ever be able to take it from him.

Behind the curtain of his eyes, the bedroom dripped into view. He could have wished it was clear like sight but for Ossacer, it was as if God had blessed him personally with a second chance and it was up to him to make of it what he could. The others and the Echelon had thought he'd been unusually quiet and reserved throughout this dusas and he was happy to let them think that way. They left him to it when they understood he was all right, just feeling low.

But what he had discovered was in the process of changing his life from one of reliance to one of renewed independence. It had been almost by chance, even though Ossacer understood that it was because he'd been forced to develop his other senses. He'd learned to listen to the minutest of sounds to build up a mental picture of what surrounded him. He habitually held out his hands, not just to feel ahead and to the sides but to gather information on the currents of air passing his body. His fingertips had developed great sensitivity, allowing him to gauge the distance and complexity of solid shapes near him.

His nose was equally sensitive, able to sort scents in fine detail. He used it to give him direction. He could smell the villa from up on the hillside; he could navigate from the villa to the forum. And he could walk unaided to the orchard up above Genastro Falls. No one was scared he would pitch over the cliff any more. To him these were small victories in a life of struggle against his disability. However, in his few meetings with other blind people, he had become aware that his senses were far more acutely tuned than were those of others.

It led him to think. The only benefit of his blindness, and it had a bitter edge, was that it gave him time to think free of the distractions of the world of light. But this time the reward had been great. Their training had focused so much on harnessing the energies of God and the earth to achieve their goals, whether it be growing plants, bringing fruit to trees out of season or identifying the seat of infections in farm animals.

They still had so much to learn, particularly about efficiency. A single use of ability left them tired and wrinkled, sometimes for days. But what they had all worked out was that, while the particular energies most closely related to the ability they were employing aided their efficiency greatly, other energies drawn from unconnected places could be used, though they drained the Ascendant more quickly.

Father Kessian had likened it to carrying water from place to place in a sponge rather than a skin. It worked but was more tiring, because more trips would be needed for the same volume of water as so much got wasted on the way.

So Ossacer had worked on, as he liked to think of it, blocking the holes in the sponge. And he had linked the effort with the knowledge that there was something more to his acutely tuned senses than effort and fortune. It was because of who he was. There was energy all around him. It fed through his fingertips, his nostrils, his ears and his tongue direct into his mind. And there he used it.

He had always been a natural Pain Teller, able to map an infection, fever, strain or break in the body of a man and to a lesser extent, a beast. But what he hadn't been able to do, what none of them had got even close to, was healing. Gorian, the first Gorian, had written about joining energies to heal but that had proved impossible because all maladies appeared as grey shades that masked energy flows and there was no way to break through. Until now.

It had come to Ossacer quite suddenly that because there were energies everywhere that could be harnessed, if inefficiently, to heal, it wasn't necessary to go through the grey shades; you could go around them. Lacking in the confidence to test his theory on an animal, or even to talk to Father Kessian or Genna about it, he had first applied it to the energies he picked up through his remaining senses. And what he found was that he could draw an energy map in his head of the immediate area around him.

Solid objects like walls, cabinets, columns and beds appeared as deep grey shapes on the bright canvas. But people appeared as moving hues of red, green and yellow, shot with deeper blues and, when they were damaged, grey shades and black. Their outlines were blurred but distinct enough to make out individuals. It was how he had hit Arducius with the snowball. In an open space, background was difficult to discern, particularly after snowfall, and so people stood out like fires in the night.

It was tiring though, because none of the energies were directly applicable. So he had to work hard to keep the map in his head. He couldn't do it for long yet but hopefully long enough to help Arducius.

He stepped out of his bed, seeing his hands in front of him, his fingers deep red and bordered in pale yellow, his legs similar but less intense and the rest of his body dulled a fraction by his nightshirt. Below his feet, the rug was a pale shadow on the cool blue of the stone and ahead of him, Arducius's head and arms were visible above his covers.

He sat on the bed.

'Are you ready?' he whispered.

'How did you do that? I was watching you. You moved like you could see.'

'I can,' said Ossacer, feeling his excitement grow. 'Sort of. I'll explain it to you all. I just need to try one more thing.'

'And I am your subject, is that right?'

'Well, obviously.'

Both boys laughed quietly, energised by the thought of doing something in secret and not wishing to wake Shela.

'What do you want me to do?' asked Arducius.

'Nothing. Just lie there. It shouldn't hurt but tell me if it does and I'll stop whenever you want me to.'

'I'll be all right.'

Ossacer let the energy map fade in his mind, satisfied he was in control of his senses. He placed his hands on Arducius's left arm.

'That's cold,' hissed Arducius.

'Sorry.'

He drew back into himself, letting the energy from his own body channel through his mind, down his arms and across Arducius. Immediately, he could see the other boy's outline in his mind and he used a little energy from Arducius to bolster his own. He traced the bright pulses that were arteries and veins, following their flow through Arducius's body. The outlines of bones appeared dull green, his heart blazed red, lungs a cooler red tint and stomach a calm yellow.

Surrounding the bright strong trails of Arducius's body were the free motes of energy. They appeared as faint trails or twinkling dull lights to his mind. He was sure he could drive them to link the two areas of broken energy either side of breaks like those in Arducius's wrists. He moved his hands down towards the damaged left wrist, letting just the tips of his fingers brush his skin.

'Don't move,' he said, feeling a twitch from his friend. 'Sorry if it tickles.'

'It's warm,' said Arducius.

'Good.'

Arducius's wrist was a mess. Ossacer almost withdrew his fingers from the splinted bandage. He'd been used to sensing bruising, typified by a wash of clouded grey, damaged lines but this was something far worse. His mind displayed to him a deep, impenetrable grey shot through with a dead blackness where the fractures were complex and the energy of life absent. Splints weren't going to help.

'What's wrong?' asked Arducius.

'These are bad breaks,' he replied.

'I hadn't realised,' said Arducius dryly.

'I don't mean that, I mean they go so deep. Your bones are set but there is nothing running through them to heal them. No lifelines.'

'Well then . . .'

'It's all right,' said Ossacer, feeling Arducius tense. 'I can bring them back.'

Ossacer knew he couldn't draw from Arducius to link the broken lines around his wrists. It was the same with most injured or sick people and animals. They were inherently weaker for obvious reasons. And while the trails in the air and carried through the hypocaust and on the slight breeze from under the door provided raw material, he had not plugged enough holes in the sponge and Arducius needed major help. Ossacer was going to have to use himself. This was going to be far more tiring than he first thought.

He gripped Arducius's wrist very gently, rippling his fingers across the bandage. He felt the depth and breadth of the damage, noted the dark lines indicating hairline fractures and the trapping or piercing of nerves and veins. Satisfied he understood the scale of the task, he placed his hands with his fingers splayed across the bandage with thumb touching thumb.

In Arducius's hands and fingers, the energy trails were haphazard, directionless, probably contributing to the aches and tingling sensations he was feeling. Ossacer felt joy wash over him, quite unexpectedly. It was exactly as Father Kessian and Genna said it should be. Exactly as the writings of Gorian and the scriptures of God described. The circle of life was interrupted. It was the flows of energy, the circuits great and small, that gave health and life. And it was their disruption that took them away. Now he knew with no doubt that his idea was right. And that God had placed him and his friends on this earth to heal and to cure. To be a force of wonder and to do God's work. The Order was wrong.

'I am going to join the broken lifelines around your wrists. Try to be still.'

'Using what?'

'Anything I can get from this room. But mainly myself.'

'Ossacer, that's—'

'Don't argue. God will return my strength to me.'

He tried to bring in the slight energies from the breeze and the warmth of the stones under his feet, opening his mind as he had been urged, like he would open his mouth to accept food. But so little came in. He could just feel it helping his focus though it was nowhere near enough to help Arducius. What he had hoped, he couldn't quite do and now wasn't the time to be experimenting. He just prayed he had enough within him to do what had to be done.

Ossacer poured himself into his task. He channelled his body's energy into Arducius's arm, feeling the boy tense beneath his fingers and hearing a grunt of surprise. In his mind, he could see lifelines from his fingers intertwining with those either side of the broken wrist. Arducius gasped as the circuit was completed, feeling the life flowing around and edging into his injury.

That was the easy part. He could stay here, relieving Arducius of his pain for as long as he could stay awake and concentrated but it wouldn't heal him. Now he had to drive the lifelines back through the damaged wrist, providing the linkage that signified healing had taken place.

Ossacer could see like none of the others could, the disruption caused by the break. Where the bone was not set correctly, where fragments still sat in his flesh and where the blood flow was interrupted.

'Here we go, Arducius. Please try to be calm. The energy needs to flow into your wrist now. I hope you aren't hurt.'

'Get on with it.'

Ossacer nodded and breathed in very deeply. He began where the lifelines were strongest in Arducius, in his forearm. He could see the energy map in his head, could see the exact points where the lines turned away from Arducius's wrist to join with his own. He concentrated and pushed down, beginning to tease the lines back to where they belonged. Fraction by fraction he went, using the artificially completed circuit to force passage through the physical damage. He moved bone fragments back into place, opened up veins again, dragged nerve endings into position. It was a terribly slow and delicate process.

He had to fight every strand of energy every minute step of the way. Like steering multiple eels through a maze that shifted and changed around them; each one only too happy to fall back if his attention wavered.

He could feel the sweat form then drip from his brow. It dampened his armpits and back. His whole body heated as he used more of himself in the effort. He had abandoned all thought of channelling the room's random energies now. It was a step too far for a young mind needing purity of focus.

And at the same time, he had to fight to contain his excitement. Because underneath his fingers with their red and yellow outlines bright with the density of energy, the black and grey were lightening; fading away.

'How do you feel?' he managed to ask through his own gulping breath.

'It burns,' said Arducius, sounding calm. 'But it doesn't hurt.'

'Good,' said Ossacer. 'I think.'

The centre of the break slowed him even further. So many hairline cracks and displacements. Arducius said it ached. It must have been agonising. Ossacer quashed the guilt that sprang into his conscience. He poured more of his energy into his work. He could feel himself weakening. And where the sweat ran down his cheeks, he could feel the dryness that came with age.

All this and more again, he reminded himself, if he was to fix both wrists. The elbow, not broken but swollen, would have to wait.

Shela Hasi awoke stiff and tired when the dawn, bright and white, found its way through the louvered shutters. She massaged her neck with one hand and blinked the room into focus. The yawn died in her throat.

Arducius, his wrist splints discarded, was sitting on Ossacer's bed holding the boy's hand in his. Ossacer's head was just visible. His face was cracked and lined, his head covered in grey hair. He barely moved but Arducius was smiling from ear to ear. The pained pallor in his cheeks was almost gone and his eyes shone with new health.

'Look what he's done,' he said. 'Look what he's done.'

Shela stared, confused, not knowing whether to cry with joy or scream in fear.

Chapter 16

847th cycle of God, 35th day of Dusasfall
14th year of the true Ascendancy

When Kessian pushed open Gorian's bedroom door that morning, the dazzling dusas sun was reflecting harsh white off the snow and blazing in through open shutters.

Gorian was sitting at his small desk, reading the Ascendancy text on the scope of the Land Warden discipline, its potential development and applications. Kessian had written it himself over four decades before. That Gorian should appear so engrossed in what he now considered inane meanderings, gave some small pleasure on a troubled day.

Gorian's tunic was slashed with the red of the Ascendancy, matching his own. His feet were bare, toes tapping idly on the warm stone under his feet. He didn't look round until Kessian had lowered himself slowly on to the end of the boy's bed.

'How did you know so long ago that we would ever exist?' Gorian asked, his voice clogged with emotion.

He looked terrible. His eyes were red and puffed where he had rubbed the tears away and the dark smudges beneath them told of a restless night. Kessian was comforted that in the quiet and dark, Gorian had found guilt and remorse. But he was concerned at the lack of either sentiment the boy had chosen to display to his mother the previous evening.

'Because your namesake saw the patterns and didn't let a single incident pass unnoted. And from such a wealth of observation, we were able eventually to trace where the potential was strongest and the logic most compelling. That is the way of discovery and advancement in science.'

Gorian frowned. 'Is this science? Or is it a blessing from God?'

'The two are inextricably linked. God shows us where to place our feet, he opens our eyes. We accept that our doctors develop their science through knowledge of the human body. But they would be nowhere without God's hand to guide them. So it is with us. We are shown the path; it is up to us to understand.'

Gorian was silent for a moment. He swallowed.

'How are Ossacer and Arducius?'

'Now that should really have been your first question, shouldn't it?'

No response. Gorian's lower lip was trembling and tears filled his eyes.

'They are both fine, fortunately for you,' said Kessian after a while. 'Ossacer has demonstrated remarkable new understanding.'

'What?' Light and desire blazed in Gorian's eyes.

'Ah well, had you waited and encouraged him, no doubt you would have found out. Gorian, why did you do it?'

The weight of Kessian's disappointment registered like blows on Gorian; every word striking a little harder than the last. The tears fell down his cheeks. Kessian made no move to comfort him though it was surely what he craved.

'Why didn't he tell me?'

'We are not talking about Ossacer, we are talking about you,' said Kessian sharply. 'He had every right to do what he did. You had none. And from the words you spoke to your mother last night, you do not understand that.'

'I do,' he wailed. 'I didn't mean to hurt him.'

'Gorian, look at me,' ordered Kessian. Gorian did so. No one defied Father Kessian. 'Do not shy away. You took Ossacer's wrist and you burned it with frost, using your Ascendant ability. He will carry the scars to his grave. I can see the regret in you now but it was not there after the event, was it? And it did not occur to you before you acted in the first place, did it?'

'I didn't want to hurt him. I didn't want Arducius to be hurt.' Gorian cut a pathetic figure sitting slouched in his desk chair, one hand over his eyes now, the tears still dripping down his cheeks. It was all Kessian could do to keep from hugging him close. He looked broken.

Kessian moderated his tone a little. 'But how can we believe that? You did what you did. And when your mother questioned you about it, you said that the strong took what they wanted and that in effect the other two were to blame for what happened and not you. Gorian? Help us to understand. To help you. You cannot let your control go like this. Not with the power you have.'

Gorian didn't know what to say, that much was plain. Kessian wasn't surprised. He waited a while. Gorian composed himself just a little but clearly wasn't going to say anything.

'Gorian, look at me.' Kessian waited until he was obeyed. 'Let's try one thing at a time. Why did you say what you said to your mother?'

A pause. 'Because I was angry, I suppose. I wanted to be right. I thought I was right.'

'Did you really? But presumably you think a little differently now.' Gorian nodded. 'But I still don't understand. Meera was quite specific about how lacking in remorse you were. Do you remember how you felt to be like that?' Gorian shook his head. 'All right then, why the sleepless night and all the tears of guilt this morning? Do you know what changed your mind? You've had enough time to think. Try for me.'

Gorian's face looked about to crumple again. 'Because I knew you would be coming in here to see me this morning,' he said. 'And I knew you would be angry and I hate it when I make you angry.'

Kessian met Gorian's gaze levelly. 'I'm not sure whether to be flattered or insulted,' he said, knowing the comment would pass the boy by. 'The trouble is, if what you say is true, that doesn't make you sorry for what you have done, only sorry for the reaction it would provoke in me. Are you truly sorry for what you have done?'

Gorian nodded. 'I know it was wrong.'

'You know now or you knew at the time?'

'I know now.'

'Well, that's honest at least,' said Kessian, though the response was not the one he wanted. 'Tell me this. Was it only the fact I would come here that made you think and realise you had done wrong?'

Gorian frowned and then nodded. 'I think so.'

'And what will happen when I am not here to make you think?'

'You'll always be here, Father Kessian,' said Gorian, his tone a little desperate. 'We need you. I need you.'

Kessian fought the urge to put his head in his hands and forced a half-smile on to his face instead. 'Oh Gorian, you and I both know how old I am. I cannot be here forever. One day, and perhaps soon,

God will open his arms to welcome me back to his embrace. Who will you turn to then, I wonder?'

Who will you respect enough to maintain your discipline . . . Kessian shook his head and stood up.

'You're leaving me?'

'For the time being.'

'What's going to happen?'

Kessian looked at Gorian, every inch the frightened boy awaiting inevitable punishment. So much at odds with the arrogance of the night before. He sighed.

'I still don't think you fully realise what you have done,' he said. 'Before you can come out of this room, much has to happen but it will happen quickly. I will talk with the other Ascendants and they will help me decide whether you should be taught with them or apart from them for the time being. And they alone will decide if they ever want to play with you again.

'And while we are talking, I need you to think about this: the works of the Ascendancy are only ever destined for help and peace. Never to inflict pain, for evil or to enforce authority. The Ascendancy is a tool of God whose mercy and benevolence know no end. What you have done is demonstrate how all that is good can be used for evil. The scalpel of a doctor can slit the throat and the hoe can be used to strike down an innocent man. And our works can be diverted to cause death and damage. They must never be allowed to do so again.

'Ask yourself, Gorian, if you want to be loved and revered as a bringer of miracles and a man who spreads life and health about him. Or whether you want to be hated and feared, and forever live in the knowledge that there are those who desire nothing more than your death, and that ever an arrow or a blade will be coming at you but you know not from where.' He nodded at Gorian's reaction. 'I hope that scares you. It is supposed to. You have within you a great potential for power, as do your brothers and sister. And if you believe in me as you say you do, you will do me one great service and swear to use that power only for the purposes your namesake gave his life for. The purposes I would give my life for too.

'We will speak again before you leave this room. But in the meantime, if you are hungry, I can ask Shela to bring you some breakfast.'

Gorian nodded and Kessian smiled in response.

'Good. Think hard, Gorian. We all love you and want you to be inside our embrace forever. But you must learn to curb your temper or you risk being a very lonely young man. Don't let me down.'

'I won't, Father. I am sorry.'

Kessian let himself out of the room and closed the door behind him. Genna, Meera and Shela were waiting for him.

'So many contradictions in that young man. I wonder about the state of his mind, I really do,' he whispered. 'We must watch him very closely indeed, even at play. There is a battle going on in that head of his and I have no idea which side will win. Shela, he can have his breakfast now.' He leant in and kissed Genna's cheek. 'This is an unexpected pleasure, my love.'

'And there's another for you in the main dining room. Arvan Vasselis is returned from Estorr. He's waiting for you.'

Kessian felt a release of anxiety he barely knew he'd been hoarding. 'Now that is good news. Vasselis alive rather than executed for heresy is surely a step in the right direction.'

Genna chuckled. 'I feel sure he agrees with you. Come on, I'll leave you there and go down to make sure Netta and Kovan are settled in at their villa.'

'I expect you'll find Kovan wherever Mirron is,' said Kessian. 'He'll be happy Gorian is out of the way just for a moment.'

'Hush yourself, Ardol Kessian.'

Kessian beamed at her. 'I still remember what it was like to be that age and smitten. Joy and pain the two sides of the coin and a whole sheaf of clumsy thoughts and emotions to battle. I don't envy him.'

'Yes, you do,' said Genna.

'Yes, I do.'

One of the two ornate marble fireplaces in the dining room contained a peat and wood blaze that sent powerful warmth into the room to augment the over-worked hypocaust. Marshal Vasselis had ridden in with a howling wind at his back that was creeping round the compass and would soon be sweeping up the bay from the sea.

He had taken off his gauntlets and was warming his hands over the fire. His fur-lined cloak was still close about his shoulders and his eyes were on the portrait of Gorian above the elegant, carved mantle. He turned when the door opened. Ardol Kessian walked in, his movement slow and heavily reliant on the sticks in his hands. His hips caused him constant pain by all accounts and the arthritis was present in every joint. Genna gave a small wave and closed the door behind her husband.

Kessian looked frail. Vasselis had been away a long time and the Father of the Echelon had moved rapidly towards death. At least he had seen the genesis of everything he had worked for all his life. Vasselis considered that he might be blessed by not living through much of what was to come.

'I've got old, haven't I?' said Kessian, easing himself into one of the chairs that had been set in front of the fireplace.

Vasselis nodded and came across to his old friend, kneeling to cover his cold hands. 'Reading my mind again, Ardol?'

'Just your face,' replied Kessian.

'I never was good at hiding my thoughts from you,' said Vasselis. He stood up and turned to the table nearby. 'They've delivered tea. Would you like some? I suppose it's a little early for wine.'

'Thank you, Arvan. And welcome back.'

Vasselis passed him his tea, a rich herb pressing, warming and sweet. 'There were a couple of days when I seriously doubted that I would ever hear you say that. These have been difficult times and I fear they are merely a prelude.'

'We had to expect that. But the fact of your presence here means that at least the Advocate is prepared to listen to us. Tell me what she said.'

Vasselis summarised his conversations with both the Advocate and Paul Jhered, concluding with his summoning to the palace to hear their conclusions.

'I went there not knowing whether I would be taking ship that evening or facing the last days of my life in a cell beneath my own offices in the basilica,' he said, remembering vividly the nerves he had experienced and the dark expressions of his friends as they faced him across a formal meeting table. Only time would tell whether he had lost them as friends even as he gained them as temporary allies.

'Why did you speak to Jhered?' Kessian interrupted for the first time.

'He represents the highest order of security in the Conquord,' said Vasselis. 'He is also a very old friend of mine whom I would trust with all of our lives. And that is what we have to do. The time for difficult choices and difficult times is with us now.

'The only reasons I was not denounced by the Advocate and handed over to the Chancellor – the only reasons the Order is not already riding here – are Caraduk's unblemished record of alliance to the Conquord; the history of the Vasselis line in ensuring that record has always been maintained; and the personal regard and trust in which I am held. I am not trying to sound arrogant, just give you the bare facts.'

'Arrogance is not a trait that taints you, Arvan.'

Vasselis nodded his thanks. 'I needed to speak them because all three have now been put at grievous risk. I care little about my personal standing but I care deeply about the reputation of my family and the close relationship between Caraduk and Estorea. I believe in what you do here, but you and your townspeople must play their part.

'Westfallen will soon become a focus of the Conquord as keen as the eastern front of Tsard or the treaty negotiations with Sirrane. We are going to be investigated very thoroughly by the highest echelons of the Conquord. We have to trust that those who come here share the mind of the Advocate and the Exchequer. We have to trust that the Order will be excluded as I have been assured. And the people of Westfallen must be one in their belief.

'The Ascendancy cannot afford to be marginalised. Not now. And I have to say that the reports of my border security are not encouraging. Word is being passed though it has not yet escaped. When the Advocate's investigators get here, that must still be the case because only their approval can give us security.'

'When will they get here?' asked Kessian, his hands wringing together.

'That I can't tell you. At least not yet. They will give us as little warning as possible because they want neither us, nor the Order, to have word what they are doing. Tell me I have not just made the biggest mistake of my life.'

Kessian sipped his tea. His hands were quivering and not just as a consequence of his age.

'We are increasingly experiencing trouble with sections of the citizens. Never mind that many of them have fathered or mothered Ascendancy strand children. Never mind that most of them have experienced fleeting or long-lasting passive ability. Our Ascendants are new, powerful and frightening. And at heart, no one really wants change and they are only too aware that we are bringing them change that will affect them all. No one speaks out against us but my welcome in the forum is not as warm as once it was.'

Vasselis nodded. He wasn't surprised. The courage of most normal people was at best transitory. But it was a problem he could do without.

'Then I will speak to them. Tomorrow midday at the oratory.'

'I'll make the arrangements.'

'It's time to let this sleepy town know what is going on beyond its fields and its fishing grounds. Time they know the Advocacy is focusing on their very lives. Now, is there anything else I need to know about?'

With great care, Ardol Kessian told him about Gorian and his heart beat chill in his breast.

'You can keep him under control?'

'For now,' said Kessian. 'He's just a child, after all. But I fear what he will feel, think and do when he is older and stronger and I am gone to God's embrace.'

'Then his behaviour must be altered now,' said Vasselis, letting his face harden and his tone become that of the Marshal issuing edicts. 'You must not let him become a maverick. It is too dangerous to us, our families and to the citizens of Caraduk. There are four Ascendants. Gorian is but one and for all the power he almost certainly will have, he is just a boy and will be just a man. Four, Ardol, can very easily become three.'

Chapter 17

847th cycle of God, 36th day of Dusasfall
14th year of the true Ascendancy

They saw Gorian in the winter garden shortly before they were all to go to the oratory to sit while Marshal Vasselis spoke. Kovan Vasselis had wanted to stay to protect Mirron but she had assured him of her safety and he had, with some reluctance, left to be with his father.

'Will he never leave you alone?' asked Arducius, flexing his elbow which was still stiff despite the efforts of Genna Kessian and Westfallen's doctors. Ossacer had not been able to do his work upon it. He only just had the strength to get out of bed after his exertions on Arducius's wrists.

'Leave him alone, Ardu,' said Mirron. 'He only wants to help.'

'I think it's a little more than that,' said Ossacer.

All three of them were sitting on the same bench, in front of a fountain turned off until genastro warmed its pipes. Mercifully not too far away now. A brazier of coals sat on a stand in front of them, its heat welcome on their outstretched hands. All had cloaks pulled tightly around them and leggings bound them from ankle to hip. Still, it was freezing though Mirron enjoyed the clouding of the breath in front of her face and the sheer vitality of the cold. If she concentrated, she could trace its signature, deep and dark.

'Oh, and how would you know?' she asked him, already knowing the answer but desiring his confirmation.

'There are few good things about being blind but one thing I do is hear better than you. And Kovan always speaks more softly and earnestly to you than he does to the rest of us, particularly you-know-who. I think you have rivals for your affections, dear Mirron.'

Mirron looked at Ossacer who was staring in her direction, no doubt seeing her through her lifelines. She smiled.

'I don't know what you mean.'

'Then you are the only one who doesn't,' said Arducius, siding with Ossacer as so often. 'They both fancy you in their own way. Who will you choose, I wonder?'

Mirron felt herself blush and the thrill of excitement rush through her. 'Neither,' she said, images of Gorian's face crowding her mind. 'I have better things to think of than boys.' Her smile widened. 'Anyway, Ardu, haven't you been bumping into Livvy by accident rather a lot recently?'

Arducius blushed as deeply as she did and rubbed a chin that was beginning to sprout traces of soft hair.

'It would be more but her parents aren't exactly encouraging our friendship.'

'She cannot be a mother of the Ascendancy,' said Ossacer. 'You are wasting your time.'

His words died harsh in the garden. Arducius turned sharply to him.

'What do you mean?'

Ossacer tapped his ear. 'You should listen harder. You know we're not here by chance. Every child born to the Ascendancy now is by design, to be like us. Livvy's parents have no abilities. Neither does she. You will not be allowed to fall in love with her.'

'I don't . . . What are you talking about? I just like her that's all.'

'And that is all it will ever be. List the parents of the tenth strand and tell me I am wrong. Gorian or Kovan on the other hand . . .' He folded his arms under his cloak and leaned back, a mischievous grin on his face. 'Both have strengths the Ascendancy needs.'

'Stop it, Ossacer,' said Mirron suddenly uncomfortable. The whole idea was ridiculous to her. They were only thirteen, all of them. Yet she yearned for the closeness of Gorian's skin. The smell of his hair and the sheer strength of his gaze.

The door to their right beneath the colonnaded passageway opened then and out he came. He was wearing a plain black cloak. The hood was thrown back and his glorious shoulder-length blond hair lit up his face. But it was a face broken and sad. Mirron wanted to run to him. To embrace him and tell him it was all right, that they had all forgiven him. But she could not. The damage he had inflicted on her brothers was still too fresh.

She felt the tension in the air like a sharp frost on a mid-dusas morning. Arducius had drawn himself up to stare at Gorian from as high as he could and Ossacer's face was blank with contempt. She didn't want it to be this way. She so loved them all. She wished none of it had ever happened but it had.

Gorian's eyes flickered from one to another as he approached. He stopped by the brazier, making no attempt to sit with them. Behind him, in the doorway, Hesther and Meera stood with Father Kessian, watching. There was a hush on the garden. No one knew what to say. No one knew if they were supposed to say anything. She focused on Gorian who now stared at the ground. It was down to him.

'Th-thank you all for agreeing to see me,' he said, the words struggling to get past his lips. He glanced back towards the door. 'I know nothing can change what I did but I am truly sorry for what happened and I promise it will never happen again.'

'Until when?' snapped Ossacer, hand stroking the bandages covering his burns. 'You never mean it but you always do it.'

Mirron saw Gorian's eyes flash but he nodded his understanding anyway. 'I can change,' he said. 'I will change.'

All their words hung in clouds of breath on the still air. Mirron couldn't find anything to say. Nor, it seemed, could Arducius though she could feel his mind working, seeking a solution.

'I am so sorry for the hurt I caused you, Ossacer,' said Gorian. 'And I never meant for you to have to break yourself protecting him, Arducius.'

'I would have done the same to protect you, Gorian,' said Arducius quietly; and Mirron felt tears pricking at her eyes.

'And I would have told you what you wanted to know,' said Ossacer. 'All you had to do was wait until I was ready. But you couldn't.'

'I understand that now,' said Gorian. 'I need you to forgive me.'

Another silence with no one prepared to say the words. Gorian looked at Mirron and she averted her gaze, staring instead at Ossacer who's anger burned bright.

'We have no reason to trust you,' said Ossacer.

Gorian breathed hard like he was about to cry. 'I know, I know. But you have to give me another chance. We have to stand together.'

'You didn't think that when you burned me,' said Ossacer.

Gorian said nothing for a while. His eyes shone wet and he shivered with more than the cold of the morning. 'Thank you for being able to fix Arducius,' he said.

'I had little choice,' said Ossacer. 'He broke his wrists so badly he would have lost his hands.'

Mirron saw Gorian react as if slapped. The shock on his face paled it more than the cold ever could. Again, she held herself in check. She could comfort him later.

'I had . . . I wouldn't have—'

'But you did,' said Ossacer. 'And look what might have happened. Then where would we be? The Ascendancy quartet. One blind, one with no hands, one with no control over his temper and one who isn't sure what she is. Pretty poor for all the love Father Kessian has shown us.'

'Enough,' said Arducius and he stood up, looking powerful and so determined. 'We cannot live if we snipe at each other forever. We were born to be together and so we must be.' He stepped forward and grabbed Gorian's collars. 'I know you are sorry for what you did and I know you would change it if you could. And we will forgive you now even if we don't trust you just yet. But we have to believe in each other like we always have or we're lost. I can't do any of this without all of you.' He beckoned Mirron and Ossacer to stand up. The gesture was too quick for Ossacer to follow in the trails and Mirron whispered in his ear and helped him.

'From now on what we do, we do together. Always. And we will never hide anything from each other however small. Swear it and join with me.'

They did and joined in the embrace. Mirron gripped Gorian hard and he responded. To her left, Arducius clung on to her, his fingers biting her flesh, demanding she agree. But across the circle, Ossacer's hand on Gorian was tentative and his face clouded. For him, forgiveness would take its long, slow time.

Though it was barely past midday, the lanterns that bordered the forum shone under the cold grey sky. From his position on the oratory, Marshal Arvan Vasselis looked out over the gathering of the citizens of his most beloved town. The Ascendants sat looking small and fearful to his right. The Echelon, with Reader Elsa Gueran, stood proudly to his left. The borders had been closed for the duration of the meeting though there was no traffic expected; the cold discouraging all but the very hardiest of traders.

There were a couple of visitors in Westfallen and they were being kept away with the reason simply that the Marshal Defender was addressing the citizens of Westfallen on a private and personal matter. True enough.

Most of those citizens knew the subject of the address. None of them knew the detail and Vasselis was going to have to be at his best to bring them to stand behind him and the Ascendancy for what was to come. He glanced up at the heavy clouds and hoped the snow would hold off long enough. Kessian said it would not snow until evening. Arducius reckoned it would be a little earlier than that. Above his head, the feeble glow of the sun was just visible as a lightening of the grey. It was time.

Vasselis stood up, took off his fur-lined gauntlets, swept back the hood of his cloak and walked to the dais. The cold bit deep into his face and hands but he could hide neither and remain honest. The murmur of the crowd, bunched tight together for warmth, died to a whisper and then away altogether. The wind whistled around the columns bordering the forum, bringing in the sound of waves grabbing at the fleet hauled high and safe on the beach.

The oratory was well-lit and coal braziers stood in eight places on the stage. They offered Vasselis precious little in the way of warmth where he stood underneath the vaulted open-fronted oratory, between the two intricately carved columns supporting the cross-beam.

'My friends, thank you for coming to listen to me at what is a critical time for Westfallen, Caraduk and indeed the whole of the Estorean Conquord. I could have wished you'd brought me warmer weather. I don't know about you down there but it is perishing cold up here.'

He waited for the ripple of laughter to subside. The faces turned to him were expectant and welcoming. He knew how much they loved him. Guilt gripped him over what he was going to have to say. It would be like the end of innocence; a rude welcome to the rest of the world.

'You know, every time I come here, I fall in love with this beautiful town a little more. My family wish we could live here and I enjoy nothing more than to walk among you, drinking in your health, strength and kindness. There really is nowhere else like this in the Conquord and I salute you for what you have built here.'

The cheers were louder this time and the applause took some time to die down.

'But it's not just what you have built that sets you apart, it is what you have nurtured here over the decades and the centuries. The great work to which so many of you have been a crucial support. A great work that is blessed by God. A work that has seen most of you enjoy abilities that will one day be enjoyed by the many, not the few. How wonderful that you have been part of it. And in a thousand years, your names and name of the Westfallen will be written large in history and legend. You will never be forgotten.'

They were with him now. Silent.

'And why is this? It is because right now, the potential Gorian wrote so much about has finally been realised. And these four young citizens to my right represent everything that all of us and our fathers before us have worked for so long to achieve. You will all have read about the trials that our ancestors faced. Keeping the Ascendancy secret from the Order; constant disappointment; deformation of mind and body in those born into high expectation. Maintaining the Ascendancy strands through illness, through war and through suspicion. Such enormous problems that it would so often have been easier to give up and consign it all to myth.

'But the belief shown then was too strong and with the support of this fine town, the Echelon have continued to the success we now enjoy. And now is the time when we must be stronger and more as one than ever before.'

His tone had hardened and as he paused for breath, he scanned the citizens. His reminder of history had worked and the pride of achievement was shining from hundreds of faces. But it was mixed with anxiety. There were too many out there who knew very well that following the building of ego and pride, came the need for belief in the face of adversity.

'Because with our success comes change. And with change comes fear of the unknown and fear of the reality with which we are faced. I have heard of your reactions to our young Ascendants and I understand them, I do. Of course you must do what you believe is right for yourselves and your children. But you must not overreact and you must always remember that you are deeply imbued with what is happening here. You cannot ignore it.

'So I am disappointed that many of you are so anxious that it has led you to remove yourselves from the Ascendants and so isolate them, shun them even. They may have extraordinary abilities but they are still just ordinary children in their hearts. And they need your help to remain ordinary. They are your friends, as are the Echelon. Do not turn away at the moment they need you most. You all know that my son is a great friend of theirs. He doesn't fear them, he loves them.'

He held up his hands, noting the guilty shifting of feet.

'But enough. I am not here to lecture you on how to bring up your children, though I would like you to examine how you think today. What I am here to tell you has far-reaching ramifications for us all.

'We have reached a crossroads. The young Ascendants have emerged and they are learning their talents very quickly. And many of you are surprised, I am sure, how fearful you have sometimes been about what that means. We have all had our moments of anxiety. But what you have to understand now is that change is upon you and your lives will never be quite the same again.

'The nature of the Ascendancy is that one day it will be announced to the outside world. That time is now.'

Consternation swept the gathering like wind across fields of corn. Vasselis held up his hands for quiet.

'Citizens of Westfallen. My friends. We none of us knew if this would happen in our lifetimes and we should celebrate our triumph though danger comes as its bedfellow. I have recently returned from Estorr where I met with the Advocate herself. I have told her what we achieved here and have begged for her acceptance.'

Shock stilled every body and every voice. Vasselis smiled as best he could though his heart was pounding in his throat. Only now did the risk he had taken with the lives of all those before him register. He fought a quaver from his voice.

'The fact that I stand here today demonstrates that she has given that acceptance. But it is conditional. To calm your fears, I can also confirm that the Order knows nothing, and for now at least, I can keep them from here as I have done for twenty years. But the Advocacy will come here to investigate and we can do nothing but answer all their questions with complete honesty. The eyes of the Advocate are on Westfallen and we must not fail now. Nothing must be hidden and none of us must speak ill of the Ascendancy in which we are all so steeped.'

Vasselis waited while the citizens digested what was going to descend on them.

'This town and all its people have been a haven of peace and tranquillity for those lucky enough to live and visit, for hundreds of years. But for now at least, that peace will be shattered. I know many of you will go back to your homes and be saddened, thinking the life you love is gone. And perhaps it has. But the measure of the truly great, the truly courageous, is the ability to grow in the face of adversity and change. To make a life better than the one left behind.

'And as I look about me today, I see greatness and courage in every single one of you. I am proud to count you among my people. I am proud to call you my friends.' The cheers began. 'Stand with me. Stand with the Ascendancy. Together we will become legend!'

Chapter 18

848th cycle of God, 30th day of Genasrise
15th year of the true Ascendancy

Genastro had been late on the ground in Tsard. And, following a deep, harsh dusas, where hypothermia had been the biggest killer in the legions camping in the occupied territories, the fresh season of growth was most welcome when it eventually arrived.

Roberto Del Aglios and the two legions and two alae under his command had been more fortunate than most. Making up half of the north-eastern front, they had been given leave to camp in the outer reaches of Sirrane, the great kingdom of wood and mountains that swept along the north of Tsard.

For Roberto, it had been a double benefit over the hundred and fifty days since the conditions dictated an end to hostilities. His mother was desperate to secure a formal alliance with Sirrane. Even now, Conquord diplomats ventured deep into the closed forest lands. Roberto played his part, maintaining a disciplined camp, foraging only in the area of forest granted to him and burning the minimum of timber.

As a result, food was sufficient and his armies were content enough. Desertion rates were low and morale reasonable. No one was happy to be marooned for dusas on campaign and there was no doubt that in Roberto's experience, Tsard was the bleakest terrain he had ever seen once the snow and ice came.

He had his discipline problems through the quiet days. Boredom was a dangerous demon and in an army of over sixteen thousand men and women, spread like disease. Drills and organised inter-manipular and inter-legion games were his most successful weapons, in addition to ensuring he rotated the foraging teams to give everyone a taste of the hunt. But arguments between lovers, over the Sirranean

whores that walked the camp, shares of food and drink, card games
. . . anything on a cold night sparked fights and insubordination.

And while Roberto had the reputation of an understanding general, he would not tolerate indiscipline. He had executed three men
and two women for serious breaches and those deaths weighed
heavily on him. But in a campaigning army of this size, he had to
make an example or face mutiny. In years gone by, loyalty to a
general was enough. But the Tsardon campaigns had been going on
for five years and patience among those who had left their families to
farm in their stead was growing thin.

This last dusas had been a busy one for the administrators. Roberto
had been visited by a senior delegation of the Gatherers to assess
manpower, morale and discuss planning for the genastro campaign.
Paul Jhered himself had visited the huge legion encampments some
two hundred miles inside Tsard from the eastern border of Atreska. It
was where the Tsardon armies had been particularly aggressive during
the last campaigning season and where progress remained tortuously
slow. The southern front legions camped by the borders of Kark had
also suffered, but more at the hands of raiders from the steppes who
targeted supply lines and ambushed marching columns.

Roberto was of the opinion that he and his fellow generals needed
no reinforcement. Rather, they needed to be utterly certain the
eastern front would remain firm so that the northern and southern
armies could advance far enough into Tsard to close the pincers.

His aim was to secure the southern border of Sirrane far enough
east to stand directly above the Bay of Harryn, which lay the best
part of a thousand miles south. Ambitious but achievable and one
brick in a year's campaign that ought to see the Tsardon broken and
pushed back into their heartlands, fastnesses and strongholds. Surrender would then be a realistic outcome and they could all go home.

It was the message he had been giving his soldiers and cavalry ever
since the Gatherers had left him. They took back his thoughts about
doubling the guard on all supply lines and manning every one of the
nearly two hundred border forts that were the defence against
Tsardon incursion into Atreska and Gosland. He had been disturbed
to hear that one in three were no more than empty shells. And one
thing guaranteed to sap morale, particularly among the Atreskan
alae under his command, was word from their countrymen that the
raids were unabated and the civil war still simmering.

Communication between the fronts had gathered pace the moment the snows began to melt. The massive campaigning force, twenty Conquord legions and sixteen alae numbering in total close on one hundred and twenty thousand citizens, had begun drilling into fighting order and fitness at the same time. Roberto loved this time of the year. Energy and belief surged through his soldiers and cavalry. Each man and woman believed that this year would see their last on campaign. Each dreamt of a return to the lives the Conquord offered them in return for their service in the legions.

For Roberto, he would swap his armour and gladius for the toga and rod of high political office. He wasn't sure how much he was looking forward to it but such was the destiny of the Advocate's eldest son. She wanted him home. Perhaps that was why he was reluctant to give up the soldier's life. Thirty-eight he might be but she would mother him like he was ten, schooling him in the vagaries of political life. She meant well but it could be so patronising.

Roberto shook his head and blew out his cheeks. He ran a hand through his close-cropped black hair and pushed himself up from his desk, taking the paper the Conquord messenger had delivered to him. He turned to look into the mirror set up in the right-hand corner of his command tent, which sat in the middle of the camp. One valuable piece of advice his mother had given him was to be aware of his appearance at all times. Five years on campaign in Tsard made no difference to that advice. Legion commanders had to be in control, had to set the standard for discipline and that began with his personal bearing.

The man who stared back at him was clean-shaven and heavy-framed. Deep blue eyes shone out of a face red from the battering of wind, snow and ice. He wore a white knee-length tunic slashed Advocacy green and cinched at the waist with a leather belt buckled with the Del Aglios crest – a rearing white horse with crossed spears beneath its front legs. His dark green leggings ended in hobnail boots, capped in shining steel.

He nodded, satisfied. Undress uniform was acceptable enough for the orders of the day. He unhooked his fur-lined and hooded black cloak from the stand on which his beautifully polished and pressed dress uniform hung, and slung it around his neck, fastening it with a Del Aglios brooch.

Roberto smoothed his hair, spun on his heel and strode out of his tent, pausing to take in the fresh, cool air of an early genastro morning in Tsard. Before him was a sight he would never have tired of seeing.

To his left, the staggering forest of Sirrane. With evergreen and new growth thrusting through the canopy, it rolled away higher and higher, up slopes still hung heavy with snow. No one really knew the full scale of the forests or mountains. Conquord agents had been two thousand miles along its southern edge and had not reached its end. Could it really be as deep north to south. Its heart was the dominating peak of Gor Nassos, at best estimate in excess of thirty thousand feet high. On a clear day the snow-capped and awesome peak could be seen from hundreds of miles distant, thrusting above the tree line.

The rumour was that the Sirranean capital city was at its feet, on the banks of a crystal blue lake but no one still alive had travelled that far. Sirrane was a nation of secrets that would be kept so long as the forest stood. No thought had ever been given by the Conquord to wage conquest war against it. Legions would be swallowed up in the dense depths of the forest, never to be seen again.

And for their part, the Sirraneans had never shown any desire to expand beyond the outer boughs. They were born, lived and died in the forest, and were rarely seen more than a few miles from their homes. None had ever visited the Conquord. Roberto found them fascinating. Accepting of other countries, trading with them, but diplomacy was as far as it went. As to their culture, it remained like their political and economic systems, an enigma. If he had his way, his first job as a Conquord politician would be as emissary to Sirrane.

Roberto let his gaze travel left to right over their intended destination for this campaigning season. It was a beautiful but worrying landscape for a general. Beyond the plateau on which they had camped, the land fell away quickly before racing away across an undulating plain that had been the scene of their last battle the previous season. A victory that had gladdened their hearts for dusas.

Beyond the plain, the Tsardon hinterland reverted to its characteristic features. Sharp inclines, steep-sided valleys and river courses winding through treacherous rock-faced gorges, all carved out by the hand of God. Crags and rock towers studded the landscape like sentinels, daring invaders to continue.

Hard terrain for marching, let alone fighting. Roberto knew he would have to work hard to gain the ground advantage when they made fresh contact with the ferocious and worthy Tsardon armies.

Looking out over Tsard, its predominant green washed with the purple and blue of early heather flowers, he felt a pang of regret that this stunning landscape would soon be stained red with the blood of thousands of men and women. It would be littered with bodies too numerous to bury and scattered with broken leather and steel for local scavengers to dart out and take once the armies had moved on. All because the King of Tsard would not hear the wisdom of Conquord unity under the Advocate. How many more lives were still to be lost before they surrendered?

Roberto acknowledged the salutes of his tent guards and strode out into the camp. It was a larger, more permanent version of a marching camp. Inside the tall, quadruple-gated wooden stockades, paved roads divided the camp into its constituent parts.

His engineers had done a sound job. Guttering and drainage had been a primary concern, with raised wooden platforms a few inches above ground on which all the tents were pitched. Only the paddocks stood on the thawing earth and the churned mud beneath the horses' hoofs testified to the master engineer's wisdom.

His cavalry, elite of the legions, were billeted close to him, along with his command staff. Legionaries and engineers circled him in order of age and experience; the triarii nearest to him, the hastati on the outer edge by the fortifications and in between them, the principes. Textbook. But then with the Conquord legions, it always was. There was no other way. Discipline, order, victory.

He walked past the legion and alae standards planted outside the command quarters, snapping in the fresh breeze. Emotive banners of veteran fighting forces. The 8th and 10th Estorean regulars, known by their legionaries as the Screaming Hawks and the Hammer Fists respectively. And the 21st and 25th Atreskan alae, cavalry-dominated and going by the names of God's Arrows and Haroq's Blades.

Ducking under the loose tent flap, he was greeted with the multiple scrape of chairs, shouts for attention and the thumps of left fist striking right shoulder.

'At ease,' he acknowledged. 'Sit, sit.' Roberto made for the angled table on which were pinned the quartermaster's numbers, the best maps they had of the surrounding area and details of the path already travelled. He brandished his messenger papers.

'Dusas is officially over.' There was a short cheer, though the twenty assembled in front of him already knew it. 'We strike camp at the earliest opportunity, which I have deemed will be in seven days. You all know what you and your centurions must do to get your citizens into battle trim. Here are your additional orders.

'The Arrows and Blades, I want your mounted scouts in the field from today onwards. I want settlements visited, provisions secured and best routes plotted. We are all aware of the potential for ambush. Get as much information from the locals as you can. Pay them well; my mother's war chest is deep indeed.' A chuckle. 'I want scouts four days ahead of us at all times on the march and I want messages daily. I will not be surprised by encounter with the enemy. I trust that is clear.' He waited for the relevant masters of horse to confirm.

'Good. Hawks, your scouts will travel the eaves of Sirrane. I will not be flanked. Distance and messaging as with my alae. Fists, your scouts will mark our rear and maintain communications with the eastern front. Supply will be difficult and I will not tolerate interruptions due to information negligence on your part. Agreed? Excellent.

'Master of Engineers, Rovan Neristus. We're rolling. We have just spent dusas next to the best source of timber in the world. I trust our supply contracts are in place. If not, you have seven days. Don't come to me on the march telling me a scorpion or wagon must be abandoned due to lack of raw materials or you will find yourself fighting with the hastati.'

The pigeon-framed engineer scowled at him. 'I am sure the hastati would be proud to have me with them, Roberto.'

'Let's pray we don't have to find out. Again, you have leave to pay. Quartermasters have my accounts. Remember, all of you, that we are not at war with Sirrane and our aim is never to be so. You will not take liberties. Except perhaps with their whores.'

Another chuckle. He held up his hands.

'Two pieces of news for you. One good, one not so. While we are not receiving reinforcements, the eastern front will benefit from four new legions. They are going to be raised from Avarn, Neratharn, Morasia and Bahkir who are all underrepresented on this campaign.

Conscription is already underway but we cannot expect them into the fight until solasfall at best. That, my Atreskan friends, means that your country is not suffering any more drain from its fields and businesses.

'But before you get too happy, I have to tell you that while the messenger service and the supply lines from Gosland and Atreska are being strengthened, both by late genasfall, the border forts will not be. I have been given no reason but I suspect it is money and available bodies.'

There was a single voice of dissent and Roberto nodded.

'I know, Goran, I know. But this is the reality. We must use it as a spur to win decisive victories early in the campaign to force raiders at our backs to join the armies in front of us.

'Make no mistake, we will win this campaign this year. We all want to see our homes again. Mind your discipline, mind your troop morale. I will not hesitate to remove command from those who demonstrate their inability to perform in the field. In the last five years, none of you have failed me. See that it remains that way. Dismissed.'

Thomal Yuran, Marshal Defender of Atreska, sat in the throne room of the principal castle in Haroq City, now called the basilica since their accession to the Estorean Conquord. The former King of Atreska was long dead, preferring to be executed rather than bend knee to the Advocate. Yuran had thought himself the rightful if fortunate successor and he had been honoured to be the first unfettered Marshal Defender of the province. Now he was not so sure.

Genastro had brought precious little in the way of warmth to his heart and bones and a brooding anger had settled on him since his frustrating visit to the Advocate the previous dusas. The freezing temperatures that had swept across the Conquord and into Tsard had matched his mood and the wait for a reaction to his demands and the investigation into his province's finances had been interminable.

But it was done now and the papers awaited him once his audience with Praetor Gorsal from Gull's Ford was at an end. She waited for him to respond to her latest plea even now. He took a moment. The throne room bore Estorean marks. White columns had been raised on which to mount busts of great Atreskan rulers and they managed to look completely out of place in the tapestry-filled room with its vaulted stone roof.

The original throne had been destroyed, a symbol of a government dismantled, to be replaced by a wide, low uncomfortable seat of office. And the uniforms of his guards all bore deep green trim, as did the Atreskan crest of a crenellated tower crossed by swords. Right now it all stood for very little. Genastro had come and the raids would begin again in earnest.

He looked across at Gorsal whom he had bade sit though it was against protocol. She was shivering from her journey, sick with fever and fear for her people whom he had been so unable to protect from the Tsardon.

'I wish I could promise more than I already have. Already, I am dragging too many away from their lives and damaging our economy to fight a war we do not want and to protect borders we should not have to protect. Unless the Gatherers outside my door now have news which surprises me, I can offer you no security barring that within the walls of this city.'

'We will not leave Gull's Ford,' rasped Gorsal, coughing violently enough to double over with the effort. 'So we will burn when they return and the deaths will be on your head. The end of the cycles of so many under God. Can you live with that?'

Yuran bit back his retort. He thought nothing of the Conquord religion, only agreeing to his Marshal Defendership when it was clear Atreskan religions, which had more in common with the Tsardon than Estorean, would be allowed to continue. The civil strife over which he presided made him wonder if that too had been a mistake. No wonder he returned to his shrine every night to beg for direction from the lords of sky and stars.

'What would you have me do? There are fifty villages in your position. I cannot defend them all, or one above another. We must hope for an end to the Tsardon campaign. Pray for that at your House of Masks.'

Yuran cursed himself for the look of contempt that crossed Gorsal's sick, pale face.

'I have hope,' he said. 'Really I do. Though I can give no more, I feel the Advocate will agree to staff the border forts with Conquord legions.'

'Another empty promise from the luxury and decadence of Estorr,' sniffed Gorsal. 'As empty as Jhered's.'

'Then come here to Haroq until the trouble is over. Rebuild when our soldiers return to the countryside,' he said.

He felt so torn. Estorea still held his respect though it diminished by the day. Its officers and politicians haunted his corridors. What choice did he have but to remain in step? Yet, at the same time, he tasted the emptiness in the words he spoke. Platitudes, no more.

Gorsal shook her head. 'We are strong in the outlands,' she said. 'We have pride in our way of life. All we ask is that the Conquord returns the loyalty we have shown in it. Defend us. Defend your people. Or one day we too will listen to the rebels and be lost to the Conquord.' She stood up. 'And we will not be alone. Bring us hope, Marshal. It is all we have ever wanted.'

Yuran sighed as he watched her go. He smacked his palm on the arm of the throne and leant forwards, wiping the stinging hand across his brow. Around him, his advisers were silent. He suspected them all of being Estorean spies. He had appointed none of them, after all. At least they could report back on his continued loyalty.

Footsteps echoed through the throne room. Three walked towards him, two men flanking a woman. Gatherers. He waved them forwards, examining their expressions. Unreadable.

'So,' he said. 'What of my books? And what of the decision of the Advocacy to grant my desires.'

The woman, a Gatherer Appros, a senior accountant and soldier, handed him a single sheet of parchment sealed with the Del Aglios crest.

'This is word from the Advocate,' she said. 'Meanwhile, our report on your books is being studied by your own accountants. It reveals little that can be construed as negligence.'

He spread his palms before accepting the parchment. 'I told you that you wasted your time, Appros Menas. I give all I can. Presumably, therefore, I will not be asked to raise more soldiers or pay more taxes.'

'Indeed not,' said Menas, her tone neutral, her face severe, scarred from an attack years before. 'Though you will also not be surprised to learn that a country that cannot give in taxes, cannot expect defence raised by the taxes of others, particularly when the Tsardon campaign is such a drain on the exchequer.'

Yuran sagged. 'What? Surely that is precisely the reason for the Conquord. Central taxation for the good of all. Neratharn is not under attack. Its people can defend mine while we need it. Are we not a family?'

'Yes, Marshal Yuran, we are. But it is the decision of the Advocacy that the remaining military budget to be spent on raising further legions to assure us of victory in Tsard. That is where the Neratharnese will go, among others.'

'Then I am back exactly where I started,' he said. 'My people will die at the whim of the Tsardon raiders.'

'Your country's defence is not my concern,' said Menas.

Yuran didn't respond. He feared arrest for what he was liable to say when his temper broke. He cleared his throat and dragged open the parchment. It was a short message. Actually it was an invitation, one of those where there was no option to decline. He read it as if from over his own shoulder, such was the disbelief and the thundering in his head. He let it drop from his hands and fixed his eyes on Menas, who flinched visibly.

'Is this some kind of a joke?'

Chapter 19

848th cycle of God, 1st day of Genasfall
15th year of the true Ascendancy

The palace was busy, far busier than the Advocate would normally allow. The halls bustled with civil servants and local specialist businesspeople going about tasks handed down to them by the organisers. The hum of activity in the wide corridors and public audience rooms only served to deepen Jhered's anger.

He had meant to bathe, having just stepped off ship from Gosland, but the banners on the streets, the air of fervour in the city and the industry on the Hill had given him a sick feeling. Instead, having discovered the reason for it all he slapped his gladius on to his desk, threw his filthy cloak across the office and strode into the palace, looking for the Advocate.

Decorations adorned every column and insulted the statue of every general who had ever brought victory to the Conquord. Worse, they insulted every legionary and cavalryman out in the hinterland of Tsard facing the enemy. His boots echoed darkly off the marble floors of the great entrance hall, which had been converted into a makeshift project office. Heads turned towards him, people so drunk with their own importance they looked on him with something bordering on condescension.

Nodding curtly at palace guards, he swept along the central gardens, down the colonnaded passage to its left and up the stairs leading to the private levels, where the Advocate and her inner sanctum lived their lives away from public gaze.

His expression as much as his rank granted him access up the huge sweeping white marble staircase with its balustrades carrying busts of former Advocates and its walls a mosaic of the defining battle of Karthack Gorge. A stunning victory where the Avarnese were finally defeated, to give the Conquord total dominion over the south of the continent and opening up the northwest to the legions. Jhered had had ancestors in that battle. One was a decorated general who had died for the Conquord in the gorge.

It was a magnificent sight but Jhered had no time for it now. He took the stairs three at a time, all but flattening two people on their way down. All fine weave togas, bright colours and garish headwear. He pulled up just in time, recognising them. Rich landowners, grown fat off the efforts of others and with no sense of the world beyond their luxurious, cosseted existence. Poison in the Advocate's ear.

'You'd better not have any part in this stupidity,' spat Jhered.

They smiled at him indulgently as one might a miscreant child. 'Ah, the magnificent Exchequer Jhered,' said one, voice affected by wine. 'Box up your temper. We are saving the Conquord from implosion, reminding ourselves of our glories.'

'You and your kind will bring us to our knees, turning a blind eye even while you burn.'

He stalked past them, shoulder connecting heavily with the speaker who stumbled against his friend.

'Beware, Jhered, lest your star should wane. Your friends may be powerful but they are few.'

Jhered stopped and turned. He was a step above them and used his height to glower down at them, pleased by the paling of their stuffed cheeks.

'Go ahead and threaten,' he said, voice cool and soft. 'It is a long while since I exercised my right to examine the finances of named individuals. Perhaps I should take time to enjoy that pleasure once more.' He leaned over them. 'Go.'

He shook his head as they hurried down the stairs, no doubt to scribe letters to the Advocate about his brutish ways. At the top of the stairway, a galleried landing made up three sides of a square. Passages and rooms led off each. Guards stood at every corner, armour bright in the multiple lanternlights, spears held at ease, eyes front.

'At least some here are still capable,' he muttered to himself. 'Where is the Advocate?' he asked of the nearest guard. He hardly need have bothered. From an open door halfway up the first mosaic-laid corridor, laughter spilled through an open door on a gentle tide of stringed music. He recognised Herine's voice.

The guard nodded in that direction. 'She is entertaining the sponsors, Lord Jhered,' he said.

'Then my face will bring welcome relief,' he said.

'I have no orders to keep people away, sir,' agreed the guard.

'Lucky for you.'

Jhered smoothed his hair and rubbed at his face while he walked the short distance to the reception room. Guards moved to attention, spears snapping in front of their faces. He stood in the doorway for a moment. Herine was lounging on a banked pile of cushions in the centre of the room. Men and women, eight at a quick count, were spread around her. Some were standing and others were too close to her feet for his liking. Sycophants.

One, a young man barely out of his teens, was draped in front of her. Her fingers traced a course over his finely muscled torso while in her other hand, a goblet of wine hovered near her mouth. Servants stood around the walls, stepping in to offer fruit and more wine. Musicians were seated to the right of him playing delicate melodies on kitharas and lutes.

Jhered shook his head, something he seemed to do a lot in the palace these days. He felt like spitting on the stone between his feet. Instead, he walked in slowly, letting his presence fill the room and silence the twittering conversation as gradually as it might. He came to rest a few paces from the scatter of stools and cushions. Those standing moved reflexively away. He didn't fit. His trail clothes clashed with their finery, the dirt and dust of the real world an affront to their fantasy.

The Advocate swivelled her head to him and smiled. She raised her goblet, spilling a little wine down the chest of her consort. Her fingers trailed in it and she sucked the end of each one in turn.

'My Lord Jhered, arrived from the wilds. What news of our far flung territories?'

She was drunk, her words a better fit for the heroic stage than to address her most senior soldier. He ignored the question.

'Games?' he said, the word like a mouthful of rotten meat. 'Which of these cretins persuaded you of that? Or was it one of those bloated mannikins I met on the stairs?'

Herine's face fell in mock distress. 'You mean you don't like the idea?'

'Don't like it? My Advocate, this is a folly more grand in the making and damaging in the execution than the building of the new arena during the rule of your grandfather. And we have all read of the lingering effects of that decision.'

A ripple of dissention ran around the sponsors. He spared them a contemptuous glance. All middle-aged, all sodden in the mind and puffed up by their closeness to the Advocate. Herine caught their mood and her expression sobered. She made to speak but Jhered got there first.

'Party's over,' he said. 'Time to go and lay heavy on someone else's hospitality.'

It upset them, as he knew it would. The self-appointed great and good of Estorr, and thereby the Conquord, spluttered and made protest to the Advocate. The wash of wine through her head had apparently cleared and she was glaring at Jhered, embarrassment mixed with annoyance. He met her gaze squarely.

'Unless you want this conversation to be more public than it should, clear the room, my Advocate,' he said into the mounting furore.

'I don't remember granting you an audience, Exchequer Jhered.'

'And I don't remember my Advocate being prey to such blind recklessness. Please,' he said. 'Now.'

Herine weighed him up. He saw the most delicate of nods.

'I will recall you all in the morning,' she said. 'My apologies for the ill-tutored interruption of my Exchequer.'

A relieved titter ran around the sponsors. Jhered bit down hard on his temper, holding Herine's gaze instead. The consort moved reluctantly from the playful embrace of the Advocate and stood up, petulant expression fixed on Jhered as he passed.

'The Advocate makes no decisions but for the benefit of the Conquord. It is right we celebrate our triumphs,' he said, voice wavering and lighter than his frame suggested. 'You should think abou—'

Jhered grabbed him under the lower jaw, pushing his mouth shut. He drove the consort backwards towards the door, speaking as he went.

'There will never come a time when I take advice from a half-man destined only to lose his balls should he surprise us all and prove fertile. I wonder if she has not made a mistake choosing you. It sounds as if yours have already been taken. Out!' He thrust the consort through the door to sprawl against the wall opposite. 'Out!'

He swung away and slammed the door, catching a poorly disguised smile on the face of a guard. The look of the consort was murderous. Let him try. He marched back towards the Advocate, expecting vitriol but seeing instead an amused expression. He knew this tactic of old and steeled himself to retain his mood.

'Oh Paul, you really shouldn't treat my new love like that. So delicate of mind.'

'He demonstrates no mind at all,' growled Jhered. 'And I will treat those morons with whom you surround yourself exactly as they deserve.'

'You'll make more enemies,' she said, a smile across her face, the wine glass by her mouth again. Jhered shrugged. 'I know, I know. Add them to the list, eh? Now, have you calmed down at all, or must I call in the guards?'

'I am not as much a danger to you as you are to yourself with this ridiculous decision. Celebratory games? What possessed you? Has that coven of empty-headed flab put something in your wine?'

'Paul, I would—'

'And as God-embraces-us-all, celebrating what?'

Herine took a deep breath. 'Sit down, Paul.'

'No, I think I'll stand.'

'You will do as ordered by your Advocate, Exchequer Jhered.'

Jhered cleared his throat. 'Aren't we past such displays, you and I?'

'You can seriously pose that question after your grand entrance?'

Jhered paused, taking a deliberate deep breath. This was why he would never settle down with a woman. Something in them burned his fuse painfully short painfully quickly. He held up his hands and sat down.

'Wine?'

'No, thank you,' he said. 'Herine, I have not come here to argue with you or to have you pull rank on me. I just want to know what on God's great earth makes you think that celebratory games will do anything for your position or the position of the Conquord in the wider world.'

'During the deeps of dusas, while you were gone, we—'

'We?'

Herine gestured at the empty cushions. 'We. It was not just the chill of the weather but the chill of the people. Spirits are low. We have been fighting Tsard for five years and have not yet struck the decisive blow. It was decided that ten days of games as solastro dawns would lift sagging hearts and remind our citizens of the glory of the Estorean Conquord.' Jhered frowned. It was clear she believed it, or thought she did.

'Paul, the battle for the Conquord must be fought in our own streets first. What use is there if our own closest citizens do not love and respect us? They need something to cheer and they shall have it. These games will be a triumph.'

Jhered nodded, fighting in vain for the words to describe how he felt. He scratched the bridge of his nose and wiped at the corner of one eye with a dusty finger.

'I disagree. In time of major campaign, austerity must hit everyone to make them feel they are sharing in the effort. And how will the treasury pay for all this? Games are a dreadful expense. Your sponsors cannot hope to raise all the funds for the scale of events I assume you are suggesting.'

Herine laughed, a light sound as if he had asked the simplest of questions.

'Oh, Paul, the treasury is deep. We have the funds.'

'No, dammit, we do not!' he thundered, temper snapping at last. He crashed a fist down on to a salver, catapulting its remnants of fruit into the air, and surged to his feet. 'I and my Gatherers have just spent dusas dragging ourselves from one frozen province to the next to wring any small levy we could to fund the raising of more legions. And small was our return. Nothing could be taken from Atreska or Gosland, nothing from Tundarra, Easthale or Gestern. And you will not ask Vasselis for more though he would probably find it. The money is not there. You and I both know it.'

'Then find it for me, Paul,' Herine shouted back. 'You're my Exchequer. It's your job.'

Jhered paused. 'You don't really expect me to respond to that, do you? You know what I'm getting at.'

'You've become blinkered by the war, Paul. The treasury has budgets for every part of Conquord business. Others can spare funds for this.'

'With respect, my Advocate, you are missing the point.' He saw Herine bristle but ploughed on. 'If you can afford to divert money for the games, you can afford to divert it for the war in Tsard or the security of Atreska. It is that simple in the minds of every general, including your own son, and I am amazed that you cannot see it.

'Admit it. You are pandering to the whims of a dozen bored rich citizens who need something new to play with. And all the while, your legions fight and die in your name. Every coin you waste on these games could have gone to helping them win. This money could secure Atreska's and Gosland's borders.'

'I'm sure Marshal Yuran will see the value of the games once he is here.'

Jhered gaped. 'You are inviting him?'

'Every Marshal Defender is summoned.'

'Dear God, that is like showing the condemned the forging of the sword that beheads them. Are you trying to start a rebellion?'

'He will not rebel.'

'No? You have not seen the look in his eyes recently. The Atreskan civil war haunts him daily. He knows how thinly we are stretched on the Tsardon frontier. One reverse and their armies will march unopposed to Haroq City.'

'Paul I—'

'And when they get there, who will stop them marching all the way to Estorr?'

'Lord Jhered, you will be silent!' roared Herine. 'I do not care who you are, I will not be spoken to like this in the heart of my own palace.'

Jhered made to respond but the look in her eyes stalled him. He settled for folding his arms across his chest and giving a curt nod.

'Oh, thank you so much for your agreement,' said Herine. 'Now you listen to me. I will not have such wild talk in my palace or in my streets. You speak as if the Conquord is under threat. It is not. You speak as if we are on the verge of bankruptcy. We are not. I have sixteen legions and fourteen alae in Tsard and I am reinforcing them with more, as you well know. This is an army larger than any the Conquord has sent on campaign and one that every right-minded citizen knows will be victorious.

'And even should the impossible happen, and Tsard threaten our borders, the weight of citizenry and standing legions we have throughout the Conquord are simply overwhelming. The Tsardon know this. They will defend as they must until forced to surrender, but they will never break us.

'You speak of joint austerity. Paul, please. It has always been that the border states face the new enemy while those at the expanding heart of the Conquord enjoy the life for which their mothers and fathers fought through history. It is the way. We are a meritocracy. We earn the right to our luxuries. When Tsard joins the Conquord, Atreska will reap those benefits too. The games we are staging are a celebration of the glory of all we have built and all we have still to build. They will go ahead and you will not undermine them.'

'And neither will I have any part in them. Nor will I or any member of the Gatherers attend. I have listened to you and I hope you are right, I really do. But it is my people who have to travel to provinces under threat and I will not have them accused of being party to wasting revenue that could have been better spent. Their job is dangerous enough as it is.'

They knew each other well, Herine and Jhered. And he knew he had pushed her as far as she would go. They glared at each other for a time. He was aware she needed his support to give the games final credibility. She was aware she had to find a compelling reason for him to be absent. Fortunately, there were plenty.

'Paul, I respect you and everything you say but you still have the capacity to surprise and disappoint me.'

'It's why you keep me around,' he growled.

She nodded. 'Perhaps you're right. But sometimes your particular brand of reality is as tainted as you believe mine to be.' She took a sip of wine and Jhered saw her reach a conclusion. 'I'm busy here as you can see and, frankly, I don't want you around here muddying the fountains and spreading your ill-humour. But neither do I want you too far away.

'We've delayed too long investigating Arvan Vasselis and West-fallen. It's plagued me throughout dusas. Where does it leave the Order? Where does it leave me as Prime Speaker? I need answers, Paul and to be honest there's no one I trust to get them except you, though I'm scared at the prospect of what you'll find down there.' She let her voice drop to a whisper. 'I've had nightmares about signing his execution order.'

'I've suffered similar anxieties,' said Jhered.

'No doubt. So go to Caraduk. Find out what's going on. And see you don't get back until the games are over. And tell Arvan he need not attend. I expect he will have other things on his mind when you arrive.'

Jhered smiled, satisfied. 'And on a more or less linked matter, how has the Chancellor taken the news of the games.'

'She's delighted, as you might expect,' said Herine. 'Games have always been stages for the Order to educate, have they not? And with so many Marshals in attendance from provinces whose native religions still flourish, she is practically drooling at the opportunity.'

'A less than pleasant image,' said Jhered. 'I'd best get moving.'

Jhered saluted, right arm to left shoulder, and turned for the door.

'Paul.' He stopped and swung back. Herine was standing. 'You are my most trusted friend. But even you are not above the law. Go carefully and mind your words. These games have already been approved by the Senate. Defamation of them is an offence.'

He sighed. 'Everything I do, everything I say, I do for my love of you and the Conquord. You should ask yourself what really drives your decisions.' He reached the door. 'Your inner circle is your only flaw. Don't let them blind you. The Conquord needs you too much.'

He left her frowning, not knowing whether she would take his words as insult or compliment.

Chapter 20

848th cycle of God, 8th day of Genasfall
15th year of the true Ascendancy

The scouts attached to the Haroq's Blades had sighted Tsardon forces seven days before and immediately, Roberto had upped the marching pace, meaning to close to within a day's march. They had moved easily deep into the Tsardon hinterland, travelling along made paths and roads where they could, and in a straight line where they couldn't. The landscape had become cluttered with valleys and clefts and more scouts had been sent out to guard against ambush. There had been three skirmishes away from the columns, all of which Estorea had won, but the chance of larger encounters was growing.

Local settlements had already been scouted and armoured foraging parties were sent out to secure supplies, under orders not to use force unless they encountered reluctance. Roberto had no doubt that some of his foragers would concoct such problems in order to swing their blades. It was the way of things and perhaps the odd demonstration of Conquord determination was not so bad.

Three day's fast march and the dust cloud that signified the Tsardon army was clearly visible at the top of every rise. Scouts reported the enemy army slowing, apparently seeking advantageous ground on which to take a stand. Meanwhile, messengers from the south and east reported both Estorean armies closing with large Tsardon forces. So soon into the fall of the season.

Roberto had returned messages indicating concern at the apparent high level of organisation and intelligence of the enemy; and more importantly, at the scale of the forces that had been raised against them. He faced numbers estimated at two-thirds his own and that was reflected across the three fronts. He urged care in picking battlefields, patience in the face of provocation and resistance of the urge to fall into the small divisive skirmishes preferred by the enemy.

Two days later and the army was moving through difficult rocky terrain, seriously impairing the movement of the wagons. Scouts had reported the Tsardon stopped and camped. Roberto decided to take his time, ordering half pace and moving four maniples back to help the wagons across the treacherous ground.

It was a tense time. The Tsardon had been here before them and the way was littered with totems and shrines. Roberto's scholars interpreted most as curses on enemy feet to bring broken bones, blisters and disease down from their Gods. But some were exhortations to withdraw, allied with threats of death should the army breast the next rise, ford the next river or traverse the next valley.

The Atreskan alae were superstitious, steeped in religious history linked to Tsard. Their concern fed back through the legions and Roberto did not hesitate to act. Leaving his extraordinarii in position, he rode through to the head of the column and halfway up a valley with sheer rock faces either side of him and a shallow tributary at his feet. There he turned and addressed the Blade's light-horse archers and any others who could hear him.

'Are we seasoned campaigners or raw recruits frightened at the scattered idols of a people who fall back ahead of us? Are we one under a God who embraces us all under sky and over stone or a fractured mass that follows every sign as if it was gospel? No one will die at the head of this valley. No one will die as a result of any of these trinkets littering our path. I will prove it to you.'

He dismounted and walked to the totem which had brought the cavalry to a temporary halt. It was a low stone tower built around a wooden stake. The stake held the single, twisted horn of a mountain ram in its cleft and the whole was splashed with its blood. It was the second they had passed but was of a larger scale, a greater warning. It read that the beast of the mountains would fall on those who attained their peak, that the rocks would tumble and the blood would run.

Roberto lashed a boot at it, scattering pebble, stone and stake. The horn bounced from the wall behind it and skittered down the slope.

'It is as fragile in construction as it is in invested threat,' he shouted. 'Blades. At my shoulder. March!'

He led them to the head of the valley, spreading his arms at the emptiness he found there and smiling down at the thousands who followed him. He heard cheers way back from those who could see little but his silhouette. He inclined his head and turned back to look out at the vista afforded him.

Conflict was close. To the north, the forest of Sirrane ran up the foothills of a low mountain range. South, the head of the valley on which he stood revealed itself as a long, unbroken ridge towering hundreds, thousand of feet in places above the floor of the narrow, tree-studded and river-run plain laid out below him. Across that plain, perhaps six miles away, the Tsardon camp rested on the lower slopes of a range of snow capped peaks. The range was cracked by passes and eventually fell away south at the farthest reaches of his vision to be replaced by gentler hills and rises. North, the line was unbroken up to and through the border of Sirrane.

Behind him, the army was coming to a halt. He was happy to stand there, alive and unmolested while he made his admittedly simple decisions. The Tsardon camp was well placed. They knew he would not attempt to march through Sirrane, hence the northern route was closed. The camp guarded all three of the easily visible passes and overlooked an army marching for the southern hills.

Up in the sky, clouds obscured the early afternoon sun. There was no sense in marching much further today. He walked back down to the cavalry and took the reins of his horse from an aide. He mounted up and spoke to the Blade's Master of Horse.

'Down slope and hard right. Three miles south and break for camp. Have a colour party and engineers ahead with you for marking the boundaries. Delay only means empty stomachs.'

'Yes sir.'

'Go,' he said and kicked his heels into the flanks of his horse, goading it into a trot down the mud and rock slope to where the tributary burst from below ground. 'Blade's Master of Sword!' He roared. 'Where are you, Davarov?'

'Sir,' came back the reply from the mass of men and women crammed into the narrowing valley sides.

'Deploy your light infantry between us and the enemy during camp build. There will be cavalry with you. You won't be troubled but showing intent never hurts.' A smile touched his lips. 'And you could use the practice, eh?'

'Might I remind my General that in the last games, the Blades infantry were the swiftest at the exercise you give us tonight?' Around him, citizens cheered. 'And if we need practice, what does that say about the infantries of the Arrows, Fists and Hawks!'

The cheering got louder, mixed with laughter.

'It means you are all slack after a dusas where you exercised only your hips and wrists,' said Roberto, clapping his hands. 'Now march. The cavalry escapes you.'

He rode back up the path and took his horse to one side to watch his army pass, encouraging every citizen that caught his eye, assuring them that each pace brought them closer to honour.

His head buzzed with excitement. Battle was close.

The camp was complete before nightfall and fires scratched at the twilight sky. Smells of cooking came from a dozen directions. The engineers had found a slightly raised plateau almost directly opposite the Tsardon. A stream ran at its base and the ground was firm for pitching tents and hammering in the stockade panels.

While the bulk of legionaries and cavalry saw to equipment and horses, carpenters and smiths worked under the direction of engineers to repair the damage to wagons resulting from a tough day's march. The surgeons too were doing brisk business on bites, blisters, sprains, twists and the odd break. The camp felt confident, loud with chatter, song and activity.

Across the plain, the Tsardon had chosen not to attack, exactly as Roberto expected. He'd long ordered the Blades back into camp and now just a few riders prowled the open spaces between the picket lines, ready to give early warning of any raid or full blown attack. Roberto was sure they would suffer neither.

He dined in his tent along with all his senior commanders that evening. Scouts weren't expected through the camp gates until the early hours and he was in the mood for a little relaxation and speculation in advance of any concrete information they brought him.

He raised his silver goblet, embossed with the Del Aglios crest and etched with the family prayer. They were almost the first words he had learned as a boy.

> When the world is dark, there is always light for us
> When the flood waters rise, there is always ground for us

When the mountain falls, there is always shelter for us
When the enemy strikes, there is always a shield for us
When God's embrace surrounds us, we need never be afraid.

'Ladies and gentlemen, welcome to your new home. For the next few days, at least.'

They drank and the army's Order Speaker, Ellas Lennart, led the prayer.

'May the arms of God be forever around this army as it performs His work in His name. May each of us be kept safe in His embrace.'

'So it shall be as dawn lightens the sky,' they responded.

'Thank you, Ellas,' said Roberto. 'Eat, eat.'

The low table around which they lounged was stocked with smoked meats, bread and sweet sauces, hot and cold. Flagons of wine and water stood in three places. Plates were filled in silence, all of them waiting for him to begin the debate. He was happy to oblige.

'We have options,' he said. 'You know them, I know them. So tell me the mind of a Tsardon commander this evening.'

'We are the invading force,' said Elise Kastenas, the 8th legion Master of Horse. She was a Caraducian from the heart of the northern plains, and born to ride. Short and powerful, she was a career soldier and bore the scars of her battles proudly on her long, striking face. 'They should want to keep us at arm's length indefinitely. But they are a curious enemy in some regards and we have been able to draw them out on a regular basis these past five years. A march towards them will prove too much temptation.'

'I agree,' said Goran Shakarov, Master of Sword for the God's Arrows. He was a great barrel-chested Atreskan with heavy features and black hair that hung almost to his waist. 'They are a proud people and our presence here on their land as invaders is an insult. I've lived next to them all my life. They aren't waiting for us to tire of war and melt away like ice under the solastro sun. They want to drive us out of their country.' He smiled, showing off broken teeth. 'I know how they feel.'

Tomas Engaard was shaking his head. The 10th's Tundarran Master of Horse was tall, blond and imposing. He was a fine archer from the saddle, the best Roberto had ever seen.

'I don't see how you can say that. It might have been the case three years ago but we've seen them cede ground to us on a regular basis over the last four or five seasons. There's two possible reasons for that and both should worry us. First, they are learning from us and we're going to find it increasingly difficult to draw them out on our own terms. Second, they might be deliberately bringing us in. What concerns me is that the eastern front is facing a stone wall again this year if our intelligence is correct. And that means we have significant Tsardon forces behind us. We are more reliant than ever on General Gesteris keeping them busy.'

'I don't think we can afford to worry about being cut off, Tomas,' said Roberto. 'I hear what you say but our enemy is ahead of us. Gesteris is not going to fold, let's be realistic. If we can defeat those before us, we can circle round and deliver the decisive blow.'

'What I'm saying is that if they continue to fall deeper back into the hinterland, chasing will leave us ever more isolated.'

'Which is why I want to know the mind of their commander,' said Roberto. 'They have camped and let us catch them. For what it's worth I don't think they'll be packing up and falling any further back. They want to fight us now. The question is, will they meet us on the plain and if they won't, where will they line up and can we force their hand? Should we, for instance, break camp and false march south?'

'Not as first play,' said Davarov of the Blades. His voice was hoarse from habitual shouting on top of a heavy cold. 'We have a sound position here. Excellent all-round vision and no chance of a surprise at our backs. Let's get across there and see if they'll join us on the flat.'

'Would you?' Ben Rekeros, a native Estorean, was well into his fifties and would retire from his position as the 10th legion's Master of Sword at the end of this campaign. He was a man of few but weighted words and Roberto respected him enormously for his brain as well as his leadership and muscle. 'Think I'd just draw up on the slopes below their camp if I was them and see if we'll break on their phalanxes or wait down range of their archers.'

'But this is where it doesn't work like we expect,' said Elise. 'I don't agree they're drawing us in, and I don't think they have the patience to match march with us to gain best tactical advantage. They've never shown that sort of will before. They need a victory early in the season and they've stopped here because they can deploy against us. It may not happen tomorrow but I bet a day's pay we'll be at them on this field and nowhere else.'

'Mind what I say,' said Tomas. 'Even if they don't move, they can hold us up here for as long as their patience holds out. That's maybe all they want to do.'

'So you're saying you're wrong?' Roberto was smiling.

'No, General, I'm saying that while I concede that they may not want to draw us any deeper into their lands, they may still be planning on isolating us from help. We are already far further advanced than the eastern front. I say again, they are learning from us. They won't just charge down the hill at us.'

Roberto drained his wine and refilled his goblet with water to wash down the rather dry bread and tough meat.

'Do we have a contract to hunt Sirrane for game?' he said.

'Quartermaster says so,' said Shakarov.

'Then I wish he would shoot us something fresh. This animal is way past its best.' A light laugh greeted his words. 'Right, thank you for your thoughts. Unless our scouts bring me very surprising news, I suggest you all assume the camp stays for tomorrow at least. We will march in battle formation all the way and see how close we can get before I order triplex acies deployment. I will not provoke assault at this stage. Tomas, I don't quite agree with you. I don't think delay is in their thoughts. Neither, Elise, do I think they'll rush out at us the moment we get within taunting distance.

'So, a nice easy day.' He chewed on a mouthful of bread, his teeth cracking a seed. 'By the way, now is the time to bring up any problems. I don't want to hear them at dawn.'

None of them had the chance to say anything. The sound of spears being snapped to attention was followed by a soldier ducking inside the tent and sweeping off his helmet.

'Yes, centurion,' said Roberto.

'Conquord rider from General Gesteris and the eastern front, my Lord,' said the centurion, a man of the 10th legion by his insignia. 'He assures me it is important.' He was holding a satchel.

'I have no doubt,' said Roberto. 'Bring it here.'

The centurion hurried across the tent, handed over the satchel and departed with a smart salute.

'One of yours, Ben Rekeros,' said Roberto, nodding at the centurion's receding figure even as he broke the Conquord seal on the satchel.

'Yes, General, and a fine one, if a little nervous in the face of his seniors. He'll do well, should he live past the hastati.'

Roberto retrieved a sheaf of papers from the satchel. They were tied with string and on top of them was a content and summary sheet written in Gesteris's flowing hand. He scanned the top sheet and felt a warmth spreading through him.

'This message was sent from the approach to the fords at Scintarit. How far away is that, do you think?'

Davarov scratched his head. 'Messenger service could get here in six days with river passage, riding at night and fresh horses for onward transport the whole way. It's the best part of four hundred miles, I'd say.'

'Then they have been as quick delivering this as they can,' said Roberto, impressed despite himself having checked the date of the message. 'It seems we are behind the game, growing fat where others' sword-arm muscle is toned. General Gesteris engaged the Tsardon seven days ago. Let's hope he is already victorious.'

'Does that change anything?' asked Tomas.

'Only in my heart,' said Roberto, 'I hate not being first into conflict. Makes me want to rip the head off the nearest Tsardon. Lucky there are so many about, isn't it?'

Chapter 21

848th cycle of God, 9th day of Genasfall
15th year of the true Ascendancy

The horns sounding at dawn were all but drowned out by the rain drumming on the tents. A weather front had swept over the ridge behind them in the middle of the night and while the winds died quickly, the cloud remained and the camp had taken a soaking for four hours straight.

Shouts rang around the camp, driving citizens from their beds. Rain set discordant music on thousands of helmets, shields and breastplates. Roberto was already up, his aide strapping on his armour. It shone in the lanternlight and he nodded approval. Beneath the polished metal covering head, chest, forearms and shins, his Conquord green clothes had been pressed and stitched with the prayer of victory first uttered at the Battle of Reeth's Pass two hundred years before. A battle that had been decisive in the fall of Tundarra to the Conquord and one in which the Del Aglios family had risen to prominence.

He raised his arms while his gladius, in its scrollwork scabbard, was belted on. His cloak, black and slashed green and carrying the Conquord crest, was fastened at his right shoulder.

'Thank you, Garrelites,' he said.

The young hastati inclined his head and slapped his left fist to his right shoulder.

'Will we fight today, General?' he asked.

Roberto smiled at him. 'How many times have you asked me that? And what do I always reply?' He clapped Garrelites on the shoulder and pointed to his bow, which stood in its protective leather in a stand.

'That if you were a betting man, you'd say that we wouldn't be fighting, just standing and shouting, sir.'

'Well, there you go,' said Roberto. He took the bow and strode out of the tent. 'Get to your maniple, Garrelites and remember not to get yourself killed. I need someone to buckle on my breastplate of a morning.'

'You always say that, too, General.'

Roberto laughed. 'Get going.'

The noise of the army coming to order was deafening close to, a wave breaking around him, harsh under the rain and lowering dark cloud. Roberto added his voice to the tumult.

'15th horse, why are you not mounted!' he bellowed. 'Where is my marching order? Hawks and Fists, you are slack this morning. It is a lovely day for a fight. And why is it that my armour is the only one from which the rain shies? Did we all run out of polish last night? Let's have you. Archers, keep those bows stowed. Conquord, we are marching. This will be an ordered deployment. I want those Tsardon pissing down their legs at our very advance!'

The wide streets of the camp were designed with formation in mind. The site of each tent meant that the maniples formed up in precise marching order. Quickly, the streets filled. Spears and pikes bristled in the air. The thrumming of rain on metal helmets increased in volume. From the paddocks, cavalry were mounting up. Horses, sensing the anxiety and tension in the air, stamped and snorted. Roberto's horse was brought to him and he stowed his bow behind the saddle before swinging smoothly aboard, giving himself a more elevated view of his fighting force.

The mass of voices was quietening now, leaving the air clear for centurions and masters to drag their citizens into tight formation. Roberto nodded. Their work over dusas had been most worthwhile. Over sixteen thousand infantry and two thousand cavalry, ceaselessly drilled in marching and deployment. Legions in competition with each other, cavalry detachments engaged in races and flanking games.

Roberto trotted to a mound of earth built for him by the principal gate. His flagmen stood on it, waiting for him. Turning his horse, he could see the army ready. It had been a decent assembly, given the torrential rain.

'Right, let's have them. Signal the gates.'

'Yes, sir.'

Flags, green and red quartered, swept up to the vertical, moved out thirty degrees, paused and swept down. On all four gates, the signal had been awaited. Orders were given. The hinged gates were dragged aside. Reinforced bridging was laid across the ditch and the army began to move. It would be the first sight the Tsardon had had this genastro of a Conquord force in battle order.

Roberto loved this moment. Fear and excitement in the faces of his hastati, weary experience in those of his triarii. The overwhelming feeling of energy of an army primed to fight. And the sound. It would always send shivers through his body. The rhythm of feet on the march, the rumble of thousands of hoofs on solid ground. Sound that spoke of unstoppable power.

The three infantry columns marched out of their respective gates, principal centre, right and left while the cavalry exited via the tenth gate at the rear of the camp, wheeling left or right depending on their flank position. From above, it would look like four great, dark snakes issuing from the belly of a scaled beast. He trusted the image was no less unsettling from across the plain.

Shouting encouragement, luck and God's protection to the principes who passed by him through the principal gate centre, Roberto let the thrill of the march rattle through him. He rode out behind them with his extraordinarii, a bodyguard made up of Atreskan and Estorean cavalry. Left and right, outside their tents and wagons, the camp followers watched them go. The traders and the whores, wondering how business would be at the end of the day.

Outside the camp, the columns formed up. Hastati left, principes centre and triarii right. Further right, the engineers led mule-drawn wagons in a line of forty, each carrying a mounted scorpion bolt-thrower. Estorean cavalry trotted on the left flank, Atreskan on the right and ahead, guarding against any sudden moves by the enemy though none looked likely. The rain and gloom cut visibility but it seemed as if they were just standing and watching, if the dark smudge in front of their camp was anything to go by.

The legions marched through the rain and mud and on down to the banks of the river that flowed across the centre of the plain. The ground was easy enough on the way down a very gentle slippery decline of rich grasses and tussocks of shrub. Roberto's scouts had identified a crossing point where rocks poked above the water course. Fording the river, they forged on. Two miles to the enemy.

Roberto rode at the head of the army, gauging distance and the time to give the order to deploy. Ahead, the Tsardon were rushing into formation and moving down the slopes to give them distance ahead of their camp without giving up the advantage of higher ground. It was a less disciplined assembly than Roberto would have accepted but was effective enough.

Roberto ordered the wheel to deploy at just under half a mile distance. A long way out of arrow range and giving him room to advance at direct provocation. Latest estimates gave his archers a little less range than their Tsardon counterparts though in rain like this, any bowman was at a great disadvantage. The scorpions would be in play before the archers anyway, sending their bolts over a range just short of three hundred yards.

Roberto rode away to the right past cavalry who had broken into archer, sword and cataphract companies for the skirmish and charge. Behind him, maniples marched into place, their centurions keeping them in close order. Wagons rattled into position, covers left on the weapons for now with the rain unwelcome on hinge and rope unless battle demanded it.

He waited at the end of the formation. It took almost an hour to build, each maniple spaced precisely from the next in classic quincunx formation. Careful positioning defended by cavalry who had eyes only for the enemy. Once complete, he rode down the line. Past archers and light infantry ready to respond in a skirmish. Past his phalanx and heavy infantry, their shields front and centre standing on the floor and their sarissas, twenty feet in length, tips almost lost in the rain. The Atreskan alae infantry made up the left and right, his Estorean regulars in the centre.

'We are the Conquord's army!' He knew his speech would be heard by relatively few, particularly given the rain thumping on ground and helmet, but its content would be passed on quickly enough. 'We are the vanguard. Virgin territory is before us. And I understand none of you have left any virgins behind you.'

A coarse cheer and a ripple of laughter spread out as his words passed through the army, maniple by maniple. Roberto walked his horse to the centre of the line and stopped, looking back over his three ranks of legionaries.

'We have our orders. This is the year when we strike the decisive blows that will bring Tsard to its knees before God and the

Advocate. And there is a greater prize on offer than the booty we already carry. This time, victory means we can all go home.'

A second cheer, louder. Spears and pikes rattled against the backs of shields.

'But you have to earn it. Respect your enemy and fight hard. Protect your friends. Discipline. Honour. Victory.'

They were ready. All they could do now was wait.

And wait they did. Through a rain-soaked day in which all their taunting, fake moves and small advances drew not a single man or arrow from the Tsardon on the slopes before them. Roberto kept them in the field until late in the afternoon and as the clouds finally began to disperse, they marched back to camp and into the setting, red sun.

It was the same for four days. The Conquord army's shows of strength, skill and determination to fight were watched by a Tsardon army content to jeer, hoot and even sing from the safety of the slopes up which they knew Roberto would not take his legions. The range advantage of the enemy bows was a problem and he would not have it multiplied by attacking uphill. He had already considered moving his scorpions ahead of the infantry. It was not a tactic he liked. They interfered with the advance of the infantry and damage or loss was a significant risk. But, ultimately, it might be the only move certain to bring out the enemy.

He had even tried a false march south and it had been immediately clear the enemy would let them go. A scout reporting back that night had given him the reason why. More Tsardon forces were building seventy miles distant. All a march would give him was enemy to his front and rear. Not a prospect he was prepared to entertain.

On the evening of the fourth day of the stand-off, Roberto had walked through the army, pausing at cook-fires, joining in songs and story-telling and leading prayers at the Order table and lawn. They might not be able to have a House of Masks on campaign but there was no reason to abandon all their traditions. The lawn grew in the bed of three wagons, transferred to the ground in front of the Speaker's tent when the marching camp was built. In these last days of sun and rain, it had grown very well and his horse had grazed on it. A good sign of things to come.

He was eating alone in his tent later on, surrounded by reports from his centurions, the quartermaster, the surgeons and veterinaries.

The army was in rude health and he was preparing a message for Gesteris on the eastern front, asking for news and reporting on his first contact. A mug of sweet tea stood steaming at his left hand and a bowl of rabbit broth was on his right on the crowded desk.

'A moment, General?'

He looked up; his Master of Engineers stood in the doorway. Rovan Neristus was a timid, balding man with a feeble physique wholly unsuited to life on campaign. How he had survived so long Roberto wasn't sure but every day was a blessing. He had a brilliant mind and a sharp wit. The army loved him. Roberto had often mentioned that even though he was the general, the last man to die in his army would be Neristus. He beckoned him in.

'What can I do for you, Rovan?'

While it was traditional for each legion and ala to have its own company of engineers, Roberto had decided to create a dedicated unit. It was two hundred strong. While each man and woman was nominally attached to a legion maniple, they were too vital to waste in combat. Farmers and potters can fight, Roberto always said, the best carpenters, smiths, scientists and masons have better things to do. Unless I'm about to take a sword in the gut, of course. Then they can fight.

Neristus swept the cap from his head and came in. His hands were filthy with grease which was smeared on his face and clothes too. He was well into his sixties and middle age beckoned him. Roberto wondered if he had ever worried about his appearance. Doubtful.

'Thanks for smartening yourself up before coming to see your commanding officer. I'm glad you hold me in such high regard.'

'It hardly seems worth it, Roberto,' said Neristus. He never had been very good at military protocol. Certainly not in private. 'I'm not finished working yet.'

'So . . . ?'

'Well, the way I see it, we'll be here 'til dusas trying to get these Tsardon off the slope unless you put the scorpions up front,' he said.

'Ah, a tactician now as well? Your powers grow.'

Neristus pointed at his eyes. 'These work,' he said. 'And I know we don't have the numbers to waste attacking upslope. Not with what's waiting for us further on.'

'Correct,' said Roberto. Something was coming. Something good or Neristus would not be standing here. He felt a surge of anticipation.

'So we need to persuade the enemy off the slope and on to the flat soon or we risk them being reinforced.'

He was a meticulous man, Neristus. A fine quality though it did lead him to state the blindingly obvious sometimes. Roberto chose not to interrupt. Otherwise they might be all night getting to the point.

'My carpenters have been working with some of the different woods the Sirraneans are selling to us. Very interesting qualities in some of the beech wood. It has great strength combined with flexibility. It means we can . . .' He paused. 'Do you have the time to come and see?'

Roberto shrugged. 'Is it worth it?' he asked a little mischievously.

Neristus stared at him. 'I never waste anyone's time,' he said.

The engineers' workshops were set up at the tenth gate and as far from Roberto as possible to keep him from the noise. The place was ablaze with light and baking hot from the forges. Hammer on metal rang out into the night sky, mixed with the sounds of saw, lathe and file.

'Don't you let your citizens sleep?' asked Roberto as they walked into the open front of the workshop.

'The body needs less sleep than we think it does. Anyway, we enjoy our work,' said Neristus. 'Over here.'

The scrawny little man led him to the right-hand corner where two scorpions sat on the ground. The teams around them hurried to their feet to salute. Roberto acknowledged them with a curt nod.

'Carry on.' He turned to Neristus. 'So, what am I looking at?'

Neristus clicked his fingers. 'Tension these two,' he ordered his team. 'Watch, General.'

Roberto watched. Two men wound each windlass at the rear of the pieces. The single iron-clad wooden arms, for all the world like oversize bows, bent as the cord wound and tightened. Wood and rope creaked, the slider dragged the bow string back along the bolt groove. One clicked into its trigger mechanism. A short time later, the other did the same. The teams stepped away. Roberto frowned. He had to look twice but there was no doubting the difference.

'You've set this trigger further back along the shaft than the other. Why?'

There was a gleam in Neristus's eyes. 'The Sirranean beech is wonderful,' he said, patting the scorpion in question. 'Look at its extra tensile capability. It is over fifteen per cent.'

Roberto smiled. 'And how much further will it fire?'

'Sixty yards easily. I have made all the new arms, General,' he said. 'With your permission, I can have them all fitted by march tomorrow.'

'Are they accurate?'

'We can experiment on the Tsardon if you like,' said Neristus.

It would make all the difference in the world as far as this combat was concerned. Roberto nodded, delighted.

'Rovan, you are a genius and your engineers a credit to the Conquord. Get it done,' he said. 'Tomorrow will be a great day.'

Tactical changes had been communicated through the chain of command before a dry and gloomy dawn broke. The army marched as it had done the previous four days but this time, unlike any other, there was the genuine belief that blood would be spilled. Neristus had walked with his wagons this morning and the sight had given Roberto even greater confidence. The scorpions were all uncovered, the fresh oil glistening on the new beech arms.

They deployed as before, but this time there was no pause. Immediately, they were in position, the advance began. It was slow and steady. Roberto put his magnifier to his eye to see if the Tsardon were reacting any differently to this change but there was no significant movement. Their infantry held its long deep single line with central phalanx. Behind, archers stood ready, with cavalry to the flanks.

Roberto's own cavalry stood back a short distance. Sixty yards meant his scorpions could fire over the heads of his infantry and into the Tsardon ranks before the hastati were in range of enemy arrows. It would expose the flaw in the enemy position. While they held tactical advantage of the upslope, they had little ground to play with in retreat before breaking on their own camp. There was only one way to go should they want the scorpions to stop firing once they had begun.

Neristus was an excellent judge of distance and it was his signal that Roberto took to halt the army. They were closer than they had been before. The hastati were within two hundred and fifty yards of the enemy, still standing defiant and tall above their shields. There was no movement in the Tsardon lines except perhaps a slight uneasy shifting at this new move. But they knew that they were still safely out of reach.

'Hold!' shouted Roberto, his orders signalled by flags and echoed through the army by his masters and centurions. 'Ready to defend. Shield wall on enemy advance, pikes front and proud.' He swung in his saddle from his position on the right flank with the Estorean cavalry. 'Engineers. Cock and load. First on my signal, then by the Master's command.'

Forty scorpion windlasses turned, operated by their two-man teams, creaking and grinding. Bolts were slotted into position, fluted pyramid steel heads on ash shafts, heavy and deadly. The ready was signalled. Roberto held up his arm, flags mimicking him. A silence spread across the plain. On the slopes the Tsardon waited. Below them. The Conquord readied.

'Do me proud, Neristus,' he whispered.

He swept his arm down and the flags came with him. Almost as one, the scorpion strings snapped forwards, dull thuds breaking the silence. The missiles whistled over the heads of the infantry. Roberto could just about track the mass of them but lost them in the background of the mountains and green when they pointed earthwards again.

The breath of every Conquord soldier and cavalryman was held. He imagined Garrelites standing with the infantry, peering out from over his shield at the bolts racing towards the enemy. The boy was anxious to fight. Today, he would have his wish.

The Tsardon moved, a violent ripple over a calm sea. Shouts of alarm echoed out and the bolts struck home. Roberto scanned the lines through his magnifier. Men were scattering from the points of impact. Some of the bolts had fallen short a good ten yards, ploughing up the earth or bouncing to fall with little force. The best of them had struck directly into the front line. Men lay dead. One, impaled on a bolt, twitched and jerked, blood spouting from his mouth. The Conquord legions were cheering.

Behind Roberto, the windlasses wound again. 'More elevation,' he roared. 'Five degrees.' The order was passed to the engineers. Handles cranked and the points of the new bolts canted upwards.

They fired again. Another brief quiet then the death whistle. This time the bolts all struck into the front three ranks. Shields had been placed in a linked defensive formation but were of no use against the heavy projectiles. Wood and hide splintered, chainmail and scale armour sheared. Roberto thought every bolt found its target and through his magnifier saw one drive straight through the body of one man into that of another, the pair of corpses cast into the comrades behind them. Conquord legionaries taunted and laughed, bade the enemy come and fight.

A third time the windlasses were wound. There was action in the Tsardon camp. The only question was, which way they would go. Again, shields were placed as a barrier, Tsardon cowering behind them, packing tight to get as many layers to the front as they could. It was an error. Neristus's scorpions spat again, strings thrumming. More Tsardons died, swept back by the harpoon-like bolts, limbs torn from sockets by glancing blows.

This time, though, the Tsardon charged the moment the missiles struck. Infantry and cavalry swept down the slopes at them. The change in the noise and atmosphere was stunning. Tens of thousands of men hurtling over the ground, baying for the heads of their enemies. The rumble of feet and the drumming hooves shook the ground. For the raw hastati in the forward maniples it would be terrifying.

In response, centurions began trotting along the backs of their maniples, all looking to Roberto and the flags. He moved quickly to a position where his standard could best be seen, feeling a thrill course through him and his heart start to pump. He dragged his gladius from its sheath.

The windlasses creaked again. Roberto had a short amount of time to assess the enemy charge. It was ordered and disciplined, its pace designed to disrupt and force back. The Tsardon would want to trigger a retreat knowing that the scorpions were slow to turn around and could easily be lost.

Their units were wider than Roberto's maniples but overall, the line was not as broad making the chance of flanking by their cavalry small. His, on the other hand, could make the attempt. But not yet. Flags and messengers were set along the battle line which was in the order of half a mile wide. Too long for him to have close control. Messengers and flagmen could relay his intent, his masters and centurions made the local decisions and he had to trust them to

make the right ones. They waited for him to signal how they would
begin the fight.

Tsardon cavalry were fast and skilled at firing from the saddle at
pace. Ranks of foot archers were also advancing just behind the front
lines which carried their trademark shields and mid-length slightly
curved swords. Strong for cutting in open skirmish, not so useful in
close ordered combat. Roberto's decision was simple.

'Signal tactical plan one. Infantry to hold close, cavalry to break
and harry. Close on thirty yards separation. Do not let them stop and
pepper us.'

The flags waved the prearranged communication. Runners spaced
along the back of the hastati repeated the orders. Over the advancing
noise of the Tsardon, Roberto heard centurions and masters roaring
commands. In the centre of the Estorean lines, eight maniples armed
with the sarissa made up the phalanx. They moved up a few yards
for the front ranks to kneel and give themselves room to bring their
weapons to the horizontal. A forest of spikes was presented to the
enemy; three ranks of them before the first hastati would be at risk
from a sword thrust. Shields were planted in front of them, leaving
tiny targets for arrow and javelin.

Right across the battlefront, the infantry maniples prepared for the
assault, shields of the front ranks right forward, those behind them
holding theirs above their heads, creating an armoured shell. Left and
right, allied and Estorean cavalry broke into attack and reserve units,
ready for the orders to move. And in the principes and triarii, composite bows were brought to bear, arrows stuck into the ground at
the feet of hundreds of calm, experienced Conquord soldiers.

The scorpions fired again, bolts clearing the front of the Tsardon
army, falling into rear lines, causing consternation and a temporary
break in the advance. The whole had slowed to little above walking
pace now, keeping close in response to the order ahead of them. They
banged swords and spears on shields as they marched, roared insults
and war cries, their volume making up for their relative lack of
numbers. They needed to break the Conquord legions quickly.

'Archers!' called Roberto. 'Ready volley.'

More flags, more runners. Bows bent. A heartbeat before he gave
his order, the Tsardon bowmen fired. Thousands of shafts arced over
the enemy front lines rattling into shields of the hastati maniples, a
rain of barb-tipped ash, dense enough to find every chink in the shield

wall. Roberto saw gaps appear, shields fall on top of the bodies of the men who carried them.

'Damn, that's a lot of arrows,' muttered Roberto, already debating signalling the advance though he knew he should not.

'Hold firm!' The shout carried along the line. The wall reformed, gaps plugged as completely as possible.

The Conquord legions answered back. A volley soared out, whispering through the air to fall among the first ranks of the marching Tsardon, clattering over shields, striking through helmets and burying in legs and arms. Men fell. There were screams but the taunts and songs didn't falter. The marching pace increased and Roberto could see shields held closer and above heads in mimic of his legions. More arrows. Shafts every count of ten from either side, the sky clouded with them, falling deeper and deeper into the Conquord ranks. His citizens were falling while the armies closed though the enemy was suffering greater loss.

'Keep your discipline,' he said under his breath. 'Don't shift, don't show any fear.'

'Ward!' barked the centurion.

Garrelites set his shield at an angle above his head and braced himself. Through the tiniest gap in the shield wall, he saw the arrows coming. A terrifying, withering rain flashing towards his eyes, whipping just overhead or thudding into shield and armour. They fell like hail on tin, the rattling scrabble of deadly claws. They skipped and bounced off the defence, found every gap and punched through any weak point.

There was nowhere to go. Nowhere to run. Every legionary stood firm. For Garrelites, it was the worst moment of any battle. The only moment when he felt genuinely helpless. His heart thrashed in his chest and he prayed to the Omniscient that this was not his day to die under a barbed shaft. He had promised the General he would be back to help him from his armour when victory was won.

The Conquord archers responded. He watched the arrows fall among the enemy, unfortunate Tsardon slain before they could strike. The hastati cheered. Another volley came at them. More prayers, more muttered luck. The metal rain fell. Arrows thumped on to his shield, the noise and vibration hideous. One slammed straight through, its point splintering the wood just under his arm.

Three ranks ahead of him on the front line, a citizen took a shaft through the eye. He fell dead. Life snatched away. Nothing anyone could do but move forward one rank and help the body back and away.

Garrelites breathed deep and moved up, desperate to hear the order to advance and the sound of sword on sword.

Three more volleys and the Tsardon were within thirty yards. Flags circled and flattened to the horizontal. Roberto's hastati moved. Kept in order by the centurions at their backs, they held shields high or overhead and paced forwards, the flanks faster than the centre. Their taunts ripped through the air, insulting the accuracy of the enemy archers, doubting the skill of their swordsmen and speaking the certainty of Conquord victory.

The Tsardon responded. Arrows still flew. Right and left, the cavalry shadowed his own. But they'd strayed just that bit too close. Roberto kept a close eye on it, an idea hatching. He turned in time to see the scorpions fire again, bolts striking into the heart of the archers, slamming men from their feet, scattering earth and blood into the air. He beckoned the nearest runner.

'Have the scorpions target the cavalry. One volley only,' he said.

'Yes, General.' The woman sprinted away to the rear of the lines, Roberto watching her for a moment and hoping his cavalry would take the hint. Any message wouldn't reach the left flank in time. Behind him, he could and did issue orders quickly.

Watching the two infantry armies march to collision always excited him. He spent so much time drilling his commanders about the work they did for themselves, their families and the Conquord. He expected every citizen to take his or her full strength and belief into the combat. He expected them to give absolutely everything, even if that meant their lives.

With barely a pause and with the weight of their fellow citizens behind them, the Conquord legions and the Tsardon army moved together at walking pace. Infantry javelins whipped across the shortening space, tipping down into the front few ranks of enemy. Swords came to ready, shields up and soldiers into fighting stance. In the centre it was phalanx against phalanx, a grinding attritional conflict. On the flanks it was the thrust and hack of the Estorean gladius against the chop and block of the longer Tsardon blade.

The first clash of weapons signalled a concerted and massive increase in the noise from every throat. Here was where it began for them. Here was where their lives would be judged.

Roberto watched, waiting for the scorpions to be moved and primed. Arrows still fell but the armies had spaced now, making targeting more difficult and with the cavalries still out of effective range too much fell in between first line and reserves.

Down on the battle front, there was no indication of either side making any headway. Perhaps the Conquord were marginally forward on the flanks but this early, the exchanges were neither ferocious, nor prolonged, with no man or woman wanting to make the mistake that led to a real gap. As he watched, the sides began to disengage, enemies pushing each other away, slashing at empty space or butting out with shields. A few bodies lay on the ground. Each side taunted and beckoned the other on while more Conquord javelins were launched from behind the front ranks.

Roberto frowned. There was no pace to the conflict, as if both sides were merely fencing in practice for some real event in the future. The scorpion strings thudded again. Practice was over. His engineers had not let him down. Bolts flashed into the enemy cavalry on both flanks, skewering horses, impaling riders through their saddles or taking them clean off to collide with comrades. Panic was instant. Horses scattered from the impact areas, riders fighting to control rearing animals. Close on the right, a whole section of cavalry stampeded away towards the Tsardon camp, riders helpless, some even choosing to dive off and roll. It was better than he could possibly have hoped.

He ordered the attack signal but hardly need have bothered. His cataphracts charged, horse archers giving support and they in turn defended by lighter sword-wielding cavalry units. In all, two thirds of his mounted force rode at the enemy, the rest defending the infantry flanks who had responded equally quickly and engaged once again.

A great wall of noise rolled around the plain. The roars of Conquord soldiers sensing victory in the stunning turn of events; the thundering rumble of hoofs on sodden ground; the snorting and neighing of horses; and the harsh sounds of metal impacting on shield and armour.

Roberto watched the first cataphracts go in. Drawn from the landed nobility, the heavily armoured riders carried the two-handed kontos lance and were trained to break up enemy cavalry units by charge, wheel and withdraw. They drove into the Tsardon horsemen, punching rents in their lines, adding to the disarray caused by the scorpion attack and engendering more panic. Scores of riders were downed in an instant.

Hard in their wake, archers rode in, releasing three volleys as they traversed the fractured line before following the cataphracts out to reform and charge again, passing the light cavalry on their way in.

As early as the second charge, Roberto saw the enemy began to buckle. A few riders had already detached and were heading for the camp and beyond. Time to push it all home. With the scorpions dumping bolts in the gap between the enemy front and reserve lines, and nervous about the coverage of their flanks, the Tsardon infantry was vulnerable.

The din was incredible. No order would be heard and none had been given beyond that to attack. Garrelites stood in the second rank now, roaring on his comrades ahead of him. In the press of shields and citizens, the heat was intensifying and the stink of blood, shit and bile was a nauseating mix. Up close, the Tsardon were a fearsome force. Curved swords slashed dripping with Conquord blood. Oval shields presented stiff defence.

He glanced at those standing to his left and right. Their faces mirrored the stress he felt. Sick with anticipation, desperate to fight but equally desperate to escape with their lives. Garrelites gripped his sword tighter and bounced his shield on his arm for the hundredth time. In front of him, the fighting was fierce. The violence unremitting. The rhyme ran round his head again and again . . . 'Put armour on a farmer and fall hard on all the Tsardon.'

Blades clashed and thrust. Sparks flew, men grunted, shouted and cursed. They fought for a better stance, the killing angle and the mental edge. Weapons cracked on to shields. The thudding impacts echoed in the confined space. Louder and louder. The hastati ahead of him screamed. His helmet flew from his head, bouncing off Garrelites's shoulder guard. He spun, showing Garrelites the rake across his throat, and fell dying.

Garrelites met the eyes of the Tsardon and leaped into the hole, denying him the chance to strike at the opened flanks of the legionaries to his left and right. The enemy carved his sword downwards. Garrelites deflected the blow aside and followed up, stabbing out with his gladius, feeling the point graze scale armour. The pair of them squared up again.

Garrelites's head cleared. This man was not his equal. This man was not worthy of life. Garrelites felt the closeness of the hastati around him. He could not let them down. He punched out with the boss of his shield, finding the enemy blade thumping into it. He hacked around with his gladius, struck the Tsardon defence.

The enemy blade came back at him, glancing from his left shoulder and sending a sheet of pain down his shield arm. Garrelites gasped. The Tsardon sensed a chance, he could see it in the man's eyes. His shield was thrust forwards. Garrelites gambled. He swayed back and left. The enemy came on, expecting the block but not getting it. His sword clashed into Garrelites's shield but it was an unbalanced strike. Garrelites saw the gap, thrust his gladius inside the enemy defence and felt the blade slide through armour and into gut.

The Tsardon's eyes widened in shock and pain. He coughed. Blood spurted from his mouth and splashed over Garrelites's face, shield and helmet. He began to fall. Garrelites kicked him backwards and shouted in relief. He heard a concerted roar from all around him and saw the Tsardon line flicker and ripple. Something had happened. Somewhere on the battlefield a major blow had been struck.

Next to him, a distracted Conquord legionary was cut across the legs and collapsed. A new gap, a new threat. Garrelites could not pause while his shield arm recovered. He shook his head to move blood and sweat from his eyes, breathed deep and moved back to the attack, praying victory was coming soon.

'Principes to the front line!' ordered Roberto. The flags signalled the advance.

The Conquord's second line trotted in, adding weight to the press that was forcing the enemy back step by step. Volleys of arrows were swapped again but the power was with him. Roberto could feel it. God-embrace-them, he could see it. On the left, a critical break-through had been made. He could see hundreds of horses fleeing back up the slope. Simultaneously, he could just make out the far left maniples of the God's Arrows pushing in at pace.

The call for more effort fed along his infantry. The taunts became louder, the thrusts of sword and shield harder, backed by the knowledge of impending victory. To Roberto's right, the cataphracts had gathered for a mass charge. Already weakened, the Tsardon cavalry were driven to tatters. And while the lighter cavalry chased the remnants away from the flank, the cataphracts ploughed into unguarded archers and infantry. The enemy scattered in front of them or were trampled beneath hoofs, battered by shield and lance.

Garrelites knew the principes had joined the battle. Hastati fell back to allow them in but he stood his ground. His gladius dripped with the blood of three victims now and he felt empowered, indestructible. The principes struck the Tsardon hard, driving their thinning line back a little. Garrelites went with them, shoving with his shield, hacking and slashing ahead of it.

He heard horses and felt the thrumming of hooves. Enclosed where he was he didn't know whose they were or how close. But the arrival of the principes surely meant the battle was turning. Surely it was Master Kastenas who rode into the heart of the enemy.

The sweat was pouring off him. His arms ached and his legs were on fire. Right ahead, the Tsardon line compressed across his vision, as if God had shoved them with one mighty hand. They began to panic. Behind him, hastati were clamouring to join the push. Garrelites looked over his shield. The Tsardon weren't looking ahead any more. He stabbed his sword deep into an enemy soldier's side and ripped it clear, moving up even as the man fell. They were breaking. The Tsardon were breaking. Through the crush of bodies ahead he could see a thinning as they began to turn and run.

Another huge roar split the air around him and the legions surged forwards, led by the solid line of principes. To his right, the infantry was curving in, snapping the jaws of the pincer shut, rotating around the phalanx which stood as anchor to the fight. Garrelites waved his sword above his head and joined the charge. Everywhere was the confusion of feet and bodies. He skidded and slithered over Tsardon bodies, using his shield as a support.

The joy of victory infused him. In front, a Tsardon slipped and fell. Garrelites crashed the edge of his shield into the unprotected back and his sword into the enemy's helmet. Blood splattered the churned earth. It was incredible. The battle should have ground out all day. He had been into the front line so quickly that it was only now he realised he hadn't really thought to live through it. He laughed, caught the excitement of the hastati crowding around him and ran on up towards the Tsardon camp.

Garrelites didn't see the blade that slid high into his thigh and up into his groin. He hadn't been looking down at the dead, only ahead at the running, routed Tsardon. He'd run on a pace before the pain hit him and dropped him to his knees. He fell on top of his shield, arm beneath him. The shock rolled over him. He struggled on to his back. Hastati ran past him.

He saw the man who had struck him. A Tsardon lying with head slathered in a sheet of blood. The sword just dropping from his hand. He fell back, exhausted.

'Bastard,' said Garrelites. 'God take you to the devils on the wind.'

He shuddered and shook off his shield. He grabbed at his leg and groin, feeling the soaking of blood. The blade had sliced through his flesh so easily, right where he had no armour. The blood sluiced out so fast. He grasped at the wound, trying to stem the flow. But it burst around his fingers.

He called for help but the noise was so loud around him. Tramping feet and thundering hooves. He held out a dripping hand.

'Please,' he said.

Someone was coming. Someone had caught his eye and seen his predicament. The world swam in front of him. There was a roaring in his ears. He was lying on his side now, his hands back groping at his wound. So much blood.

He wondered if he could wash it off before he had to help the general with his armour.

Roberto could not just sit and watch. He shouted his pleasure and turned to his extraordinarii, all of them staring in delight and triumph.

'What a victory,' he said. 'What an unbelievable victory. God love Rovan Neristus. God love the Conquord.'

He raised his sword above his head.

'Estorea!' he called. 'Let's chase these bastards down.' He kicked his heels to his horse's sides, the extraordinarii all around him. 'I want their commander's head in a bag and on its way back to the King of Tsard by nightfall.'

Whooping, he galloped away after his victorious army.

Chapter 22

848th cycle of God, 40th day of Genasfall
15th year of the true Ascendancy

The road to Westfallen had not only a fine surface, excellent lodging facilities and sound security, it also afforded its travellers peaceful and beautiful scenery. It was in every way the perfect antidote for Jhered's foul temper since his falling-out with the Advocate.

Her decision to absent him from Estorr for the lead up to, and performance of, what had been infuriatingly entitled the 'Glory of the Conquord' games was a slight in the mind of every titled citizen of the Conquord. But they had no idea of the real reasons for his absence or its potential ramifications for their faith.

The journey to Port Roulent, Caraduk's principal port on the Tirronean Sea, had been terrible. He'd been laid low with a stomach infection that had robbed him of strength, appetite and his sea legs. He had never been so sick in his life and stepping off the *Hark's Arrow* was blessed relief.

He'd been weak and had travelled to Cirandon by carriage, a herb-scented kerchief to his nose most of the way. Vasselis had been his typical honourable self and had insisted he stay at the Marshal Defender's grand three-storey villa, with its stunning gardens and luxuriously appointed private baths.

Jhered's condition had improved quickly with the added help of Vasselis's skilled doctors and their herbal and vegetable drink preparations. But his mood had not. He had found himself suspicious of Vasselis's motives and had spoken to him very little throughout his brief stay. It was not until now, with the sun warming his body as he and his friend rode a pair of excellent horses, that he felt himself begin to relax.

The road to Westfallen ran bedside long stretches of the River

Weste. It was as well-prepared and surfaced as any in the inner Conquord outside of the highways. Plenty of trade came through Westfallen on the route between Easthale and Cirandon and there were few times when they were alone for more than a couple of hours at a time.

The vegetation running along the banks of the wide, slow-moving and shallow river was a riot of colour and clogged with new life. The road ran along the south bank of the river, leaving the north bank to nature.

Marshland was the dominating feature, running almost a hundred miles wide in some places and finishing at the towering Dukan Mountains. The marshes were peerless for the student of wildlife but hopeless for much else. It was a flat, featureless area, striking for its bleakness. Jhered enjoyed its hostility, the haunting calls of hunting birds and the mournful cries of animals strayed in too far, never to escape. They were a fitting reminder that the land must always be respected. God held unshakeable dominion and not even the most peaceful of countries was safe everywhere.

To the south was where the real beauty lay, to Jhered's eyes. Plains of heather and long grass blown by the prevailing east winds giving way to gentle, tree-covered hillsides dotted with small settlements, isolated farmsteads and the villas of the rich, retired Advocacy hierarchy.

He knew the countryside well. Easy to lose yourself in the hunting and fishing, or just walking through the glades and along lakesides that rippled with light. He was planning on building a villa there himself in the next decade or so, to be completed when his days as a Gatherer were over. He was supposed to enter the Advocacy political system but the idea repelled him. He liked neither crowds nor sycophants. Retirement and silence were infinitely more attractive. Assuming there was a Conquord to retire from when the time came.

'Have you staked out your land yet?' asked Vasselis, reading his thoughts.

Jhered pointed along the line of a valley that he knew ended in a broad expanse of prime fishing ground.

'On the north ridge above Lake Phristos,' said Jhered. 'Good pasture land for my horses and the best view in Caraduk.'

'And you can have the marble quarried and brought upstream

from Glenhale. A lovely spot, though I take issue with you about the view. Second-best perhaps.'

'Assuming it hasn't been sacked and burned by the time I get there to rest my old bones,' said Jhered, surprising himself with the meaning in his tone.

Vasselis looked at across at him, a frown forming under his broad-brimmed hat.

'You're being over-dramatic,' he said.

'Really?' said Jhered sharply. Since that night in Estorr his respect for Vasselis had been so much lessened and the disappointment still pained him. 'You base that assumption on what, exactly?'

'I do travel to Estorr regularly, Paul.'

'But you don't see what the Gatherers see.'

'So enlighten me.'

Damn the man but he was so understanding.

'We are under pressure. Victory in Tsard is by no means certain, despite the presence of some fine generals and veteran legions. The front on the Omari-Dornos border has stalled completely. Add that to the naval presence we must maintain in the Tirronean Sea, Gorneon's Bay and the Great North Ocean, and we are stretched far too thin. The raids in Atreska and Gosland are serious drains on morale and loyalty and Gestern is coming under more and more pressure. And if that wasn't all, Yuran still cannot cure his own internal struggles. One day we will get a real bloody nose, or worse. What then? One thing is certain, games are not the answer.'

'We agree there.'

'Tsard is strong and determined and we have little meaningful defence,' said Jhered, relieved that he was getting the sort of hearing he didn't get in Estorr.

'Against what?'

'Against serious defeat.'

'That's a bold and rather worrying statement coming from you,' said Vasselis, his expression severe.

'You haven't been to Atreska or Tsard.'

There was a pause. 'This is serious, isn't it?'

Jhered almost laughed. 'See me smiling, Marshal?'

'No,' said Vasselis. 'No, I don't.'

Jhered hadn't meant it that way. The mood had cooled just as he was cheering up. He let the silence rest for a while.

'How long before we can see it, then?'

'What?'

'Westfallen, of course.'

'Sorry,' said Vasselis. 'I was thinking of something else.' He scratched at his head under his hat. 'Not long at all now. Just up this last rise and it'll be laid out below us, looking the perfect picture of peace it undoubtedly is.'

Jhered saw the glitter in Vasselis's eyes and felt a welcome smile warm his face.

'Is there anything you care about more than this apparently peerless town?'

'Apart from my wife and son? Not really.' He chuckled, relaxing. 'You've never actually been there, have you? Always sending minions to do your gathering despite my best advice.'

'Perhaps I always harboured anxieties about what was hidden beneath the surface,' said Jhered, wondering if he actually believed what he'd just said.

'You have no need to,' said Vasselis.

'That is yet to be seen.' Jhered rubbed dust from his eye. It was becoming a very hot day. The sky was a startling blue, the air hot and still in the shallow valley they were climbing. 'How long since I was in Cirandon?'

'A couple of years, something like that,' said Vasselis.

'I swear your son has doubled in height in that time,' said Jhered.

He glanced back at Kovan, who was riding and chatting with his investigation team while Netta rode in a covered carriage out of the heat of the sun. Kovan wasn't just here for the break. He was a useful witness and, Jhered was aware, a potential conspirator. His mother, too.

'Promise me you'll find the time to spar with him,' said Vasselis. 'And don't take him too lightly. He's top-ten ranked in Cirandon these days and only just seventeen.'

'I'll be glad to. I could do with the practice.'

'How do you rank these days?'

Jhered growled. 'Well, after the games, I'll be nowhere but right now I'm third. I don't get much time to challenge these days. Much to do outside Estorr.'

'*Third?* Perhaps you shouldn't spar after all. Don't want you hurting him.'

'I'll be gentle, I promise.'

'That would be a first.'

The two men fell silent while their horses climbed the last of the rise. Jhered felt the breeze growing and could smell the coast on the air. Vasselis reined in and stopped.

'Well, there you are,' he said. 'Tell me I've been exaggerating.'

He had not been. Westfallen was beautiful. From the fishing boats in the bay, to the stunning waterfall. From the golden sanded beach to the clean white of the houses built around the forum and fountains. From the fields swaying with wheat and vegetables to the water mill whose gentle slapping wheel set the slow pace of life. It was an absolute picture. Hard to believe that the heresy Vasselis admitted it harboured really ran through its cobbled streets leaching into every brick.

Jhered looked to the right as his team drew up beside him. He had been granted just two but they were of the highest quality. Captain Harkov of the Advocate's personal guard whom he had managed to prise away from his family and duties. He would cast a sceptical eye over the affair, uncluttered by religious beliefs. And the Advocate's Master Engineer, the anxious ageing genius that was Orin D'Allinnius. He wanted the view of a scientist and engineer and there was none better in the Conquord. Barring Rovan Neristus who Roberto kept with him in Tsard.

Behind them, the wagon had stopped. Vasselis's twenty guardsmen and Jhered's own unit of levium, the Gatherer's elite, waited for the order to move on.

'I expected something darker,' said D'Allinnius, his small eyes almost buried in his scowl. 'You painted this place as some evil stronghold. I think I might retire here rather than recommend it be razed to the ground.'

Jhered shook his head and spoke for Vasselis's benefit more than his own. 'I think you might recall that what I actually said was that heresy can paint the view white while inside the heart beats black and determined.'

'Very poetic,' muttered Vasselis, unimpressed.

'I just don't want people's view changed because everything looks pretty, all right?' He stared squarely at D'Allinnius. 'Clear?'

The engineer shrugged. 'Science is not confused by appearances.'

'Captain Harkov, anything to add?' Jhered had noted the captain was frowning down on Westfallen.

'I was wondering where that cloud came from,' he said, pointing to the far side of the town where, in the otherwise pure blue sky, a dark grey smudge appeared to be growing over a field of wheat.

'Steam or smoke, I would presume,' said Jhered.

'No,' said D'Allinnius. 'It has none of the properties of either.' He paused and cleared his throat. 'More likely it's an illusion brought on by the heat and proximity to the sea. Nothing heretic in that, I suspect, Exchequer Jhered. Now.' He paused. 'Hold on. Isn't that . . . ?'

Vasselis was laughing. 'Yes it is. Amazing, isn't it? And a miracle after twenty days of unbroken sunshine, wouldn't you agree?'

Jhered felt his heart racing and he muttered a prayer to God to keep them safe within his embrace. It was a solitary cloud, it was not moving across the sky and it was disgorging rain.

'You have it, you have it,' said Kessian from his chair.

Mirron could just about hear him and drew huge confidence from his words. She pushed her fingers that little bit harder into their positions around the back of Arducius's head. He was kneeling on the ground outside the villa on the hill, where the irrigation had failed and crops were at risk from the dry spell. One of his hands was in a bucket of water, the other palm upwards towards the sky.

Their abilities had opened up this past season, like the mist parting to give the first view of a new land. They had learned to contain themselves while using the energies of the elements around them, amplifying them and shaping them before delivering results that had been both wonderful and terrifying.

Mirron had been scared by what she had been able to do. They all had, she thought, except perhaps Gorian though even he seemed changed. Quieter and more studious, less quick to anger. She pushed the thought of him away; it made her pulse beat faster and a heat build deep in her gut. Concentrate, she said to herself in the Father's voice.

She could feel Arducius channelling the natural energies of the water through their bodies, he as Wind Harker and lead in the work, she as added amplification. It was something they had tried in the stillness of the villa but now it was needed by Westfallen farmers.

The chance to further rehabilitate them in the eyes of the citizens excited her.

Arducius tensed and gasped. 'Keep still, Mirron,' he said. 'We're doing it, can you see?'

Mirron looked up. Her body was alive with the rush of water energy, smooth and constant. Like earth energy but cooler. She let it fill her and grow within her, then directed it through her fingers into Arducius. She could see the lines streaming out of his splayed fingers, high into the sky above them. The cool energy hit the hot air and became instantly visible as a rapidly forming cloud. Arducius used the new energy to contain the cloud, stop it dispersing to nothing but mist and be burned away.

She was amazed at his skill. While the cloud wasn't huge, it was the fact that he could read the energies in the sky like any great Wind Harker but then use them to his advantage too. She wondered if she could adapt his ideas for her experiments with fire.

Above them, the cloud bubbled and filled. It darkened and spread a shadow across the ground that covered them, the villa and the fields around them. It was hundreds of feet above them, lower than a cloud should be, and the size of half the hillside.

'It's beautiful, Ardu. Keep building.'

'As long as you're with me.'

They were both tiring. The drain on her energies was giving her a tremble in her legs and she could feel Arducius wobbling under her hands.

'Care now,' came Kessian's voice. 'Don't push too hard. You've already done so much.'

'Time to release, Mirron,' said Arducius. 'The bucket is empty. Ready?'

'Yes.'

Mirron saw his hands clap together and then drag apart claw-like as if he was tearing through cobweb. She felt a drop of water on her forehead, another and another and then it was pouring from the cloud, soaking the ground. And she was hugging Arducius and they were laughing and dancing in the downpour despite their tiredness.

She saw Father Kessian staring in delight up into the sky, the rain making him blink hard. Standing nearby, the farmer, his wife and two of his workers all had their hands out, watching the water hit their palms and believing neither what they were seeing nor feeling. But they couldn't keep the smiles from their faces.

'All right you two, a little calm now,' said Kessian, pushing himself from his chair with the aid of his sticks. 'You should go and rest, you must be tired.'

Mirron beamed at him and both of them ran across to hug him.

'Look what we can do,' said Arducius, a little breathless.

'You make a very old man very happy indeed,' said Kessian.

'And next year, I'll be able to cover the whole sky from a single bucket, just watch me.'

Kessian laughed and Mirron watched him glance up at the cloud that was thinning quickly now though the rain still fell hard and dense, drenching the fields and bouncing from the limp stems of wheat.

'I don't know what to say,' said the farmer, coming over to them. 'You might have saved my crop. It's . . . well it's, I don't know.' He gestured at his fields and wiped a hand through his sodden hair.

'I'm glad we can help you, Farius,' said Arducius.

He nodded and ruffled Arducius's hair. 'I'm glad you can too. We've all learned a lot this past season or so, haven't we?'

'So we have,' said Kessian. 'I hope you can get your irrigation going. Just a broken pipe somewhere I expect. Hmmm.'

Mirron knew that sound. It was the Father having an idea.

'I wonder if young Ossacer could help find such a break,' he said.

'Like he does in a bone?' said Mirron, seeing the thought quickly. 'He might be able to sense the water flowing out of a break, mightn't he? Because it would leave relative darkness because the water energy would soak into the earth around it.'

'Clever girl,' said Kessian. 'We'll talk to him later. If that's all right with you, Farius?'

'Your help is more than welcome,' he said. 'I just wish you'd let me pay or do something in return.'

'When the investigation arrives from Estorr, speak well of us, that's all I ask,' said Kessian. 'Remember we are not to be feared and that God has not forsaken Westfallen. He has given us gifts and miracles.'

Farius nodded. 'You know I was one that thought otherwise. I'm sorry I doubted you.'

Kessian put a hand on his shoulder. 'There is no need to be. We have all been scared of what we have seen and we have all searched our hearts to learn if we act against God. Trust in us. Trust in Elsa Gueran. We only want the best for Westfallen, for God and for the Conquord.'

Mirron sighed. She hadn't let go of Father Kessian and she was glad. The belief in what he said ran through him and gave her such comfort. He would see that only good came of the Ascendancy. He could do anything.

'Look,' said Arducius.

Everyone turned where he pointed. Riders had appeared on the rise at the edge of town on the road in from Cirandon. They began walking down into the town at a gentle pace. Behind them came a carriage and at least thirty or forty more people on horseback. They had all known the investigation was on its way but to see it sent a shiver through her, the Father and Arducius.

'It looks like I'll get the chance to repay you very soon now,' said Farius.

'Indeed it does,' said Kessian. 'Come on children, time to go home and prepare.'

'God will protect you,' said Farius. 'Good luck.'

'Thank you,' said Kessian.

Mirron smiled at Farius. 'Thank you for letting us help.'

'Anything for the Ascendancy,' said Farius.

And she could see in his eyes that he meant it.

Chapter 23

848th cycle of God, 40th day of Genasfall
15th year of the true Ascendancy

Gorian felt more special, more important than he ever had before. Like an actor perhaps, only this was better because an actor merely entertained. What he was doing could affect all their destinies. Ossacer had been selected too, but he had been almost too scared to do any work. Lucky they had selected easy tasks for him or he would have failed and made them all look foolish. Gorian determined to show them something far better.

Father Kessian had asked him to go slow and explain everything as he went but he wasn't sure they'd be able to hear that much. The noise in the shed was terrible. The cow was in extraordinary pain, the calf inside her was a breech. She was dying and so would her young one unless he did something quickly. Surgery would only help the newborn. He could save them both.

Gwythen Terol was with him. She had taught him everything she knew about the skills of a Herd Master and still she could help him. But by the time he was nine, he had known more than she ever would. The moment they had walked into the barn, the heifer's legs had collapsed beneath her, unable to take her body weight now the pain had become so intense.

She had turned her head to Gorian, recognising his aura and pleading with her eyes for him to help her. His calming touch allowed the herdsmen to place ropes around her body and over beams above to haul her upright when the time came. Her head was turned away from him and held by two men to keep her from damaging herself. Her body rippled with the effort of staying alive. Her lungs heaved and she was soaked with sweat.

Gorian moved to one side of her while Gwythen went to the other side. Both placed hands on her flanks.

'Can you feel the calf?' she asked.

Gorian nodded. He let the wildly pulsing energies in the heifer enter him and filtered out the pain to leave two beats. One, frail and terribly fast, was the calf's.

'It's still alive but very distressed,' he said. 'What I've done is allow the mother's lifelines to run through me. It means I can feel much more than Gwythen who is only able to work out general physical states. I can tell you things about every individual muscle, nerve and vein.'

'How is that possible?' asked one man, voice only just carrying over the din of the heifer.

Gorian looked round at him briefly. He was quite old and had only ever frowned since he'd got off his horse. An engineer or scientist apparently. 'Because I am connected to the nature of all living things. And if I concentrate, I can feel and change anything I want to. I don't expect you to understand because you will never know what I see through my senses.'

'Gorian, concentrate on the job in hand,' said Marshal Vasselis, whose proud and pompous son stood next to him, hand on a sword he could probably hardly use. 'We all agree that this cow will soon die along with her calf. What we are here to see is the result of your intervention.'

'Yes, Marshal,' said Gorian. 'I need to establish the exact position of the calf. We know it is breech but it might be possible to turn it and so save them both.'

He leaned in closer to the heifer. The animal stank of sweat, faeces and fear. Its hide rippled and in the enclosure, Gorian felt a few nerves. Should it buck or shift with any remaining mote of strength it could crush him. But it seemed able only to bellow its pain and its helpless rage. He breathed in the strong scents and tried to shut the stench from his mind.

'Not long now,' he whispered to them both.

The heifer's life energies were uneven and they pulsed stress and fading strength through him. He traced back along them to where they were sheared or trapped. He drew in a sharp breath. At that moment the heifer shuddered violently and vomited bile and blood.

'What is it?' asked Gwythen. 'I can feel strain in many muscles. There must be some torn.'

'Yes,' said Gorian. 'And it's worse, too. They are all in spasm around the womb. The calf is not quite breech. She is lying with her lower back across the birth canal and the mother can't relax to let her move.' He raised his voice. 'I can trace all the individual lines of energy that signify the womb muscles and the way they are reacting with each other. What I must do is use myself to force the cow's own energy through those lines so the muscles relax and contract in the correct order. I hope you understand what needs to happen even if not the way I will make it happen.'

'You will use your mind?' asked the tall, severe man, Jhered. The Gatherer who scared them with a sharp look.

'Not exactly,' said Gorian. 'My mind understands what my senses can see and makes pictures in my head of it all. I use my whole body to change or amplify the energy I bring into myself from outside.'

'Good enough for now, lad,' said Jhered. 'Get on and do what you must. This noise and stink is making my head spin.'

It was quite easy, really. Gwythen kept her eye on the heifer to make sure he wasn't causing her too much more pain while he worked out the way to use the animal's own body to move her calf. There was a rhythm to it and the moment he began it, the heifer did a great part of the work herself. The calf reacted too, jerking to point its nose down, seeking its way out.

Gorian could feel the mother relax as the pain eased and the birth neared. He fed energy into the last of the lines and the calf entered the birth canal. The heifer reacted the way nature intended she should, and tried to stand.

'Gwythen, move!'

Gorian dived out of the front of the stall. The cow shifted and struck the side where he'd been crouched. Strong arms pulled on ropes and dragged her upright. She lowed, long and pained. Gorian could feel the strain of her body through the air itself and saw the rippling in her flanks.

The calf was born in a tremendous rush. It spilled out in its sac, bringing blood and slime with it and sprawled in the hay. Gorian rushed forwards and took the slithering new born in his arms, freeing its nose, mouth and eyes. The owner reached in to free it from the umbilical cord and immediately, the calf tried to rise while its mother sought to turn to lick it clean and push it to suckle.

'All safe now little one,' said Gorian, stroking its slimy, quivering body. 'I had your life in my hands there, didn't I? Lucky I wanted you to live, eh?'

He stood up and wiped his hands down his tunic. It was covered in sludge and blood. He smiled at Kessian and the Marshal. Everyone seemed to be frowning back at him.

'I did it,' he said, in case they'd failed to see his triumph. 'They would both have died without me.'

'What did you mean, "Lucky I wanted you to live"?' asked Jhered.

'Just that,' said Gorian, irritable that his work had been taken so lightly.

'And does that mean that you could have killed it just as easily with your . . .' He waved his hands searching for the words. 'Abilities.'

Gorian frowned. 'I just meant that because I wanted it to live, it lived. I was here, I could help, I gave it its life. No one else could have done that. What's wrong with you, can't you see that?'

'All right, Gorian,' said Kessian. 'He has to ask his questions. Try not to get upset.'

'I gave it its life,' he said, staring at Jhered and finding himself unafraid. 'And I would do the same for you, too, if you asked me. Would you be so suspicious then?' He looked for his mother. Meera was there nodding at him, telling him he'd done well. 'I need to rest. I'm tired.'

They parted to let him go but he could still hear them talking after him but not about him. Already, they'd forgotten what he'd done. None of them could do it. Why weren't they amazed?

'Where to now, Lord Jhered?' Marshal Vasselis asked the Gatherer.

'Your Reader, I think. She has some questions of a difficult theological nature to answer. Then, uh, Kessian, isn't it? Kessian, I will want to talk to you. Don't go far.'

Their voices became indistinct.

'What will they do?' Gorian asked his mother.

'I don't know, my darling,' she said, holding him close to her. 'But you have shown them how much good you can do. So have Ossacer and the others but you saved two lives. They cannot congratulate you, they have to suspect you. That is their job. Try not to worry. Get some rest instead. They'll want to talk to you more, I am sure.'

'Why can't they just accept us like everyone else here?'

Meera sighed. 'Oh, love, that is a hard question. The world is a big and mistrustful place and people are scared of things they don't understand. Most of Westfallen were too for a time. The Order doesn't see things quite the way Elsa Gueran does. One day you'll understand.'

'So why aren't they here asking questions?'

Meera's face clouded. 'Because they are not interested in asking questions, only in making judgements. Be happy we are under investigation by the Advocacy and not the Order.'

And though he pressed her, she would not say more.

Elsa Gueran did not know whether to be scared or relieved, quiescent or defiant. She faced Jhered, Harkov and D'Allinnius alone in the House of Masks. If any here were truly guilty of heresy then surely it began with this woman. Pretty, even beautiful in her facial features but a woman who had systematically abused the teachings of the Order for her own and Westfallen's purposes. Such was Jhered's assumption when he faced her. Could she convince him otherwise. Or perhaps it would be Harkov who would do that in the analysis that would follow.

'I know you will think little of me, Exchequer Jhered. All I ask is that you question me fairly and listen to my answers. Everything I do I believe to be God's will.'

'Let me assure you I think nothing of you whatsoever. That you wear the robes of a Reader and sit proud in a House of Masks is an affront. And that you must have had complicity within the Order to maintain your deception makes me sick to my stomach. How far does this go towards Estorr, I wonder?'

'Do you want an answer to that question?' she asked, trying not to show her nervousness at his vehemence.

'It is as good a place to start as any and perhaps the easiest question you will have to answer today,' he said. 'Go ahead. I'm listening.'

'Whatever my feelings towards the Order as an organisation and the disbursement of its strictures, I will not implicate it in any way in the extraordinary things we are doing here,' said Elsa. And she surprised Jhered by smiling. 'After all, why should they take the credit?'

'You have not answered my question,' said Jhered.

Elsa met his gaze squarely. The light of late afternoon streamed in through the open double doors. It shone from the polished root scrollwork that embossed every inch of wood in the House and the masks that covered the walls, low domed ceiling and racks of shelving. The cooling sea breeze ruffled the stacked volumes of the Chronicles of Memory, exposing the early pages of the topmost to reveal flashes of colour, intricate design and likenesses of the dead in detail laden with emotion.

'Westfallen's Reader has always believed in the truth as presented by the banished strand of the Order because we are not scared of what it represents. We do not believe it will undermine our authority, quite the reverse. But this means the Reader is chosen from a small pool of Order acolytes, many of whom have never been granted the keys to a House of Masks or the lawn on which to preach.

'We are in careful contact, building what must be built because it is the true word of God as we see it.' She held up her hands. 'But I know most do not agree with us so we do not seek to force our views on any to whom they are unwelcome.

'And because we do not want the interference of the wider Order, Westfallen is kept apart. If you have the allies, it is easy to dissuade others from travelling here. After all, I can just as easily report on such a quiet and faithful place by making the journey to Cirandon. And as you know, we have one very powerful ally.'

Jhered's hands had been cupping nose and mouth. It had been an unconscious move and he removed them slowly. The woman's arrogance was breathtaking. He had expected her to hide behind the scriptures, quote obscure passages that justified her heretic views. But she was brazen, confident in those she assumed would protect her because the Order was not there to deliver its justice. Jhered might have had little time for the zealous pronouncements of a Chancellor in pursuit of control but this was surely just as bad. Innocents would have been misled, perverted from the path of faith and God.

He looked across at Harkov and D'Allinnius. The latter was impassive, the former regarded Gueran with apparent respect and a slight smile. He quashed his immediate anger. It was why he had picked them to help him after all. Vasselis deserved balance if nothing else.

'What you have said is an admission of guilt under the law of the Order,' said Jhered. 'You mock the place in which we sit and the title before your name. Your actions should see you burn. You're lucky it is me you will answer to.'

'I am,' agreed Elsa. 'But then that is why you are here without the Order, isn't it? You are supposed to represent reason and impartiality, aren't you?'

'No,' said Jhered firmly. 'I am here at the request of the Advocate, following admissions from Marshal Defender Vasselis, to assess whether your . . . experiments, are a crime against the Conquord, the Omniscient or both. I am not impartial and you will do well to bear that in mind. Now. Questions and straight answers.

'The Order discredited and outlawed the splinter faith hundreds of years ago. Its observance is forbidden to followers of any faith as a perversion of God's teachings. What right do you have to preach it here?'

'I preach the teachings of the scriptures. The splinter faith, if that is how you want to describe it, is not preached. It is everywhere, in all our lives. I do not need to tell what all here already know.'

'You're saying that none in Westfallen reject your beliefs?' asked Harkov.

Elsa smiled and shook her head. 'I don't think that any of you have the remotest conception of what you have come to investigate. The splinter faith, which we term the Ascendancy by the way, has been part of the life of Westfallen for centuries. Ever since it was rejected by the Order. It is the natural order of life to us as it should be to all who follow our faith.'

Jhered scoffed. 'You are pushing your luck, Reader Gueran. I have studied the scriptures at great length. I am a true follower, a faithful believer in the Order of Omniscience. You play with heresy just as you play with nature. How can it be the natural order of life to bring rain where God has brought blue sky. Or to take control of the body of a cow to bring a life into the world that God had clearly decided should not be begun? Where in the scriptures is this written?'

Elsa placed her hands on the books in front of her.

'Much we now know was not known when the scriptures were written. Merely because something is not officially sanctioned in

Order law does not make it forbidden. Your argument would stop us using man-made implements to treat our sick, would it not?'

This was where he wanted to be. Tackling her on the core of the faith she purported to support. It was where he would undermine her and expose her naivety.

'I would agree, were that my argument. But you know it is not. Our advances in science and medicine allow us to give our sick and injured the means to recover should their wills be strong enough and their bodies desire it. Such is stated as God's will, isn't it?'

Gueran nodded. 'The natural cycle of life is inviolate. Medicine must seek to counter only that which attacks the body or the crop or the beast against the will of man or God.'

Jhered slammed his fist down on to the table that separated them. Leather-bound volumes juddered and Elsa jerked backwards.

'So how can you believe in your Ascendancy and similarly remain true to the Order you so casually denounce?'

'I denounce no one and nothing, least of all the Order,' said Gueran after a pause to gather herself. 'The Order is the faith that I have known and loved all of my life and that will never change. It is my life. Evidence of God's blessing overwhelms my senses with every breath I take. But the Order's eyes are closed to the evolution of man and it fears for itself should its grip on the Conquord faithful ever be loosened.'

Jhered laughed. He had heard it all now.

'You think the Order is blind? My misguided woman, it is you who needs to see what stands before her. Your Ascendancy uses you to justify its existence under God when surely all you have learned must be crying at you that these children represent an abomination, innocent as they may be as helpless participants in the crime.'

'I see the growth of man to levels where he is better able to do God's work and bring peace and comfort to the world.'

'But they put themselves equal to God,' shouted Jhered. 'They assume God-like powers and hold fire and water in their hands. They challenge the very centre of our faith, even as you try to hide them within it.'

'They do nothing of the kind,' said Gueran, maintaining her calm under some duress. 'God is the Omniscient. These are but four people doing his work wherever they find it. They will be no more equals of God than I will be. We are all His servants. Please understand, Exchequer Jhered. This is progress. It is wonderful and we should embrace it, not hate it. I am a Reader of the Order. If I felt it in anyway insulted the faith I love, do you really think I would countenance it in the fields over which I preside?'

'Heretics forever seek to wound true faith from beneath the cloak of piety,' said Jhered.

D'Allinnius spoke up, his cracked voice quiet and careful. 'The ox, the mule, the horse and the pig are all bred selectively as we strive to improve their health and their abilities to serve their appointed purposes. This is merely a matter of benefitting their owners. Who will own your bred humans?'

'No one . . .' Gueran paused, irritable. 'With respect, you are missing the point. Our Ascendants prove that man or woman can be closer to nature and hence to God – something for which all followers of the Omniscient strive. And a breeder who produces prime cavalry stock merely proves observation and selection can produce a horse suited for the purpose rather than trusting to nature and fortune. We are no different in that regard and the will of God is such that we should seek such improvement.

'But in all these cases we believe the result will occur naturally, given time.'

Harkov cleared his throat. 'Sorry, but are we to understand that you feel that children with these abilities would have occurred without your intervention?'

'Eventually, yes,' said Gueran. 'The Ascendancy believes fundamentally that one day, all those born will display such abilities to a greater or lesser extent. This is so important because it means that it is the will of God and we will not go against that will.'

'But there are no obvious raw materials,' said D'Allinnius.

'I don't understand.'

'They are the first and only thus far,' he explained. 'They have come seemingly from nowhere, through your selection of parents based on measures we are yet to understand. There have been none like them before, occurring at random. What is the pool from which they have been drawn?'

Gueran frowned. 'Well, Westfallen, of course.'

'I see,' said Harkov. 'So there are some here that exhibit some form of these abilities naturally, are there?'

'Well, obviously.' Gueran could not suppress a smile. 'Almost everyone for some part of their lives.'

Jhered sat up, feeling a jolt through him as if he had been struck. 'I *beg* your pardon?'

Chapter 24

Roberto Del Aglios woke at a wail from outside his tent and felt immediately lost. It was hot, despite the hour of the night, and sweat was soaking his bed. He couldn't recall going to bed. He listened to the camp while he tried to remember what had happened. It didn't sound right at all. The quiet had a dead quality to it and the wail had echoed off the sheer rock walls at their backs.

He tried to sit up but felt so weak. Every muscle ached. The merest movement sent nausea chasing through him. There was a cloth on his forehead. He dragged it off and heard it slop into a bowl of water at his bedside. Oh yes, now it was coming back.

'Garrelites!' he called, his voice feeble and hoarse. He coughed violently, almost vomited.

He heard footsteps and his tent flap snapped. He didn't feel strong enough to turn his head so he waited until a face appeared above his.

'You aren't Garrelites,' he said, recognising his head surgeon: Dahnishev, the tall, stick-like Goslander miracle-worker.

'At least your eyes work,' said Dahnishev. 'Garrelites died in the battle. Don't you remember? He's dead. Same as you should be.' He placed a hand on Roberto's brow, his cheek, neck and chest in turn. 'Your fever has broken.' He smiled. 'You're a lucky man. God still requires your presence above the earth.'

'Fever,' repeated Roberto, struggling to force the pieces of his memory together. His head was pounding. 'Are we secure?'

'Calm yourself, General,' said Dahnishev. 'One step at a time.'

'Garrelites dead?' said Roberto. 'A good man. Friend.'

'Yes,' said Dahnishev. 'Now, tell me if you can, how you are feeling.'

'A little vague,' said Roberto.

'I gathered that,' said the surgeon. 'Aches?'

'Everywhere. Worst in my head. And my stomach feels like my horse is lying on it.'

'At least you have feeling. That's a good sign. And your delirium has ceased.'

'How long?' asked Roberto.

'Eight days,' said Dahnishev.

'God-embrace-me,' breathed Roberto.

He felt faint, his heart thumping in his throat. He tried to push himself up but Dahnishev restrained him easily.

'I don't think so,' he said. 'You do not have the strength. Tomorrow you can sit up, and the day after you can stand. Maybe.'

'I have duties. The Tsardon—'

'Are nowhere near us. Please, General . . . Roberto, listen to me.'

Roberto nodded. The sudden panic eased a little and he focused on Dahnishev. The surgeon's piercing blue eyes were hooded with an expression of fatherly concern. He felt tired and his concentration was already threatening to wander.

'Sorry. I'm sorry.'

'No need to apologise, General.' Dahnishev sat on the bed next to him. 'We've had a plague of typhus through the camp. It's on the wane now. We've rid the camp of fleas and rats, dug the trench very deep around the stockade and instituted a bite examination regime. We have it beaten but we are seriously weakened. I will bring numbers to you when you are stronger but what you must understand before you rest again is that we are not under threat. We sent messengers to General Atarkis and his legions now defend us beyond the quarantine zone.'

Roberto sank back into his pillow. 'Are riders going to Estorr?'

Dahnishev nodded. 'Yes. We have requested reinforcements. I will send Elise Kastenas to you tomorrow to brief you and take orders. But right now, you need some small sustenance and plenty of sleep. And I will tell the legions that you are going to live. It will be a massive boost to them all.'

'Good medicine,' said Roberto weakly.

'The best,' said Dahnishev. 'We have been praying for you, Roberto. You are the heartbeat of this army.'

'You're embarrassing me.'

'Deliberately. Because you need to be up and walking through the camp as soon as you can. And if you listen to what I say, you will be. Do you understand, General?'

Roberto nodded, weary. 'Never go against what the doctor says.'

'Sound advice. Food then sleep. Don't get up. You can piss into bottles.' Dahnishev rose. 'I'll look in on you later.'

'Thank you, old friend.'

'Praise God you have been spared.'

The cheers spreading around the camp accompanied him back to a peaceful sleep.

Roberto didn't know how long he slept but he awoke with a clarity of mind that was truly double-edged. He had been returned to himself from the prison of his fever and for that he was relieved. But the memories and the knowledge that came with it were unpleasant and depressing. It had begun just a few days after the victory against the poorly commanded Tsardon forces. They had returned their dead to the ground and the embrace of God, the surgeons had treated the injured, and they had celebrated for two days.

Detachments of Hawks cavalry and Blades light infantry were harrying the remnants of the Tsardon army, scattering and capturing as they went. Prisoners were being marched to the camps near the Gosland borders in their thousands. The army was set to reform fifteen days later on the far side of the mountain range into which they had chased the vanquished enemy.

The battlefield had been cleared of useful weapons and armour and the Tsardon camp similarly picked clean. In keeping with the traditions of the war, the Tsardon dead were moved into rows and left for their own people to deal with according to their bizarre religions and laws.

Spirits were high when they broke camp in the dark of early morning, five days after the victory, and set off south and east around the mountains, shadowing the legions commanded by General Atarkis. Scouts and messengers reported scattered towns and settlements in their path, all of which were searched and supplies bought for the march.

There were also reports of a new army gathering ten days from them. They were well-positioned across a mountain pass, commanding the only route to Khuran passable by an army for three hundred miles in either direction. Roberto and Atarkis would join forces to defeat this last major obstacle before securing the territory they had won. The assault on the capital would begin the following spring, assuming Gesteris from the centre and the garrulous old Goslander, Jorganesh from the south, achieved their goals.

The first infections had begun to appear three days into the march. Admittedly, the valley they travelled was part swamp, overrun by rodents and home to clouds of mosquitoes but they had camped carefully each day, with trenches dug, palisades erected and all tents pitched by late afternoon. The typhus had taken hold all the same. Fleas on the backs of rats and mice, so Dahnishev said. One flea would infect everything it bit and with ten rats to every legionary, there was a plague of the carriers before the typhus itself.

Roberto accepted disease as a hazard of campaigning. Diphtheria and dysentery were relatively common and containable with wagons to carry the sick in quarantined conditions. However, the scale of the epidemic which had engulfed his army had taken him completely by surprise. And ten days after they had begun marching, and with the southern edges of the mountain range within his grasp, he had been forced to stop.

Five days later, barely enough soldiers had been fit enough to carry out all the camp duties. The Atreskan cavalry and infantry had been ordered to stay away and to make urgent contact with Atarkis. The Del Aglios legions had been lame sitting ducks.

Roberto sat up in his cot and clutched its sides while the world swam in front of him. He was shivering again, though not from his fever. It was all too easy to recall his own rising desperation and the anxiety in his troops as the typhus began to claim lives at an alarming rate.

By the twentieth day of their enforced halt, with the weather alternately baking and soaking them, he had lost more to disease than he had to Tsardon blade and arrow. Panic and a sense of impending doom were spreading through the army and it threatened to break them. Whole maniples would lie sick and dying while others were untouched. Eight men in a tent would die while two remained fit and healthy, praising God for their fortune while they wrestled with their guilt.

Roberto was forced into increasingly severe measures to keep his army from falling apart. Along with Dahnishev he had implemented the plan to exterminate every rat, mouse and flea, a massive task in an army of sixteen thousand. He had ordered the horses picketed away from troops, to be handled only by the stable duty officers and their teams. They would carry fleas and he could not risk his allowing cavalrymen to touch them while the epidemic raged.

When the first desertions were noted, principally from the Atreskan legions, he had doubled the guard on the gates and palisades and strengthened his outer pickets. A stockade had been built just outside the main camp, near the followers, who were also suffering badly. When he was last aware, it had held seventy men and women who had felt running was their only chance of survival. He had news for them the moment he was up and walking.

And finally, with genasfall at its height he too had succumbed. The memory of his own descent was hideous. The fever that had gripped him without warning, leaving him feeble and sweating, barely able to walk. Almost worse was the headache. An unremitting pounding as of hammer on rocks, slamming through his skull. He had heard men and women crying out for mercy and respite and had thought them weak willed. How he had craved their forgiveness when he suffered their fate. He knew he had moaned in his agony too, feeling as if his head was going to shatter, his brain rupture.

By the time the rash, raised and red, had begun to appear on his body, to smother his skin everywhere but his face, palms and soles, he had already begun to lose his senses. He knew the itching drove him to further distraction and that Dahnishev had bound his hands to stop him tearing at his flesh but it had seemed distant somehow,

And finally, on his way to blessed unconsciousness, he had been aware of his breath rushing in and out of his lungs so quickly his vision, already double from the headache, fogged and darkened. Dahnishev had tried to calm him. He remembered that. The last thing he could recall was the slow tolling of his heart, so slow that it robbed him of the last remnants of his strength.

All thought of leading an army had gone as the fever and delirium had swamped him, taking his mind and imprisoning it inside his weakening, sick body. He could recall nothing of that time. Eight days lost to him.

He shook his head and the quivering subsided. A smile touched his lips and sudden relief cooled him. The fact was, he still had an army out there. From what Dahnishev had told him, they were over the worst of it. Recovery would begin in earnest and perhaps they could march from this awful place in a few days. His smile faded. After all, how many would still be alive to march behind him?

Roberto shouted for attention and a legionary, carrying a spear and wearing full armour, polished to perfection, walked into his tent.

'Bring me Elise Kastenas. And have some food sent in too,' he paused and thought. 'But before that, help me up and dressed.'

'Yes, General.' The legionary leant his spear against the door pole. He was a young Estorean hastati, of average build and with deep brown eyes matching his hair.

'What's your name, citizen?'

'Herides, my Lord.'

'Proud of your armour and weaponry?'

'Yes, my Lord. It is all that keeps me alive.'

'Good. It shows. Consider yourself attached to my personal guard as aide replacing poor Garrelites.'

The young man smiled and blushed under his tan. 'Thank you, my Lord Del Aglios. I am truly honoured.'

'And thank you for remaining faithful through the disease. I need men like you close. Now, help me up and to my dressing table.'

If Herides felt embarrassed at the support he had to give Roberto, he didn't show it. Roberto felt incredibly weak, his legs barely held him up and he leant heavily on his new aide. Herides was efficient and smart and in a shorter time than he had anticipated, Roberto was seated at his map table, dressed in a light toga bearing the Del Aglios crest. Elise Kastenas and the food arrived together. The latter looked tempting and smelled devilishly good. Elise looked exhausted, careworn and ten years older.

'Sit, sit before you fall,' he said. 'And eat, for God's sake. You look worse than I do.'

Elise's smile was bright and warm. 'It's good to hear your voice, General,' she said, sinking into a recliner next to him. 'And you should study yourself more closely. I may be a little tired but you are just skin and bone. And you could do with a shave.'

Roberto rubbed his chin, surprised at the growth of beard.

'Didn't they keep me clean while I was sick?' he said, only half irritated.

'Garrelites wasn't there,' she said.

'No. No, indeed.' Roberto recalled the man's professional bearing and good humour. 'At least he escaped the plague. Died a hero in battle instead.'

Elise nodded, dropping her head and swallowing hard.

'It's been bad, hasn't it?' said Roberto. 'I'm sorry I wasn't there to help you. But I need you to tell me what I have left. The command team. Have they all survived?'

'No,' said Elise and there were tears in her eyes. Roberto's heart sank. 'Ben Rekeros and Tomas Engaard are both in God's embrace. The tenth legion has taken a fearful beating. And in the alae, Shakarov and Davarov are both still sick. Surgeon Dahnishev thinks either will be lucky to survive. The rest of us are all right. I have not been touched and Ellas Lennart came through it while you were fevered. I think his death would have been a terrible blow. The legions needed to know God was at least sparing His own Speaker. Elsewhere the commanders and masters are still walking.'

Roberto sighed. Amongst the citizens packed in their tents more tightly and so much more vulnerable to fleas, the story was going to be a hard one to take. Poor Rekeros. So close to retirement. God had deserted him too soon.

'My numbers then, broadly.'

Elise took a deep breath. 'The tenth has suffered by far the worst. Almost three thousand infantry have been lost.'

'*Three thousand?*' Roberto's breath caught in his throat and he felt physical pain. He sat back, unable to comprehend the scale for a moment.

'And in the cavalry, one hundred and forty are gone.' Elise wiped at her eyes. 'In the eighth, we have lost a thousand infantry so far but our cavalry have been largely spared. Twenty gone and another thirty still sick. The alae have fared much better. The cavalry and light infantry sent out to harry the Tsardon are complete. And in the camp, they seem to have been more resistant. The Arrows have lost three hundred infantry and forty cavalry. The Blades five hundred infantry and a hundred cavalry. The numbers will rise but not by much.'

'May God preserve those who still walk,' whispered Roberto. 'I had no idea it would be so bad.'

'Almost seven out of every ten in the camp have been sick. Dahnishev says that we have been lucky.'

'Lucky?' Roberto's laugh was short and bitter. 'I would hate to see ill-luck then.' He thought hard for a moment. 'What is the mood out there?'

'Morale is low,' said Elise. 'A hundred and thirteen stand in the stockade. The gulf in fatalities between legion and alae has led to trouble. Atreskan shrines have been set up and they are saying that it is these that spared their people and will save Shakarov and Davarov. And even some of our own speak of God abandoning us in an evil land. The tenth is a cursed legion now. So many deaths. But belief in your survival has kept the army together in the main. When you walk among them, pray God it is soon, spirits will lift.'

Roberto felt sick. The food in front of him smelled sour. He took a sip of water and forced his attentions on a piece of bread smeared with honey sauce.

'We will do what must be done,' he said. 'I'll be well enough to walk tomorrow, I promise. In the meantime, prepare the papers for disbandment of the tenth legion and the burning of the standard. We must do this in the right way. All those in the legion must be released and be invited to join the eighth or the curse will continue. I am sorry for its demise. Such a proud history. The alae will stay as they are.

'Send messengers to Estorr and to the other commanders in the field of my decision and our latest numbers. When we meet Atarkis, I will assume overall command of the entire force until our reinforcements arrive. Anything else that comes to me, I will send for you again.

'Elise, this is already a disaster. It is by the efforts of you and the command team that it has not been a calamity. I will be commending you all in my papers. But more than that, I want to thank you personally. I am in your debt.'

Elise smiled. 'We do it because we believe in you. There was never a thought to the contrary.'

'Now eat, eat. And when you have written the orders, you will sleep until dawn tomorrow. That is also an order.' He looked her in the eye and saw the relief there. 'Now, let's speak of something a little more uplifting. I feel the need.'

'The Games start tomorrow.'

'Games?' Roberto bellowed a laugh. 'Games! Dear God-around-us. We die of typhus and they celebrate our glory. My mother has done many stupid things in her time as Advocate but this surely is the crowning folly.' He paused. 'Mind you, it gives me an idea . . .

Something to raise the spirits and engender a bit of competition after sitting around and getting blunt.'

'You aren't serious?'

'Never more so, Elise. Never more so.'

Roberto was humbled by his reception when he walked through the camp the next morning. So much genuine affection, relief and joy at his survival that he had to keep focused to stop the tears forming in his eyes. Clean-shaven and in his dress uniform for the unpleasant business he had to carry out, he walked with ten of his personal guard along every street of the camp. He stopped to talk to as many as he could, took hundreds of salutes and thanked everyone he met for their solidarity through the plague.

Not unnaturally, the camp was a mess but there were signs of it being brought back to something approaching full working order. Quarantine had been lifted around the horses now the rats and fleas were gone and the cavalry was able to reacquaint itself with its animals. And that was not the only boost to morale. There was laughter around the camp for the first time since before he had succumbed to the infection. Cookfires roared in the late morning heat but a breeze kept the temperature very pleasant.

Roberto had gulped the fresh air greedily when he had first stepped out of his tent. He drew in more deep breaths now, reminding himself of the odours of the camp, both fair and foul. It was all like the scent of new life compared to the stale, herb-soaked air in his tent.

But as much as it was greeted with excitement by his legions, every pace hurt him. There was none of the cluttered bustle. The noise he was so used to was muted though the mood was light enough. And the energy he associated with his army was missing. Too many had died for that. Too many good men and women in the arms of God when they should be polishing armour and sharpening swords ready for battles to come. How fragile even the strongest were in the face of the smallest of enemies. How delicately God held them that one judder should cause so many to fall.

The massed tents of the 10th legion, empty of their original incumbents now, had been turned over to the surgeons as makeshift hospital dormitories. Roberto headed for them to see the extent of the disease still threatening his army. As he approached, Dahnishev walked out of one of the tents, rubbing his hands on a cloth. His face was grim but it cracked into a smile when he saw Roberto.

He strode across and clutched his general on his upper arms. 'It lifts my heart to see you walking,' he said.

'And I to *be* walking,' said Roberto. 'You look awful. When did you last sleep?'

'Don't ask me to lie to you, Roberto,' replied Dahnishev. 'Trust me to look after myself.'

'As you wish. How many are still sick?'

'It diminishes by the day. I have two hundred still in fever, a further fifty or so recovering. We are approaching the finishing line but you can expect a hundred more to die, though we might be luckier and lose fewer.'

'Work your miracles, my friend, we need them more than ever.' Roberto shook his head. 'It's so quiet here.'

'A quarter of your force has died,' said Dahnishev. 'But those who survived are stronger of will than ever before.'

'Most of them,' said Roberto, nodding in the direction of the stockade. 'Now, will I be a help or hindrance to your patients?'

'What do you think? Come with me.'

Dahnishev took him on a tour of every cot in which the sick lay. Some were lost to the fever and had no idea he was passing them. Those on the road to recovery he could see take heart from his visit and he stopped by each one to give what comfort and strength he could. And in a tent of their own lay Shakarov and Davarov, both men still fevered and unconscious. Their cots were positioned close together because Dahnishev believed the old friends would take strength from each other. Roberto walked the narrow space between them and knelt so he could put a hand on either raging brow.

'Dear God who blesses this earth and all that grows upon it and walks across it, spare these fine men for the work they must do in your name. Let them feel the sun on their faces again and know your mercy. I ask this as your humble servant.' He closed his eyes for a moment before moving his hands down to their shoulders. He gripped them hard.

'Come on you two. Lazing in bed while there are still Tsardon out there. I don't know if you can hear me but I need the pair of you. Not one or the other. Both. If you must die, don't do it here. Do it in battle and reach God on the waves of glory. Come back to me. Let's drink wine and laugh as we have done for years. That's an order.'

He pushed himself to his feet. Shakarov stirred but did not awaken. Roberto wondered if anything he had said would sink through the fever and bring them back. He turned to Dahnishev.

'Time to do what must be done,' he said. 'Then I can pray over the Chronicle of Memories.'

The stockade was a simple wooden construction of sharpened wooden stakes fifteen feet high with a single door, guarded night and day. Steps ran up to a parapet which overlooked the patch of mud and filth on which the one hundred and thirteen deserters ate, slept and walked. No shelter barring that of their prison walls. Bread and water once a day. They looked as they should, broken and ashamed.

Roberto climbed the stairs and at once, every face turned up to him in expectancy. He stared down in contempt. Atreskans, Estoreans, Tundarrans, Caraducians. He shook his head.

'What possessed you?' he asked. 'Why did you think your chances were better away from the legions? What sort of fool have I been commanding who would entertain such thoughts?' He looked around them again, recognising some. All were infantry, all hastati. Raw in the harsh truths of the campaign. 'I cannot have panic and I will not tolerate disobedience. This is my army and it operates under my rules.

'While you sought to run away from the disease, thousands of your comrades who needed your help were sick and dying. You turned your back on them as you turned your back on me. What you have done is unforgivable. You might have thought I would hand you back your swords, such are the numbers we have lost to typhus.

'But if you know me at all, you will know that I would rather face the Tsardon hordes with one strong man than ten thousand cowards. You do not deserve the embrace of God and you do not deserve to breathe His air or walk upon His earth. My army will be the stronger for your absence.' Roberto paused. Not one of them was looking at him now. They all knew what was coming.

'You will all be executed at dusk this night and your bodies burned and scattered to the devils that live on the wind. And if you feel that harsh punishment, then think on this in your final hours. There are those in this army granted less life than you who showed courage you did not. There are those who will die after you who go to the embrace of God, taken too soon.

'Don't pray for yourselves, it will waste precious breath. Pray for those on whom you turned your back in their time of greatest need. Pray for those of us who trusted you and who now stand betrayed. You may die but your shame will live on in your families. Think on that. Die thinking on it.'

He turned on his heel, hurried down the steps and away.

Chapter 25

'This is the core of everything,' said Kessian. 'This is not something you can teach any child to do. It is something they are born with. All we can hope to do is train them to use it wisely, if they posses it at all.'

Jhered sat in the ancient man's villa, among the ruins of a splendid dinner and in the presence of all those who termed themselves the Ascendancy Echelon. They represented he ages of man from youth to near death and had given him the first inking of the true scale of the project. Vasselis had barely scratched the surface with the knowledge he had imparted in Estorr.

Jhered had come here ready to hate these people. But they accepted him, presumably because Vasselis said they must, and he was fighting hard not to begin liking them.

The door opened and the youngest of them returned under the weight of books she had been sent to retrieve from the library. Some of them were clearly very old indeed, dating back as far as the Conquord itself and perhaps even further.

'Ah, Jen, excellent,' said Kessian, this fervent, passionate man whose failing body was no cage for his enthusiasm. A man who could predict the weather more than twenty days hence absolutely without error. 'Put them down here by me.'

'So, can you put a figure on exactly how many of the population of this place have, or had, some ability?' Jhered asked, keen to keep to the subject at hand before the books were shown to him.

'At least eight out of every ten births, I would say,' said Meera Naravny, the mother of the difficult one, Gorian. She had demonstrated her complete imperviousness to fire during those moments when he had arrived and been overwhelmed by the presence of their abilities and their apparently casual acceptance of them.

'Eighty per cent?' He gaped momentarily. 'How can this be? How can we not have heard about it before now?'

'One thing at a time,' said Willem Geste, another very old man, a Firewalker like Meera. Well-spoken. 'It is no accident, at least not now. A master cavalryman and woman who produce a child would be disappointed if that child had no aptitude for riding, yes? So it is here. The density of display of abilities in newborns has grown with every generation. It is natural selection.'

There was that phrase again and it was beginning to sound horribly plausible.

'But we don't trumpet the gift we have been given,' said Genna Kessian, the charming wife who could identify the source of any pain in the human body with a single, effortless touch. 'The Order would not see things as we do, as you are very well aware. No one would display their ability in the presence of a stranger. No matter the temptation to boast and gain profit. Successive generations here have learned loyalty and understand the price of indiscretion to themselves and all whom they love. And those strangers that have seen what they shouldn't, well . . .' She glanced at Vasselis. 'We cannot have careless mouths whispering dissent in the wrong ears.'

Jhered raised his eyebrows and caught Vasselis's eye. Even paradise had an iron border. He nodded minutely. He understood the need for security as much as he thought he understood the reasons why the veil had to be lifted now.

'But why here?' he asked, unsure for a moment whether he had spoken aloud.

'Because this is where Gorian lived,' said Kessian, his eyes alive with his passion,. He patted the books at his right hand. 'It's all here and I leave these with you to read during your stay which can be for as long as you have questions to ask.

'There have always been people born with ascendant abilities, mostly transient in nature. Gorian wrote all their stories, brought them together. People shunned by their own citizens and needing a new home; those who felt apart from their families and friends and needing an explanation; or those scared by the strangeness they felt and wanting comfort.'

'Gorian?' asked Jhered. 'Not . . . ?'

'No, no. Our young Gorian is named after the man who started it all around five hundred years ago,' said Kessian. 'And everything he learned, he recorded. The Order killed him when they caught him but they couldn't destroy his work, much though they believed they had. You have never heard of him, have you?'

Jhered shook his head.

'It isn't a surprise,' said Kessian. 'Dangerous information for them and something that gives a lie to their determination that the Ascendancy is a perversion or witchcraft. It is not. It is as natural as the turning of the tides or the leaves on the trees.'

Jhered shook his head. 'Be careful with your words, Father Kessian,' he said. 'Whether or not the law should have been passed by the Order, it is on the statute. I am sworn to uphold the laws of the Order and the Conquord.'

'Then what is the purpose of this investigation, if not to expose whether the Ascendancy is heretic or should be accepted?' asked Willem. 'Surely you need us to be honest with our feelings and our opinions. Unjust laws need to be repealed.'

'As I explained to your Reader, I find myself in an invidious position. I am not impartial. A crime has been committed, about that you should have no doubt. The question is, what will we do with you and what have you learned? I am here to try to uncover your purposes and your desires.

But that doesn't mean you are without allies. Orin D'Allinnius is fascinated by your processes and Captain Harkov sees only the pure thought in everyone. I, on the other hand, am troubled that you have developed your Ascendants under the banner of the Order. There is your crime and it is serious. Should it be turned over to the Order, you would suffer severe penalties.'

Silence. But Kessian was not a man to be cowed. And his enthusiasm was infectious. Jhered could not help but warm to him.

'Then read what Gorian has written. Speak to the town and to any of us. The root of everything we have done is in nature and so is the will of God. It is the repression of the Ascendant strand that is unnatural. That is a decision taken by men and women for their own ends, pure or otherwise. I might ask you where in the scriptures the repression of nature is deemed either necessary or acceptable.'

Jhered smiled. 'The Order leads as it sees fit and is given that responsibility by the Advocate. A fracturing of the Conquord's central faith would be a disaster.'

'We do not wish that,' said Genna quietly. 'We have never wished that. It is an enduring sadness that we know the Order would have us all burned for our work.'

'How wonderful it would be if everyone could feel what our Ascendants feel,' said Kessian, his fervour boiling over. 'Think, Lord Jhered, of the joy of being able to feel the growth of your crops. To understand your horse so minutely that you would never cause it harm. To open your eyes on the new day and experience the energy of the earth beneath you throughout your body. To be one with nature and the elements. To come closer to God.'

Jhered leaned back and let Kessian's words sink in. And through the glory of his suggestions there came dread.

'But what, Father Kessian, if the powers of all are so great that they can control the sea, the weather and everything that grows. It is a gift to evil, should they choose to use it as such. How far will your Ascendants be able to reach?'

Jhered didn't meet the Ascendants alone until the fifth day of his investigation. It had been the most extraordinary time. Westfallen was unlike any place he had ever been despite being in the heartland of his favourite country. He felt like he had been inside a bubble, cosseted from the rest of the world. But a bubble in which events potentially as important as those in Tsard were unfolding.

The citizens and Ascendancy of Westfallen had been honest, welcoming and after the first couple of days, unafraid. He had seen at first hand how careful they were around traders and visitors to the town, and how naturally those with fledgling abilities accepted what they had. He talked to so many of them, along with those whose abilities had faded with time.

There was no doubting their belief in the purity of their intentions but he couldn't shake off the worry that the naivety that their insular lives had brought them had blinded them to the ramifications of what they were doing. Jhered was a career soldier and understood that for every good intention there was an enemy who would reverse it for you. The Ascendants were dangerous, no question.

He had wrestled with the conflict in his discussions with Harkov and D'Allinnius, and had written of it extensively in his notes. Was it nature or was it design disguised as nature? And more pertinently, what should the Advocacy do with them . . . with the whole of Westfallen, for that matter?

It was difficult, though, to consider anything but acceptance and mercy, sitting where he was right now. Marshal Vasselis's walled garden was in its pomp. Flowers of every colour decorated walls and beds. Ivy had climbed to adorn the statues of the greats of Caraduk and cascaded across the roof of the marble shelter in which they sat, away from the punishing light of the sun. The fountains bubbled happily, carp in their pools rising to grab flies before returning to the shade of white-flowered lilies.

In an arc around the bench on his left, sat the Ascendants themselves, all smartly dressed in pale-coloured tunics, slashed with the Ascendancy red and cinched with white rope. They were a fascinating mix of anxiety, teenage cocksure arrogance, and a touch of real maturity.

With great interest he had watched them come in through the gate at the bottom of the garden and approach him. The blind one, Ossacer, had his arm on that of Arducius, the gentle-faced one. At he other side was the girl, Mirron. Pretty. Ossacer hardly looked as if he needed their help, so sure was his step. And just apart from them was Gorian. He was studying Jhered as they came close, his eyes penetrating and slightly disconcerting.

'You can learn a great deal about people before you utter your first word to them,' said Jhered, when they were all seated and comfortable. Their maid, Shela Hasi, had supplied welcome cool drinks before withdrawing. 'Their bearing; how they walk; in which order they look at you; who looks you in the eye without fear; and who with interest or trepidation.'

They were silent, waiting for his prompt to speak, he supposed.

'You do know why I am here, don't you? They've told you all about me and my colleagues and the seriousness of our investigation.'

Nods and the odd muttered 'yes'. He smiled.

'No need to fear me. I am not your judge today, merely your observer. So please feel free to speak at any time.'

'Are you really a hard man?' asked Gorian suddenly.

Jhered was taken completely by surprise. 'I—' He paused and chuckled. 'And I was supposed to be questioning you. Let me say this. It is the nature of my job that I take taxes and levies from people who sometimes do not agree with how much I want or are reluctant to part with what they must. These people will find out that, yes, I am a hard man. They also find out that I miss very little indeed. Something you might remember while we talk, eh?' He let the smile fall from his face. 'Why did you ask me that?'

'Because we have heard lots about you. You run the Gatherers and so no one likes you.'

'No one likes the tax man,' he agreed.

'But you don't seem so bad,' said Gorian.

'That's because you have given me no cause to be. See it remains that way.' Jhered steepled his fingers. 'Tell me why it is the other three don't like you as much as each other.'

All four of them stared at their feet for a time. Good. Best they understood who was in control.

'I would have thought you'd stick closer together. After all, you are the only four so far, even though I understand more potential has been born and yet more is expected.'

Gorian was looking at him now but wasn't about to say anything. Jhered was disappointed.

'You see, I have a problem. Your Echelon, your Reader and in fact anyone else I have spoken to has been terribly keen to tell me about the great and good things that you can do now and that you will be able to do in the future. Apparently, you might be the saviours of us all, the vanguard of a new human race that uses its powers to the benefit of all.

'But I do worry about what you think. After all, you have minds of your own and for a brief moment at least, you threatened to be inquisitive. You must have considered your futures. Are you all of one mind? From your approach, I suspect that you are not.'

This time the silence was irritating. The fact that he was unused to dealing with children was becoming painfully apparent. He coughed.

'Do you want me to pick one of you to break the ice on this rather warm day? Mirron?'

'I knew you'd pick me. Just because I'm the girl.'

'Or perhaps I think you're the brightest among you,' he said sharply. 'Just say something in response. Think about it, young lady. When you look forward in your life, what do you see?'

'I see myself here in Westfallen. I will join the Ascendancy Echelon as we all will because it must develop to help new Ascendants learn more quickly than us. I expect I will be a mother of the Ascendancy in time, just as my brothers will be fathers. And I'll use my skills to help people where I can. Why would I want to do anything else?'

'You don't feel that you'll be able to dictate what you want because of the power you have?'

She frowned. 'I don't understand.'

Jhered raised his eyebrows. She really hadn't considered it. She was only fourteen, he supposed. Still, she should have been more aware. He already knew his skill with a sword would take him high in the Advocacy well before he was her age.

'Do you see yourselves as separate from the rest of the Conquord?' he asked, an idea sparking.

'We're citizens of the Conquord,' said Arducius. Jhered noted how Mirron and Gorian looked at him and Ossacer squeezed his forearm. 'And the Conquord will find tasks for us if it wants us. Or we will choose for ourselves. Either way, the right decision would be to let us develop the next generation of Ascendants.'

'In your image?'

'What other image is there?' said Gorian.

'We are only as separate from the Conquord as any farmer or fisherman in Westfallen. We will serve if drafted, we may volunteer if the wars are still going on. When the time comes, God will show us the right path,' said Arducius.

'You really think you would be asked to don armour and march with the hastati?' Jhered was amused at the image.

'No,' said Ossacer. 'We would be doctors and veterinarians. That is where our skills would lie on the battlefield.'

'Really? Nothing more? Gorian, what do you think?'

Gorian shrugged. 'Ossacer is right. Mostly. But perhaps we can have other effects too. We can stop or start the rain too. And we can make the wind blow. Maybe our generals would want that in preference to our skills with injuries.'

Jhered nodded. 'I agree,' he said. 'And do you think that is how you should be used? Gorian?'

'No, of course not,' said Gorian. 'We are different. We should master our own futures. Do what we want to do.'

There it was. The others looked askance at him and, if it was possible, leaned away from him. Gorian had already begun to see where his powers could lead him. And for Jhered, the spectre of their manipulation by a general seeking much greater power for himself. The others still swallowed the limited view offered them by the Echelon. A view for which Jhered had respect. But in Gorian there was a brief exhibition of the problems they would inevitably face when these young minds all began to stretch.

And they clearly could not see the danger.

'So,' he said. 'you've answered my first question about how you approached me, haven't I? You three disagree with him. But is he not the more realistic one?'

Arducius was shaking his head. 'We must only use what we have to do God's work. That is in healing and creating growth, not in making a field slippery for the feet of our soldiers.'

'Oh Arducius, you don't understand,' said Gorian. 'We could make it rain when our armies charged because then the enemy's arrows would not fly straight and true. And we could direct the lightning against our enemy's armour to save the lives of our own people. I thought you all liked Kovan. At least I listen to him.'

'Always so clever, Gorian,' said Arducius. 'I don't know why you don't just leave since you know it all already.'

'Why do you say that? I listen and I learn. Don't be jealous just because you don't do what I do.'

'I am happy not to do what you do,' snapped Arducius. 'Who'd want to have your mind?'

'Stop it,' said Mirron. 'You're embarrassing me.'

She looked up at Jhered, her cheeks red and her eyes moist. Ossacer was once again hanging his head.

'I don't want to do my work in a war,' he whispered.

Jhered's heart missed a beat and he fought the urge to place a comforting hand on the boy's shoulder. Arducius was already there.

'It will be as God wills it, Ossie,' he said.

Jhered watched them. The three closing ranks and Gorian apart, confident in himself. They were a fascinating quartet. Jhered wasn't sure what he'd learned. In so many ways they were just young people like any others running the streets of the Conquord. In others, they understood the weight of their talents. And one of them had begun to understand their potential for power and influence too.

They chattered in ever widening circles while the afternoon waned to a glorious fiery dusk. When Jhered rose to leave, he knew he would spend the night awake, trying to decipher how he felt about these children. He thanked them all for their time and patience and began to walk down to the gate.

'Exchequer Jhered?'

He turned. Arducius was standing, the others grouped around him.

'Yes, Arducius.'

'We are not evil. We didn't ask for the abilities we have but we were born with them. All we can do is make the best we can of them and see that we live out our lives as God would wish. Don't call in the Order. We would burn and we don't deserve that.'

Jhered nodded curtly and spun on his heel. He took a long walk on the beach before going back to his rooms in Vasselis's villa.

Vasselis rode with Jhered to the top of the rise where, ten days before, they had looked down on the tranquillity of Westfallen. And for his part, the Marshal was happy that tranquillity remained intact for however brief a period. It was the fiftieth day of genasfall though it was hard to distinguish the blistering heat from a day in the middle of solastro.

Vasselis had ridden out without any of his guard. There was no danger here and Jhered's levium were an honourable legion, professional and exemplary. He felt safe in their company, no matter the current relationship between the two old friends. D'Allinnius and Harkov had been respectful guests and had made new friends among those they were investigating. Vasselis respected both of them for their objectivity and their delicacy.

'You are going to ask me what I'm going to say to Herine Del Aglios aren't you?' asked Jhered as they approached their parting. Vasselis was staying in Westfallen for the time being.

'Of course. I'm bound to.'

'It's going to be the question on the lips of every single citizen in Westfallen, isn't it?'

'Don't play with me, Paul. That's beneath you.'

Jhered reined in and motioned everyone else to carry on. Vasselis stopped with him, trying to read his expression and failing.

'It had always been my plan to think on all I had seen and heard, and then review all I had written on my way back to Estorr. To take the views of my team and discuss every single item of evidence. And I will still do that. But I'm equally aware that to leave you with no notion of my thoughts is tantamount to cruelty against the whole of that—' He gestured back towards Westfallen '—extraordinary little town of yours. I can see why you love it, by the way.'

'Thank you for your concern,' said Vasselis. 'You really should be building your villa there.'

'You'll understand why I think that a poor decision at the moment,' said Jhered.

'Your loss,' said Vasselis.

Jhered wiped a gauntleted finger under his nose. 'Arvan, I will say these things to you and you can interpret them as you will for your people. I am not going to go home and announce what I have found to the Order. If I have my way, the Chancellor will be kept out of this for as long as is practicable.

'But I can see no way the Advocacy can leave these people under your control. Your love of them has kept you from seeing the truth. They are a weapon. Dangerous if they fall under the wrong influence.'

Vasselis started. 'They're just children, learning the boundaries of their abilities.'

'How distant are those boundaries, have you asked yourself that? Gorian already sees destructive potential and I'll wager he's experimented, hasn't he?' Vasselis couldn't hide the truth from his face. 'I thought so. They need control and the Echelon doesn't know how to exercise it.'

'You mean military control,' said Vasselis. 'Paul, don't do this. They are vulnerable children. They need the security Westfallen gives them. Don't take that away from them.'

'What choice do you think you have given me?' said Jhered, anger in his eyes. 'I cannot go back to the Advocate and report a clean slate. Think about it. Not only are they a weapon, they are a gale through the fabric of the Conquord. People will be frightened of them. God-around-us, so was I when I saw what they could do. And there are five-year-olds and babes in arms even now who could be the next. How can we not be involved? When you came to me you must have known what could happen.'

Vasselis sighed. 'I know. I know. But you always hope, don't you?'

'Look, Arvan, this is better than you could possibly have hoped for when I arrived here, believe me. I'm still going to have to consult more widely about the theological implications. I'm still not convinced it's not heresy. But one thing more than anything else has given me pause for thought. While you and your Echelon might be criminals under God, your Ascendants are not. And because you are their protector, at least for now, I feel honour-bound to stand with you. And I am confident the Advocacy will agree with me, and that means the Order will be kept from you.'

'Thank you, Paul,' said Vasselis. 'Thank you.'

'Don't take it as acceptance, because it is far from that. Some day in the future, there will be a case to answer. For now, don't go far and make sure your Ascendants do not leave Westfallen. Life has changed for all of you.'

Chapter 26

The fords at Scintarit had become a major irritation to General Gesteris. The season of genastro was deep into its fall. Warmth had given way to oppressive heat and the Tsardon were not to be moved or lured. Almost thirty days since the first skirmishes and he had not been able to draw his enemy into a pitched battle.

Scintarit was a broad, marshy plain through which the bedrock pushed in a multitude of places, sometimes in flat slabs above the level of grass and sod, and at others like fingers reaching for the sky and soaring hundreds of feet into the air. It was bleak and windswept even in the heat, which did little to burn off the moisture underfoot. The water table was very high and it made marching, riding and drawing wagons problematic.

And slicing across the centre of the plain in long slow curves was the River Tarit. It was fed by underground courses that rose at the base of the Halorians, a huge range of mountains that bestrode the north east of Tsard, and was bolstered by the magnificent Halor Falls during the wet seasons. The river was never less than a quarter-mile wide. It was held in by steep, rocky banks that were impassable to wagons along practically the whole of its course through the plain and into the staggering Gorge of Kings seventy miles away to the south.

The Tsardon had destroyed the two bridges that had spanned the river north and south but they could do nothing about the triumvirate of fords in the centre of the plain. Treacherous, slippery expanses of smooth, moss-covered rock between one and three feet below the surface. Each was wide enough only for a single column to approach and cross. But such was the care with which that had to be attempted that defenders would have their pick of helpless targets.

The tactical importance of the plain could not be underestimated. Ceding it to the Tsardon would leave them unhindered access over easy ground all the way to the Atreskan and Goslander borders. And a Conquord victory would open the central heartland of Tsard, and bring ultimate triumph and the fall of the Tsardon capital of Khuran a huge step closer.

So it was that while Del Aglios and Atarkis north, and Jorganesh south, took their smaller armies into striking positions on Tsard's flanks, occupying good numbers of the enemy while they did, Gesteris held and pushed the centre with the largest single army ever despatched from the Conquord. Over eighty thousand citizens facing an enemy perhaps sixty thousand strong.

His was the glory of command, but his was the task of greatest difficulty and risk. Naturally a cautious man, he was only too aware of the pivotal role his army represented. Conquord territories had been stripped of large numbers of men and women to build what he saw before him each morning at dawn. They were an experienced force but cumbersome to command even with the chain he had established.

Logistical problems were huge, and not the least of them was the necessity to make camp around five miles from the banks of the River Tarit. It ate into every day's marching and deployment. Gesteris typically roused his army three hours before dawn and occasionally earlier in an effort to gain surprise. But the Tsardon picketing and forward scouting either side of the river was comprehensive and defensive units could be mobilised quickly to block any potential strike.

So, the sixty days had seen little more than cavalry charges, quick raids and some pickets destroyed, only to be rebuilt almost as quickly. Most of the time, as had been the nature of this war, the two sides marched out to stare at each other across the water in lines spreading over five miles to cover the fords. And at the end of each day they were marched back as the sun fell behind the Tarit Plateau.

Both sides knew the other could not afford rash moves that might lead to defeat. And for their part the Tsardon were entirely happy to wait. They knew that even should they be attacked by flanking Conquord armies, their numbers would be great enough, along with forces from elsewhere in their country, to be comfortable. They also knew that without Gesteris, Khuran would never fall. It was stalemate and it drained the morale of the Conquord army, who wanted little more than to see their families and their homes again.

Gesteris rose to the same routine as he always did on campaign. The reveille in the camp shattered the calm of dreams. The shouts of centurion and master mixed with the neigh of horse and the thunder of tens of thousands of citizens dragging themselves from their bedrolls.

He lay in the dark and listened for a few moments before his aides came in with lanterns and breakfast. He ate while he dressed. In the half light of the wicks, he examined his reflection in the mirror, noting the sheen of his polished armour, the clean dark green of his clothes and the deep grey of his cloak, embroidered with the Estorean crest and bounded in root motifs.

He smoothed down his similarly grey hair and stretched the skin of his face with a hand to remind him of his youth, three decades gone now he was in his fifties. Finally, he secured his green-plumed helmet, chin strap tucking in with familiar tightness.

Gesteris's force was separated into three, one to march to each ford. Latterly, he had separated the camps to make the march more efficient and had kept himself attached to the centre of the three, nominally with the 2nd legion, the Bear Claws of Estorr. However, movement among the three was fluid and he placed light infantry and cavalry in heavy concentrations on the flanks for quick dispersal to another location, feinting to push the left or right ford. It was the nearest he had come to forcing a critical breach and triggering the battle he craved.

He walked through his troops and cavalry, wishing them luck for the coming day and sharing prayers with the Speaker on the lawn outside her tent. He walked tall and proud, letting the belief that they would soon force battle and win the day sweep from him in waves. And inside he didn't doubt it would happen. It was the when that bothered him, and whether he would be forced to send messengers to the flanks, telling them to camp and hold for him. He didn't want that. It would shame him.

Gesteris inspected a maniple of the 30th ala, the Firedragons from Gosland, and a cataphract of his own legion. He mounted his horse, signalled the horns to sound and led the triarii from the principal gate. It was an efficient and unspectacular march along route seven, which was currently the least churned on the approaches to the water's edge, though the mud was still ankle-deep in places.

Firmer ground was marked and flagged across the marsh. His engineers had laid temporary stone and hardwood roads on all exits to the camp and out along every route for a mile at least. The retreat routes were clear and pristine, unused should the worst occur and they be forced to fall back to defend the heavily fortified camps.

Everything correct, everything in its place. All that was missing was the fight and he was running out of time and ideas. He knew he wasn't as imaginative as some of the younger generals. He heard mutterings, or at least thought he did. But he'd see the moment. He always had in the past. And his return to Estorr would be triumphant once again.

The army had deployed in a deep triplex acies formation covering the centre ford by mid-morning. Peace descended after the barrage of the march. Thirty thousand soldiers and cavalry stood with barely a sound to mark their presence bar the whinny of a horse, the flap of strap and cloth in the wind, the snap of a standard against its pole and the chink of metal on metal.

In front of them across the river, the Tsardon stood in a mass, their heavy complement of archers and crossbowmen forward most as always and their poor catapults drawn up close to the ford. There was barely even a shout or a taunt any more. It was a scene replicated left and right. Between the armies, flagmen and riders waited for orders.

Gesteris looked up at the sky before urging his horse into its slow, daily walk along the front of his lines. There was not a cloud in sight and the sun was hot, mocking his impotence to act. His Master of Horse, Dina Kell, accompanied him. An aggressive cavalrywoman, he had felt her silent discontent grow by the day and her suggestions were leaning towards excessive risk for questionable gain. Nevertheless, he respected her skill and experience. He would not have another commanding his cavalry.

The only thing he wished he'd done at the outset was build artillery towers on the river bank. That might have given his scorpions and ballistae the height to reach the enemy. Too late to try it out now. By the time they'd finished construction, he would have had to force his way across the fords.

Something caught his eye in the southern sky, away towards the

Gorge of Kings. Like a stain in the heavens, a dark smudge on blue canvas. He frowned. There was nothing down there. The land was dry but the way south and east was impassable for an army along the eastern side of the gorge. Hundreds of miles of deep clefts, sharp rocks and crags sprinkled with coarse heather, fit only for the most tenacious of goats.

He pointed. 'Master Kell, tell me what you see over there.'

Kell's deep brown eyes gazed out from under her plumed helmet. 'Dust in the air,' she said, her voice thick with her Tundarran accent. 'Probably reinforcements coming up from the Toursan Lakelands.' She shrugged. 'It won't be a large force. Jorganesh has most of them tied down, doesn't he?'

'So we are told,' said Gesteris. 'Do we have scouts down there?'

'Not at present,' said Kell. 'There's no crossing now the bridge is down. But I can have riders despatched.'

'Do so.'

He looked at the dust cloud again. So hard to gauge how distant it was or how large. Gesteris wasn't sure why but he didn't share Kell's confidence in the likely meagre size of the reinforcements. Under the shimmering heat haze accuracy was all but impossible.

He stopped his horse, reached round and fetched a map from his saddle bags. He unfolded it and squared the drawings with what he could see in the distance. The sides of the gorge reared high into the sky, tumbling east into the rocky terrain that, with the Toursan Lakelands, secured his southern flank. The river's course meandered for fifty miles, becoming arrow-straight for the last twenty before it fell into the gorge. Arrow straight.

Gesteris squinted, trying to place the dust, which would already give an inaccurate position of the reinforcements, the scale of difference dependent on the wind strength at the gorge mouth. The direction of the breeze where he stood was almost directly north, meaning the dust would probably be in advance of whoever was creating it. But it might then identify their lateral position more accurately.

He gripped his reins tight, trying not to betray sudden fear. He wanted to fetch out his magnifier too, but that would draw unwanted attention to the problem.

'Get those scouts down there now,' he hissed at Kell. 'And tell them to take care. The Tsardon are this side of the Tarit.'

*

The raids had continued and the Conquord did nothing but take more of his defence to bolster the clearly struggling armies in Tsard. He had manned as many of the border forts as he could and cycled his troops among them to keep the raiders guessing where they could safely cross into Atreska. But it did little except delay the inevitable.

Now, in his hand he held the message he knew he would receive from the Advocate, and he read it with disdain. His refusal to attend the Games had been greeted with fury and threats. His stewardship hung by a thread and Herine Del Aglios was looking for the final reason to have him replaced.

'But why should I care when my people are dying and my cities are burning?'

'My Lord?' his aide sounded startled.

'Sorry, Megan,' Marshal Yuran said to her. 'Thinking aloud.'

She was sitting behind him, reading the petitions of the day. He knew what they would contain and had risen to walk on to a balcony in his castle to stare down with deepening dismay at the state of Haroq City. It had begun with the populations of border towns beginning to trickle in behind the city walls, many bringing with them tales of Tsardon atrocities. But equally many had brought ultimatums such as the one he had heard from Praetor Gorsal at Gull's Ford. Too many of them exhorted him to abandon the Conquord and declare independence.

For them it was a simple choice. The Tsardon way or death. For him it was considerably more complex. Conquord troops were all across his lands, whether marching to or from the battlefronts, on defensive or assessment duties. Rebellions across Atreska took up as much of his time. His senior advisers were all Estoreans, loyal to the Advocate. And for his part, he still clung to the belief that the Conquord would triumph in Tsard quickly and the promises made by the Advocate would come to pass.

Yet he understood the desperation of his people and he saw in their eyes, the accusation that he was impotent to help. It hurt him, cut him to the quick. He had sold them the glory of the Conquord and so far it had led to little but fear and death for too many.

He really believed he was doing everything that he could. He had sent patrols to the Tsardon border and they had scored some fine victories. But it seemed that raiders were deeper into his country than

he had guessed and there were not enough troops to cover everywhere they might strike. The Tsardon ability to hit almost anywhere
they chose was spreading panic to all parts of Atreska. Surely they
were working with the rebels. And when the population of Haroq
had reached bursting point and he had to house refugees outside the
walls, the rioting had started.

The city's citizens had joined with the displaced and marched to
the castle in their thousands to demand action. They had wanted
more soldiers in the field and an ultimatum sent to Estorr concerning their loyalty if the Conquord failed to protect them as the
constitution decreed.

Yuran had seen the leaders of the popular movement and had
explained to them all that he could. He had urged them to remain
faithful and to pray to whichever gods they chose to see them
through this time. He had said how it looked dark but that victory
was at hand in Tsard and this was to be the penultimate campaigning
season.

He had pacified them for the time being but when food became
short with too many fields and farms empty, patience had run out.
Demonstration had become looting and he had been forced to send
out the Haroq guard to quell the trouble. Martial law was in place. A
curfew from dusk 'til dawn kept trouble to a minimum but each day
he saw fires in new parts of the city and heard the muted shouts of
mobs.

Slowly but surely, civil law was disintegrating in Haroq City and
even the Order of the Omniscient could not keep their faithful from
taking up arms.

'What can I do?' he asked. 'I am threatened with dismissal as
Marshal Defender. But my title insists that I do my job rather than
fawn to the Advocate at games which mock every hungry child in my
country and sneer at every drop of blood spilt by innocents working
their fields on the Tsardon borders.'

'You must do right by your people,' said Megan softly, unsure
whether she was requested to respond. 'Which is what you do
now.'

'Small comfort when those people I am sworn to defend turn on
me and each other. The cells are full of agitators, many of them
Tsardon sympathisers and they have dragged the heart from the city
like they have from its farmlands. But they don't understand the

implications of returning to independence. If we did, Atreska would become a battleground and I will die before I see that happen.'

'Can I speak freely, Marshal?' asked Megan.

'Please. Any solution is better than the mess I can see from here.' He sighed.

There was a pall of smoke hanging over the north of the city, scene of the latest unrest. The streets were quiet now, the early afternoon sun sapping the will of even the most fervent protestor. But it was another blot. Another memory among witnesses of Yuran's Conquord troops putting down revolt by force of arms in their capital city. It could not go on.

'It is time to take greater risks in defence of Atreska. Do what Estorea would do. Conscript every refugee. Arm them and train them and take them out to defend their country. Give them a purpose. And in so doing you will remove the impetus to riot. Take the money from the levy to pay for it. The Exchequer will respect the necessity.'

'Really? Exchequer Jhered is a notably difficult man to negotiate with.'

'What do you care, Marshal Yuran?' Megan blushed. 'Forgive me but if you are to be removed, the burden of taxation will no longer be on your shoulders. If the Tsardon succeed in their intent, the result is the same. And if you succeed, the people will be foursquare behind you and the Conquord will not be able to replace you and remain credible. You will be a hero, even more so than now. And your negotiations on the levy will be from a position of great strength.'

Yuran looked at her, feeling as if the sun had broken through the cloud to warm his face. Whether it would solve the Tsardon and rebel problem or not was very much dubious. But it would most certainly solve the civil unrest in his city and relieve the pressure on its inhabitants. Perhaps elsewhere too. Normal life could return. And most crucially, it would buy him time. Precious time.

'Bring me the leader of the city guard and the general of the legion defence. By the Gods of Atreska's glorious past, girl, that is a plan worth pursuing. Why did it not occur to me before?'

'Sometimes we do not see that which is closest to us,' said Megan, trying hard not to be delighted at her success.

'Thank you for having the courage to speak out,' said Yuran. 'We might get out of this mess yet and if we do, I will see you rewarded.

Now go. There is a great deal to be done if we are to save Atreska from all-out civil war.'

The lookouts had seen them coming this time but it was clear the Tsardon had no desire for the element of surprise. This was the third raid. Everyone in Gull's Ford knew what it meant and was ready. The meeting in the basilica had been long and bitter at times but ultimately, the desire to live and work in the place of their choosing outweighed any other consideration.

Praetor Lena Gorsal walked out to where the Tsardon would enter the town and waited. She watched them pass the outer farms and drop their speed to a trot and then to a walk. They had been seen and, more importantly, they would have seen the shrines to Juni, the Atreskan god of fertility. This was the season of heat and harvest and Juni was in her pomp, basking in the glory of her creations across the land.

Gorsal stood under the blue sky and beating sun, the flag of parley idling above her head. Her administrators and magistrates stood with her. All wore the clothes of solastro, none were armed though they blocked the road.

The Tsardon approached, confident enough to keep their swords sheathed. Pennants fluttered from fifty or so spear tips in the force of approaching a hundred and fifty. Because of the heat, they were lightly armoured for riding. Bows were slung unstrung across their backs. Their horses looked fit if tired from a morning's ride.

Their leader dismounted when they had come to within twenty yards, six guards at his shoulders. Gorsal was glad it was him again though he strutted as if lord of all he saw.

'Praetor Gorsal,' he said, bowing minutely.

'Sentor Rensaark,' she acknowledged, recalling his rank which was similar to a centurion.

'You are still here,' he said in heavily accented Estorean. 'I respect that. I presume therefore that you were successful in your pleas to your Marshal. Unless, that is, you desire death.'

'Neither,' said Gorsal and she indicated the parley flag and noticed Rensaark scowl and stiffen. 'Hear me if you have any respect for me.'

Rensaark shrugged for her to continue.

'Our pleas and demands to Marshal Defender Yuran were turned aside. Your statement which we relayed to him was laughed away.

But we are a town with no desire to die for those who refuse to protect us in our homes and offer us vague sanctuary in tented encampments in Haroq City.

'We want to live here in Gull's Ford, in peace. We want to trade with our neighbours, be they Conquord, Atreskan, Karku or Tsardon. A simple life with simple demands. So we have come to a decision.'

She turned and raised her hands towards the settlement, beckoning with her fingers. On every rooftop in Gull's Ford stood a flagpole and at each one, stood a citizen armed with a bow. At her signal, flags were unfurled. Gold and white halves on the diagonal with a golden sun on the white half, a white sun on the gold half.

They were the flags of the old Atreskan monarchy.

She turned back to Rensaark. 'We no longer consider ourselves allied to the Conquord. In this small enclave we are independent, a reformation of the old Atreska. You have seen the shrines that the Order would destroy standing proud in our fields once more. And now you have seen our flags. We are of one mind here and so it is up to you, Sentor of Tsard. Slaughter us or trade with us. Return to how we were or be our enemies forever. What say you?'

Rensaark stared at the flags then back down at Gorsal. He barked a command that made her flinch. His men dismounted and began walking their horses towards her. Rensaark's face broke into a wide smile, showing off broken, rotten teeth.

'Fear is at an end for you and friendship with the Kingdom of Tsard can begin again. By your step, the death of the Conquord begins. This day is history. This day is victory without blood. '

He held out his hands, palms up. Swallowing her revulsion for the man's past deeds, she laid hers upon his. The deal was done. Destiny was set.

Chapter 27

They marched out four hours before dawn and their songs and prayers shattered the peace of the night. General Gesteris was at the head of his army, marching south to meet the new threat. He had begun it, bellowing out an Estorean anthem that had been taken up first by his extraordinarii and passed quickly through the columns of soldiers and cavalry under his command.

The sound sent a shiver though him. Thirty thousand voices lifted in praise of their country, their Conquord.

> *Estorea, Estorea,*
> *The jewel of the world,*
> *How great the march, how great the fight,*
> *How great the Conquord might.*
> *Each one of us is all of us,*
> *Each one of us fights true,*
> *Our enemies will bow their heads,*
> *The Conquord grows anew.*
> *So fill your heart for love of God,*
> *For Advocate, for me*
> *For Estorea as one true heart*
> *Will sing their victory.*

Fires were burning in the Tsardon camps to the east and across the river to the north. The answering chants, when they came into earshot, had set up a cacophony that had bounced across the plain. Gesteris was uplifted. The first skirmishes would be settled by word and song. And he did not underestimate their importance.

Gesteris was surprised but content that the Tsardons had forced the fight. Presumably, it meant that the flanking Conquord forces were progressing well but whatever the reason, he had had to respond to a breathtaking move by his adversary.

There was another army coming up the eastern side of the River Tarit. They had retained scouts all along the southern marches but not at the gorge head since the bridges had come down. Gesteris wasn't sure whether their original destruction had been an elaborate ruse or not but he respected the move nonetheless. What embarrassed him was that he had exhibited neither the wit nor the imagination to execute it himself.

The Tsardon had laid a pontoon bridge sixty miles south, taking it slowly and working only when the armies were facing across the river. They'd moved new forces up from the centre, avoiding Jorganesh and Del Aglios, and staged them in a dark camp on dryer ground where woodland grew up the outer slopes of the gorge.

With two days to redeploy his forces following confirmation of the new threat, Gesteris had met with the command teams of all three armies. Now, on the third morning, he was ready. The Conquord citizens were going to have their fight at last. He was split four ways, with the heaviest weight on his right and under his command. It was a gamble. He had to break the Tsardon army on his side of the Tarit quickly and hope his depleted forces at the fords would hold.

To the right, the problems were significant. Fifteen thousand foot warriors were marching, backed by four thousand archers and, critically, six thousand of the awesome steppe cavalry. Gesteris had drawn off all the cataphracts from the three armies, set them with light infantry and two thirds of the horse archers and placed them at his flanks. In the centre, he was operating two phalanxes and meant to break through around the flanks using hastati swordsmen to force the pace. Principes and triarii under local command would to be used as shock troops to back the front line.

Gesteris didn't like fighting on fronts at right angles to each other and he'd separated his force from those at the fords by a mile. If the enemy broke through, he should have time to bolster the rear and clear a retreat to the camps.

Approaching his marks, and with the morning sun beginning to build heat under a thin layer of cloud, he could survey the Tsardon forces. They advanced in their battle line, making an imposing spectacle. Over a width in excess of a thousand yards, they moved quickly across the plain, flowing around fingers of rock. The crump of their feet sounded the rhythm for their songs.

Cavalry rode wide on both flanks, their order impressive even from a distance of well over a mile. Gesteris's words to Master Kell, who was in command of all cavalry on this battlefront, had been well chosen. These were not recent conscripts. The steppe cavalry hailed from the lands north and east, on the borders with Sirrane and the rocky lands just north of Kark. They were well-trained, funded by rich lords, and a worthy enemy for the Conquord. One day, they would make an ally he would be proud to command.

Gesteris watched units of his horse archers and light infantry in the field ahead, deterring attack on the column by Tsardon forces. Skirmishes had been joined on four occasions already, signalling the intent of both sides to fight hard on the day. So far, the Conquord had come out on top. His horse archers were better skilled and on faster, fresher horses.

He signalled the right wheel and the army began to deploy in exemplary order. In an hour, his formation was complete and his skirmishers were back on the flanks or behind his lines. The Tsardon continued to close, upping their pace, while on the far bank of the river, attack was imminent.

Gesteris saw flags communicating orders and heard the rumble of foot and hoof as his commanders moved to their initial positions. He rode down the front of his line, shouting over the taunts of the advancing enemy. This was not the time for grand speeches. This was the time to be seen and to bring courage to those in the front line who had never experienced battle before.

'Strength!' he called. 'You are the Conquord. Fight hard, win well. Never take a backward step.'

He repeated his words along the line, taking the cheers of his soldiers and the salutes of his cavalry. They were ready. He rode around the right-hand edge of his army and galloped to his viewing position. It was not a great one. The land was flat but at least he was on bedrock, unlike the majority of his troops. That was a problem that would only worsen, though at least the enemy would be suffering the same way

His runners, riders and flagmen were waiting. His standard stood tall.

'I want all information relayed more quickly than you've ever done it before. I want updates from the fords and I want them accurate and comprehensive. Don't let me down.' He nodded at their acknowledgements. 'Good. Be ready.'

A battering noise swept across the plain. The Tsardon on both fronts clashed weapons against shields, voiced their battle cries and moved to the attack. There was going to be no squaring up at short distance. No baiting, no prolonged exchange of arrows and crossbow bolts. There was to be no tactical advance.

Gesteris felt the thrill course through him.

'Phalanx set. Archers ready,' he called, the orders relayed by flag to the field. 'Cavalry to respond at will.'

The Tsardon were marching hard. Cavalry moved at a slow trot either side of them, champing to be set free to gallop. Down to his left, Master Kell deployed a cataphract in front of a detachment of horse archers, ordering them to angle in to the enemy right-hand and hold for the order to charge.

Behind the hastati swords and sarissas, archers stood with arrows in the ground at their feet, bows strung and ready. On came the Tsardon, into arrow range, meaning to hit the Conquord armies hard and fast. Gesteris glanced behind and to his left. It was the same situation across the near ford and, he assumed, at the two out of sight.

Orders rang out. Arrows flew in clouds, hammering into the Tsardon ranks. Gesteris saw men stumble and fall, helmets spring from heads, and arms and legs jerk back under strike. They did not falter. Tsardon crossbow bolts and shafts answered from behind their front lines, rattling into the hastati shields but it was not a concerted barrage, inaccurate on the move.

The Tsardon were within fifty yards when their cavalry charged. Around half of it as far as Gesteris could see. It was an extraordinary sight. Three thousand horses and riders thundering on. Sweat steamed from hides and the mud churned and spat from beneath hooves. They drove hard around the flanks of their infantry, undaunted by the arrows directed against them.

Horse and sword commanders reacted quickly. Kell's cataphracts levelled their lances and moved to counter, armour glinting in the sunlight. Across the flanks, gladius maniples closed their shields into fighting order and waited for the wave to break across them. And in the centre, the dual phalanx crouched and angled their sarissas into a forest of deadly spikes.

Arrows came over their heads in volley after volley. The noise reached an incredible crescendo. Conquord forces bellowed to bolster their courage, yelling in the faces of the enemy, who held a tight line even as they raced in the last few yards. Gesteris heard the sounds of multiple artillery weapons firing behind him.

Cavalry and infantry collided and thunder rolled across the plain. Horses bucked, swung sideways or ploughed ahead. Riders hacked and slashed. On the fringes, more were galloping in. At the centre, his cataphracts drove a wedge, allowing horse archers to fire over their heads. Riders and horses died in their dozens. The sound of screams was terrible, equine louder than human. Blood was a mist in the air, clouding in the intense heat generated by the battle. Kell fed in more units, giving others the chance to withdraw, reform, wheel and come in again. The violence of the conflict was shocking even to a seasoned general like Gesteris and he knew it couldn't be kept up for too long.

The relative contrast in the infantry lines was startling. The initial collision had been signified by a rippling back of the Conquord forces followed by an immediate steadying. In the centre, phalanxes faced each other in a grinding conflict that would barely move all day. But that was not where the day would be won or lost. Out on the infantry flanks, both of which Gesteris could see by standing on his saddle, the fighting was fierce. Javelins and arrows still fired overhead, cutting down soldiers on both sides.

Down on the fighting line, the Conquord held close order against the wider stances of the Tsardon warriors. His soldiers used their tall rectangular shields as battering tools, thumping them forward, opening them up to allow the stab or slash and closing again, giving the target little time to strike back. The Tsardon were more lightly armoured than his. Their metal-banded leather allowed them quicker movement than the scale, breastplate and helmet of the Conquord. Wood and hide shields were effective blockers and their swords, carrying a slight curve, were longer and better for the slash.

Gesteris watched on. 'Keep them holding,' he said. 'Wear them down. Drain them.'

Flags responded to his words. Riders were flying along the back of the lines, carrying messages. He dropped back into his saddle and took a longer look at the fords. Archers in wide arcs were firing on the fords themselves. Onager rounds soared high to crash down into the river. Spouts of water were flung high into the air. Scorpions thudded. And down on the front, on the banks of the river and out of his eye line, his soldiers held a solid line with sarissa, gladius and shield wall deployed in defence.

He let the scene, the energy and the deafening row roll over him. He felt that curious moment of peace he always experienced when battle was joined. Neither side had broken, neither could be said to be winning the conflict. The battle had settled. It was now that the master general could make the moves to win the day. Dimly, he thought he could hear the bark of dogs.

Gazing out, Gesteris saw the cavalry forces begin to separate with the initial clashes done. Here was where it would happen. The steppe cavalry held the morale of the Tsardon in their hands, he was sure of it. And to expose just one flank would be a devastating blow. He kicked the flanks of his horse and, with his extraordinarii behind him, rode in search of Master Kell.

The splendour of the games impressed even Herine Del Aglios. And as Advocate, and Advocate's daughter, she had seen them often enough. The official opening of ten days of games was blessed with beautiful warm sunshine across Estorr. It bathed the principal arena, sending the shadows of columns, arches and flags over the concrete oval track and the sanded inner field.

Herine had ridden in her chariot at the head of the palace cavalcade through the Victory Gates. She had paraded along the processional drive and past the Gardens of the Advocates, where her predecessors' statues were decked with flowers. Crowds lined the route. Above them, painted banners related the story of the rise of the Conquord in images, the names of heroes blazing out from their borders of classic root motif. She had taken their applause and their cheers, seen the lines of 1st legion guard keeping order and waved graciously and gratefully back.

In the gardens as she passed, qualifying for the arena finals was in its fourth day. Stands had been built around temporary courts and crowds had flocked to see the best the Conquord had left to offer display their skill with sword, spear, arrow and javelin. But so many were absent on campaign or, in Jhered's case, on more solitary service.

Elsewhere, runners competed in sprints and endurance qualifying races; horses and riders were going through their paces over jumps and in displays of close control; chariot racers tore around the oval at the north end of the gardens; and teams from all corners of the Conquord tackled the obstacle courses which would be replicated in the arena later in the games.

Everything was in its place. The Advocacy scientists had promised displays unsurpassed, the traditional and the modern. On the last day, the arena floor would be cleared and the scale model of the Tirronean Sea surrounding Kester Isle would be built and flooded. Nothing in Herine's experience came close to the spectacle of the reconstruction of the Siege of Kester Isle, back in the 633rd cycle, just before the fall of Gestern.

The sheer feat of engineering required to produce model miniatures of ships, the castle and artillery never ceased to amaze her, though she had seen it unfold half a dozen times since her childhood.

She climbed the stairs to the grand balcony at the first level of the arena and stepped out on to the deep green carpet that ran around the plush throne at its centre. Chancellor Felice Koroyan was already in her seat, along with the Speakers of Winds, Seas and Earth. And to the right, sat her inner sanctum of sponsors and two of her children; Adranis, her son of seventeen and Tuline, her daughter of fourteen. The latter looked grumpy and no doubt would rather have been anywhere else. Adranis, on the other hand, gazed out at the spectacle in unabashed wonder.

Herine walked forward and sixty thousand citizens roared and chanted her name. She breathed it in, certain now that her decision to hold the games was absolutely the right one. How could anyone doubt that the desire to relive past glories still burned bright in her people. How could it be a waste of time and funds when it brought everyone to such passion and energy.

The chanting continued. Fists punched the air, scarves waved, their multiple colours a dazzling display and a fitting opening. The fervour washed over her and she closed her eyes while the power swept through her. It was worth all the organisational pain just for this. She opened her eyes and raised her hands. The audience quietened and she spoke loud, her voice carrying clear across the bowl, echoing from the precisely carved architecture.

'Citizens of the Conquord of Estorea, welcome to the glory of your world. The glory we shall celebrate in these, the greatest games ever seen!'

Cheers erupted around the arena, the noise staggering and marvellous.

'Everything we have built has been by our own hands and through the blood and toil of our legions, who even now work to make our Conquord ever greater. In these next ten days, you will see wonders from a dozen countries. You will see the finest athletes, riders and warriors compete for the coveted Gilded Leaves of the Conquord. You will see the strongest teams ever assembled vie for the champion's trophy, the Golden Lances of Ocetarus. And you will see acted out for you the greatest victories the Conquord has ever won.

'Watch, my citizens, and know that your work, your sacrifice and your wills are what make our Conquord great. And that through you, we will become greater and greater.

'Let the Games begin!'

Fanfares rang out, all but drowned by the renewed cheering and chanting. Herine stepped back to her chair, waved to all corners and sat down. The noise bounced around the arena, uplifting and energising. With the first athletes taking the arena, the tumult began to subside and Herine felt a touch on her arm. She turned to her left and smiled at Chancellor Koroyan.

'A stirring speech, Herine,' she said. 'And a crowd desperate for entertainment. The drudgery of war has sapped the will of the citizenry and even the Order cannot hold them all up. These games are a master stroke and we will preach the glory of the Omniscient to a revitalised people. I thank you on behalf of us all.'

Herine was taken aback by the admission as well as the gushing enthusiasm. Quite uncharacteristic. There was surely an agenda behind it.

'Well, thank you, Felice,' said Herine. 'I am heartened by your approval.'

'What other response could I give? I can feel the people as if they have found new life. And the glory of the Conquord is the glory of God.'

'Let's hope the games live up to their billing.'

'It makes it all the more surprising then that Exchequer Jhered is not by your side, lending his support as I do.'

Herine kept her expression carefully neutral.

'The affairs of the Gatherers cannot stop even for games such as this. The Games celebrate glory but we are still at war. Taxes have to be collected.'

'And the word of God has to be spread through the Conquord and into our new territory as a matter of urgency. But still we have made the effort to bring a senior delegation to the Games. The citizens need to see us. They need to see the Gatherers too.'

'Are you sure?' asked Herine, piqued. 'Most people would welcome the absence of the levium. They are hardly a force loved throughout the Conquord.'

'And the Order has its opponents—'

'—diminishing daily—'

'—but if we are to be accepted as the force for good we undoubtedly are, then we must be seen to be beneficent. Able to enjoy the pursuits of the ordinary citizen. After all, if we do not understand the people, how can we lead them?'

'The Gatherers do not seek to be spiritual guides,' said Herine shortly. 'Perhaps we should enjoy the fact that we are here and not be concerned with those who are not.'

Koroyan smiled indulgently. She was wearing her robes of state, a deep ochre toga over which was placed a sash of gilt-edged Conquord green. Twined in her hair was a circlet of gold, of woven roots, closed at her forehead with a spray of leaves. It gave her a proud look and powerful appearance in which she revelled.

'It's just that I had heard that when he left Estorr it was in poor humour.'

Herine eyed her. 'Perhaps because he was annoyed his duties would stop him challenging for the Gilded Leaves in swordsmanship.'

'Perhaps so. Though I had heard it was as a result of a discussion with you when he voiced his opposition to the Games. That it was an exclusion rather than a necessity driven by his duties.' Herine said nothing. Koroyan pressed further. 'And such odd travelling companions too, I understand. Harkov of the palace guard and D'Allinnius your chief scientist. The latter would surely be of more use to you here, don't you think?'

'Lord Jhered requested those companions for his trip and I agreed,' said Herine.

'But still . . . an odd delegation to collect a levy. Is there trouble in Caraduk? I understand that was where he was headed.'

'You understand a great deal, Felice. And not all of it should you be concerned with. Have your Speakers in Caraduk reported any problems?'

'They have not.'

'Then there is your answer,' said Herine.

'But Caraduk always concerns me. Information from some of its more remote corners is difficult to come by. Almost as if it is desired that I should not hear what goes on.'

Herine laughed but knew it was unconvincing. 'And what might go on that would worry you in such a loyal state as Caraduk?'

'What indeed.'

The two women's eyes met and held. Below, the quarter finals of the chariot racing had begun to the roars of the crowd. Herine turned to watch, aware that Koroyan had not shifted her gaze.

Chapter 28

848th cycle of God, 1st day of Solasrise
15th year of the true Ascendancy

Master Kell watched the horse archers of the 9th ala, the Rogue Spears of Atreska, drive in behind a break forged by the second cataphract, attached to the 2nd legion. Her legion, the Bear Claws of Estorr. They poured arrows over the steppe cavalry who were in temporary disarray, trying to gather themselves for retreat and reform.

'Signal the first heavy!' she yelled at her flagman. 'Let's force that breach.'

Flags whirled and dipped, three in unison. The cavalry watchers relayed the information to her first cataphract, drawn from the 34th ala, Tundarran Thunder. They gathered and charged, riding hard for the centre of their infantry flank defence. Simultaneously, the Rogue Spear archers wheeled and galloped away, the Claws hard on their heels, escaping being dragged too far into the belly of the steppe cavalry.

The enemy had no respite. The first cataphract slammed into the part-broken line, driving it further back. And in their wake, the archers came in again to down disoriented riders and cripple horses. It was a textbook assault and the Tsardon were weakening.

Back behind the infantry, Gesteris was feeding maniples of principes into the left-hand infantry lines, forcing the Tsardon to retreat. And while the right was tasked to hold and skirmish, the left made inexorable progress. She felt so alive. The sun was past its zenith but still baked down hard, sapping the strength of any whose morale was weakening.

Beneath their heavier armour, she knew the Conquord legions would be suffering but the evidence of their superiority would see them stand all day. Gesteris had been careful to cycle his hastati as best he could and the tactic was beginning to pay off. The phalanxes held easily. Very few casualties on either side. But anxiety was eating slowly into the Tsardon ranks. News of the slow push filtered across their lines. If the flank broke under pressure, the Conquord would be in behind.

'Time to make it happen,' said Kell. She turned her horse and spurred the mare towards the commander of the left flank maniples. 'Keep them backing off,' she ordered her second. 'I'll be back.'

She rode through units of resting cavalry, congratulating and demanding more effort to ensure the day was won. Across the back of the lines she went, with the noise of battle rolling over her and around her. Behind her, the fords were being held comfortably enough though casualties were high on both sides with the narrow battlefronts concentrating the fighting.

'Nunan!' she shouted, voice loud in the din.

She could see the Bear Claws' Master of Sword in the thick of his command. He was standing forward of the triarii, sending in maniples of the principes in response to Gesteris's flagged orders. His green-plumed helmet marked him out though his armour, polished and shining that morning, was covered in mud and blood.

'Nunan!'

He didn't hear her until she was practically on top of him. His sharp-featured face was spattered with filth.

'You're a long way from home.'

This close to the battle they were yelling at each other. A hundred yards away, the two lines had engaged again. The clashing of weapons and shields thudded around her head, a noise she was able to blank out when she rode into battle herself.

'We can win this here and now.' She leant out of her saddle as he approached and lowered her voice a little. 'We can break the steppe left and be in behind them. But I need your help and I need you to back me up with Gesteris.'

'You don't think he'll see it himself?'

'You heard him, he only wanted gentle pressure and wearing down. He's too cautious and it's too hot for your infantry on the front. It could turn the other way. I can make sure it doesn't. You in?'

Nunan scratched some mud from his face. 'Well, I don't want to cook in my armour any longer than I have to.'

Kell smiled. 'Get up behind me, then.'

Nunan hauled himself up on to her horse. 'Keep the pace up,' he ordered his second. 'Don't take a backward step. New orders coming.'

Kell pushed her horse hard across the churned ground, shouting soldiers from her path. Behind the lines, the scene was no less chaotic. Messengers and stretcher parties rode and ran in every direction. Light infantry redeploying from the fords were marching to the right flank. Some of Kell's cavalry was heading in the opposite direction, tired horses being walked, blood streaking coats. There was mud everywhere.

Gesteris saw her coming and cleared a path. He raised his eyebrows when he saw Nunan.

'I trust the battle is going exceptionally well for you both to leave it to speak to me,' he said.

Nunan dismounted, uncomfortable on horseback. Kell stayed aboard.

'We've done as you ordered, General,' said Kell. 'We've got them stepping back and wavering. But we can do more. We can break them. Draw off the right flank reserve and give it to me. Let Nunan commit more principes and even triarii on the far left in the space I make. They can't hold us, they won't have the discipline.'

'Unless they move and shadow us,' said Gesteris. 'And I think you are making a mistake underestimating the steppe cavalry. They won't break and rout.'

'I don't underestimate them, sir, there just won't be enough of them if they are forced to defend their infantry. And it's the infantry that will break.' She bit her lip. Gesteris didn't respond. She continued. 'Who will they commit from their reserve? Look along the line. It's mainly archers and light infantry. They aren't heavy enough to get through the principes' gladius line. And the steppe cannot afford to come left or we will have them on the right instead.'

Kell watched Gesteris scan the battle with minute care. Every muscle in her body tensed in frustration. He stood on his saddle and turned a slow circle, taking in the fords where fighting had all but ceased for the moment it seemed, such was the drop in noise.

'Nunan, what say you?'

'They are uncomfortable with the close form of our line and the skill of our soldiers, General,' said Nunan. 'I agree with Master Kell. We can break them here and now.'

'And if they have placed reserves below the lip of the river bank and behind the rise ahead that we cannot see?'

'Then we are in the correct order to counter them,' said Kell. She blew out her cheeks. 'General, the moment is now. The day is already long and if we do nothing more we risk not forcing the breach and having to fight on tomorrow with no surety of securing the same advantage.'

Gesteris eyed her from beneath his helmet. He appraised her carefully, his grey eyebrows arrowing in.

'I will not risk the army,' said Kell, urging his decision.

'No indeed you will not,' said Gesteris.

He fell silent. Kell stared at him while the din of battle washed over them. Volleys of arrows whistled through the air. Centurions bellowed orders. Soldiers responded, pushing, defending, withdrawing, engaging. Cavalry charged, wheeled, regrouped and charged again. She didn't understand this caution. The battle was tipped in their favour. One small shove . . .

But Gesteris was no doubt adding up every citizen he had and their current positions. If nothing else, he was meticulous. No life was ever wasted. Not even one in eighty thousand. His citizens, conscripts and allied legions loved him for it; his commanders less so.

'They are already strengthening the left,' he said at length. 'And you have them uncertain. Surely a push at the weakened right would bring better result.'

'They are more competent there,' said Kell. 'They are into the rhythm of the battle. All I need is one more cataphract, two units of sword cavalry and one of archers. Trust me.'

Gesteris's eyebrows disappeared beneath the brow of his helmet. 'Trust you? Of course I do, Master Kell. That is not at issue.' He fell silent again, a thought having struck him. A maniple of hastati marched past, withdrawn to rest and tend wounds. 'Keep up your pressure. Perhaps we don't need to adjust our lines here at all. There is stalemate at the near ford, after all, plenty of horses standing around idle. We'll try it your way. Await the reserve and engage at will.'

Kell smiled and nodded but her words were lost in shouts of alarm that swept across the Conquord lines. She snapped her head round. Whining and whistling filled the air.

'What the—'

The sky was studded with stones.

In blank disbelief, Kell watched the artillery rounds fall into the midst of the Conquord legions. Heavy onager rounds smashed down on the rear ranks of the hastati. Thirty or forty of them up to three talents in weight obliterating the soldiers they struck, sending up massive plumes of mud and scattering citizens in all directions. She could see the movement of infantry like waves through the close-ranked maniples and heard sudden uncertainty in the tenor of the noise around her.

She had sympathy for them. Those stones should be too large to launch, their projectors too heavy to be dragged across the sodden ground. The heavy Conquord onagers were defending the camp for exactly that reason, their wagons not up to the task. Somehow, the Tsardons had solved the problem and the effect was enormous. All they had to counter this were scorpions whose ammunition was all but spent.

'Back to the lines!' shouted Gesteris. 'I'll get you your reserve. I want those catapults in pieces.'

He was in a state of some shock. Down at the front, centurions urged a greater push. The legions regrouped and roared their comrades on. Arrows fell more thickly.

'How under God have they done this?' asked Gesteris.

'It doesn't matter,' said Kell, though she was equally desperate to know. She helped Nunan back on to her horse. 'Send that reserve, General, I'll do the rest.'

She saluted him, dragged her horse around and sped off along the back of the lines, hearing the triarii yelling encouragement to those in front of them. Approaching the left flank, she saw the stones arc in again. Their trajectory was high and there was plenty of warning the missiles were coming. But the legions had nowhere to go. Shields were raised; futile defence against the stones that plunged into helpless bodies, driving some into the ground, battering others aside like skittles. This close, the sound of impact was sickening, a bass thud followed by the splintering of shield, armour and bone.

Nunan slid off her horse and ran into the midst of the growing chaos, calling for order, for a steadying of the standards. Trying to make himself seen and heard. Kell did the same, galloping down to the front of the defensive cavalry lines where riders struggled to calm nervous horses. So far, the artillery was trained on the foot soldiers but the screaming noise was enough.

'Hold!' she shouted. 'Keep order, keep going forward. Remember we're still winning the day.'

The scorpions responded, bolts tearing into the Tsardon reserve behind their front line. The Conquord renewed their fight. Out at the battlefront, the cavalry captains were pushing hard, responding with typical courage. She could see the first cataphract deep in combat, flanked on the left by a sword unit and from the rear by archers.

The Tsardon had steadied and were defending their infantry effectively if not comfortably. Far left towards the river, Tsardon reserves were occupying Conquord forces headed by the second cataphract. They were not engaged, the opposing sides vying for tactical position.

She sucked in her cheeks. She needed a point to break through and get at the artillery. Her flagmen were waiting by her.

'Signal the reserve archer and sword units to attack far left. I will lead.'

'Yes, Master Kell.'

Kell put her heels to her horse again and the mare sprang forwards. She rode the animal hard across the muddy ground. She could see the reserve answering her orders and moving from their positions outside of missile range and heading in her direction. She raised an arm and waved it forwards along the course of the river.

Exhilaration flooded through her. Eighty cavalry swept up to her, the sounds of hoofs rattling in her head. Mud flew up around them, spattering her face and armour. She wiped it away from her eyes and urged her mount on, leading the two units into the fight. The captain of the second cataphract saw her coming. She watched him wheel his forty heavily armoured horses and riders, set lances and charge, knowing she would back him.

Kell drew her sword and held it up. The slim blade glinted in the sun. Sweat was running down her face and her heart thudded in her chest. To her left, the Tsardon onagers thudded again. This time she could see them and she cursed and spat. They sat atop what looked like wheelless wagons, their great arms thumping into their stops and sending their deadly missiles high and long, three hundred yards and more.

These were not field weapons, more like siege artillery. Dragged across the marshy plain on heavy sleds then anchored to rock. Another smart move and one that provided a growing problem for the Conquord. The stones fell on the legions. More died, crushed, broken and hurled aside. The legions would not stand forever without seeing a counterattack. Kell was going to provide just that.

'Claws for the Conquord!'

She pointed her sword forwards, spurred her horse to full gallop and crashed into the steppe cavalry, feeling the shock of the impact rattle through her. The cataphract had driven a wedge into the enemy and was looking to wheel and reform. There was a confusion of horse flesh and steel. Kell swung right, her sword biting into the arm of a Tsardon rider. He raised a defence and blocked her next thrust but a lance pierced his shoulder and took him from his horse. Kell spurred on deeper into the melee, her cavalry behind her. The cataphract was withdrawing, leaving her clearer vision. Arrows carved through the sky, falling ahead. Tsardon volleys answered, steppe cavalry came at her.

Kell turned her horse left and struck out right, her sword catching her enemy a glancing blow across his metal-stripped leather helmet. He wobbled in his saddle. She stabbed straight, taking him under the arm, her sword ripping out and carving deep into his horse's shoulder. It reared and threw him. Conquord riders came to her left and right, pushing hard into the enemy. Blood sprayed into the air. One of her riders was driven from his saddle, a spear in his chest. Ahead, the wall of steppe cavalry was deep and dense. Both sides slowed.

'Wheel!' she yelled, not wanting to lose momentum. 'Archers, keep them back.'

She turned her horse sharply, hurrying it away and shouting her order again. The archers had spread in front of her, firing quickly and accurately from the saddle, guiding mounts at the canter with thigh and heel. She nodded her approval, rode through their line with Tsardon shafts falling about her, came about, gathered her citizens to her and charged again.

Herine had just watched a breathless chariot final and had to restrain herself not to jump up and roar the Estorean team on to victory. After all, an Advocate must be even-handed in her approach to her Conquord. But now she stood with the sixty thousand in the crowd to applaud one extraordinary move after another by the 1st legion, the Estorean Legends, cavalry and infantry.

Seamless formation to phalanx, to turtle, to wedge. Shield walls snapped into position as arrows rained down from the platforms all around the arena. Metal-tipped, she was led to believe, but you never could quite tell. It hardly mattered. To see them bounce and snap off the gleaming Conquord green and gold barriers placed against them was utterly thrilling.

Circling the infantry as it advanced in perfect form towards her position, was the cavalry. The cataphract had skewered moving targets following a charge and break that had drummed in her blood. The horse archers shattered clay discs from galloping horses. The sword cavalry clashed in mock battle with Tsardon-garbed forces, driving at them, scattering them and defeating them.

They had leaped from horse to horse, stood on their saddles while their mounts chased across the sand. They had somersaulted over horses, jumped into saddles, balanced horizontally at right angles to their animals' motion and leaned out and down to pluck the smallest gleaming coins from the ground, faces inches from hoofs.

The announcers had been drowned out long ago by cheering citizens and at last the legion was drawn up before her, the dust clearing from the stadium to reveal the standard bearing the rearing white horse and crossed spears of the house of Del Aglios. She bowed to the legion general and the roars of the crowd took up again as the Legends departed the arena. Herine turned to the Chancellor.

'Can we ever doubt the superiority of our armies?' she said. 'No country can stand against such skill.'

'Would that every soldier and rider was so well trained,' said Koroyan.

Herine flapped a hand at her. 'Years of campaigning under my generals and centurions is training enough. What's next to feast upon, I wonder?'

'The hunting archery finals,' said Adranis, consulting the order of the day.

His face was flushed with excitement and his whole body was bunched and leaned forward to the edge of the balcony as if he were about to spring down and join in.

'Oh, wonderful,' said Tuline, rolling her eyes. She was sprawled in her chair, her legs dangling over one arm. 'Grown men crawling through sand and shooting at stuffed animals.'

Herine smiled at them. 'Thank you for being with me,' she said. 'Roberto would be proud of you both.'

'I expect Roberto is having much more fun,' said Tuline. 'At least what he sees isn't made up and fake.'

'You'll let me join the cavalry, won't you, mother?' asked Adranis.

Herine chuckled. 'Of course. Fine young horseman like you? I'll probably give you to Master Kell. She'll make you great.'

Adranis beamed.

Gesteris's words sounded loud in Kell's head. The steppe cavalry were testing her severely. They were excellent horsemen. Quick on the turn and accurate with spear and arrow from the saddle. If anything let them down it was sword work but you had to get close enough to lay a blade on them first.

Kell's units had seen off the regular Tsardon horse quickly and she had thought the break was hers. But the reserve Gesteris had sent to her had been matched by a large detachment of steppe cavalry, perhaps three hundred strong. And all the while, the stones, each as heavy as a man, still fell. The onagers were so far unchallenged and Kell was aware that Gesteris would be fretting as his infantry died without raising a sword against their foe.

Trotting towards the enemy, she looked left and right and saw the spread of her forces. They had built one cataphract from the three and it stretched across her vision. Three deep, they would punch into the steppe horsemen. Behind them the swords would come and over their heads the arrows would fly. But it was a formation forced on her by the enemy.

Facing her, the steppe had broken into units of twenty or so and were weaving in and around each other. Their horses were covered in bright red-trimmed yellow cloth under which light armour was fixed. The riders were dressed in dun-coloured leathers, yellow pennants snapping at the heads of spears, yellow cloth strips from sword pommels and bow tips. All designed to draw the eye and distract. And that wasn't all. Kell could feel it in the air around her. Anxiety brought on by reputation. But the steppe cavalry weren't the only feared riders on this battlefield.

'Cataphracts, remember who you are!' she shouted from her

position just behind them. 'We are the Conquord. We are Estorea. We are the Claws, the Thunder and the Dragons. Never defeated.'

The cavalry came to a canter, closing to within two hundred yards. The flanking lancers moved up to form a shallow crescent. The steppe cavalry paid them no heed. Kell was concerned at this new tactic. They trotted and cantered in their small units, seemingly at play with one another while their opposition came on. She wondered how they would reveal themselves at the charge.

Kell urged her horse up to the cataphract captain. He faced her, his full helm obscuring all but his eyes, his armoured fist tight on his reins.

'Charge at fifty yards. Travel straight. Do not be deflected by them. We are behind you for those that pass you.'

'Yes, Master,' he said, gruff Goslander tones muffled by his visor.

'God protect you.'

'And you. For the Conquord and for me.'

'The Conquord and for me.'

The captain's orders rang across the line, repeated and returned for confirmation. The gap closed. Arrows started to fly from both sides. At seventy yards, and with shafts beginning to find their targets, the pace upped further. Sixty. Fifty.

'Conquord! Tear their flesh.'

Horses spurred to the gallop, the cataphracts surged away, lances coming to ready, gripped in both hands. Riders leaned forwards against the expected impact. What a sight they made. Three hundred driving headlong. Kell called her swords and archers to her and galloped after them.

Through the churning, flying mud and the flanks of the charging cavalry, she saw the steppe cavalry react at last. Every other unit turned and charged, leaving holes in their line. The others scattered, sweeping out to the flanks and further dividing in to threes and fours. Kell shook her head, confused.

The cataphracts collided with the steppe cavalry. Horses sheared left and right at the final stride, lances smashed Tsardon from their saddles, Tsardon blades slashed into horse and rider. But more than half of the Conquord lancers went through unchallenged. At the flanks, the steppe cavalry had already started to turn.

'God-surround-us,' breathed Kell. 'Archers! Flanks. Bring those bastards down.'

The enemy were racing around behind their slower-turning quarries. She should have seen it, she should have seen it. Bows bent, arrows flew. Cataphract cavalry fell, too many and too quickly. Kell galloped into the battle, racing past the fake front and through to the skirmish. In front of her a steppe rider took an arrow in the throat and dropped from his horse. She searched for a target. Arrows whipped around her head. Men fell either side of her.

She looked left. It was chaos. The steppe had broken the Conquord advance into small units and still they had more out on the flanks. She saw them join and charge in. She saw swords glint and arrows in the sky. Behind her, the onagers sang again. She could hear the fretful noise of dogs barking. Hundreds of dogs. She glanced right and saw the mass of them streaming forwards through the Tsardon army like they were chasing the catapult stones.

Hoofbeats, loud. She swung forwards. The Tsardon mace was already on its way. She got her sword in front of her but it was beaten aside and the weapon struck her breastplate. The metal bent inwards, the pain intense and shocking. She was lifted from her saddle. Out of control, she went backwards and down. The last she saw was the rear end of her own horse before the uprushing ground knocked her senseless.

He was just an ordinary citizen but his skill with the bow was exceptional. A potter by trade and a hunter for relaxation. He had struck every target square in the middle as each was moved from behind cover by the wires laid across the arena. Even Tuline had propped her face up on one hand to watch.

As was his right, he was shown to the Advocacy balcony to receive his prize; the gilded leaves of the Conquord, embossed with bow and arrow. Herine slapped Tuline's leg and waved her to a properly seated position as the man came through the curtains, dusty and delighted. He received his prize with an extravagant bow.

'A most impressive display,' said Herine.

'Thank you, my Advocate,' he gushed. 'I never thought I would be standing here before you. So many are more skilled.'

'And most of them are in Tsard,' muttered Tuline.

Herine shot her a dangerous glance. There would be words later. 'Ignore my ignorant daughter.' She smiled. 'Though General Gesteris could use a man as skilled as you to help him.'

The man blushed crimson. 'He needs no help to secure victory for the Conquord,' he said. 'Though if I am called I will be proud to serve you.'

Herine kissed his forehead and the cheers began. 'You are a credit, citizen. Enjoy your moment.'

Nunan stood with his hastati, keeping them strong though the fear was building within them and their confidence draining. Next to him, a youth of no more than eighteen stood shaking, waiting to enter the fight. All day he had been standing and watching while his comrades fought hard, were injured, killed or withdrawn to rest. His time into the front line was soon and he wore his fear like a mask under his helmet. He cowered behind his shield.

And now the stones were falling, the ground was shaking and men were being dashed to fragments behind him. The smell of vomit and piss was mingling with sweat, leather and blood. Nunan could see it was all the boy could do not to run.

'You know me, citizen?' he said. He had borrowed a shield from his triarii and had set it before him against the arrows that fell at random.

'Yes, Master Nunan.'

'Then stand with me and we will fight side by side. Have courage. The cavalry will break the onagers and we will have victory.'

'Yes, sir.'

The noise here was deafening. Nunan had forgotten what it was like and felt the strains of stress in his own muscles too as he waited. In front, three ranks ahead, Conquord shields punched forwards, forcing space to open and allow the gladius thrust. The Tsardon with longer swords and oval shields, blocked and countered. Casualties were still relatively light but blood sluiced around their feet, mixing with mud. The sound of sudden death chilled the heart as it always would.

'Wall!'

The word carried across the lines. Shields flew up to cover the sky. Stones whistled overhead. Nunan held his breath. Beside him, the boy prayed through clenched teeth. The stones hit. Immediately to his right, daylight and devastation. Nunan was rocked on his heels. Men and women screamed. Mud fountained into the air and sprayed sideways. He turned his head away reflexively, feeling wet impacts on his helmet.

He looked back to the boy who had dropped his sword and was staring at his hands. They were covered in gore. His face was drenched in it and those eyes were the eyes of a man ready to break.

'Leave the field,' ordered Nunan. 'Go with my blessing.'

But the boy just stood while the maniple rippled around him and the hideous calls of the crushed wounded laid over the clash of steel on shield.

'Press!' Nunan yelled. 'Strength and order.'

His shouts were taken up by the centurions but more cries were filtering across the field. He heard panic and rumour in them and for the first time in his career, he felt the army waver. The phalanx had been broken.

'Hastati, hold and defend.' He spun and ran out to give orders, praying that Kell would break through. 'Three maniples of principes to the fore, triarii to the phalanx. Don't take a backward step, don't turn away.'

But at the back of the lines he could see soldiers breaking off and moving backwards. The Tsardon were throwing everything at them now. Arrows were thick in the air and the enemy taunts began to ring true. Nunan sprinted for the centre, surrounded by gladius-wielding triarii. He rallied centurions to get faltering citizens back into the fight, to force the legions to stand fast. He moved triarii forward, needing their experience and sheer courage. Fear would sweep through the army and take hearts and wills more surely than any plague.

'We're still winning this,' he called again and again. 'Fight for the Conquord. Fight for me. Fight.'

But the phalanx was in real trouble. The centre had been hit by stone after stone, the front ranks were under pressure from Tsardon who had dropped their spears and were forcing through the forest of sarissa tips with sword and shield. Triarii were sprinting in to bolster its collapsing core while to the right, cavalry were pressing hard to alleviate the infantry pressure.

Nunan looked for the phalanx's commander but he was nowhere to be seen. He caught the collar of a frightened young woman.

'Where's Keita?'

'Gone,' she said, shivering. 'He was hit square on. There's nothing left of him. We're losing this fight, Master Nunan.'

'No, we are not,' snapped Nunan. 'Get back in. Stand with your citizens. We will win.'

He shoved her away, back to the phalanx rear division. The sarissas held high were wobbling, not bolt upright as they should be. Alarm. More stones. More fear. Nunan prayed for fortune. He didn't get it. Forty missiles slammed into the legions once again, ploughing their furrows through the mud and slaughtering and maiming where they travelled. Three more hit the phalanx. Immediately the Tsardon pushed harder, archers poured arrows into the mid and back lines. Nunan heard them rattling over shields.

'Hold!' he bellowed. 'Hold!'

Uncertainty threatened to swamp the legions. The onagers were still firing and the Tsardon were ferocious, sensing victory. He would not taste his first defeat. Not while he had strength in his limbs and breath to shout. Further forward he went, into the thick of the jostling, stinking line. His presence brought people back from the brink, made them believe again. He raised his gladius and led the rally.

The next stones came in, cascading down behind him and covering at least the four maniples either side of him. But the expected impact vibrations and screams didn't come. Instead a curious silence passed briefly through the ranks. Nunan felt liquid splash across his back. He turned briefly. Blood and gore was everywhere. Some were covered head to toe in it. No one had escaped the splatter. They hadn't been stones. They'd been blood sacks.

'God-spare-us,' breathed Nunan. He swung back round. 'Brace, brace, brace! Dogs. Dogs coming in.'

And in the next heartbeat they could all hear them. Snarling, barking and howling. In front of the Conquord, the Tsardon stepped back a pace and through came the dogs. Dozens, hundreds, thousands of hounds. Driven by hunger and crazed by the scent of fresh animal blood. The blood that covered the legions.

The dogs, a powerful hunting breed, boiled over the front ranks that went down under the tide of fang and claw, their shields and gladiuses rendered useless. They burrowed into spaces no Tsardon could go, seeking the blood and the flesh they craved.

Nunan lashed out, slicing one across the back. It yelped and turned to bite him, missing his hand by a whisker. He hacked again and again. Dogs were all around him now, swarming by him and driving deep into the Conquord ranks. The Tsardon roared them on.

'Fight, Conquord, fight.' His shout was taken up by centurions and triarii alike.

Throughout the forward maniples, weapons stabbed down. They slashed and ripped into dog flesh, filling the air with squeals, cries and screeches. But for every dog they downed, another two leaped to bite and tear at every spurt of blood.

Legionaries went down with jaws clamped around their throats, over their faces or deep into arm, leg or side. The blood sacks came down like filthy rain but were now interspersed with stones, both cold and flaming, adding to the chaos. Nunan spun to strike out at an animal and another knocked him from his feet. He dragged his sword in as he fell. The dog bared its teeth and darted in to grab at his back where blood had sprayed over his armour. He arced a cut deep into its flank and it jumped away. He got to his knees. The animal came back at him and he speared it through the chest.

Regaining his feet, he looked about for order. There was little. Blood was slicking the mud. All around him, the hastati lines were fractured and the problem went into the principes behind too. The dogs had caused confusion everywhere. Tsardon arrows flew thick once more and their infantry charged across the short divide.

Nunan yelled men to him, urged them back into the front line and ran in himself. Triarii were about him. Senior soldiers, seeing the danger and cutting swathes through the dogs that still ran around in their hundreds, scattering hastati, too many of whom had turned to run.

'Stand!' he bellowed. 'Stand with me, Conquord.'

The arrow caught him through the shoulder, having come down a steep arc. The impact was as surprising as it was agonising. He felt the point slice through at the joint of his breastplate and shoulder guard. He staggered and clutched at it, his gladius tumbling from his hand as the strength left it. The weight drove him to his knees and men running behind him knocked him further down.

Nunan squeezed his eyes shut against the wave of pain. He felt hands around him, trying to pull him away. When he opened them again all he could see was the blood sluicing from the wound. He shuddered. Surrounding him, the faces were anxious, frightened and uncertain.

'Fight,' he managed. 'Fight. For me.'

He wasn't sure which way they were moving when his world dimmed away.

Gesteris saw it begin to unravel and flagged orders for the triarii to take the front line. He had to get a steadying influence at the crisis point. But the Tsardon artillery had been awfully effective and on the left flank, Kell's cavalry were scattered and fighting small skirmishes against steppe riders perfectly suited to such combat.

Through his magnifier he had seen his finest cataphracts picked apart by the steppe cavalry. He had seen stones tearing great rents in the guts of his infantry while too few enemy died on the sword or the arrow tip. He had seen the phalanx break at its front and in its heart. He had seen the blood sacks drop and the dogs swarming like ants. And he had just seen Nunan fall.

For a moment, there was a hiatus. The battle raged along the front and arrows clouded the sky. But Gesteris was running out of options. Forty more stones hurtled down, smashing everything in their path and, finally, the hastati broke and ran. Through their dying comrades, through the fighting triarii and principes, chased by dogs biting at their heels. It began in the centre of the phalanx and swept out like a wave across the shore. The Tsardon saw it and poured forwards.

'Damn you, no,' he said. 'I will not lose this.' He drew and raised his sword. 'Extraordinarii, with me. Raise the standard.'

He kicked his horse to the gallop and charged at the enemy. Conquord cavalry came from the right to help him. He raced right across the front of the Tsardon, heedless of arrow or sword. His own blade licked out. He took the sword arm from one man, slashed backwards into the shoulder of another and battered the helmet from a third.

He chased them back, fifty extraordinarii and a hundred cavalry with him. He pulled up where the line had already fractured completely and wheeled around hard, meaning to run back the way he had come.

'Fight on,' he shouted at any who could hear him. 'Get them running.'

He began the second charge. He forced his mount into the faces of Tsardon who stumbled back in front of him. The horse reared, its hoofs taking a soldier in the face. Behind him, triarii were following him in, bringing wavering hastati and principes with them. And for one glorious moment, the enemy looked uncertain.

But more and more infantry were chasing round him, determined not to let the pressure off. For all he forged a gap, it was just forty yards in a battle line ten times that length. And everywhere, the Conquord standards were wobbling. His citizens were being cut down like weeds and the surge was unstoppable. Steppe cavalry moved across his vision to the right. They slammed into unprotected maniples trying to keep some semblance of a fighting line together. They didn't stand a chance.

Gesteris wheeled again and began to gallop away from the shattered battlefront. Ahead of him now, all pretence at legion order was gone. Hastati were pouring past his more experienced units. Helpless to halt the tide, they ran too. The rout was headlong. Tsardon mixed with Conquord soldiers, keeping them running or hacking them down. Here and there knots of his cavalry tried to defend their legionaries but the steppe cavalry were approaching in droves from both flanks.

'General!' someone shouted. 'General!'

He looked around. His extraordinarii were around him.

'We have to get to the first ford. We have to turn the reserves round. Break the Tsardon advance.'

He urged his frightened horse to another gallop. He ignored friend and foe alike, hoping against hope to reach the fords while the armies there still held. But there were tens of thousands of men and women swarming across the plain now. The noise was indescribable. The ground resounded to running feet. The air was full of shouts and screams and cries of triumph.

And at the fords, they had watched it coming with complete helplessness. From across the river, the Tsardon had launched an all-out assault, engaging the Conquord with renewed ferocity. Already, Gesteris could see reserve maniples starting to turn and run back towards the camp.

'No, no,' he muttered. 'You have to stand.'

They would not. He had not reached the first ford before the steppe cavalry had bludgeoned into the open flank of the reserve and the few cavalry not committed in defence on the river bank. He watched the army move and ripple like fields of corn in the breeze. Hundreds of heads turning, their focus on their task lost. All the

Tsardon had to do was push a little harder. They executed the move perfectly.

Gesteris let his horse begin to slow. It was hopeless. The army at the first ford unpicked like a poor weave, whole legions turning and running away west. And as quick as brush fire, the rout spread to the second ford and then the third. Hastati led it. Breaking away from the front line, leaving the Tsardon free to run at unprotected, unprepared legionaries and defeating all attempts at formal retreat.

Gesteris saw flags waving. Commanders trying desperately to inject some order but getting nothing whatsoever. And in moments, they too were forced to turn tail and flee in the face of the Tsardon rush that threatened to overwhelm them all.

'General,' shouted an extraordinarii riding by him. 'We must turn now. The day is lost. We can hold them at the camps if we can get there before them.'

He nodded and pushed at his horse, the tears building behind his eyes. How had it been so easy? Where were his forward scouts to tell him?

The noise was awful now and whistled in his ears like wind around rocks. Conquord forces running blindly for the camps. Tsardon warriors striking out with blade and shaft at unprotected backs. Cavalry trying to buy space and being cut down.

At least the onagers were silent.

Gesteris was powerless. It was over five miles to the camps and the steppe cavalry was coming up fast. Conquord losses would be huge. Gesteris did the only thing he could. He spurred his horse and joined the stampede. And the only songs of glory that found his ears were in a foreign tongue.

Chapter 29

848th cycle of God, 1st day of Solasrise
15th year of the true Ascendancy

When Dina Kell regained consciousness, the battle had moved past her. She pushed herself up on to her elbows. She felt completely disoriented. Her helmet had come off and was lying in the mud a few feet away. Through the trampled grass she could see the still mounds of horses and the crumpled tragedy of people, Conquord and Tsardon, littering the ground. There was a concerted roar behind her and a curious, breeze blown silence surrounding her. Nothing moved but mane hair and helmet plume. Distantly, dogs were barking.

She had no idea how long she had lain on the battlefield among the stamping hoofs of cavalry horses, the arrows, the blades and the tumbling of bodies. She supposed she was fortunate to be alive but the overwhelming sense of despair that gripped her obscured even her own physical pain and made a mockery of any notions of luck.

She groped for balance and pushed herself up on to her haunches. The world swam before her eyes. She was aware of a stabbing pain in her chest and that her right arm was hanging at her side. A brief look confirmed the mace blow had staved in her breastplate, no doubt cracking and breaking ribs. She presumed she must have landed on her arm when she hit the ground. It hardly mattered.

Kell fought her mind into focus and looked around her. Figures moved in the heat haze to her left and there was a dark mass away ahead of her. The armies. But they weren't fighting any more. There were none of the sounds she associated with the battlefront. The myriad clash of steel on steel, the rumble of horses, the thud and whistle of artillery. She didn't want to believe it but there could be no doubt what had happened. Her shoulders slumped and she hung her head.

Now she was moving, the pains in her chest and arm intensified. She tried to keep her breathing shallow. She had to move. She was too close to Tsardon positions and a long way from her own people. Behind her, the river flowed on unconcerned at the disaster that had unfolded on its shores and the blood that would mingle with the waters once it had soaked through the ground.

Kell dragged herself painfully to her feet. She really was alone and for that she had to be thankful. She tried not to think about the chaos of eighty thousand citizens running across the mud, trying to get to the relative security of the camps. They were six miles and more from her position. If there had been no organised retreat, the carnage could be terrible, the numbers taken captive enormous.

Damn the Tsardon, their stones and their dogs.

She began to move back towards what had been the battlefront, picking her way between bodies. She veered towards the river, aware of her vulnerability. Alone behind the enemy. Every pace jarred pain into her ribs and though she tried to hurry, the ground was difficult. Her feet slithered in mud and blood and caught in deep hoof imprints. She stumbled repeatedly, gasping each time as if struck. Her vision wouldn't quite settle and she saw mirages of people and dark shapes that resolved into spears of rock or nothing but tricks of her mind.

Blood and bodies. Everywhere. Kell stumbled once too often and fell to her knees. The waste of war was laid out in front of her. Some of them were still moving feebly. Hundreds across her unfocused field of vision, scattered like seeds from the hand of God. Torn cloth fluttered. Weapons glinted in the mud. All was dark stained and stinking. Kell was suddenly very afraid.

She forced herself to look around. There were figures, Tsardon doubtlessly, moving among the dead. Concentrating on picking through the bodies lying across the field; aiding their fellows, hastening the ends of their enemies. Soon she would be seen too and she did not want to die. Not here and not like this.

She slipped down on to her left-hand side, hoping the lie of the land and the confusion of bodies would obscure her progress, and began to grope her way to the river bank. She dared not look back. Beneath her, the mud was slick. Above her, the late afternoon sun was boiling her inside her armour. Sweat mixed with blood and covered her skin. Every movement was torture. She guessed it to be no more than fifty yards to the bank and cover. It took her an hour of desperately slow movement to get there with the thought of a sudden hand on her shoulder picking at her courage with each passing moment.

She crawled through puddles of blood, across the corpses of her comrades and through the innards of horses split with steppe blade lances. By the time she dragged herself over the lip of the bank and slithered painfully down the slope to rest in the cooling water's edge, tears of loss and despair had already soaked her face.

Kell rolled full on to her back and let the water drench her while she wept. She kept a hand tethering her to the bank and stared up at the sky. The sun was below the bank and a cool wind was blowing along the river. Kell's body chilled quickly and she hauled herself out onto the mud in the lee of the bank.

The lip overhung the river above her head. She was safe here for now. Roughly level with the battle line of the day, she was out of sight of the whole field. It was about a mile to the first ford around a bend in the river. A long way from the camps she doubted were still standing. Two thousand miles from Estorr as the bird would fly.

Images of the day played out in her head though she tried to stop them. How arrogant they had been. How certain of their ultimate victory. And how comprehensively they had been out-thought. How many of those who had marched out singing the Conquord anthem now lay under God's perfect blue sky? Friends, lovers and great soldiers. So many would be gone. Hopeless exhaustion swept over her and she closed her eyes. At least the tears stopped.

It was the songs that woke her. Her eyes snapped open onto a starlit night. Confusion gripped her momentarily before her parlous situation forced itself on her mind. They had not been Estorean songs of glory. They had not been sung on a lush green field by the Bear Claws of Estorr. The dream faded beyond her grasp.

The night was warm and humid despite the clear sky. Kell waited until her eyes had adjusted to the dark before she tried to move. She did well to stifle the scream. Her arm and chest had stiffened while she slept and she couldn't move her hands far enough to unbuckle her crushed breastplate. When the sweep of pain had faded she moved again, more slowly this time.

The despair she had felt when she had passed out was gone, replaced by a desire for knowledge. She knew the defeat had been total but she also knew that thousands of her people would be scattered and running away from the battlefield, trying to pick a way home in front of the Tsardon army. Some would reform and organise as best they could. Others would run and hide and be lost forever, victims of their terror. She had to get amongst them, help them, try to find information about the magnitude of the disaster.

Kell slipped and slithered along the river bank as quietly as she could, looking for a place where she could more easily climb the lip. Every move was a sickening jolt to her injuries and even the most shallow climb she could find was a trial. Looking out across the marshy plain towards the camp, the tears, the dread despair and the grief threatened to overwhelm her again.

Tsardon songs of victory rolled across the open space. Their laughter mocked her. Their fires covered the ground, a macabre carpet of flame illuminating cavorting silhouettes. But none was bigger than the blaze that marked the position of the once proud Conquord camps. Home to eighty thousand. Now pyre to how many, she wondered.

She stared at it all until her eyes fixed on the dancing flames. The enemy were all around her. Along the plain in either direction, choking the ground between her and the camp and ahead of her at the fords. She stood little chance of escaping them by attempting a crossing of the plain now. Even less so given her injuries.

But at least when they marched she would have certainty of their positions and direction. And if she could find a horse, she would have more speed than a marching army too. She could afford to wait them out but one way or another, she had to get to Estorr. To Atreska or Gosland even. It was the duty of all Conquord citizens from the routed army.

Someone had to tell them what was coming.

Kovan Vasselis found Mirron walking alone in the orchard. The day was peaceful with the sound of gulls echoing distantly up the cliff sides from the bay. It was bright and the sea breeze kept the temperature bearable. She was dressed in that simple blue tunic dress that seemed to enhance her beauty so effortlessly and Kovan felt overdressed in the formal toga his father made him wear when they visited Westfallen. It was slashed with Conquord green and Vasselis blue. His gladius in its gold weave sheath hung from the leather belt at his waist.

She was sitting with her back to a tree and gazing into its sick-looking branches while her hands were planted firmly in the grass. He noticed the green stems had grown around her fingers as if in response to her presence.

'I didn't realise that happened,' he said, thankful of a way to open the conversation.

He found his mouth dry and his stomach full of nerves. Silly really. She was three years his junior but she had always had the same effect on him. Only latterly had he fully realised what that meant and he was determined to win her despite the competition. She started and looked round at him sharply, her face melting into a smile as she recognised him.

'Sorry, I didn't mean to startle you,' he said, standing a respectful distance from her.

'It's all right,' she said, sounding soft and musical. 'I was miles away, lost in the tree. I'm trying to find out why it's dying. What did you say?'

Kovan pointed to her hands. 'The grass. I didn't realise it just grew like that around you.'

Mirron looked down and nodded. 'We're getting closer to every-thing that grows,' she said. 'I love it that the plants respond to me like this. Like I spread health wherever I go.'

She spoke quite without arrogance and her voice was full of wonder and joy. Kovan smiled and moved closer.

'It's amazing what you can do,' he said. 'Is it all so natural now?'

'No,' she said. 'Any Works take concentration and energy like always. But Father Kessian says our latent energy is what does things like make the grass grow if we rest our hands on it for any length of time. It's the same energy that helps us renew ourselves and takes the wrinkles away.'

'Do you mind if I sit by you?'

'Of course not.' She patted the ground. 'Plenty of grass to spare.'

That close to her, he was almost overwhelmed. He could hear her breathing, see the turn of her mouth and smell the freshness of her scent and clothes. He was desperate to touch her and terrified at the prospect. She might recoil, after all, and he didn't think he could stand that. He kept his hands in his lap

'So what's wrong with the tree, then?' he asked.

There were curled dead brown leaves and twigs at the end of each branch and the bark was flaking and split.

'I don't know yet.'

'Oh.' He paused. 'So why are your hands on the ground?'

'Because I'm starting with the roots. Seeing if they're diseased.'

Kovan nodded. 'I see.'

A sudden panic gripped him. His mind had blanked and for the moment, he couldn't think of anything to say. He felt the silence stretch out and become heavier with every passing moment and all he could think to do was nod and say, 'I see' again. His relief when Mirron spoke was written on his face he was sure.

'I was about to start on the trunk when you came along. I think it might be rotten inside though I don't know why.' She stopped and turned a smile on him that tipped his heart on its head. 'That's my excuse for being here. What's yours?'

'I.' Kovan stalled. His face felt terribly hot. 'I just. Well I just wanted to be sure you were all right here on your own.'

'Why wouldn't I be?'

'Oh, no reason. But, you know, what with all that went on with the investigation . . .' He trailed off, knowing he wasn't being at all convincing.

'Kovan, that was ages ago. Well, twenty days and more. But thank you. It's always good to know I have a protector.'

'Always,' he said.

Her expression sobered. 'Can I ask you something?'

'Of course,' he said and a thousand possibilities clamoured in his head. Her words didn't match any of them.

'We were talking and—'

'We?' he asked quickly.

'Gorian and me.'

'Oh.' His heart sank.

'Has your father said anything to you about what might happen to us?' She looked across at him, so vulnerable and afraid for a moment. 'We don't want to leave here. Will we have to?'

'God-surround-us but I hope not,' he said. The thought of her in Estorr so far away was a pain in his chest that would not go away.

'You know what Exchequer Jhered said to my father though, don't you?'

She nodded and stared at the ground. 'Father Kessian told us. But we thought your father would be able to make them see it wasn't necessary. That if they wanted to watch us they could do it here.'

'It isn't that simple,' he said, echoing his father's words. 'Nothing in the Conquord is ever that simple. And it isn't just to watch you, remember, it's to protect you as well. The Order will hate you.'

'But why? We haven't done anything. And we aren't ever going to.'

Kovan shrugged. 'They won't see it like that.' He tried to smile but it wouldn't come. Gripping his courage tightly he placed a hand over hers and his heart sang when she did not try to move them. 'You've never seen the Order except Elsa Gueran, have you?'

She shook her head.

'Most of them aren't like her. They don't understand that it's God's will that you were born to be what you are. And they seek to destroy anything they don't understand.' Kovan squeezed her hands. He knew he'd scared her but he was happy. He was going to be able to say the words he had planned to say when he walked up here. Words that he was certain would win her heart. 'But I won't let anyone hurt you. I will always be there to protect you. Always.'

She beamed at him and moved her hands to hold his. He felt a thrill rush through him.

'Thank you, Kovan.' She got up and he with her. 'Now I really should work out this tree or Father Kessian will be annoyed with me.'

'How is he?' asked Kovan. 'Really, I mean.'

'He's old,' said Mirron and she swallowed. 'And he gets ill all the time. And though he tries to hide it, I think he struggles to breathe. But he won't let Ossacer examine him. One day soon he won't be there to guide us. I don't know how we're going to cope with that.'

'I'm sorry,' he said. 'It'll be hard for us all but you the most.'

She nodded and turned to face the tree. 'Shouldn't waste any more time.'

She placed her hands on the cracked bark and Kovan saw her jolt violently. She gasped and gripped the trunk tightly. Her eyes closed and she leaned her forehead against it, a low, pained moan escaping her lips.

'Mirron, are you all right?'

She didn't respond. She was shuddering and a line of dribble ran down her chin. Her teeth were grinding together. Kovan took a pace towards her and stopped, staring at her hands. The tips of her fingers were discoloured grey-brown like the bark. And as he watched, the colour moved up her fingers, rippling her skin. Veins in the backs of her hands swelled and pulsed, green mixed with the sick grey and brown.

Mirron cried out, an anguished squeal. She was trying to speak but was incoherent. Kovan didn't know what to do. He was transfixed by her hands which appeared cracked and split now as if extensions of the bark itself. He wanted to drag her away but wasn't sure if it would do more harm than good. And he wanted to shout at the tree that it was killing her while she tried to heal it.

'Mirron, pull away,' he said. 'Pull away.'

He moved closer and reached out a hand. He touched her shoulder. She jerked, her hands sprang from the tree and she fell into his arms. He clutched her gratefully and they sank to the floor together. She was breathing hard and he could feel her hands grasping his back and toga. Her heart thumped against him, the pulse rapid with her fear.

'It's all right,' he said, stroking her sweat-sodden hair. 'It's all right. I've got you.'

He glanced back at the tree. Where her hands had gripped the trunk, the bark was gone and he could see the shape of her hands as if she'd dipped them in paint and printed them on. And where her feet had been, the grass was long, some of it wilting and brown.

'What happened?' he asked. 'What happened?'

Mirron pulled back from him. Her body was shaking. She stared down at her hands as if they'd betrayed her. Nothing of the bark colour remained though the skin was wrinkled and dry. Aged.

'Mirron?'

She turned scared eyes to him and tears were starting to run down her face.

'Get Father Kessian,' she said. 'Get the Ascendants. Please hurry.'

Kovan laid her on the ground in the shade of another, healthier tree and ran for Westfallen, shouting all the way.

Chapter 30

848th cycle of God, 2nd day of Solasrise
15th year of the true Ascendancy

It was night and Kovan was still shaking. He'd tried to sleep a little that afternoon but the shock had settled on him and all he could see in his dreams was Mirron transformed by bark. Sometimes it was just her hands but in others she had leaves growing from her body and her face was sick wood.

The only thing he could do was talk about it but that seemed futile too. He'd been comforted by his mother and then accompanied by his father to the villa where Father Kessian and the Echelon had spoken with him at some length, trying to understand what had happened. At first they didn't believe him, thought it some adolescent fantasy. But when Mirron had managed to speak, they had all begun to panic.

Much of it had passed Kovan by in a haze but he had seen them scouring their books and breaking into hot debate and argument. They asked him over and over to make sure he hadn't left out any detail and he'd even had to sit by while an artist sketched his words.

Finally, they'd finished with him though it didn't seem to have solved anything. Mirron wasn't able to explain herself. She remained confused, apparently. Kovan had refused to leave the villa until Father Kessian said she was all right. And so it was late when the old man came to the library where Kovan was trying to distract himself with books. He rushed to his feet the moment the door opened.

Kessian shuffled in, leaning heavily on his two sticks and looking exhausted. He had a sickly pallor from a chest infection he was unable to shake off and his hands quivered as he tried to grip the sticks. Genna Kessian walked in behind him. Her concern was for her husband, not Kovan.

'It was good of you to wait,' said Kessian, his voice quiet and full of phlegm. 'No need to get up.'

'I couldn't leave,' he said. 'How is she? Is she all right?'

'She's fine as far as we know,' said Kessian. 'Neither Ossacer nor Genna can find anything wrong with her.'

'Has she said more about what she felt, what happened?'

'This and that,' said Kessian. 'She's confused. Though it does seem certain that your touch halted whatever was going on. Now, whether that ends up being the right thing to have done or not, we don't know yet because we don't know if Mirron was genuinely in danger or not.'

'But she was in pain. I heard her,' said Kovan, shivering. 'I will always be able to hear that.'

Kessian smiled. 'I know, Kovan, and we were very lucky that you chose to go looking for her today. However, if there is one thing that our Ascendants have learned, it is that pain in their work is not always a danger sign. Sometimes it is shock as the body reacts and then adapts to something new. And perhaps that is what happened today. Only time will tell and Mirron can explain it all to us.'

'So have I done her more harm by touching her and stopping it happening?'

'I very much doubt it,' said Kessian. 'Now go back home and get some sleep. And remember this. You acted out of pure honour because you heard Mirron was in pain. And she is grateful to you. We all are. And you were there to come and get help. Most importantly, it meant Mirron was not alone when she went through this new experience, and there is no price you can put on that.'

Kovan smiled, comforted and was suddenly struck by how very tired he was. He felt small and fragile, not tall, strong and seventeen at all.

'Thank you, Father Kessian.'

'Come back and see Mirron tomorrow,' said Genna. 'I'm sure she'll want to see you.'

Kovan said his good nights, walked out of the library and headed across the colonnaded gardens. They were beautifully lit tonight, illuminating the fountains and flowers. Small lanterns at ground level highlighted the paths.

'Running off home now, are you?' came a voice from the gloom.

Kovan stopped and turned towards the sound. He could see a shape beyond the lights that was not part of the gardens.

'It's late, Gorian,' he said. 'Time I was in bed. And way past time little boys were asleep.'

Gorian walked into the light and onto the path in front of him.

'Couldn't leave her alone, could you?' he said, sauntering towards Kovan, his sandals whispering on the stone.

'What?' Kovan stared back. Gorian was as tall as him and would be a stronger man in a couple of years. But not yet.

'Do you think she went up there so you could be alone with her?' Gorian walked up to within a pace. 'She needs space and peace to understand herself and her work. We all do. We understood and respected that. Why didn't you? You just interfered.'

'She went through something none of you have experienced,' said Kovan. 'Father Kessian says it was lucky I was there.'

'Lucky?' scoffed Gorian. 'When you're in Westfallen we're lucky if you *aren't* hanging around like a cloud of dung flies. And what could you really do to help? You are not part of the Ascendancy. Why don't you just leave her alone? She went up the hill to the orchard to get away from you, don't you get it?'

Kovan did not blink. He knew it unnerved Gorian. It was a duellist's tactic. 'She could have asked me to leave. She did not. Perhaps she was trying to avoid you.'

That stung him, took the words from him. 'She doesn't need your interference. None of us do.'

'Then who do you think will protect the Ascendancy when my father is gone?' Kovan sneered at him. 'I will hold all of your futures.'

Gorian laughed. 'No you won't. God-look-upon-us, you have no idea, do you? And you're supposed to be the older, clever one. Don't you see, when Exchequer Jhered reports, we will be called to Estorr to see the Advocate. And while we're living in the palace, continuing our learning under the protection of the Advocacy itself, where will you be? Lying dead in some Tsardon field probably, having had to go to war to prove yourself a worthy Marshal Defender.'

Kovan couldn't find the words and Gorian ploughed on.

'Forget her,' he said. 'You can never have her. That is for others.' His smile was full of malice. 'That is for me, should I so choose.'

'She will make that choice,' said Kovan. 'And your arrogance will prove your undoing. She will care nothing for your tricks because she can perform them all herself. I offer her so much more.'

Gorian shook his head. 'I've told you before, it won't happen that way. You know something, Vasselis? There will come a time when I will be able to kill you with a touch or a whim of the elements under my control. Your fancy sword play won't help you then, will it?'

'Are you threatening me, Gorian?'

'What does it sound like?' It was Gorian's turn to sneer. 'In the end, your influence will stop at the borders of Caraduk whereas mine will reach to the heart of the Conquord.' He paused and his voice softened. 'Let it go, before it gets you hurt. There are people in this town I care about. Become the good Marshal Defender you are destined to be and look after them. Then perhaps we can be friends.'

Kovan was genuinely surprised by what he had heard. He watched Gorian for new signs of mockery but there were none. 'Only life isn't that simple, is it? And one thing you'll learn is that a Vasselis always shapes his own destiny. No one lays it down for him.'

'Then perhaps we won't be friends,' said Gorian.

Kovan shrugged and walked past him. 'I can live with that.'

Mirron awoke to a changed world. It was a while before she could put her finger on it. She knew she felt different when she went to sleep the evening before. Her fear had been replaced by an unsettling calm and she had slept undisturbed until the sun pouring through her open shutters brought her round.

She lay with her eyes open, staring at the ceiling which was reflecting sunlight off a pond outside her bedroom window. She could hear the sound of fountains and sense the heat of the day rising quickly. In the sky, she could feel the thrill of wind through the feathers of the birds that swooped over the ripening crops or gathered on the dockside.

Westfallen was busy, the market open and thriving. Vitality pulsed, though here and there the grey stain on her mind signified sickness of mind or darkness of mood. Right outside her window, the gardens grew strongly, their roots working down, swelling and building. The grand old beech tree in the far corner, though, that was dying. A disease was in its trunk, killing it from the inside while outside, a few curled leaves were the only visible evidence. It was exactly like the tree in the orchard yesterday—

Mirron shook her head violently, her heart pounding. She was hot and the fear was back. She tried to focus on the dancing reflections on her ceiling but she couldn't keep the outside from her head. Every time her mind slipped just a fraction, she felt or sensed – she wasn't sure which – the life beyond her window. She knew the strength and direction of the wind, she knew the state of the tide in the bay.

'Calm down, calm down,' she said to herself. 'It'll go away.'

She concentrated on her own breathing and pulse, using the relaxation exercises Hesther had shown them all in the early days before they emerged and the world was still closed to them. But all that happened was that her body spoke more loudly to her than it ever had before. She could feel the blood in every vein and artery, the movement of her bowels and the air in her lungs. And there was a crackling that she wasn't sure if she could hear or not. If she could hear it, it sounded like the growth of roots through the earth.

It didn't go away. She did manage to quieten her heart but the relaxation brought only stronger feelings across her, all vying for her attention. She couldn't shut it out. She felt the edges of panic on her skin. Her hands gripped the sheet below her and tightened into fists. The tree was suffering, the shrubs by it were healthy and reaching for the sun above and the water below. In the marketplace, not far from the villa, the crush of life threatened to overwhelm her completely.

'Mother!' she shouted, her voice cracking a little. 'Mother!' More of a wail this time though she hadn't meant it.

She didn't know if anyone would hear her but she didn't think she wanted to get out of bed to find out. She wasn't sure her legs would carry her despite the fact she knew with absolute certainty that there was nothing physically wrong with her.

'M—'

There were sandalled footsteps on the marble, getting louder. Mirron dragged in a huge breath and sighed it out, feeling the air energising her body. And she heard, if that was what it was, the roar in her lungs. The door opened and Gwythen Terol stood there. Her face was full of concern.

'What is it, darling? Are you all right?' She came into the bedroom and moved across the wooden floor onto the rugs by the bed. She sat on its edge and put a hand on Mirron's brow. 'You're hot, young lady. And a little flushed.' She frowned. 'Are you sickening?'

Mirron shook her head. 'I can't shut it out, Mother,' she said. 'It's in my head and it won't go away.'

'What do you mean?' Gwythen's frown deepened.

Mirron wasn't sure how to make her understand. Her mother's concern was in the heat of her body, the heightening of her pulse and the focusing of the energy trails that ran through her. She watched the trails for a moment, her mind automatically seeing them and comprehending them. Those she could shut away with a blink of the eye.

'The world is speaking to me,' she said, fighting for the right words. 'It's just there all around me and I can't make it stop.'

Gwythen got up. 'Hang on, Mirron, let me get Father Kessian. He needs to hear this.'

'Don't leave me,' said Mirron, tears behind her eyes.

'Shh shh. It's just for a moment. He's not far.'

Mirron watched her mother go. And when the door closed, the world shouted for her attention. She was helpless to stop her mind seeking out the roots of every feeling. She wasn't actually hearing it all, but the sensations expressed themselves to her as sounds. It was the only way she could make sense of them.

With every passing moment, it got louder. Insects flashed by, revealing themselves by a whine in her head. Their energy burned quickly, dying even as they sought life, such was the shortness of their span on the earth. And at the other end of the spectrum, the ponderous sensations of deep-rooted plants and trees.

'Leave me alone,' she said, her voice little more than a whimper. 'Please.'

But it just got worse. There was a low rumble that seemed to come from beneath her, the very movement of the earth. Crackling and snapping from all around her, the growth and death of leaf, bloom and root. Scratching and creeping, animals large and small in the ground below her, the air above and the gardens outside. And the hum, growing and growing, of the citizens of Westfallen.

By the time Father Kessian walked in, slowly and painfully, her mind was so crowded she could barely focus on him. His voice calmed her a little and she found she could fix on his face, its lines and wrinkles, its care and love. She burst into tears.

'Oh, my child, don't cry,' he said.

'Please make it stop,' she said.

He was helped to sit by her and he, like her mother had, put a hand to her brow. His reaction told her he could feel the heat surging from her.

'Try and tell me how you feel,' said Kessian. 'Is it like you felt yesterday with the tree and the bark?'

Mirron nodded, feeling a little relief. Like always, the Father could make them stop, think and see.

'When I touched the tree it spoke to me so strongly,' she said. 'And now everything speaks to me.'

'And what did you do with the tree? Try and think about that.'

'I don't know . . . I understood why it was sick and I tried to fix it. But it was more than that. I felt like I was part of it.' She stopped. 'I joined with it, became one with it just for a time. Until Kovan broke the contact.'

'And could you still feel it speaking to you after that?'

'So loud it hurt.'

'And could you shut it out?'

'I don't remember. It went when I was taken from the orchard.'

'Well that makes sense,' said Kessian. 'You were too far away to feel it.'

'But why can I feel people in the marketplace now?'

Kessian's eyes widened. 'Are you sure?'

Mirron nodded and the noise got louder again. Much louder. 'I don't need to see the energy paths to know they are there. And I don't need to see the paths to know the beech in the garden is dying. Cut into the trunk if you don't believe me.'

'Oh, we believe you, Mirron. Nothing you can sense should be too farfetched for us to believe. And can you concentrate on me? What do you see?'

'I don't want to,' she said, but she found her mind reaching out anyway, unbidden, seeking him.

'Because you don't want to feel a body that is dying?'

She nodded and the state of the Father was revealed to her. She could see the grey and dark in his lifelines and the paucity of the energy available to him. She tried to shut it out. Before long, she would be able to guess how long he had left and she didn't want to know that. But she couldn't keep out the feelings that flooded her. They were the feelings of life ebbing fast and the sounds that represented them were tortured and wrenching, the sounds of a struggle that could not be won.

'I don't want to have to feel it,' she said, beginning to cry again. 'Help me make it stop.'

'My child you are connecting to the world around you at a new level,' said Kessian gently. 'You can sense everything from the elements that make up all of us to those that make up this earth, be they man, animal or flower.'

'Why?' she wailed. 'I don't want this. It's too loud.'

'You will learn to control it like you did the visions of the energy paths. It is part of your development, though one that is not written about. Try and welcome it, try and understand it.'

'I can't!' she shouted.

The sensations poured over her like a wave on the beach. Louder than ever before, every individual thing clamouring for her attention. The rumble in the earth set her teeth on edge and the screaming of the wind in the bay rattled in her head. The energy of the marketplace was a roar now and she couldn't pick out any of the individual elements that had spoken to her when she awoke. She gasped at the power of it all and squeezed her eyes shut. It hurt. It hurt her so badly she thought it would shake her apart.

'Help me,' she whimpered, staring past Kessian at her mother. 'Help me.'

'Try and keep calm,' said Kessian.

Mirron's body convulsed.

'Help me!' she screamed.

The tide washed her away from them.

Chapter 31

848th cycle of God, 3rd day of Solasrise
15th year of the true Ascendancy

The Tsardon army came to order and marched from the fords at
Scintarit two days after their victory. It was a huge movement of
men, horses, farm animals and wagons broken into three columns to
ease congestion on the roads as well as their supply chain.

Master Kell had watched them whenever she could. They had
scoured the battlefield, taking weapons, armour and mementos from
the dead. Their own fallen they had laid in lines and performed
religious rites before burning them on pyres. The Conquord dead had
been left to the heat, the rodents and the carrion crows. Already the
stench was growing and the air hummed with clouds of insects.

She had watched columns of prisoners marched towards the fords
and away. Thousands of them heading to slavery, execution or for
ransom. Even from a distance, she had been able to see the bowed-
head shambling of the vanquished. But she could not be concerned
with them. Not yet anyway.

Kell kept herself concentrated on her own survival. She had plenty
of water but her hunger was growing acute. Her chest was a problem.
It would be painful to ride or fight. It was a mass of purple and black
bruises, swollen round the damaged and probably broken ribs over
her heart. Her right arm, though, was not broken. Torn and bruised
certainly but it would recover unaided and that was a blessing.

It was not long after dawn on that second day that the last of the
regular army left Scintarit, marching away while the air was still
relatively cool. Kell waited until the middle of the morning just to be
sure. People still moved in the thickening heat haze. These were not
soldiers but the first scavengers on the search for scraps. Nothing to
be concerned about.

Her time was now. The battlefield would fill with people from settlements located at every point of the compass. Despite the sweep of the army, there were always pieces to be found if you had the stomach to scatter the rats and search the pockets of putrefying corpses. Sightless eyes would stare at you, daring you to go on. And broken limbs would slip suddenly, mimicking brief life. Kell needed to be clear of it before the frenzy began.

She stood up and stretched in the sunlight for the first time in what seemed like an age. Her body was stiff and her gut achingly empty. She used river water to wash away the mud she had plastered on her armour to dull its shine, scrubbing hard at the Conquord crest until it gleamed afresh. Under cover of the moving army, she'd battered the breastplate a little flatter, relieving the pressure on her ribs.

Kell clambered up the bank and began to walk across the plain. The stripping of bodies had been comprehensive but she kept her eye open for anything she could use. She bent to rotting corpses often and kept her cloak about her despite the heat in an attempt to look to the casual observer like just another scavenger.

She found nothing to augment her meagre kit. Her helmet and sword were lost on the field, leaving her with only her twin daggers. They had been a gift from Gesteris in recognition of acts of bravery early in the campaign. With heavily carved hilts and script on the blades they were ornamental pieces, though she kept their edges sharp.

Her journey across the stained mud showed her the tragic tableau of the rout. So many men and women with wounds in their backs, cut down as they ran. Bodies were densest close to the battle lines and spread in a wide arc away from it. She could see where people had run towards the fords looking for the safety of another army, only to trigger it to rout as well. And she followed the thinning line of bodies that led towards the ashes of the camps. Most had run there seeking sanctuary or a rallying point. The Tsardon had simply overrun them.

She wanted to hurry but knew it would draw attention to her. So she made her walk a deliberate one, muttering prayers over all those she passed. She was stunned at the violence at her feet. She had experienced defeat in her time in the legion cavalry, most notably in her first year in the wars of Gosland before she joined the Bear Claws. But nothing like this. Then, retreat had been the granted option. This had been a slaughter of all those not fast enough to outrun the Tsardon blades and arrows.

It was midday by the time she reached the ruins of the Conquord encampments. She had been barely able to take her eyes from them ever since they had resolved themselves from the haze. Smoke still spiralled into the air from fires that would smoulder for days. Parts of the central camp palisade still stood defiant, jutting blackened from the ground. But inside, the destruction was complete. She crunched across the ashes of the principal gate and stopped. Not an inch of tent canvas remained. All that had not been taken had been burned. Scattered across the open space, she saw the bones and skulls of those who would never feel the embrace of God and she wondered who they were.

From her right she heard the whinny of a horse. It was behind a line of standing timbers. She walked carefully towards it, putting her back to the wood and edging her head around to see. It was her first piece of fortune since she had awoken on the battlefield. A Tsardon rider, a messenger by his lightweight clothes, was relieving himself against the palisade. He was partially concealed by his horse which stood as a disinterested sentinel, turning its head to look at her.

Kell slid a dagger into her left hand. It felt uncomfortable and clumsy there but it would have to do until her right was healed. She paced across the mud, praying to tread on quiet ground and hiding her weapon and armour beneath her cloak. She almost made it too but the man's bladder was empty and he turned and saw her when she was still six paces from him.

He said something and waved his hand impatiently back towards the scavengers. He showed no fear of her, seeing on her face the filth of the plain and in her stance the hunch of the poor. Kell smiled at him and continued to walk carefully towards him, her cloak edges held together by her sore right hand. He frowned and spoke again, more harshly this time, pointing back over her head and reaching one hand to the hilt of his sword.

Kell knew it would hurt her but it was her one chance. She sprang at him, letting her cloak fall open. His eyes widened at sight of her armour. Her dagger swept up and he wasn't fast enough to dodge it. It struck him below the ribs and she drove it in hard and vertical, dragging him on with her right arm around his neck. They both gasped. She at the pain flooding her chest and he at the shock of the blade slicing through his body.

He tried to fend her off but did not have the strength. The dagger point pierced his heart. He jerked and fell limp. She let him slump to the ground. Blood had poured down her hand and covered her right leg. She knelt to clean what she could on his clothes before unbuckling his sword belt and sorting through his pockets. She found flint and steel and a few coins.

She stood and spat on his body, steadying herself against the wave of faintness that swept through her head.

'You are just the first.'

She strapped on his sword, discarding her own scabbard. His was a slightly curved blade, typical of the Tsardon. She drew it with her left hand and made a couple of gentle sweeps, feeling its balance and weight. It wasn't bad but was no match for her cavalry sword. Some Tsardon bastard would be carrying hers now. She hoped he died on it.

Kell glanced around her. She hadn't been seen. There was no one near. The horse had backed away to the extent of its tether at the scent of blood. She walked slowly towards the gelding, a hand outstretched to smooth its bold black cheek.

'Shh. It's all right. All right. You have a better master now.'

The animal responded to her gentle tones, nuzzling at her shoulder. She unhitched the tether and threw the reins back over his head, moving down his flanks still speaking softly. The horse nickered and tossed his head. She opened the saddle bags and all but cried in relief. Trail rations. Bread and dried meat. And animal skins brimful with water. She knew she shouldn't stay here but for the moment didn't care. And when she rode away from Scintarit, it was with the sweet taste of food still on her tongue.

The horse was fresh and strong, bred on the steppes. It was a responsive animal, sure of foot and comfortable with the terrain. A joy to ride. Kell rode west at speed, pausing to walk only when the pain in her chest became too much to bear. She had begun her ride a good half day behind the last of the Tsardon infantry but expected to come across them camped before nightfall.

The sun had lost its power and was setting in a blaze of red behind Kell when she crested a rise a couple of miles from the Conquord-built road along which the Tsardon now marched. The futility of her situation was made plain. Not for nothing had the Conquord legions built the highways where they had and opened battlefronts in the three places they had chosen.

A vast cloud of dust covered the sky ahead of her and beneath it, the Tsardon army was at rest. Hundreds of fires dotted the ground which was carpeted dark with men. She guessed the rear of the camp was something approaching five miles from her but she could see the spread of it disappearing outside of her vision left, right and ahead.

There was no getting round them in time to reach Atreska before them. They would sweep through the Conquord supply lines and along its roads to the border knowing that only those who had got away in front of them could carry warning of their coming. To the south, any escapee risked the swamps that bordered the Toursan Lakelands and the cannibals rumoured to live there. And to the north, the Khur's Teeth ranged north and then east, to merge with the Halorians. It was no place to march an army with only the treacherous ice-covered Ruin's Pass as a crossing.

For Kell, the pass would have to do. She had no choice but to try and make it to Gosland and travel south from there. She kicked at her horse and set off north, stopping only when dark covered the land and tiredness overtook them both.

Kell walked and rode for five days, eking out her rations as best she could. She was unwilling to enter any of the settlements she saw and instead kept off trails and the few roads she encountered, preferring the solitude of the wilds. Travel was relatively easy and every day, more strength returned to her arm and the bruising on her ribs yellowed and faded. There was still a sharp pain every time she drew breath. No doubt a cracked rib rested on her lung. This long after the injury the pain to reset it might not be worth enduring.

On the sixth day she was riding at an easy trot through the gentle sloping hills that led up to the Tarit Plain. Another day of unbroken sunshine beat down and she had stopped often to water her horse and take shade where she could find it. Riding up a shallow valley along a drying stream, she caught movement only a moment before the arrow thudded into the ground just in front of her. Her horse backed away and she reined in to stop him.

'Not another pace or the next one will stop you for good.'

Kell laughed aloud. It was an Estorean accent.

'It's me,' she shouted. 'Master Kell.'

She realised her cloak hood was still over her head, protection against the fierce sun on the back of her neck. She swept it back.

'God-embrace-me, we thought you dead on the battlefield or taken for a slave,' came the answering call. 'Ride up. We'll meet you.'

Kell had not expected the joy she felt at hearing a friendly voice, though she did not recognise to whom it belonged. Riders were heading down a slope to her left. She saw the insignia of their legion and her smile broadened still further.

'Claws!' she cried, unable to contain herself. 'It sends my heart high to see you. God has shown mercy at last. How many are we?'

The pair of riders, horse archers, came alongside her. They were grim-faced and her joy faded.

'Very few,' said one. 'Follow us, Master Kell, Master Nunan will tell you all that has happened.'

'Pavel Nunan alive, too?'

'Barely,' said the other. 'Come.'

Ten days following the defeat and these survivors had their wills so firmly battered down that they could find no reason to chat or even to properly acknowledge her authority and presence. It was as if she were a stranger and they did not trust her.

On any other occasion she would have said that the campsite was beautiful. A glade of trees spread across a small grassed plateau, sheltered on three sides by hills. The stream she had ridden along rose bubbling from the bedrock in the centre of the camp.

Here, though, she was confronted by misery, desperation and suffering. It was impossible to estimate accurately the numbers of Conquord soldiers and cavalry here. Two hundred, perhaps a few more. Most were lying down. Many were still. Some moved among them and she saw one field surgeon for which she was very grateful. She counted twenty who stood or rode guard including the pair who had intercepted her. Though a breeze blew around the plateau, the air reeked of vomit and excrement.

She dismounted and handed her reins to a young woman barely able to raise a smile at her appearance. She certainly made no attempt to salute.

'Where is Nunan?' she asked.

'At the head of the stream, underneath the beech tree,' said one of the Claw horse archers. 'If you'll excuse us, we need to be back on patrol. The Tsardon are still searching these hills and we must be vigilant.'

'Of course,' she said. 'Dismissed. And thank you.'

She took their salutes and walked quickly through the makeshift camp. Most of those she passed didn't seem hurt, just resting. She frowned. There was no structure here, nothing that spoke of true organisation. She hoped Nunan could explain. He was sitting with his back to the tree, heavy padding strapped to one shoulder. His breastplate rested next to him and he sweated in the heat, drips running down a pained, pale face.

'Pavel Nunan, I might have guessed you would evade capture and find yourself a beauty spot in which to rest,' she said, smiling and squatting down in front of him. 'It's a little messy, though.'

He looked up and grinned back. 'The cleaning detail had no news of your arrival, Dina,' he said. 'I'll have them flogged the moment I am able to raise my arm above my head to give the order.'

'How bad is it?'

'Me or them?'

'Let's start with you.'

Nunan scratched his nose. 'Took an arrow as the army collapsed and was carried off the field. I think I was one of the lucky ones. The dogs were everywhere. So many bite wounds, so much infection. The arrowhead is out of my shoulder and the wound is clean enough but it's sliced me up plenty. Not sure I'll score too well with the sword next games.'

'As long as you live,' said Kell.

'As long as any of us do,' said Nunan.

'Let's hear it then.' She gestured at the camp.

'It's a little hazy for me but as I understand it, most of those who made it here ran on past the camp when it was clear it was going to be surrounded before we could get there. There was mass confusion at the fords and some were holding long enough for us to get past them and run dead north.

'Don't ask me why we weren't chased down, I can't tell you but when we got clear and hidden the next day we were able to organise a little. All you see here are those too sick to be moved and those who refuse to leave them. And then there's me, somewhere in between and in charge of the lot.'

'So how many escaped?' Kell understood the state of the camp now at least.

'We'd swept up almost two thousand by the time the Tsardon started moving out. No doubt many thousands more have made straight for Atreska or Gosland but I couldn't risk assuming that. So I've sent as many horse and light infantry as I could to take messages to both Haroq City and Goscapita via Ruin's Pass. As long as the pass is kind to them they should make it before the Tsardon.'

Nunan coughed and a spasm of pain flashed across his face. He groaned and put his hand to his shoulder.

'Are you sure you're all right?'

'Never better,' he grumbled.

'What news of Gesteris?'

'No news,' said Nunan. 'The last we saw of him, he had taken his extraordinarii across behind us to give us room to escape. He was trying to keep the ford armies standing but he wasn't ever going to succeed. Let's pray he didn't leave it too late for himself. We saw the flames of the camps that night, you know. Would he have been in there? That's the question.'

'God will protect the great, and he is one of them,' said Kell, surprised for a moment by her lack of genuine concern for her general. She knew why immediately. The man led a charmed life. God smiled on him every day. Barring one, perhaps. 'Are messengers on their way to Del Aglios and Jorganesh?'

'In a manner of speaking. Word isn't going to reach Jorganesh for some time. I've got a platoon of cavalry hidden overlooking the Tsardon. They'll head south as soon as it's clear – probably have done by now. As for Del Aglios, there are a few at the Halor Falls. There's supposed to be a pass there. I don't trust them, Kell. There's not a will among them to do anything other than hide. Part of me agrees with them. But someone has to get word north.'

Kell shook her head. 'I've heard lame and obvious set-ups before, my friend, but none as glaring as that.'

'You will do it though, won't you?' Nunan frowned. 'You're hurt too, aren't you?'

'Nothing that stops me riding,' she said. 'But I'll check in with the surgeon before I go.'

Nunan smiled again. 'Thank you.'

'And what are you going to do?'

Nunan shrugged and wished he hadn't. 'Patch ourselves up well enough and keep on searching for survivors. Either cause trouble around here or head back to play some part in the defence.'

'Hmm. You should consider carefully which way you head. There's what, two hundred of you here at the moment?'

'Thereabouts.'

'You're easy meat for any sizeable raiding party. Make sure you have scouts ahead even for so few of you. And if it's looking bad come and find us. Del Aglios and Atarkis will both be heading south when they get the news. Better you're part of a larger force, eh?'

'I'll bear it in mind.' His expression sobered. 'Kell, there's one other thing. I don't know how much credence to give this but my scouts only report what they see. The prisoner columns going east are full of Tundarrans, Estoreans, Caraducians, the Phaskar . . . you name it but not a one from Atreska.'

'Coincidence?'

Nunan raised his eyebrows. 'And it's reported that Atreskan infantry and cavalry are marching west with the Tsardon.'

'Separate prison camps?'

'They don't appear necessarily to be prisoners at all,' said Nunan.

'Are you seriously suggesting mass defection?'

Nunan sighed. 'I don't know what I'm suggesting. But Del Aglios has two Atreskan ala with him. I just think he should know what we've seen, that's all.'

A thought rose unbidden in Kell's mind and she excused herself and hurried back to her horse. What had that man been doing at the burned-out camp? She found the saddle and bags and went through them. There was a message. Hardly surprising for a messenger. She walked the camp, looking for an Atreskan or Goslander, finding several before one who could read the Tsardon scrawl.

The man, with a patch over the eye that he had lost, read the message in halting fashion. He gripped it harder with every sentence and Kell's heart almost blotted out his words.

'It can't be,' she said. 'It can't be.'

'That's what it says, Master Kell. I'm sorry.'

'But will he turn, I wonder?' said Kell.

'Who, sir?'

'Yuran. Dear God protect us if he does, we could have war on Estorea's doorstep before dusas. And nowhere near enough there to defend us.' She stood up and looked down at the Atreskan. 'Pray our messages make it before the Tsardon do. Pray I reach Del Aglios quickly. And pray the guts of this message do not come to pass. Or you, my friend, will shortly be my enemy and all our lives will have been a waste of time.'

Chapter 32

Orin D'Allinnius was glad to be home. Not the best of sailors, he had endured rather than enjoyed the *Hark's Arrow*'s voyage to Estorr and had set grateful if unsteady feet on the dockside.

The full signed report was in Jhered's hands following their exhaustive discussions first in Cirandon and later on board ship. Jhered had dismissed both he and Harkov and had ridden away with his levium guard through the dark streets. He was on his way to the Hill, there to deliver their combined and, D'Allinnius thought, enlightened verdict.

Harkov had offered a horse to take him home but D'Allinnius had declined. The night was clear and warm, with a breeze from the sea keeping the humidity low. His villa was not far from the harbour anyway and he took a leisurely stroll home along lively streets. His bags would follow him the next morning.

With the games just over, the banners and friezes still adorned the streets and the verve in the city was palpable. D'Allinnius could feel it in the air and hear it in the hubbub from taverna and bar. He raised his eyebrows in new respect for the Advocate's decision.

D'Allinnius was a well-known figure throughout the city and particularly in his home quarter. His walk was interrupted by all those enquiring after his health and whereabouts these last days. Had he enjoyed the Games . . . wasn't solastro glorious this year and did he want to stop for a drink . . . He answered politely and refused any invitation, citing tiredness after a long day. Inside the gate of his villa, looking out across the manicured shrub gardens to his front door, D'Allinnius stopped and breathed deep and slow, soaking up the peace.

His staff knew to expect him and there were lights inside. There would be food on the stove and water heating for a wash. If he was lucky, they would also have found him a companion for the night. He could do with it. Abstinence didn't agree with him.

The villa was cool inside. Marble shone in the lantern-light and the sound of fountains echoed from the hall beyond his porch. Walking quietly through the hall, he saw movement in the colonnaded garden at the centre of his modest but comfortable dwelling. He greeted the servant who looked at him with an expression of some concern before directing him to his larger reception chamber. Apparently, he had visitors.

Feeling irritable, he bustled into the room with its rugs covering an austere stone floor and its windows open to the night. Three people sat together on straight-backed chairs opposite his own recliner. Food and wine sat untouched on the table between them. He felt a chill through him and a hard shiver of fear.

'Good evening, Orin. I trust your voyage was an uneventful one.'

'Chancellor Koroyan,' said D'Allinnius. 'What a pleasant surprise.' He found in himself the courage for acidity. 'Come to bless my safe return and continuing health, I presume. You really shouldn't have put yourself out.'

Koroyan didn't smile. She adjusted her robes while the two that flanked her, dressed in Speaker garb but looking nothing more than hired muscle, stared at him with undisguised menace.

'Sit down. I do not want to crane my neck to look at you.'

D'Allinnius thought to retort but instead responded meekly, nodding and sitting. He squeezed his hands together to mask their shaking. Now he faced her, his anxiety grew still further. There was a cold contempt in her eyes, mixed with a burning fervour. It was a dangerous combination and one he associated with denouncement or speeches on the evil of heresy.

D'Allinnius had always kept out of her way in the past. He was uncomfortable with the enforcement of Omniscient doctrine favoured by the Chancellor despite official sanction of alternative religions and atheist beliefs like his own.

'Let's be absolutely clear,' said the Chancellor. 'I don't like you or the meddling with God's earth you are permitted in the name of science and engineering. I have no respect for a calling that openly questions my faith as part of its remit. And as you will be aware, I am a very busy woman as my position demands.'

'I think the Advocate—'

'The Advocate is not here. I am.' The Chancellor paused and stared at him for a moment. 'You look scared, Orin. I find that disturbing. After all, I am only the Advocate's appointed representative of God on this earth. Surely you have nothing to fear from me.'

D'Allinnius's throat was tight. He reached out for the water jug and found himself pressing his lips together with the effort of keeping his hand steady.

'I did not expect you, that's all,' he said through dry lips. 'I don't know why you're here.'

'And that scares you, doesn't it, Orin? Someone of my importance sitting in your house awaiting you. I expect servants to be scared of me but the Advocate's Master Engineer? What must you have done to be so worried?'

D'Allinnius took a sip of his water. He was sweating. His mind wouldn't settle. He tried desperately to calm himself. But the more he focused, the more the reasons for the Chancellor's presence reared in his head. And he had been sworn to secrecy by the Advocate herself.

'I have done nothing,' said D'Allinnius. 'Barring carrying out my duties as ordered by the Advocate, who is my ruler. Not you.' That last was a whisper.

The Chancellor leaned forwards slightly. 'Do not attempt to hide behind the Advocate's toga. The laws allowing practice of other religions are there for political expediency in ill-educated border territories only. They do not apply here as they do not apply in Caraduk. And I will root out and destroy heresy against the Omniscient where I find it. That is my prime motivation.'

'Those laws apply across the Conquord, Chancellor Koroyan. You, like I, cannot choose when and where they are enforced.'

'Hmm.' The Chancellor's smile was ice. 'I think you will find you are mistaken in that, Orin. As you are if you think you can refuse my demands now. I should remind you that you are very much alone here. I am suspicious and I want answers.'

D'Allinnius took a deep breath. 'I have nothing to say to you.'

'Another mistake,' said Koroyan. 'I don't want to have to use coercion or, God-embrace-me, force but you make it so difficult.'

'There is nothing you have that would force me to speak against the vows I have made to my Advocate.' But he was quaking inside at the promise in Koroyan's voice.

'You think yourself immune because of your position but you are wrong. The Advocate might turn a blind eye to your proclivities but that does not make them any the less abhorrent.'

D'Allinnius crumbled inside. 'How could you—' He said before clamping his mouth shut.

'Oh, Orin, how naïve you are. I am the Chancellor of the Order of Omniscience. Only the Advocate is closer to God than I am. No one denies me anything. Not for long. When I ask, people answer. Always.'

The Chancellor straightened her back and made a single gesture with her left hand. The two men rose and strode round the table to stand behind D'Allinnius.

'Abuse of minors is a crime against God and the Conquord,' she said. 'But I will do as the Advocate does if you tell me what I must know. I am charged with the sanctity of the Omniscient. Therefore I must know if heresy is being spoken or practised. I know you journeyed to Caraduk with Paul Jhered. I know you undertook an investigation. That the Order was not involved leaves me deeply concerned. Tell me. What did you find fluttering under the Vasselis banner?'

'It is not for me to tell you,' said D'Allinnius, swallowing at the constriction in his throat. 'And you cannot scare me with your threats. I am protected. Ask the Advocate.'

'But I am asking you.'

'I will not tell you.'

He felt hands, strong hands, clamp on to his shoulders. He smelled sweat and violence in the air. The Chancellor looked at him in mock concern.

'Please don't make me hurt you, Orin.'

He shook his head, scouring the depths of his dwindling courage.

'I will not tell you,' he repeated.

'Yes, Orin, you will.'

Herine was surprised at how pleased she was to see Paul Jhered. The Exchequer had breezed into the palace, demanding an audience. He was not changed and had indulged in little more than a perfunctory wash. He stank of the sea. She untied and dismissed her consort, whom she had been enjoying very much, but found herself smiling as Jhered's eyes followed the beautiful young man out, the growl on his lips hurrying him along.

'Oh, Paul, you are an impossible man. Scaring my consort and barely letting me cover my dignity before you burst in.'

She lay back on the bed in what she knew was a decorous fashion while she watched Jhered move to a recliner and sit down to pour himself watered wine and heap a plate with fruit.

'Then you need faster servants. I told the woman to run. Clearly she did not.'

'She did and she was out of breath when she spoke to me. Can it really be so important, what you discovered in Westfallen, or have you come to wreak revenge for your punishment?'

'On the contrary. I thank you for what was a fascinating, if disturbing, trip. And yes, it is that important, as you well know. Come and join me here, Herine. I'm uncomfortable staring at you on your bed.'

Herine laughed, wrapped her gown more tightly around her and gathered it at the waist with a leather cord.

'I've missed you,' she said. 'You and I should not be falling out.'

'You don't seem to have despaired too deeply,' said Jhered. 'The Games were a success, I am told.'

'Yes, they were. And I note you have timed your return impeccably,' said Herine sharply. 'Not even you can have failed to sense the mood of the city.'

'I am sure the citizens are very happy,' said Jhered. 'Perhaps not our Atreskan and Goslander friends, though.'

'My latest reports have our armies north and south scoring significant victories and the east holding firm against the mass of the enemy. Victory is close.'

'I pray that you are right. How long until the next reports?'

Herine shrugged, bored of the discussion. 'In the next seven to ten days.' She beckoned for Jhered to pour her some wine. 'So, is it witchcraft and heresy or is Vasselis sinking into delusion?'

Jhered opened a leather satchel he was carrying and pulled out a bound document. He handed it across the table. Herine took it and opened it to the first page.

'There are two documents. This is the shorter one. It contains a summary, recommendations and detailed accounts of what we saw and understand. The longer version contains genealogy and speculation on ability and development. It also contains the sworn statements of every man and woman in Westfallen, plus all those involved from the house of Vasselis. I will leave it in the satchel for you.'

'I see.'

Herine began to read. She scanned the summary and flicked on into the accounts, finding herself drawn deeper and deeper into the content which read like fiction. Outrageous, dangerous fiction from warped minds. She heard Jhered speaking to her. Words like 'custody', 'weapon', 'observation' and 'control' filtered through but she was barely listening. She could scarce believe the words before her were signed as truth by the man opposite her. She felt her eyesight funnelling and her skin crawling. The blood ran hot in her veins and her palms were clammy.

She had no option; she read the whole report then and there, trying to see a way out and searching for the falsehoods and trickery that would show it to be an elaborate ruse. Jhered's recommendations spoke of careful education and later, introduction to the Order and thence the populace. They discussed likely fear but balanced that with the potential for progress and advancement of the human condition. All of it under the auspices of the Advocacy. But he had missed the most fundamental fact.

'This is abhorrent,' she said when she felt able to speak with any strength. 'I asked you to travel with an open mind but not without the guidance of God. This is an affront to the Omniscient. What were you thinking?'

'That is exactly what I felt when I first saw the Ascendants and spoke to Westfallen's Reader. But you have to divorce yourself from the scriptures and see this for what it is. An experiment on the edge of acceptability but one that would have been replicated by nature and hence God over the course of time. Is that heresy? It's the question that has been plaguing me.'

'How can you even ask that, Paul?' Herine shook her head, disappointment seeping through her. 'Maybe I shouldn't have sent you. Vasselis has obviously influenced you.'

'Don't say that until you have read every word in both reports. It does disturb me, yes. But these are the facts . . . for the people of

Westfallen, it is literally their everyday life. All the Ascendants are for them is the next step. The fire is alight.'

'Then it must be extinguished,' said Herine. 'Paul, I am Prime Speaker of the Order of Omniscience. I am His representative on earth. I allowed the investigation to go ahead without the Order out of respect for you, Vasselis and the knowledge that there would be no balance from Felice Koroyan. But what I've read here . . . I don't know how you have reached the conclusions you have reached. A weapon? They will be uncontrollable. I don't see how they can be allowed to survive, I really don't.'

Jhered tensed and frowned. 'You cannot unleash the Chancellor on them. Not now.'

Herine shook her head. 'However it is dressed up, what I read here is a crime, nothing more. And it is a crime that has been being perpetrated for a very long time.' She sighed. 'I cannot have such flagrant breaches of the laws of the Conquord. People must be brought to trial for this and be found innocent or guilty by the Order and the magistrates.'

'All I ask is that you consider this more fully before making such a decision. Read what we have presented. Think. Meet them.'

'I will meet them. Here. In Estorr. And in chains. Do I make myself clear?'

'You are talking about Arvan Vasselis here, Herine. Think what that means.'

'I know,' she whispered.

Herine stared at Jhered, watching him consider his next actions. She knew he was torn. God-surround-them but she felt a dread weight on her as she spoke the words. She would read tonight. After all, there was no prospect of sleep. But in the morning, she could not imagine her mind would have changed. And that meant Arvan Vasselis would stand before her, in all probability to hear her pronounce death by fire.

'I will receive my orders from you in the morning,' said Jhered, standing, his voice flat. 'And if you wish me to organise the custody of all those involved, I will do it for you, my Advocate.'

'No, Paul. I'm sorry but no. Harkov will go. This is a job for the palace guard, not for you.'

'And I just walk in circles here until he returns with my friend bowed under the weight of his bonds?' Jhered shook his head. 'Thirty days at the very least. It will drive me mad.'

'You have other duties that will occupy your mind, my Exchequer. Marshal Defender Yuran refused to attend the games. I want you there because he must be removed and the levium can oversee a bloodless change with you at their head.'

'And who will rule in his place?'

'Consul Safinn, naturally. Had I listened to my head, he would have been sitting on the throne since accession.'

'And are you not interested in the reasons Yuran did not attend? Perhaps he felt his absence would be a blow to morale with Tsardon raiders swarming his borders and his country in uproar.'

'His message of refusal mentioned nothing but his contempt for the Games and their timing.' Herine shrugged. 'It is the final insult.'

Jhered inclined his head. 'Whatever your wish, my Advocate.'

'I'll have the orders ready for you at dawn. Bring Harkov with you.' She watched him nod and turn to go. 'And Paul?' He stopped but did not turn back. 'Thank you.'

'Don't. This is not a time for gratitude.'

She bowed her head and it was a long time before she felt able to face the night.

Chapter 33

848th cycle of God, 14th day of Solasrise
15th year of the true Ascendancy

Words had been muttered during the night. Jhered had been informed and at dawn had gone to his bedside. He'd been unconscious since being found and the search of his villa had revealed that he had been the only survivor. All of his staff were dead. Not tortured and beaten like him; executed. Their necks broken and their bodies laid out to be found and accorded their burial rights.

Jhered looked down on D'Allinnius and almost wished he had died too. His injuries were appalling and Jhered could only respect the courage he must have shown in trying to resist revealing the secrets his attackers had wanted. The surgeons were not at all sure he'd survive but Jhered was desperate that he confirmed the identities of those who had done this to him. Jhered was certain he already knew but against the Order, there could be no action without witnessed testimony. Hence Harkov sat by him.

D'Allinnius was almost unrecognisable. His face had been systematically battered. His jaw was smashed, his teeth gone or chipped. The swelling was awful around his eyes and mouth, one ear had been sliced from his head and his hair had been ripped or burned from his scalp. His arms were broken, he had lost three fingers and all his remaining nails were torn away. Similar treatment had been meted out to his legs and feet.

Bruising was extensive all over his body and his genitals had been branded with hot metal. Salves and lotions were smeared over those parts of his body not covered by bandages. Jhered's fury threatened to consume him. Nothing excused this cruelty and if he was right and it was the Order, it was a crime against God that they would have to answer.

D'Allinnius's eyes were moving beneath his blackened lids and periodically a whimpering escaped his lips. Jhered wiped a hand across his mouth and looked up at the surgeon in attendance.

'You're sure you don't remember what he said?' he asked.

'No, my Lord. I was too far away when he began to mutter and I couldn't get him to repeat himself.'

'You're sure he was conscious?' asked Harkov.

The surgeon nodded. 'He looked at me. Eyes full of pain and fear. Who would do such things to this man? *This* man?'

'We'll find out,' said Jhered. 'Don't concern yourself with that, just with keeping him alive.'

'That depends as much on Orin as it does on me now,' she said. 'He is splinted, his pain is lessened and he is as comfortable as I can make him. He lost a lot of blood lying in his villa for God knows how long but if he wills it, he can live. Though how his mind will be is another question.'

Jhered breathed through fingers that were across his mouth and leaned his elbows on the bed. He felt completely responsible. It was he who had persuaded D'Allinnius to join him and Harkov. He who had assured the scientist that he would be safe and that the Advocate would protect him. So much for the assurances of the Exchequer.

He had to assume D'Allinnius had been broken eventually and that preparations were being made for the torturers to travel to Westfallen. He had ordered a small fleet be readied to carry two hundred levium south on the morning tide and his spies were all over the city, looking for information. There didn't seem to be any unusual Order activity on the docks or in the Chancellery but he had been unable to find the Chancellor herself and that did worry him. She could be hard to locate but this was beginning to be too much of a coincidence. The Advocate was being unusually tight-lipped. Jhered didn't like it at all.

'Come on, Orin, speak to us,' said Jhered gently. 'Give us the means to catch who did this.'

D'Allinnius coughed. Jhered wiped the spittle from his lips with a cool wet cloth. The chambers in which he was being kept were attached to the palace. Vaulted ceilings held up by pristine white ionic scrolled columns. Soft light streamed in through huge expanses of netted glass which looked out on to fountains and gardens. Inside, his was the only bed but every other flat surface was covered with fresh-cut flowers and green leaves, their scents a balm to the nostrils.

'That's it, Orin. All over now. You're safe. Really safe this time. No one can touch you here. No one can hurt you.'

'He's waking,' said the surgeon.

The scientist stirred. Limbs moved feebly and the whimpering was pained. Jhered wished he could do something more than mop his brow, practically the only area on his body not bruised or burned.

'Don't move, my friend,' said Jhered. 'Rest your body. Speak if you can.'

D'Allinnius's eyes flickered and opened a crack. His face screwed up against the light and there were tears in the corners of his eyes. Jhered smiled.

'I'm sorry this has happened to you,' he said.

D'Allinnius almost smiled but the bruising and his cracked, burned lips stopped him.

'Price . . . of . . . fame,' he managed. Jhered was amazed he could summon the desire to attempt a joke.

'You need to rest, Orin,' said Jhered, briefly resting a hand on his shoulder. 'For now, just tell me who did this.'

'They know everything,' wheezed Orin. 'I tried.'

'That much is obvious,' said Harkov. 'Your bravery is incredible.'

'Who?' prompted Jhered.

'Chancellor,' said Orin, around mumbles and gasps of pain.

Jhered's jaw dropped and he glanced around quickly. Only he, Harkov and the surgeon could have heard that.

'Personally?' he asked, unwilling to believe it. Orin nodded, an agonised gesture. 'Why didn't she kill you?'

'She thought she had,' said Orin. He pushed his tongue across his lips. 'I assume.'

'It would have been easy for her to think so,' said the surgeon. 'When he came in here, his breathing was so shallow I thought he was gone. We needed to use a mirror to be sure he was worth tending.'

'Glad you had one handy.' Orin coughed violently and shuddered with the attendant torment.

'Quiet now,' said Jhered. 'Sleep, Orin. And thank you.'

D'Allinnius's eyes bored into his with a sudden energy. 'Save the Ascendants. They are only children.'

'I intend to,' said Jhered.

D'Allinnius nodded, apparently satisfied, and closed his eyes. Jhered watched him for a moment to be sure he hadn't slipped away. He rose and his anger began to surge.

'Harkov, looks like your job in Caraduk has just become a lot more pressing. And you.' He grabbed the surgeon's arm and squeezed. 'You say nothing of what you have just heard. Nothing.'

She stared back. 'A surgeon never discusses her patient with any other.'

Jhered let go. 'Be sure you don't. It's too important, believe me.'

'You can trust me.'

'See that remains the case.'

Jhered strode for the door and hauled it open. He marched fast across the gardens and into the palace proper, entering through the administrative offices. He passed ranks of desks and piles of papers and scrolls. People picked their heads up to watch him go by. He kept his eyes fixed ahead and his gladius tight to his side. Through the offices he went and into the central hallway from which ran corridors to the colonnaded gardens, grand reception rooms and the Advocacy hall. He didn't break stride all the way to the Advocate's private chambers. The hour was early and unless she was ill, she would still be asleep.

With Harkov in his boot prints, he ran up the broad stairway and barked aside the guards at its head. Outside Herine's door he was blocked by two personal bodyguards crossing their spears in front of his face.

'The Advocate is still at rest, my lord,' said one.

'Then it is time she was awake. The Conquord struggles without her.'

'We cannot grant you admittance, Exchequer Jhered,' said the other.

Jhered drew himself up and glared down at them. 'Your diligence does you credit,' he said. 'But I am ordering you to stand aside. I will speak with the Advocate.'

'We cannot,' said one nervously.

'Fools,' hissed Jhered. 'I mean her no harm. It is your delay that will cause it. Oh, dammit.' He unbuckled his sword belt, dropped it to the ground and snapped his fingers at Harkov to do the same. 'Watch over me if you must but I *will* see her now.'

The delay was short. The guards glanced at the intricately designed scabbards on the ground and then back at the Exchequer. Their spears moved aside.

'Good decision.'

Jhered threw open the double doors and walked into the heavily scented and draped gloom. A small sliver of light fell across the bed in which he could just make out two forms. It was his boots ringing on the marble of the apron that woke the pair. Herine shouted in surprise.

'Don't worry, my Advocate, it is Jhered and Harkov.'

Jhered said nothing more while he walked to the bed. Its fine weave sheets and Conquord green coverings were knotted and dishevelled.

'What the hell do you think you are doing, bursting in here like this?'

'Trying to save your Conquord,' said Jhered. 'From those who would undermine your authority to satisfy their own warped ethics.'

'I beg your pardon?' she said.

Jhered's eyes adjusted to the dim light. Herine was sitting up against a pile of cushions. Her hair was held in a net and she was wearing a sleeveless gown. The consort had retreated to the far side of the bed and was trying to look inconspicuous. Jhered stabbed a finger at him.

'Do I *really* have to tell you what to do?' he growled.

The consort, lithe body muscled and toned, leapt from the bed like a startled cat and ran for the doors, grabbing a cushion to cover himself on the way.

'You will go that step too far one day,' said Herine. 'Even you are not above the law of the Conquord.'

'And is the Chancellor?'

'No one but me,' said Herine, regaining a little composure.

'Then you must have her arrested now. It was she who tortured D'Allinnius. Personally.'

Herine was quiet. 'He didn't die, then?'

'What? No,' said Jhered. 'Though how he didn't, I have no idea. But he has identified her. I can't order her arrest. You can.'

Herine moved to the side of the bed and got up. She took a wrap from a chair and covered herself more completely. She spared Harkov a glare and walked to one of her recliners. She sat and poured herself some water from a jug.

'It's too late for that,' she said.

Jhered frowned. 'What do you mean? She's already in custody?'

'No, but she's already left Estorr.'

Jhered went cold. 'What? When?'

'Two days ago, late in the evening.'

'I'm confused,' he said. 'We spoke of who we felt might have committed this crime on Orin and yet you didn't tell me she was leaving, let alone stop her yourself?'

Herine spread her hands. 'It seems to me that justice will be done under God.'

Jhered opened his mouth and shut it again straight away, turning instead to Harkov. 'Captain, would you wait for me in my offices, please?'

'My Lord,' he saluted, right fist slapping into his chest. He bowed to Herine. 'My Advocate.'

When he was gone, Jhered turned his ire on the Advocate. 'Justice? Have you taken leave of your senses?'

'I will not be spoken to—'

'Dammit you will listen to me, Herine. Does nothing we talked about mean anything to you? The Chancellor will go to Westfallen and the justice she will mete out will leave that town burned to the ground along with everyone in it, innocent and complicit alike.

'What happened to your desire to see them tried in Estorr? The laws of this Conquord, which you apparently hold dear demand that happen. You cannot let the Chancellor do this.'

'Cannot?' The Advocate raised her eyebrows. 'There is nothing I "cannot" do, Exchequer Jhered. And why would I not decide that this clear case of heresy be judged by the Chancellor of the Order of Omniscience?'

'Because you know the violence of the judgement she will make. Because you know that she will act outside the laws of the Conquord and hide behind the face of God.' Jhered put his face in his hands. 'Herine, what have you done?'

'What I should have done at the outset,' she said. 'Were I not blinded by my allegiance to you and Vasselis.'

'You are making a very grave mistake,' he said and paused, another uncomfortable thought in his mind. 'Did you know she had tortured Orin herself?'

Herine stood up and stalked towards him. 'What happened to

Orin was very unfortunate and I am saddened the Chancellor was present. I pray he will recover and if you for one moment suggest that I condone such actions I will have you removed from office, believe me.

'You are walking a very fine line. Don't push me any further, Paul. I have a Conquord to run and my decision is that matters of heresy will be dealt with by those with the experience and the knowledge to make judgement under God. That, if you are feeling slow, means the Chancellor.

'But if you feel you should be present to maintain justice, if you think Vasselis is unable to do that for himself, then you have my permission to return to Westfallen. See if you can catch the Chancellor.'

Jhered stared down at her. He couldn't understand what had happened. This woman knew the excesses of the Chancellor better than any of them. A year ago she would have been rebuked, controlled. Now the shackles were off and Jhered felt unable to change the Advocate's mind. So much in their relationship had changed.

'No,' he said. 'Harkov is entirely capable. And I will serve the cause of the Conquord better by travelling to Atreska.'

Herine nodded. 'This'll be twice I'm happy you aren't here.'

'Yes,' said Jhered. 'And when I return, we will sit and talk about whether I can still work for the Advocacy. Because these days, my views on how we should best serve our citizens seem to differ fundamentally from yours.'

She shrugged. 'Your voyage will give you time to think. Go.'

Jhered bowed but paused before leaving. 'Is there something else I should know? Is there trouble you're hiding from me?'

'I run a huge Conquord. There is always trouble. But none of it is as close to my heart as that standing in front of me now. Go.'

Jhered walked out of the palace and into the warm morning sunshine. He collected Harkov from his offices and the two men took horses and rode to the docks to oversee the preparation of their respective fleets. He was taking two ships, all he had available. Conditions for horses would be tight but not impossible. Many of the riders would have to sleep on deck as a consequence. Harkov's fleet was three ships and on the way to Port Roulent, his men at least would sleep more comfortably.

There was the best part of a day before they sailed and Jhered was not going to waste it.

'Captain Harkov, I know you're well connected with the messenger service,' he said.

'Yes,' said Harkov cautiously.

'While you're sending your messages to your wife and family about your next absence, I want you to ask a few questions. Who has come in and where are they bringing messages from. Talk to the individuals if you can. There's trouble somewhere and we need to know about it. I don't know what it is but I feel uncomfortable. The Conquord faces more than the crisis about to hit Westfallen and I want to know what it is.'

'Sir, surely the Advocate would have told you of all people,' said Harkov.

'Do you love the Conquord?' asked Jhered.

'I would die for it,' said Harkov.

'Then trust me as I trust you and do as I ask. The Advocate is not herself and we must help her despite her. There are times when citizens such as you and I must act at the boundaries of law to save those who rule us and the places we love. And my instinct tells me that now is one of those times.'

Chapter 34

848th cycle of God, 20th day of Solasrise
15th year of the true Ascendancy

Felice Koroyan, Chancellor of the Order of Omniscience and beholden only to the Advocate on God's earth, stood in the prow of the *Everlasting Truth*. She could smell the evil of heresy on the wind.

The galley rowed gracefully into the harbour of Port Roulent, sail furled against a buffeting offshore wind. A seven-day journey of prayers for strength and courage had passed on a sea blessed calm to hurry them to their work. From Port Roulent, it was four days by horse and carriage to Westfallen. Then the cleansing could begin and those who could be saved for God would be so. Those who could not would dance with the devils on the wind for eternity.

The Order flag fluttered proudly from the mast. Its stylised 'O' was made up of clasping hands and surrounded a quartered tableau of sun, tree, horse and embracing lovers. Its gold on green colouring signified the Chancellor was on board. It would be seen through the magnifiers trained on every vessel that passed the harbour castle and moved to berth against the deep-water dockside. There would be honour that she had chosen to visit. If only it was with cause to celebrate.

Horns announced her admission to the harbour. Flags marked the berths for her ships. Flurries of movement indicated hurried preparations for her landing. With her vessel closing on the harbour wall, Koroyan searched the fast-growing crowd for her representatives. She had sent two pigeons when a day from land. It would be a matter of some inconvenience if they had not found their targets.

'Your Grace.'

She turned to Horst Vennegoor, Prime Sword of the Omniscient, commander of all her forces. He had agreed to take personal charge of the security of the trial that would take place in Westfallen. He had at his disposal, one hundred of the Armour of God, 3rd legion of the Omniscient. They were a skilled guard for what would be a difficult task. All the riders were able with bow, sword and spear. All were dedicated warriors of God, sworn to police the instruction of right and truth on His earth.

'I didn't hear you approach, my Prime,' she said.

Vennegoor inclined his head. He was a narrow-faced man, well into middle age. His sparse grey hair was oiled flat on his skull and his warm brown eyes gazed reverentially into hers. These were eyes that, when allied with his gentle tones, had persuaded many a criminal to give themselves away.

'Silence is a weapon that should never be underestimated,' he said, smiling. 'But I would wear steel-shod boots if you desired it.'

'I'm not sure which I would fear most were I your target; knowing you were coming or turning to find you there,' she said. 'You wanted me.'

'Merely to point out our welcome party,' said Vennegoor.

Koroyan chuckled. 'Then I lose my bet on the abilities of your birds. Good.' She looked out once again at the harbour side. 'Where are they?'

'Coming down from the Principal House of Masks.'

Vennegoor pointed to the House which stood apart from the rest of the thriving port, on a hill that overlooked the south bay where the fisher fleet was drawn up. She could see Order flags and pennants spread through a short column of riders with three carriages. Exactly as she had requested. She watched their progress while the *Everlasting Truth* nudged into berth. Her Prime Sword stood by her, hand ever on his weapon's hilt. Others of the Armour were in attendance, bows strung. It was inconceivable that she would face an attempt on her life in Caraduk but there was never any excuse for laxity.

They flanked her down the gangplank and she walked, arms tucked in at the elbows and palms spread out to take the observance of the citizens. She smiled to the left and right, nodding her acknowledgement of prayers from workers blessed by her presence among them. Thirty yards ahead, Port Roulent's Principal Speaker waited at the head of her column. She had dismounted her horse, holding its reins while the stiffening breeze blew her robes about her legs. The crowd was standing a respectful distance from them and Koroyan could hear prayer chants being taken up. A glorious sound in a province of great piety. But one with a rotten core.

'Blessed Chancellor, this is honour without measure,' said the Speaker, dropping to one knee, one hand to her forehead, one planted claw like on the ground in the symbol of root in earth. She was grown fat on the bounty God provided. Her round face was taut and sweating.

'Come, stand up, Speaker Lotheris. It is too long since I've journeyed to this southern gem. The honour and pleasure are all my own.'

She spoke for the crowd and felt the waves of gratitude roll from them. She took Lotheris's slick and hot root hand in her own and kissed her damp forehead, conferring her blessing.

'I'm glad you received Vennegoor's pigeons,' she said quietly. 'It will make our unpleasant task that much more simple.'

'Everything is in hand,' said Lotheris.

'We'll speak in my carriage,' said Koroyan. She made quick estimate of the time of day. It was not long past noon and the heat was intense despite the breeze. She addressed the crowd. 'Spread the word. I will take service at the House of Masks at dusk. All are welcome to hear me and glory in God.'

An excited babble of conversation broke out. Koroyan indicated Lotheris precede her into the carriage. As soon as the door closed behind her, the carriage turned, shouted demands clearing a path. Vennegoor would look after himself and the rest of the deputation of speakers and warriors. This most trusted of men would never let her down.

'I have prepared rooms for you at my villa,' said Lotheris. 'Your people can camp or be billeted throughout the port, should you so desire.'

'No,' said Koroyan. 'As soon as the service is over, I shall take a ceremonial meal with you and the deputation and we will then leave for Westfallen. Now, tell me before you ask the questions you must, what of my requests?'

'I have positioned warriors on the roads to Westfallen, Cirandon and two other minor tracks. Those we suspect might carry word will be detained.'

'Carrier pigeons?'

'Everything is being done that can be. I have watchers at the lofts and falconers on the routes. At the least, we will see if birds are sent but we are applying pressure for messages to be held up for a day at least.'

'Good. Do you have news of Arvan Vasselis?'

'Our information is that he is in Cirandon, though his wife and child could still be in Westfallen. It is a favourite retreat of the family. I have no certain information, though.'

'Interesting,' said Koroyan, seeing the possibilities. 'And that is where we shall leave him for now, at least. This situation must be handled in the correct order. Better he is absent for its beginning. Good.'

'But there are problems, nonetheless,' said Lotheris. 'The security on the road to Westfallen is tight. Word has been that it is a standing exercise against an animal plague but it has been in place for too long, I feel, for that reason to remain credible.'

'I have one hundred of the Armour of God at my back, Speaker Lotheris. Wayposts will not prove a stumbling block.'

'Chancellor, I must ask. All of this comes as a shock, though I have acted on every request in your messages. What has happened in Westfallen? And why is Marshal Vasselis involved?'

Koroyan nodded. 'What is the name of the Reader of Westfallen?'

'Elsa Gueran, my Chancellor.'

'And have you ever seen her or heard her utter a word?'

'No,' said Lotheris. She frowned briefly.

'And no doubt when you talk with the Principal Speaker of Cirandon, you find that he has similar problems, and indeed feels obstructed.'

Lotheris nodded. 'That's true as I recall but—'

'Then gather God close and listen to what I have to say. It is a lesson in why vigilance must never be allowed to slip. There is evil being perpetrated in this most beautiful of countries, and it is so close you can all but touch it.'

By the time they reached the House of Masks, Lotheris's bloated face was dark and angry.

It happened to them all one after another and the days had become long and bleak for the Ascendancy Echelon. So much at odds with the glorious sun shining down upon God's earth. The crops ripened, the fruit swelled on the trees and young animals strengthened and grew. Even the fish seemed to shoal in increasing numbers, waiting to swim into the nets as soon as they were cast.

In every way it was a solastro season that God blessed. Westfallen basked in heat tempered by a sea breeze. The weather was set fair, of that Ardol Kessian was absolutely certain. Trading was brisk and profitable and crops had already been sold at good prices, well in advance of an excellent harvest. Public festivals and prayers around the House of Masks were fervent and covered in smiles and laughter.

Yet in private, away from the prying eyes and cocked ears of visitors, traders and strangers, prayers were offered for the Ascendants. The whole town knew of their struggle and behind closed doors, the concerted will of the citizens was bent on beseeching God to grant mercy. Well-wishers kept up a steady stream to the door of the villa. Gifts and words were welcomed. None would ever be turned away. Sometimes, the solidarity was all that kept them going.

Hesther saw little of it, just as she saw little of sleep, food and thought for anything other than the Ascendants. When she did rest, images of them crowded her mind and she often cried out as loud and frightened as they sounded, lost in whatever battle was taking place inside their bodies.

From the third day of solasrise it had taken them all so quickly. Hesther could not shake the memories. The three boys had sat around Mirron's bed, watching her writhe, wail and moan. All of them had laid hands on her, tried to comfort her, but their words had lacked conviction and Hesther had seen the fear of anticipation on their faces as plainly as if it were being played out now. In their development as Ascendants, what happened to one of them happened to all of them.

So sad. That youthful male excitement and wild imagination about soon being able to take on the form of tree, horse or anything they touched was shattered so quickly. Replaced by a dread knowledge of what was to come.

It was no surprise that Ossacer had succumbed first. Always so sensitive, his understanding of the state of Mirron's body gave his mind the knowledge to move him parallel with her. And with his constitution so poor, their fear for his life was great. Arducius and Gorian supported each other as best they could in the day they were alone together before Arducius collapsed quite suddenly in the colonnaded gardens.

But by the time Gorian fell into unconsciousness, he was no longer scared but angry. He was certain that this was the path to greater power and understanding and he felt helpless because it was something over which he had no control. Kessian had spoken to him at great length but it did little but force him into impenetrable introspection. He was a troubled boy, beginning to believe his ability was about to desert him.

When, three days after Arducius, the pain of his sensations began to overwhelm him, he had smiled and cried in relief.

'But what relief is there now, my nephew?' whispered Hesther, smoothing away the damp hair from his raging brow.

All the Ascendants were in the same room, deep in the villa. Here, their occasional screams would not worry Westfallen's people or alert suspicions in strangers. In the sixteen days since all of them had been like this, fighting with themselves and beyond the help of man and God, there had been no change in their condition.

In the calmer moments of their torment, when their every muscle had not been tensed and their faces contorted and frightening, they could be cleaned and cared for. Water and liquefied foods, vegetables and bread mainly, could be encouraged down by stroking throats. Limbs could be exercised against muscles cramping and withering. Genna Kessian and the surgeons had established strict routines and all of those charged with watching the children knew them minutely.

'Hesther?'

Hesther glanced across at Shela Hasi. Poor Shela, who was sitting in a chair by Arducius's bed. She had driven herself harder than any of them, almost blaming herself for their condition. Their words of comfort did little to appease her guilt.

'Sorry, just talking to Gorian. I wonder if speaking to them helps them.'

'Anything's worth trying,' said Shela.

It was late afternoon and a quiet period for the Ascendants. They had been fed, had their limbs manipulated and had been changed into fresh clothing. Yet even while they weren't moaning or speaking gibberish, their rest was uncomfortable, disturbed and worrying for all who watched them. Genna Kessian and Andreas Koll had withdrawn to try and rest. Meera Naravny and Jen Shalke were due in soon.

It was almost impossible to keep Meera or Gwythen away from their children. Upsetting too for the mothers of Arducius and Ossacer. Ordinary folk touched by lasting ability who trusted their children to the Ascendancy Echelon as all who participated did. The identity of their fathers was, and always would be, kept secret from the children. It was knowledge unsafe for them to know.

Hesther looked back down at Gorian. His head was laid to one side, his mouth was moving and there was a line of drool running on to his pillow. She wondered where he was. Whether he was really in pain or whether his loss was in confusion of the mind and body. An inability to understand and control the sensations that poured through him.

The door to the scented room opened and Kessian walked in. His movement was terribly slow and pained. His face was drawn and white. His eyes were sunken and dark and his frown perpetually deep. The Ascendants were killing him as surely as his long, long years. Willem was with him, another old man looking so much more aged than his years but finding in himself the strength on which Kessian relied to get around when Genna was sleeping.

Hesther's heart went out to him and she rushed across the wooden floor to him.

'Oh, Ardol, you should be resting. Here, lean on me. Willem, get to a chair. You look exhausted.'

'Resting?' Ardol's eyes were damp and his expression desperate. 'How can I do that? How can any of us?'

He moved his hand from Willem to Hesther and let her help him into the room. Its brightly decorated walls depicting animals, flowers and fish still smelled of fresh paint. His sticks rattled on the floor. Hesther tried to direct him to a chair but he resisted.

'Let me look on them all. Let me see if there is any sign.'

Hesther shepherded him along the line of beds. She felt the sag in his body and heard the sigh on his breath. And like every day when he visited, the tears rolled unchecked down his cheeks. It was the worst part of each day for any who walked with him.

Kessian stood on the precipice. Not knowing if he was about to lose all for which he had worked all his life. These four represented his final chance to see a true Ascendant. Those born since were showing no signs of breakthrough. Finally, he let her guide him to a richly upholstered armchair into which he folded with a desperately tired breath.

'You have to believe this is part of their growing. You have to believe this will conclude with true emergence and that everything we have seen before was a mere prelude,' she said, kneeling in front of him and placing her hands on his knees.

Kessian looked at her, imploring. 'When will it end?' he said, all power gone from his voice. 'How can we believe this is right, good and proper? How can God be putting them through this? How can we stand by?'

'We stand by because we can do nothing else. We have entered the unknown and we must have faith. God will not desert us and we, the Echelon, will not desert you. We are all prey to despair but we must not let it consume us.'

Kessian covered her hands. 'Hesther, you are so strong. At least I know I leave the Echelon in the best of hands.' His eyes moved to the beds. 'I so want to see them smile just once more.'

Hesther forced a smile on to her own face. 'You will see so much more than that. Your return to the earth is not quite so imminent and well you know it.'

A knock on the door, quiet and respectful. Shela rose and opened it. There stood Kovan and Netta Vasselis. Son and mother. He was tall and handsome in the image of his father, she graceful and still so beautiful. Both had been of such unwavering support in these awful days. Days in which the Marshal himself had been detained in Cirandon on urgent Conquord business before travelling to Glenhale. They waited on the threshold, carrying fresh flowers from their walled garden.

'Is it convenient to visit?' asked Netta.

'I hardly think the wife and son of our beloved Marshal need permission,' said Hesther, getting to her feet and smoothing her dress.

'You overstate our importance, Hesther,' said Netta, smiling. 'And you know what I mean.'

'Come in,' said Hesther. 'You know you're always welcome.'

Netta walked to the nearest bed to stand by Shela, who was once again with Arducius. Kovan ignored all the boys, walking the length of the room to where Mirron lay, currently very still. He grabbed yesterday's flowers from the vase and thrust the new ones in rather crudely. He sat on the wooden chair at the head of her bed and laid the discarded blooms on the floor.

'No change?' he asked, picking up one of her hands and stroking it.

Hesther shook her head. 'No, Kovan, I'm afraid not. But I'm sure somewhere inside, she's the better for you being with her.'

Kovan blushed and smiled. Netta walked over to Hesther.

'You should let me take my turn here,' she said quietly. 'You all look so tired.'

'We couldn't possibly,' said Kessian, not rising from his chair. 'The Echelon must deal with this, though where we'd be without your support, I don't know.'

'I do understand,' said Netta. 'But if you change your mind . . .'

'You'll be the first to hear,' said Hesther. 'But we pray every day that this nightmare will end.'

'We are at the House of Masks each dawn and dusk doing the same.'

'And that is where your presence is most valuable,' said Kessian. 'The fact you are here and public in your support keeps our people with us.'

'I'm sorry I brought this on you.' It was Kovan's voice carrying across the room in the hush.

'Don't blame yourself,' said Kessian. 'We've been through this, Kovan. This isn't your fault.'

'I've been thinking,' said Kovan. 'If I hadn't done what I did in the orchard, perhaps she could have learned a little more and dealt with it better. I feel like I triggered the change.'

'Change?' asked Kessian. 'You think it so, do you?'

'What else can it be?' He shrugged. 'If it were not, then we should all be scared for their lives, shouldn't we? Rather than waiting for them to awaken.'

Kessian chuckled. It was a sound that filled Hesther with warmth and hope.

'Your uncluttered vision is a blessing, young man,' said Kessian. 'And be assured you didn't trigger this. It was surely a coincidence, something to do with their age and the stage of their development we had reached. After all, if you did trigger it as you imagine, then why are the other three not still standing, eh?'

'We know so little,' said Hesther. 'For all Gorian wrote, he didn't see this in any of his subjects, nor in himself. This is uncharted in all our existence.'

Kovan looked over at them dubiously. 'I don't know. Coincidence, accident or destiny. The distinction is slight.'

Hesther turned to Netta and whispered. 'He's a deep thinker, isn't he?'

'He has a sharp mind, if a little frivolous yet,' said Netta, pride shining from her.

'He will make a fine Marshal, when he is called,' said Kessian.

They fell silent for a while, all watching Kovan speaking quieter words to Mirron and cooling her forehead with a dampened scented cloth.

'You know he paces the gardens just waiting until he can come here again,' said Netta eventually.

'Does he know he can never be a father to her children?' Kessian's voice was barely audible.

Netta shook her head. 'We've spoken to him but he's seventeen, Ardol. What does he care for the demands of the Ascendancy? He thinks he can change anything and everything that he wants. But he'll understand as he grows up.'

'Poor lad,' said Hesther. 'Forbidden love.'

'Don't worry about him,' said Netta. 'He doesn't see it that way. And when his infatuation wanes, she'll be left with the closest of friends and he with an understanding of the Ascendancy better than any outside of Westfallen. It may prove invaluable in future years.'

Hesther watched him. His face was full of his adolescent passion for Mirron. She couldn't agree with Netta, not with her assumptions of the future anyway. This didn't look like a love that would fade easily. It was a while before she realised what she was seeing. Kovan was speaking quietly to Mirron, his face close to hers and both his hands covering one of hers. Mirron's free arm rose sleepily from her side and her hand stroked his face. He gasped a laugh.

'What are you doing here?' she asked, voice clear and even.

'Hello, beautiful,' he said.

Hesther and Shela were both running to Mirron's bedside. Netta had stayed to help Kessian up and he was shouting hoarsely for someone to get Gwythen. Mirron looked completely bemused. She had stayed staring at Kovan, whose smile would have lit up the darkest night, but she focused on Hesther now. A frown creased her face.

Hesther looked down at her. 'Your eyes,' she said, unable to help herself. 'They're beautiful.'

And they were. They seemed to shine and they modulated through every colour of the rainbow. It was quite extraordinary.

'What's going on?' asked Mirron.

She looked about her now, tensing when she realised she was not in her own room and seeing the three boys to her right.

'Do you remember what happened when you were awake last?' asked Kessian, coming to the foot of the bed.

'I— What are we all doing here? What's wrong with them?'

'In a moment,' said Hesther. 'Answer the Father.'

'I couldn't make it stop,' said Mirron. 'It wouldn't go away and it washed over me. You were there, you must have seen.'

'We did,' said Kessian. 'And do you recall anything of what you have been through since then?'

Mirron giggled. 'I've only been asleep. And I feel fine now.'

'It's been much more than that.' Kessian's tone stifled her laughter. 'You lost consciousness on the third. It's now the twentieth.'

Her jaw dropped and after a moment she mouthed the phrase, 'Seventeen days?' Kessian nodded.

'And your brothers are still suffering. Did you suffer, Mirron? What do you remember?'

Mirron looked again at the other Ascendants. She shook her head. 'All I did was learn how to make it stop. No. I don't mean that. It never stops. I mean, learn how to bring it under control, like the fire and the rain I already can. But it seemed like a short time. Seventeen days? And what about my eyes?'

'We'll show you a mirror in a moment,' said Kessian. 'Tell me how you feel now?'

Mirron paused and thought. A warm yellow chased across her irises before settling to a gentle, pulsing blue. 'I can feel it all, like warmth here. ' She touched her stomach. 'And here.' She touched her head. And then she moved her hand from Kovan's and held them both up, wiggling her fingers. She stared squarely at Kessian. 'And I can hold it all here. All of it.'

Chapter 35

*848th cycle of God, 20th day of Solasrise
15th year of the true Ascendancy*

The first of Yuran's hastily assembled citizen militia had already left Haroq City with the brief to defend their own lands. They had armour and weaponry supplied free by the Haroq City armoury. The money in their purses had been taken from the levy chests. The Marshal was delighted with the immediacy of the results. It was a risk, he knew but the easing of the tension in the city had been reason enough.

He had given back the defence of his country to its people despite the weight of manpower under the Conquord banner in Tsard. And while his militia didn't have the newest armour or the keenest blades, what they did have was a renewed belief in their Marshal. And because Yuran had sent each unit out with well-trained guardsmen, they felt they had the means to make a difference.

The riots and demonstrations had quickly subsided and Haroq had returned to a calmer state. Now would be the testing time. He awaited militia reports on how deeply the Tsardon raiders had penetrated and in what numbers. He needed them to encourage the people back to their homes to harvest the crops before dusas froze the ground once more. He needed them to see wider civil disobedience subside.

Yuran was enjoying a late supper with Megan. He had broken the seal on some fine wines and ordered his cooks to make classic Atreskan and Tsardon delicacies. The windows of the grand vaulted dining hall were all thrown open on the night and Yuran was enjoying the air free of the sounds of dissension and violence.

Try as he might when the Estoreans came to visit, he could not get on with eating in the reclined position, so he faced Megan across a proper table with high-backed straight chairs. Candelabra burned aside the night and servants stood at the tapestry-hung walls awaiting his signal. It was the Atreskan way. Throat-of-the-goat, it was practically everyone's way, barring the Estoreans and the puppet Caraducians, wasn't it?

'Marshal?'

'Sorry, Megan, I was miles away.'

'You were shaking your head. Is something wrong?'

'No. No, of course not,' said Yuran. 'How could there be anything wrong?'

Megan wasn't just bright, inventive and intelligent. She hadn't merely saved his city and maybe his whole country from the price of continued civil war. She was also quite, quite lovely. Perhaps it was the wine clouding his vision but this adviser seemed genuinely happy in his presence. Not nervous or awed. And she hadn't reacted with anxiety when he had requested she join him. More like she expected and looked forward to it. Perhaps it had been part of her plan all along.

Yuran would be happy if that proved to be the case. He raised his goblet and sipped again.

'How are you finding the goat's heart flambé?'

'Interesting,' she replied. 'Not what I'm used to, my Lord.'

'Please,' he said. 'This is an informal supper. My name is Thomal.'

Megan blushed and nodded. 'Thank you,' she said.

'It is the least I can do for the saviour of my nation.'

'Oh, I think you're going a little far,' she said. 'Perhaps just the city for now.'

Yuran roared with laughter and Megan joined him. He wagged a finger at her. 'That is what I always saw in you. You are honest and you are unafraid.'

'I am a proud Atreskan, my L— Thomal. Anything that keeps our country safe, I will do.'

'Then perhaps I should send you to speak for me at the Advocacy. Perhaps the Del Aglios woman would listen to you more seriously than she does me.' He realised halfway through that he was serious.

'If you wish it,' said Megan.

'Though I would not wish you to be far from me for too long,' he said, almost whispering.

Megan's head dropped and he was speared with regret.

'I'm sorry. I've gone too far.'

But she shook her head and looked back at him, the tears rolling down her face. 'No, you haven't,' she said. 'But it isn't often that the words you hear in your dreams are spoken to you when you are awake.'

Yuran felt a surge of relief and a pure happiness. He leaned back into his chair, unsure what to do next. He gazed at her, aware that they were both grinning like imbeciles. The hammering on the door to the dining hall was most unwelcome.

'Dear-God-of-the-sky, can I not have a moment's peace!' he yelled, thumping his fist on the table. 'Sorry, Megan.'

He pushed back from the table and rose. He indicated brusquely his servant open the door. A senior aide almost fell over the sill on his way into the room, such was his urgency.

'This had better be extremely important,' growled Yuran.

'It is, Marshal.' He paused, looking across at Megan.

'Speak. Megan needs to hear it too, whatever it is.'

The aide nodded. Yuran frowned. The man was sweating and there was a quiver to his hands as if he'd undergone heavy and prolonged exercise.

'There's a rumour sweeping the city,' he said. 'You'll hear it through the windows soon. Legionaries from the war have arrived. They're a mess.'

'We've seen them before. Deserters, refugees from a setback.' Yuran shrugged. 'What's the rumour?'

'Actually, it's not a rumour. I've spoken to one.' The aide took a deep breath. 'The entire eastern front has collapsed. Conquord forces have been routed. The Tsardon are marching on Atreska.'

'What?' Yuran refused to believe what he had just heard.

'If they are to be believed, as many as fifty thousand.'

Yuran sat back into his chair and threw up his hands. 'I don't . . . What did I say? What have I been saying since this campaign began? Too much reliance on the fronts, nothing in reserve.' He shook his head, the enormity cascading through him. 'Oh dear God-of-the-sea, we are defenceless.' He looked back at his aide. 'How long before they get here?'

'The survivors that have reached here so far have all been on horseback. Part of the Rogue Spears, the 9th Atreskan ala. They have outpaced the marching force comfortably but it is likely that the first Tsardon cavalry is no more than five days behind them, possibly as few as three. The main body of the army can be expected in ten days, no more.'

'Using our highways,' whispered Yuran.

'They will speed the enemy's progress.' The aide inclined his head. 'Marshal Defender, your orders?'

'Orders . . . orders.'

Yuran felt a crushing weight on his chest. His vision fogged. He felt the damp heat of sweat all over his body. His mind raced to no end and all he could see was doom. His head felt like a furnace had been laid inside it.

'Marshal?'

Yuran shook his head violently to clear it and held up a hand, aware it was shaking but not caring. He looked down the table at Megan.

'My destiny is not to enjoy a life of peace, is it?' he said.

'We will follow you whatever comes,' said Megan. 'Just tell us what you wish us to do.'

Her face, full of love and belief, rescued his will. Yuran sat taller in his chair.

'Bring me my commanders. I would know what strength I have that I can bring to bear in our defence. Perhaps we can hold them near the border. I will write a proclamation to be posted throughout the city, telling the people what is about to befall us. And light the beacon fires. Atreska is at war again and we must protect as many as we can inside the walls of our cities.' He turned his head to his aide, feeling a sudden fury replace his earlier despair. 'And I want the Estorean consul standing in front of me right now. Go.'

The aide ran from the room. Yuran listened to his footsteps echoing away along the stone corridor. From beyond the windows, he could hear the city coming to fearful wakefulness. And when the beacon fires were lit it would be the same across Atreska. The families of those on campaign in Tsard would wait to fall on any survivor who came through the gates, demanding information about their loved ones. Looking for any scrap of hope that they had escaped the disaster; the stories of which would race through the country like a fire, fanned by the winds of invasion.

Megan rose and came around the table to him. He stood and they embraced, both clinging hard, faces buried in each other's shoulders. Eventually Yuran pulled back.

'It's a sad fate that our first embrace is one of goodbye,' he said.

'My Lord?' Megan frowned.

'You of all of us will be safe, at least for now. You are ready for higher office and you will go to Estorr to take my messages and sue for massed reinforcement. If we cannot keep them at our borders, even if we cannot save our capital city, we will not lose our country without a fight. It is time for the Conquord to stand up for its peoples.'

He traced a finger down Megan's cheek. She grabbed his hand and squeezed it tight.

'You can take a boat down the Teel to Byscar at first light. With fair weather, you can be in Estorr in thirteen days. I will give you a note and seal for use of a ship and crew.'

'I should be at your side, Marshal,' said Megan.

'You will serve me and Atreska better in Estorr, Megan.' He leant in and kissed her lips. 'The fastest way for us to be together again is to work apart for now.'

Megan nodded. 'I will do my best.'

'I have grown to know nothing less.'

They embraced again and Yuran watched her go, unable to dispel the feeling that the Conquord had robbed him of something else he loved.

This time, Sentor Rensaark crossed the Tsardon border into Atreska with an army all but marching in his hoofprints. His work of years had not been in vain. He gazed into the breaking dawn to watch Korl's eye rise above the mountains, knowing that the ultimate victory for his King was at hand. He rode at the head of five hundred steppe cavalry, more than half of whom were fresh from the glorious victory at Scintarit. Down the rise on which he had paused, one of the two hundred border forts that studded the Atreskan border was plainly in view, its Conquord flag lazing in the heat.

He held his spear horizontally above his head and the cavalry began to trot the last mile to the fort, a deep rumbling of hoofs and a cloud of dust indicating their approach. That they had been seen was apparent when the Conquord flag was lowered and that of the old kingdom of Atreska raised in its place. Rensaark smiled. As it had ever been.

They reined in practically under the shadow of the fort. He dismounted and walked towards its iron bound doors. One of them swung open. A grey-haired man in a dented, tarnished breastplate over a cream woollen tunic strolled out. A pipe was in his mouth, smoking gently.

'I see you have not spent any of your earnings on fresh equipment, Centurion Danler,' said Rensaark.

The man, scarred and cynical even for an Atreskan, shrugged. 'It doesn't do to let any inspector think our pay is anything more than the pittance it officially is. And I see you have brought rather more than your normal raiding party. I presume this increases my purse.'

Rensaark laughed. 'Ever you try, Centurion. No, it does not mean that.' He snapped his fingers and one of his men dismounted and brought across a small wooden chest. 'But here is the gold we do owe you. It'll be the last.'

Danler raised his eyebrows. 'Oh?'

'You have been a loyal servant of both our countries,' said Rensaark. 'But surely you've seen survivors of the Conquord armies running for safety here.'

'Deserters pass here regularly,' he said. 'Who am I to stop them, eh? There may have been more than of late but the reality of battle falls harsh on the coward, doesn't it?'

'Then let me tell you that the Conquord was routed at Scintarit. That its forces are beaten and scattered from here to Sirrane in the north and Kark in the south. That we have scored the greatest victory in the history of our kingdom and that Tsard is marching to Estorr to break its walls. And that you have secured your future by seeing that we would be victorious. You and the supply chain we have already built deep into Atreska will speed us to the sundering of the Conquord. It will be so in Gestern and Gosland too.'

There was fear in Danler's eyes as he accepted the chest. 'Are you laughing at me?'

Rensaark shook his head. 'We were once friends and we will be again. You know what we want from Atreska and I have come to ask you for one more favour. Speak to the forts that flank you. Get the message passing along your borders. The Tsardon army will cross into your lands and they must be as friends to us. Make sure we are not delayed.'

Danler sucked his lip but he nodded.

'You have nothing to fear, my friend. And everything to be thankful for. The army will be here in two days. Make sure you have the proper flags flying.'

Rensaark's eye was caught by movement on the horizon. He saw smudges of smoke climbing into the sky, their intervals too regular to be a coincidence.

'What are those?' he said.

'Beacon fires,' said Danler. 'Atreska believes she is invaded. Should I light the fire on my roof, then the border will believe it too.'

Rensaark smiled. 'Believe me, not your fires. You are not invaded. Not by Tsard. Your invasion took place a decade ago. Our mission is liberation.'

'Don't make me look a fool, Rensaark.'

'Time will banish your worries,' said Rensaark. 'Now, I must go. I have business with your Marshal. It's time he understood too.'

Yuran had the simpering, patronising consul pinned to a wall in the throne room. His men kept the Conquord bodyguards back. Yuran had been kept waiting while the fear in his city grew by the moment and the beacon fires spread the word across the country. By the time the consul had deigned to appear, Yuran's eyes saw but one colour.

'The legions will reform in advance of the enemy. The Tsardon will never reach Haroq City.'

Yuran pushed a little harder, seeing the consul cough. He was a small man with close-cropped black hair and a belly that had seen too much luxury.

'Your precious army is gone,' he shouted, his spittle peppering the consul's face. He shook him with every phrase. 'They are leaderless, they are terrified and they are beaten. You have left me and my people defenceless through your arrogance and your deafness to my words. Where do we have to go now?'

The consul raised his hands in a pathetic, placatory gesture.

'I understand your concerns.'

'You have no idea of my concerns. You never leave your villa but to gorge yourself at my expense. You see nothing, you know nothing. There are fifty thousand Tsardon approaching my borders. And I have three legions. Three! And none of them are battle hardened, nor within a hundred miles of use.'

'And of course, you shall have more defence,' said the consul. 'I will return to Estorr immediately with my advisers and appraise the Advocate of—'

Yuran laughed loud and right into his face. 'Oh no, my weasel you will do no such thing. If I am to die at the hands of the King of Tsard then you will be standing at my shoulder.'

The consul displayed real fear for the first time. 'I—'

'You thought to escape. Even by the standards of Conquord consuls you are supremely gutless. I have already sent a delegation to Estorr. Most of the Gatherer unit has gone with my people to add credence. If nothing else, at least they have courage and the respect of the Advocacy. You, I am sure, have neither. You will not leave the city. Indeed, you will not leave your villa unless I so request it.'

The consul blustered incoherently. Yuran pushed him into the wall one more time.

'War is at my borders. And you, my spineless mentor, will face it with me.'

Chapter 36

848th cycle of God, 25th day of Solasrise
15th year of the true Ascendancy

It was dawn and Chancellor Koroyan was angry. Her wagon trailed behind Prime Sword Vennegoor and the Armour of God riders while they swooped on a guard post set out of sight of travellers heading away from Westfallen. Leaning from her window, she could see men running. One jumped onto the back of a horse and galloped away in the direction of the town in a clearly pre-arranged move.

Vennegoor pointed three fingers and a trio of riders upped their pace further in pursuit. The rest rode around in an arc to cut off any other attempt to run. Before them were eight men dressed in the livery of Marshal Vasselis, his personal army not a Conquord legion. Sensibly, none had drawn their weapons or nocked arrows into bow strings.

Vennegoor dismounted when her carriage rattled to a stop. He opened her door and the pair approached the guards. All looked experienced soldiers. None displayed any particular fear. It was testament to their loyalty to Vasselis and their belief in the Order, whose crest they could not have helped but see. It made no difference.

'You stand accused of heresy and protecting evil in the town of Westfallen,' she said, watching the anxiety cross their faces. 'Furthermore, you stand accused of obstructing the Order in its ordained duties, and of complicity in harbouring and protecting a heretic Reader. I, Felice Koroyan, Chancellor of the Order of Omniscience, lay these charges. How do you plead?'

Felice kept her tone deliberately neutral and matter-of-fact despite the fury inside. For the third time, she had been forced to lay charges against those merely acting on orders from Vasselis. And for the third time, the fear before her was palpable.

Seven of the eight dropped to one knee, hands placed palms down on the ground. Their captain swept off his plumed helmet and held it across his chest. He was a man still in his early years. His bearing was professional but he, like his guards, stared back at her in mute shock.

'Speak,' said Vennegoor. 'The Chancellor has asked you a question.'

'We are not guilty,' said the captain, plainly struggling to believe who was facing him. 'We guard as ordered. Westfallen has suffered an outbreak of bovine flu and is quarantined. Respectfully, my Chancellor, I must ask you to turn back.'

Felice knew her expression was bleak. 'And we were asked the same by the first two guard posts we encountered. So do you know why we are still here? It is because God's work cannot be obstructed by lies. Bovine flu . . .' She shook her head. 'Do I look an imbecile to you?'

'No, my Chancellor.'

'No,' said Felice. 'Then why do you peddle this untruth before me. This flu outbreak you claim has gripped the unfortunates in Westfallen has been going on longer than science and knowledge can persuade. It would by now have taken the life of every animal in the town or long been cured. If you can come up with no other response, I can only conclude your guilt.'

'Please, my Chancellor, we are ordinary soldiers and citizens. We follow orders and display the loyalty demanded by our Marshal Defender.'

'Even if that means turning your back on your God?' Felice let her anger take her. 'Even if that means evil is born and blossoms before your eyes? Does not your God, do not I, also demand and deserve respect?'

'Of course, my Chancellor.'

'Then show it,' she spat. 'Tell me the truth.'

'I do not question the orders of my Marshal. Please, Chancellor, we are innocent.'

'Liar,' said Vennegoor smoothly. 'We know the questions you ask of those journeying to Westfallen. And we know what you ask of those who leave. Quarantine for the propagation of evil. You are as guilty of heresy as surely as your Marshal and your Ascendants.'

The word dripped like rot from his mouth. Felice saw the captain react and his head drop fractionally.

'Oh dear,' she said. 'Guilty.'

Behind her, a hundred bows were drawn back. Panic took the guards. Shouts for mercy, pleas for clemency, exhortations of faith. She shook her head.

'Your God asks of you only that you do His bidding and keep His earth free from those who would corrupt it. You did not do this. You provide no credible defence, you are aware of the presence of evil and so I find you guilty of the charges laid before you. You are sentenced to death and you will never feel the embrace of God.'

'You have no authority to carry out such sentence.' The captain at last found his courage.

'In that, as in many things, you will find you are wrong,' said Vennegoor.

One of the guards broke and ran. Vennegoor's arm rose and fell. From the flanks of the arc of riders, bow strings thrummed. Arrows clouded her vision for a moment, thudding into the guardsmen. Multiple shafts pierced each body. All the men died instantly. Felice shook her head.

'Burn them. Let the devils have them. Sentence has been carried out.' She knelt on one knee. 'Let us pray.'

Arducius walked through Westfallen towards the sea. His friends were with him. Ossacer had a hand on his right arm though he could have chosen not to; seeing through the trails was easy enough now but still an effort of mind. Mirron walked slightly ahead of them, chatting with Kovan, who strode proudly with his hand rested casually on his sword pommel. Gorian was on his left, sauntering in that way of his. He was chewing a stalk of grass and every time he looked at Mirron and Kovan, a small smile touched his lips.

It was afternoon on a God-blessed day and the life of the earth surged gloriously through the Ascendants. Arducius felt it as a rumble through his entire body. He remembered the pain of his connection with all around him and the relief in the faces of the Echelon when he came round. And to think they had thought that the playing with the elements they had done was emergence. It was not. It was just the preamble. Everything they had learned had been moving them towards the ability to accept the real energy, the real lifelines.

And what they felt now was an order of magnitude so much larger than before. No wonder their bodies and minds had fought to be able to accept it and control it. No wonder they could still barely contain what they felt and were so careful in preparing their Works. Even now, they did not dare try and examine their full potential. It scared them all and Father Kessian wanted them to tread carefully. And so they did.

Today they had a break from their studies and had decided to go swimming and sailing. Kovan was going to officiate in some races above the water and use the hourglass to time them on dives to collect a set of coloured stones he would drop himself. Arducius loved games like these. They brought the Ascendants closer together and, he hoped, helped repair the divide that existed between Kovan and Gorian. Perhaps that was too much to expect. Particularly when the object of their disagreement was right there with them. He wished Mirron would take it more seriously but she seemed to revel in it.

The fishing fleet was out in the bay when they arrived at the beach. Only a handful of boats were pulled up on the shore. Kovan's single-masted boat had been prepared by members of the household staff and, as always these days, some of the Marshal's soldiers were present. Still, Kovan was in a fine mood. His father had unexpectedly arrived the evening before from some business over at Lake Phristos and Glenhale. Actually, it gave the whole town a lift. There had been an air of worry over the place ever since the investigation and having him here made people feel safer.

Gorian knelt at the water's edge and placed his hand in the water. Ripples fled away against the inward tide and wavelets. Arducius went to stand beside him.

'Is he out there?'

Gorian turned to look at him, a smile on his face and his eyes a steady deep blue. 'Yes,' he said. 'He's coming in.'

The dolphin broke the surface thirty or so yards out and swam into the shallows, occasionally lifting his head from the water to chatter at them.

'He's happy,' said Gorian. 'I can feel a surge through him, like new life. Perhaps there's a big shoal out there.'

'Well, no doubt Jen has found it if there is,' said Arducius.

'No doubt,' replied Gorian. 'One day they won't need a fishing fleet. We'll be able to bring the fish straight into the shore.'

Arducius laughed. 'I don't think so, Gorian.'

'Believe it,' said Gorian and his face was serious once more.

Just down the beach, the staff had launched the boat and held it in a couple of feet of water. Kovan was already at the tiller.

'Come on,' he said. 'In you get. The contest won't wait.'

The sound of bells shattered the peace of the afternoon. In the water, the dolphin dived and disappeared. On the beach, the Marshal's guards shot to their feet and looked away to the rise on which the watchtower stood, looking down on the road to Cirandon. Kovan scrambled from the boat and the Ascendants gathered together.

'What's going on?' asked Ossacer, clutching at Arducius's arm.

'It's the alarm,' said Kovan. 'Nephis, take the detachment from our villa. Get my father, he's up at the lake. I'll get the Ascendants to the Echelon villa.'

'Yes, sir,' said Nephis. He and two of his comrades ran away from the beach. The other two came to flank Kovan.

'Come on,' said Kovan. 'You need to get under cover.'

'Well, why don't we just swim out to sea?' said Gorian.

'No,' said Kovan. 'You know the arrangements. You can't stay out there forever. Come with me.'

'I don't take orders from you,' said Gorian.

Arducius felt Ossacer's hand tighten on his arm. He looked round and caught the look on Mirron's face too. She was staring up at the rise where the bells still rang and soldiers were running. He swung round to Gorian.

'This isn't the time. They're frightened. We will do what Father Kessian wants or the Echelon won't know where to find us.'

Gorian glared at him for moment but nodded. Kovan relaxed.

'Let's go,' he said.

'They're coming,' said Mirron, pointing up to the rise.

Arducius looked up. Riders were pouring over the rise. So many of them.

'Who are they?' he asked.

'It doesn't matter,' said Kovan, his voice assuming the tone of command. 'Let's go. Hurry.'

He began to run up the road that led up to the left of the forum. It was the quickest way to the villa and what they hoped was safety. In front of them, confusion was taking hold. People crossed their path, running, walking, shouting. Most were heading home but many were just moving away from the riders, heading down into Westfallen and towards the beach.

Arducius made sure the others were with him. Mirron's face reflected the fear he felt. Ossacer was using the trails in the air to guide him now and had left the security of Arducius's arm. Gorian's face was dark and angry, his eyes flicking to the invaders, whoever they were. Arducius prayed they were Advocacy forces. If it was the Order, they were in serious trouble.

Heat and the run was making him sweat. He felt it down the back of his tunic, under his arms and on his face. He ran just ahead of the other three, with Vasselis's soldiers bringing up the rear. People got out of their way, shouted for them to hide, to run and to disappear.

They turned left away from the forum and ran up a steep cobbled street with houses tight on either side. Kovan kept the pace up and the Ascendants followed him. Arducius could hear the sound of the soldiers' boots ringing on the stone. His fear grew. They left the street to head through fields to the villa. A dark line appeared on the horizon, spreading quickly to their right.

'Oh no,' said Kovan. 'Faster. Faster.'

It was more riders. They had ridden off the road and through the farmland, cutting off escape towards the lake and the river to Glenhale. Arducius's heart was thundering in his chest. He could sense the waves of uncertainty that had gripped the town. Through the ground, the rumble of hoofs could be clearly felt. The clash of sensations was uncomfortable within him, like a churning unhappiness of life lines. His chest tightened.

They had climbed above the level of the town now and were close to the villa. Riders had already made it into the heart of Westfallen and a quick glance showed them on the way to the House of Masks, around to the Vasselis villa and moving to completely encircle the town from the land. There was panic in the air and Arducius felt Mirron beginning to breathe too fast.

'Steady, Mirron,' he said. 'It'll be all right.'

'They've come for us,' she said. 'They've come to take us.'

'They will not get you,' said Kovan over his shoulder. 'Keep going. I'll keep you safe.'

They were in the open now, sprinting hard. The villa was only a couple of hundred yards away and Vasselis's soldiers could be seen in the grounds and around the walls. As he watched, three ran out of the front gates and turned right. Up the track towards them came five riders. There were barked shouts to stop that went unheeded.

Swords were drawn and steel glinted in the sunlight. Arducius caught his breath. The horsemen rode on. The soldiers came to ready. There was a blur as the two sides passed each other. He saw a blade sweep down into the face of one of the soldiers. He was plucked from his feet and tumbled into the ground, rolling to lie still in the wake of the horses. Blood. There was blood all over the sandy ground.

Mirron screamed and came to a stumbling stop, her hands over her mouth. Arducius felt sick. Around the other side of the villa came more riders. They seemed to be everywhere and on each horse was the same branded mark of a circle of arms with hands clasped.

Kovan stopped running and held his arms out left and right to stop the Ascendants running past him. The two soldiers came to his side and drew their swords. Ahead, the survivors of the rider attack ran to their comrade. Horses wheeled and came back towards them. Arrows were in tensed bows and they backed away, arms raised.

Arducius saw other riders coming down the road towards them. Yet others dismounted and ran in through the gates of the villa. Down in the town, the shouts were loud and scared. Horses whinnied and snorted. Hoofs stamped on cobbles.

'Stand with me,' said Arducius, bringing the Ascendants to him. 'Keep your heads down. Don't let them see who we are.'

'It's the Order,' hissed Gorian. 'They have come to kill us.'

'You don't know that,' said Arducius.

'We can stop them,' said Gorian.

Arducius glared at him. 'We will not use our power for violence. Our only chance is to prove we are a force for good. It is what Father Kessian demands.'

The clop of hoofs was so close and loud now. Arducius looked out from under his brow. Four riders came towards them. Two had bows, the others swords. Beside him, Mirron was shaking. This was beyond any of them. The violence they had seen, the blood on the ground, the weapons pointed at them.

Ossacer gripped his arm again. 'I can't concentrate,' he said, his voice small and terrified. He coughed. 'I can't focus.'

'It's all right,' said Arducius. 'Lean on me. Gorian, see to Mirron.'

Gorian enveloped her in one strong arm and she clung to him.

Arducius wasn't sure which one of them was the most scared. And then one of the riders spoke and confirmed all their worst fears.

'Citizens of Westfallen, you will gather in your forum. There is evil here. Heresy against God. Your Ascendants will be unmasked and will be tried. All those complicit in this crime will be tried. Put up your swords. Move.'

Chapter 37

At least the Order didn't know which of them were the Ascendants but it wouldn't take them too long to narrow it down. Right now, they seemed content just to herd everyone they found into the forum. The heat was oppressive, the anxiety more so. Bewildered citizens stood still and silent, or turned round and round, looking at the riders that had secured the forum's every side.

Standing on the oratory stage, under cover from the sun, were six people. Four were soldiers. Warriors of the Armour of God. The other two were Horst Vennegoor, the commander of the riders, and Felice Koroyan, the Chancellor. She was a proud figure, tall and slender, staring down at the people with a sneer on her face. She already hated them and she knew nothing about them.

The Ascendants were standing with Kovan in the middle of the crowd. The soldiers had been taken away somewhere else. Kovan had managed to conceal his gladius under the folds of his light cloak. It gave him some comfort at least. Gorian and Arducius had been arguing, hissing at each other. Gorian wanted to act. To bring on a storm or a gale. Rush the stage and get the Chancellor. Arducius had told him to keep calm but it was getting increasingly obvious that Gorian would not be tamed forever.

'You don't even know if you can do these things you suggest,' said Arducius.

'Don't be stupid, Ardu,' snapped Gorian back at him. 'You can feel it the same way I can. We all can. The energy of the wind thrills your body like it does mine. More so for you as Wind Harker. You know the power that lies under the stone of this forum. We can harness it.'

'And what good would it really do? You cannot scare them all off. There are too many. And when you are done you will be wrinkled and exhausted, unable to run. You will have identified yourself to them and left yourself helpless. Wait.'

'For what? For them to find us anyway just by looking in our eyes?' Gorian's were a livid swirling brown as he felt the power beneath his feet and let it feed him. 'We can't stay here and do nothing. We may as well cut our own throats. Don't you see that they know all about us already? They knew where the villa was, they knew where the Marshal's villa was and they knew where the House of Masks was. Someone has told them everything.'

Kovan turned on him. 'Listen to Ardu,' he said. 'Be calm and wait. We are not helpless. My Father and the Echelon are not yet here. That means they haven't been found.'

'And then what? You think Father Kessian and Willem are going to scare them? They are old men. And your father doesn't have enough with him. It's down to us.'

'But not yet,' said Arducius. 'Please Gorian, don't give us all away.'

Gorian looked at Mirron and she nodded her agreement.

'Please,' she said, reaching out a hand to him. 'Listen to them.'

But Gorian was right in his assessment of the Order's knowledge. Dread clutched at Mirron's heart. Order warriors moved through the crowd. Consternation spread. They were moving in from all sides. Just a handful of them but they missed no one, looked at everyone. And try as they might to look away, Mirron could feel the eyes of the townspeople on them. Not in blame or accusation, but in sympathy. She wished they wouldn't, it would draw attention.

'Eyes down,' whispered Arducius. 'Just look at the ground. Whatever happens don't look up.'

Whenever she glanced around, Mirron could see warriors grabbing people and pushing them towards the oratory and the Chancellor. There were angry words, even the odd scuffle and one screech of pain. People jostled and she caught metal in the sunlight again. She shuddered. It reminded her of the man she saw killed outside the villa. Such violence in her home. Something she never dreamed to see.

The soldiers were coming closer to them.

'Don't struggle,' said Arducius. 'Do what they say. Gorian, that means you.'

'All right,' hissed Gorian, voice still full of anger.

She felt a hand on her shoulder.

'Get to the front,' ordered the warrior. 'Now. Stand with the others.'

She nodded, fixed her gaze on his boots. He put a hand on her back and shoved her. She cried out.

'Get your hands off her,' said Gorian.

'Don't talk back to me, boy,' barked the soldier. 'Go with her. And you. All five of you. Run or you'll feel my boot in your backsides.'

The Ascendants and Kovan breasted through the crowd which parted to let them through. A dog ran in front of them and Arducius stumbled over it. Other hands touched them. But these were friendly and encouraging, as were the words that accompanied them. Mirron muttered her thanks. In front of the crowd, a line of warriors stood across the face of the oratory.

To the left, more Order soldiers separated a small but growing group from the rest. They were beckoned over to join them. Mirron dared a quick glance. Kovan would be about the oldest there at seventeen. Some were as young as ten. Too many of them stared at the Ascendants with the accusing expressions not shown by their elders and parents. Kovan saw it and moved through the group, some thirty or forty strong so far, whispering what he wanted them to do. One loose word and the Ascendants would be unmasked.

'I'm sorry,' whispered Mirron to a girl near to her, feeling a cat brush against her legs. 'You'll be all right. Don't worry.'

Up on the oratory, the Chancellor stepped forwards. Around the forum, her soldiers bellowed for silence.

'Some of you might wonder why I am here and why you are gathered before me,' she said, staring all the time at the youngsters to her right. Mirron could sense her revulsion. 'But I doubt that number is very high. I expect some innocent visitors have been caught up in this and let me assure you that you have nothing to fear. God is with you although He has surely forsaken the place in which you now stand.

'To all those who choose to dwell here, I say this. You have a beautiful haven here. A paradise, some might say, that God has blessed with strong earth and bountiful seas. A gift. And yet you have let evil rot it. And that evil has pervaded to every corner of every villa. You have allowed to be created children who you would seat above God. People who you think will be able to manipulate the elements and the earth, the skies and the seas, animals and trees . . . other people, whether they will it or not.

'Nature in all its glory and terror is for us to enjoy, respect and maintain. It is not in our gift to dictate, alter or control it. That is heresy.'

She paused and let her eyes pass over the crowd. The silence was total among the people. No one even dared to shift their feet. Only the cicadas in the fields and the birds in the sky continued to call and sing.

'And I will uncover all of those who are guilty and bring them to justice under God. And what will that mean, I wonder? Perhaps those who revealed their fears of the crimes being committed here are exaggerating. Perhaps I am only seeking a handful of criminals and four tortured individuals whose bodies contain power they cannot hope to understand or control.'

Mirron shrank back against the comforting frame of Gorian. His hands slid around her waist, holding her close. She tried not to cry but it was so hard to contain her fear. Surely the Chancellor was staring straight at her, speaking into her heart to make her confess. She clamped her lips together to stop them trembling.

Around the group of young citizens, dogs and cats were beginning to gather. They were focusing on Gorian. How long before one of the Order remarked on it. She tried to focus her mind to send them away. Gorian should be doing the same but his barely suppressed rage was aimed squarely at the Chancellor.

'Make no mistake, I will discover the perpetrators of these crimes. Who it is that sanctioned the creation of these Ascendants and who it is that protects them now. And let me remind you that should you shield them, or even should you refuse to identify them when so demanded, you will be as guilty as they are.

'I will leave you to think on that. God looks down with benevolence and mercy on those who repent and return to the true faith; those who renounce the corruption they have experienced. Some of you will resist in a misplaced desire to protect these heretics. I will demonstrate why that would be a very grave mistake.'

She indicated to Vennegoor.

'Bring them up!' he barked.

A ripple ran through the crowd. There was movement left and right of the oratory. From the right the Echelon were moved onto the platform. All of them except dear Jen Shalke who would still be out with the fleet. Father Kessian led them, looking terribly old and fragile.

'Oh no,' said Mirron, feeling the tears running down her cheeks. 'How can they do this to him?'

He tried to look proud but he tottered on his two sticks and had to be helped to where they wanted him. Next to him was Genna, then Willem, Andreas, Hesther, Meera and Gwythen. They didn't look as if they'd been hurt but in their faces was all the stress of their capture. They were all made to stand.

'I won't let them hurt him,' muttered Gorian.

'Nor me,' said Kovan from next to them. 'Not him. They daren't touch him.'

'They would not want us to give ourselves away,' said Arducius. 'Remember that. We must not sacrifice ourselves.'

'I will not stand by,' said Gorian. 'And if I give myself away, so be it.'

Mirron heard a gasp from in front of her and followed the fingers that were pointing to the left of the oratory. Someone was being dragged on to the platform between two Order warriors. A name was shouted out and picked up by the crowd which bunched in singular outrage. Mirron looked hard and knew it to be true.

Through the mask of blood on her face under the tangle of her hair, and in the dishevelled, torn and bloodied robes, she could see it was Elsa Gueran. Elsa who did nothing but smile, love and preach the true word of God. There were shouts of anger and fists punched empty air. Bows were bent all around the forum and here and there, Order soldiers waded in to deliver kicks and punches to quell the unrest.

'And why are you enraged?' shouted the Chancellor. 'This woman took vows of piety and loyalty only unto God. And yet she has not merely turned her head from the heresy in your midst, she has taken active part in it. You should be cheering me for uncovering her crime and punishing her for it. You have to have faith in your Reader. How can you have faith in one who presents her back to God?'

There was renewed silence across the forum. Mirron, like all of them, knew with a sick certainty that there was going to be no justice. There were going to be no hearings and trials. There was going to be killing under the veil of God and with the approval of the

Chancellor, the one person charged above all others with the protection all who walked His earth. And up on the stage, the first act of a hideous drama was being played out before its frightened, captive audience.

'And what did you ask, I wonder?' Kessian's voice was trembling but full of passion. 'Did you care for the truth or did your thugs merely demand justification to beat an innocent woman? How is it that the most ignorant among us stands in judgement over us? How is it that you who should be seeking new glories of God feel so threatened by them that you would kill His people to hide them?'

Mirron's heart sang at the sound of his voice and for one moment, she felt the mortal fears of Westfallen lift. But the whole time he had been speaking, Koroyan had been sauntering easily towards him. She stood in front of him now. He did not flinch.

'So eloquent are the words of evil,' she said. 'So seductive are you tones, Ardol Kessian, father of this heresy. Always, those who seek to destroy God disguise their desires in the clothes of righteousness.'

'Destroy?' Kessian's face was dismayed. 'Will you not listen to us, Chancellor? Will you not see what is being done here and that all who are involved believe utterly in the sanctity of God?'

'I do not need to see. I dare not face it,' said Koroyan.

'You dare not face it for risk that you would see the truth.'

Mirron gasped. It was Elsa who had spoken. Her voice was thick with blood but she was holding her head up, her arms still held by her captors. Koroyan spun on her heel and strode back across the oratory, pointing an accusing finger at Elsa all the way.

'See!' she shouted to the crowd. 'See the corruption that evil brings? The confusion of the once pure mind.' She grabbed Elsa's chin. 'I almost pity you, girl. Because it is you who does not see. I have no need to confront your truth. I *am* the truth.'

'Then you are blind,' said Elsa. 'Because only the blind could fail to see the faith and love of God in this town.'

Koroyan stepped back, her face pinched with contempt. 'It is one insult too many,' she said. 'You have already confessed to crimes that carry the penalty of death and the scattering of your ashes to the devils of the wind. And now you seek to question my faith?'

'I only ask you to see,' said Elsa.

'It is not my eyes that have failed.'

'Don't let her take you!' Elsa was suddenly calling to the crowd, to anyone that would hear her. 'Don't let her persuade you we are ungodly. Don't let her turn you away from—'

Almost too quick to follow, the Chancellor grabbed Elsa's hair and pulled back her head. Her robes billowed and Mirron caught a glint of silver, moving left to right. And when she stepped back, the blood was pumping from Elsa's throat and Koroyan's robes and hands were stained red.

'Bring me water to wash away this filth,' she said. 'Sentence is passed.'

From the silence came a storm of rage. Everyone was yelling abuse. The word 'murderer' echoed around the columns of the forum. The crowd surged again and the Order soldiers pressed in, swords drawn, bows bent back. Kovan and Arducius restrained Gorian. Ossacer was clinging to Mirron, who in turn stared at the oratory platform where the Echelon was being pushed back by soldiers. They were gesticulating, crying, trying to force their way to Elsa whose life ebbed away in front of them all. She had been dropped by the soldiers and died alone.

Genna was holding on to Father Kessian who was wheezing as he tried to speak. He clutched at his left arm as if in some pain. It was his voice again that rose above the quietening tumult. But he could barely get the words out, such was his struggle to breathe.

'This is not trial nor justice,' he said, gasping between almost every word. 'This is murder born of ignorance and fear. For all the evil you denounce us for, the only person harmed is dead by your hand.' He stopped and sagged, held up by Genna and now Willem, who came to his other side. Both were whispering to him.

A bolt of fear speared Mirron and around her the Ascendants tensed as one. Koroyan was on him again, striding the stage like some heroic actor.

'I would stop its spread even if that meant burning everyone in this town,' she said.

'You have no authority,' said Kessian, his face red and agonised. 'Where is the Advocacy seal?'

'I act under the authority of God.'

'You act for your own ends. I do not recognise you as my Chancellor.'

Koroyan backhanded him across the face. He jerked backwards and then pitched forwards. Genna screamed. This time, no one tried to stop Gorian. They were all with him, knowing what they must do.

Barring their way were two soldiers. The air was hot and dry, the energy trails livid before Mirron's eyes. She drew it into her, feeling the scorching race through her veins and burgeon under the focus of her mind. She channelled it through to her hands, pressing her palms together to keep it cycling within her. In front, Kovan and Gorian had pushed other children aside, shouted them down. And in the confusion and in her rage, Mirron opened her palms and the flame spat out. It slammed into their helmets and breastplates, attracted by the metal, and knocked them both from their feet.

The Ascendants were past them in a moment, racing towards the oratory. A wind bore down the forum, picking up a cloud of sand and dust. Arducius was walking with his arms out by his sides, channelling the gale that blinded and confused the bowmen ahead of them. Shafts were loosed but they flew harmlessly into the teeth of the wind.

Up on the stage, it was all those there could do to stay on their feet. Gorian and Kovan had reached the side stairs. Kovan faced an Order warrior, blocking his thrust aside easily and thumping the hilt of his sword into the man's face, downing him. Gorian went past him, ignoring Vennegoor on his way to Father Kessian and the Chancellor.

Mirron went after him, Ossacer too, and when Kovan had his sword point at the Chancellor's neck, Arducius stilled the gale. Silence, punctuated by the sound of approaching horses. The crowd gaped as the sand and dust fell and uncertainty returned. Mirron had no idea what to do next. She wondered if any of them did. All the Ascendants were round Kessian now. The soldiers had backed off. Through fear or confusion she didn't know.

Bows were trained on them from all sides. She looked around the oratory. At Koroyan, who ignored the sword point and stared at them in utter disbelief. Vennegoor had his hand on his sword hilt now.

'Don't,' said Kovan. He was behind the Chancellor with a hand on her shoulder. 'Take your hand away and order your men to stand down. I don't want to hurt her but I will. If one arrow is loosed—'

'Keep calm, young man,' said Vennegoor. His voice was weak, his eyes wandering to the Ascendants like his Chancellor's. He made a downward gesture with his hands and the bows were relaxed. 'No one needs be hurt.'

'It's too late for that,' said Gorian from where he sat, cradling Kessian's head in his lap. The Father was breathing but it was faint. Ossacer had his hands on him and was trying everything he could to help him. 'You have already caused more hurt more than you can imagine.'

'So, here you are at last,' said the Chancellor. Her face was white and she too had a trembling voice. 'Those who would depose God and sit as lords over us all. Your display has merely confirmed your guilt. This is an abomination. A terrifying, shocking abomination. And it shall be stopped. Here, today.'

The horses were getting closer and Vennegoor gathered himself.

'What will you do now?' he said, addressing Kovan. 'We are a hundred. And you can hear others approaching. You are but one sword and those who can create a gale against all reason and faith. You cannot win. Put it down, lad. Let what must be done, be done.'

'You will all die before I let you hurt one more of us,' said Gorian.

'And demonstrate your evil to all present,' said the Chancellor.

'I am protecting my own,' he said. 'You have no idea what I can do.'

Kessian's hand reached up and gripped Gorian's. His eyes opened and Mirron felt a rush of relief. But it was brief. There were tears in Ossacer's eyes, escaping down his cheeks.

'Don't do it, Gorian,' whispered Kessian. 'For me, don't do it. Don't give them the reason they need. Help is coming.'

'For you, Father,' said Gorian nodding, his voice beginning to break. 'But only for you.'

'Good lad,' he said. 'Good lad. Remember your destiny.'

His hand slipped away and his eyes closed. And all the Ascendants sensed it; grey fading to dark. Lifelines blinking out. The passing of blessed life.

'No!' screamed Mirron. 'NO!'

She buried her head in Genna's chest, wailing, her whole world tattering. She could hear the shouting around her. Kovan strong and steady. Gorian raging and accusing. Arducius trying to keep them together but unable to make himself heard through his sobs. The wind came again. Thunder cracked in a sky darkened by gathering cloud. There was noise and running feet. The sounds of swords clashing and a single dominating voice demanding order.

Chapter 38

848th cycle of God, 25th day of Solasrise
15th year of the true Ascendancy

Vasselis knew he had to keep himself and his soldiers calm. Riding hard from the lake where he left Netta hidden and under guard, he brought ten with him. Approaching the town he could see the crowd in the forum and was certain that the Order had come to Westfallen. The forced gathering for denunciation was ever their method. How they had found out about the Ascendancy would have to wait.

Galloping towards the head of the forum and the oratory, he split his force to take both sets of steps. Three guards stood by each. He rode right. Arrows took down two and he leaped from his horse to confront the other. He drew his cavalry blade.

'Drop your weapon,' he said.

Above them on the oratory he heard harsh words. Then it was a scream of grief. Ahead of him, the Order warrior stood resolute. Vasselis lunged at him. Their blades clashed. He forced his enemy's right and lashed in his left fist, feeling the steel knuckled gauntlet splintering his cheek. The man fell back. Vasselis drove his blade through his gut and jumped over the crumpling body and up the steps.

Out on to the stage he came. His son, *his son,* had a blade to the Chancellor's neck. Horst Vennegoor stood rigid near them. Across the oratory, the Echelon and the Ascendants were grouped together. There was screaming and there was crying and he could see the raw fury in Gorian's face. In the sky, storm clouds gathered. And out in the forum, the citizens of Westfallen cheered at sight of him and his men.

'I will have order here!' he roared. 'I will have order.'

The skies began to clear and the wind dropped away. And now all he could hear was weeping. He stalked towards the Chancellor, a drop of blood falling from the tip of his sword. His men had pushed her warriors on the oratory away, disarming them, and were protecting the Echelon and the Ascendants.

'Unbuckle your sword belt, Horst. I don't want your blood on my blade as well,' he said. 'And signal all your warriors to withdraw. You are all leaving.'

Vennegoor inclined his head and moved his hands to his belt. Vasselis stood before the Chancellor, seeing fear behind her proud expression. Not fear for her life but what she had seen.

'It's all right, Kovan. You can relax now. I'm more proud of you than I can say.'

'You implicate your son as well,' said Koroyan. 'Is there no end to your selfishness?'

Vasselis watched his son put up his sword and move over to stand with the Ascendants, a man this day. In its way it was an emergence as important as for those who he protected. And in the face of such aggression and violence. Another day, Vasselis would smile about it. Not today.

'Kovan, they are your responsibility now. Take them, you know what to do.'

'She killed Father Kessian,' shouted Gorian.

'And that is where it will end,' said Vasselis though his heart was breaking. 'Go. While you still can. It isn't safe here for you any more.'

'They won't get far,' said Koroyan. 'We know their faces. Their eyes are evidence of their guilt. And you will burn with them, Marshal. Your time is almost up.'

'I would not say another word, if I were you, Felice. You have done enough damage for one day.'

He looked to his left and saw Elsa lying in her blood, her hair ruffling in the breeze. And to his right, Kessian. Still and dead.

'I am here to—'

'Silence!' Vasselis vented all his fury into the one word. 'Unless you have the seal of the Advocate you have no authority to dispense justice here. This is my country and these are my people. And I will not hesitate to cut down any who threaten them.'

The cheer from behind him was loud and long. He nodded but didn't turn to them. Instead, he leant into Koroyan.

'Felice, you can have it your way if you want and I will humiliate you in front of all these innocent, law-abiding people. Or you can leave now and we will both stand before the Advocate to explain ourselves another day. Which is it to be? Either way, the Ascendants leave unharmed.'

Koroyan looked at the Ascendants having to be dragged away from the body of Ardol Kessian. She smiled ice.

'You are a heretic and you will burn,' she said. 'How many men is it you have here, I wonder?'

'Damn you, Felice. Damn your ashes to the wind.' He turned. 'Run, Kovan. Run!'

Arducius could barely see for the tears clouding his eyes. He had been pulled to his feet by one of Vasselis's soldiers and bundled down the stairs to the back of the oratory along with the rest of the Ascendants and the Echelon. Arrows had begun to fly from the sides of the forum, clicking into stone and whistling overhead. Only Genna remained with Father Kessian, his body stretched on the stone stage in the heat of the afternoon. Mirron's screams as she was dragged from his side and rushed away would live with him for ever. He had no idea what had happened to Marshal Vasselis.

The air was full of shouts and violence. He and the others were in the centre of a mass of sprinting legs and flailing arms. Vasselis's men ran ahead of them and behind them. Hesther, Meera and Gwythen ran with them while Willem and Andreas, too old to keep up, sought shelter where they could. But they were not the target, not for now.

The Order warriors had broken from their ring around the forum and were trying to force their way through a crowd that obstructed them at every turn. Kovan led the Ascendants along an alley and then right down a narrow street that would take them parallel to the forum and back to the beach. He ran hard, flanked by his father's men. Gorian ran just behind him.

Ossacer was struggling, unable to focus on the trails in the sky to help him run. He was being held steady by one of the soldiers; a gloved fist grabbing the back of his tunic and all but lifting him from the ground. It was the same for Mirron. She had stumbled more than once and had been swept over a soldier's shoulder where she stared behind her at Arducius, her face blank with shock and covered in her tears.

'I'm here, Mirron,' he managed. 'I'm here.' But he didn't think she heard him.

They were being chased. The Order was after them. An arrow smacked into the buildings to the left.

'Faster!' shouted a soldier. 'Don't look back.'

Three men spilled out into the street ahead of them. More arrows flew. One caught a soldier in his face and he was pitched from his feet to go crashing into the wall at his left. Kovan and the other soldier closed to attack. Both had gladiuses and used them two-handed. Arducius could barely register it all but there it was, happening right in front of him.

Kovan didn't hesitate. His blade swept down left to right and a bowman fell, a great slash through his light riding armour and deep into his body. Vasselis's man batted aside a blade and returned his sword into the neck of his enemy. Blood fountained into the God-blessed blue of the sky and sprayed across Arducius's face as he ran through, having to jump a body still moving with the last of life. The third enemy loosed another arrow which missed its target. Kovan chopped down into his hands. The man howled and fell, an anguished sound that speared Arducius. He felt the surge of energy as the man's body tried to compensate for the wound. The street was running red.

Arducius was breathing hard. He wiped at his face as he went. More arrows came from behind, none coming too close with the archers having to fire on the run. But he could not pause or slow. The roar of the crowd in the forum reached them here but was dulled by stone. His ears were full of the echo of boot on cobble, too. So much clamouring for his attention when it was all he could do to keep placing one foot in front of another.

They emerged from the end of the street and into the glare of the open space that ran down to the harbour, the beach and the open sea. Dogs ran beside them, barking in frenzied fury. There were people running in from the right-hand side. Order warriors, Vasselis's men and ordinary citizens. The direction of the Ascendants had been obvious from the start; it was their only real chance of quick escape.

The arrows hadn't stopped but now the soldiers at the rear did. Yelling the Ascendants on, they turned and rushed the Order archers heading towards them. Arducius only had eyes for ahead. On the beach, Kovan's boat was ready and prepared. Five of Vasselis's archers stood around it in an arc, composite bows bending, releasing.

Arducius tried not to look but couldn't help it. So many of the Order seemed to be running at them. They had cleared the last of the houses on the far side in front of the forum and were tearing across the coarse, brown grass that separated the town from the beach. After them came the enraged townsfolk.

Kovan led them on to the harbour concrete, racing for the boat. They weren't going to make it first.

'Into the water!' shouted Arducius. 'Ascendants, let's go. Kovan, you'll have to pick us up off shore.'

He saw Kovan nod and indicate his men continue with him. Mirron was put down and Ossacer released. The soldiers turned and ran after Kovan. The Echelon gathered around the Ascendants.

'We haven't much time,' said Hesther, her face creased with stress and the effort of running.

'You should be coming with us,' said Gorian.

'We can't do that,' said Meera, enveloping her son in her arms. 'You have to get away from here. We'll be all right, the Marshal will protect us.'

'I don't want to go,' sobbed Ossacer. 'Please don't make me go.'

'It won't be forever,' said Hesther. 'You'll be back before you know it.'

'I'm not going,' said Mirron. 'I won't leave you. Any of you.'

An arrow skipped off the ground too close by for comfort. The sound of swords clashing rang out across the water. The Echelon crowded round the Ascendants. Gwythen hugged Mirron hard.

'It's too dangerous,' she said. 'Come on, young lady, we've spoken about this. We knew it might happen.'

Arducius felt the same fear that he saw in their faces. But they couldn't stay here at the moment. That much was obvious.

Hesther glanced behind her and clapped her hands. 'Come on, go. Arducius, look after them. Gorian, keep hold of your temper. Mirron, remember where your heart lies. Ossacer, everything can be healed. Now go. We'll shield you.'

Arducius nodded, kicked off his sandals and led them into the harbour waters and out of sight.

Kovan didn't look back. His boat seemed terribly far away and the enemy was closing in. He was running along the harbour wall with three men. The archers guarding the boat still fired but had to let their arrows fall short for fear of hitting innocent citizens.

'Swords and shields!' shouted Kovan.

Ahead of him, his men had heard him. Bows were discarded, rectangular shields were picked up from the sand and gladiuses drawn. They spread around the stern of the boat while Kovan's aides stood in the water at the bow, keeping it ashore but ready to launch.

There were at least six Order warriors well ahead of the main mob of enemies and allies who would reach the boat before Kovan. Behind them, another two slowed to loose arrows. One was felled by a haymaker punch to the back of the neck from one of Westfallen's powerful farmers. The other was enveloped by the crowd to the unsettling sound of cheers.

Kovan felt sand crunch beneath his feet. 'When I get away, stop this fighting as soon as you can. Too much blood already.'

'Yes, sir.'

The Order reached the boat, bucklers on arms, cavalry swords in hand. The defenders braced, ducking behind their shields to take the first blows. Blades thudded on to shields. Immediately, those shields punched out and opened, forcing opponents back, freeing space for the stab. Gladius blades licked out; none found flesh.

'Keep them back,' shouted Kovan.

But from the far side of the beach from the direction of the House of Masks, more warriors were running in unopposed.

'Your left, your left,' called one of the soldiers with Kovan.

But those at the boat couldn't hear them, deep in their engagement with the swordsmen facing them. There was nothing that could be done bar pray the arrows missed their targets. Kovan was only twenty yards away, a target himself. He saw the enemy stop, steady, aim and release. Half a dozen shafts whipped across the clear blue sky. Kovan heard himself muttering 'miss, miss'.

One found its target, taking the soldier through the side of the neck. He was punched from his feet, colliding with the man next to him. Three Order warriors were past them immediately and at the men around the boat. They backed away from the swordsmen, holding up their hands in surrender. They were cut down where they stood in the shallows, blood splashing into the water.

'No!' screamed Kovan, then muttered. 'They were unarmed. Unarmed.'

He stuttered to a stop, the shock overwhelming him momentarily. But his father's men did not. They raced into the attack and Kovan watched them go, wanting death for the enemy. Retribution. Vengeance. He felt sick.

One of his men hurdled the bow of the boat with a roar and crashed his sword two-handed into a poorly prepared enemy soldier. The blade bit deep into the enemy's hip and drove him sideways off his feet to splash hard into the water. Another Order guard deflected a blow with his buckler but was off-balance, slipping on the sand beneath his feet. The next blow came in underneath his guard, chopping into his side and up into his ribs. The third man turned and ran.

Back at the stern of the boat, the defenders were holding off their men comfortably. Kovan had seen enough and he found himself suddenly fighting back the tears. There were dark stains spreading across the clear blue water and bodies floating face down. He ran straight into the side of one of the Order warriors, bowling him from his feet.

'Enough!' He stood in between the opponents. 'No more, no more.'

He found the words hard to speak and he was gasping for breath. One of the Order warriors picked up the tip of his sword. Immediately, Kovan's men flanked him.

'Put up your blades,' said Kovan. 'They've gone and you will not stop me taking this boat.'

'You will burn, heretic,' said a warrior. 'And your father will not help you because he will be at the next stake to you.'

'You will show Lord Vasselis respect,' snapped a soldier.

Kovan shook his head. Away towards the town, the stampede was losing its focus. Knots of his father's men were running to face larger groups of Order warriors. The citizens' anger was beginning to dissipate and town leaders were shouting others to stop or ushering them away. And back towards the forum, horns were sounding. Two distinct tones.

'Keep them back while I launch,' said Kovan.

The boat had drifted and was side on to the beach, rocking under the gentle waves. He splashed into the shallows, and dragged the bow out to sea, wincing as the hand of a dead man brushed his leg. He tried not to look at the blood slicking the water while he moved down the side of the boat and climbed in astern. He grabbed the main sheet in one hand, drew it across his body and tautened the sail. His other hand was on the tiller. The boat moved away from the shore. He glanced back at Westfallen and wondered whether he would ever see the town or his parents ever again. Trying to remain strong he sailed into the bay, searching for the Ascendants.

Vasselis and three men kept the Chancellor and Vennegoor under guard until the horns blared to call off both his and their forces. He listened while the sounds of panic faded gradually to be replaced with impotent anger and grief. The floor of the forum was more akin to a battle ground that that of a solastro trading day in Westfallen. Vasselis found it terribly hard to believe his own eyes.

He counted twenty bodies on the ground, most with people tending to them. A couple were Order warriors caught in the brief frenzy that had overtaken the place when the Ascendants broke to run. But the rest were ordinary citizens, standing in the wrong place at the wrong time when the swords and arrows began to fall.

'I should see if I can help them.'

The voice almost tore him in two. It was empty, lost and terribly alone. Genna Kessian. Vasselis dragged his gaze to her. She was standing up, supported by one of his soldiers. She was rubbing her hands down her tunic dress and staring at him, imploring him to give her the help no one had the capacity to offer.

'The surgeons will see to them, Genna. Please, let us help you now. And Ardol.'

She nodded and he saw the strength flood from her. She wavered and the soldier pulled her to him, holding her up.

'Take her and Father Kessian to the House of Masks. Find the Lay Reader to organise the service.'

'Yes, Marshal.'

The Chancellor made a dismissive sound. He turned on her.

'Something to say, Chancellor?'

'He will desecrate the House by his presence. As will you all.'

Just for a heartbeat, Vasselis thought to strike her down. She saw the twitch in his sword arm.

'No,' he said as much for himself as for her. 'Or all I would be is a common killer like you.' He nodded his head at Kessian. 'All in the name of God? You have murdered him as surely as if you'd plunged a knife into his heart. I loved that man. He and Genna are my oldest friends. I can name every one of the people who lie on the floor of the forum. These were peaceful, faithful people.' His voice rose to a shout. 'What have you done?'

Koroyan stared at him as if he was an imbecile. 'I have exposed a heresy and was delivering justice,' she said.

'That is a word you are not fit to use.' Vasselis shook his head, trying to hold in the emotions boiling through him. Kessian one side, Elsa the other. Both dead. 'Want me to walk you through the forum? Show you the Tundarran cloth merchant lying dead there?'

'Sometimes the innocent die in the cause of the greater good.'

'Your God damn you, Chancellor Koroyan, whoever he is. Everyone here is innocent.'

'No, Marshal, they are not. And I was discovering the truth through confession and prayer until you interfered. All this blood is on your hands. You were supposed to be in Cirandon, overseeing the last days of your command.'

'Yes, didn't expect me to be here, did you? You should know by now that I make it a rule never to let your spies know all of my plans. You know what sickens me most? It's that you think you can get away with this. You have no authority from the Advocate. Your actions are illegal and all your protestations about the sanctity of the Order will not save you this time.

'I would take you into custody myself but it might interest you to know that Captain Harkov is coming here with two hundred levium and palace guard so I can hand you and your thugs over to him, can't I? He should be here later today.'

Koroyan chuckled. 'How little you really know about the workings of the Advocacy, Marshal Vasselis. He hasn't come here to protect you from me. He has come here to arrest you. All I did was get here before him. I will prevail.'

And Vasselis could see in her eyes that for the first time in their conversation, she was telling the simple truth.

Chapter 39

Neither Ossacer nor Mirron would stop crying. The heat of the sun on their backs had dried them out quickly after they'd hauled themselves into Kovan's boat but they were all shivering. Arducius held Ossacer, Gorian held Mirron and they stared at each other or at Westfallen shrinking behind them. There had been no talk besides first words of encouragement and thanks when they were out of the water. Now all that broke the silence was the sobbing, the lapping of water against the hull of the boat and the thrumming of the breeze in the taut sail.

Kovan had left them to it. He felt as pale and scared as all of them. The weight of his sudden, unexpected responsibility was making itself apparent and he gazed at them in some perplexity. His hand was still confident on the tiller, though, guiding them on a long tack out into the bay and leading to the sweeping channel that opened eventually into the ocean. There was a galley waiting for them out there somewhere. Permanently on station for this eventuality as well as for the defence of Genastro Bay. They would have no notice of the Ascendants' arrival.

The Ascendants had hidden by Genastro Falls until they'd sensed the movement of Kovan's boat across the surface. Gorian had called the dolphin to them as well and it still swam alongside, one eye on them, its chittering anxious.

Ahead of them, the cliffs that bordered the channel rose dark and imposing hundreds of feet into the air. Sea birds circled high and the wind was picking up, funnelling along the channel and speeding their progress. Behind them and making for the harbour as quickly as they could, went the fishing fleet and Jen Shalke. Unaware of what had befallen their town until they encountered the solitary boat. They had left food, water and extra clothes with the Ascendants and had hurried on their way with violence in their minds. Jen Shalke had left them only reluctantly, her innocence like theirs, crumbled away. In one of the skiffs was a fabulously coloured coral fragment she had collected for Father Kessian. All it would do now was adorn his grave.

Ossacer shifted under his arm and Arducius looked down at him. His tear-stained face was racked with incomprehension and anguish. Arducius's heart went out to him. There was a dread hole that had been torn in his body when the Father died but for Ossacer it must have been worse. His hands had been on the Father when he slipped away.

'Why couldn't I save him? I tried to feed my own life energy into him but it wouldn't go in.'

'There was nothing anyone could have done,' said Arducius.

'He was grey all around his heart,' sobbed Ossacer. 'And I felt him go. I tried to keep him but I couldn't. I couldn't.'

Arducius hugged Ossacer tightly to him. He felt helpless. The thing he wanted to do more than anything was to cry himself out but he had to be strong.

'It isn't your fault, Ossacer,' said Gorian.

Arducius shuddered. It was the first thing Gorian had said and his voice was cold and emotionless. Mirron sensed it too and looked at him.

'Now we know who our enemies really are,' continued Gorian. 'Everyone who worships the Omniscient.'

'Oh, come on, Gorian, that's not true,' said Arducius.

'Isn't it? I'm not talking about Elsa, the Echelon or the Marshal. But we aren't living in Westfallen any more. And the world outside doesn't like us.' He looked around them and didn't get the reaction he wanted. He raised his voice. 'Are you stupid? The Chancellor came personally to see us burn. She brought a hundred warriors. How much more proof do you need? We are lucky to be alive and the only way we'll stay that way is if we assume everyone we meet is our enemy. We'll probably find more friends among the godless in Tsard.'

Arducius stared at the floor of the boat.

'You saw them,' said Gorian more quietly. 'The warriors and the

Chancellor on the oratory. They were terrified by what we did. The wind, the heat-wash. Word travels fast. The Marshal says it every time he comes to talk to us. Soon everyone will know about us. They'll know about our eyes. And they'll be frightened of us too because the Order will tell them we are evil and they will believe the Order. And you know what people do with things they fear, don't you?'

There was a pause before Mirron spoke. 'They destroy them,' she whispered.

'I'll be here,' said Kovan. 'No one will hurt you if I can help it.'

'You can't stop them,' said Gorian, not unkindly. 'No one can.'

'I'll get you to safety,' said Kovan. 'I promise.'

'And then what?' Gorian spread his arms. 'What happens when the Order finds us in Gestern or Sirrane or wherever you think we should be? What's your father's plan then? That we spend all our time on the run, never having a home and always scared in case we get caught and burned?'

'You have to be safe first and then we can work to persuade people that you are not evil,' said Kovan.

'How?' Mirron's question was a cry. 'Their minds will be poisoned and they will all want us dead.'

'Everything we have is gone,' said Ossacer. His voice was like ice over the heat of the day. 'We can never go home and we will never see our friends and families again.'

Arducius felt a shiver throughout his body. He was connected to everything around him. The sea, the wind, the energy in the air and every living thing. But he felt isolated and hopelessly alone.

'It won't be like that,' said Kovan. 'The Echelon will survive. There is already another generation of Ascendant potential. And my father is powerful and influential. He will speak to people. Make them understand.'

Gorian snorted. 'You know nothing of this.' He waved a hand angrily towards Westfallen. 'It could all be burning right now. Your father might be dead. We might be the only Ascendants that there will ever be.'

'We have to have hope,' said Kovan. 'We have to trust those we left behind.'

'No,' said Gorian, and that chill was back in his voice. 'We have to assume we are all there is. It is the only safe way. So, Kovan, son of

Arvan Vasselis, that makes you the protector of the four most important people in the world. We are unique. Better not let us get hurt, had you?'

Arducius looked over at Kovan. His hand had tightened on the tiller and his eyes were fixed ahead towards the channel. He was shaking his head and moving his mouth soundlessly; trying to sort out the confusion in his mind.

'It'll seem better when we are on the ship,' he said and he became the seventeen-year-old son of Vasselis once more, rather than the swordsman who had saved them. 'They'll know what to do. My father will have told them and everything will be all right.' He turned his gaze to Mirron. 'You'll see. It'll be all right.'

Mirron buried her head in Gorian's chest and began to cry anew. Arducius focused on the horizon and wished that he had never been born an Ascendant.

Marshal Thomal Yuran stood on the walls of Haroq City. The gates were still open and the depressing tide of refugees showed no signs of abating. Inside the walls they were being channelled to parks and warehouses where makeshift camps and kitchens had been set up. Others were being herded on to every available ship for dispersal down the River Teel that led south-west to Byscar, Atreska's principal port on the Tirronean Sea.

In the five days granted him, he'd done all he possibly could. Megan had left with messages for the Advocate. The beacon fires had been lit across Atreska, alerting the populace to invasion. Birds had been sent north to Gosland, south to Gestern and Estorr. Horse and ship-borne messengers took the same news.

His military commanders had confirmed with him that much of his country's defence was scattered along the Tsardon border with reserves camped on the central plains. From the dust cloud in the hot solastro sky, it was clear that the enemy had not been stopped by his outer defences. And his latest scouts reported that five hundred steppe cavalry were approaching, presumably to demand his surrender.

He had pulled back every legionary he could to defend the city and the lakelands to the south-east that let into the River Teel. It was his only escape, his only defensible supply line and he would exact a heavy price before conceding it. Haroq was a difficult city to take, as the Conquord had discovered a decade ago. So it would be again. He had seven thousand in two reduced legions at his disposal. With courage, luck and skill, they could hold out until reinforcements arrived from the outlying regions of Atreska, and from Neratharn and Estorea, Phaskar and Avarn.

But he questioned whether there truly was the will to stand against what was reportedly a force in excess of thirty thousand. Gosland could be facing a similar-sized army, which would bypass Del Aglios's last known position. Gestern, assuming Jorganesh still stood, might have some sort of chance of bringing enough defence to bear.

There was panic in the city. Food was rationed, space to lay your head was at a premium. And while some refugees had managed to bring a good deal of their possessions with them, those he saw walking in now had little more then the clothes they wore. How would he care for them all? Everywhere, the old shrines had been rebuilt or reopened as native Atreskans sought solace in their old gods and spirits. Everywhere he looked, it appeared that the ways of the Conquord were being deserted.

'See what your policies have brought us,' he said to the Estorean consul, Safinn, who was standing by him.

He was wearing his formal toga, slashed with the green of the Conquord, and had adopted a proud bearing for the good of the citizens of Haroq. But beneath the veneer, Yuran could feel his fear, just as he could feel that of all the Conquord dignitaries and the handful of Gatherers trapped in the city. None would be allowed to leave until the conflict was resolved, one way or another.

'You have no words for me, do you?' Yuran chuckled and shook his head. He was hot under his polished armour and plumed helmet but he would not now be seen out of it until battle was done. 'And you cannot deny what every citizen in my city can see and what every refugee running through the gates below our feet fears. Never mind the handful of riders approaching. Under that great cloud of dust on our horizon march tens of thousands of Tsardon infantry and cavalry. Just think, Safinn, that your rulers in Estorr don't yet know they are invaded. Not until my carrier birds reach them.

'They will sit and drink their wine and delight at their fortune while you and I die on these walls. Uncomfortable, isn't it? Where is your confidence in your might now, eh?'

'Gesteris's legions will reform and regroup. They were scattered, not slaughtered, and the Tsardon are naïve if they believe they have broken the Conquord with a single victory. Hold your walls, Marshal, and help will come from every direction.'

Yuran stared at the consul whose own gaze was fixed steadfastly on the approaching dust cloud.

'As that dust cloud covers the sun so you close your eyes to reality,' he said. 'Have you not listened to the legionaries who have staggered through the gates, bloodied and beaten? Scattered, they most certainly were. And taken prisoner in huge numbers. How many are there out there with the will or the wit to reform for another fight against an enemy who beat them so comprehensively?

'You have never stood under the weight of battle and you have surely never tasted the crushing bitterness of total defeat. I have. And it has taken me years to build the courage to stand as I do now. You are a fool, Safinn. You were born one and you will die one. Watch and learn.'

When the sun reached its zenith and the heat became all but unbearable, Yuran moved into the shade of the gatehouse. Men, women, children and broken soldiers still streamed through the gates. His city militia and the 1st Haroq ala, the Stone Warriors, marshalled them on their approach.

Close now, no more than an hour away, the Tsardon cavalry rode on. They were flanked by his own cavalry and riding under a flag of parley, just as he had expected. He gave the order for the refugees to be sent around to the eastern portal and felt the satisfying, deep clang as the huge iron gates closed under his feet and the portcullis rattled into position.

He signalled his flag of parley to be flown from the gatehouse and he walked out on to the balcony over which an awning was stretched to keep the heat at bay. How incongruous it was. The balcony was beautifully carved, depicting victory celebrations from the accession to the Conquord. It had been designed as a stage from which to welcome dignitaries and allies from across the empire. Now he stood to await the vanguard of an invading army who would see it cast to the ground forty feet below.

Archers stood along the length of the gatehouse and stretched away around the walls. From turrets studding the walls at intervals of three hundred feet, ballistae, onagers and double-springed scorpion bolt-throwers were in position and ready to fire. None would do so without his express order. He knew the Tsardon. Some demonstration of superiority was likely. He would not be goaded and his artillerymen and archers were under no illusion as to the costs of independent retaliation.

'You have never seen an enemy this close, have you, Safinn?' Yuran found in himself a streak of contempt he hadn't known he possessed. 'I can smell your fear. Like shit festering in the heat. Pathetic. Nowhere to run, is there? Nothing to do but face your enemy and defeat him, or pray for your God to deliver you a quick death. After all, what will the Tsardon do to the emissaries of their mortal enemy?

'I should show you the scar across my back. Inflicted by the same gladius I now wear at my waist. An inch lower and I would not be standing here.' He let his breath play over the consul's face. 'Inflicted by an Estorean intent on excising my kidneys.'

'What is the point you are trying to make?' asked Safinn, his body already shaking.

'That your days of comfortable luxury are long, long past. That you will have to be the man that your Advocate thinks you to be. I am the Marshal Defender here but you are the Advocacy's most senior dignitary. Do you have it in you to face your enemy down much as I did a decade ago? And are you prepared to pay the ultimate price, as I was?'

'I will do what my Advocate expects,' said Safinn.

'We'll see very soon, won't we?'

The Tsardon steppe cavalry rode up in disciplined order and deployed with an expert precision that Yuran could respect. He hadn't seen steppe cavalry in a long time. Their skills had clearly not diminished. They finished with six riders in the centre within shouting distance of the balcony. The rest were ranged in a wide arc around them. Bows were in the hands of one in every two. The others held pennanted lance blades upright.

In the centre, Yuran saw the sentor who led the cavalry. He was flanked by bowmen. The sixth rider carried the parley flag; white and yellow halves divided by a diagonal slash. The sentor did not dismount. He scanned the balcony and the walls left and right. Yuran could see the slight smile on his face.

At the same time, he became aware of a silence spreading across the city. Voices stilled as word was passed that the Tsardon were at the walls. Outside, where most could not see, the enemy waited. Their destiny was about to be decided. There would be few that believed any other outcome than war was possible. The silence was scared, laden with inescapable fate.

'I presume I address Marshal Defender Yuran, ruler of the kingdom of Atreska,' said the sentor, speaking in common Tsardon.

'You do,' said Yuran, choosing to respond in kind. Safinn's discomfort was justification enough. 'I would have your name, sentor.'

'Rensaark,' he replied. 'Adjutant to the King of Tsard, his Highness, King Khuran. And by my presence here you know he will long remain king.'

'That remains to be seen,' said Yuran. 'One victory does not complete a war.'

'Your parley flag,' said Rensaark, indicating the cloth that hung from the front of the balcony. 'It is that of Atreska, is it not? A sign of your past.'

'The Conquord does not believe in the parley,' said Yuran.

'No,' said Rensaark. 'And this man at your right hand. A Conquord man?'

'The consul. Safinn of Estorea.'

'I am not at parley with the Conquord,' said Rensaark.

He muttered a couple of words Yuran could not catch and made a small hand gesture. One of his guards had nocked a shaft and loosed it faster than Yuran could truly follow. The arrow struck Safinn in the throat, driving up into his mouth. Safinn groped at the shaft, his mouth open, disgorging blood. He could not speak. His tongue was pierced by the arrow head. He stared at Yuran, pleading as he fell to his knees.

'The ultimate price,' said Yuran. 'May your God embrace you.'

Safinn fell on to his side, hands clutching uselessly at his throat, choking on blood, wood and metal. Yuran held up both his hands against retaliation by his people.

'Then talk to Atreska,' he said. 'What is it you want to say that I would want to hear?'

Rensaark inclined his head. 'But let us not shout our words at each other. Meet me at your gate. Let us talk like civilised men.'

'Are you sure that is what we are?'

'Hear me and know it,' said Rensaark.

Chapter 40

They sat alone across a simple table in the gatehouse guard room. Both were unarmed. Some food and water had been brought in. The Tsardon stood by their horses in front of the gate, which was open in deference, though filled with heavy Atreskan infantry. Rensaark had not wanted a guard with him.

'If I do not walk from these gates at nightfall, the Tsardon army will tear down the walls to retrieve my body. Where then would you be?' he had said.

Yuran had said nothing for a long time and Rensaark was happy for the silence.

'Do you know how long it has been since I didn't hear the sound of a horse? Either beneath me or stamping in the paddock in the night. I haven't felt the chill inside thick strong stone like this for many days.'

'It's a city that is difficult to take,' said Yuran, a little confused by what he was hearing.

'Only been done once,' said Rensaark.

'The Conquord legions are a formidable enemy.'

Rensaark smiled. 'Maybe once but the Tsardon are more so. We warned them as we have been warning you these past years. Do not fight us. We are too strong.'

'Sentor, I would hate to think you were toying with me because of some misplaced belief in the inevitability of your victory,' said Yuran. 'You have come here to talk with me. Make your demands.'

'Marshal, I understand the conflicts that rage inside you,' said Rensaark.

'Really?' Yuran raised his eyebrows. 'I was not aware I had any that were so obvious.'

'Ten years ago, we would have met as friends, trading partners. Tsard was no threat to you.'

'Of course you weren't,' said Yuran sharply. 'You needed us as a buffer against the Conquord. Until the Conquord attacked us, our history was littered with border conflict. Estorea didn't finance the building of every fort, did they?'

'You exaggerate,' said Rensaark.

'You have a short memory,' said Yuran. 'But I hardly think you have come here to debate our history.'

Rensaark shrugged. 'In a way I have. The fact that I have not marched in here to demand your surrender has everything to do with our history. Our relations have not always been smooth but we have never been at open war either. And we would not be now but the Conquord has attacked us rather than extend the hand of friendship. A hand we would have taken to our hearts.

'What choice did we have but to fight back against all of the Conquord? You don't think it hurts us to raid your lands to make our point?'

'Don't take me for a fool,' said Yuran. 'I have seen the results of your pain. Stolen people. Burned villages. Decapitated bodies. Burned Readers and Speakers. You have turned more cruelty on my people than the Conquord ever did.'

Rensaark's expression hardened. 'Because you ignored our emissaries and our pleas to talk.'

'What choice did I have? We are at war with you. Atreska is part of the Conquord. I was forbidden to speak by the consul.'

'Well he is not here now.' Rensaark's voice was a growl. 'And I am talking to you as an Atreskan. The Conquord must be stopped. This reckless expansion threatens us all. If Tsard does not stand, where will its eye turn next. Sirrane? Kark?'

'All that you see is war,' said Yuran, keeping his voice measured. 'Yes, I am unhappy that Atreska is on the front line but if Tsard is defeated, I am closer to the heart of the Conquord. And that heart beats in peace, and wealth and security for its citizens. No one in Phaskar, Caraduk or Bahkir has to wonder if raiders will ride to burn their crops. For all I fought the Conquord a decade ago, our accession to it brought a fledgling stability to my country that we had never experienced before. A stability that Tsard has undermined ever since.'

'Because Estorea decided to make your borders the new battle-front,' said Rensaark. 'Against the wishes of many of your people and opposed by Tsard. Where is that fledgling stability now? It is dead in its nest. Where is the defence now that your campaigning armies are beaten? Where do you think the next battle will be fought?'

Yuran let his gaze drop. Rensaark was right. How brief peace had been in reality.

'Have your people really benefited from accession to the Conquord? Their religion, our religion, is suppressed. They are taxed so heavily they can barely feed themselves and their young men and women are conscripted into the legions. And for what? To feed the ego of your Advocate and her desire to preside over the greatest empire this world has ever seen. This is personal ambition.'

Yuran shook his head. 'No. You have never met her. I have. And for all her faults and blindness, her desire is truly in providing peace and comfort for her subjects. She understands the necessity of war to achieve that goal.'

'As she understands the need to subjugate her conquered territories,' said Rensaark. 'Marshal, I know your desire. And I know it matches the will of your people. I talk to them. There are villages all over your country flying the flag of independence. We bear you no malice. We merely want to give you back what you crave. Your freedom to rule your own people.'

Yuran gazed into Rensaark's hard face. The sentor had struck to the very core of his dreams and he knew it.

'There are over thirty thousand marching to Haroq,' said Rensaark. 'We have no desire to spill the blood of one more Atreskan. Help us. Help Tsard return this world to its natural balance. Help us break the Conquord.'

Yuran sighed and rubbed his hands over his face. 'This is very difficult,' he said. 'I need time to think.'

'There is little to think about bar protecting your people, keeping them from the ravages of a war that should not be fought on their lands. But it will be if you refuse me now. My generals are not in the mood to pause and debate.'

'You must give me some time,' said Yuran.

His heart was racing. He felt like he was being torn down the centre of his skull. A headache was building. An enemy that wanted to sack his city he could understand. But this . . . He studied Rensaark, wondering if his words were sweetened lies or honest assessment.

'You have a day,' said Rensaark. 'And in that time I will show you why you should trust us. This is not invasion, it is liberation. I will prove it to you.'

Yuran watched him ride away with his cavalry and walked in silence back to his castle, wondering if he lived in a city he could defend or in a prison, awaiting his execution.

Throughout the rest of that day, he wrestled with his choices. How could he turn from the Conquord now, after a decade of investment in all it stood for? How could he abandon them when to stand shoulder to shoulder would make him a hero in Estorea? How could he not, knowing that to stand against the Tsardon would see his fields run red with the blood of his own people? Rensaark could so easily be lying. The war could be fought on his doorstep whatever decision he made now. He could merely be trading one governing empire for another. Hemmed in by people on both sides who made almost identical promises about the long-term future of Atreska, he had nowhere to go. He was alone. He cursed the fact that he had sent Megan away. She would have been able to clear the paths in his mind for him. But now she might be sailing to the heart of a new enemy.

Outside in the gathering dusk the city was calm. He had reopened all four gates for refugees and had stood down the bulk of his army from the walls. When the Tsardon cavalry had ridden away, there had been no general call to arms. It gave them some little hope but underneath it was confusion. A hiatus. Because the enemy would be in sight the next day. They were still coming.

Yuran felt unable to do any more. They would have to wait like he did for Rensaark to make good on his promise if he intended to do so. But even he was unprepared for the scale of the Tsardon gesture.

He was woken at first light and hurried to the walls in a carriage while the citizens of Haroq City cheered and chanted his name. No one would tell him what his talk with Rensaark was supposed to have secured. They all assumed he knew and he was too long a politician to disabuse them of such notions. Perhaps it wasn't anything to do with the Tsardon at all. Perhaps the Conquord legions were approaching to keep his city safe.

When he reached the balcony, he gazed out on a sea of Atreskan soldiers and cavalry. Rensaark was with them and more were marching up all the time. They cheered when they saw him. Legion banners waved. Fists punched the air. A wave of emotion broke over him and it was all he could do to stop a tear falling from his eye. He ran from the balcony, ordered the gate opened and went out to meet them personally. Rensaark dismounted and met him in front of his people.

'We mean you no harm,' said the sentor. 'Here is my proof. Join with us. Win back your independence.'

'How many?' asked Yuran.

'Soldiers and riders of the 9th ala, the Rogue Spears and the 8th ala, the Shark's Teeth. Over six thousand men and women. We are sorry for each one that had to die at Scintarit. These we return to you freely and fully armed.'

Yuran started at that last statement. Rensaark noticed and nodded.

'You cannot beat us,' he said. 'Any of these brave citizens will tell you that. There is no risk in freeing them into your care. Don't let more Atreskan blood be spilled on behalf of a Conquord that is incapable of defending you. Send your people back to their homes and villas. Have them work in peace in their fields and in their workshops. Declare your independence today. Do it, Marshal. Because we won't turn away. War is coming to the Conquord. Don't let it be your war.'

Yuran had awoken with the knowledge well before he had been urged from his bed. In the end there had really been no other choice. Yuran looked past Rensaark at his citizens. They were there. Ready to be released back to their homes and their families. Armed and armoured.

'If I do this, I will need the most secure of assurances from your king. I will be hunted from within and without my borders by the agents of the Conquord, as will all who stand with me. And I invite you in with no certainty that you will ever choose to leave.'

'Your concerns are natural and respected,' said Rensaark, bowing and smiling. 'And that is why I and my general will sit down with you in your castle before the Tsardon army takes one more step into your territory. This is the first step on your path to liberation for you and all your people. Open your shrines. Smell the freedom on the air.

'We are your friends. Your allies. Together, we can bring down the Conquord.'

'Together?'

'Oh yes,' said Rensaark. 'Tsardon and Atreskan will march side by side to Estorr. Independence is your gift. Bringing it to others is your destiny.'

The River Teel was a wide free-flowing river, tidal at its outflow into the Tirronean Sea. Paul Jhered and the levium paused only for essential supplies at Byscar, where the bulk of the Atreskan navy was at anchor, before entering the river delta. They made excellent use of the tides in the lower reaches of the river and the strength of their crews to move them quickly through the upper flows towards Haroq's deep-water docks.

Under the flag and embroidered sail of the Gatherers, making speeds of up to eight knots under a wind that allowed them to ship oars and enjoy a full sail, the *Hark's Arrow* and her sister ship, the *Hark's Spear* were unmistakable vessels. Jhered was used to the steady gaze of those they passed in the dozens of riverside settlements and on the busy river itself. But two days from the docks, that traffic had increased dramatically. Likewise, activity on the riverside had been overtaken by build-ups of Atreskan legionaries and in the distance, cavalry could be seen patrolling plains and lake lands. Smoke from beacon fires smudged the horizon.

Jhered had watched it while an inevitability built up inside him. He'd seen this sort of thing before. He'd been through it in his own country as a boy. Atreska was invaded; or at least they thought they were. All the signs were there and it made sense of the abuse that had been thrown their way. Eventually, he'd ordered a detachment of levium take a long boat and intercept one of the overladen river craft heading south-west. He'd seen the short exchange on board and heard the report from his addos. He could scarcely believe it. At least messages were already being relayed to the Conquord and Estorr; it gave him leave to continue his journey.

And now with the largely empty berths in sight while the dockside was full of men and weaponry for transport, he addressed his command team of ten.

'Whether or not Atreska is facing an invasion is still open to debate. Rumours of rout are often exaggerated. But whatever the true picture, the city will be on edge and we are not liked at the best of times.'

'Perhaps a disguise for you, my Exchequer,' said Appros Harin to general laughter.

Jhered nodded the best-known face in the Conquord at him. 'And perhaps I should strap my legs up and walk on my knees to further fool them.' He held up his hands for quiet. 'But the point is well made. Do not wear your cloaks or carry your badges of office more prominently than you need to. We must do everything possible to avoid arousing the anger of the city.' He paused, allowed his expression to harden.

'You have all travelled with me to Haroq and wider Atreska before and that is why you are with me now. We were here to remove Yuran from office and see Consul Safinn take temporary control. This may now not be possible so not a word of it must pass. Here is what must be done.

'Harin, take the ninety and split around the city. The basilica, the hospitals, the garrison and the legion complex. Find out what you can, preferably from battle-front refugees if such are to be found. If you can find none, it tells its own story. Make yourself known to the commanders of local forces. They'll be less likely to panic, more so to give you a balanced picture.

'I will take the ten and go to the castle to make contact with Appros Menas, her team and our soon-to-be-erstwhile Marshal. Ladies and gentlemen, we will be travelling on foot. It isn't too great a distance from the dockside to anywhere and I don't want a flurry of horses giving us unwanted attention.' He scanned them, checking they had understood.

'Communication will be via this ship or messages passed through to the Gatherer station at the castle. Keep an eye on the harbour. Should we lower the Gatherer flag, it means we need to leave fast. In any event you are all to report back aboard by nightfall.' He paused. 'It may not be as desperate as we have heard but there is no doubting something has spooked Haroq and Yuran badly. Keep your eyes open. Don't ignore anything. Trust no one but your levium and the armour of the Conquord.

'Prepare your people.'

Barely had the ships nudged berth and the gangplanks thudded down than the Gatherers were running into the heart of the city. Jhered led them out, nodding at some of the soldiers lined up along the dock. He heard many a comment but few were worthy of response or even acknowledgement. He was used to it.

'Here to collect the taxes, Exchequer?'

'Think the Tsardon might have got to them first, Exchequer.'

'Either that or we've spent them on ourselves for the first time in a decade.'

'If I were you I'd sail away right now, my Lord Jhered.' The tone of this one made him pause. He looked into the eyes of an old soldier. Well into middle age and sitting on a barrel. 'Nothing to be done here.'

'There is always something that can be done,' said Jhered.

'And in your case, that is leave, and alert any that you can, sir,' said the soldier, a centurion in poorly polished armour. 'Nothing can save Atreska for the Conquord now.'

'Stand up when you address a superior.' Jhered shook his head. 'You are a poor example for your men.'

The centurion spread his hands. Jhered frowned. Every other soldier they'd passed had been an Atreskan. This man wasn't. He was badly sun-burned and his accent too light. He was a countryman, a Tundarran. Jhered waved Appros Harin to continue.

'I was there, my Lord. At Scintarit. I escaped because I was guarding the camps that day. I'm sorry but this is as good as my armour gets these days.'

'What happened out there? What's become of Gesteris?'

The centurion glanced left and right, aware others were paying too much attention to his conversation with Jhered. He beckoned the Gatherer closer.

'It was a disaster of a magnitude that will shake the Conquord, Lord Jhered, but you don't have time to hear about it, not now. Something's not right with what the Marshal is doing. He's been parleying with the Tsardon.'

'They're here already?' Jhered gaped.

'A few of them. Steppe cavalry.'

'What is there to talk about?'

The centurion raised sun bleached eyebrows. His scarred forehead wrinkled untidily. 'Old friendships?' he suggested.

Jhered straightened.

'Name and legion,' he said.

'Autin, my Lord,' he replied, standing at last. 'Of the Tundarran Thunder.'

'You're relieved of all duties.' Jhered indicated to one of his levium. 'Take the centurion back to the ship. I would hear his stories on our voyage home, whenever that might be.'

Autin saluted. There was a slightly wild look in the man's eyes. He'd seen too much already. It was eating at his mind.

'Thousands of Atreskan soldiers were released back to the city this morning, my Lord,' said Autin before he moved. 'Armed and unharmed, prisoners from Scintarit. In advance of the weight of the Tsardon army. Why do you think they'd do that?' Another raising of the eyebrows.

Jhered turned to his nine remaining levium. 'It seems we have urgent work to do.'

Haroq was a classic walled and defended Atreskan city, and for that Jhered was grateful today. He could lead his people quickly along wide main thoroughfares kept clear for troop movements to and from the docks. And always he could see the castle set on a rise in the land and dominating the city from its centre.

Passing the western edge of the forum, he caught a glimpse of the real Haroq of today. Thronged with citizens who had nowhere else to go. Frightened, meandering and lost. Sleeping under the stars and waiting to hear the first thud of artillery. Jhered's mind was bleak. Perhaps they would not have to.

The Gatherers marched purposefully through the castle's courtyard gates. They did not pause for the horn announcing their presence to the keep. The place was in uproar. The courtyard rang to the sound of horses and the shouts of soldiers. Packed carts rattled over the cobbles. Messengers ran in a dozen directions. To the left, behind a cordon of legionaries, ordinary citizens waited to make their demands. Jhered did not think they would get a hearing today.

He spared the turretted, crenellated keep a glance as he strode beneath the gate house. It would ever be an ugly structure. Some efforts had been made to reflect Estorean architecture. Carved marble overlaid stone in places and carved columns had been erected from which hung the banners of the Conquord nations. It was supposed to be a glory walk but the banners were tatty and the marble unwashed. Yuran had otherwise clung to many traditions of old Atreska. Perhaps that should have worried the Advocate more deeply.

Beyond the gatehouse the untidy inner courtyard greeted them. A central fountain was being constructed about ten years too late. Like the hypocaust which Jhered doubted would ever be installed. The courtyard was a wide, circular, weed-grown cobbled space. The unbroken inner walls presented an imposing grey face, studded with veined glass and shutters.

Jhered pointed ahead. 'Stalos, you are coming with me to see Yuran. The rest of you, secure the Gatherer station. We will take any chests we have. Tell Menas and her team that they're leaving with us. Wait for me there.'

'My Lord.'

His hand on the pommel of his cavalry blade, Jhered trotted around the fountain towards the wide marble steps up to the Marshal's lavish living quarters. There was an uncomfortable quiet here. None of the activity they had witnessed in the courtyard that would reflect a ruler preparing for war.

'He'd better be here,' muttered Jhered.

'Exchequer?'

'Nothing, Addos. Just keep your eyes open and your hand to your sword. This doesn't feel right at all.'

Jhered knew the route well. He nodded to the guards on the steps, feeling their eyes on his back on his way into the cavernous, flag-hung hall. Inside, colonnades bordered mosaic pathways set on original stone. He headed left and up a wide flight of stairs and onto a carpeted landing.

A broad lantern-lit passage stretched away on a left-curving arc. Guardsmen stood outside the double doors to Yuran's dining hall. Their faces registered their anxious surprise at who approached them. Their spears crossed in front of the carved wooden doors.

'Tell the Marshal I am here,' said Jhered. 'I'll speak with him now.'

'He is in council, my Lord Exchequer.'

'Evidently,' said Jhered. 'Interrupt him.'

The guards shifted. 'He cannot be disturbed, sir. Please?'

A burst of laughter came from within.

'I won't ask twice and your spears will not stop us. Now, one of you will tell him I am here or I will announce myself.'

The guardsmen failed to stare him down and removed their spears. He nodded.

'I'm sorry,' said one.

'I beg your pardon?'

The guard shrugged and opened the door. Jhered strode in.

'Marshal Yuran,' he said as he walked inside. 'I'm anxious to share your joke. I—'

The room was full of Tsardon.

Chapter 41

Ten Tsardon. Yuran. Six of his council. Every head turned to him. The Tsardon didn't recognise him of course. But that was as far as his fortune went. Yuran swore and stood, his chair squealing backwards and rocking, almost falling. It was enough to have the nervous Tsardon do the same. Hands went to sword hilts. One of them said something, a question.

'I am very disappointed,' said Jhered. 'I didn't ever dream you'd turn traitor.'

Yuran stared at him, the ghost of regret passing across his face. 'Guards. Take him.'

'I don't think so.' Jhered turned his back on the dining hall and the concerted move in his direction. The guards blocked his passage out. 'Time to choose.'

A fragment's hesitation. Jhered smashed his forearm into the head of one. The guard's skull thudded into the doorframe and he crumpled. The other gasped and fell forwards. Stalos dragged his dagger clear. It was always a mistake to ignore a Gatherer.

'Run,' said Jhered.

The two men raced around the curve, steps echoing from the walls. Behind them the shouts were growing. They clattered down the stairs, through the hall and past the stunned gate guards. Jhered came left around the fountain.

'Levium!' he roared. 'We are betrayed. Let's go.'

One of his people was at the door to the Gatherer station. He turned and bellowed something through the opening. Jhered came to a halt, recognising him.

'You're the fastest man we've got. Straight to the docks. Don't look back. I want the flags down, oars ready and the sails up. We're leaving. Go.'

'My Lord.'

A bell sounded. It was the rapid clang of an alarm call. From the Marshal's quarters, soldiers ran into the circular courtyard. There were footsteps behind him too. Levium. Four carrying chests between them.

'We're out of time,' said Jhered. 'Go. Drop the chests. The treasury will have to do without them. Free your hands to fight.'

He ducked as an arrow glanced off the wall to his right. Levium returned fire. Two men were downed.

'Good to see you, Menas,' said Jhered.

'And you, my Lord Exchequer,' she said, reloading her bow and firing again.

'And now all I want to see is your back ahead of me,' he said. 'To the basilica. We need to get the others.'

About twenty Atreskans were in the courtyard now. Shouts were ringing out from other directions too. The bell was taken up by others out in the main courtyard. The Gatherers ran headlong under the gatehouse. Jhered came last, urging more speed.

The confusion of movement in the main courtyard gave them brief advantage. The alarms were going but no one knew who they were looking for. And the Gatherers were an unlikely target. People stood and watched them go by and they were most of the way across the cluttered space before the order to close the gates was understood.

There was too much unwanted attention now. Jhered glanced behind and saw the pursuit building, people swinging up on to horseback. He lengthened his stride and ran around to the front of the levium. Menas came to his right-hand side. In the castle gatehouse, men put their shoulders to wheels and the gates began to swing shut. Counterweights rattled on chains, wood creaked and groaned.

'Buy me some time,' said Jhered.

Menas and another of her team stepped aside from the run to shoot. Jhered didn't pause. Drawing his sword he went hard at the handful of guards at the bottom of the gate.

'Levium! For Estorea!'

The rest took up his shout. Arrows flicked by his head. One sank deep into the throat of an archer at the gate. Another took a gateman in the back of the neck, sending him tumbling across the wheel. Jhered held his sword in front of his body, only moving it in the last pace before contact. He took it round in an arc down and right, using the pace he generated to continue the swing up and left. The powerful move struck the spear from his target's grasp. The man had the speed to reach for his sword but not to draw it. Jhered chopped back across his body, his blade biting hard into the guard's side and sweeping him from his feet.

Levium were left and right of him now, facing four remaining guards. Jhered could hear running footsteps and horses on the gallop. Shouts and screams had filled the air, almost drowning out the alarm bells which tolled as if at great distance. He sensed a shadow above him and stepped back sharply. A body struck the ground before him, an arrow protruding from his eye.

The fall had surprised the Atreskans more and the levium drove forward into the space. Jhered cracked a left-hand punch into the side of a guard's head. He knocked the man down with a sword pommel into his nose. Blood sprayed across his vision. Another body fell across his path, the man gasping his last breath.

'Clear!' he shouted and they ran through the gates and out into the city.

On the wide stone parade ground outside the castle, people were standing and staring. Alarm bells were sounding across the city and the unmistakable sounds of a building panic echoed across the clear sky. Twenty or more soldiers were running towards them.

'Keep it tight,' shouted Jhered. 'Attack on my word only.'

He identified the leader of the section.

'Centurion, trouble in the castle,' he said as they approached. 'Tsardon infiltrators.'

'What?' The man clearly recognised Jhered but didn't believe what he'd heard.

'We're going to get help from our ship. Yuran is safe for now. Go.'

'Yes, sir.'

Jhered glanced back over his shoulder to see him go. The gates had closed behind them and he heard men yelling for them to be reopened. Yelling for people to stop the Gatherers. The centurion came up short and turned. He was thirty yards distant. It would have to be enough.

'The basilica,' he said.

He took the levium away at a sprint down the wide empty main street leading back towards the dockside. Menas ran alongside him.

'They're through the gates, sir. Riding hard. They'll catch us easily.'

Jhered nodded. They'd passed two side streets already, both packed with confused, frightened citizens. At the third, he took his levium right. Keeping his sword high above his head he shouted and pushed his way through the crowd which ebbed and flowed in front of him. In the mass of citizens around them, he lost the sounds of pursuit. Horsemen would be seriously hampered through here but would have guessed where they were headed. Foot soldiers would still be after them.

He took the next left turn which sloped down to the back of the oratory. It was lined with businesses, mostly closed and boarded. People were sitting beneath awnings where they could find space. Some had obviously chosen it as their place to live during the expected siege. Jhered couldn't spare the time to wonder how most of these people would react when they found out their Marshal Defender had betrayed the Conquord. He felt like giving them the rope to string him up.

A celebratory arch put in place when the Conquord accepted Atreska made the north entrance to the forum. People Jhered knew were depicted on its sculpted faces. People who had given their lives to bring Atreska to the glory of Estorean rule. Beyond it, two flights of stone stairs. He took them three at a time, barging people aside, the last of his patience in tatters.

The basilica ran almost half the length of the eastern side of the forum. Jhered could see it was heaving with refugees seeking respite from the sun, which shone down with unremitting goodwill. It was open-sided like its sister structure in Estorr. The levium flew up its steps in a line.

'Levium!' roared Jhered. 'To the Exchequer.'

He saw his people detach themselves from knots of refugees, officials and battle-weary legionaries. At second glance the place seemed more hospital than camp. It would have been a mine of useful information if they'd had time to glean it. He was happy to see Appros Harin among those coming to him. The pursuit was closing in. Soldiers were coming down the stairs and riders were entering the south of the forum.

'No time to explain. We have to get out now. Get runners to anyone elsewhere in the city. They are not to identify themselves as Gatherers to anyone, it'll get them killed. If the ships are gone, they all know the pick-up point on the lake. We'll wait as long as we can.' His shoulders sagged. 'Harin, we are in a city of traitors.'

Harin was desperate to ask questions but held himself in check. He turned to the growing number of Gatherers in the basilica and called a few names.

'The rest of you, here,' said Jhered. The noise outside the building was growing. People were hurrying from the centre of the forum. He could hear screams and angry shouts. The bells still rang out. Fear mingled with the smell of sweat and disease inside.

'Assume every Atreskan soldier to be an enemy. There are Tsardon in the city. Stalos, take twenty down to the ships. Set up a perimeter. The rest, let's give them the way out then defend their backs. Any of you who had the sense to bring your bows, use them on horsemen. We're attacked north and south.'

He estimated seventy of the Gatherers were with him. He watched pairs of runners heading off in three different directions, all of them diverting enemy attention. Harin took ten out to cover the soldiers approaching through the celebration arch. Jhered took the rest and moved to the edge of the basilica, forming up just inside the first line of columns.

The atmosphere was changing quickly. Citizens were scattering from in front of the riders. There were twelve horsemen at a quick count, leading about twice that number of soldiers towards the basilica.

'Keep an eye out behind,' said Jhered not turning from the enemy. 'How many bows?'

'Six, my lord,' said Menas.

'Excellent. Stay under cover. You'll have clear sight any time. On my mark. Riders first. At first volley, we will rush. They won't be expecting this many of us. The twenty, don't engage, keep running. Any questions? Good. God keep us safe for greater deeds.'

The Atreskans were overconfident, cantering towards them with shields on their backs. Jhered kept a hand raised, waiting. Behind the riders, some of the soldiers carried bows but most had spears in hand. They were castle guard, little more than ceremonial with their brightly polished armour and deep red and green cloaks. He let them get within twenty yards before he dropped his hand.

Arrows whipped away. Jhered ran down the steps, leading thirty levium. Moments later, the arrows hit home, taking man and horse alike. One reared, throwing its rider. Others began to pull up, a couple tried to wheel away. Order was lost. When Jhered was five yards from them, more shafts struck. Two further riders were taken from their saddles. Another animal felt the barb deep in a shoulder. The levium engulfed them.

Jhered hacked up two-handed, striking the sword arm of his target. The man pitched off the other side of his horse. Jhered didn't stop. He shouldered his way through panicked horse flesh. A blade swept at him. He blocked it easily, turning it aside and thumping a riposte into plate chest armour. The Atreskan grunted and gasped as the metal compressed into his ribs. The flat of Jhered's blade slapped the rump of his horse and it sprang away.

Two paces later and he was through the flimsy cavalry line. He glanced left and right. The levium were with him.

'For the Conquord!'

His cry was taken up in all their throats. He ran at the foot soldiers. He saw spears levelled, bows turn and swords drawn. Arrows showered down on the enemy. Two of the bowmen died. The spearmen tried to bunch close. It was a woeful effort at a phalanx-style defence. He ducked under the single rank of spears, his blade sweeping above his head. He rose, chopped down on a wooden shaft, spun on his heel and carved his blade into the neck of a terrified guard. The man screamed and fell sideways, tripping up the guard next to him. Jhered vaulted them both.

The next man to face him had gladius and oval shield. Jhered opened his stance and beckoned the man on.

'Teach you how to fight levium, did they boy?'

The legionary was well trained but unused to fighting outside of a solid line. He kept his body tucked behind his shield and his gladius tight to his right. He half-crouched and moved in. Jhered was waiting. The soldier punched out with his shield but Jhered wasn't there. He'd stepped left already, bringing his blade across his body and chopping back out and up to the right. The blow was blocked but the legionary was off balance.

'Not good enough,' said Jhered, stabbing him under his arm and into his lung.

The levium were rampant. They tore through the Atreskans. The last of them turned and ran back towards the castle. Jhered ignored them. Looking back he saw Harin engaged with the soldiers he'd duped outside the castle gates. Menas had turned her bows on them now and they were being worn down. The forum itself was clear of citizens. They stood in a packed ring at its borders, staring mute at what they witnessed. The why would be known to them soon enough; and the Conquord would show them no mercy.

Jhered led his levium out of the forum and back towards the docks at a run. He could see the twenty ahead of them, forcing a path through streets onto which the forum population had been forced. There were bodies lying in the street, too. Soldiers and citizens who had made the mistake of getting in their way. Jhered had no sympathy. Atreska had turned.

In the wake of the twenty, Jhered's passage was easier. He crested a rise in the road and saw the docks laid out before him. The panic hadn't reached there yet but it was just a matter of time. At their berths, the ships sat calm, flags still fluttering serenely from masts.

'Eyes left and right,' said Jhered. 'Tell me what you see.'

'West along the docks,' said one of the levium immediately.

Jhered looked and cursed. Riders and plenty of them. Worse, they were unquestionably Tsardon steppe cavalry. The twenty were going to be caught by them before they reached the ships. A quick glance over his shoulder told him that Menas and Harin were still engaged in the forum. He ran harder, taking his thirty with him.

The bells had stilled and the city was alive with a frightened confusion. No one was getting in their way but the eye of every citizen was on them. They'd seen Gatherers cutting down Atreskans and they had no idea why. The hatred and aggression directed at them was growing. Jhered would have shaken each one by the shoulders and told them what their Marshal had done but he had more pressing matters. His sense of injustice burned in him. The city was against them because most of them didn't know the enemy was being given free rein to ride their streets. By the time they knew the truth it would be too late. He feared for this beautiful country and its peaceful majority.

At the entrance to the deep-water berths, the twenty had seen their pursuers and had stopped to form a defensive line. Simultaneously, the flags began to move down the masts. And just before he lost sight of them behind the buildings ahead, Jhered saw his crews running down the gangplanks.

Curiosity overcame fear and people were crowding down to the docks ahead of them, drawn by the atmosphere of imminent conflict and violence. Jhered found himself jostled as he tried to force his way through the deepening crowd. He was only forty yards from Stalos and the twenty but the steppe were going to reach them first. He could hear the rattle of hooves on the stone of the dockside but he couldn't see them clearly.

'Out of the way,' he shouted, keeping his sword high above his head.

The levium shouldered through the crowd, which had turned like the tide and was beginning to bunch back towards them, thickening like a city fog at dawn. Jhered felt his frustration growing. He rattled his sword pommel against the head of a man ahead of him who had turned to shout for help.

'I'm right behind you,' said Jhered. 'You want help, get out of my way.'

'The Tsardon,' he shouted into Jhered's face. 'The Tsardon.'

'I know,' grated Jhered and shoved him roughly aside.

The fact of the levium behind them and the Tsardon in front of them flickered through the press of people in the street. Unbelievably, more were running in behind them and the confusion of movement caused falls and panic. The levium tried to keep their blades away from the people but it was becoming increasingly difficult to move with any concerted direction when they did so.

And then, above the shouts and the clamour, Jhered heard the unmistakable sound of swords clashing. All he could do was turn his left shoulder to the crowd as it packed and ran about him, screaming as it tried to distance itself from what it had come to see.

'Hold, levium,' he called into the tumult.

He gritted his teeth and took blow after blow to his body from jostling elbows, feet and knees. He was forced back pace by pace but still held his sword away from them, knowing that to let it fall would be to hurt an innocent.

The crowd dispersed and Jhered had sight of the twenty once again. He began to move forwards, calling the levium on and pushing himself through the few hardier souls that hadn't fled at the first sight of metal and blood. The steppe cavalry, and there had to be thirty of them at least, had driven into his people and were turning to ride out and regroup. At least five were down but behind them, the crews were lining up with bows strung and ready.

'Get the injured away; let's reform that line.'

He ran onto the dockside. The steppe were wheeling their mounts. They paused, assessing the renewed force against them. Jhered knew what they would do.

'Archers! Keep them back. Let's make them pay for every shaft they fire.'

Bows were dragged from backs, arrows nocked and the steppe began to gallop across them at no more then twenty yards separation. A volley of arrows came from the crew, ripping into the Tsardon. Two were turned, one was struck from his horse but the others did not pause. With legs controlling their horses, the cavalry tore past, turned in their saddles and fired. Jhered felt shafts whistle past him and heard the cries of the wounded behind him.

Already, the steppe were slowing to turn again. Another volley came from the crew but they were not as accomplished as their enemy. Not enough arrows fell in the target area to even give them pause for thought. This was not a skirmish the Conquord would win. Jhered turned.

'Run for the ships. Do it now. Crew fall back. One more volley.'

Levium helped their wounded up and began to hurry them towards the triremes still sixty yards distant along the docks from which every seaman was scattering. Jhered grabbed a shield from an Atreskan legionary standing with his mouth open.

'Fight!' he yelled into his face. 'You've got a bow, idiot. Use it.'

He swung back to the Tsardon, ramming his arm through the shield's loops. They were riding in hard, heading directly down the dockside five abreast. Behind them and rushing down the hill were Menas, Harin and their levium. Arrows ripped into the back of the Tsardon charge, deflecting a little of its intensity. But those at its head came on oblivious to the new trouble. Bows were bent and arrows flew. The levium had not been prepared for this. How could they be?

Jhered ducked behind his shield and stepped smartly to the edge of the dock, scant inches from a tumble into the water. An arrow thudded into the shield. He heard hoofs close to him and lashed out with his blade, feeling it bite into flesh. A horse screamed and a rider was catapulted from his saddle. He let the weapon go lest he be dragged off his feet with it. The horse plunged right off the dockside and into the sea. He crouched low, his shield above his head. Horses thudded past him and he felt the swipe of a blade nick into the shield. Beside him, the legionary was less fortunate. He'd stretched his bow and taken a sword in the neck for his efforts. He sprawled on the stone, blood flowing from his body.

Jhered peered right. Levium ahead of the charge were fighting amongst the steppe. Left, Harin and Menas had reached the dockside and came on at a charge. And behind them, more riders, more soldiers. Tsardon and Atreskan. They were running out of time.

Jhered drove to his feet in the shadow of a trailing steppe horse slowed by the weight of comrades ahead. He reached up and dragged the rider from his saddle. The man struck the ground on his back and the last he saw was Jhered's shield crushing down on his face.

The remainder of the steppe were disengaging. He heard foreign orders shouted and saw the concerted wheel away. Heels dug into flanks. The riders surged back along the dockside. Menas and her team fired into their midst, dropping another three, before dodging left and right. He saw Harin duck a flashing blade and leap onto the deck of a merchant vessel. He rolled once and regained his feet. Jhered beckoned them on.

'Let's get aboard. They're regrouping.'

It was a blind run now. The crew had fallen back to the gangplanks and had bows trained over their heads. Thirty yards to run. Jhered dropped his shield and stooped to drag a wounded woman to her feet. She'd taken an arrow through her shoulder and had a deep cut in her side.

'Come on, up and run,' he said.

She gasped in pain. Another levium came to her other side and the three of them half-ran along the dockside. They skirted the bodies of their people on the way, each one registering in Jhered's mind for the revenge he would extract from Yuran and the Tsardon. His mind was blank with fury and he glared at the Atreskan soldiers stationed on the docks. None had moved to their aid bar one and now they could see their own men riding with the Tsardon. He had no words for their cowardice and indecision.

Through the stone, he felt the rumble of hoofs. Arrows flew over his head from his crew.

'Get on board!' he yelled. 'Get that damn sail deployed.'

It was already happening. The skippers of both vessels were as ready as they could be. Jhered could see oars positioned ready to push off the quay and men stood ready at the fore and aft ropes. Archers stood on the deck, shield men in front of them. Arrows fell. One ripped through the flesh of Jhered's left arm where it supported the wounded woman. The pain was extraordinary. His grip threatened to loosen but he forced himself to clutch harder.

He dared a glance behind. The Tsardon had pulled up still in arrow range. Atreskan swordsmen were running past them. He upped his pace a little more, dragging the woman with him, realising that the arrow had punctured her back, pinning them together.

He ran through the thin line of his own archers and thumped onto the gangplank. Crew tried to take the woman from him.

'No, no. Leave her.'

He moved to the stern and knelt down below the gunwale. Levium were racing up both gangplanks. Most were on board now. He saw Menas fire one last arrow before shouting for the lines to be loosed. Oars pushed at the dock wall. The *Hark's Arrow* moved away. The sail was deployed, wind taking it immediately and beginning to move the vessel towards the centre of the lake. Menas dropped her bow and leapt for the side as the gangplank fell into the water. Harin was there, gripping her hands where they clung to the rail. Others grabbed her back, pulling her into the ship. Arrows whipped across the deck, thudded into plank and mast. Harin was thrown back, a shaft embedded in the top of his shoulder.

Jhered waited until the Appros moved again before he ducked his head down and looked at the woman in his arms. She too was still alive but her breathing was ragged and her face sweating and pale.

'Hold on,' he said. 'Help is coming.'

He turned them both and sat with his back to the gunwale. He breathed in the sea air and looked back along the ship. Atreskan and Tsardon arrows still flew and he gestured for the levium to keep down until they were out of range.

'Keep to the centre of the channel,' he ordered the steersman who crouched over the tiller. 'We don't want to face their artillery as well.'

'Yes, my Lord Exchequer.'

'Get us home,' he said. 'We have a Conquord to save.'

But it wasn't just Estorea that he had to contact. What he'd seen was a disaster that could sweep the Conquord aside. They needed a weapon the enemy did not know existed and could never possess. And he knew where to get it.

He stroked the woman's head and prayed Harkov had reached Westfallen in time.

Chapter 42

The new day dawned beautiful and clear. The sun quickly warmed the air and the earth. A light breeze rustled ripe crops ready for harvest. It brushed across the surface of the water. Moored ships bobbed gently and wavelets caressed the shore. Westfallen was as much a picture as it ever was during solastro.

A visitor would have thought the population had disappeared, such was the emptiness that echoed around every corner and the blank front of every closed business. The forum was deserted. The fishing fleet drawn up on the beach. The fields empty. A single voice rang out across the town. It came from the House of Masks and every citizen of Westfallen was grouped on the grass in front of it to hear the lay Reader speak.

Arvan Vasselis stood with Netta among the citizens, joined with them in their grief and loss. This was the first of too many commendments to be made this day and it was the one which dragged at the heart as no other truly would. A commendment of a return to the earth was a time to celebrate the life just passed and the rebirth that would follow. It was a time when the loss suffered by those the dead loved was tempered by the knowledge of a union between the dead and God. Or so it should be. But this day there could be no true celebration and there could be no mitigation for the cold that swept the hearts of Westfallen's citizens.

Ardol Kessian had been returned to the earth, wrapped in a deep green woollen cloth and placed in a grave in the woodland behind the House. A private ceremony that only Genna, the Echelon and Vasselis had witnessed had taken place as dusk fell the night before.

Now his mask, along with those of Elsa Gueran and the seventeen others who had died during the horror in the forum, was displayed outside the House with attendant flags. Vasselis could not take his eyes from it. A thin clay mould taken from his face on the day of his death and decorated by his loved ones with messages and symbols. The mask would hang in the House for a single year from this day before being returned to them for the family shrine.

Vasselis fancied he could see the laughter lines beneath the bright colours and words covering the mask and it brought him the briefest moment of levity. Around him, he could hear crying and muttering as the lay Reader intoned the words of commendment. Each phrase merely heightened the sense of injustice they all felt, and the intolerable harm done to their community and all of their lives. He hugged Netta close and listened to the Reader, a fisherman's wife thrust into the role following Elsa's murder.

' . . . we are all of us called by God to return to His embrace and be at one with His love before our cycles continue on His earth. And we that remain are left to celebrate all Ardol Kessian gave to us and to God during his wonderful life among us. God will call in His way and in His time.' She looked up from the scriptures, closing them and shaking her head. 'Though it is impossible to conceive that He would have called dear Ardol in this way, nor any of those whose commendments I am desolate to be making.'

A tear fell from the corner of her left eye and rolled down her cheek as she reopened the scriptures.

'Let Ardol Kessian's Mask hang in the House to watch over us for a single cycle. Let him look out over us all and give us guidance and support. And let all those who would seek his counsel come here free of prejudice and ask it of him. Let his life just passed warm all of our hearts in the seasons to come. Let it be so.'

'As it always is,' intoned the crowd.

'And now I invite all those who wish it to place gifts in Ardol's travelling chest, that he may have fresh food and clothing for his journey into God's embrace.'

She knelt and opened a small wooden chest, carved with roots and the sun. It would be filled with gifts from the citizens and buried at his feet. Vasselis walked first to the chest and squeezed the Reader's arm as he knelt by the chest.

'Thank you, Elena. Your words are those of the true God.' He placed a hunting knife in the chest. 'For you, Ardol, my dear old friend, to help you hunt that which you need on your journey. God will smile on you.' He felt a constriction in his chest. 'And I, left here in your wake, will dedicate my life to bringing justice for the crimes committed here in the name of God by a fake priestess.'

He rose and held out his hand for Netta. The two of them led the procession away from the House of Masks. A place where they would all be returning, time after terrible time, in the next days, to commend those that should not have been taken.

'I have to go to Harkov, now,' he said, feeling the weight crush him again. 'Talk to him. Make him understand.'

'Don't let him take you,' said Netta, her expression desperate. 'You have to be here. You have to keep the fires lit for the return of our son.'

Vasselis all but broke then. Kovan. Catapulted into the wilderness. Unprepared and so young to take on the responsibility that had been placed upon him. He was a strong young man but this . . . Vasselis could only pray that those in place for this eventuality and those they met at random would help him. Help all of them. There was nothing he could do now other than keep their home safe for the day they came back. Should that day ever come.

He walked with Netta to their villa and released her into the care of his men before mounting up. He rode up the slope out of Westfallen towards Caraduk, where Harkov had made his camp at a respectful distance. One hundred and sixty levium were with him. The forty palace guard had escorted Koroyan, Vennegoor and the survivors of the Armour of God away from Westfallen.

The Chancellor had gone only reluctantly, all but accusing Harkov of collusion with Vasselis and the heresy of Westfallen. He had held his calm admirably and in his capacity as a captain of the Advocate's palace guard had written assurances to her concerning the independence of the enquiries he was making. In the same capacity, he officially recorded her accusations against named individuals but also noted Vasselis's counter-accusations. There would be trials, he had said. And they would take place in Estorr, not Westfallen.

He had given leave, finally, for Vasselis to remain at liberty during the commendment of Ardol Kessian and for his part, Vasselis wasn't going to abuse that trust. Harkov was an honourable man from the same exemplary mould as Paul Jhered. He was a man on his way up in the Advocacy.

Harkov rode out to meet him and the two men walked their horses down a slope in the vague direction of Lake Phristos.

'She'll be back, you know,' said Vasselis, once the pleasantries had been dispensed.

'She will be returned to Estorr and my deputy will read the charges you have laid to the Advocate. I don't think she'll be going anywhere.'

'You're being naïve, captain. We both know the Advocate won't detain her, leaving her free to act again. And she only has eyes for one place.'

'I cannot imprison the Chancellor of the Order,' said Harkov. 'And I have to respect her word. All I can do is release her into the authority of the Advocate. Anything else is beyond my powers.'

'You didn't see her,' said Vasselis. 'I did. I saw the zeal in her eyes blinding her to her actions. She cut the Reader of Westfallen's throat in front of the entire town. There are hundreds of people here who would bear witness. If you were in her position of power, what do you suppose you would do?'

Harkov regarded him for some time while they walked across sun-baked grass.

'Marshal, you know the feelings of the three of us who came here. And you now know what happened to D'Allinnius and why the Chancellor came here in the first place. But ultimately we all answer to the Advocate and she has ordered your arrest.'

'You cannot remove me. We may as well burn Westfallen ourselves.'

Harkov raised a hand and Vasselis calmed. He relaxed the grip on his horse's reins.

'Please,' he said. 'With the Chancellor gone, I can speak freely. I am not here at merely the behest of the Advocate but of Exchequer Jhered. He blames the Advocate's fear on the Chancellor feeding her untruths about the risk to her rule the Ascendants represent. He fears that in killing them and you, she would be killing something that could potentially save the Conquord.'

'Is that not a little over-dramatic?' said Vasselis. 'Our Ascendants' Works are all based in peace, not war.'

'I know what he said to you about their capacity for destruction. And he believes further that the Advocate and through her, the Chancellor, cannot be allowed to destroy this weapon. He will be very unhappy that I was unable to take the Ascendants into my custody.'

Vasselis stopped. 'He is acting against her?'

'He fears for the Conquord. You've heard his concerns about the war. His only concern is for the Conquord and though he loves the Advocate, it's the Conquord he serves, and all the peoples it contains.'

'And what about you, Captain Harkov? Where do your loyalties lie?'

'They lie in truth and justice and the desire for Conquord unity.' Harkov cleared his throat. 'They lie, in this case, with the Exchequer.'

Relief cascaded through Vasselis. 'You will not regret this, my friend.'

'I have agonised about this, Marshal. I am with the palace guard. I have a young family and I am betraying the orders of my Advocate and making myself an enemy of the Chancellor, just like you. It is no accident that the levium, not my own riders, are still with me. I will not implicate them.'

'And what happens now?'

'What happens is that you are in my custody. That much has not changed. But I have been given no set date by which to deliver you to Estorr.' He nodded his head at Westfallen. 'Tragically, I suspect this place is to become a battleground of Conquord faith and we must be ready. I cannot let you leave Westfallen but your deputies and I will make free use of the messenger service.

'Bring your people here, Marshal Vasselis. Bring your soldiers and your engineers and your scientists. Because when the Chancellor realises I have no intention of bringing you to trial, she will be back, with or without the Advocate's blessing. And we must be ready or we will all burn.'

'Why are we going there? I don't want to go there. I don't. I want to go home.'

Mirron's misery was complete. She was seasick on top of everything else. She stood apart from the rest of them at the port rail, looking away back towards Westfallen. Below her, the oars of the trireme were silent while the wind pushed the ship forward at a healthy pace. They had found the ship, *Cirandon's Pride,* as light had

faded the evening before. Their initial relief at being on board was
short-lived and the fact of their situation intruded on them harder
now, a day later.

Arducius had done his best to be strong for them all but he felt as
Mirron did, though he was not as vocal in opposition. Ossacer was
sick too, shock having taken his strength from him again. He
was below the deck being tended by the ship's surgeon, while the
skipper, a woman called Patonius, tried to explain her orders.
She was a powerful woman. Not tall but with muscled shoulders,
close-cropped hair and a face red and rough from years at sea.

'Sirrane is a secretive, closed country,' she said patiently. 'And the
Marshal has been keenly involved in the negotiations to secure trade
and proper diplomatic links with them. They know him and they
trust him as far as they trust anyone. You'll be safe there in a way
you'll not be safe anywhere else right now.'

'It's so *far*,' said Gorian.

'Another reason it's so safe,' said Patonius. 'You'll leave ship at
Byscar and take the Conquord highway all the way through Atreska
and Gosland. Some of the Marshal's best people are on board and
will be with you.'

'But I don't want to go there,' wailed Mirron.

'Well, you must,' snapped Patonius. 'God-embrace-you, child, you
should be grateful you have such powerful friends. You do not know
how lucky you are.'

Gorian opened his mouth but Kovan was quicker.

'Gorian, don't,' he said. 'Captain, to these Ascendants this doesn't
seem like luck. They've been hounded from their homes, seen their
beloved Father die in front of them and seen more blood than anyone
ever should. These are true innocents. Give them time to adjust,
please.'

Arducius found himself staring at Kovan with renewed respect.
Mirron was doing much the same, though Gorian merely frowned.

'So don't tell us we're lucky,' he said, tone sullen, eyes sunken from
lack of sleep.

Patonius nodded. 'Innocents, are you? I don't know who you are
or what it is you are supposed to be able to do, but let me tell you
this. It is over twenty days to Byscar, if the wind is still. If it blows
from the south up the Tirronean at a steady six knots we could make
it in twelve. Then it's another twenty-five days by horse, boat and on

foot to Sirrane. At the very least. That's travelling without a break because your enemies might be behind you. Enemies that want you dead or you wouldn't be on board my ship.

'You are in for a hard time and no amount of crying over what you have lost or where you want to go will change that. You are under my care, as ordered by Marshal Vasselis. And I will deliver you safely to Byscar. That means you stay out of the way of me and my crew or you'll find yourselves swimming to Atreska. Do I make myself, clear? This is the open sea and I am in charge. Innocence is over.' She turned and inclined her head to Kovan. 'Complain to your father about me when you next see him if you want to. Right now I have greater concerns.'

She walked away to the stern and the tiller, glancing up at the sail as she went.

'Why did you let her talk to us like that?' demanded Gorian.

'Because she runs this ship. My father considers her among his best skippers, and that's good enough for me. She isn't really that bad. I just think she doesn't like anyone who isn't a sailor.'

Mirron was noisily sick again over the side of the ship. Her hair trailed in her mouth and vomit mixed with saliva hung in strands from her lips. Kovan went to her but she shrugged him away.

'Ossacer will stop it when he's able to,' said Arducius.

'If, you mean,' said Gorian.

'And you'll leave him be.' Arducius glared at Gorian, already tiring of his sharp comments. They were the only words he spoke. 'You know how hard it hit him.'

'And it didn't hit me hard?' Gorian had tears in his eyes again. 'I watched him die, too. We all did. And now he's gone, and we are alone and lost and going to some foreign land, and we don't know when we're ever going to be able to go home. Probably never. What can we do, Ardu? What can we ever do?'

Beneath his anger, Gorian was as scared as all of them. There was a pleading in his eyes mixed with the brooding Arducius recognised only too well. He'd never be able to read him properly. There was always something else there within him.

'We can continue to study and learn and improve,' said Arducius. 'You saw what we did at the forum and that was almost without thinking. There must be so much more we are capable of.' He shrugged. 'Perhaps we can speed this boat on a little, eh?'

'What's the point?' said Gorian.

'The point is that we can't stop now. Or the Father will have died for nothing. You don't want that, do you?'

Gorian shook his head. 'Never.'

'Good. Neither do I. So let's try and make the best of this. Make sure that everything we do, he would have wanted and do it all in his memory. What do you say?'

Gorian nodded. 'I say that I will never forget him. As I will never forget who has killed him. One day I'll get her. I'll make her sorry and her God won't be able to save her from my fire.'

Arducius sagged where he sat. 'Don't waste your time hating her,' he said. 'You'll never get close to her.'

'Yes I will,' said Gorian.

'And what will it prove? That you are a killer, just as she is?'

'No,' said Gorian. 'That she should have listened to us rather than try to kill us. That her time is over and the time of the Ascendants is here. That we are the new power in this world and her God is no longer the master of our earth. We are.'

Arducius was gaping but he could do nothing about it. Next to him, Kovan had stopped sharpening his sword and was staring. Even Mirron had turned from her misery at the rail.

'It is God who has granted you your abilities,' said Arducius eventually. 'We do the work of God.'

'Think what you like,' said Gorian. 'You can be hunted all your life if you want but I won't be. And the only way to stop them is to make them see that it is we who are in control.'

Chapter 43

The woman thrashed and spat her fury. It took three men to hold her down while Dahnishev examined her. Her face was filthy and cracked, burned so deeply by the sun the scars would never heal. Her hands were ragged beneath her torn gauntlets and when they had removed her roughly repaired breastplate to ease her breathing, they'd found a livid bruising where at least one rib was pressing on her lung.

The scouts who had come across her had thought her dead. Her horse, hardly in better condition, had been nuzzling her body. But she had flown at them with the strength of the insane. They would have killed her but had seen the Estorean crest on her armour. Instead, they had tied her across her horse to bring her back to the camp for treatment.

'Is there nothing you can give her to calm her?' asked Roberto.

The noises she made were disquieting. Her eyes would snap open and would always fix on him. Then the stream of babble would come. Completely incoherent but with a repetitive urgency that worried him deeply.

Dahnishev indicated a mug next to him. 'I've got a decoction of white mandrake here and it would knock her out if only I could get enough between her lips.' He straightened. 'She's in a poor state.'

'That much I can see,' said Roberto.

'She's terribly dehydrated. I doubt she's eaten enough for many days but it's her exposure to the sun that is her main problem.' He looked up at his General. 'If she hasn't cooked her brain, I'd be surprised. Listen to her.'

'We need to know what happened to her. She's a refugee from somewhere.'

'Or a deserter,' said Dahnishev.

Roberto shook his head. 'She's a senior Estorean cavalrywoman.' He paused. 'Someone here must know her, mustn't they?' He snapped his fingers at a guard. 'Get me Master Kastenas.'

Roberto looked down at the woman and her eyes opened again. Dahnishev tried to force more liquid between her lips but she coughed and spat, trying to speak. Her hands clenched and she frowned, pleading with him to understand her.

'Shh,' he said, placing a hand on her brow. 'Shh. Let our surgeon help you. You are among friends. Rest. Talk tomorrow. There's plenty of time.'

She shook her head violently, almost knocking the mug from Dahnishev's hands.

'Whatever she wants to say, she doesn't want to wait,' he said. 'I think you should leave. She clearly recognises you, probably from some coin or other.'

Roberto smiled. 'All right. Just don't let her die.'

He ducked under the surgeon's tent flap and out into the late evening. He couldn't shake the doom-laden thoughts from his mind. He hoped he was wrong and she was a survivor of a Tsardon raid on a transport column but that explanation just didn't ring right. There were quite a few soldiers hanging around the tent.

'Nothing better to do?' he said, recognising the livery of the 15th ala. 'Master Shakarov doesn't require your presence for camp duties?'

They looked at the floor. All but one.

'We were wondering if there was any news, General,' he said.

'I am well aware what you were wondering.'

'It's just that we heard she was from Scintarit and there's been a defeat there and that the Tsardon are heading north to us now.'

'Really?' Roberto tried hard not to laugh. 'Remarkable that you've heard so much. Perhaps she fell into her delirium just for me, eh? There is no news. We do not know who she is or where she is from. And let me assure you that when I know something you will be the very last to know. Now go away and find your centurion. Tell him from me that you are desperate to muck out your cavalry's horses. Go.'

He shook his head and turned away. Kastenas was approaching.
'You wanted me, General?'

'Yes, Elise. Go in there and tell me if you recognise our guest.'

'Yes, sir.'

Roberto looked around the camp. It was all but complete and the evening meal was being prepared. He didn't like the buzz of rumours that floated across to him. He couldn't stop it and he needed accurate information so he could deflect the worst of the speculation.

Since he had linked with Atarkis's legions there had been a change in structure. He had assumed overall command of the army with Atarkis as his second. It had led to some dissent among Atarkis's people but he had assured them of their relative independence in battle. But, in the end, an army could only have one leader.

They had continued to march into the heart of Tsard, moving south away from the border with Sirrane. The countryside was lush and productive and they had eaten well and travelled quickly. They had not made contact with any other Tsardon army and hope was rising that they would reach their mark for the campaign season without further battle. But raids by steppe cavalry had increased and his supply line was under constant pressure, as were his pickets. He had lost too many scouts for his liking and the guerrilla nature of the Tsardon tactics was unsettling. Every day, he lost men. The Tsardon were not suffering likewise.

The raiding had forced him into unpleasant choices. He had sent armoured foraging parties ahead of their route with instructions to leave nothing for others to use. They had carried messages of intent to local populations ahead and behind the march about the consequences of supporting cavalry raids and had made examples of three settlements already. The necessity disturbed him but the effects on morale of his inaction would be more severe.

At current pace, they would reach their mark by the middle of solasfall and he would be in the happy position of being able to relieve some of his longest serving legionaries to return to their homes for the winter. That assumed, of course, that the highways being built and the defences being put in place were of sufficient strength. Further, it rested very much on his mother agreeing to his request for reinforcements following the effects of the typhus plague.

He shuddered as he always did when thinking back on that awful time. And to think how much worse it could have been. Both

Shakarov and Davarov had survived. God had spared his most capable Atreskan field commanders for greater deeds. His friends.

'General?'

It was Elise Kastenas interrupting his reverie. He turned to face her.

'Well?'

'I know her all right and so should you. Delirious, burned and bedraggled, that is still Dina Kell, Master of Horse of the 2nd Estorean, the Bear Claws.'

'The *Bear Claws?*'

Kastenas nodded. 'I trained with her. Served with you both in Dornos.'

Roberto looked around to make sure they had not been overheard and ushered her back inside the tent.

'The Claws were at Scintarit. It's Gesteris's legion.' Roberto pushed a hand through his hair. 'If she's here . . .'

'It isn't going to be by accident.'

'God-embrace-us.' He looked down at her. She was sleeping now under the white mandrake and Dahnishev was tending to her wounds.

'I know what you're going to say,' said the surgeon. 'I'll do what I can. We'll get water into her, cool her down as much as we can and drag this rib out of her lung. After that, it's up to her.'

'I need her, Dahnishev.'

'I know,' he looked round, scowling. 'What did I just say, Roberto?'

'So earn your reputation.'

Dahnishev chuckled. 'It's one bound to tarnish.'

'Not today, eh? Wake me if she wakes. We aren't moving until she's told us what happened to her. Time we all prayed that we still have an eastern front.'

Roberto sat alone in his tent after he'd eaten with his command team. They knew as much as he did now and had been tasked to come up with disaster strategies. Shakarov and Davarov looked haunted as they left and Roberto had assured them of first information. Until then, there were to be no rumours spread, despite the fact that talk would be rife following the announcement that there would be no march the following day.

Dahnishev sent word in the cool hours before dawn. Roberto

found him at the door of his tent, having scattered the legionaries that had gathered there.

'She's coherent but whether she's sensible is another matter for you to judge. She will only speak to you.'

Roberto nodded and walked to the cot on which Kell lay. She tried to push herself up onto her elbows but had barely the strength. Dressings obscured much of her head and neck and balms covered what little was exposed. Her chest was heavily strapped and blood was soaking through where Dahnishev had cut her to reset her damaged rib.

'I am General Roberto Del Aglios. You wanted to speak to me. Take your time. We have plenty of it.'

'No. No, we don't,' she rasped, her voice sounding like it was being dragged over gravel. 'We were smashed. The Tsardon are marching on Atreska, Gosland and Gestern. The Conquord is in desperate trouble.'

Roberto sat down heavily, his mind buzzing with her words. 'Gesteris? What happened?'

Kell shook her head. 'Gone. They are all gone.' She stopped and wheezed. 'We're scattered, running. Leaderless. But it's worse.' A single cough sent a violent spasm through her body.

'That's enough,' said Roberto. 'Rest.'

'No. I'll be all right. General, you have to know. The Tsardon aim to release all the Atreskans. They want to turn the country from the Conquord.'

'You're sure?'

'All the evidence says so. All I've seen, all I've heard on my way here. You've got two Atreskan legions out there. They are the enemy, I'm sure of it.'

Roberto sat back in the chair, struggling to take it all in. What he had heard was impossible, surely.

'You'd better have the strength because I want to hear everything right now.'

Herine Del Aglios stood on the private balcony of her chambers and felt lost for the first time in her reign as Advocate. No one she needed right now was with her. Jhered was on his way into mortal danger. The Chancellor was probably still engaged in her duties in Caraduk.

And Gesteris. Well, her most senior general could quite easily already be dead.

She watched Yuran's emissary walk across the inner courtyard garden and away to the Atreskan state rooms in the palace. She was a bright girl and Herine had warmed to her immediately, even if the message she carried was one of unmitigated disaster. Yuran might well have unwittingly presented her with his successor. Once she had disappeared from sight, Herine returned to the papers in her hand. They were written by her son and for that she had to be grateful. At least he was still alive. But for how long?

The path to conquest had been so smooth but now it was all unravelling before her eyes. She didn't think she was overreacting. The Conquord was suddenly big and unwieldy. Tsard was going to invade. Her own son's army had been decimated by plague and her largest army was gone. Just gone.

She had to arrange a defence across many thousands of square miles of land and sea. She had no idea how. That was the work of her military but the war in Tsard had taken so many of them away and she had no faith that those behind the desks in Estorr's armed forces headquarters had the experience or the wit to work it for her. She had no option but to trust them. But in doing so, she could be placing her Conquord in the hands of incompetents.

She leant on the rail and breathed hard, determined not to let the tears begin. She should have listened to them. Years ago, Gesteris and Jhered had both told her that the men in charge of her armed forces were unworthy because they were not career militarists. Jhered had wanted Roberto in charge. Gesteris had wanted the job himself. And for the Conquord navies, it should have been Vasselis. A man who might also be dead.

'What have I done?' she whispered.

It had been so easy. Victory had followed victory and the treasury swelled, as did her legions and navies. She was happy for her best people to remain on campaign to ensure the continued glory of victory in battle. It had been the perfect time to reward her closest allies in the political and business spheres with figurehead positions. Giving them offices that would cement their reputations forever. They were capable administrators and sound accountants.

But they knew nothing about how to organise a defence of the

Conquord. And she could not remove them from duty without seriously damaging her own credibility. Besides which, there was no one better in Estorr to take their places. The worst thing was that she had been warned and she had chosen to ignore the warning, preferring to surround herself with people who agreed with her every decision. It was a crime of the ego no less damaging than that which had seen her invade Tsard in the first place. Jhered had tried to tell her. She had refused to listen.

'Oh, Paul,' she said. 'What am I going to do if you don't come home?'

'My Advocate?'

She turned sharply. Her consort stood there wearing just a cloth around his waist. His fine muscled body was oiled and shone in the lantern light and his cheeks were reddened with a little fine clay. He smelled fresh from his bathing. His smile was easy on his handsome face and it irritated her more than she could say.

'What do you want?'

'I thought I heard you speak, my lady.'

'So?'

He shifted, slightly nervous. 'Were you speaking to me?'

'Is your name Paul?' she asked sharply. He shook his head. 'Then I did not call you, did I?'

He paused, trying to size up her mood. For all his physical prowess, he was dull of mind and she required intellect and insight this evening.

'You're troubled,' he said. 'Perhaps I can help you.'

She pushed herself from the balcony rail and strutted towards him, happy to let her anger wash over her and see him back away, pace after pace.

'Help me? Are you of hidden military expertise? Can you tell me the positions of every legion under Conquord control and advise me where they must be repositioned to best counter the threat we face? Are you capable of identifying the best patrolling zones for my navies such that they might intercept invasion forces? Are you by some happy chance of a tactical mind so keen that your every order will be followed without question and so secure our borders? Have you seen so much war that you can weight our counter attacks to leave the enemy no option but to return to the defensive and leave the lands they threaten even today?'

He held out his hands in a pathetic calming gesture and tripped on a low table, falling over its marble surface.

'No, my Advocate.'

'No.' She shook her head. He got to his feet. There was a little blood on his heel. 'I need men around me who can save my Conquord.'

'I can calm your mind,' he said, voice so high it almost whined like a scolded dog's.

'Dammit but Paul Jhered was right. I wonder whether your balls have already been removed such has been your inability to impregnate me. Why do you think you are allowed in here, if not to provide me with the next child for my family?'

'One day—'

'One day is not and never was, soon enough. Your time is over now. I am tired of your body as I am tired of the wheedling tones of your voice. You have given me nothing but insignificant satisfaction in bed and my womb lies empty of all but the impotent seed you provide. Although your mind is so dim, perhaps it is a blessing. Any child you fathered would be of no use to me.'

All the colour had drained from his face. Behind him, the doors had opened and guards were in her chamber in response to her shouting. She saw him trembling as he reached out to her.

'Please, my Advocate, do not dismiss me.'

'You have nothing to offer me,' she snarled.

He winced. 'But I love you.'

'Love? Ha. What use do I have for such an emotion when I look at you? Get out and be happy you are not dragged in chains to my prison. Out!' She pointed from the room.

'The palace at Phaskar, my Advocate?'

'Is for the fathers of my children. Not for seedless imbeciles. OUT!'

He scurried from the room and the guards followed him. She wiped her hand across her mouth. Her bed looked large and empty.

'No. That didn't help.'

There was wine on the table and sweet indulgences on a plate next to the flagon. She sat down on her recliner and poured herself a brimming cup. She felt unable to concern herself with events beyond her door any more this night. She'd call the advisers she had to hand tomorrow, when God's sun warmed the earth and sky once more. Now she would toast those she wished were here to help her. She hoped she had enough wine to do them all justice.

Chapter 44

Roberto looked out over his camp when dawn lit the eastern sky and wondered how many of those sleeping within its stockade could be trusted when they knew all there was to know. And what he might do to pre-empt the problems he was liable to face. Inside his tent were all those he had chosen to draw into what amounted to an inner sanctum for his conscience. He had delivered Master Kell's reports to them and had left them to read and digest his full account after giving them the summary. He could hear them beginning to speak, so walked back in to face them.

General Atarkis and Elise Kastenas. Surgeon Dahnishev, whose own country of Gosland was under clear threat. Rovan Neristus, his brilliant engineer. Goran Shakarov and Master Davarov. Atreskans whose loyalty was beyond question. All sat on stools in a loose circle around a low table thick with mugs of steaming herbal infusions.

'Do you believe her?' asked Shakarov, his heavy features dark and brooding.

'There is no reason not to,' said Dahnishev. 'She is lucid if exhausted. Her sickness is not in her mind. And her account, in my opinion, is too detailed to be fabrication.'

'I agree,' said Roberto.

'Then the Conquord is all but lost. Gesteris's army represented two-thirds of our fighting force,' said Davarov. 'There is no effective defence. Certainly not in Atreska. Not against such an army ranged against them.'

'You are seeing doom where there is none,' said Roberto. 'And even if what you said was true, we must still make the right decisions for the Conquord we defend.'

'But Kell believes there will be no fight in Atreska because the legions and Yuran will turn,' said Dahnishev. 'The implications for Gosland, Neratharn and Gestern are immediate and terrible.'

'What do you make of that?' Roberto directed his question at the two Atreskans. 'If what Kell says is right, the Tsardon have separated Atreskan prisoners from all those of other nationalities and marched them towards their own borders. What other conclusions can we draw?'

'I think you assume Atreska and its people weak of will and loyalty if you believe this act will lead to our turning,' said Davarov, his thick accent edged with anger.

'Please,' said Dahnishev. 'No one is questioning the loyalty, strength or courage of the Atreskan peoples. One look at this army is evidence enough. But what of its Marshal? A man famed for his allegiance to the luxuries of the Conquord but his mistrust of paying the Exchequer for them.'

Roberto was fast enough. Just about. Shakarov launched himself at Dahnishev, fists bunched. He collided with Roberto who was surging from his stool while Davarov clung to his waist and Atarkis his shoulders.

'Bastard Goslander weasel,' he spat. 'He has guts and loyalty. Something your own arse-licking coward Marshal would never understand.'

'Sit down, Goran,' said Roberto, staring him in the eye.

Shakarov jabbed a finger over Roberto's shoulder. 'He insults my Marshal.'

'Sit.' Roberto pushed him back hard. 'Down.'

Roberto remained standing until he saw the tension ease from Shakarov's shoulders. Davarov, angry himself but under far more control, kept a steadying hand on his arm. Shakarov tried to shake it off but Davarov merely tightened his grip.

'I am sorry if I caused offence,' said Dahnishev, unruffled by the attempted attack. 'But I feel this is a time for honesty.'

'Indeed,' said Roberto. 'But your honesty sometimes lacks tact.'

There was a chuckle around the group, not shared by Shakarov.

'But in this instance it points out rather accurately the problems we face as a command team.' He leant emphasis on the final word. 'We are marching into a very difficult situation. The best we can pray for is that Atreska has accepted the gift of the repatriation of its legions and turned them round to head the defence of the country. But at worst, we will be faced with marching into a country to attack the Tsardon and find that some of those in Conquord livery are standing against us too. I do not have to draw you a picture of the stresses that will cause among our own legions.'

'I will fight for you and for the Conquord,' said Davarov.

Beside him, Shakarov was nodding.

'I would expect nothing less from either of you. But I suspect that not all of those under your charge will feel the same. There is conscription throughout your infantry forces.'

'So what do we do?' asked Elise.

'We have little option but to split the army, Roberto,' said Atarkis, speaking for the first time. 'Give me back my command and I will take my legions back to Gosland. If the Tsardon force heading north is as large as we fear, their defences won't be strong enough. You should march south towards Atreska.'

Roberto nodded. 'I concur. We face an immediate and great threat. Our most direct route is to the south of the Halorians to follow the Tsardon across the fords at Scintarit. It's risky but it does provide us more options for our own deployment.'

'But it'll be slow-going until we reach the roads laid down by Gesteris's engineers,' said Davarov.

'But we'll be moving towards Atreska from the north through Gosland,' said Atarkis. 'I'll be able to build strength of arms on the march. Communication will be better and we can get messages of intent through to Estorr unhindered by Tsardon or – excuse me, you two – Atreskan rebel forces.'

Shakarov grunted his contempt at the possibility.

'Messages will go back from us too, but we will not follow them directly,' said Roberto. He fetched their campaign map from his angled desk. They cleared the mugs and he spread it out on the table. He pointed out their current position. 'All right, here we are. Haroq City is twenty-five days fast march away, taking the Scintarit route. It is the faster way though we will be alone because General Atarkis will seek to engage the Tsardon force moving north.'

He leant back. Nodding at Davarov who wanted to speak.

'I don't know your intention, Roberto, but for me as an Atreskan of the Conquord, it is our duty to disrupt the invasion at the earliest opportunity. We aren't going to be able to catch the Tsardon northbound army before General Atarkis engages. And I don't think we should try.' He traced his finger down the map. 'So we must hope that Atreska's standing legions can hold up the westbound force while we come at them from behind, sweeping up any of Gesteris's people we find on the way.'

'I think encountering thirty thousand Tsardon as soon as possible is not advisable in any instance,' said Elise. 'I agree that we must split our forces to defend both countries but we must take care we don't engage the Tsardon before we have to. If Atreska's standing legions cannot hold them, I question the wisdom of simply running into the back of them. We do not have the numbers unless our element of surprise is total.'

'True enough,' said Roberto. 'So tell me one other thing, any of you. We are agreed that if Kell is accurate in her account and her dates, the Tsardon will have been at Haroq City for some days now. If the Atreskans have been surprised, Haroq may even have fallen and the route to Byscar and the coast opened.

'You all know the size of my army. Is our duty to a country that could quite easily be lost, or is it to the wider Conquord? And are these two one and the same thing in this case?'

'What are you suggesting, Roberto?' asked Dahnishev.

'That we could instead continue south to Gestern where the Tsardon are also bound. But there, at least, we know Jorganesh will retreat through Atreska to join Gestern's border defence. And of course, there's Kark.'

'We cannot abandon my country,' said Shakarov quietly.

'But how best can we serve it, Goran?' asked Roberto. 'We will total fifteen thousand against a marauding army at least twice that size. An army that has tasted recent victory and might, just might, be bolstered by those we considered allies only yesterday. They will be stopped in Neratharn by winter, if not the Conquord standing legions.'

'So we should bypass the Atreskan conflict?' asked Davarov. 'Surely not, Roberto.'

'It is an option. I'll tell you what worries me most is that while defences can be brought to bear relatively quickly to slow the Tsardon advance through Atreska, and Gosland for that matter, the same cannot be said for Gestern. And if I was the Tsardon commander, I would wish very much to take Gestern and annexe Kester

Isle. From there, I would have my pincers locked around Estorea. And I would have at my command all routes to Kark for minerals and metals.'

The room fell silent. He watched them while they stared at the map in front of them.

'Big place, isn't it?' he said. 'And we have a responsibility that encompasses the whole of it.'

Shakarov and Davarov both had their heads in their hands.

'Goran, you indicated that you would fight for me and the Conquord,' said Roberto. 'And that is not going to be in your home country. Not yet, though I promise you we will have a part in Atreska's liberation, should she fall. This is hard for you, I know, but that is my decision. We'll damage what we can of the Tsardon effort on our way south but we will not risk getting trapped between the enemy advance and its reinforcements. Neither will I risk marching this army blindly into a country that is surely descended into open war.

'Do I have your support?'

Davarov and Shakarov looked at each other.

'Unconditionally, as always,' said Davarov.

'Good,' said Roberto. 'We march tomorrow, three hours before dawn. Brief your citizens. Make them understand. This is a change. We are no longer marching to victory. We are marching to save our Conquord. Nothing will feel the same. And one other thing. Shakarov, Dahnishev. I do not tolerate dissent in my command team. One more transgression and, friends or not, you will be removed from your positions.

'Dismissed. Neristus, stay behind, would you? I need to talk to you about transport for heavier artillery pieces. No one is doing to me what the Tsardon did to Gesteris.'

The breeze was upstream and the Gatherer vessels had sails furled against masts on the approach to the fortifications at Byscar. Below, the stroke beat out a punishing pace; the oarsmen would earn their money this day. The *Hark's Arrow* and *Hark's Spear* were in line astern, moving at upwards of seven knots against the sluggish tide.

Ahead, the Teel delta and the Byscar sea defences lay less than three miles distant around a spur of land. Jhered had not been alone in seeing the birds flying high overhead, way beyond arrow range. He

could guess the content of the messages they carried and the
Gatherers had to be ready for anything from blockade to fast pursuit,
to stone and bolt fire.

The closer they approached, the more the risk of a blockade
diminished. Indeed Jhered, standing in the prow with his shield
leant against the rail, expected to have seen one already at the head
of the Teel. It was a good sign. The Atreskan navy, much of which
was stationed in Byscar, was either at sea or did not have the crews
on stand-by to respond. Even so, the Gatherers lined the decks,
bows ready. In the half-deck below, the small-bore bolt-firers were
winched and loaded.

Jhered scanned the land to either side of the Teel, which widened
dramatically on the approach to the delta. Flood plains ran away
north and south, with the land rising to the spectacular cliffs on
which Byscar's castle sat, dominating the skyline ahead. The port
nestled in an inlet at the bottom of a steep incline and Byscar's
businesses and homes were built all the way up the cliff side, accessed
by snaking roads.

In hollowed-out points on the cliffs facing into the river, across the
delta and out to sea, stood the port's defences. Reached by tunnels
dug through the rock, they were heavy-bore artillery, capable of
delivering two-talent stones that would shatter keels and sink vessels
in a single strike. The natural defence of the rock made them almost
impossible to hit from sea level. Jhered feared them because shallow
water and a turn in the river drove every ship into their range.

At less than a mile distant, the Gatherer ships began their forced
swing to port. Jhered watched men appear on the ramparts and
stand by the Atreskan republican standard which flew from the
castle towers. Signalmen. Dual flags in hand, they sent out their
messages. Bells sounded, their chimes bouncing off the rock faces and
echoing dully across the river. Without a choice, the Gatherer ships
came on.

Jhered trotted back down the length of the ship, feeling its smooth
movement across the calm water.

'Keep low until you fire,' he said as he passed his archers. 'Look to
the cliffs. Shout the attacks. Brace, levium. Stand firm.'

He reached the stern where the skipper stood next to the tiller
man. On the port rail, a young lad was working a plumb line, calling
out the depths.

'Hug the port shore as close as you can, Captain. Let's not give them more angle than we have to.'

'I'm already there, Exchequer,' said the Captain. 'Any closer and we'll be brushing the sand. And worse.'

'Can you get anything more out of them down below?'

The captain bared his teeth in what passed for a smile on his thin face. 'If I do, we'll have little left for running when we pass the harbour. Exchequer, with respect, I know what must be done.'

'Just get us past here in one piece.'

The Captain's reply was lost in a ripple of sound from the cliffs above.

'Ward!'

Jhered saw the stones arc out. Huge dark shapes crossing the cloudless sky, moving quickly. Falling, falling. Great plumes of water and spray spouted from the river. Jhered couldn't count them all. Over a dozen certainly. Mostly ahead in an arc thirty yards off the starboard bow. Others fell to port. Jhered was sprayed with water and the wash rocked the ship.

Immediately, the captain ordered an increase in pace and a slight change of course, heading for the impact areas of the first starboard stones. Jhered frowned.

'Sighters. They'll be bringing their angles back a little,' he said in response. 'They won't see our movement. Trust me.'

Jhered nodded. He moved ahead along the ship to stand by the mast. On a promontory of bedrock above a rocky shore at the apex of the turn, he saw soldiers running. Behind them, a horse and cart on top of which stood a scorpion bolt-firer.

'Ahead left!' he indicated the new threat. 'Targets approaching.'

It would be at the extreme edge of their range. The ship ploughed on, her sister in her wake and fifty yards behind. Jhered watched the scorpion being prepared. He saw the angle, saw the bolt being loaded. They fired. He couldn't track the trajectory, it came too fast. The bolt struck, thudding into the gunwale in the ship's front quarter. Wood splintered and the head rammed through. The levium behind it was struck in the midriff and pinioned to the deck, jerking spasmodically. Jhered closed his eyes.

'Fire!'

The levium answered him. A volley of arrows soared high. He lost them as they crossed the cliff line. By the scorpion, he saw two men fall. His own lightweight bolt-firers sounded too, but their shafts fell short, splashing into the shore.

'At will,' he called.

A second ripple from above. Onager stones breached the sky. He tracked them, hearing another volley of arrows flick away. And another. The stones fell. His heart missed a beat. They loomed large. Too large. The captain had misjudged. He took an unconscious pace backwards and saw some of his levium do the same. But in the last moments, the balls dropped short, splashing down no more than ten yards from the tips of the oars. Water washed across the deck. He turned his back to the spray, seeing other stones fall the other side and behind. At the stern, the skipper was smiling.

The *Hark's Arrow* drove hard into its port turn, rounding the promontory and giving the archers clear sight of the scorpion crew. They loosed another bolt which flashed across the deck and fell harmlessly into the brackish waters of the delta. The answering arrows silenced its taunting crew. Straightening the tiller, the skipper aimed them beyond the harbour and out into the Tirronean Sea.

Jhered saw the masts of three vessels moving beyond the harbour wall, heading out to intercept. Their sails were full and the old Atreskan flag flew at their mastheads. Whatever Yuran had said in his messages, his navy had been only too happy to turn from the Conquord. He wondered if Atreska had ever been truly loyal.

Ahead and behind now, the artillery spoke. Stones rolling apparently lazily across the sun and falling around the helpless vessels. For the second time, the slight change in course and pace fooled the enemy and the stones missed. But the density of artillery surely meant that it was only a matter of time before their luck ran out.

The only way to stop them was to get close to the harbour and the enemy ships. The captain clearly thought the same. Jhered could see him studying the pennant atop the mast and gauging if the sail could be deployed. But the wind still held against them. Instead, the oars dipped a little more quickly and the rhythmic songs of the crew sounded a little louder.

'A bonus to the crew if they keep this up for an hour!' called Jhered.

'I'll set the glass,' answered the skipper; and Jhered had no doubt that he would.

Edging around the harbour wall came the enemy ships. Triremes all, smaller and quicker than the Gatherer vessels, and set with ramming spikes on the bow. The skipper sailed directly at them. Byscar's defences fired again. Jhered turned his head to watch the hypnotic approach. The stones made a beguiling sight on the upswing of their arcs. They were on a wide spread and falling now. He could hear the whistle of their passage. It was the sound of the wind devils, calling men to their dooms.

Impact. Water sprayed across the deck again. One stone landed perilously close to the portside oars. Two were clipped and shattered. Below decks men were thrown from their seats. Jhered heard them scream. The ship faltered, its rhythm disrupted. It rocked from the wash.

From behind a crack ricocheted across the water. Jhered spun round, hand on the mast to steady himself. The *Hark's Spear* had been hit. A stone had struck her mast halfway up, breaking it in two. He watched the great beam topple to port, showering down wood shards. The whole ship rocked violently. Men were pitched over the side or sent sprawling across the deck, some helpless under the falling mast, rigging and furled sail.

The mast thudded down, destroying the rail and splitting timbers. Crushing levium. He could hear the cheering echo from Byscar's cliffs mixed with the shouts, orders and agony of his people. He looked to the skipper who shook his head and instead of going to their aid, asked for more speed from his crew.

Tearing his eyes from the *Spear* Jhered focused ahead.

'Archers,' he snapped. 'Targets ahead. Let's do some damage.'

The enemy were under sail and oar. Spaced apart from each other by seventy yards or so, they came on in a single line. The *Arrow* steered at them, unflinching, giving them no clue. They closed quickly. Jhered could hear the drums of the Atreskans beating out time. He saw archers gathered on deck.

At less than a hundred yards, his skipper changed course. The tiller swept to port and drove the rudder starboard, angling the ship into the gap between two of the enemy. Simultaneously, the starboard oarsmen lifted, accelerating the turn. Even so it was a slow adjustment of a large ship. Jhered saw the enemy respond. Both triremes ahead began to turn in. The distance between them decreased.

'Down and drive!' roared the skipper.

The starboard oars dropped and stroked. The tiller straightened. Pace increased.

'Archers ready!' called Menas. 'Let's take first volley.'

Jhered was suddenly horribly aware of his vulnerability. His shield was still resting against the bow rail. He ran down the ship against all natural instincts, seeing the enemy close the gap ahead. Arrows flew. His levium loosed dense volleys both sides and ducked down as they were answered. Jhered dived flat to the deck. Arrows whipped and skipped above him, striking wood and metal. He didn't hear a single cry. Good.

Rising, his heart missed a beat for the second time. There was barely enough space for the ships to pass now. They were within thirty yards. The ramming spikes angled in more and more with every stroke but now at least he could see the captain's gamble. He grabbed his shield and crouched at the bow, peering over the rail, directing his nearest archers and wishing he had learned the art himself to any reasonable level of skill. Too busy with the sword the whole of his youth.

The air was thick with arrows and the shouts of his levium. Metal tips rattled like hail on timbers. He could almost smell the oil and paint on the Atreskan vessels but even as his levium were wounded and died on the deck, he could still raise a smile.

'Ship oars!' the skipper's thundering voice rolled across the deck.

'Down! Down!' ordered Jhered.

Through the smallest of gaps they came. The crew dragged their oars in, leaving their momentum to carry them through. On the Atreskan vessels the order had been the same but they were neither as disciplined nor as swift. Jhered heard the splintering of wood and felt it beneath his feet. The enemy archers fell silent, struggling to keep their feet.

The *Arrow* moved past them, forging into open waters. Jhered looked back down the ship. The skipper was standing tall, his tiller man crouched behind him, hand steady. They had no more than three yards either side at the stern. He saw the skipper turn to his opposite number and make an obscene gesture. He said something too but whatever it was got lost in the panicked shouts of the enemy.

Tillers were pushed hard port and starboard. The ships began to angle away. But twenty yards behind the *Arrow*, they collided, brushing against each other and destroying what few oars were left to them, grinding timber against timber. The two vessels lurched apart and kept going. Through the gap would come the *Spear*. Wounded but very much afloat, her oars bit into the water and moved her gratefully along after her sister.

The third enemy vessel was turning but it would not catch them. Jhered would be surprised if they had any desire to do so.

And at the stern, the skipper clapped his tiller man on the back and roared with laughter.

Chapter 45

848th cycle of God, 32nd day of Solasrise
15th year of the true Ascendancy

'Say it,' repeated Arducius. 'Speak it with us.'

Gorian sighed dramatically and nodded that he was ready to intone with them. It was the sixth day of their voyage north and the second day since Ossacer had awoken, nervous but apparently all right in every other respect. He had settled Mirron's sickness and pointed out a weak joint in the ship's hull to Patonius. The skipper had only half-believed him at first but, on discovering he was right, had reacted with a bemused suspicion. She had kept the knowledge to herself but the rumour had spread through the crew nonetheless.

The Ascendants sat below decks in the cramped quarters Arducius shared with his brothers. Kovan bunked with the first officer. The two were apparently friends from school in Cirandon, though the sailor was a few years older. Mirron was using the Marshal's cabin.

The looks she had drawn from the crew had escaped none of them and Arducius had been forced to recognise for the first time that the girl he thought of as his sister was almost a woman. And a very pretty one at that. He could no longer deny the reasons for Gorian and Kovan's sparring for her attentions. He didn't like it much and had been close to her ever since.

Arducius was determined that they should keep up the ways Father Kessian had shown them, though every lesson, every practised work and every recital had brought them fresh pain. And after discussing it long with Kovan, they'd also agreed to practice below decks in their quarters. It was altogether no fun at all and spirits were very low. God-surround-them but they had not even been able to swim despite the entire ocean about them and the presence of the dolphins Gorian was able to summon at will, even without water contact. He wouldn't tell them how.

'Ready?' Arducius asked the others. They nodded.

'Our God who blesses this earth, all those who walk upon it, all the creatures who run across it and all the fish that swim in the seas, warm our hearts while we study to do your work. By your grace are we blessed. By your wisdom are we Ascendants born to serve you and to bring greater comfort to all those we touch. Let your hand guide our minds and our bodies as we grow each day to be more able to serve you. You are the Omniscient. We are your servants.'

They dropped their heads for the moment's quiet contemplation. Each one of them consulted their inner senses and delved into their strengths. Their lifelines burned bright in the stuffy air of the quarters. The energy of the world coalesced about them through every breath, every flicker of the eye and every touch of their hands. Arducius glanced at Gorian. He knew why he was reluctant to pray. Arducius didn't think he really believed in it any more. Not where his place in it was anyway.

'One by one, tell me what you see this morning. Mirron?'

'I see the energy of the sun warming the air above our heads and I feel the cook fires burning in the galley. They use poor fuel which burns unevenly. I could help them if you'd let me.'

'Maybe later on. Ossacer?'

'There is a grey surrounding the energy maps of at least half of the crew. It is an infection that may or may not grow. It would be easy to kill but the surgeon does not even know it exists. None of them feel sick.'

'Is it dangerous?'

'No,' said Ossacer. 'It's like a cold or something.'

'Then we can let it run its course. Gorian?'

'I see everything. Is there anything you want me to bring out in particular for this pointless exercise? Arducius, we can make this voyage better for everyone. And at the same time we can show them what we can do. What power we have.'

'You want them to fear us?'

'No,' said Gorian, frowning. 'I want them to see us for who we really are. We're like prisoners in here.'

'You heard what Kovan said. This is a small ship and the crew are superstitious like all crews. It doesn't matter that they are the Marshal's. Out on the sea, we are alone and at risk.'

'I'm not scared of them,' said Gorian.

'Respect them instead,' said Arducius.

'You're beginning to sound like dear, obedient Kovan,' said Gorian. 'Perhaps you should bunk with him if you don't want to be an Ascendant any more.'

'Don't be so stupid.'

They all turned to the door in the instant before Kovan knocked on it. They knew it was him by the change in the energies his lifelines forced on those that surrounded them. It was a realisation that had come upon them slowly. At first, Arducius thought it just quick reactions. One time, though, he had his eyes closed and saw as well as felt the shift in energy through the changing of colour in his mind. He had known then it was one more thing they had at their disposal.

'Come in,' said Ossacer.

Kovan entered. 'Come up on deck before you start. You've got to see this.'

'What is it?' asked Arducius.

'Kester Isle.'

They followed him through the ship and up the small flight of stairs to the slightly raised foredeck on which sat the ship's single scorpion bolt-firer. Its cold dead metal was unsettling. But for once they forgot its presence. Because off the starboard bow was Kester Isle, the defender of the Conquord, so they had been schooled. The sight took Arducius's breath away.

Through the night, they had been approaching it and Kovan had requested they sail close to get the first view. Patonius had smiled, a rare event, and had agreed. They were no more than a half mile from its western edge. The beauty and the terror of man and nature, the Marshal had described it. Arducius hadn't understood at the time but he did now.

Kester Isle was a towering dog leg of ancient rock, hundreds of miles long. At its southern end it was a sheer black cliff better than two thousand feet high. It was often lost in cloud during dusas when the waves crashed against its base, trying in vain to scale it. Myth had it that God had sent a bolt of lightning that cracked the land in two as a demonstration of his power and so created the cliff. Father

Kessian had said it was probably a volcano beneath the sea or an earthquake. Arducius didn't know which to believe.

It didn't matter. They had already sailed beyond it and the teeth of rock that kept any boat from getting too close to it. The western cliffs were hardly less impressive. The whole of Kester Isle sloped down south to north where it ended in a series of jutting spikes of rock called the Lances of Ocetarus, the name of an Atreskan god of the sea. The tidal eddies they produced made approach to the northern beaches treacherous and had led the Conquord engineers to build harbours further down its flanks.

Arducius stared at the rock, letting his eyes travel up the cracked, pocked surface, home to countless thousands of seabirds. Waves rumbled at its base. The water breasted not far below the first of innumerable numbers of fortifications. They jutted or had been carved out of its sides at almost every level on which his eyes lingered. They appeared to drip there, like the heavy blossom on a willow tree, lighter in colour than the rock to which they clung. He saw the sparkle of lights in the gloom, the sheen of metal brackets on onager and bolt-firer and the glint of tripod-mounted magnifiers. Every angle was covered. There had to be hundreds of them studding the pitted walls.

He had read that behind them all was a maze of passages linking armouries, workshops and barracking for thousands of men, and all leading to the top of the isle, whose natural covering of grass and trees was dominated at its centre by a vast man-made plateau. And on the plateau rested the great palace, city and fortress of the Ocetanas, the Conquord navies.

Even from this angle and distance, better than fifteen hundred feet below, the buildings were awesome. Watch towers studded the perimeter of the plateau which stretched the width of the isle. Each tower was linked by ramparts from which the arms of artillery pieces jutted and were covered by canvas. Beyond them, he could see the topmost stories of the palace hung with the flags of the Conquord and the Ocetanas. The latter, displaying the profile of a ship under the sun and over the rolling oceans was set just below the level of the Conquord standard.

Every piece of stone was a dazzling white, every roof tile a bright fiery red. And the towers that sat at each corner of the plateau were masters of all they saw on the surface of the sea. They bulged out in their centres, in mimicry of classical Gesternan architecture.

One day, Arducius resolved to himself to go there. Walk the long paths that wound up to the plateau or ride the sequential lifts that were strong enough to move building slabs. He'd walk through the city gates and see the vast fields that made the isle self-sufficient. And he'd see the pumping stations where the water from the rivers deep in the bowels of the isle, or caught in the rain catchers was fed to the irrigation and fountain systems. The diamond city. The place where, if even the whole Conquord fell, no enemy could hope to take.

He felt a grab on his arm. It was Kovan.

'Look, Ardu, look.'

The ship rounded a rock and cement wall that made up the southern barrier of one of the four great harbours that Kester Isle possessed. Inside it at anchor, at berth or just visible through the huge sea gates that let into the vast caverns, were ships. Ships everywhere. Trireme, galley, artillery platform, and spiked corsair. He smiled for the first time since he'd seen Father Kessian fall. He never thought to see one spiked corsair, let alone a cluster of a dozen and more.

They were the vessel of the Ocenii Squadron, the navy's elite. They looked evil. Garishly decorated, particularly the ramming spike, they sat low in the water. They had a single purpose: to propel the Ocenii hard and fast into the enemy. To hole their ships at the waterline and to bring the Conquord's best onto the decks of their foe. They carried sword, composite bow and pitch fire. Their reputation was unparalleled.

'Have you ever seen them?' asked Arducius. 'The Ocenii?'

Kovan nodded. 'Just once, my father brought me here to see them train. You've never seen anything so fast across the water. And when they strike their target, they slice the binds that keep them in their seats for impact and climb up their oars so fast you cannot keep up. And to see them fight, even in sparring is something you cannot describe.'

Arducius wasn't sure how much Kovan was exaggerating. Mirron was.

'They sound like monkeys with swords,' she said dismissively. 'And the painting on the sides is so ugly. As ugly as the boats.'

'Ships.' Kovan and Arducius spoke together.

'What's the difference?' asked Mirron, plainly uninterested.

Arducius shook his head, staying Kovan's attempt to explain. 'You're wasting your breath.'

He looked back down the deck. There were a handful of crew topside. Riggers and the boy that operated the plumb line. Patonius was on the covered aft deck with the tiller man. They kept on staring like they had ever since Ossacer had identified the weakness in the hull. It made Arducius uneasy. He could feel the animosity through their energies. The ill-feeling was like a chill breeze on his body. He wished he could shut more of it out sometimes but then he wouldn't be able to experience the wonders and glories of all God's creatures, the seas and the earth.

'What are you staring at?'

'Gorian, don't,' said Mirron.

Arducius sought the object of Gorian's belligerence. It was a rigger. A sinewy man with long, lank hair tied in a ponytail. He was stripped to the waist, showing off his corded, dense muscle. He said nothing but continued staring. Other activity on the deck halted immediately. Patonius leant on the rail and watched. There was a smirk on her face. Arducius felt the mood cool around him.

'Do we look strange or something?' Gorian pressed.

The man shook his head and walked towards them. Kovan moved a pace forwards in front of Mirron.

'Leave it, Gorian,' said Arducius. 'It doesn't matter.'

'It does,' he said. 'I don't like being stared at.'

'I'm not staring at you, boy,' said the rigger, only a handful of paces away now with his mates gathering under the mast to watch him. 'But your pretty sister is worth a closer look.'

'I think that's close enough, though,' said Kovan, holding out an arm. 'She's just a girl. You'll frighten her.'

'Oh, a protector,' the rigger said, his smile broadening unpleasantly. 'And a high-up one too. Don't worry, little marshal, it's just a bit of fun.'

Ossacer had come to Arducius's side and was clutching his arm nervously. Arducius patted his hand, happy that Kovan would handle it. He had his father's calmness about him.

'Only for you, not for her,' said Kovan. 'Go back to work.'

'Come on, little one. Come and see the ship with a proper man. I'll take you places you've never seen before.'

Mirron stepped back and towards Gorian. He stepped in front of her and next to Kovan.

'Don't make me hurt you,' he said, his voice cold.

'Gorian,' warned Arducius. He looked to Patonius in appeal. She merely shrugged and carried on watching. She didn't understand.

The rigger laughed. 'What with? Your little boy fists and your funny eyes? Do you really think we believe the stories we heard? Don't insult me, boy or I'll put you over the side.'

'Fun's over,' said Kovan, glancing at Gorian. 'Let's not get angry. It isn't worth it.'

The rigger leered at Mirron. 'Young and firm. Just the way I like my women. Come on. Just a walk.'

'No,' she said.

'You heard her,' said Gorian. 'Now turn away before you never see anything ever again.'

'That's it, I warned you.'

The rigger stepped forwards, a determined look on his face. But he had misjudged Gorian. He was quick and strong for fourteen. Arducius felt the change in the energy trails on the hot breeze. Ossacer tensed and Mirron began to mouth 'no' but it was all too late. Gorian ducked under the rigger's grip, straightened and slapped a palm over his eyes. There was the briefest flare and the rigger fell back, screeching, his hands to his face.

'No,' said Gorian. 'I warned *you*.'

'He's blinded me, he's blinded me,' wailed the rigger, dropping to his knees.

His mates bunched and ran, shouting their threats and promises. Kovan drew his gladius.

'Halt your movement!' bellowed Patonius.

Down on the oar deck, voices called up and the rhythm was interrupted. Oars clashed before the stroke man brought them back under control.

'Nobody take another step,' continued Patonius. She strode up the ship towards them, pausing briefly by her crew. 'You, get Anthus down below to the surgeon. The rest of you get back to your work. Do it now. I'll handle this.'

Arducius could see Gorian standing proud and defiant. Behind him, Mirron was staring open mouthed at the rigger, Anthus, who was helped sobbing to his feet to be led away.

'I could help him,' whispered Ossacer.

'I don't think this is the time,' said Arducius.

'Put up your sword, young Vasselis,' said Patonius, stepping up to the bow deck. She stood square in front of Gorian. 'There is only one person who dispenses discipline on my ship and that is me, not some stupid little boy.'

'I told him to stop and he wouldn't. He deserved it,' said Gorian.

Patonius's face was bleak. 'He was having a little fun. Had he laid a finger on you or Mirron, I would have stopped him and I would have administered any punishment I saw fit. What you think does not matter on my ship and it never will. Tell me, is he permanently blind as a result of this devilry that my Lord Marshal is so keen to protect?'

Gorian shrugged.

'He doesn't know,' said Ossacer quietly. 'He never knows.'

He was massaging his wrist where the frost-burn scars were.

'I have a crew behind me who will demand retribution for what you have done,' said Patonius. 'Our rules out here are very simple. Like for like. Should he be blinded, so shall you be.'

Mirron gasped but Gorian merely shook his head. It was Kovan who spoke.

'I'm sorry, Captain, but I cannot let you do that,' he said.

'I beg your pardon?'

'My father has placed the Ascendants in my care and they are not to be harmed.'

'In your care but not under your control,' she said. 'Nevertheless such an act cannot go unpunished. I'm sure your father would agree. But for now, my judgement is this. All of you are confined below. You, Gorian, will be lucky ever to see the sun again. Mirron, this is for your own good. The blood of fertility has run from you?'

Mirron nodded, blushing.

'It's a sign from God,' said Patonius. 'And grown men can smell it on you as if it were freshly squeezed juice from ripe fruit. Keep yourself out of the way. Now all of you, get out of my sight until I order otherwise. Never mind what you possess, you are a long way from enough protection should my crew seek vengeance.'

On his way past Patonius to the ladder below, Arducius paused and squinted at the trails in the air emanating from the south-east, beyond Kester Isle. He frowned.

'Something wrong?' she asked.

'You might want to steer us closer to shore. The first of the solasfall storms will be here in seven days.'

Patonius turned a slow circle, staring at the unbroken blue sky. 'I hardly think so, Arducius. This is the Tirronean Sea and we are a long way from the turn of the season.'

Arducius shrugged. 'Seven days,' he said.

She glared at him, insulted. 'Ridiculous notion. Get below.'

Chapter 46

848th cycle of God, 39th day of Solasrise
15th year of the true Ascendancy

Arducius was pitched from his bunk and struck the wall opposite. He checked himself over quickly. He'd been lucky. Nothing was broken but he'd have some bad bruising. Ossacer would need to look at it later. Assuming they didn't sink, of course. It was pitch black, the candle having long since toppled over and snuffed out. He shook his head and opened his mind to the energies surging about him. It was like a cascade of ice-cold water through his mind, washing away everything else.

He could see Gorian and Ossacer's energy maps with stunning clarity. Both of them were sitting up, clutching the sides of their cots and sampling the power that thundered around them. Beyond the walls of their tiny room and away beyond the confines of the ship, was the thrashing life of the storm that had boiled out of the southeast exactly as he had predicted, and rapidly overtaken them. It presented itself to him as a blaze of yellow-white light, coiling, spinning and spitting out strands and sheets of energy that had huge force but which dissipated the next instant.

Arducius had felt it approaching like a steadily increasing weight on his back. The others had sensed it too, though not as keenly or for as long. He had no idea whether Patonius had decided to move inshore but it didn't feel much like it. Pushing his mind out, he couldn't sense the steady rhythms of the land anywhere nearby, though that might have been because the storm obscured all else.

'It's incredible,' breathed Gorian.

'It's making me feel sick,' said Ossacer.

'Surprise, surprise,' said Gorian. He was very much back to his old self following the brief remorse that had gripped him the day after he'd blinded the rigger. Arducius had wept too when he'd heard Gorian begging Father Kessian for forgiveness in his prayers.

'Shut up the pair of you, I'm trying to concentrate.'

'What is it?' said Ossacer.

'It's getting stronger. Can't you see the energy being dragged from the top of the sky?' Arducius could. Like water sucked down a plug hole. Coursing into the heart of the storm. 'Oh no.'

'Where are you going?' demanded Ossacer.

Arducius pushed himself up the wall as another wave clattered them port and aft. The mess on the floor was rearranged and he heard someone's head strike wood. Gorian grunted.

'There's a bigger wind coming. Much bigger. I have to warn Patonius. We have to turn into the storm.'

'You can't go out there,' said Ossacer.

'I'd rather get flogged than sink. Stay here.'

The door slammed open. Patonius stood there with a crewman who held a lantern. Both were drenched from head to foot. She grabbed the collar of his night shirt.

'Come with me.'

'Careful,' he protested.

She dragged his face right to hers. 'Stow it, witch-boy. Time to prove to me you're of use to this world.'

Patonius hurried him along the lurching ship, past a blur of oarsmen trying to keep the ship travelling. It was a cacophony of shouts, creaks and grunts mixed with fear and the battering of water against timber. Water beat into the deck and sloshed around the floor beneath their feet. No one sought to clear it. Arducius felt the weight of their efforts as a solid presence in his mind, a wall of determination made up of the energy maps of their straining bodies.

He stumbled up the stern ladder as the ship pitched into the guts of the swell, hands dragging him through the hole and out into the storm. In the open, the world was black and bucking. Beneath them, the sea rolled and gathered to fling itself at the tiny ship that was alone in the darkness. Arducius could see the froth on the water and above, the clouds so low they seemed close enough to touch.

He grabbed the rail, planted his bare feet on the soaking, slippery deck and looked forward. There was no one ahead of him. The sail was down and furled rattling and slapping against the mast. Three men fought to keep the tiller steady and the ship moving ahead of the storm while the rain drove horizontally along the ship. A sheet of lightning split the night, offering Arducius a terrifying sight of the ocean, white-capped and huge above him.

The energy release of the lightning acted like a heavy slap across his face. He turned to Patonius. Their heads were almost touching.

'What do you expect me to do,' he yelled at her, his words tattered on the gale.

'You sensed this thing,' she shouted back. 'You tell me where it's going. When it will pass us.' She paused. 'Tell me which way to point my ship.'

Arducius already knew. 'You have to turn around into the storm. The wind will get worse.'

'I can't turn. Broadside we'll be capsized. I have to run ahead.'

Arducius shook his head, not knowing how he knew but seeing the pictures in his mind. 'The waves will sink us unless we are facing them.'

She stared at him. 'Then we will be lost. Look at the swell. We cannot turn.'

He felt the power above and below. The extraordinary energies nature threw together. And his mind, a calm oasis where they could rest.

'Wait. Bring the others up here,' he said. She frowned. 'Please, you have to trust me.'

The ship fell off the crest of a wave and slammed onto the down surge. The whole vessel shuddered. Wood flew across the deck, the remnants of a shattered oar blade.

'What do you have to lose?'

She gritted her teeth and nodded.

There was no fear in them where they knelt facing each other on the aft deck. Nervous crew stood around them, stopping them from sliding while the ship plunged and yawed around them. Patonius stood by the tiller, watching. Arducius had seen her mouthing prayers and making the symbol of the Omniscient over her chest.

The Ascendants linked arms around shoulders to keep themselves tight and their heads close together so they could hear Arducius speak.

'Feel the storm. Ignore the power in the water which feeds from it. Accept it in. Channel it through your bodies and back into the sky. Tell me you can do it.'

One by one they did and Arducius could see in his mind's eye, the circle completed. Together with their bodies linked by the lifelines surrounding them, they became as one with the storm.

'Gorian, you wanted to know what calling a storm would feel like? Remember this night.'

To create such power from the slight energies of the wind and sun on a cloudless day was still a dream to them. But the knowledge of the storm's magnitude told Arducius, told all of them, that they could create such a thing one day. It was not uncontrollable within them.

'Flatten the energy map in your minds,' said Arducius. 'Push it out just a little way.'

The effect was instantaneous. The Ascendants changed the nature of the energy cycle immediately around them. The twisting, bulging spirals and spikes were calmed in their linked consciousness and through their bodies, like teasing wool into thread. The wind about their heads died away. The rain stopped beating on their bodies Arducius was dimly aware of shouts of shock from around them and the shifting of feet.

'Good,' he said. 'Now push out further. Use the wild energy to create the calm and keep the circuit unbroken. Gently. We have to get this right first time.'

It was a time when he understood how far they had developed in the years since first emergence and the scant days since full emergence. Their minds and bodies were so much stronger. So much more capable of accepting energies and manipulating them in greater mass than before.

Together, they expanded the bubble of smoothed energy. Pushed it out towards the sides of the ship and into the space beyond. In their minds the bubble appeared as a flat neutral circle with frayed edges. Surrounding it were the clashing whites and darks of the storm beyond.

Beneath them, the ocean subsided. Not completely. The rhythms of the waves beyond their control fed into the deeps far below. And above them, the gale dropped to a stiff breeze and the rain fell straight down. Arducius smiled. Their minds were steady but the drain on them was huge, dragging the energy from them to feed the bubble and keep the storm at bay in direct proportion to its power.

'Turn the ship, Captain,' said Arducius. 'We cannot keep this up for long.'

The silence that had fallen on the *Cirandon's Pride* gave way to order, beat, action and song. The ship turned into the face of the storm and moved on to the cheers of the crew. The fear would come later with the return of the gales.

'They are saying it was coincidence. They are saying God showed us mercy and the eye of the storm and so we were able to turn,' said Patonius.

The Ascendants and Kovan were in Mirron's quarters. The wrinkles on their faces and hands had already faded. It was three days since the storm had passed and they had resumed their course. Arducius had assured the captain that there was not another storm within ten days of them but even so, she had set them near enough to the Gesternan coast for quick shelter should they need it.

'If it keeps them happy,' said Kovan.

'No, that's not it at all,' said Ossacer. 'We saved them. We made it possible for the ship to turn.'

He was staring straight at Patonius, his sightless eyes making her uneasy.

'Next time, we'll let the ship sink,' said Gorian. 'Let God save them then if He can.'

'And you would go down with it,' snapped Patonius. 'Where is your sense, boy?'

'Where is yours?' he retorted. 'We can't drown.'

Patonius stared at him and shook her head. 'I will not talk to you. Petulant brat.'

'None of this really matters,' said Arducius. 'What do you think, Captain?'

'I know what I saw. So do those who were standing around you and on the tiller. I know you forecast the storm and I know there was a weakness in my hull.' Her head was shaking again. 'But still in my heart, I cannot believe it's really you that is doing this. And the crew do not want to believe, and so they don't. I see God's hand in this, all of it. And I would believe in coincidence faster than in witchcraft.'

'It isn't witchcraft. It is inside us, part of us,' said Mirron. 'God works through us. We do what we do only by His grace and gift. Please, we only want to be accepted. We only want to be free to do good.'

'I'm not sure I believe that of all of you,' she said, looking askance at Gorian for a moment. 'I don't know. I've got a crew of grown men and women out there and they are frightened of four children. There is mistrust and there is hatred too. What would you have me do?'

'Let us prove to you and your crew that this is not coincidence,' said Arducius. 'We can manipulate the elements and the energies of life at will. We're sorry for what Gorian did. But we can help your crewman.'

'I can make him see again,' said Ossacer. 'I'm sure of it.'

'You cannot even see yourself,' said Patonius, not unkindly. 'How can you cure another?'

'Let him show you,' said Mirron.

'Anthus would not let any of you within a mile of him if he had the choice. Every rigger wants you put over the side. And while you might not be able to drown, you can certainly starve to death so don't push me.'

'Please,' said Ossacer. 'You must let me try. The nerves in my eyes have died and I will never see. I think his are burned so the life energy can't get through them. I can heal the burns inside and take away the scars. Then he can see again.'

'I have no idea what you're talking about. How can you know what is wrong with him?'

'I'm guessing but I'm good at guessing,' said Ossacer. 'Please, captain.'

She addressed herself to Arducius. 'If he causes Anthus any more pain there will be nothing I can do to save any of you, do you understand?'

'Of course.'

'Then I will speak with him.' The slightest of smiles crossed her face. 'What has he got to lose, right?'

Arducius accompanied Ossacer to the surgeon's area later that day. Ossacer could have walked there by himself using the trails in the living wood but the captain didn't think it wise. The surgeon's area was just a table and chests with drawers fixed to the floor and curtained off from the hammocks in which the off-duty crew rested. It stank of old blood and the sweet aromas of herbal preparations. He couldn't count the hammocks that swung from the beams on three levels, the bedrolls on the floor and the belted knots of belongings. And Arducius had thought their temporary home to be tight and sparse. These people always had nothing.

The walk made him sad. It would have made Gorian proud. The crew who saw them backed away from them. They made religious signs and muttered protective words. He saw keepsakes and charms around their necks that hadn't been there before. And he heard them spit on the floor behind them and rub their feet on the deck. It would have broken Father Kessian's heart.

They were ushered through the curtain by the surgeon herself, a short-bodied woman who seemed somehow out of proportion. She had long limbs and powerful looking hands with long fingers. Probably good for a surgeon. He couldn't work out how tall she was because she was stooped in the cramped space. She was very pale skinned and he thought he could see a layer of downy hair on her face and the backs of her hands. He was aware he was staring and blushed. She chuckled. A hard sound from deep in her throat. And then she spoke and her voice was like the grumbling fall of rocks.

'You have never seen my like, younger,' she said.

'I'm sorry,' he said. 'I didn't mean—'

'I am Gorres of Kark.'

His mouth dropped open.

'That's them, isn't it?' said Anthus from within. His voice was over-loud, frightened.

'Yes,' said Gorres, sparing Arducius any further embarrassment. 'No need to worry, I'm sure.'

She waved the Ascendants forward. Anthus was sitting on a stool near the table. His eyes were bandaged and his hands were clamped to the seat, his knuckles white.

'Who's that?' Anthus's head twitched round.

'My name is Ossacer. I'm blind too.'

'Don't come any closer. Blind or not, you've got those eyes changing colour all the time. Not right. Will I have those eyes if you fix me?'

'No,' said Ossacer. 'Only we have those.'

'Gorres?'

'Yes, Anthus, speak.'

'I will get better on my own, won't I? Eventually?'

'I think not. You cannot even tell light from dark. I cannot help you.' Anthus was silent. 'Let the younger try. Do you want to spend the rest of your life in shadow? And on shore?'

Anthus shook his head. 'Just don't make it worse.'

Ossacer took that as agreement. Arducius watched him. His delicate fingers reached out. Gorres was rapt, licking her lips in anticipation.

'I'm going to lay my fingers on your bandages above your eyes,' said Ossacer. 'You'll feel warmth. Perhaps a tingling. If you feel any pain, tell me.'

Anthus breathed deeply. 'This isn't right.'

'It wasn't right what Gorian did to you. This will put things back where they should be,'

Ossacer's fingers touched and Anthus started violently.

'It's all right. Try to relax.'

'Relax. Don't think so.'

'It'll be done quickly. Do you feel warmth?'

'Yes. It itches. In my head. Make it stop.'

'It will. Just a moment.'

Gorres whispered in Arducius's ear. 'What happens, younger?'

'Ossacer will detect where the energy lines are blocked and he will remove the block by forcing a little of his own life energy in. That will clear the scarring in his eyes and let Anthus's own lifelines complete their circles and let him see again.'

'He doesn't cut him?'

'He doesn't even move the bandages.'

'Done,' said Ossacer.

'You've done nothing,' sneered Anthus.

'Keep your eyes closed,' said Gorres, stepping up quickly and placing a palm over his bandages. 'Snuff the lantern, younger.' She began to unwind them. A couple of layers and then soft pads soaked in balm. She peeled the pads away. Anthus gasped. His hands reached up and his eyes flickered beneath their lids. 'Keep shut. Let me clean you.' She wiped away the slight weeping that had gummed his eyes. 'Now. Put your hand over them. Open slowly.'

'I can see light,' said Anthus but there was no joy in his voice.

'Fascinating,' said Gorres. 'Amazing.'

'It doesn't scare you?' asked Arducius.

Gorres laughed. 'Now why would it do that? I am Karku. I was born into wonder.'

Arducius looked back to Anthus. His eyes were open and he was squinting against the light, even in the gloom below decks. He prodded around their edges.

'The pain around the sockets will fade,' said Ossacer. 'You should have as much sight as you ever had.'

Anthus retched suddenly and Arducius saw he was shivering.

'Go away,' he said. 'No one can do this. No man. No woman. I'm dirty. Touched. This is devil's sight.'

Gorres got to him before he could scratch his eyes out. Her strong arms bound him tight and she whispered for him to calm. Ossacer backed up. Arducius held him.

'I helped him,' said Ossacer, voice trembling. 'I helped him to see.'

'Best you leave, youngers,' said Gorres, holding the writhing Anthus hard. 'He'll come round. Maybe you should too. What you have, people will shy from. It's too different and men scare easily. Hide what you are when you can. Estorea isn't ready for you. It might never be.' She smiled rather sadly. 'I'm sorry for you. I know what you feel you can be.'

Arducius led Ossacer past the staring, suspicious eyes of the crew in the open quarters and around the oar deck. They could all hear Anthus's cries. His denunciation of Ossacer's act to restore his sight and his assertion that he had been cursed. Ossacer himself was on the verge of tears and Arducius hurried him back to Mirron's quarters and called Kovan and Gorian in. Before he had the chance to tell them all that had transpired, the shouting had begun.

'Why now? Why when we've cured him? Why not when Gorian hurt him?' asked Mirron.

'Until now they could fool themselves,' said Kovan. 'Even what Gorian did could have been a fluke, poking his eyes out or something. But now . . . well it's there for everyone. He couldn't see and now he can.'

There was a loud thud from outside. Kovan drew his sword and ushered the Ascendants behind him. Gorian stood at his shoulder.

'I won't hesitate,' he said.

Kovan glanced at him. 'I wouldn't ask you to.'

'The more good we do, the more they hate us,' whispered Ossacer.

He was sitting on the bed, Arducius with him. Mirron stood behind the two others, not knowing where to put herself.

'You should listen to me more often, then, shouldn't you,' said Gorian. 'Stop snivelling. It makes you sound weak.'

'You didn't hear the hate in his voice,' said Ossacer. 'He thinks me evil.'

'So we have to defend ourselves against these unbelievers,' said Gorian. 'We can do it. We have power they can only dream about.'

'You cannot think like that, Gorian,' said Arducius. He had closed his eyes when he heard Gorian's words but was clinging on to the possibility that they were said in fear, nothing else. 'Just because they don't understand doesn't—'

There was a thump against the door. Mirron screamed. Gorian jumped back a yard. A woman's loud voice stilled the shouts. Patonius. It was confusing. They couldn't hear what she was saying but the responses were hard and angry. But it seemed she was holding sway. Then another voice. Distant, perhaps from above. And everyone fell silent. They heard the running of feet and the clatter of men against ladders.

Inside Mirron's quarters, they were too scared to say anything. Each of them strained to hear some clue. And the Ascendants all pushed out with their minds to see if they could sense anything in the trails through the air.

'More life is coming,' said Gorian.

'Above or below the sea, I can't tell?' said Mirron.

'Above. Other ships I suppose.'

'What do we do?' asked Ossacer.

'Wait,' said Kovan. 'Patonius isn't going to give us up and the crew won't mutiny. Not against her. All I'm worried about is who is coming. I didn't like that silence.'

'Who do you think it could be?' asked Ossacer.

There was furious activity up on deck. It sounded as if the sail was coming down. And presently, the unmistakeable rumbling of oars being shipped.

'Well, whoever it is wants to come and say hello,' said Ossacer, trying to sound bright. 'Think we've got any friends out here?'

Even Gorian chuckled. 'Only if dolphins have learned how to sail.'

The laughter was over-loud and Kovan shushed them. They could hear strange voices echoing from distance. There was a thud which had to be a gangplank going down. More feet. Determined, ordered. Plenty of them. Arducius felt a trickle of pure ice down his back and the dread realisation of complete helplessness. Well, not quite complete.

'Be ready,' said Kovan to Gorian. 'And any of you. I'm sorry but this sounds bad. It could be the Order.'

'They've betrayed us, haven't they?' said Arducius.

Kovan nodded. 'My father's own people.'

Footsteps approached. Heavy boots thumping off boards. The door handle turned and the door opened. A man ducked in under the lintel. He was tall. Very tall.

'Well, well, well,' he said. 'The Conquord's new weapon. Now this is a happy coincidence. I've got work for you.'

Arducius didn't know whether to laugh or cry.

It was Exchequer Jhered.

Chapter 47

848th cycle of God, 1st day of Solasfall
15th year of the true Ascendancy

Herine Del Aglios looked long out of the grand arched window in the palace conference room from her seat at the head of the long oval table. Dominating the skyline on the hills above the city were the great beacon fires. Ordering their lighting fifteen days ago had been the single worst moment of her life. And they would burn until the threat to the Conquord was gone.

Or until the Conquord was lost.

The beacons had not been lit in three hundred years, when the last mortal threat to Estorea was felt. That the next should occur during her tenure was a shame she would never truly shed and it weighed heavy on her.

All across the Conquord, from Dornos in the north to little Easthale in the far south, to Bahkir and Tundarra in the west the sight of the fires would cause fear, confusion and even panic. That sight meant invasion and it meant that the citizens of the Conquord were being called to arms.

In every corner, the standing legions would be leaving their peacetime posts and travelling to the muster points. They could not know what they might face. The marching and dispersal orders had gone by bird and via the Conquord messenger service the same day the first beacon was lit in Estorr. Some would not yet have arrived. And all Herine could really do at this stage was pray that she had made the right decisions and that her orders would be followed by the marshals, consuls, praetors, aediles and generals on whom she now relied.

She'd quipped that on seeing the beacons, most of her command structure would have had to dig the emergency orders out of their deepest trunk and blow off the dust of ages. No one had laughed at the time and right now, her words sounded hollow. The reality was that it was not at all certain that the beacons would be burning across her lands. And even if they were, there was no guarantee the emergency orders in advance of those she had despatched would be read, understood and acted upon.

Assembled before her were those diplomats and senior military officials who had been in Estorr at the time, in addition to the recently arrived consuls of Easthale, Caraduk and Avarn. Nineteen people in all, who had been thrust into position as the war council. Jobs that none present were qualified to do. Only a handful even had first-hand knowledge of conflict on their borders.

'So, can we hold them?' she demanded of the table once the preamble of welcome was done. 'And let's drop the protocols. Just speak. We are all equals here today.'

'With respect, I am not sure that is the first question we should be asking,' said Propraetor Cisone, head of trade. An old man steeped in the workings of the Conquord. 'I would rather hear, in best case, whether we can get our legions into their designated holding positions before they are overrun by the enemy. I know I am repeating old lines but we are deaf and blind to the actual situations on the borders of Atreska, Gosland, Dornos and Gestern. Everything we know is at least ten days out of date when we read it.'

Herine spread her hands. 'Yet that is our position. We cannot send messages at the speed of thought, only react to the information we do receive. Yes, Consul Hathones.'

Estorea's lead representative in Neratharn was recently arrived and she was glad of his presence.

'Neratharn has been on a state of high alert for years, ever since civil strife surfaced in Atreska. We have significant defence on our borders and that is going to be reinforced by the standing legions. We are confident we can hold the Tsardon.'

'But Atreska is abandoned to ruin,' said Megan, whom Herine had invited to the council as Atreska's most knowledgeable ambassador. 'You assume our legions cannot halt the advance and because of that refuse to place more forces at my Marshal's disposal. A conclusion I don't understand. I came here to ask for help. You are leaving my people defenceless against a ruthless enemy.'

'Perhaps this is why you have not achieved such high office earlier, young lady,' said Hathones.

'Don't patronise me,' said Megan.

'I apologise,' said Hathones and Herine raised her eyebrows. 'But your legions have not even been able to quell their own rebellious people for the last ten years. Conquord legions marching through your country have been subject to attack from the very people they seek to defend by defeating the Tsardon. To place a defensive line in Atreska now is pointless. The Tsardon were on your border twenty days ago. They are deep in your country now. We have to make a stand where we have the tactical advantage and that is not inside Atreska. It is on the border with Neratharn where our defences remain strong.'

Herine watched the wider meaning of Hathones' words sink in. Megan was staring at him, apparently unable to comprehend that Atreska was, in all likelihood, as good as lost. But the ramifications went far wider than that.

'We are fortunate, are we not, that there has been unrest in Atreska these past years,' said Cisone. 'It is a shame there has not been such disobedience in Gosland.'

'I think you had better explain that comment,' said Herine into the silence.

'I will lay it out for you,' said Cisone. 'And refer you back to my original remark about being overrun before we reach our positions. Atreska's civil war has ensured Gestern's northern borders are heavily defended. It has also ensured that Gosland's southern borders are patrolled and secured. Both these concentrations of forces will ensure Tsardon advances are slowed dramatically. And let me remind you that if we do lose integrity along the Gesternan border, we risk losing access to the metals and minerals of Kark on which our armies so heavily depend. Having to ship them from Kark's south-eastern coast would be ruinous to our war effort.

'But should the Tsardon be in contact with the Omari, or should the Omari decide now is the time to exact revenge for our incursions into their territories, then it is surely from the north, not the east, that we suffer the greatest threat. The distance for communication is huge and the only battle-hardened legions are those we are going to have to draw away from the Omari border to meet the Tsardon threat.

Only the Tundarran navy keeps the Omari navy from landing anywhere it chooses along our northern and eastern coasts.

'If I were you, I would be sending a diplomatic team and some overflowing revenue chests to the Omari right now.'

Herine regarded Propraetor Cisone, looking for any hint that he might be exaggerating. He clearly thought he was not.

'Ambassador Tharin, what do you say to this?' she asked of the Dornosean diplomat.

'I am minded to agree with my learned friend here,' said Tharin. His resonant voice commanded instant attention. It was as deep as the frown driving his huge, grey bushy eyebrows together. 'Your orders, as I understand them, will remove the two reserve legions from our border and place them on Gosland's south and east borders. This is in addition to the three legions already withdrawn and who were to be used as additional reinforcement in Tsard. These legions, are of course, still in Omari and organising their detachment from the campaign. This leaves us with just four forward legions, the stretched support of the Tundarran navy and our own limited border defence. Should the Omari choose to march on us, we will not hold them for long.'

'You feel we have taken too much from the Omari campaign?' asked Herine. 'You did have an opportunity to object at the time the orders were drawn up.'

'I feel our chess board is ill-stocked with pieces,' said Tharin. 'And there is no doubting the greater threat is from the Tsardon we know to be in Atreska and rumoured to be attacking Gosland and surely Gestern. If you're asking me if the Omari can be pacified, well I doubt it. Whether they feel strong enough to move on to Conquord territory . . .' He blew out his cheeks. 'They might. They just might.'

'Then talk with Cisone after this meeting. Take who and what you need and organise diplomatic overtures with the Omari. Their accession will have to wait, I fear.'

'Of course, my Advocate,' said Tharin.

'Thank you. And now, with apologies to all those who know this, but for the benefit of those just arrived who do not know everything we are asking of their countries, Marshal General Niranes will outline our position. Marshal General.'

Niranes stood holding a sheaf of papers. The businessman turned politician appeared nervous and uncertain. For him, the figurehead position was one that secured him contracts and great wealth. Now, he was paying for the patronage and friendship of the family Del Aglios. Herine doubted he'd slept much these past days.

'I draw your attention to the map in front of you,' he said, reedy voice jarring on the ears. Around the table, delegates stood and leaned over. The lanterns suspended from the ceiling lit the carefully drawn and highly detailed relief map of the Conquord.

'Take a good look,' said Herine. 'This is a map I do not wish to redraw.'

Niranes sniffed. 'We have identified three defensible positions based on our calculations of likely Tsardon speed and Conquord resistance to enemy advance. They are Neratharn's border with Atreska, Gestern's border with Atreska, and in Gosland, a line from Goscapita and slightly south-west along the Alane Range and the Tharn Marches.'

Megan sighed. 'How easy it is to give away a country from the safety of the Conquord's heart.'

'None of the decisions made have been easy, my Lady, I assure you,' said Niranes. 'And we are ceding large swathes of Gosland too. The Atreskan problem isn't merely its state of unrest. We just don't have the reserves to organise an effective counterattack. And it is also your unfortunate geography. Beautiful though your flat lands are, and wonderful for crops, they are terribly hard to defend against a large army.

'Neratharn has the huge advantage of a line of border forts never dismantled after Atreska's accession and because of your constant troubles. It also has significant natural defence as does Gosland. I am sorry, as we all are, that your country will suffer as a result. But the wider health of the Conquord must be my primary concern.'

'People I love are there. Marooned. Abandoned.' She turned to Herine. 'My Marshal has for so long pleaded with you for the lowering of levies and the building of internal defence. And you have consistently refused. We will all pay. Atreska is only the first.'

'Megan, please, you are becoming emotional,' said Herine.

'And you are surprised?' Megan was shouting now, her face reddening but her voice strong. She stabbed a hand at the map. 'You have casually crossed off my home to protect yourselves. Left my people at the mercy of the merciless. The Conquord swore to defend us. It sickens me that we are now so inconvenient.'

Herine stood. 'I will point out two things and then you will leave to compose yourself. First, your endless civil unrest was and is the responsibility of the Marshal Defender.' She emphasised the final word in what she was aware was a patronising manner. 'I will not be held accountable because so many of your citizens chose to fight against the Conquord when it was always plain they would prosper under our government. They are reaping the consequences of that resistance and it is tragic that innocent Atreskans will also suffer.

'Second, any level-headed citizen will tell you that before you can beat an enemy on the march, you must first stop that march. For that, you must pick the best battle grounds. We have done that and when the Tsardon are stopped, they will be beaten back and Atreska will be released from their grip.' Herine took a breath and paused.

'Megan, you are here because I thought you possessed of a keen mind untarnished by national prejudice. Please don't make me change my mind. You may go.' Herine waved her hand and turned away. 'Marshal General, please continue.'

Herine sat back down and found her mind wandering. Niranes was going on to recount the name of every legion which should be mustering to march to any one of the three designated fronts. To list numbers of infantry, cavalry and artillery. To explain how the Tundarran navy was going to maintain its watch over the Omari. And he would outline how the Conquord navies would mobilise to blockade the Tirronean Sea against the Tsardon fleet at anchor in the Bay of Harryn.

But the trouble was that all his numbers were based on complete complements and on every reserve citizen answering the call. The facts might be very different and there was not the military mind here to be able to redraw the plans should the numbers be down by ten per cent, twenty, maybe even a third.

She needed more information. More than that, though, she needed Paul Jhered.

'I didn't think Harkov would get there in time,' said Jhered. 'I'm sorry. I truly am.'

He had listened to the harrowing accounts of all five of them. The exaggerated versions of the Ascendants and the far more measured and factual report from Kovan Vasselis. It had served to stoke his fury and confirm his worst fears.

'We don't know what happened after we escaped,' said Kovan. 'My father was outnumbered.'

'But the town was with him.' Jhered nodded. 'He'll be all right. And Harkov will have made it. He's a good man and he knows what must be done. But what you did there and on board *Cirandon's Pride* changes the route I was going to take. We also need to avoid a war zone.'

He looked at the Ascendants, gathered on the side of the cot in his quarters while he sat on a chair in front of them. Kovan rested his backside on the desk. All of them looked tired, anxious and dishevelled. He'd had them fed and then clothed in the best his crew could find and spare. But that hadn't taken the pinched looks from their faces. Their last hours on Vasselis's ship had been hard. They were still floating near the Caraducian vessel.

'What were you going to do?' asked Mirron. 'And what do you think we're going to do? If Harkov is there, why can't we just go home? It's safe now, right?'

Children. One breath, a thousand questions. And no answers they would fully understand.

'First of all, believe that what I choose to do, I do for the good of the Conquord. Not you, and not me. If our good is served as a consequence, all is well. Next, understand that we don't have to like each other for our companionship to continue. You will come with me and you will do what I say.'

'You didn't expect to meet us out here, did you?' said Gorian.

'Did you work that out all by yourself?' replied Jhered sharply. He blew out a breath. 'Look. The world outside your so recently ruptured cocoon is in very bad shape.'

'Well, it can't be that bad,' said Gorian. 'Or we'd have heard about it.'

'Want to wear my uniform?' snapped Jhered. 'No? Then be quiet and listen to me. Say nothing unless I ask you, am I clear?' He watched them all flinch back but found he hadn't finished. 'Did you notice how one of my ships has no mast? That's because it took a two-talent stone fired from an Atreskan onager. They have turned against us. Civil war is now outright rebellion. I have people trapped in there who will probably not survive. Sixty thousand Tsardon are at this moment marching into Conquord lands. I have seen the vanguard myself and if you want go next door, you will see the wounds their arrows and swords caused us when we escaped them. Do not dare tell me it can't be that bad, because it is. And it gets worse hour by bloody hour.'

Jhered pushed a hand across his tied-back hair. They just stared at him, waiting to understand.

'Oh, there's no point to this. Menas!'

The door to the small cabin opened almost immediately.

'Yes, sir.'

'Take a longboat to the *Spear* and give them the sealed messages. They are for the Advocate's eyes only. She must hear of Atreska's betrayal.' Jhered clicked his fingers and turned to the leader of them, the thoughtful one. What was his name . . . 'Arducius. You can predict weather. I've a ship rowing due west to Estorr across the open sea.'

'The weather is set fair for four days. There will be another storm from the south after that.'

'Good, they can make it.' He turned back to Menas and took some parchment and a quill and pot from his desk. He gave her the pot and dipped the quill in it. 'Get Harin on board as well as any of the other wounded who can't get on the *Pride*. Tell Harin to talk to the Advocate. Give him my seal and tell him to deliver these messages. Again, to her alone.' He wrote as he spoke. 'He must tell her that I have the Ascendants and I will keep them safe from harm. Which includes hostile Conquord forces. That she must on no account allow further attacks on Westfallen. That we are going to join with Roberto. And she must trust that what I do, I do for the Advocacy and the Conquord.'

He handed her the paper. 'Understood, Appros?'

'Yes, sir. And Patonius?'

'*Cirandon's Pride* goes to Kester Isle to carry the news that the Atreskan navy cannot necessarily be trusted. After that, they are to take word of the Ascendants' safety to Westfallen. I'll speak to her myself but you need to get Harin going now. Time is pressing.'

Menas saluted and left the room. Jhered turned back to the Ascendants and Kovan. Their expressions had cleared of their suspicion and anxiety. Mirron was even smiling.

'Glad you were listening,' he said. 'A lesson learned. Now, I need to apprise you of a few facts concerning why you must hide yourselves and those eyes from the Order. Why I want you to practise as hard as you can every day you are with me and why whether I or my crew think you are a force for good or a heresy against God has absolutely no importance whatsoever.'

Ossacer put a hand up, his sightless eyes boring into Jhered's face.

'Yes, young man.'

'Will people ever accept us? Even when we help them, they hate us.'

'Well,' he said, feeling a little good humour steal over him at long last. 'Win the war for them and they'll have no choice, will they?'

Chapter 48

848th cycle of God, 5th day of Solasfall
15th year of the true Ascendancy

The wind was picking up out to sea and clouds were gathering over Estorr as night began to fall. A storm was on the way and people would be rushing around in the stifling muggy streets, anxious to get their business done before the rains came. God, as always would provide. The lakes and rivers would swell to fill the aqueducts and the filth would be scoured from the cobbles to rush down the drains, into the sewers and back into the earth. Estorr would sparkle when the clouds eventually parted.

But, once again, Herine Del Aglios sat in her private audience chambers and wondered if those she trusted most implicitly were actually working against her. The throne in these chambers was as uncomfortable as that in the basilica from where the impending war was being coordinated. She had returned from there to a private audience with Appros Harin. He was before her, seated at her order, his shoulder heavily strapped and his face pale with the pain of the arrow that had struck him. Down in the harbour, the damaged Gatherer vessel was already being steered to dry dock for repairs.

She had read the papers Harin had given her with a growing sense of inevitability. When it went wrong, it didn't stop. At least her decision not to confront the Tsardon in Atreska had been vindicated. It was cold comfort. As for Jhered's personal decisions . . . all in good time.

'You are certain of Yuran's defection?' she asked.

'He was hosting Tsardon in his castle, my Advocate,' said Harin. 'I saw them with my own eyes. And we were attacked by Tsardon and Atreskan forces during our escape.' The memory of it was plain on his face.

'And the betrayal is total?'

'That is impossible to establish,' said Harin. 'It's reasonable to assume that significant forces from Scintarit are back in Atreska. We don't know their designation or loyalty. And there will undoubtedly be some, in the military particularly, that will resist Yuran's call. But his people are very loyal to him. Even those who opposed him during the civil war did not wish him removed from power but to be the ruler of an independent Atreska.'

'What a mess,' said Herine. 'I must get word to the Neratharn border.' She stared at Harin a while before asking the question she knew she must. 'I am relying on you for honesty over loyalty to your commander. Tell me, is the Exchequer still with me?'

'His loyalty to you and the Conquord is, and has always been, unswerving,' said Harin immediately. 'What he does, he does because he believes it in your best interests, though he knows you might not agree or understand. And if I was not injured, I would be with him still.'

She leaned back against the deep green upholstery. 'So, if I do not believe you I would be forced to arrest you.'

'That is so, my Advocate,' he replied.

'I think instead I will use your talents in the administration of this war we find ourselves having to fight. As soon as you are able, report to the basilica and find Marshal General Niranes. He will be in great need of your help. We are short on field knowledge in this city.'

'Of course, my Advocate. I'm honoured.'

The two of them shared a brief smile before the door to the chambers opened and in swept Chancellor Koroyan.

'Dismissed, Appros Harin. And thank you.'

He saluted and walked stiffly from the room. Koroyan glared at him on his way out and strode up to the throne. Herine put down one sheaf of papers and picked up another. This set was recently delivered to her by the palace guard who had escorted the Chancellor back to Estorr via Cirandon. Harkov hadn't travelled back as he had been instructed, choosing to stay in the little port town. Jhered's influence, it seemed, was everywhere.

'I had no idea it was such a long journey back from Caraduk, Chancellor.'

'I had unavoidable business in Cirandon on my return from the evil I witnessed in Westfallen,' she said, her tone haughty and patronising.

'And the fact of the beacon fires that you would have seen across the whole of that country, summoning you back here with all speed, didn't hasten your decision to leave at all?'

'I felt the Conquord best served by my presence in Cirandon until my business concluded.'

Herine sat upright and waved the parchments at the Chancellor. 'And what, in God's good name, am I to make of all this? Charges have been laid against you and your people. Murder. Brutality. Imprisonment.'

'Exaggeration by the hand of evil. The charges are laid by Vasselis who is more deeply involved in this crime than you could possibly imagine.'

'You deny the beating of Elsa Gueran, the Reader of Westfallen?' Herine read from the parchments. 'That you yourself cut her throat in front of the entire town?'

'She was guilty of heresy. She was executed as the law allows.'

Herine slapped her hand on the arm of the throne and shot to her feet. 'Damn you, Felice the law does not allow for barbarism. Even against heretics. Where are the trial papers? Where is the confession? And where was the proper conduct of execution? You are my Chancellor. What did you think you were doing?'

'I was doing your bidding, my Advocate.'

Herine gaped. 'I beg your pardon?'

'You asked me to clear Westfallen of heresy.'

'I asked you to *investigate*,' shouted Herine. 'Big, big difference.'

'You told me there was evil there. You told me it couldn't continue.'

'Yes, and I told you to discover its scale and to bring to justice, those who had perpetrated it.'

'And so I—'

'My justice, Felice!' Herine slapped her chest above her breasts. Her voice choked. 'My justice. The justice of the Conquord on which we rely to keep our cohesion. Not the summary dispensation of Order law.'

'With respect, Herine, you were not there. The stench of it was everywhere. The whole town is involved.'

'I know,' said Herine. 'I have read the report. How does this excuse you from murder?'

'I saw with my own eyes, these . . . these Ascendants call heat from the sky and a gale from the lightest breeze. And Vasselis and his son threatened me in order to let them get away. This evil must be utterly destroyed. It has no place under God's earth. My charges have been documented. Westfallen should be razed to the ground along with everyone in it.'

'And that is exactly what I wanted you to ascertain for me. I respect your opinion and your position. Or I did.' Herine paused and waved the parchments again. 'This is a detailed account. As I understand it, the Ascendants did not reveal themselves to you until after the murder of the Reader and the striking down of an old man. By you. Vasselis also did not interfere until that time. And in the mayhem following, which you sanctioned, seventeen unarmed citizens were killed. One of them a Tundarran cloth merchant. Surely an innocent.'

'I was being threatened,' said Felice.

'It happens a lot to people who murder and assault others, you'll find.'

'By a heretic and criminal whom I demand you bring to justice,' she continued. 'Or I will do so myself.'

Herine shook her head, exasperation breaking over her. 'Have you no inkling of what you have done here? Are you really that ignorant, blinded by your zeal? I am the Advocate. I am the embodiment of God on this earth and you are sullying my reputation. What I have here in my hand is more than enough to see you locked up and tried for murder. A crime that brings a burning of the body and a scattering of the ashes to the devils on the wind. *You*. The Chancellor of the Order of Omniscience.'

The brief fear on Koroyan's face disappeared beneath contempt. 'You cannot believe the word of a heretic and consort of evil.'

'But you have as good as admitted your guilt,' raged Herine, unable to control herself for the moment. 'These are officially laid charges and I must hear them answered. As I will those you have lain against Vasselis and Westfallen's people. That is the law and I will uphold it.'

At last, the Chancellor calmed enough to be worried. 'Herine, you can't lock me away. You can't. Not while Vasselis runs free.'

Herine shook her head. 'There at least we agree. No, I can't. But not for your reasons. You will walk free because the Conquord is under threat and the leader of the Order must be present. The effect on morale if you were jailed would be incalculable. But don't take this as release, merely reprieve. There will be a reckoning one day.'

'And Vasselis?'

'For him too. And for now, he too will remain at liberty. He may indeed be heretic to the Order but I cannot do without the legions he will supply to the Conquord's defence.' Herine saw the anger return to Felice's eyes. 'Chancellor, you will confine yourself to aiding the efforts to save the Conquord. Neither you nor any members of the Order or its armed forces will go within a hundred miles of Westfallen unless I so demand it. Do not cross me on this or, so help me, I will have a new Chancellor, war or no war. Felice. I mean it.'

The Chancellor nodded. 'But it is already too late, my Advocate. The word is spreading through Cirandon and Caraduk and it will spread through Estorr and into the Conquord. The faithful citizens of this great land will not let this evil prevail. I do not need to go back there to know they will be destroyed.'

'Then you have more belief in our citizens' desire to see the Order's will done than I do. There is a Tsardon army coming. Backed by rebel Atreskan legions under Yuran's command. I think they will have more pressing matters, don't you?' Herine sat down, feeling suddenly tired. 'Act for me, Felice, not against me. The Conquord cannot afford you to be divisive.'

'The Ascendants are still out there,' muttered Felice. 'We cannot let them run free.'

'They too are out of your control and will remain so. They are not to be touched until I command otherwise.'

'You know where they are?' Felice's eyes widened.

Herine smiled. 'I am not the Advocate for nothing.'

Felice turned briefly towards the door. 'That was what Harin was here for. They are with Jhered, aren't they?' She spat the Exchequer's name.

'Who they are with and where they will go is no longer any of your concern.'

'Have them brought here. Have them tried. Found guilty. They above all must burn.'

'No,' said Herine quietly.

'You cannot say "no",' protested Felice, her volume rising. 'They are an affront to your person as they are to the God you represent on earth. They have to be put to death.'

'No,' she repeated. 'They will serve the Conquord.'

Felice jabbed a finger at her. 'That is not in your gift as Advocate. Those who act against God may not act for His people. I knew this of you. You would call yourself "Emperor" and make your rule inviolate.'

'Enough.' Herine clapped her hands once. 'I have heard enough of your wailing and your blasted piety. We are at war. And I would do anything to save my people from our enemies without and from the traitors in our midst. Anything.'

'Even if that means tilling the earth with evil that rails against God?'

Herine met the Chancellor's gaze. 'Even that.'

'Then you have my undying contempt.'

'When the Conquord is saved, we will return to this discussion. Until then, I am watching you, Chancellor Koroyan. Now, get out before I change my mind concerning your liberty.'

It was revenge but there were days when indulgence in such an undisciplined and dangerous emotion was the only way to ease the memories of the past. The life and desire had returned to Master Dina Kell's eyes, under Dahnishev's care. Her breastplate had been beaten back into shape and polished to a glorious shine by the smiths and she had been furnished with new weaponry and a Conquord-bred stallion.

And now she had been given temporary charge of a hundred cavalry from the 8th Estorean, the Screaming Hawks. Roberto rode with them, under her command, and was immediately impressed by her skills as horsewoman and leader. She had taken a short time to brief them on her signals and commands and had trusted them to understand her first time. The Hawks cavalry responded.

Breaking into two, the Tsardan cavalry cantered down the low rise behind the enemy and moved smoothly up on either flank of the supply train heading towards the fords at Scintarit. They were precisely where the scouts had said they would be. Tsardon scouts lay dead a day to the rear, giving them no clue what was coming at them.

It was the sound of their approach that had finally alerted their quarry. A few Tsardon riders turned to face them and the men who walked beside the wagons began to form up a defensive line while the carriages tried to escape. Pointless.

Kell raised her spear, tied with a pennant, and pointed forwards. With a roar, the Conquord cavalry spurred their mounts to the full gallop and charged. Roberto felt the thrill course through him. He led the second group, riding hard up the enemy left. In front of them, Tsardon archers fired on the run, the shafts high and wide. There was no cohesion in the defensive line and when those same archers turned to run, most of the swordsmen went with them.

Roberto had one hand on his reins. The other gripped a javelin. Riding down the line of fifteen wagons, he cocked his arm and threw. The javelin struck one of the few who still faced them in his chest and knocked him from his feet. Spears flew to their right and head on, taking wagon drivers from their seats or biting into the backs of fleeing Tsardon.

Faster horses overtook Roberto, their riders turning in their saddles to fire. And when they wheeled away, they revealed foot soldiers just a few strides ahead. Roberto drew his sword, leant from his saddle and chopped down on the head of the first man who could only raise his bare arms to protect him. Another two strides and Roberto's sword swung back up, glancing into the helmet of another, sending him tumbling into the side of a wagon.

To his left, his cavalry had spread out and were shooting and cutting down runners. Across the train, Kell's riders peppered wagons with arrows and spears while others cruised around in a wide arc to sweep up escapees.

Roberto galloped past the lead wagon, pointed his bloodied sword to the right and began the wheel. Behind him, he heard the shouts and screams of the Tsardon about to die, and the whisper and thud of arrows, the thrum of bowstrings. He pushed his horse back to a run and made for the lead wagon. Driver and guard were still aboard.

He surged beyond them, executed a tight turn and raced up beside them. It was like his first days on campaign under General Gesteris. He hacked out with his sword, forcing the driver to sway away from him. An arrow flicked past him and into the chest of the guard who fell under the wheels. The wagon bucked and rattled. Roberto put a foot on the kicking board and swung his other leg over his horse's head. His weight carried him across the short gap. He grasped a wooden strut with his sword hand and thumped his fist into the driver's face. The man's nose bloodied and he fell back, scrabbling for a dagger. Roberto followed him, and a single sword thrust up under his chin finished him.

He grabbed the reins and slowed the wagon, turning it to the right and forcing those behind to slow and stop. He could only see a handful of the Tsardon still on the ground and fighting. And now to his rear, the cavalry fell on helpless drivers and guards. There were to be no prisoners. No witnesses.

'Victory!' called Kell. The cheer was taken up by the Hawks and rolled across the open plain ahead of them.

Roberto steadied the horses in their traces and dropped to the ground, tying off the reins. He walked back along the line of stationary wagons, congratulating his people. It had been a textbook attack. He found Kell examining the captured artillery. Other cavalry were in the covered wagons, searching their contents.

'Exemplary, Master Kell,' said Roberto.

'Hmm,' she said, barely looking up from the ballista that had caught her interest. 'The Hawks cavalry are an excellent unit. No more than I would expect from Elise Kastenas.'

'What's wrong?' he asked.

'This,' She patted the arm of the ballista. 'It's been refurbished but they haven't removed the maker's mark.' She turned to look at him. 'It's one of ours, taken from Scintarit.'

'Really?' Roberto looked back the way the supply train would have come. 'Seems a cumbersome thing to do. Are you sure you mean refurbishment, or modification?'

'I'm not an engineer,' she said.

'Fortunately, I have a very good one.' Roberto smiled. 'I wonder what's in the rest of these wagons.'

The haul was valuable. Very valuable indeed. Eight heavy onagers, enhanced or not Neristus would be able to tell him. And four in two covered wagons that would fascinate the Conquord engineer. They were lighter pieces but each was mounted on a single axle and pair of wheels like a chariot. A design the Conquord had not made work. The other five wagons were weighed down by weaponry, repaired Conquord infantry armour and onager stones of eight different calibres. No wonder they were so slow-moving.

'What does this tell you?' asked Roberto.

'That we've been underestimating them ever since the start of this cursed campaign, General,' said Kell.

'Political statements later, Master Kell. What else?'

'That they are over-confident. These wagons were vastly under-protected. The situation in Atreska is probably worse than our most lurid nightmares.

'Right. Work to be done.' He turned and shouted. 'Hawks! I want these wagons drawn up to the fords. We'll camp there tonight. I want a messenger to the army. They are to march to our position. And I want three scouts to report to me immediately for work ahead and into Atreska.

'For the Conquord! Move.'

Chapter 49

848th cycle of God, 6th day of Solasfall
15th year of the true Ascendancy

The morning was dull and cloudy, providing welcome respite from the recent days of blistering heat. It was the first indication they'd had of a changing of the season towards dusas. And Roberto, for one, was praying for an exceptionally hard, cold season. It was probably the only thing that would truly stop the Tsardon advance.

They had broken camp three hours before dawn, taking with them every piece of timber. There was no second Conquord force coming behind them and he was damned if he was going to leave anything for the Tsardon to use. Armoured foraging parties were also travelling east and west of their position, taking everything they could find. The rules of the war had changed. On the way in, they had bought goods, avoided marching through settlements and begun to build relations with the local populace. On the way out, they destroyed buildings, burned crops and killed any that resisted them. It was a sad necessity.

'Refugees are expensive,' he had said to his command team. 'They are a drain on morale and they get in the way. Just ask Thomal Yuran.'

The raid on the supply train the day before had lifted the spirits of the army. Scouts were ahead, looking for information on the situation in Atreska and would report back in a few days. But he was not going to wait by the River Tarit for the reports.

He rode at the front of the column as he had most days of their hard march south. His extraordinarii were around him, significant forces of cavalry were guarding the flanks, and scouts were in the field, looking for any sign of the Tsardon.

Roberto marched his army straight across the battlefield. It was pitted, torn and tough going. Wagons were driven slowly. Everywhere, the remnants of the rout were a reminder of what had happened here. Tattered cloth clinging to rock or grass. Shards of metal glinting in the daylight. And still the odd corpse, stripped by looters and eaten by rodents, lying dishonoured under God.

He would not let his people touch them. The plague was still a raw memory. But he wanted them to see the cost of defeat. He wanted them to feel the desire to save the Conquord from those who had done this. He wanted them never to forget that they represented civilisation. The Tsardon represented barbarism that had to be put down.

Beside him in his saddle, Neristus yawned. Lights had burned in his workshop the entire night.

'Sorry to cost you your night,' said Roberto.

'And for making me ride here?' asked Neristus, a smile on his lips. 'I was sleeping in my wagon.'

'There's things I need to know. Like everything you learned from your examination of our new artillery pieces.'

'Well, I'll start with those that began life as Conquord weapons,' said Neristus. He sniffed and wiped a grimy finger under his nose. 'They are not much changed but the bracketing shows skilled metalworking. Strong and yet quite light. And on a piece that can throw a three-talent stone, that could make a difference of two or three miles an hour when they are being brought in for deployment. It's significant.'

Roberto nodded. 'Undoubtedly.'

'But it's an enhancement of our own design,' said Neristus. 'And that means they have had such weapons in their possession a long time. Years. Unless they stumbled on the development by accident, they have surely had our weapons to look at since before the campaign began.'

'Atreskans and Goslanders selling on after their accessions?'

'It seems likely.' Neristus raised his eyebrows.

'I suppose I shouldn't be surprised. Costing us now though, isn't it? And them.'

'That depends whether the traders are Tsardon sympathisers or not.'

'Let's stick to your report.'

'Very good, General. Where was I? Oh yes. Finally, the timbers have been replaced with the same Sirranean wood we are now using on our scorpions. And that is not a surprise at all.'

'No indeed. And the single axles?'

'Amazing,' said Neristus, and Roberto had to laugh at his obvious respect for his fellow engineers. 'Our problem hasn't been so much the fixing of a single axle on these pieces but the fact that the pressure of the firing action flips the piece and tends to buckle or break the axle after a few rounds. Remember?'

'I'll take your word for it,' said Roberto.

Neristus waved a hand impatiently. 'Well, anyway, they've developed a metal spring and again, they've kept it remarkably light. It's a mimic of the wooden assemblies we've developed and that adorn every wagon in your army. A great piece of work. It allows quick deployment, quick movement, and can be dragged by a team of four men quite easily if necessary. And the wagons carry ingenious counterweight arms as well as fixing spikes. Clever stuff.'

Roberto whistled. 'And can you copy it?'

'Of course. Not instantaneously but we're already working on it.'

'Good. You've got half the time you think it'll take you,' said Roberto.

'You should get one back to the Conquord engineers in Estorr,' said Neristus. 'Put in on a ship out of Kirriev Harbour.'

'You have read my mind, dear Rovan,' said Roberto. 'Now, get back to your wagon before you fall asleep and off that horse.'

'Thank you, General.'

'If she bolted, we'd lose a valuable mount.'

They rowed north about a mile off the coast of Gestern, enjoying calm water but little wind. Jhered had sent birds to Marshal Defender Katrin Mardov in Gestern's capital city of Skiona. The city lay three hundred miles south of his chosen landfall but if he was fortunate, she or some of her representatives would be available to him when they docked at the port town of Kirriev Harbour, at the end of its namesake inlet. Kirriev was only a couple of days from the Atreskan border, and, in combination with the proximity of Kark, offered them their best chance of finding their way north to Sirrane and Roberto unmolested. It was a bizarre twist of fate to have to consider Tsardon lands safer than those of the Conquord but these were changed times.

Jherd was standing in the stern of the *Hark's Arrow*, watching Mirron and Gorian playing in the water behind, sporting with the dolphins that appeared whenever the latter was close by. He'd thought it was coincidence the first couple of times but now he had no doubt the boy could summon them like Jhered could his horse. Extraordinary. Kovan Vasselis stared down at them too, his hands gripping the aft rail, an expression of pure frustration and helplessness on his face. Jhered hadn't tried to help him. Nothing could be done for a young man chasing something he would never catch. He had to work that out for himself.

Jhered had maintained an air of confidence and normality for the sake of his crew while the Ascendants had practised their art over the last few days. All of them had seen sights they never thought to see and he was proud of how they had reacted. And the Ascendants had responded in kind.

Indeed, the only reason Arducius and Ossacer were standing with him now rather than swimming was that the one had overdone it bringing up a wind earlier in the day to speed them along and give the rowing crew a rest. Ossacer had also conducted a surgery for the many minor ailments that befell sailors on long voyages. Blisters, infected cuts and the odd broken bone. Nothing serious. Consequently, both were tired and looking drawn.

'Tell me again why you get like that,' ordered Jhered. 'Old-looking, I mean.'

'It's because everything we do is based on the lifecycles of the energy we manipulate,' said Arducius. 'If you think about it, if we make a tree grow, we are also making it older, forcing its lifecycle to speed up. It is the same if I draw a breeze into a wind, or form cloud from a little moisture in the sky. It is forcing the potential of the energy into reality and hurrying it along. Because this is all channelled through our bodies we inevitably use our own life energy as catalyst. The more we use, the older our bodies get. Though at least for us it is a temporary effect.'

Jhered frowned. 'Why is it temporary for you?'

Ossacer shrugged. 'Because the unbound energy in everything that lives replenishes us.'

'Obviously,' muttered Jhered.

'Don't you understand?' asked Arducius, his eyes sparkling mischief.

'Don't task me, boy,' said Jhered, though his chiding lacked any real weight. 'I understand a great deal more than you think. Though perhaps in this instance, Orin D'Allinnius should have been here. He would have enjoyed your explanation more than I did.'

Arducius nodded and his expression sobered. 'Will he be all right?'

'I don't know,' sighed Jhered. 'He was very sick when I saw him but he's got a strong mind.'

'It's a shame,' said Ossacer. 'I liked him.'

'Everybody does,' said Jhered.

'Not everybody,' said Kovan, tearing his eyes from Mirron and Gorian. 'The Order has a great deal to answer for. And answer it will.'

'No,' said Jhered, raising a finger. 'Not the Order. Just certain of those who wear its robes and hide behind its scriptures. And yes, she will be held to account, have no doubt. You know, young Kovan, if you are to follow in your father's esteemed footsteps and achieve high office in the Conquord, you need to learn to choose your words with greater care.'

Kovan shrugged. 'If you say so.' He turned back to the sea.

'I think he has other things on his mind,' said Ossacer, chuckling.

'Shut up, Ossie,' snapped Kovan, a blush spreading around his neck.

Jhered smiled broadly at Kovan's back but at the same time, was piqued by unease. He looked at the blind youngster.

'How can you know that, Ossacer?' he asked.

'It's been the same for years,' said Ossacer. 'And anyway, I can see his shape in the trails if I want to. And whenever he looks at Mirron his map pulses very bright in my mind. That's how.'

'Really. And what does mine tell you?'

Ossacer looked at him briefly. 'You'll live a long time because you don't waste your energy. But you don't know what to make of us. We make you nervous and you aren't used to being nervous. I can see that because your map ripples whenever you are around us and it is normally so still and controlled. And you don't like children much, do you?'

'What?'

'That wasn't anything to do with the energy map. That's just what I think,' said Ossacer.

'Well, thank you for your insight into my mind.'

'True, though, isn't it?'

Jhered shifted and cleared his throat. 'I'm just not used to being around children, that's all.'

Damn the boy but he was accurate. That unease was much in evidence right now and the fact Ossacer could see it just made it worse. Jhered cast around for a change of subject. Away atop the Spine of Gestern, smudges of smoke reached high into the sky. At night, the blazes had studded the darkness; mute alarms that he still found himself staring at.

'Can you see the smoke?' he said, pointing away landwards.

Kovan and Arducius followed his hand. Ossacer curled his lip.

'What do you think?' he asked.

Jhered closed his eyes briefly, cursing himself a fool. 'Sorry, Ossacer.'

'It doesn't matter. What is it, anyway?' he asked. Good lad.

'As far as any of us can see from north to south along the mountains, the beacon fires are lit,' said Jhered. 'They are to call the citizens to order because the Conquord is invaded. I've been very happy to see them here. Gestern is remote.'

'What will happen, Exchequer Jhered?' asked Arducius.

'In Gestern or the Conquord?'

'Anywhere,' said Arducius.

'Well, in the wider Conquord I don't know. In Gestern, it means that the standing legions will muster. And when the orders reach them from Estorr, they march. All the threat comes from the Atreskan border so we might find Kirriev Harbour very busy. At least, I hope we do. The citizens will all have to work for the war effort. There will be traders buying as much metal and raw materials as they can from Kark. There will be smiths, artillery makers, armourers . . . all have to do what the Conquord requires. People will watch the coasts. There is an emergency signalling system that the beacons are central to. And every man, woman and child who can, will be expected to bear arms on demand.'

Arducius shuddered and turned anxious eyes to him. Jhered continued.

'War is a terrible thing, violent and frightening. Whether you are on the front line and fighting, or in your home, wondering if the war will come to your doorstep. That's why we have to be ready. That's why everyone is taught about the beacons when they are at school. Sometimes the unthinkable happens. Like now.'

'Will it work, I wonder?' asked Kovan. 'My father has often said that because no one believes we can fall, no one will pay attention to the alarms. Or even really know what they are for.'

'He said the same to me,' said Jhered, smiling. 'Mind you, he also said that he wasn't sure the tinderboxes would be dry at the beacon posts. But there are fires across Gestern and that gives me heart and hope. But we all have to do our part in war. Whatever we can to protect the place we live and the people we love.'

'I think you're lecturing us,' said Arducius.

'There are some things you can't hear too often, young man.'

Two days later, they rowed through the last deeps of the Kirriev Inlet and into the harbour. It bristled with activity. Through his magnifier, Jhered could see soldiers clogging the docks. Ships of the Gesternan navy were in port as well as those flying the flag of Estorea. That was no surprise. No doubt they had been carrying the orders to Marshal Defender Mardov. But it confirmed how careful he would have to be in getting the Ascendants off the ship.

He had no idea when Chancellor Koroyan would have reached Estorr on her return from Westfallen or what she would have said to the Advocate. It could have been in time to catch the ships and birds. One thing he did know was that his messages would not have got there in time to be worked in. It meant that every Conquord vessel and soldier, Order Reader and cavalryman, was a potential spy. At least Koroyan wouldn't have known he had the Ascendants when she reached Estorr. Just that they had escaped her clutches. Unfortunately, Gestern was a likely destination.

The Gatherer berth was empty. Wanting everything to appear as normal as it could under the circumstances, he ordered them dock there before ducking quickly below to speak to his charges.

'We have advantages,' he said. 'No one here can possibly know what you look like unless the Chancellor herself has decided to gamble and travel here. Something I would bet my reputation she has not done. You are on a Gatherer ship and in the company of the Exchequer. And believe me, my presence is enough to make people look the other way.

'But your eyes will always give you away. They set you apart and you know what being unusual does for you. So when we disembark, whether we have the Marshal's escort or not, you will keep your heads down. You will be surrounded by my people but on no account be tempted to lift your heads until I say it is safe to do so. We cannot risk someone seeing you. News travels too fast and I do not have enough swords to protect you.'

Up on deck, the skipper's orders sounded out as the ship approached dock. They could hear the hubbub and chaos of the dockside and the sloshing of water as oars were backed to slow and turn the trireme. He heard his name called.

'Right. Wait here until I call you up.'

He clattered back up the ladder and out into the cloudy morning once again. There were a pair of carriages and a chariot on the dockside waiting. All flew the colours of Gestern, a vibrant red background on which were depicted lions rampant either side of a snow-capped mountain. It was a legacy of their past under the rule of Kark. He nodded his pleasure. Katrin Mardov was waiting for them, her long brown hair blowing about her head.

'I had no idea I was due for accounting,' she called.

'I think I may give you a reprieve this once, Marshal,' he said. The gangplank slapped down. He turned to an appros. 'Bring the Ascendants. See that they keep their heads down.'

He trotted down on to the dockside, the concrete feeling strange and still after his time at sea. He greeted the Marshal with a salute which she returned. Mardov was a key Conquord loyalist. Gestern had prospered enormously under the empire's auspices and her family had fully embraced its framework. Respected throughout her own country and the wider Conquord, Katrin Mardov was a tall, slender woman in her middle years. She was an administrator, not a soldier, and was possessed of a keen mind. It was a mind that was ever being used to its fullest extent. She studied him with her soft brown eyes.

'Your message was rather cryptic, Paul,' she said. 'And it's not a common occurrence for you to bring cargo. Certainly not valuable cargo. Normally you're taking it away.'

Jhered smiled but knew the joke was forced. 'War changes most things, doesn't it?'

'So, get your cargo off. What is it? I've got other transport if it's bulky.'

'It's people, Katrin. Five of them.' He held up a hand. 'Trust me. Take us to your palace. I'll tell you all about it then.'

Chapter 50

848th cycle of God, 8th day of Solasfall
15th year of the true Ascendancy

Pavel Nunan, Master of Sword for the 2nd legion, the Bear Claws of Estorr, met Roberto's army two days after they had crossed the fords at Scintarit and turned south to skirt the Toursan Lakelands on their way to Gestern. He had approached their marching camp on horseback late in the afternoon, riding pillion behind one of thirty of Master Kell's cavalry, and shadowed by Roberto's forward guard.

Kell had enveloped him in a long hug and brought him personally to Roberto's tent, where the next stage of their operation was being planned. Roberto stood for Nunan's salute before pointing him towards an empty stool among his command team.

'Sit, sit,' said Roberto. 'And help yourself to food.'

'Thank you, General,' said the sharp-featured Goslander.

Roberto studied him. The effects of a shoulder injury were still apparent in the way he carried himself and his uniform was a maze of repairs. But his breastplate and helmet were polished and in fine condition. The scabbard at his waist without doubt held a sharpened gladius.

'She found you. I knew she would.' Nunan looked fondly across at Kell.

'And so here we are,' said Roberto. 'How many are you?'

'We are still finding survivors from Scintarit,' said Nunan. 'Escapees from the Tsardon prisons, those who were lost in the Halorians or down towards the Toursan Lakelands whom we have contacted through our foragers and forward scouts. We'll never know how many are lost and never to be found. But we now have three thousand, four hundred and seventy-three, as of the day I left our camp. Many are not fit to fight. Some never will be. But we are making a difference. We have been disrupting supply to Atreska though we are coming under increasing pressure from steppe cavalry who are patrolling the area from the Tarit Plain south to the fords.

'They'll know you are here and marching south and it will worry them. But I don't believe you will meet significant resistance until you reach Gestern or at the very earliest, cross the Atreskan border in the south.'

'I don't understand,' said Davarov. 'If they know their supply lines are being raided, why do they guard them so inadequately? The one we took down could never have stood up to a concerted raid, whether they saw it coming or not.'

Nunan spread his hands. 'And in their overconfidence they are not unlike we were until very recently. I'm guessing but the fact that they marched so much of their army north, south and west suggests they are confident of victory despite supply disruptions. And that they have Atreska to supply them anyway.' He scanned those assembled in the tent, his eyes resting on the two Atreskans, Shakarov and Davarov. 'You don't know, do you?'

Roberto felt a sudden chill. 'Know what?'

'The supply train you attacked. I'm surprised it was crossing Scintarit at all. We haven't seen one for twenty days. We had assumed any reinforcement would be diverted north or south, particularly because of our presence here. And because they don't need to supply their armies in Atreska.'

'What are you talking about?' demanded Shakarov.

'Atreska has turned,' he said. 'They fight with the Tsardon, not against them.'

Davarov and Shakarov were on their feet in an instant. Kell and Nunan followed them, she standing in front of him.

'You lie,' spat Shakarov.

Nunan faced him evenly. 'Strike me for a liar if you believe it. But I have been here trying to stay alive for over fifty days, with Tsardon around every bend of every path and river. I'm here because I believe I must gather all the information I can and disrupt the supply as best I can. And I have seen with my own eyes the flags of old Atreska flying on every fort along the border. I have seen Tsardon standing on their battlements with their Atreskan allies.' He pushed Kell aside. 'Strike me for a liar.'

Roberto didn't look at them. The ramifications of what he had just heard were falling through his mind like rock from a mountainside. He kneaded his forehead with his left hand.

'Sit down, sit down. All of you.' He waited until he heard seats being retaken. 'Good. Now, I understand the emotions but we've been here before, haven't we?' He looked meaningfully at his Atreskan commanders. 'Please, let us think about this in a balanced way. Half the citizens outside this tent are Atreskans. And what Nunan has said affects them all.'

'How far have your scouts penetrated my country?' growled Shakarov.

'All the way to Haroq City,' said Nunan. 'The flags are flying on Yuran's towers.'

Shakarov and Davarov were both hunched forwards. Big strong men, both of them, but both with eyes that shone damp in the lantern light.

'There must be resistance,' said Davarov quietly.

'Yes,' said Nunan. 'Throughout the country as far as we have seen. There is good news within the gloom, my friends. It is easy to cross the border if you are a native Atreskan and I have plenty with me from the Rogue Spears who remain loyal to the Conquord. We have had contact with legions fighting a rearguard all the way to the Neratharnese border. Across the country, loyalists strike at them but their numbers are overwhelming and Yuran's legions are with them. The Conquord forces cannot hope to stem the advance and the fact of the civil war played into our enemy's hands. For every citizen who would strike them down, there are three who will feed and heal them.'

'Is it organised, this resistance?' asked Roberto.

'Barely,' said Nunan. 'But if the rumours are right, General Gesteris is there, somewhere in the south-west. We are going to find and join him. Take the fight back to the Tsardon at Neratharn. Reform the Bear Claws.'

Davarov turned to Roberto. 'General. Roberto. Please, we must join this fight. We still have eleven thousand in our force. We can break them.'

'Wait,' said Roberto, raising a hand. 'Nunan, what do you know of the forces moving south to Gestern.'

Nunan's face was grim. 'They've diverted at least seven thousand more to that front. It's clear that they don't expect significant resistance until they reach Neratharn and the force going north to Gosland I suspect to be a holding one only.'

'Then they will get a bloody nose from Atarkis,' said Roberto. 'Good. I don't think they've accounted for us at all. At least, not properly.'

'Don't say it, Roberto,' said Davarov. 'It makes Gestern the critical front for the Conquord, I know.'

'Nunan? What of Gestern?'

'I have very little information, General,' said the Master of Sword. 'But you aren't going there for no reason, are you? There are now upwards of twenty-five thousand Tsardon on their way there. Jorganesh was already having trouble in the south with steppe cavalry and Tsardon infantry. If he retreats, as is likely, it will add pressure on the Gesternan border. If he stands, he risks being cut off.'

'And whatever his decision, it has surely already been taken,' said Elise Kastenas. 'Assuming he received your messages or has been contacted by the Gesternans.'

'I think the point is this,' said Roberto. 'Whichever direction we take, we will be chasing the Tsardon. But there is clearly more risk to the Conquord through the loss of Gestern than Atreska, simply because of the weight of defence that exists in the wider territories. We will continue our march as planned. And you, Nunan, still determined to head into Atreska?'

'Absolutely,' said Nunan. 'General Gesteris is my commanding officer. It is my duty to try and find him.'

'And mine,' said Kell. 'I am a Claw.'

'I respect that,' said Roberto. 'Gesteris is a lucky man. We could do with soldiers like you. But before you and Kell go back to your people, tell me how you've managed to keep your Atreskan legionaries from deserting or betraying you. I think Davarov and Shakarov would be fascinated to know.'

'It's quite simple,' said Nunan. 'I and the Rogue Spears Master of Sword have questioned each one separately about their loyalty to the Conquord or to an independent Atreska. Those who speak the former have removed their Atreskan insignia. Those who speak the latter are no longer with my army.'

'You let them go home?' asked Shakarov, frowning.

'Oh no,' said Nunan, eyeing the two Atreskans warily. 'We have too many enemies already. I will not willingly add to them.'

'War begins to bite,' whispered Davarov. 'The Conquord must prevail.'

'Lift your heads, Ascendants,' said Jhered. 'You are among friends here.'

They all looked to Arducius who nodded, though he felt suddenly anxious. Their heads came up to look at Marshal Mardov, and the small, luxuriously appointed reception room in which just she and they stood. His heart fell and he wondered if they would ever really have friends outside of themselves.

The Marshal saw their eyes and covered her mouth with a hand to hide her gasp. She took a step backwards. She made the encircling sign of the Omniscient over her chest and stared. Her eyes eventually dragged to Jhered.

'What are they?' she asked.

'Ask them yourself,' said Jhered. 'Please, they are just children.'

She turned back to them and her look was reluctant, suspicious. Beside Arducius, Ossacer had returned his sightless gaze to his lap. Mirron took her lead from Gorian who was staring at the Marshal with a mixture of pride and anger. She struggled to frame words.

'We are the future,' said Gorian. 'And Lord Jhered says we will win the war for the Conquord. That is what we are.'

Arducius found a smile crossing his lips. Mardov was taken aback by Gorian's confidence. And for once, the fiery Ascendant had not chosen belligerence.

'How?' she asked.

So they told her, Arducius mainly, but by the time they had finished, all had had their say. Mardov was seated by then, caught in the tale they were telling. And if he didn't mistake it, Jhered was actually proud of them.

'Please,' said Ossacer in conclusion. 'If there is one thing you believe in all that you have heard, it is that we are not against God, we are with God. We serve Him and the Conquord.'

'Manipulation of the elements?' Mardov shook her head. 'Can it really be true?'

'Think of the possibilities,' said Jhered. 'Do you want a demonstration?'

'I'm not sure I do. Does that make sense? Maybe later,' said the Marshal. 'You understand this is all rather difficult to take in. I'm not surprised the Chancellor has reacted the way she has. This is . . .' She blew out her cheeks, unable to string the right words together.

Arducius regarded her, wondering what she really thought about them. No doubt her friendship with Jhered had swayed her to listen to them. But in her eyes remained the look that was becoming all too familiar to him. Misgiving. Anxiety. And the unhappy wariness that led so quickly to fear and hate. Funny. He had been desperate to feel dry land beneath his feet, the security of walls around him and a comfortable bed on which to sleep. He had been here only a few hours and now he wanted to leave.

'I will help you, though, Paul,' she said. 'I don't know where you're going with this but I know you well enough to trust you.'

'It's all I ask,' said Jhered.

'And it's all we ask too,' said Arducius. 'Just to be given a chance. Not judged before the act.'

'Very well,' said the Marshal. 'So. Where are you going? Despite what I've just said, I don't think you can fight your battles here. We are desperate but not so much that my people will take on something this new, this . . .' She waved a hand ineffectually.

'Different,' said Gorian.

'Uh, yes.' The Marshal smiled, embarrassed.

'How are you desperate?' asked Jhered. 'I thought your borders well defended. And with Kark to your east . . .'

'The Tsardon are marching south very quickly. There is no real resistance in Atreska, as you well know. Their numbers and equip-ment suggest they mean to breach us, not hold us. Again, not a surprise. I need Jorganesh. We hear nothing from him. He has four legions and they were up against lesser numbers, though the steppe are a real handful as always. With him at my forts, I consider myself content. Without him, I won't last long into dusas.

'The Tsardon have a lot of ships in the Bay of Harryn. I can't take my legions or my navy from the east for fear of invasion from the sea. There is no reinforcement coming from the mainland. You know the problems, Paul. Overstretch. Scintarit and Atreska were the lynch-pins. Both are broken. Whatever you think you can do, it needs to be done quickly.'

Arducius looked at Jhered. Plainly the news was a surprise. He had spoken to them about the pressure that Gestern would face but something was not as he expected.

'I had thought Jorganesh to be here by now,' he said quietly.

'No,' said Mardov. 'And my scouts cannot find him, nor will my Karku contacts give me anything. I am praying he is in Atreska, perhaps engaged with an enemy I had no knowledge of. Out in the harbour, we aren't supplying, we're evacuating. This town is being made into a barracks.' She looked at the Ascendants dubiously. 'They are but four, however powerful you think they are. If Jorganesh is gone, over thirty-five thousand Tsardon are coming here and I cannot defend against such numbers. Not even if I had a wall across my northern border. Paul, where are you going with them?'

Jhered took a deep breath. 'I need to find Roberto Del Aglios. I have to get him to accept the Ascendants. It is the only way to ensure they can be used without the Order or the armies railing against them. I have to get up towards the Sirranean border and his last known position. I'd thought to track along the Karku border and skirt the Lakelands.'

'Dear God-who-embraces-us-all,' said Mardov. She glanced again at the Ascendants and Jhered motioned her to continue. 'Are you mad? Sirrane is a lifetime away, and that assumes Roberto is still there. If he has word of Scintarit he will either be on his way back through Gosland or heading to the fords himself.'

'And that would truly be a blessing.'

'One that you are counting on, I suspect.' Jhered raised his eyebrows and inclined his head. 'I understand your thoughts, Paul, but it isn't realistic. You can't travel in Atreska now. My best scouts are being picked up. The Tsardon forward riders are everywhere. And even where they aren't, the Atreskan traitors are.'

'Then what do you suggest, Katrin?'

'You only really have one choice if you want to get into Tsard but you couldn't take the numbers that you have brought on your ship. You, these four and a couple of others at the most, if you aren't to be deemed a raiding party and slaughtered before you have travelled a mile.' She shrugged. 'You'll have to go through Kark.'

The forum in Gull's Ford was full of Tsardon soldiers. There was not enough ale and wine to go round, it seemed, and there would be trouble again. Like there had been night after night since Atreska's so-called 'liberation'. The Tsardon slept where they felt like, used the basilica as an administration office and officer's quarters, took everything and paid for nothing. And this was supposed to be preferable to Conquord rule.

Han Jesson was hearing the same excuses Yuran had been giving them for a decade. How peace and plenty would follow war and austerity. He stood on the steps of the forum with Praetor Gorsal, whose words he heard but whose smile was brittle.

'You have to give them time.'

'To do what?' he said. 'Destroy the rest of the town that escaped the raids? Look about you. This isn't liberation. This is occupation.' A familiar knot of cold loss gripped his stomach. 'And where is my family?'

'In time,' said Gorsal. 'In time.'

Jesson stared at her. 'Not good enough.'

He walked down the steps and onto the forum floor. The place stank of sweat and alcohol. Citizens reduced to little more than servants. All pretence at a working economy was gone. And when the food was exhausted, they would be abandoned. Jesson had only agreed to defect because he had been assured his wife and son would be returned to him. That had been almost sixty days ago. But no one had been returned to the homes from which they were snatched those six long years past.

The Tsardon commander was drinking with his men at the corner taverna. He was an arrogant man. Overconfident in his authority and ignorant of the feeling Jesson could sense building in the town. He barely spoke the Atreskan dialect and they had been forced to adopt a halting border language none of them had used in a long time.

Jesson breasted through the Tsardon warriors, trying to keep his courage afloat. They paid him no heed. After all, he presented no risk. The Tsardon commander, a sentor named, Hareshin, looked up a little blearily as he approached. Dusk was hours away and this man was drunk. Jesson feared the darkness.

'You come to offer me something?' he asked, straightening a little. 'Some word of thanks or a prayer for our Gods?'

Immediately, attention was focused on them.

'No,' said Jesson. 'I come to ask you to prove that you are really my ally.'

'Prove it?' The sentor smiled and raised his cup. 'That we are here is proof enough. That the Conquord is banished from here, and soon the face of this world, will be more proof than any should need. Go away. Better still, get me another drink. This one is warm.'

He slopped wine in a puddle on the table and poured the rest away very deliberately.

'Your raiders took my wife and son from me,' said Jesson, finding courage at the end of his despair. 'Prove you are better than the Conquord. Find them for me.'

Hareshin laughed in his face. 'Back. When were they taken?'

'Six years ago. Sentor Rensaark took them.'

'Six years?' Hareshin looked to his men and the volume of the laughter increased. 'Did the Conquord take your mind as well as your country? They are gone from you. Sold on.' His smile became a sneer. 'Your son is a slave, if he is not dead already. And your wife. Imagine. She is moaning under the man she now worships as he thrusts inside her willing body. The man whose seed swells in her belly. The man who will not let others take her. A Tsardon man.'

Jesson stared straight back at him. His rage burned inside and he kept it there.

'She is happy. Now.' Hareshin sat back in his chair. 'Let that be good enough.'

'Well, it's not,' he said quietly. 'It's not good enough at all.'

Chapter 51

848th cycle of God, 8th day of Solasfall
15th year of the true Ascendancy

Jorganesh spurred his terrified horse back down the long single column of his army and yelled for order. Futile or not in the barrage and the panic, he had to try.

'Shields overhead. Set defence up the slopes. I want to see sarissas, I want to see walls of steel and timber. Show them the Conquord crest!'

The rain of fire was unceasing. From high up on the tree-lined slopes of Lubjek's Defile, the flaming arrows and stones fell. The jaws of the trap snapping on the helpless Conquord army below. The air was hot and full of the screams of men, women and horses. Smoke was filling the narrow path at the bottom of the defile and floating up to obscure the trees behind which the Tsardon were so effectively hidden.

Onager stones whistled down. Smeared in burning pitch, they crashed down all around him, exploding on the valley slopes either side and thundering into his legions. The stones shattered shield and bone, drove gashes in his defensive lines and battered wagons to flaming fragments.

'Hold!' he shouted. 'Hold.'

At either end of the column, his cavalry were chasing up the slopes and into the trees, riding hard at the unseen enemy. Arrows rained down from thousands of bows, rattling on shields and finding every chink in the wall. Jorganesh could feel the fear in his army. They would not hold for long.

A burning arrow thudded into his horse's neck. The animal reared and screamed. Jorganesh was pitched off backwards, cracking his lower back onto the sun-baked ground. He rolled aside. Hands grabbed at his shoulders and weapon belt, dragging him further from the stamping animal. She bolted away up the slope, turned a right angle and fled back towards the head of the column.

He was dragged to his feet and taken inside the shield wall among scared but determined triarii infantrymen. A blood-streaked face was thrust into his own. Master of Sword, Tord Parnforst from the 17th ala, the Bahkir Thunder, yelled at him in the deafening roar.

'We have to get out of here, General.' A flaming stone splintered the defence just to their right. Both men ducked. Fire spattered out through the triarii. A dismembered arm thudded against Jorganesh's helmet, splashing blood down his face and dropping at his feet. A ripple of anxiety that ran away through the infantry. 'We're being taken apart.'

'The defile is ten miles long,' Jorganesh shouted back, spitting blood from his mouth. 'We'll be slaughtered if we try and run. We have to give the cavalry time to quiet the artillery.'

'We must attack upslope.' Parnforst gestured away into the wooded sides of the defile. A rattle of arrows on the shield wall. A renewed roar from their right. 'In maniple order.'

'I—.'

'Sir, you cannot hold us here. The hastati will break before long.'

Jorganesh stared at him, knowing he was right. Lubjek's Defile was always going to be a gamble but one he had been forced to take, against all their better judgements. When word had reached them from Gestern of the force approaching through Atreska, he had disengaged from his enemies and force-marched his soldiers back along the border with Kark.

Time was against them and in the open, the steppe cavalry were a menace he could barely contain. Lubjek's Defile had offered a chance to gain respite from the enemy riders and take four days off their journey back to Gestern. None of his scouts had seen the danger coming. And now he was stuck in the centre of the valley, his army stretched out over three miles.

To run would be to sacrifice artillery and the injured. To stand risked a rout on to the enemy swords. To attack uncoordinated carried a similar death sentence.

'General. Please.'

Jorganesh nodded. 'Form them up. Get runners down the lines.

Alternate maniples left and right. Keep the wall solid front and rear. We all move together on my signal.'

Parnforst grinned. 'We'll take them.' He turned to bellow for volunteer messengers.

Jorganesh stooped and picked up a damaged shield from a dead citizen. He whispered a short prayer for her continued cycle while he loosened it from her arm. The whistling of onager rounds and the whine of arrows surrounded them. He waited for the dread crump, trying to count the impacts. Twenty, thirty, it was hard to tell.

He pushed through the crowded, sweating knots of fear that surrounded him. He shouted for strength and solidarity, promised them revenge and victory. Holding the shield high and right, he ran back down his lines, shouting for centurions to form their maniples up. He meant to make it back to the head of the column, pick up another horse and lead the advance himself.

'I need a horse,' he said to a member of the extraordinarii come to protect him.

Heedless of his own safety, he ran part way up the side of the defile. He had to see what was going on further down the line. He had to know the army was together. Above him, he saw his cavalry-men hunting in packs, further and further up. Forty and fifty yards up where the sides grew steep and rocky and the trees began to grow out at angles. He could neither see nor hear if they were finding targets, such was the noise from the valley floor.

Finding a vantage point where he was at least partially hidden from above, Jorganesh turned and gazed down at the disaster unfolding below him. He could see a clear mile and more down the defile before it turned a right hand bend and out of sight. The floor of the valley was a sea of shields glinting in the sun that scoured through the clouds of smoke overhead. Coils of black and grey spiralled into the air from the most recent impacts and he saw myriad tracers of arrows crossing the sky. Onager stones followed them, crunching down on to his army or burying themselves amongst the rocks either side.

The army was a rippling, moving snake. He could see the passage of his orders passing down it, the maniples switching to adjusted formations. He nodded, impressed. Under the weight of fire, still there was discipline. The sound of his army straining for order rose to him and he knew they would not fail him. But there were so many bodies down there. So much blackened death smeared across the valley floor. How many thousands were already gone from his four legions?

He made to move back down but something caught his eye higher up the slope, beyond his cavalry. He could see movement low to the ground. The undergrowth was rippling, sleek shapes moving within it.

'What is that?' he whispered.

There was sound, too. He could just begin to start making it out. And by the time the cavalry horses above him had started to rear and bolt he was sprinting back down to the army.

'Brace!' he roared. 'Brace! Shields to the ground. Blades low. Crouch, crouch!'

They couldn't hope to hear him and the message wouldn't get through the long, line miles out of his sight. All he could do was hope that his centurions saw what he had before it was too late.

Charging back down the slope, legion cavalry tried to control scared horses through a mass of animals biting and snapping at their fetlocks. In amongst the incessant fall of arrow and stone, the first of the dogs broke from the undergrowth and crashed into poorly prepared infantry. They bit, barked and scratched on their way deep into the army. They were small, ferocious hunting dogs. Lithe and vicious.

The sound of collision echoed up the valley, the army descending into chaos. Jorganesh punched his shield out into the face of a snarling animal. Slicing his sword through its gut with his gladius. The next barrelled straight into his feet, knocking him off balance. He slashed out sideways, catching its hind quarters. The dog yelped and turned. A second gladius drove down behind its neck.

Jorganesh climbed to his feet again. Panic was everywhere. Citizens were burning, fighting hand to hand with animals, for God's sake. Here and there, his cavalry swept past, those that could striking out, trying to drive them away.

'Hold position!' he called. A futile shout in the tumult.

He looked around him for Parnforst but the Master was nowhere to be seen. There were breaks in the defensive line as far as he could see. Dogs lay skewered on the end of sarissas. Men wore gashes on their faces and hands where the tide had rolled across them. Fighting still continued unabated. More and more of the dogs rushed down the slope and into the Conquord troops, searching out prey.

Jorganesh turned to face the slope, standing with hastati of the 42nd Estorean, the Golden Lions.

'With me, Lions. Let them break over us.'

But there was renewed shouting all around them. And he could sense the terror in it. The Tsardon were coming. A forest of spears sailed down the slopes at them. Heavy, short-range shafts that punched through shield and armour. Down the sides of the valley flooded the enemy, cries of death and victory on their lips. As far as he could see in either direction, the tree-line disgorged their foe, chasing the last of the dogs before them.

Thousands of them. Thousands. Surely there were not this many in the south. Surely the kingdom did not have this many warriors at its behest.

'Stand! Stand!' called Jorganesh, his shield once more ahead of him, in the front line with the rawest of his troops, giving them the belief to stay.

Regrouped Conquord cavalry was galloping along the lower slopes of the valley to his left. Tsardon bodies tumbled and twisted, struck by arrows fired from the saddle or by those in the terribly thin Conquord line with the wit to string their bows. Legion standards still flew proud along the column, muster points for the fearful.

The Tsardon broke across them, a wave of steel and muscle. It was like the old days of Tsardon attack except this time, their massed undisciplined charge would not stall on a forest of pikes or sarissas. It would not meet the implacable triplex acies. Jorganesh's column was only ten ranks wide and attacked from both sides.

Jorganesh took a first impact full on his shield, feeling the damaged wood and metal give just a little. His gladius licked out from behind it, stabbing deep into Tsardon flesh. The enemy fell back and three more took his place. There were hands dragging at the shield, blades whispering through the air above his head. He ran his blade across his vision, slicing through knuckle, hearing the howls of agony. To his right, a hastati fell under the weight of enemies. Jorganesh stabbed out sideways, taking one in the back, He slashed up, biting into another's face.

Left, the line fractured and broke. There were Tsardon in amongst them. Bowmen were cut down where they stood with no time to loose another shaft. He backed away. Tsardon followed him. The deep-tanned oval faces of steppe warriors glared at him. Brown-eyed and black-haired they were, with fearless expressions speaking of the insult of their invasion by the Conquord and their determination to see it broken. A blade thudded into his right-hand side. He partially deflected it but his armour was dented, knocking the wind from him. He pushed his shield out hard, striking one in the face. The Tsardon's nose splintered, driving bone up into his skull and killing him.

The roar was everywhere. A hurricane around him. He could barely see another Conquord citizen but still they fought. He could hear them shouting, struggling and dying. Tsardon still poured down the valley sides. His eyes were clouded with blood and his nose was full of the stench of the enemy. He clubbed left, right and ahead. He kept his shield moving, searching for men to stand by him.

Horses galloped past. Tsardon were cut away in a swathe.

'Hold position!' he shouted into the moment's breathing space.

But the hastati were not schooled for this. They ran into the space the cavalry had given them, frightened by the fighting at their backs. They broke up the defile chasing down Tsardon and were being picked off, one by one.

Jorganesh bellowed for order and for his standard. The pressure was enormous. Into the hole rushed the Tsardon. Still the arrows came from behind him. Still they took down the enemy. Jorganesh clashed blades with a Tsardon, forcing him back. The man tripped over a root and fell. The general struck out and took him in the throat.

Another blade came at him. He ducked and raised his shield, deflecting it. There was fighting right behind him. He glanced over his shoulder. Not long now. He roared his fury. His gladius came overhead with everything he had and carved deep into the neck of an enemy who had thought to kill him. He dragged it clear, paced back and opened his shield to the left, knocking another down. Jorganesh stamped on him on his way to a third, stabbing him under his guard. A blade thundered into his shield, knocking him backwards.

He found himself looking down his line for a heartbeat. They were lost. Tsardon were covering the valley floor. He saw a standard topple and fall and heard the Tsardon exult. Hastati fled to nowhere. Principes in a tight circle fought hard. Triarii still stood five deep but the press on them was overwhelming. Cavalry ran the flanks, trying to drive the enemy away but with every pass their numbers dwindled.

Jorganesh called for a rally around him. His standard bearer still stood by him but he was otherwise isolated. Men fought their way towards him. He kept his shield close and his sword tucked in, defending against the blows that came at him. The Tsardon had picked him out. Their sentors demanded his blood. Beneath him, the ground was slick with blood and treacherous with the bodies of his army. It would be the same along all three miles of Conquord troops. They had to regroup. Had to stand tall.

'To the triarii,' he called to any that could hear.

He had about twenty hastati around him. Citizens destined for honour, should they live. Those that had stood while their comrades fled. He dashed his shield into the back of a Tsardon who had just struck down an infantryman. He speared his sword into the back of his neck and ran over him, back down the line. Left and right his hastati hacked, stabbed and pushed. But there were Tsardon everywhere. They ran hard into the small standard-bearing unit, desperate to bring it and the general down.

Jorganesh called for strength and for power. A blade from nowhere splintered the top of his shield and bit down into his arm. He grunted at the pain and lashed out with the broken shield, feeling it strike flesh. Tsardon rushed into a gap between him and the triarii. In front of his eyes the world was a forest of blades and bodies.

He heard someone calling his name from ahead. Parnforst. Still alive. Then there was still hope. Jorganesh drove on. His blade took another Tsardon in the lower back. He brought the remnants of his shield in front of him, ducked his head and ran headlong, shouting his hastati with him. But at his left, a young man took a sword in the gut and tumbled into him. Right, his guardsman was felled by a blow at his legs.

'General Jorganesh!'

Parnforst's face was close, so close. Jorganesh felt an exquisite pain in his hip and his right leg failed him. He dropped to his knees, slashing as he went down. The Tsardon couldn't get his blade in front of him fast enough. Something connected with the back of his skull and catapulted him forward. He was lying on his shield. He tried to roll onto his back.

'Jorganesh!'

Fainter now. Above him and around him, legs and bodies and sky. He saw the standard of the Golden Lions break and fall. He heard the shouts of the enemy. All he could see were the backs of his few men trying to surround him. He tried to call for them to run. To get word to Gestern. He tried to rise but something was pinning him back. He felt faint and grasped on to his consciousness.

Jorganesh.

Perhaps no one had said it. Or perhaps Parnforst was being dragged away so distant was the call. He coughed and tasted salt. Someone stood above him. Tsardon. One of so many. He prayed for the life of the Advocate and begged for the mercy of God.

Pain. Brief pain.

Chapter 52

848th cycle of God, 11th day of Solasfall
15th year of the true Ascendancy

Thirty days and the sense of loss had not diminished. The light of life had failed on the twenty-fifth day of solasrise and it would not return. People still carried on, of course. But everything about them was changed, inside and out. The blessed had become the cursed.

Hesther Naravny opened the shutters on another day of uncertainty and anxiety. So empty. Devoid of laughter. Of all the elements that Westfallen once had. Now no more than a garrison town full of grey and scowling faces. Did they blame the Ascendancy? Probably. But there was a steadfast refusal to show it.

Hesther turned away from the shutters and walked out of her room and into the vast emptiness of the villa. She still fancied she could hear echoes of the young Ascendants in its deepest corners. She still expected to hear Ardol Kessian's voice booming out from the library or the dining room. Or floating above the sound of the fountains. But in reality, it was just the sound of her sandals on marble that reached her. Strange how none of the Echelon seemed to find each other any more. It had seemed so effortless before but Kessian's death had broken the rope that bound them and they were all lost in the same space.

Nothing gladdened her heart any more. Not even the sounds of the five youngsters that could easily be the next strand of the true Ascendancy. They were almost seven years old now and developing well. Andreas had been taking their training and consequently they didn't feel Kessian's loss so acutely as the emerged had done. And the current babes in arms would never know his smile and his strength. Such a tragedy. Perhaps when they were old enough, Kessian could be spoken of with the warmth of love rather than the bitterness of loss.

Hesther gathered her courage to her and walked out into Westfallen to make her daily pilgrimage to the House of Masks. It was a ritual that gave her the will to carry on another day with the burden she now bore as Mother of the Ascendancy. It was not a long walk but ever it renewed her sadness and forced questions into her mind.

The sounds of sawing, hammering and the shouts of men rang around the town's periphery. Everywhere she looked, there was new construction under the keen eyes of Vasselis and Harkov. All of it ugly though she cared little for the aesthetics either way. Not when the necessity of it all shouted at her far louder, questioning everything she had believed in all her life.

Out beyond the boundaries of the town, five watchtowers overlooked every land approach to Westfallen. They stuck up from the landscape like accusing fingers, their dark wooden structures strong and practical. Each could house bolt-firers and twenty archers if they had to, so Harkov had said. If only it had ended there. But such was the perceived threat that Vasselis had ordered Westfallen be encased by wood and stone.

The reinforced stockade was well advanced already. It was being built all the way from the northern shore of the inlet, round to where the cliff path wound up to the orchard. It was twenty feet high. Thick and heavy wooden planks, treated to be resistant to fire, built between stone towers on which would sit ballistae or bolt-firers. It was a prison of their own making and every day she saw it, Hesther shook her head, denying the necessity. Could there really be enough hate to threaten them this much?

They had had no right to bring all this to Westfallen. No right to subject these fine people to a daily ration of fear and uncertainty. She fought back the anger and strode up the slope to the House of Masks where, as on so many days, she found Genna Kessian.

Hesther knelt by her on the lawn. Genna turned and buried her head in Hesther's chest, clinging onto her while she wept. She had become so old and frail, Ardol's death killing her as surely as any cancer. It would not be long. Eventually, Genna composed herself and withdrew. Hesther barely felt the weight of her go, so thin had she become.

'I had him for so long. Longer than I could ever have dreamed, so blessed he was with his ability and the life it gave him,' Genna said, her voice tiny and faint. 'Yet I still feel he has been stolen from me too soon.' She looked at Hesther, her eyes searching and desperate. 'I so want to be able to celebrate his return to the earth and sleep happy because he is in the embrace of God. She denied me that. She has taken my joy from me.'

'Oh, Genna,' said Hesther, finding nothing else to say.

'I don't want to hate,' she said. 'But it's all I have left in my heart.'

Hesther was crushed. What was the sense in denying for Genna what she felt in herself every day she awoke. New anger blossomed inside her. That these were to be the last overwhelming feelings of this wonderful woman.

'Don't be hateful when you go to lie with Ardol,' whispered Hesther.

Genna almost smiled then. 'I'm counting on him to be able to lift it from me.'

'He will,' said Hesther. 'He gives us all the strength to go on. That's why I'm here.'

'He'll be glad to know the Echelon is in your hands now,' said Genna. 'He was always so proud of your strength.'

Hesther sighed. She didn't feel strong at all. 'Where are they, Genna? Are they safe out there? Are they even still alive?'

Genna patted her knee. 'On their way to Sirrane and out of the Order's clutches. It is the only blessing we have.'

But Hesther couldn't share Genna's confidence. High in the Dukan Mountains, the smudge of smoke and flame that was the invasion beacon blotted the perfect day. Word had reached Vasselis that they had been lit because of a disastrous reverse in Tsard and an invasion of Atreska. Genna's grief had blinded her. The Ascendants would be journeying through a war zone. She prayed that whoever was with them was as capable as the Marshal Defender said.

She listened to Genna's quiet words for a time, added her own prayers and messages and stood to touch Kessian's mask. There hadn't been enough space for everything that people wanted to say and the lay Reader had allowed both the inside of the mask and a specially noted page in the book to be used. It was against the scriptures for such a volume of outpouring but as the Reader had said, she wasn't the only official in the Order making up the rules to suit them. She had not attempted to keep the bitter edge from her voice.

Hesther squeezed Genna's shoulders and walked back down into the town. The forum was quiet these days. No traders had visited since the Chancellor's cataclysmic appearance. Vasselis had assured them that no one would be out of pocket as a result and many businesses that relied on passing trade had closed up and lent their muscle to the security efforts. The town might have been empty of joy but it was brimmed with the determination to survive.

Hesther wandered up to the hub of the building. A quarry barge of stone had arrived from Glenhale the previous day and the masons were hard at work erecting another of the towers that seated the stockade. She was looking for Vasselis and found him with Harkov under a canvas shelter nearby. Both were studying plans but there was a map on the table too and that worried Hesther for reasons she didn't understand at first.

Vasselis came around the table to kiss her forehead and cheeks and usher her inside. Still as authoritative as always, he cast around orders and advice with great heart. But Hesther could see further into him than those at his command. He was haunted by his last sight of Kovan, running away to a fate as yet unknown. And though he had hidden it under a welter of effort and work, much as Netta had, it ate at him, undermined his confidence. Kovan, he had said in the first days after, was a work so nearly complete but one still in progress.

'Come to check on your workforce, Mother Naravny?' he asked, using the title that still sat so uncomfortably on her shoulders.

'Just trying to fill up the hours, same as every day,' she replied. 'Think you'll have it done before dusas bites?'

Vasselis shrugged. 'I'd like to say yes. But the weather is getting a little unpredictable.' Her head dropped and tears threatened afresh. 'I know, Hesther. Nowhere else in the Conquord has there been the capacity to predict the weather with such accuracy. We have taken it for granted for so long that now it has gone we feel helpless, staring at the sky and wondering when it will darken to snow.'

'Ardol would have known,' she said, trying to be bright. 'He loved this time of year. The storms sweeping up the inlet from the south. The cold fronts coming across the Tirronean Sea from Gestern. He used to say it was guesswork when it all clashed together around the turn of the season but he never got it wrong, did he?'

Vasselis's eyes sparkled. 'No, he didn't. And until Arducius returns, we'll have to muddle through.'

'I don't much like opening my shutters these mornings,' she said. 'I'll never get used to being surprised by cloud or cool on a solas day. Will he ever come back, do you think?'

'You know, I really believe he will. That they all will.'

Hesther studied him. He refused to face any other eventuality. The belief burned bright in him. She wished she had the same capacity.

'I'm glad your son is with them,' she said. 'They trust him. They love him.'

'All except Gorian.' Vasselis chuckled.

'They're just young boys. They'll work it out. Out there, they'll have no choice.' Hesther glanced at the map. It took in much of Caraduk, Estorea and parts of the Tirronean Sea. 'Thinking about expanding your empire, are you?'

'Some matters of state can't wait,' said Vasselis. 'Harkov was helping me decide where to move my defensive legions.'

Hesther frowned. 'I thought the orders from Estorr had done that.'

'They only told me to send three legions to Neratharn. With what little I have left, I have to worry about a Tsardon threat from the east, directly onto my lands, should Gestern fall.'

'But surely Kester Isle . . .' Her frown deepened.

Vasselis glanced about him. The shelter was empty barring the three of them.

'Hesther, it isn't getting any better out there. My roll-call of loyal troops is getting short. I am starting to make enemies among my own people.'

'What are you talking about?'

'This isn't just going up to thwart the Chancellor,' said Harkov, waving at the fortifications. 'She has sown dissension among the Omniscient faithful on her meandering way back to Estorr. The reports I'm getting suggest that volunteering for the Order legions is at an all-time high. The war seems a very long way away from most in Caraduk but they are scared instead by the threat they think is blooming here in Westfallen.'

Vasselis scratched at his head. 'I've divided my own people.'

'No you haven't,' said Hesther. 'The Chancellor has done that.'

'The result is the same. And now it is the flip of a coin whether the

Armour of God are the first to test themselves on these walls or whether it will be the bakers and farmers of Cirandon.'

'You're certain we will be attacked.'

'It is the only thing on which I would stake my life right now. But at least this time I will be able to guarantee your escape.'

And when Hesther walked back to the villa, her eyes fell on the three triremes anchored in deep water and wondered how long it would be before she would be calling one of them her home.

'Cosseted cretins,' muttered Jhered, stamping up the short stairway to the open deck and closing the hatch on the whingeing and bickering below. 'If they want ceiling height they can sleep up here.'

'My Exchequer?'

Jhered turned to the captain of the small pleasure boat put at his disposal by Marshal Mardov. He was a pleasant enough young man but had limited skill beyond river navigation. He was also in awe of the tall Gatherer. The cruiser was a twenty-four oar affair with a single mast and brightly decorated sail. Its bow and stern were swept up in the Gesternan style. Forward stood a canvas-canopied private deck for entertaining that was bordered by an intricately carved wooden rail. All the luxurious furnishing had been removed.

The sides of the boat were painted with mountainscapes which the Ascendants had loved but the vessel itself was a day ship and had precious little space below deck, barring crew bunks. There were only two cabins. Mirron and Appros Menas were in one, leaving all the boys crammed into the other. Jhered slept under the canvas on deck. Something he was entirely happy to do. The cooler air sweeping off the mountains of Kark was wonderful on his face when the sun set, and the ripple in the sail he found much to his liking.

It was only a three-day trip upriver to the border town of Ceskas but on this the second morning, Jhered was already wondering what he and Menas had let themselves in for. The captain had clearly been told to ask no questions about his young charges and for that if nothing else, Jhered was grateful.

'Nothing. Just the trials of travelling with brats,' he said. 'Is there any chance you can raise the height of each cabin and put feathers in the pillows, do you suppose?'

The captain laughed. 'You don't have children yourself, my Lord?'

'And below are four perfect reasons why not. They have short tempers, even shorter memories and an endless capacity for saying absolutely the wrong thing at will.' He shook his head.

'We were all young once.'

'Not like that, I bloody wasn't,' growled Jhered, feeling his mood lightening. 'My father would have beaten me raw for talking back the way they do.' He walked to stand by the young skipper. 'You do have children, I take it?'

'Three,' he replied.

'Brave man. Think I'd rather face a Tsardon horde in a loincloth than that bedlam every day.'

'I'm not a sailor for nothing. Peaceful out here, isn't it?'

'Brave and wise,' said Jhered. He shook his head again. 'They hate it down there but they spend most of their time there. I don't understand it. Look at what they are missing. Actually, that gives me an idea.'

He stalked to the hatch and pulled it open. The bickering was continuing unabated.

'Right. All of you. Not another word. Get up here now. Time I talked and you listened. A little geography lesson is in order.' He paused. 'Do not mutter about me under your breath, Gorian. You may not be able to drown but it's still a long swim to the nearest hot meal. Get up here.'

The captain saw his face and decided not to smile. Jhered walked under the canopy and waited for the five of them to drag themselves to where he stood.

'If you want this to be torture in addition to it being as hard as it will inevitably be, I will oblige,' he said without looking at them. 'I understand you are feeling lost, hurt and are suffering grief. I know Mirron gets sick on water but I also know Ossacer can cure that. I know Gorian and Kovan don't get on too well but that's life. I know you are growing into power that no one can help you understand but yourselves and for that alone, I have real sympathy for you.

'That is what I have learned. Now it is your turn. But unlike you, I will be brief and state each fact just the once.'

He turned to them and pointed forward to the stunning snow-capped peaks of Kark that ran the horizon from left to right and loomed larger with every hour that passed.

'In two days we will be landing in Ceskas. It is a frontier town where people have only ever known tough lives. It perches on the top of what you might well call a mountain but that these people and their Karku neighbours would call a hillock. The atmosphere is rarefied and you will tire quickly. However, we will be there only long enough to buy mules and supplies for our trek through the borders.

'We will take high passes because the flat lands are too dangerous to travel. Not because the Karku will kill you but because where they haven't forged a pass, there isn't one. Death lurks under every careless step. Up there in the heights, dusas will have jaws of wind so cold they can take the fingers from your hands and freeze the breath in your lungs. The snow and ice are so deep and so white they can blind you. And we will be so high you will fight for every breath.

'The Karku themselves are a secretive, powerful people. Just like the Sirraneans. They do not suffer incursion by large forces and will shoot first and ask your business later. They have rituals and religions to which they are bound more tightly than any Order Speaker. They have sacred grounds that none from the outside are allowed to see, let alone set foot upon. It is a country where a word or a gesture out of place can bring you pain and death. Nevertheless, they are honourable and they are allies. Respect is everything.'

He paused and glared at Gorian before continuing.

'We will be in Kark for a minimum of ten days unless any contacts I make give me new information. From there, we will strike north through eastern Atreska and into Tsard. In a straight line it is a journey of well over a thousand miles to Sirrane but we cannot travel straight. We will be travelling lands torn apart by war so our journey might be slow. We could find ourselves travelling near the Toursan Lakelands where the cannibals still live and the marshes suck you down in moments. Through the steppe lands where the horsemen are quick, skilled and deadly. We will not stop. We will not turn back.

'If we are lucky, hugely lucky, Roberto Del Aglios and his army will be marching south and you will have escaped the worst of the journey. Only then, of course, you will be required to do your bit to save the Conquord. If you do not, you stand to lose everything you love and the grief you feel now will be as a genastro day to that you will experience.

'You and I cannot afford to fail. You can halt armies with your power. You can bring fear so deep that enemies will turn and run from you. That is what I expect of you, and all your bleating about peace will fall on my ears so deafened. The Tsardon are coming and our allies turn against us.'

He looked at them all one by one, at the pallor in their faces and the fear in their eyes.

'I know you are all scared. You should be. You have lived lives of comfort and care in Westfallen but those are over. Now you are in my world and it is at war. And war takes everything from you. Even those vestiges of hope and love to which you cling. It takes them and grinds them underfoot. There will be nothing left if we should fail. Nothing.'

Chapter 53

848th cycle of God, 12th day of Solasfall
15th year of the true Ascendancy

Roberto Del Aglios grabbed his scabbarded cavalry sword and flew out of his tent and into the muggy, still night. He was in the lightweight tunic and sandals he'd fallen asleep in. Praise God for tiny mercies.

Down by the principal gate, hastati tents were ablaze. He could hear the clash of weapons. Garish shadows danced in the harsh half-light. Soldiers were pouring down to the flashpoint from all across the camp. He shouted for them to get back to their tents. He shouted for his extraordinarii. He had no idea if anyone heard or heeded him.

Barking legionaries aside, he ran across hard packed ground, hurdled the embers of cook fires and stands of shields and swords. Closer to the fighting, the mass of people slowed him and he elbowed and shoved his way through infantry, cavalry and engineers. His temper shortened with each stride.

The conflict was extensive. On a road between the 8th Estorean and the 15th Atreskan, citizens fought with sword, spear, dagger and fist against a backdrop of flaming canvas. It was a confused mess of a melee. Hundreds of them sparring or sprawling and more were edging to join all the time.

Roberto stood and watched for a few moments while his extra-ordinarii gathered about him and the more intelligent members of his army began to back away having seen him approach. A few of the combatants disengaged under his glare but too many more were lost in the passion of their dispute. There were injured lying on the ground and he could see at least one corpse. Enough.

'Get between them,' he ordered. 'Get them back across the road. Follow me.'

Roberto ran into the fight, forcing his way between two men with fists bunched. He pushed them aside, yelling at them to stand back. Further in, swords clashed and sparks flew.

'Get back,' he shouted. 'Stand aside. Weapons down now.'

His extraordinarii, thirty of them and more, moved past him, placing themselves and their blades between groups of trouble. Roberto put his shoulder into a legionary, sending him sprawling. The man came up again, sword raised. Roberto flicked off his scabbard and placed his blade to the man's chest.

'Don't even think about it,' he said. 'Back off, soldier.'

He turned at the sound of more swords and the thud of metal on cloth. Blood sluiced from a wound. Friends came to the aid of the stricken man, angry voices raised. The blow had been struck by a huge Atreskan. He swung round, looking for another target. He saw Roberto in his way. His gladius came up and down. Roberto parried easily, stepped forward and crashed the pommel of his own blade into the man's face, putting him down. He made to rise again, blinded by his fury, but a sword point nicked his neck. He let his own weapon fall from his hand.

'That would have been a very big mistake,' growled Davarov.

'I want this stopped now!' roared Roberto into the lessening din. 'I will have order in my camp.'

And slowly, he got it. Senior soldiers joined with the extraordinarii, pushing the two sides apart. Silence spread out from the centre of the conflict. Abuse still carried from both sides and the tent fires still crackled, despite the efforts being made to extinguish them.

'I will have quiet,' said Roberto.

He looked around him. The camp road was stained dark with blood in a dozen places. Injured and dead men and women lay on the ground. He counted thirty and there would be more damage among those hidden by the faces that stared back at him. Angry faces. He walked up and down between the lines of hastati. No one would meet his gaze. He handed his sword to Herides, who had appeared at his left shoulder.

'I am glad you were not involved in this stupidity,' he whispered to the young man, then raised his voice. 'Surgeons and stretcher parties, clear the wounded. I will talk to them later. As for the rest of you—'

'They called us traitors,' came a voice from the Atreskan side accompanied by gesticulating and more abuse.

'Quiet!' Roberto stalked across to the speaker. 'When I want to hear the reasons for this waste of blood, I will demand them.' He turned away. 'The next one who speaks before I order it will be flogged. The one after that will be executed. Am I clear?'

Silence.

'If the Tsardon are watching, they are surely celebrating victory tonight if they were not before. After all, they do not need to raise a blade against us and yet we shed blood and die. And this is how you, in all your wisdom, feel we should defeat the threat to our homes and families? Perhaps I should remove myself from this army and let the hastati decide where we march and when we fight.'

He let his voice swell to a shout.

'How dare you spill the blood of your comrades. Men and women with whom you have fought side by side these past years. How dare you lessen the reputation of this army. My army. Do you really want me to demand you leave your swords at the gates when you enter the camp? Are we children or are we the Conquord's finest?

'Well?'

There was a roar of assent.

'Yes. Yes we are,' said Roberto. 'And what you few have done is damage the wills of all. And you have disappointed me.'

He walked the lines again, saw the heads hung and the regret creep into the faces of those who dared look towards him. Around his feet, the surgeon teams were moving the injured and dead.

'I know some of you by name. I have heard your pride at serving in my army. Where is that pride now? Are you so delicate that you cannot take jibes? Is your mental constitution really so frail? Any who think so know where the gates to this camp are. I will not have you in my army. I will not have you fight under my mother's banner. You disgrace it, you insult it, you sully it.

'Do you think I care where your individual personal sympathies lie? You march as one under the Conquord banner. I will not have dissension. And I will not have any of those under my command raise a blade against another. We will build a ring for those who wish to fight over their petty grievances. And that is the only place it will happen.

'Anyone who breaks that rule from this moment on will be executed. No trial. No appeal. We are at war and I do not have the time for the unworthy.' He shook his head a final time. 'Idiots. All of you. Pathetic, posturing idiots. Look forward to long years in the hastati because neither the principes nor the triarii will have you. Get out of my sight.'

He spun and marched back towards his tent, calling his command team to him. Both Shakarov and Davarov were at his side in moments, both speaking into his ears. He ignored them until he reached his tent by which time all eight he expected were with him.

'Sit down, Goran, Davarov. Sit, sit.'

'General, you cannot let these slurs—'

'Goran, I will not repeat myself. This is already a long night, please do not make it any longer.'

Davarov put a hand on Shakarov's shoulder and the two of them sat. Elise, Dahnishev and Neristus were there. His masters of horse for his Atreskan legions were there too and the Master of Sword for the 8th Estorean.

'No one sits here without bearing a measure of guilt,' he said.

'General, there was pr—'

'I won't hear it, Goran. I just won't. Do not whine at me. You and I and all of us share this problem. We knew there would be tension when Nunan confirmed the Atreskan rebellion. We knew the alae would be torn and their morale hit. We knew the Estorean legion would feel under threat and outnumbered. We sat here in this tent and discussed all these things and how we would avoid them boiling into conflict.

'But it hasn't worked, has it? There were bound to be taunts and insults. Boys and girls do it at school and they never grow out of it. But we're running an army here, not a playground, and a punch on the nose is replaced by a spear in the gut. Dahnishev, how many are dead?'

'Seventeen,' said the surgeon. 'And eight more will never fight again. The other ten will not fight again this campaign year. I don't know how many are too ashamed to come forward with anything more minor.'

Roberto shrugged and shook his head. 'We are throwing away lives in advance of fighting for them. I expected tension, I expected fist fights. But I didn't expect sword fighting. This will be nipped in the bud. And I will execute transgressors, make no mistake.

'We're in a very difficult position here. We have no room east because the Toursan Lakelands and marshes will swallow us whole.

We know the Atreskan border is compromised and we need to stay away from it as long as possible to avoid courting trouble. And my outriders are busy killing more Tsardon scouts than you have had nights' sleep.'

'Do you think it was organised or an argument gone too far?' asked Neristus.

'Davarov, any thoughts? Goran? Anyone for that matter,' invited Roberto.

'There was no armour,' said Davarov. 'People just grabbed what they could. It was not premeditated.'

'I agree,' said Shakarov. 'It will have been sparked by one slur too many from an Estorean mouth.'

Roberto bit back his first thought. 'Or the first stab of an Atreskan blade,' he said. 'You were not there, Goran. Perhaps if you had been, this could have been avoided. Blame is an irrelevance in this instance. None who picked up a weapon is innocent but I will not conduct a witch hunt. We cannot afford the time nor the tension. Short-term, though, I want you organising cavalry captains and centurions from across the legions to sentry the infantry tents.' He held up his hands at the protest. 'Just until we see a little more calm in the daily routine.'

'We need a fight to take everybody's mind off it,' said Davarov.

'Nothing unites us more than a sight of the Tsardon,' said Shakarov.

'Does it?' asked Roberto, finding himself at the heart of his fears. 'Or does it remind those that still dream of an independent Atreska that they can strike a blow for it by turning on us?'

'How can we ever know that?' asked Dahnishev. 'There are over seven thousand Atreskans out there.'

'Yes, and I do not want to see a quarter of them marching to stand with the Tsardon at our next encounter. That, Goran, is what taxes the Estorean soldier's mind. Can they trust the maniple they stand beside?'

Shakarov stared at the floor. 'You are suggesting a quarter of our people are traitors?' he asked quietly.

'Do I really need to answer that question, Goran?'

Shakarov raised his head. 'Well how many do you think it might be?'

'I don't know,' snapped Roberto. 'These are men and women

under yours and Davarov's command. You tell me. What I saw out there tonight was not rebels fighting loyal Estoreans. It was people whose passions and fears had got the better of them to the detriment of us all. But none of us can afford to discount the fact that disaffected legionaries will have been amongst them, and may have struck the first blow. Tell me I'm wrong.'

The silence was answer enough.

'So what next?' asked Davarov.

'We march south. But we do so searching for an answer to these two questions. Do we have an army that will fight as one, side by side? And if we don't, how do we return it to that state? Because if these questions are not answered by the time we encounter significant Tsardon forces again, we might very well all be killed.'

'Sleep well.'

But no one did. The shouts and taunts rang out throughout the remainder of a still night. Roberto gave up trying to sleep four hours before dawn and ordered the camp roused for the march. So much had changed over so short a time. From victorious campaigning force, through the closeness they'd forged in the wake of the plague, to this.

'It takes years to build an army's heart and a day to break it,' said Elise Kastenas.

She was riding by Roberto who had chosen to lead the marching column. Estorean scouts were in the field after the failure to return of six Atreskan riders. A foraging party from the 15th Atreskan, the God's Arrows, was also overdue. More additions to Roberto's bleak mood.

'Proving we have failed at the most critical of times,' he said. 'I cannot believe I am having to place maniples of triarii in between bickering hastati of the 8th and 21st. Where did I go wrong?'

'You haven't gone wrong, Roberto,' said Elise a little sharply. 'The betrayal of Atreska cannot be attributed in any way to you.'

'But I should have seen the problems it would create. Taken stronger measures.'

'Your army is built on the independence of its command. It has worked for five years and we have never experienced anything close to defeat. But the fracturing of the Conquord rule in Atreska has ripped open old animosities.' She looked square at him. 'Don't doubt yourself. No one here doubts you.'

Roberto nodded. He knew she was right but couldn't shake the feeling that God was testing him now. He had experienced a smooth run to the generalship. His army had worked almost seamlessly. He knew he could take credit for much of that and the victories that followed but here and now was a challenge that outweighed any enemy he had faced.

'I don't doubt myself,' he said. 'But I am seriously disappointed that the biggest problem I have faced doesn't brandish a sword in my face, it creeps up behind me wearing the uniform of the Conquord.' He blew out his cheeks. 'I might be able to stop them killing each other but I can't stop them talking. It's like a virus, Elise. You can feel the discontent. Tell me, did you consider my questions last night?'

'I thought of little else.'

'And right now, how does it look to you?'

Elise checked behind to make sure they were not being overheard. She pointed towards a rise in the ground ahead. It was flanked by steep-sided hills that ran east into the Toursan Lakelands and west into the plains of Atreska.

'If we meet an enemy on the other side of that ridge, we will be in serious trouble. A Tsardon army of equal size could well take us. We've all been speaking to our listeners in the army and there is little doubt that the trust between legion and ala is gone. Certainly in the hastati, and it goes further up the chain. In the cavalry, things aren't so bad. We are not an effective fighting force. I don't think they will turn against us but Atreskan hastati will not die for the Conquord today.'

Roberto took off his green plumed helmet and pushed a hand through his hair. 'Then we are not an army at all, but a column of citizens. How do you think we can win them back?'

He already knew the answer but wanted to hear it from another.

'We can't,' whispered Elise. 'We are marching past their country and their families are there fighting for their lives and their futures. They can't understand why you haven't ordered them in to counter the invasion. They will not see the larger picture. We might be fighting for the Conquord but they have always been fighting to keep the Tsardon away from Atreska. It's the risk of the alae system.'

'You don't think the problems will calm once we approach Gestern.'

'They'll get worse,' said Elise. She smiled. 'Why are you asking me this? You already know. We'll be marching through southern Atreska. We've enough desertions now. Roberto . . .'

'I know. I know.'

The crushing weight of his disappointment grew. He turned in his saddle and looked back over the marching column, snaking away over miles of flat ground in the early dawn light. The sky was smudged with dust, alerting any watcher that an army was on the move.

'How many will we keep, do you think?'

'So many love you as their general. Davarov and Shakarov are wonderful commanders. In the end it's down to their desire to fight for you versus their desire to see their families safe and, for some, the desire to see Atreska liberated from the Conquord.'

'So it's a popularity contest.'

'I'm glad you're joking,' said Elise.

'Only just,' said Roberto. 'Yuran has much to answer for.'

'And he will.'

Roberto sat straight in the saddle, his decision made. 'Find the command team. When the camp build starts, I want you all with me. This must be handled correctly or we'll have more bloodshed to-night.'

'What do you suggest?'

Roberto met her gaze and felt his brooding anger threaten to overwhelm him.

'Every Atreskan will be given the same choice. To hold to the oath they swore when they joined the legions or to run back to their homes as cowards. And those who wish it will be stripped of their Conquord arms and put out of the camp. We will shadow them to the Atreskan border and leave them there. And I hope every man and woman who deserts this army is dead by dusas.' He looked back to the path ahead. 'I've got a war to win and I won't suffer such vermin in the uniform of my family.'

Chapter 54

848th cycle of God, 18th day of Solasfall
15th year of the true Ascendancy

Pavel Nunan and Dina Kell presided over a stitched-together legion that its citizens had named the 'Gesteris Revenge'. They had no artillery, fewer than two hundred cavalry and a ragbag of weapons and repaired armour. But they had fire in their bellies, an anger their joint commanders were only too happy to stoke.

Nunan marched alongside infantry from the Atreskan Rogue Spears and Shark's Teeth; the Tundarran Thunder; the Gosland Spear and Firedragons; and the Bear Claws and the Hurricanes of Estorr and the Estorean Lightning. They made up the bulk of those who had mustered in the Tarit Plain. Just shy of three thousand in all. There were messengers and fast riders moving ahead of the scouts. Those still too sick to move were being tended by volunteers in the original hiding place. No room for sentimentality. Those injured did not expect to be rescued and those that left them did not promise to return.

General Gesteris had entered the fords at Scintarit with eighteen legions. All were represented in this tiny band, comprising less than five per cent of the massive erstwhile conquering army. They had no real idea what they could achieve but following contact with Roberto Del Aglios, now was the time to move.

If Nunan was honest, he'd waited in the hope that Kell would return to them. He was happy to have her guile and leadership alongside his. They had marched for ten days straight, moving light and fast and covering up to thirty miles a day, mostly on the Conquord's deserted imperial highways. The scout network was efficient and they travelled unmolested to within two days of the border.

Nunan had taken them north at that point and they had crossed into Atreska by the old road a day later. The border forts they passed were deserted and had clearly been that way for some time. It had felt good to be back on soil they considered the Conquord's own and Nunan had called for calm.

He was glad for continuing warm weather but even so, he and every citizen who followed him craved hot meat and drink. As it was, all they had was dried and cured meat and the crushed herbal drinks they'd invented during their long period in hiding on the Tarit Plain. The dark camps enforced on them to avoid detection were becoming tiresome.

The camp was quiet and Nunan sat with Kell on a fallen log in the woodland that had presented itself as the perfect hiding place for the night. The horses were picketed close by and he could hear their gentle nickering as they settled to sleep.

'We're going to have to cross the river near Gull's Ford or we'll be forced too far north. The Tsardon and Atreskan rebels will fight their way to Neratharn's south coast border. It's the only realistic point to cross such a force and the place where the Conquord will mass to repel them.'

In the light of a bright moon, and with their eyes adjusted to the gloom, Kell was scratching lines in the sandy soil with a stick.

'If Gesteris is still alive, you think he'll head there?' asked Nunan.

'I can't think of anywhere else. He'll know the situation in Atreska inside out by now and I can't imagine him mounting any form of guerrilla defence. It's not his way. He and whoever's with him will get somewhere they can stage a pitched battle and halt the enemy. Neratharn has to be it. We've all read the stories about how hard it was for us to get into Atreska that way. Let's hope it's the same on the way back, eh?'

Nunan smiled. 'Then perhaps they'll use the sea, much as we did.'

'Fortunately the Atreskan navy isn't of sufficient size and the Tsardon have no ships in the Tirronean at all. Besides, the Ocetanas will already be on station.'

'Could get interesting there,' said Nunan.

'Very.'

Their conversation was interrupted by a brief commotion and some angry whispered words. There was a scuffling of feet and a man in a light cloak, tunic and sandals was thrust into their circle.

Around them, heads rose from bedrolls to look at the new arrival. A pair of scouts stood behind him, blades in hand.

'How dare you treat me like this,' spat the man. He had a wild look in his eyes, fervent and driven. 'This is my country. You have no right.'

Nunan put a finger to his lips. 'A moment,' he said. He addressed himself to the scouts. 'What's this all about?'

'We found him striding up the trail back there, heading to the border by the looks. He said he was going to find his wife and son in Tsard.'

'On your own?' said Kell. 'It's a dangerous place for an unarmed man. And if you don't mind me saying, you don't have the footwear for dusas.'

The four Conquord soldiers chuckled. In front of Nunan, the man dusted himself down.

'Don't laugh at me. I don't deserve it. Not from you. Not from the Conquord.'

Nunan gazed at him with the genesis of interest. 'Where are you from? Not far, by your clothing.'

'I killed the last man who laughed at me. He was Tsardon but perhaps you are my enemy too. I'm beginning to think that everyone is.'

'He's rambling.'

'I had to leave. No one will help me so I am helping myself.' He held out his hands. 'I'm telling the truth. Let me go.'

Nunan looked at his hands. They were filthy. Stained.

'Am I supposed to believe this is blood? I'll ask you again. Where are you from? We aren't going to hurt you.'

'Gull's Ford.'

Kell raised her eyebrows and Nunan smiled. 'Get this man a drink and some food,' he ordered a scout. 'Sit down. I am Pavel Nunan, Master of Sword. This is Dina Kell, Master of Horse.'

The man didn't know quite how to react. He looked around for somewhere to perch and found a legionary had rolled a log up for him. He smiled nervously.

'Go on,' said Kell. 'Take the weight off those sandals. Perhaps we can find you something more suited to your road ahead.'

'You would help me?'

'We'll help anyone who kills Tsardons. It makes us allies does it not?' said Kell.

'But first, an exchange of information,' said Nunan. 'Tell me about Gull's Ford and more particularly its river crossings. Then perhaps we can advise you in return, maybe persuade you from your quest. What's your name?'

'I am Han Jesson and nothing will keep me from finding my family.'

'I can respect that,' he said. 'Tell me. This Tsardon you killed. Who was he?'

'He was the sentor of the garrison occupying my village,' said Jesson. 'He insulted the memory of my wife. I found him drunk on the street when I was leaving and now his own knife lies among his entrails.'

Nunan saw Jesson's hands trembling.

'Never killed a man before?' he asked.

Jesson shook his head. 'I've never thrown a punch before and now I am a murderer.'

'If you're worried I'll see you stand trial,' said one of the scouts, bringing up a plate of cold food.

'Hey,' said Nunan. 'Enough.'

'Thank you,' said Jesson.

'How many of them are there?' asked Nunan.

'A couple of hundred, at most,' said Jesson. He brightened, seeing Nunan's expression. 'You don't mean to skirt the town, do you?'

Nunan shook his head. 'Where's the next nearest Tsardon garrison?'

'Don't hurt the people. They let the Tsardon in but they had no choice. They didn't understand.'

'Where is the next nearest Tsardon force?'

'Most towns have them but most of them are moving towards Neratharn or occupying Haroq. There is resistance in the Grand Central Plains but they have marched round it, most of them. That's what I've heard.' Jesson fidgeted. 'Don't hurt my friends.'

Nunan shrugged. 'We'll do what we can. But if there are sympathisers we cannot let them prosper. Look where you are now. Tsardon crawling all over your town.'

Jesson's eyes darkened. 'No one was a sympathiser until the Conquord ignored our pleas for help. You have brought this on yourselves. It is we who are the victims.'

Nunan raised his palms. 'Calm yourself, Han Jesson. This is not the place to be airing your grievances however justified you think they are. Not everyone will understand.'

Jesson sat back a little. 'They are not sympathisers,' he said quietly. 'They had no choice.'

'Most of the people sleeping in this woodland were once citizens just like you and the good people of Gull's Ford. They learned to fight.' He stood, looming over Jesson. 'There is always a choice.'

He walked away to find a place to rest, leaving Kell to tell the man about the folly he was so determined to undertake. Tomorrow. Tomorrow the Gesteris Revenge would taste first blood.

Arducius put his head down, hunched his shoulders and let the mule pick its own path. The wind howled along the valley, driving icy sleet and snow into their faces. It whipped in gusts that threatened to pitch them off their mounts and found its way inside their furs, chilling their bodies. The snow under the mule's hoofs was at least a foot deep and covering a layer of ice on which it often slipped, sending his stomach cart-wheeling.

Try as he might, Arducius couldn't keep his eyes fixed ahead or on his animal's head. And every time he looked left over the drop he felt sick, deep in his gut, and his head spun. Jhered had said that morning that they were twelve thousand feet up. It felt more like twelve thousand miles. Nothing had prepared them for this.

They were eight days out of the horrible border settlement of Ceskas. Arducius was sure only Jhered's sheer presence had stopped them being attacked. They had only spent one night there while the two Gatherers bought animals, furs, supplies and whatever else they thought they would need but it had been a long and sleepless one.

Out here, the Conquord technically held sway but there were no legionaries, no House of Masks and no basilica. A clutch of a couple of hundred wood and stone dwellings clinging to a barren hillside. Their only purpose, so far as Arducius could tell, was to overcharge prospectors travelling into Kark from the west and to buy goods from the Karku cheaply and sell them on into Gestern at huge profit.

Jhered had shrugged when Arducius had told him and repeated that line about the reality of life outside of Westfallen. But he'd also seen Jhered talking closely to Appros Menas and later on Gorian had said that the Gatherers would be coming to call when the war was done.

No one smiled in Ceskas. All they did was stare and calculate what profit they could make out of the new arrivals, dead or alive. Arducius was glad to leave, as they all had been. Now he wasn't so sure. Now he'd do anything to see another face and know there was civilisation of any sort around the corner.

Beneath him, his mule swayed sickeningly as it walked along the narrow path that climbed inexorably higher and higher into the Karku mountains. Arducius couldn't believe anyone lived here, let alone that an entire race apparently thrived in this desolation. He dared another look around him, trying to convince himself that he wasn't as scared as he felt.

The snow had abated for a moment and through the narrow slit in his scarves, the world was white and terrifying. He could brush his right hand along an ice-covered rock face that soared much further than he could see. Ahead of him, peaks galloped away into the distance, getting higher and higher, dominating the land and lowering down, daring them to come further. And looking down past his left boot, the ground fell away onto the endless teeth of rocks.

He was behind Jhered, his mule blinkered like all of them, plodding on stoically in the tracks of the Exchequer. Ossacer rode behind him, then came Mirron, Gorian and Kovan. Appros Menas brought up the rear. All of them were covered in snow. Ice was building in the fur trim of their heavy coats and over the front of their thick, wool-lined leather mittens.

And this was one of the principal routes along the Karku border, so Jhered said. Others that went deeper into the country were easier but much longer and the Karku guarded them jealously. That was where they lived in great numbers so the stories went. In beautiful stone-built houses, set around high mountain lakes where the air was crisp and fresh and the grass green and hearty. It sounded idyllic. And a ridiculous notion.

Arducius sighed. The only vegetation he could see were a few gnarled trees clinging grimly to the mountainsides, and short brush and heather flattened by the wind and ice. How it lived here was a marvel but there it was. Arducius could feel the life energy pulsing slow and determined through the roots and into the leaves. They were like oases of light in the dead, cold, bleak rock. The only other energies he could sense around their small party were the fleeting lights of birds and rodents.

Ahead, Jhered pushed them on as fast and as far as he could each day. Arducius had watched him get ever more serious and concerned as they made their slow progress. He said little whenever they stopped, consulted his maps, gazed out at the ranks of mountains that hemmed them in on all sides. It all looked the same to Arducius. Awesome, but still an unending canvas. How easy it would be to enter here and never ever find the way out.

Like every morning they had risen before first light, eaten a hot breakfast and been on their way as dawn crept over the eastern peaks. They rode without further food, pausing only to rest the mules or walk them if they could, until the sun began to set. It was a short day and a long night here. Further up, where Jhered appeared to be heading, they would enjoy more light.

They had travelled up steep clefts, over broad plateaus, through staggering gorges and across bleak low plains where the wind had battered the vegetation into submission. They had been on this path, winding higher and higher up, for two days now. Last night they had slept in a tiny alcove that had been hacked out of the blank mountain side by someone ages past.

Today, they had been more fortunate. An hour or more before the sun set, they came across a wide natural cleft in the rock. It was sheltered from the worst of the weather. Tough-barked trees grew up its sheer faces, heathers dug their roots into the thin layer of frozen earth and moss grew on every rock surface. The southern face was covered in snow and ice. The northern face was a riot of colour, quite at odds with almost everything else they had seen in the last few days. Jhered had not even paused to consider moving on and it was not long before their bivouac leather was staked to the walls and a fire was roaring in the lee of the cliff.

The Ascendants and Kovan had climbed gratefully from their mules, which were now tethered to trees at the back of the cleft, and had huddled together around the fire to thaw slowly. Jhered had set a pot over the flames Mirron had created and a thick vegetable and mutton soup was bubbling away.

In front of them, the snow was thickening again, blowing past the entrance to the cleft in a cloud of huge flakes. Jhered was staring at it from beneath his perpetual frown. Arducius saw that Gorian and Mirron were looking out at it too and the reason why had never changed.

'Just think,' said Ossacer. 'Thirty days ago, we were swimming under Genastro Falls and Father Kessian was helping us understand how to harness the wind energies.'

Gorian was smiling sadly, his head nodding at the memory. Mirron's eyes had filled with tears just like Ossacer's, and Arducius felt loss pulling at his heart.

'So short a time and it seems like forever,' said Mirron.

'And it's still hot in Westfallen,' said Gorian, rubbing his hands together harder over the crackling flames.

He, like all of them, had experimented with keeping himself warm by drawing on the energies around them. But high up here that meant using the mules or the scattered life of plants; and the former made the mules scratchy while the latter made the Ascendants too tired. It had been a great disappointment to Gorian not to be able to get one up on Jhered, who felt the cold like all of them. Of course he and Menas never complained.

'Get used to it,' said Jhered, not turning. 'Wishing yourself back home won't get you there. Winning the war will.'

'So you keep saying,' said Gorian.

'Because you refuse to accept what is front of your faces.'

'We've only got your word we should be doing this. Vasselis's men had it all worked out and it wouldn't have meant us freezing to death.'

Jhered turned and his gaze on Gorian was baleful. 'No, it would have meant you blundering into Atreskan rebels or Tsardon armies instead. If you think that a better path, then take your mule and go back.' He stirred the soup. 'Your argument is single-tracked and tedious. I don't care if you trust me or not. I don't care if you hate me or not. But you will do your duty to the Conquord as directed by me.'

'Why you?' said Gorian. 'What makes you so special you can order us around?'

Arducius saw Jhered's hand tighten on the spoon but his face didn't twitch a muscle. 'Because I am the commanding officer of any I demand. And I demand it of you.'

'Do you think we can really make a difference?' asked Arducius. 'How can we win a war that all the legions cannot?'

Jhered looked at him, at all of them, and his frown lifted for a moment. 'I really don't know. All I do know is that we have to make an attempt. We have to try. The Omniscient will welcome us into His embrace if we do so. If we do not, we deserve nothing and will get nothing.

'What part you will play and when, I can't see yet. But I do know this. What you have causes fear. And fear is the greatest weapon an army possesses. We could lose the Conquord unless we can turn the tide of the Tsardon advance soon. We have to try anything we can. We have to take their belief and turn it into fear.'

'I won't hurt anyone,' said Ossacer. 'That is not what I was born to do.'

'Perhaps you won't have to,' said Menas, coming to the fire from tending the mules.

'How can we avoid it if we are to beat the Tsardon?' asked Mirron. 'How can you ask us to do this?'

'Because you are part of the Conquord and you must fight to save it!' shouted Jhered. 'God-embrace-me, girl have I not got through to you at all? If you ever want to return to the peace you knew in Westfallen you have to act now.'

Kovan stood. 'Exchequer Jhered, please. We've had enough. We're tired and cold and hungry.'

Jhered nodded and a brief smile crossed his face. 'All right, young Vasselis. Let's talk of anything else if it'll make you happier. But think on this. There are many ways to win wars and only one of them is to strike your enemy down and kill him. Think of your powers. Think of what they can do—' He stopped suddenly. '—what's wrong, Ossacer?'

Arducius turned round. Both Ossacer and Gorian were distracted, sampling the trails. Arducius couldn't sense anything out of the ordinary. His head and body were full of the power of the weather that he knew would not abate for days if they stayed here in the heights.

'There's something . . .' began Ossacer, clutching Arducius's arm.

The mules began to buck and strain at their tethers, catching some scent on the wind that howled like a thousand wolves around the opening of the cleft. Jhered, Kovan and Menas were on their feet in moments, swords from scabbards, shields grabbed from the ground.

'Get behind us,' said Jhered. 'Keep behind the fire.'

Arducius beckoned the Ascendants to him. Glancing back, he thought he saw shapes moving on the sheer faces of rock but it had to be a trick of the firelight.

From both sides of the path, creatures padded in, crouched low to the ground and ready to spring. There were four of them and at first, Arducius thought them dogs. But they were more like lions with the bulk of bears. They were completely white, from the tips of their snouts to their long tails, which were cocked like scorpions' stings above their backs. Their legs were powerful and their jaws packed with yellowed teeth for tearing and crushing. They had large eyes hooded by heavy brows and long hooked claws gripped the ice.

'Gorthock,' said Jhered. 'Get your shields in front of you. They'll work in a team so if they go for you, cover yourself. The other two of us must work fast and clean. Those jaws crush armour. Don't hesitate.'

Arducius caught the fear in Jhered's voice and knew they were in real trouble. He heard more skittering behind him and looked again but the walls were empty. It must be the sound of branches on rock. He turned back and Gorian was walking forwards.

'Gorian, stop.' Mirron's voice was panicked.

Jhered glanced left. 'Gorian, get back. This is not the time.'

'It is always the time,' said Gorian.

The gorthock had switched their attention to him now and he was already in front of the swords, too far from defence. Arducius heard low growls and the scratch of claws on rock and ice.

'What's he doing?' asked Mirron, clutching Arducius's sleeve.

'Watch,' said Ossacer

With his heart pounding, Arducius fixed on the scene in front of him and prayed that Gorian wasn't demonstrating fatal over-confidence. There was nothing Jhered or the others could do now. Gorian was kneeling on the ground, his arms outstretched in the direction of the gorthock. If they chose to strike, he would be killed.

Gorian was speaking but Arducius couldn't hear him properly. He was facing the nearest gorthock. The beast was staring at him while the others closed in on him, trapping him. The furthest animal twitched and feinted a move. Gorian didn't flinch. He held out a hand and the lead animal came towards him, rising from its hunting stance.

'It's beautiful,' said Ossacer.

'I can't see through the weather trails,' said Arducius, sensing only the blaring life energy maps of the gorthock in the midst of the snow and wind.

'He's linking with them. Forcing his calm on them. His will.'

The gorthock put its snout in his hand then licked his palm. It growled again. Gorian moved his hand and massaged the loose folds of skin and thick fur under its throat. It nuzzled his shoulder. He stretched out his other arm and a second gorthock began to walk to him, as did the third. Their tails relaxed and fell to trail along the ground. The first one was sitting now, nothing more than a puppy under Gorian's control. He was moving his attention between them, calming them, taking their aggression from them.

Arducius saw the others watching on in admiration and amazement. Not Jhered, though. He was fixed on the last gorthock which had not moved from its striking stance. It was absolutely still but for a slight quiver along its flanks. Whatever control Gorian had over the other three, it had not affected the fourth.

There was a momentary pause that seemed to stretch to eternity. And in it, the path of fate was laid out. Mirron had started to scream the same instant that the gorthock leapt. Gorian hadn't seen it, so wrapped up was he in the warmth of the other three.

Its guttural roar split the dusk. Its body was a blur through the air. But it was still not fast enough. Jhered dived at it, shield outstretched, colliding with its flank and driving it towards the edge of the cleft and towards the path. It turned and scrabbled at the shield, locking claws on to it and trying to bite over the top.

The two slithered on, their momentum carrying them onto the ice. Jhered turned his body and jabbed his sword into the slick surface, trying in vain to slow them.

'Oh no,' said Arducius.

Kovan and Menas had moved with Jhered and were after him now. Menas grabbed at the back of his cloak and struck her heels into the ice, sending up shards in a spray. Kovan ran for the gorthock's head. He'd abandoned his shield and was holding his sword in both hands. Jhered and the beast cleared the cleft and slipped on to the path. The gorthock bit again, its jaws splintering the shield, its claws still gripping tight. Its tail was whipping above its head, searching for purchase.

They were slowing, but not enough. Menas grunted with the exertion, Jhered tried to shake the gorthock free and the animal, sensing its peril, howled for help. In the moment it cleared the lip, Kovan's sword crashed down on its neck, all but severing its head. Its grip slackened and it fell over the precipice. The sudden change in weight took Menas by surprise and she fell hard on her backside. Jhered's sword bit again and he slowed to a panting, grateful halt, his legs dangling into nowhere.

The other three gorthock barked fury.

'Stop!' commanded Gorian and their throats were silent.

Jhered climbed to his feet, helped Menas to hers and nodded his thanks to Kovan. He scabbarded his sword and clapped the young Vasselis on the shoulder. Looking beyond the fire, his expression chilled and his hand was at his hilt again. Arducius spun round to see six figures emerge from the back of the cleft and walk into the firelight.

'Karku,' he said.

They studied the Ascendants closely, moving past them to Gorian and the gorthock. Jhered, they ignored completely and he motioned to Kovan and Menas to lower their weapons.

The Karku were dressed in fur and leather. Like the surgeon on the *Cirandon's Pride* they were short in the body but with long arms and legs. Their feet were bare but covered in a thick hair and their toes, like their fingers, were unusually long, with thick nails springing from their tips. Their faces were dark with hair too and their heads heavy with tight curls or hidden beneath fur skull caps.

They grouped around Gorian and one knelt by him, reaching out a hand to touch him. Others looked to the animals which Arducius could now see wore thick leather collars.

'They're pets,' he said.

'Hunting animals,' said Mirron, the fear gone from her voice. 'I don't think you could call them pets.'

'Can we go to Gorian?' asked Ossacer.

'No,' said Jhered. He walked back to the fire. 'Let's see what happens. The Karku won't hurt him.'

'Where did they come from?'

'Down the walls, I expect,' said Jhered. 'They are remarkable climbers.'

Arducius looked at the blank, sheer faces, shrouded in shadow. So he had seen them. He still didn't believe it.

'What are they doing?' asked Mirron.

'I have absolutely no idea,' said Jhered.

'They sense something about us,' said Ossacer.

'I'm not surprised,' said Kovan. 'How did Gorian do that?'

Ossacer didn't have time to answer. The Karku next to Gorian was talking. His Estorean was halting but coherent. The language of trade made it even here to the far reaches of the world.

'You are of the Haran-gor. A Parack-al.'

'What is that?' asked Gorian. 'What does that mean?'

The Karku shook his head. 'I cannot . . .' he said.

'Exchequer Jhered?' asked Gorian.

'Roughly translated, Haran-gor means Watcher of the Mountains . . . like a warden, a keeper, something like that. Like your name in a way. Gorian means "Man-of-the-mountain" in Karku.'

'Gorian,' said the Karku. 'You?'

'Yes,' said Gorian.

'You are blessed. Another Gorian lived here when the mountains were younger.'

'The first Gorian hid here when we was chased from Caraduk,' said Gorian. 'I'm named after him.'

The Karku nodded and rose to his feet, holding out a hand which Gorian took.

'What does Parack-al mean?' asked Mirron.

Jhered raised his eyebrows. 'Herd Master.'

'How can they know that?' asked Arducius.

'There's plenty we don't know about the Karku,' said Jhered. 'Perhaps the first Gorian stumbled on something he didn't ever record.'

Three of the Karku had leashed their gorthock and were walking them away. The beasts strained to remain with Gorian but their masters' strong words turned them. The other three walked back to the fire.

'Haran-gor.' They nodded to the Ascendants. 'Welcome to Kark. Exchequer Jhered, your name is known. Your passage with your friends is assured.'

'Thank you,' said Jhered, bowing. He spoke slowly and deliberately. 'I am sorry for the death of your beast. It attacked and I had to defend.'

'It is forgiven. He was old and his mind dull and slow. Gorian could not penetrate it.' The Karku paused. It was impossible to tell his age but Arducius got the impression he was quite old. 'What takes you through Kark? This is poor season for travelling the high passes.'

'I must reach a man fighting for the Conquord in Tsard but our way is blocked by the enemy through Atreska. Time is short. I had no choice but to come this way.'

The Karku nodded. 'Rest. Wait for us. There is help we can give and things you must know.'

Arducius watched the Karku. They walked to the walls and began to climb almost without pause. They were quick, their fingers and toes finding every tiny crack and giving them the purchase to move. In no time, they were lost to sight in the darkness and snow which, unnoticed, had begun to fall heavily once more.

Menas spooned soup into bowls and handed it round along with some bread. The soup had caught on the bottom of the pan and tasted a little burned but to Arducius, it was nectar.

'Tell me something, Gorian,' said Jhered. 'How many animals could you control that way?'

'I don't know. If it was cattle or sheep, maybe a whole herd. Those gorthock were more intelligent, more difficult to will. Why?'

'Just a thought. Now eat up and let's get some sleep. There's been quite enough excitement for one night.'

'Exchequer?'

'Yes, Gorian.'

'Thank you.'

Chapter 55

848th cycle of God, 19th day of Solasfall
15th year of the true Ascendancy

Nunan and Kell had roused the Revenge five hours before dawn and moved them the couple of miles to Gull's Ford in half-maniples of infantry, sections of archers and small companies of riders. The cavalry had all stopped well out of earshot while the infantry advanced to encircle the town at a half-mile distance.

Gull's Ford's occupiers were lazy and overconfident and the Conquord legionaries disciplined and skilled. With Han Jesson's detailed and accurate advice on the lie of the land surrounding his town, they had completed their manoeuvres in good time for the attack. First light was imminent and Nunan was stood ready to signal the horns.

The time for silence was done. There was a fire in his belly. Raiding and skirmishing were fundamentally unsatisfying. Brief though this might be, it was a blow for the Conquord. A retaking of land. A statement of intent.

'We'll take this town like in the old days,' he shouted to his infantry in earshot. 'House by house, street by street to the forum. Leave no Tsardon free. Let's round them up or cut them down.'

A cow lowed in a field down slope. He heard the bleating of sheep. Peace for a heartbeat. He swept his arm down. Horns sounded, the blaring taken up in relay and shuddering away across the plains.

'Reckon they'll be awake now,' he said. 'Revenge! Let's do some damage.'

They double-timed the short distance, Conquord songs in every throat. Nunan was at the head of the forces coming in from the east. Kell was around the other side of the town. The rumbling of feet and hooves blew away the quiet of dawn. Nunan saw his first sight of Gull's Ford, lying sleepily in its shallow river valley and saw figures running in amongst the tenements and villas. He hoped they were scared.

Conquord infantry poured into the streets of Gull's Ford. Half-maniples broke into units of five to make the house-to-house searches while others ran the streets. Archers headed for the rooftops around the forum while cavalry patrolled the borders for runners on foot or horseback.

Nunan's two hundred surged across the ford and up into the town's main street. They were running in close form, shields up in a wall and over their heads against the few arrows fired at them. Exactly as ordered, his legionaries peeled off from the back of the wall to take each house. He heard timbers splintering as doors went down.

Ahead, the forum was alive. Stalls had been set up for the day's trading but the basilica was busy with Tsardon, not traders. People were running directionless while the Revenge closed the net. Nunan scented battle and ordered his infantry to the charge. Many of the Tsardon were billeted in the basilica and they were boiling out onto the floor of the forum. Most appeared only half-dressed, perhaps groggy after a night's drinking. So much the better.

Nunan led his troops in. A hundred at his back now, the rhythmic sound of their feet sending confidence soaring through their bodies. They slowed and moved to a wider front. Twenty across, five deep and with a handful of archers covering them from behind and from the buildings ringing the forum. The Tsardon knotted into a loose formation. Someone was barking orders and more were hurrying from the basilica. Nunan guessed he faced fifty.

'Space!' he yelled. The fighting line spread to give room to strike.

The Tsardon backed away, unwilling to commit. A few began to break off from the back, heading for the northern and eastern exits of the forum. Conquord archers began to fire over Nunan's head. There was a concerted move away by the enemy; then they broke and ran. Straight into the path of more Revenge citizens. The net closed.

'Fight!'

Nunan charged at the remaining Tsardon who had moulded into a small and determined ring. He kept his head down behind his shield, only his eyes showing above it, and bulled into them. He felt them give. He stabbed out with his gladius, feeling the blade slip deep into flesh. There was a warm rush of blood over his arm. He dragged it back and stabbed again. Further right this time but he was blocked down. The counter came in. He pulled his shield round and took the blow full on. He took a short pace back.

A body fell at his feet. One of his own men, skull smashed. He jabbed his shield forward and up, butting the enemy under the chin. Nunan moved in, butted again and stabbed right to keep others away. His men closed in around him, the noise increased as more joined the press from the far side. Blood fountained into the air on his left. A Tsardon throat ripped out by a slashing gladius.

Nunan felt a blade rake down the front of his shield. He responded, opening his defence and powering his gladius forwards. The Tsardon hadn't laced up his armour and the blade pierced his heart. Enemy numbers were diminishing rapidly but they wouldn't stop fighting. Once more he stepped up, his elbows tucked in and his head low. His gladius licked out again, to be deflected off a mail shirt. He followed it up with another shield drive.

Such inevitability. There was no gap for the Tsardon to exploit. Just a wall of shields, embossed with the Conquord crest to remind them who it was they faced. Who it was defeated them. The last of them died in a welter of thrusts and the cheer rang out around the forum.

'Let's clean up!' barked Nunan. 'Sweep this place. Ten with me to the basilica and two archers.'

He was in no mood to pause and bask just yet. Elsewhere in the forum, citizens were herded into groups and guarded. A ring of his archers stood around the open space. It was nearly done.

'Let's not be casual,' he said. 'Never trust a Tsardon.'

His ten brought their shields in front of them and walked in a single row towards the basilica. Beyond its columns, darkness was punctuated by the light of lanterns and torches in its depths. They walked up the wide marble stair. Nunan heard movement within.

'Keep moving,' he said. 'Archers, keep it close. Flanks, do not ignore the shadows. Be sure.'

Their boots rang out in the vaulted space. Inside, the ranks of benches were empty. Behind them, the noise of the town dulled to echoes. There were doors left and right at the head of the basilica, leading to the administrative offices. A large Atreskan flag hung at the back wall. Tsardon flags and banners stood in stands around the magistrates' chairs and table.

'Tsardon warriors. It is over.' Nunan's voice was loud in the colonnaded chamber. 'The Conquord has reclaimed this territory. Show yourselves. You cannot win.'

The basilica was empty. Nunan motioned six men to the left hand door and took the others right. The door opened inwards. He nodded to a legionary. She unlatched it and pushed, stepping back smartly behind her shield. Three arrows whipped out. None found flesh.

'There's no way out,' said Nunan. 'Put your weapons down and come out.'

'There is always an escape,' came a voice, thickly accented, unafraid.

'Take a look through the windows or the side doors. The Conquord is everywhere. Gull's Ford is ours.'

'Pitiful,' said the voice. 'Your resistance is beaten. We march on Neratharn. What is one small town? It is we who are everywhere.'

Footsteps. Nunan peered from behind his shield. Figures were approaching from the deep shadows along a passageway. He held up a hand to stay his archer. There were five Tsardon. Three carried bows, arrows nocked and ready. They walked behind two who held blades to the throats of women in front of them. Behind Nunan, his other six came running, presumably having found nothing.

'This is the true face of the brave Tsardon warrior,' said Nunan. 'Let them go.'

'You would slaughter us the same way you did those who faced you in the forum.'

'I will cut down no man who surrenders. We are the Conquord.'

The Tsardon came to the doorway. Nunan could see that both women were middle-aged. Their robes suggested high office in this town. Neither struggled. The one on the left, the town's praetor, had a proud bearing.

'What is your name?' he asked.

'Gorsal,' she said.

'And you preside over a town given without a fight to the Tsardon.' He looked to the man holding her. 'Let them go. I will not ask again.'

'They will die before you strike me down.'

Nunan shrugged. 'So be it. I bear them no respect for what they have done.'

Uncertainty flickered in the Tsardon's eyes. Nunan turned to his archers.

'Best shot,' he said.

They fired. Gorsal's captor had no time to carry out his threat. The shaft took him through the eye and he dragged her to the ground as he fell. The other woman was not so lucky. The arrow pierced her neck and she dropped clutching and gasping, leaving the enemy open.

'Take them,' said Nunan. 'Kill them.'

The Tsardon loosed their arrows even as they begged for mercy. But Nunan just watched as the weight of his infantry forced them back inside the passageway. The clash of swords was brief and the sound of sword driving through armour into flesh satisfying.

He gave his shield to an archer and knelt by Gorsal. 'You are unhurt?'

'Yes,' she said and looked to her right where her companion was being tended by one of Nunan's people. 'Will she live?' The legionary shook his head.

'I'm sorry,' said Nunan. 'I had no choice.'

Gorsal's face hardened. 'No, indeed. Those with no respect deserve little else.'

Nunan stood and held out a hand for Gorsal. 'That was for Tsardon ears. We know what happened here.'

Gorsal took the hand a little reluctantly and hauled herself to her feet. 'How?'

'A citizen of yours passed through our camp last night. Han Jesson.'

'Han? They were looking for him. He killed the sentor.'

'So he said. He's beyond them now but he won't succeed in his search for his family. Tsard will claim him.'

'Poor man. It would be a blessing,' said Gorsal.

Nunan nodded and strode back out towards the forum. The legion was gathering. Cavalry were at its borders and Tsardon prisoners were herded and penned in its centre. He raised his gladius.

'Victory!'

The answering roar rolled on long, more relief than triumph. Nunan held up his hands for quiet and felt a flash of nerves. Was this how a general felt? He had never addressed this many people before. Legionaries, cavalry, enemies, ordinary citizens.

'People of Gull's Ford. You have tasted the reality of allegiance with Tsard. You have experienced their diplomacy. Burning, kidnap, murder and execution. Any who feel their lives are better under Tsardon control, the border is that way.'

He jerked his thumb behind him. In front of him, his legionaries laughed and cheered.

'This land belongs to the Conquord. Go back to your homes, take down the flags they made you unfurl and take up arms against the common enemy.' He pointed at the Tsardon, perhaps forty of them, standing dishevelled and beaten. 'There they stand. Your so-called liberators. Men who use women as shields to save their own pathetic lives. Men who would rather be hiding behind their mother's skirts than face their foe with courage.

'The people of this town were subjected to decimation. So shall you be treated. And the rest shall be released to these people's mercy. I will be praying as we march to destroy your armies that they find they have none for you. Revenge, prepare to march.'

Roberto rode out of the principal gate shadowed by thirty of his extraordinarii. Behind him, the abuse rained down on those gathered in front of the gates and surrounded by Elise's cavalry. Taunts and threats which Roberto had no desire to quell. Every man and woman who had chosen to leave his army was another scratch across his heart. But among the almost seven hundred, *seven hundred*, who had chosen to return to fight in Atreska, none had wounded him more than Goran Shakarov.

The former Master of Sword of the 15th Ala, the God's Arrows, stood with all the others. Stripped of sword and armour, stripped of all rights as a Conquord soldier. Roberto still couldn't believe it. The Atreskans stood and formed into ranks as he approached, Shakarov at their head. Behind Roberto, the taunts began to die down on the packed ramparts; everyone strained to hear what their General said.

'There is no honour in what you do,' he said. 'There is no sense in such foolish action. None of you have considered the future and now none of you have a future. When the Conquord retakes Atreska, your part will not be acknowledged. You think you go to protect your homes and families? You do not. You go to fuel the fires of rebellion, whether you wish it or no.

'That I have not labelled you deserters is a gift to you, granted only because you have all served me well in battle. But your decision marks a lack of faith in the Conquord that I can neither forgive, nor forget.

'To those among you harbouring joy that you can return to what you think is an independent Atreska, I wish you nothing but death at the hands of the Conquord's loyals. To those of you going to stand alone in front of their homes against the tide of Tsard that comes before the cleansing of the Conquord, I say this. From myth and legend of ancient kingdoms and empires come many sayings that resonate even today. One is particularly pertinent: there are no tears shed by the mother of a coward.

'And who is he who returns home before the battle is done? I hope you are shunned by your families as I shun you now. If you should die, I would not miss one beat of sleep. Your shame will bear you down with a weight you can never hope to shake.' He stared at Shakarov.

'You mean nothing to me now or ever. I do not know you.'

The big Atreskan met his gaze but there was no regret in his eyes.

'One day we will shake hands as friends again, General,' he said. 'We do not disrespect you. But there are times when loyalty to our country must come above loyalty to the leaders we love. Do not leave us with hate.'

Roberto's despair threatened to overwhelm him. He wanted nothing more than to beg Shakarov to stay. To bring the passion of these people four square behind the Conquord. A passion that could sweep the Tsardon aside. But behind him, he sensed a new trust. A new belief. And he would do anything to nurture it.

He kept his head steady, turned his horse and rode back to the camp to the cheers of his army. He didn't pause until he had reached his tent, where he dismounted, swept inside and threw his helmet across the space. Herides stooped and picked it up to place it on its stand.

'Out,' said Roberto. 'Find me Davarov and Kastenas.'

They had followed him from the gates and at the sound of their names ducked into the tent even as Herides scurried out. Roberto slumped on to his cot and put his head in his hands. Tears were threatening. Tears and rage. He could afford neither.

'You did what had to be done,' said Elise.

'Spare me your damned understanding,' he snapped. 'It is a failure.

A failure of my leadership and a failure of the Conquord system.' He raised his head. 'Sorry, Elise, that was unworthy.'

She said nothing but nodded acknowledgement. Davarov was struggling with Shakarov's decision.

'They have betrayed us, like Yuran has,' he said. 'You should have had them all killed.'

'But there's the rub. They believe they are going back to save their country from Tsard and the rebels. Do you really believe Shakarov a traitor?' Roberto pushed himself up from his cot and went to a table set with wine and goblets. He filled three and handed them round.

'At every turn, the curse on this army strengthens,' he said. 'But never did I think my own soldiers would turn against me in such numbers. It will not be allowed to happen again. How many are we now?'

'Desertions have been high these last days,' said Elise. 'But today you still command in excess of eleven thousand.'

'I came to Tsard with almost twenty.'

'But those that remain will follow you anywhere,' said Davarov. 'You've felt the mood.'

'It has been the only blessing these last days,' said Roberto. 'There have to be changes to the way we operate. I can't have Atreskan and Estorean lining up as separate legions. Not now. Davarov, I'm placing you in charge of all the infantry. Elise, you have all the cavalry. Pick your personal command teams well. We will drill together on the march to Gestern. Forget those who have gone. We've wasted too much time. Thirty miles a day from here to Gestern or we won't have a Conquord to save when we get there. And when we do, we will fall on the Tsardon with a violence they will not survive. We are the fist of God and His punch levels mountains.'

Dawn's light was growing and the Karku would be back soon. The snow had not let up and the wind howled into and around the cleft. They were all awake now and waiting. Mirron felt low this morning. She was sitting apart, her hands playing in the flames of the fire. She let the tongues lick up her fingers and warm her. There was comfort in the chaotic energies. They were hypnotic too and she had to take care not to let the fire reach her clothes.

'Here. Something to warm your insides, too.'

Mirron looked up. It was Menas. She was holding a steaming tin mug. Mirron didn't really need it but it wasn't Menas's fault she didn't understand. She took a hand from the fire and accepted the drink.

'Thank you,' she said. 'Want to sit down?'

Menas smiled. 'I'd like that very much.'

Mirron shifted along the log a little way. She sipped her drink. It was sweet herbs and tasted great on a freezing evening.

'What's your real name?' asked Mirron.

'You already know it,' said Menas.

'No, your first name. The one the Exchequer never calls you.'

Menas laughed. 'He does sometimes. When he thinks no one else can hear. It's Erith.'

'Pleased to meet you, Erith Menas.'

'And you Mirron . . . ?'

'Well it depends,' said Mirron. 'My mother is Gwythen Terol but my Ascendancy name is Westfallen. All of us are the same.'

Menas smiled. 'And which do you prefer?'

'Westfallen,' she said. 'It reminds me of home.'

Mirron looked away in case a tear fell. Menas was quiet but she was watching. Mirron felt a hand on her shoulder.

'It seems so far, doesn't it?' she said.

'Every time I open my eyes, I don't believe what I'm seeing,' said Mirron. 'Just for a moment. It's the best bit of the day. The only bit when I can fool myself I'm still at home.'

Menas knew she was going to break and hugged her to her chest.

'I'm sorry,' Mirron said. 'I'm sorry.'

'What for?' asked Menas. 'I'm just amazed it's taken you so long. Let it out,'

'It's not right.' Her voice was muffled by Menas's cloak. The smell of wool was strong in her nostrils. 'I shouldn't be here. This isn't how my life was supposed to be.'

'Shhh. I know. It's hard but not even you have power over your own destiny. None of us do.'

'You do,' said Mirron. 'You decided to join the Gatherers. You chose your own path.'

Mirron pushed away and wiped at her eyes. Menas smoothed loose hair back behind her ear.

'And you think the path I chose was a frozen mountain pass in Kark?'

'No.' Mirron laughed. 'I see what you mean.'

'And these?' Menas touched the scars on her face. 'I didn't chose these either.'

'How did you get them?'

Menas smiled though it didn't touch her eyes. 'Not everyone wants to pay their taxes. Look, Mirron—'

'Are you all right over there?' It was Gorian.

'Yes, thank you,' said Menas. 'Nothing you can understand. This is woman talk.'

She winked at Mirron, who laughed again. 'It's so easy for them. It's like some big adventure.'

'I think it might be harder,' said Menas. 'That's what they want you to think but their fears take them in the quiet of the night. Don't let them fool you. At least you can admit your feelings.'

'It doesn't seem to help much.'

'Believe me, it does,' said Menas. 'Look, Mirron, it's hard for a woman in the wilds. Even a legion woman. Most men will assume weakness in you in their arrogance. So you need to see through it and be able to prove yourself. You can do it with your ability. I do it with my bow and my sword and with the crest I bear. But it's a long time earned.'

'That isn't fair. The Advocate is a woman.'

'No, it isn't, and yes, she is. And she had to earn her respect harder than any male Advocate, believe me. And some men will never believe we should attain positions of influence and responsibility because they say we can't deal with the pressure. They conveniently forget that countless men crumble under pressure and point at those few women who have done the same. Like the Chancellor. Hardly a role model for anyone.'

Mirron felt the chill of memory through her.

'Sorry,' said Menas. 'I shouldn't have said that.'

'It's all right, Erith. I understand what you mean. Don't worry. I'll try and be more like the Advocate. Or you.'

Menas blushed. 'Oh, I'm not so great.'

'I think you are. I'm glad you're here.'

'Well, that's down to a man so I suppose there are exceptions. The Exchequer understands more than we all think he does.'

'Is he really as good as all the stories Kovan tells?'

'I expect so,' said Menas. 'And for all he can be rude and brutish sometimes, he's staking his reputation and his life on what you can do. He believes in you and that is a powerful thing to have on your side.'

Mirron stared out at Jhered, who was talking to Kovan and going over some sword moves.

'I wonder if he'll ever admit it?' she said.

'What's that?' asked Menas.

'Nothing. Nothing at all.'

Chapter 56

848th cycle of God, 20th day of Solasfall
15th year of the true Ascendancy

There were paths through the mountains. Jhered had always suspected it but the Karku concealed them from any unschooled eye. He
didn't much care. Just to be inside, away from the deepening freeze,
and to hear the Ascendants begin to relax was enough.

And while they rode or led their mules under lantern-light, deep
into the mountainsides, he knew they were travelling fast. The crow
could not fly straighter towards the Tsardon border. Their three
Karku guides, like the entire race, were an enigma. The metal and
minerals they discovered and mined with such skill were at the root
of their trading power and their diplomatic strength and yet they
were clearly uncomfortable below the ground.

'I will not believe they are a race of claustrophobes,' whispered
Menas.

Her voice echoed loud in the passage they travelled. It was wide
enough for two mules abreast and would probably have taken a
small cart. Its ceiling was only a few inches above Jhered's head as he
rode but then he would be a giant among the Karku. The passage was
rough-cut but smoothed by the movement of people and animals
over the ages since it had been made. For the most part it was
unadorned but periodically, they'd seen paintings or symbols etched
into the rock, depicting sun, mountain, tree and water.

Ahead of them, one of the Karku turned. Jhered tried to recall his
name. Harban-Qvist, that was it. The first name a given, the second a
traditional tribal identifier.

'You think us all miners, cave rats desiring to exist in the confines
of the living mountain,' he said, irritated. Menas tensed. 'Is every
man in your Conquord a soldier?'

'No. But I didn't mean that, I was just—'

'No man, no Karku, would desire to exist beneath the mountain. It is necessity. The glory of the lords of the mountains, the sky, the air and the beasts that roam is all above. That is where our joy and our hearts lie. Do not speak until you understand. You will see.'

'I'm sorry, I meant no offence,' said Menas.

'Every mark on these walls is a reminder of where a Karku should walk.'

Harban turned back to the way ahead, muttering to his companions who walked either side of him.

'Grumpy, isn't he?' said Mirron from behind them.

'People make assumptions about you too, don't they?' said Jhered. 'How does it make you feel?'

'But they are the mountain men,' said Gorian. 'Everyone knows they are all miners.'

'Harban would disagree with you,' hissed Jhered. 'And I prefer to take the word of a Karku than a young pup who has spent his life coddled in Westfallen. Watch and learn. That's what Father Kessian used to say to you, isn't it?'

There was a pained silence and Jhered bit his lip.

'You shouldn't speak of him,' said Arducius quietly.

'I mean no disrespect to his memory, Arducius.'

A light was growing ahead and Jhered welcomed the distraction. They'd been travelling much of the day inside the mountain and the weight above pressed on his mind as it did on them all. It had led to many taut exchanges and long, uncomfortable silences. The Karku began walking faster, standing taller. The mules, dogged travellers, pricked up their ears, sampled the air and brayed contentment.

Jhered found himself cheering up too. The dank chill of the passage had leached through his furs and into his bones. The sun beyond would be cold but it would feel wonderful on his face. Harban glanced over his shoulder.

'This is land forbidden to the outsider. Remember you are honoured.'

Jhered emerged into the bright late afternoon sun and shaded his eyes with a hand. Below them, down a gentle snow-covered slope, was all the explanation Harban would ever have to give them about why they chose to live outside the mountains. It made him question the location of the villa he was building back in Caraduk.

Completely encircled by mountains was a lush, undulating grassed plain. He guessed it at two miles across at least and more than double that in length. A river ran straight through the middle of it, cascading from a cave mouth high above them to the right and disappearing into the maw of the mountain to the left. Every rock face he could see was covered in bright painted friezes up to a height of twenty feet and more. Multiple paths ran away up the slope to disappear into the snowline or into the mountains.

To the east and west, huge ice-laden slopes began hundreds of feet above their heads and led further up into the sky, dividing the mountains. Jhered felt a jolt of awe. They were surely not natural features but Karku-made. Their positions were too precise for there to be any other explanation. Without them, the plain would already be deep in late shadow. But the angle of the ice face caught the rays of the sun and drenched the whole extraordinary scene in light.

There was a small town built on the plain. On either side of the river, circular stone-walled buildings of one and two storeys were spread among wide plots of land planted with vegetables or grazed by sheep, goats and long-haired cattle. The roofs of the houses were domed and made of wood. Each had a chimney in its centre. Most were smoking gently.

To the north end of the town, larger buildings were grouped around an open area. It too was circular and laid with stone. There was a well in its centre and Jhered saw others dotted through the settlement.

'Oh, it's beautiful,' breathed Mirron.

Jhered nodded. Indeed it was.

'Small wonder they want to keep it secret,' said Menas.

'We have many faces,' said Harban. 'The outside sees only one. Welcome to Yllin-Qvist.'

He led the way down the slope and broad steps from the passage entrance. Down in the town, people had begun to stop and stare at the strangers being brought into their midst. Children ceased their play and were called to the skirts of their mothers. Groups of adults gathered, many carrying weapons, including short blades, staves, spears and a single-handed weapon that looked like a miniature crossbow.

Harban's two companions ran ahead, speaking to people, calming anxieties and telling them who had come. Caution turned to reverence. Jhered heard a whisper pass through the people. He smiled at them as he passed.

'Thank you,' he said in his imperfect Karku. 'Thank you for allowing us into your home.'

He wasn't sure if they understood him. Frankly, most of them ignored him to stare unabashed at the Ascendants travelling behind him. He looked back.

'Try and smile,' he said. 'God-around-us, you look like you're going to your own executions.'

'What's happening?' asked Ossacer.

'They are staring at us, Ossie,' said Arducius.

Ossacer studied them with his sightless gaze. He smiled. 'They like us,' he said. 'They want us.'

'You can feel that?' asked Jhered.

'Their thoughts bring warmth and calm to their energy maps. They aren't afraid.'

'Feels good, I expect,' said Kovan.

'It feels wonderful,' said Mirron, favouring him with a huge smile. The boy blushed almost purple.

Jhered looked past the others at Gorian. His expression was severe, even unhappy.

'Worried someone is going to accept you for what you are?' he asked.

Gorian stared at him. 'What is it they know? I don't like people knowing things I don't.'

'Then you must dislike an awful lot of people,' said Jhered, feeling a familiar impatience. 'Alternatively, you could decide to treat them with respect and ask them once we've stopped. It's one way to a longer life, I've found.'

'They shouldn't know so much about us,' he said.

'You have no idea what they know,' said Arducius. 'It's probably about as much as we knew about the Exchequer before we met him. Rumour and reputation.'

'Why doesn't it make you happy?' asked Ossacer. 'These are the first strangers who don't hate us.'

Kovan muttered something and Gorian snapped round in his saddle.

'What did you say, boy-marshal?'

'I said it's because you are paranoid,' he said. 'Only it's worse than that really, isn't it? You want people to hate and fear you. It makes you feel powerful. Father Kessian would be so disappointed if he knew.'

'If you ever mention his name again, I will burn you, Vasselis. He was our Father. Nothing to do with you and none of your business.'

'He did know,' whispered Ossacer, almost too quiet for Jhered to hear. Then again, louder. 'He did know. That's why he made you promise what he did on the oratory when he died.'

'Right, that's it,' said Gorian.

'Gorian,' warned Arducius.

Jhered heard the tone in his voice and was off his mule in a moment, striding the short distance to Gorian, who had already raised a hand. He grabbed the boy's wrist.

'I did not save you in order for you to demonstrate your petulant immaturity, boy,' he said. 'You will put your hand down and you will behave or it will not be Ossacer or Kovan who is hurt.' Gorian made to retort but Jhered closed his grip, making the boy wince. 'Do I make myself clear?'

He slapped Gorian's hand back down into his lap and did not wait for his response. He walked back to his mule but did not remount, choosing to walk the animal.

'Don't take your eyes off him,' he whispered to Menas who rode beside him. 'We cannot trust him and I don't think Arducius can control him.'

The people of Yllin-Qvist had watched the exchange without apparent comment. Harban was looking at Jhered in some bemusement but he continued, leading them to the centre of the stone-paved circle and the well, where he bade them dismount. Karku were waved in to deal with the mules. Harban pointed to the town's dominating building. It was a high-domed structure atop a two-storey circular wall that was studded with small windows. It was painted with a mural of mountains and blue sky and its main doors stood open, revealing a roaring fire at its centre.

The buildings either side caught Jhered's attention. Both were low, not much taller than him, with steps leading down into gloom. Chimneys disgorged steam, not smoke. He asked the question of Harban.

'They are the baths,' he said. 'You have such things in your Conquord, I understand. But we are blessed. We sit on a natural hot spring here and the waters are warm and soothing after a day on the mountains. Or under them.' He stared pointedly at Menas. He indicated each in turn. 'This is for the relaxation and easing of our ills. This for the celebration of life and the worship of our lords. You can enter neither.'

Jhered made sure the Ascendants had heard before he ushered them into the domed hall. He grabbed Kovan's sleeve as the young man walked past.

'I know it's difficult but try not to anger him,' he said. 'We need him. He is the power. You know it, he knows it.'

'I'll do my best.'

Inside, the lattice of timbers that held up the roof were lost in shadow. Lanterns were set all around the walls of the single room and the fire smoke was channelled up and out through a chimney, the opening of which was just a couple of feet above the highest flame. The hall was set with ring after ring of benches facing inwards to the fire. A stone apron surrounded it.

Four Karku sat together on the inner ring of benches and the outsiders were gestured to join them. Jhered sat to their left and the Ascendants, Menas and Kovan ranged next to him. Harban stood behind Jhered to translate.

'Who are they?' he whispered.

'We are the Gor-Camas,' said one. He was old. His face and head were pale and almost hairless, his body wrapped in heavy furs though it was warm in the hall. 'The guardians of the mountain for Yllin-Qvist.' He thought for a moment. 'You would call us quaestors or magistrates, I think. I am Icenga-Qvist. Welcome. Welcome, all of you.'

'We are honoured to be invited into your town,' said Jhered. 'It is an act of friendship unexpected but very welcome. The mountain passes are cold and difficult.' He tried to speak in Karku but Icenga waved his efforts away.

'It is best you don't,' he said and Jhered saw the smiles on all their faces. 'Your inflection gives some of your words - uh - alternative meanings. But thank you.'

Icenga and the other Gor-Camas looked long and hard at the four Ascendants, studying their faces. Jhered sensed them begin to fidget and spared them a sharp glance. Arducius was whispering to Ossacer, telling him what was going on.

'Your great Conquord has shunned its future just as Gorian said it would,' said Icenga eventually.

Gorian lifted his head. 'Did you know him? Gorian, I mean?'

Icenga laughed, a warm friendly sound that boomed around the hall. 'No, younger. Do I really look so old? I am afraid stories of our immortality are just another falsehood among many.'

'Oh,' said Gorian, disappointed.

'But he was the first outsider we allowed onto our hearths. His words were like echoes of our forgotten past and we remember them in verse, spoken story and myth painting. He said others would come one day, chased from their homes by the very people that should have taken them to their hearts.'

'Did he,' began Mirron, pausing when the Gor-camas swivelled to face her. 'Did he find others like us here in Kark?'

Harban's low spoken translation brought nods from all four of them.

'Oh yes,' said Icenga. 'It was why he stayed here so long. We have forever been at the mercy of capricious elements. Our animals and crops exist on the edge of life. Nature dictated that there would be those among us who understood these things more intimately, just as the Lord of the Mountains dictated that some of us can divine copper and iron and gold.

'But they are not quite like you, though he said some with your knowledge would come, at risk to their lives. None can tame the gorthock like you, on a whim from your mind.'

'I'm confused,' said Jhered. He turned to Arducius. 'I thought the Echelon said that everything Gorian knew was documented in Westfallen. This is an enormous omission.'

Arducius had no answer.

'We made him swear that he would not reveal our secrets,' said Icenga, and there was the light of excitement in his eyes. 'The spirits of our ancestors that shield us from harm will be joyful today that their trust in him was not misplaced. It is the same trust we are placing in you. Nothing that you have seen or heard here can be spoken of to the outside.'

'Why should it have been a secret from the Ascendancy?' asked Ossacer.

'Because the risk of outsiders knowing too much is too great. We do not need interference and we do not need questions. If the word escaped, as it has that you exist, people would come. And we are not so numerous we could stem the tide of invasion forever.'

'Anyone would be mad to attack Kark,' said Kovan.

Icenga nodded. 'Yes but it would not stop them, younger. Like it does not stop those outsiders who think they have the right to mine our mountains for themselves. They might not succeed in conquest but it would change our lives forever. That is not the right of anyone to decide but our lords and our canas-u.'

Jhered cleared his throat. 'Harban said that there were things we had to know. It's getting late, the Ascendants . . . all of us, are tired.'

Icenga nodded. 'Of course. We have tracked you since you entered Kark, wondering if your journey was to escape the war but it is not, is it?'

'No,' said Jhered. 'We—'

Icenga raised a hand. 'This war must be ended. Yuran is foolish but your Advocate equally so. And now our friends in Gestern are under threat from an army too great for them to defeat. We cannot enter the conflict. Tsard has ever been a peaceful ally, much like the Conquord, but we find our borders pressed. Tsardon have attempted to use our paths to escape Conquord scouts. Conquord armies travel as close as they dare. We fear the battles that are to come, Paul Jhered. Should the Tsardon take Gestern we are isolated and they will be confident in their power.'

'And we are travelling to stop them. To turn back the Tsardon.'

'Much as we assumed.'

'You mentioned an army travelling close to your borders. The northern I presume. Is it Jorganesh? You know of him, surely.'

'He is long a friend of the Karku,' said Icenga. His head dropped and he studied his feet.

Jhered felt a chill through his body. 'What's happened, Icenga? What's happened to Jorganesh?'

'We will eat now,' he replied. 'Then you should rest. You have heard what you must. Tomorrow we will take you where you will also see what you must.'

'But—' said Menas.

Icenga shook his head and motioned to the open doorway where the last rays of the evening sun disappeared behind the mountains, dazzling the high peaks but leaving the town in darkness.

'With the last light of the day goes the time for talk of strife and pain. You will see what you must. It is more eloquent than any words I can frame in your language. Eat and sleep.'

But Jhered could not sleep. And the clouds that travelled across the darkening sky disgorged another snowfall.

Chapter 57

848th cycle of God, 21st day of Solasfall
15th year of the true Ascendancy

Sizzling slices of lamb, eggs taken from the nests of mountain birds, and thick root vegetables made a start to the day that left Mirron feeling she would never have to eat again. Beside her, Gorian belched so loud it echoed off the mountain side. She jabbed him but he just laughed.

'Just my food saying thank you on my behalf,' he said.

She smiled back at him. They were sitting together around a small fire laid outside the house in which they'd spent the night sleeping under huge mounds of furs. Dear Kovan had snored so badly he'd been banished to another room where the fire had died and it had grown very cold. Now he sat wolfing down his breakfast and glaring at Gorian. Arducius and Ossacer were on a bench across the fire from her. There was a chill wind blowing down the plain but they were sheltered and the sun was rising above the eastern slope, sending light cascading into the town.

Away to the south of the settlement, she could see Jhered and Menas in conversation with Harban and Icenga. Jhered was clearly frustrated and Mirron guessed he was not getting the answers he wanted.

'I wonder what they want to show us,' she said.

'It's nothing good,' said Kovan.

He'd put down his empty plate and was sharpening his sword on a whetstone. Around them, a small crowd of children was gathering as they were pushed outside their front doors to play.

'How would you know?' asked Gorian.

'Because Jhered is worried, and in my experience that's never a good sign.'

'He doesn't know any more than you do, Vasselis,' said Gorian.

'He's a soldier, Gorian,' said Kovan with exaggerated patience. 'And a Gatherer. He knows when people are trying to hide a problem.'

'It's not in our control, that's what I don't like,' said Gorian, quietly. 'We're just shoved here out of the way while he decides what to do with us. Don't you feel lost in all this, any of you? Doesn't it make you feel helpless?'

Mirron was taken aback. She put an arm around his waist instinctively, wondering what had led to this sudden dropping of his guard.

'All of us feel the same, Gorian. That's why we have to stick together,' she said.

'Spoken like Arducius,' said Ossacer.

'We have to trust him,' said Arducius. 'He needs us alive.'

'We're just pawns,' said Gorian. 'It isn't because he likes us. He just wants to use us. So long as you all understand that.'

There was a titter of laughter and some high-pitched whispered words.

'Hello,' said Mirron, smiling at the gaggle of children, eight in all.

They looked incredibly sweet, swathed in furs and peering out from under caps and hats, with downy hair on their faces and covering their feet. They backed away at her attention.

'Don't be afraid,' she said. 'Look.'

She bent her hand to the grass and brushed away a little ice and snow from its surface. Beneath the topsoil, buried in the cold hard earth, was the bulb of a genastro bloom. A crocus, she thought, or something like it. It was a bundle of potential life, just waiting for the spark.

Mirron applied it, feeding a brief pulse of her own life energy into the bulb and prompting it to grow. She sensed its roots searching the earth below and its bud forging to the surface. She fed more of herself in, a tiny amount in reality, and watched as the bud and stalk burst from the grass and grew a few inches. The children were staring in mute amazement. Mirron finished the job, bringing the bud to flower. It was a beautiful soft purple in colour. She plucked it and handed it to the nearest little girl.

'There you are. For you.'

The girl squealed in delight and set off with the flower clutched in her hand, her friends in hot pursuit. Mirron laughed and clapped her hands together. She felt warm inside.

'They have no idea what's happening outside their borders, do they?' she said, sobering a little. 'Cocooned like we were in Westfallen. I wonder if that's right.'

'They'll learn soon enough,' said Kovan. 'They're young yet.'

Menas was striding up the path towards them. She shouted at them when she saw them notice her. They thanked the cook for their breakfast and left her looking a little confused, holding a stack of plates and forks.

'Time to go,' said Menas when they reached her. 'Come on.'

She led them down the bank of the river. It was a sluggish flow until it reached the mouth of the mountain where it seemed to narrow and rush into the dark.

'Which way are we going?' asked Ossacer.

'That way?'

Menas was pointing into the blackness of the mountain. They could hear the water course, loud like a drain. There were two open boats moored where Jhered and Icenga were still talking about something or other.

'You are joking, aren't you?' asked Kovan.

'Apparently, it isn't as bad as it looks,' said Menas, though she was not convincing.

'What about the mules?' asked Mirron.

'They'll be safe here,' said Menas. 'Come on. The sooner we start . . .'

Mirron looked into the boats. All their gear was already stowed under leather in the bows. Each had two sets of oars and also three poles with moulded hand grips at one end, bulbous and flattened at the other. She asked what they were for.

'To keeping us away from the sides where they close in around us,' said Harban. He was smiling, enjoying their discomfort. 'You have not been on a boat trip like this in your Conquord. Inside, the river splits. To the right, the path is steep and fast and feeds the heart of the mountain, where you may not go. We will go left. It is the easier route. Just.'

Mirron shuddered and looked round at Gorian for support. He was looking as white as she felt.

'Why can't we go the other way?' asked Gorian.

'Because it leads to Inthen-Gor, the heart of the mountain. The most sacred domain of the Karku. No outsider has ever seen it. No outsider ever will.'

'What does it look like?' Arducius was gazing into the mountain. Mirron could see his imagination already running wild.

'It is beautiful,' said Harban. His tone became soft and reverent. 'A great cavern and lake that we call the Eternal Water. At its centre is an island where our ancestors built the Heart Shrine. Both are as vital to us as the air we breathe. They govern all our lives and bind us to the mountains and the air and to all the creatures that walk the paths of the living and the tunnels of the dead. Every Karku must take this journey to achieve maturity and be assumed into their tribe.'

'I would love to see it,' said Gorian.

'It can never happen,' said Harban, though he smiled. 'But you'll see enough on our journey through the skirts of the mountain.'

The image of Inthen-Gor shattered and Mirron remembered she was scared. It must have shown on her face.

'You will be fine, younger. A little danger is exciting, no?' said Harban, chuckling away to himself.

'No, not really,' said Mirron. 'Do we have to, Lord Jhered?'

Jhered walked over to them and the look on his face was not unkindly though there was a sadness in his eyes.

'Are you all right?' she asked.

'I'm fine, thank you,' he said. 'Look, we have to get somewhere very quickly and this is the only way. Believe me, I'd go another way if we could. But Harban says it's safe enough.'

'Yes, well, they all have harder heads than us,' said Ossacer. 'They probably bang them off rocks all the time.'

Jhered looked at him hard. 'You aren't joking, are you?'

'Their skulls are thicker,' confirmed Ossacer. 'You can see it in the way the energy flows around them.'

'I see.'

Mirron watched another hurried and hissed conversation in Karku, with Jhered gesticulating angrily, pointing to his head, to the water and the rocks. Finally, he threw up his hands and turned back to them.

'It's fine,' he said. 'Apparently, should any of us, including him, strike our heads, he assures me we will be killed outright. I trust that makes you feel more at ease.' He was shaking his head. 'This isn't good enough.'

'And there's no other way?' asked Arducius.

'If we want to waste thirty days and probably freeze to death, then yes,' said Jhered.

Mirron was bored with this. The boys and Jhered were all looking particularly serious and severe. Hands were on hips and frowns were deep in angry faces. She walked quickly over to Menas.

'Perhaps we should show them some courage,' she said. 'And get in first.'

'You'll be the master of men with thinking like that,' said Menas.

'What do you mean?'

Menas opened her mouth to speak but paused and stroked Mirron's nose with a finger instead. 'I expect you already know,' she said. 'Come on, let's do it.'

They walked to the front boat and climbed in.

'All we've got to do is keep our heads down, isn't it?' she said into the their stares. 'Are you scared or something?'

For three days, they journeyed beneath some of Kark's mightiest mountains and despite the wonders around them, the mood changed. Arducius wasn't sure he wanted to know why. Jhered had become even more introverted if that was possible, and their Karku guides looked sombre and drawn, like they weren't sleeping very well.

Arducius remembered the screams that had burst from Mirron's lips when the descent had begun. The feel of rock whispering past just above her head and so close to her hands where they gripped the gunwales so hard her fingers must have ached. The lanterns set fore and aft lit the journey with harsh light and garish shadow. But here and there, the lanterns had showed beautiful luminescent lichen that glowed a gentle green.

More than that, when the river levelled and the pace of the torrent slowed, they saw things that even their dreams could not have created. They had seen arrays of stalactites that were so beautiful they had stopped just to sit beneath them and stare up until their necks ached. They had seen pools lit by that luminescent lichen that had cast gentle greens and blues over the walls of deep caves. Underground beaches laced with natural columns and caves that would have shamed Westfallen's coast. Jhered had hurried them as much as he could but all of them, even Ossacer, had braved the freezing waters to swim and explore. It had been magical.

After the terror of the descent, Arducius had felt disappointed to leave the underground wonderland, as Mirron had described it. He'd wanted to see one last tributary leading away into a mysterious dark so that they could debate which hidden land it would lead to.

Early on the fourth morning, the river slowed and the passage widened dramatically. A great cave mouth revealed itself in the distance and the Karku began to row faster, wanting the freshness of the open air and the light of the sun on their faces.

Their emergence into light was startling. The brightness of the light dazzled their eyes and the warmth of the sun was delightful, even this soon after dawn. Arducius breathed in air that had lost the taint of damp rock and had gained the scent of grass and trees. The energies clamoured for his attention, almost overwhelmed his mind until he forced some control on himself. Inside the mountains had been amazing but out here . . . out here the world was truly *alive*.

The river ran through endless mountains studded with meadows on which lay settlements. They travelled gorges that were dark almost the whole of the day, so steep and tall were the sides. And they saw rank upon rank of snow-capped peaks stretching away into the distance and beyond sight in every direction, at once desolate, dangerous and unbelievably beautiful.

The Karku brought them to a deserted landing. The river bent away, west towards Gestern, so Jhered had said. North of them a tree-lined slope led away up into yet another range of mountains. This one marked part of the northern border of the country. They were helped ashore.

'Why isn't anyone living here?' asked Mirron. 'It's lovely.'

'It is a place that the lords have deserted,' said Icenga.

Jhered was glancing up at the sun and the land and water around them. It was mid-morning and the sun was strong over their heads.

'The other side of that range,' he said, pointing north. 'Lubjek's Defile, yes?'

'Yes, Paul Jhered,' said Icenga and that haunted look was back in his eyes again. 'You should come with me. The Ascendants will stay here.'

'Why?' Gorian's voice rose in complaint. 'What's so bad that we can't possibly see it? We aren't so young and delicate, you know. Well, I'm not.'

Jhered looked along the line at Gorian and Arducius feared the worst.

'For once, Gorian, I am forced to agree with you. Your eyes will tell you more about the truth of war than my words ever could.' He turned to Icenga. 'They're coming with us. All of them.'

No one said anything all the way along the passageway through the mountain. Not Mirron's wheedling, nor Gorian's arrogant insistence they be told what was there for them to see, made any difference. At one stage, Ossacer who was holding on to Arducius's arm said that he felt like he was being led to a funeral. Arducius didn't like the look Jhered gave him in return.

The path they took moved up a gentle incline for several hours. They stopped for lunch at a waypoint that was the junction of three passages and it was here that Jhered finally deigned to speak to them.

'Up there, an hour from here, we will come to Lubjek's Defile. It is a lovely treelined valley that marks the border between Kark and Tsard. It is the quickest and best escape route from the southern Tsardon steppe lands back through Atreska and into Gestern. It is therefore the natural, and indeed only possible, route for an army to take if given the word to return to defend the Conquord. It is the route General Jorganesh took.'

Jhered bit his lip and let his head drop just a little. A deep frown crossed his face and he cleared his throat.

'He entered the defile with four legions. He didn't ever leave.'

An hour later, they stood at the head of the passage, waiting to move out from the hidden entrance. The heat of the afternoon was still strong outside and Arducius was aware of a low buzzing in the air. A breeze blew about the entrance and the smell was sour, like a fire long dead and staining the atmosphere with its ash.

'Nor did any of his army. I'm sorry for what you are about to see. I'm sorry anyone ever has to.'

Arducius didn't really understand. Next to him, Mirron was rubbing her arm nervously and Gorian too, was playing with his old burn scar.

'How many were there?' whispered Ossacer.

Jhered set his jaw and followed Icenga and Harban from the passage.

'More than sixteen thousand.'

Arducius emerged into a scene of devastation. At first he thought it must be winter because the trees were denuded of their leaves and the ground was covered a dirty white. But then he looked again and had to put his arm against a boulder to stop from falling. The trees had no leaves because they were blackened burned stumps. And it wasn't snow that covered the ground. It was bones.

They lay deep and jumbled on the valley floor and were scattered up the sides before they were lost in the higher trees where the fires had not reached. He could see whole skeletons of men, dogs and horses only a few yards from his feet. And he could see where animals had tried to drag them away, breaking them and leaving limbs, skulls and shards of bone covering the burned ground.

He moved a couple of paces down the slope and looked left and right. The defile stretched away further than he could see in both directions. And the only breaks in the carpet of bones were where the wheels or timbers of wagons jutted out.

Arducius swallowed. At his feet was a rounded stone. It was smeared with filth. And now he looked a third time, he could see that the forest of twigs he thought had fallen from the trees when they burned were arrows. Broken buckles, shards of blades, twisted hilts, torn shields and snapped spears reflected the harsh sunlight. As useless and dead as those who had carried them.

His eyes misted with sudden tears. 'So much waste,' he said.

He pushed out with his senses. He was surrounded with the grey and dark of a scene shorn of the energies of life. It was cold and rotten. But there were lifelines here. Countless thousands of them just below the dead surface. Tiny energy packets among the debris of the slaughtered. Mirron had seen it too and with a gasping voice, she said:

'They're moving. The bones are moving.'

Arducius shut away the power and stared down at the thick carpet of skeletons and bones. They were shifting. It was slight but it was there, like they were being pushed from beneath.

'Don't get too close,' said Jhered. 'The gorthock might have picked the bones clean from above but the rats are still doing their work beneath.'

'It's so dark,' said Ossacer. He had his back to a tree and his sightless eyes were flickering everywhere, while his face screwed up and his fingertips sampled the air. 'Like the Omniscient has turned His back on this place.'

'But there is still power here,' said Gorian.

'What?' Arducius turned and stared. Gorian was crouching near the edge of the sea of dead.

'Something I can't describe but there's something, isn't there? Can't you feel it?'

'It's just the rats,' said Arducius.

'No,' said Gorian quietly. 'The dead have their own energy.'

'What are you talking about?' said Arducius. 'It's grey. It's dark and it's cold. Your senses are playing tricks.'

Gorian straightened. 'Perhaps you're right.' He smiled and wiped his hands on his tunic. 'It's probably the shock of all this.'

'Two legions, two alae,' said Kovan. 'What must they have felt?'

'Goslander, Gesternan, Estorean, Tundarran, Caraducian.'

Arducius started at that. Jhered saw it.

'Yes, my Ascendants,' he said. 'People from your own country. Slaughtered as they did their duty. Like rats in a trap. No mercy, no prisoners. All they wanted was to return to their families. Just like you.'

He let the words hang in the air. They were as uncomfortable as the clouds of flies buzzing over the remnants of rotten carrion.

'Was General Jorganesh your friend?' asked Mirron.

Jhered nodded. 'Twenty years and more. A great general. But even the great can be ambushed. He didn't deserve this. No one does.'

'Why didn't they surrender?'

'You cannot surrender to a rain of firestones, a thousand dogs and an enemy thirsting for your destruction,' said Harban.

Arducius felt sick. He tried to imagine the horror and the terror. The noise and the panic. He stared again at the tumble of bodies and the skulls with empty sockets. The hair that still clung on, ruffling in the breeze. A mass of citizens plucked from their lives and abandoned. Lost and godless. An endless march of the dead.

'It's time we were moving,' said Jhered. 'The Tsardon that did this are heading for Gestern.'

'They are mustering in central southern Atreska,' said Harban. 'Waiting for the Tsardon marching in from Scintarit.'

Jhered frowned. 'Mustering? That doesn't make sense. Why wouldn't the army that did this not move to attack the eastern edge of Gestern's border and let the second force attack elsewhere? Why are they waiting? They must know the Gesternans can't hold them on two fronts. Not with Jorganesh gone.'

'It is our belief they will all attack on the western seaboard,' said Icenga. 'But we don't have confirmation. Our scouts and watchers have not travelled that far into Atreska.'

'Still, that's some scout network you have,' said Menas.

Harban shrugged. 'Our mountains are high and our magnifiers are powerful. And we must know what passes our borders.'

Jhered shook his head. 'This doesn't make sense,' he repeated. He turned to Icenga. 'I must see.'

Icenga nodded. 'Our route will grant you that opportunity.'

They shouldered their packs and set off. Arducius turned his back on Lubjek's Defile with a shudder but the nausea did not pass.

'How does it make you feel, soldier-boy?' Gorian asked Kovan. 'Bet you don't want to join the legions now.'

Arducius's heart fell but Kovan did not snap back. Rather, he looked across at Gorian with an expression bordering on pity.

'That is how I would expect a coward to think,' he said. 'But it makes me even more determined to fight for the Conquord and stop it happening to those I love.'

'Well said, young Vasselis,' said Jhered.

They retreated up the valley and walked back inside the mountain.

Jhered pushed their pace hard. He felt too far from being able to help There was something he was missing and it irritated him. He didn't know why but he felt that a view of Atreska's southern plains would give him inspiration. Or bring him fresh dread. The war was outpacing him and he hoped he hadn't made a monumental mistake by believing in the Ascendants. God-embrace-him but at the beginning of this year, he would have believed only in the sword and the horse to beat back the Tsardon armies and bring Yuran to justice. A madness had possessed him.

And yet there was something about them. About their growing willingness to follow him and their unspoken belief in their largely untested powers that gave him heart. They could make rain and fire and bring growth to trees. It was extraordinary. But with the heart he took, there was anxiety. Because it was a huge step from bringing a flower to bud to stopping an army in its tracks.

Harban and Icenga took them higher again. Inside the mountain paths, the air chilled and the passages themselves became plain and rough. They were forced to make climbs up rock ladders and traversed two deep caverns within the mountains on narrow stone and wood bridges.

This was the furthest edge of the Karku domain and the sudden cold when the paths ended was a shocking reminder of the coming of dusas. It took them three days. Days in which the Ascendants at last ceased their complaining about the paths they took and the blisters on their feet. Days in which Kovan Vasselis drew into himself as the shock of what he had seen, and the reality of the fate of the legions for which he had trained, hit home. He had walked apart from the Ascendants for much of the time. He had hardly even spoken to Mirron, let alone the others.

Jhered left him to it for a while. But when their furs were gathered about them tightly once more as the passage climbed to a freezing grey opening, he sought out the boy's state of mind.

'They can fool themselves Jorganesh's army is somehow not even real. It is far enough removed for them to ignore the fact of individual suffering in others. But you. It isn't the same for you, is it?'

Kovan didn't speak for a while. Seventeen years old and young enough never to have heard of the slaughter of a Conquord army, let alone seen it for himself.

'It just makes me so angry. They don't understand and they're already smiling again. All that's happened . . . Kessian, the Chancellor as well. How can they ignore it all? This is reality and they don't seem to care.'

'It's a hard lesson, Kovan,' said Jhered. 'And they do care, but they feel the need to hide from it all. Remember, they have been torn from their lives and they are so much younger than you in so many ways. They are still children, despite all that they have learned. You are a man. And a soldier. Don't let their reaction upset you. Tell me how you feel.'

Kovan glanced behind him. The Ascendants were chattering. Jhered had learned to block out the incessant noise that resounded like the scratching of rats in the passageways.

'I am scared and it shames me,' he said. 'Gorian was right. It does make me fear joining the legions.'

Jhered stopped and waved Menas and the Ascendants past them. He took Kovan's shoulders and made the young man look at him.

'There is no shame in fear,' he said. 'Your father has told you this, I am sure. Fear makes us wary, keeps us alive. And you should fear joining the legions and serving your time. It is harsh and hard. Men and women die in battle. Death on the field might be glorious in song but it is hideous when you are standing in its midst.

'True courage comes when fear is faced, understood and accepted. You fear death. We all fear death. But we fear more the price that failure would bring our families and our Conquord. That you admit your fear shows courage. Only a fool denies it. And fools are always the first to die. You are young and brave, Kovan Vasselis. I am both glad and proud that you are with us.'

Kovan's face beamed his pride and relief. He nodded and his heaving breath clouded deep in front of his face.

'Thank you. Thank you.'

'Ask Roberto Del Aglios what happens to him even now after every battle.'

'Why?'

'Just ask him.'

Outside, the freezing air of the early morning seared into Jhered's lungs. The sun was strengthening and the snow that they had seen as they climbed had all but stopped. By midday, it would be a glorious, late solas day. The passage emerged on to a tight ledge above which steps were cut into the mountain, climbing to the peak that was still several hundred feet away.

They looked out and down onto the sweeping plains of Atreska ten thousand feet below them. Much of it was obscured under a thin layer of cloud but Harban was confident that it would burn away. He and Icenga were already climbing above them, their energy boundless, their feet sure on the icy surface.

They were sheltered here, behind a jut of rock. But the peak was exposed and the wind was howling around them, ready to pluck the unwary from their path and cast them down. Despite their acclimatisation, the air felt very thin and Ossacer looked pale.

'You go no further,' said Jhered.

'I have no intention of doing so,' said Ossacer. 'I just wanted to breathe the mountain air.'

'Well, now you have. Now get back to the intersection. All of you.'

Ossacer shook his head. 'We're all right here. Anyway, I'm going to help you.'

Jhered raised his eyebrows. 'Oh, really.'

'I'm going to try something.'

'Up here? Must you?'

Ossacer had a determined look. 'You want us to try new things. You said so on the ship.'

'Well yes, but that was storm, barrier and fire. I don't think this is the place.'

'It isn't dangerous. It'll give us more eyes. Closer to where you want to look.'

'If it works,' said Jhered.

'It'll work,' said Arducius.

Jhered shrugged. 'Fine. Fine. Just don't get careless and fall. And don't tire yourselves out. We aren't staying here long. Menas, stay with them. Kovan, come with me. I could use your opinion.'

He saw Kovan's smile and Gorian's scowl and sighed inwardly. He jabbed a finger at the errant Ascendant. 'Don't go running off.'

The trip to the summit was a slog of over an hour. The Karku had kicked footholds in the deepest ice and saw them up the hardest sections but still the ascent was painfully slow. The wind was far stronger than Jhered had imagined and he was forced to keep his head down and his body close to the ground. Behind him, Kovan's pace was dogged and determined.

The peak itself was a small sloping plateau on which the Karku had built a circular stone shelter. Jhered and Kovan slumped gratefully inside it, gasping in breath and reaching out their hands to the small fire that Icenga had prepared from a stock of wood. The flames guttered in the thin air but the warmth was wonderful.

'Our highest peak is twice this size,' said Icenga. 'You would not reach the top alive.'

'Forgive me if I don't ever try,' said Jhered. He felt faint and weak. The exertion and the altitude were taking serious toll. 'Good idea to build this shelter.'

'The watchers would freeze without it.'

Jhered was reminded of the reason they had climbed up here. 'Right, let's get this over with. Show me where I should look and give me your best magnifier.'

He could see for hundred of miles. With or without the magnifier, just two pieces of shaped glass in a wooden frame, the sense of scale was amazing. Like surveying the whole world. But the feeling of wonder didn't last long. Atreska's green, fertile plains were stained dark with Tsardon away to the west and south. Dust hung in the air and the tracks of marches were plainly visible, snaking away into the distant north.

He couldn't get the angle to see the Gesternan border defences. And to see clear across the country to the Tirronean Sea was a dream but no more than that. One thing that he could see was that the Karku had been right. The Tsardon were marching west and not directly south. And there were at least three forces massing. It was far too much for the Gesternans to repel. He sat back and handed the magnifier to Kovan. He watched the young man studying the distant enemy.

'Why are they doing it?' Jhered asked. 'They are ignoring the highway to Skiona. It's just not the right place for an army from the east to attack. Why march right across the face of the enemy, showing them your route so they can reinforce? What do they hope to achieve?'

'I don't know.' Kovan didn't turn from his search. 'Unless they think they will get reinforced from the sea.'

'That's it.' Jhered felt the blood drain from his face and a clamour set up in his chest. 'They don't want to annexe Gestern. Only her coast.'

Kovan sat back down. 'Why would they do that?'

'Because they can always come back for Gestern. What they need is Estorr and the quickest way is straight across the Tirronean Sea.'

'Yes but they won't be able to do that, will they? The Ocetanas will be on station and the rebel Atreskan navy are no match.'

'Not on their own, no.' Jhered looked across at Icenga. 'You overlook the Bay of Harryn from your north-eastern borders. What news from there?'

'The Tsardon fleet has sailed south,' he replied. 'They will be in the Tirronean before long.'

'And the Ocetanas have been forced to commit strength north. They may not have the ships to counter them.'

'There is good news, though,' said Harban. 'We had scouts in Tsard recently. Roberto Del Aglios is marching south. We can put you on a path to meet him.'

Jhered smiled. 'Good old Roberto. I knew you wouldn't let me down.'

*

Jhered's sudden and rapid reappearance stopped the argument in its tracks.

'Shut up and get up. We're moving.'

'But we can make it work,' complained Ossacer.

'Not now.' Jhered frowned. 'What was it anyway? And don't stop clearing up while you're telling me.'

'Gorian can control the minds of animals,' said Arducius. 'We all can to a certain extent but not over such distance as him. And Ossacer can read the energies of its senses and translate them into images.'

Jhered paused. 'You're saying he can see through another animal's eyes?'

'Or smell through its nose or hear through its ears,' said Ossacer. 'We were going to try it out on a bird. Gorian makes it fly, I see what it sees.'

Jhered was stunned. 'You can do that?'

'It's theoretically possible,' said Mirron.

The possibilities were extraordinary. Jhered calmed their activity with a hand.

'Sit back down. Theoretically. You've never actually done it?'

'No,' said Gorian.

'And what were you arguing about?'

'Which sort of bird we should use and what we should call it,' said Arducius, having the decency to look embarrassed.

'For three hours?' He stared at Menas, who nodded confirmation. 'Give me strength.'

'Well, it wasn't just that,' said Mirron. 'We didn't know where to find it, either.'

Jhered closed his eyes briefly. This was a very long shot but it was worth the attempt for a couple of hours.

'Right. Change of plan. We'll stop here to eat. And while we're doing it, you lot will find me a bird. Eagles see well. And you will fly it north of here and find me a Conquord army marching south. Think you can do that?'

Chapter 58

848th cycle of God, 32nd day of Solasfall
15th year of the true Ascendancy

Icenga and Harban made ready to turn from them at the furthest reach north of the Karku border in Atreska. Their descent had been quick and clean and the only regret Jhered had was that there were no horses to speed them on their journey.

Gorian and Ossacer hadn't managed to find Roberto, though the experiment hadn't been a complete waste; they had achieved control of a bird in flight. The Karku reported the army marching down the course of the River Gull, south and then west deep into Atreska. He was keeping the river between them and any Atreskan rebels and Tsardon invaders from the central north and west. Without confirmation, Jhered had to trust the reports on his position and direction.

'They are an amazing gift,' said Icenga. 'Keep them safe.'

Jhered looked across at the Ascendants, grouped together like they always were but, unusually for them, silent. Perhaps Jhered's message about what they faced had finally got through. Kovan and Menas were comparing their blades for heft and balance.

'I'm just beginning to realise it.'

'But watch Gorian. I don't like the way he thinks.'

Jhered nodded. Icenga pushed the tips of his fingers together in a peak and bowed his forehead to touch them.

'Journey well, friend of Kark. May the lords of stone and sky bless your journey.'

Jhered put his right fist to his heart. 'My arm and heart are yours, Icenga. We would not have got this far without you. Harban, I am honoured to know you.'

'Travel well, Paul Jhered,' said Harban. 'Stop this war before it shatters the mountains.'

Jhered inclined his head. 'With every breath available to me.'

The Karku trotted away back into the mountains and were lost from sight.

'Men of honour and integrity,' said Jhered. 'They've put their trust in you lot. Don't let them down. Don't let me down.'

Jhered assessed their position. Icenga had left them next to the bamboo-shrouded banks of the River Gull where it plunged underground and, he had been assured, fed the Eternal Water. He had to smile. According to the Karku, almost every waterway fed the Eternal Water. He wasn't sure they believed it themselves but it made a good myth.

The mountains were at their back and ahead were the gentle rolling plains of southern Atreska. The change in landscape could hardly have been more stark. To the west, he could see woodland, settlements, and the splash of late solasfall colour across the hillsides. The green and yellow of crops awaiting harvest, the blue and red of late flowering shrubs. Still a beautiful country and so difficult to believe that tens of thousands of soldiers were marching across it.

Their route would take them along the course of the river and hopefully into the path of Roberto's scouts and so to the man himself. He would be marching quickly and unopposed, probably wondering why he had not been attacked. Jhered knew the answer. The Tsardon had no need to. After all, marching towards the nearest Gesternan border crossing, Roberto was heading the wrong way.

But while the Tsardon wouldn't attack Roberto's army until pressed, they would certainly sweep up a small party travelling north to meet it.

'We must be careful,' said Jhered. 'We will travel slowly and keep out of sight as much as possible. Menas, I need you to work to our east. If there are Tsardon this side of the river, we need to have warning to hide. We're fortunate with cover in the river valley but we could be surprised and we are in no position to take on a raiding party.

'The rest of you, I know I keep saying I want quiet but now it's important. Keep your voices down. Particularly at night. It's warm so I expect we'll be doing without fires. You were safe in Kark. You are not safe here. Understand?' The Ascendants nodded. 'Good. Kovan, any scouting in your training so far?'

'I've hunted stag and boar with my father,' he said. 'Tracking but no scouting.'

'It'll do. I need you to sweep behind us. Only a short distance. Tsardon scouts might well be mounted. Check for tracks east and south too. Don't take them on if you see them. Come to me.'

'I won't let you down.'

'I don't doubt it.' His gaze fell on the Ascendants once more. 'Come on. We'll stay near the river bank. The bamboo should curtain us from eyes the other side and the trees on the slope will mask us from the east. Trust Menas and Kovan. Listen to what I say and act on my orders without question. Menas, Kovan. Go. Report back every three hours.'

'My Exchequer,' said Menas.

She placed her hand across her heart and trotted away into the woodland ahead. Kovan nodded and broke away to the rear. Jhered led the Ascendants down the shallow slope almost to the river's edge. The bamboo that grew thickly along its bank was a comfort but he had to guard against complacency. It was a hot day in the open with only the trees that studded their path ahead to provide cover from the sun.

They walked at a steady pace. The ground was dry and easy. The river's moisture fed the lush grass and gave it a comfortable spring underfoot. Their furs were rolled and tied about their waists and their packs were stocked with Karku trail rations of dried meat and bread.

Jhered found himself relaxing in spite of their circumstances and it was almost an hour before it occurred to him that there were a lot of birds here. They weren't flocking but either it was his imagination or they sat in the bamboo or trees to watch them pass, or soared and swooped overhead while the path ahead and behind was clear.

He said nothing until they paused in the shade when the sun was at its hottest for a quick bite to eat. The Omniscient was giving them memories of solastro to take into the long cold of dusas. The grass around the Ascendants was growing. Not quickly but it was undeniable, like a fringe around their legs and feet.

'You're bringing the birds, aren't you?' he said.

'We don't mean to,' said Arducius. 'It just happens. Actually, it's mainly Gorian. He's the Herd Master.'

Jhered gestured at the grass. 'And this. Does it just happen too?'

'Yes,' said Mirron. 'Ever since full emergence.' She smiled beautifully. 'It's lovely. Things grow where we walk if the pool of energy is there.'

Still, Jhered couldn't square it with the Omniscient. It sat uncomfortably with him though he had already used their powers himself when it suited him. He tried not to feel a hypocrite but that was what he was. A man sworn to uphold the Conquord's faith, protecting those who threatened it the most. Yet these children were not evil. They were innocents. Jhered felt a pang of guilt add to his inner confusion. If anyone was going to turn them from that innocence, it was him.

He smiled back at Mirron. 'Do you feel the life as it grows?'

'We cannot shut it out,' said Ossacer. 'Life is everywhere. All we can do is sort and suppress the lifelines and energy maps so they don't overwhelm us.'

'I don't pretend to understand,' said Jhered. 'But tell me. How easy is it for you to see the, the lifelines, is it? The lifelines of, say, a horse or a rider. How far away can you sense them?'

'You want us to stand guard at night,' said Gorian.

'The thought had crossed my mind,' said Jhered. 'So?'

'If we concentrate, we can see something that large moving through a forest quite easily, I should think. Despite the mass of energy in a place like this,' said Gorian. He looked to the others for confirmation.

'You think?'

Arducius shrugged. 'We've never done it before.'

'Well,' said Jhered. 'Nor had you controlled an eagle before but that was extraordinary. How do you feel about trying to impress me again?'

'We don't do it to impress you,' said Ossacer. 'We do it to learn.'

'Whatever makes you feel better,' said Jhered. 'Come on, eat up. Let's get moving.'

Night fell quickly this late in solastro. Gorian sat with his back to a tree while the others slept behind him under the furs that had served them so well in Kark. They had camped on the bank of the river. It was a chill night, another sign of the coming of dusas, but Jhered had stuck to his word and had not let them light a fire. Of course, all the Ascendants could use the energy around them to keep themselves warm but it was a wasteful exercise and didn't help when they were asleep.

Menas had returned to the camp at dusk, reporting that Tsardon scouts were patrolling ahead a few miles away. Groups of riders between eight and ten strong. It was a scary thought and had made whispers of their conversation that evening. As a further consequence, Jhered was awake too, shadowing his watch in the darkest hours of the night.

Gorian let his mind open to the energies surrounding them. They were duller; the world was at rest. He traced the slumbering life maps of the trees around them, gentle pulsing greens and browns; and the river behind its curtain of bamboo. It was shot with the life of the fish that traced its course and remained a stunning, shimmering kaleidoscope.

Out on the ground, nocturnal creatures snuffled and crept. He could just about make out the low shambling shapes of badgers, the fleet colours and energies of mice and rats and the smooth lines of foxes. But it was difficult to track them for long. All of them could sense him but he focused his mind on projecting darkness, tweaking their fear reflexes and keeping them away. These were creatures of such small mind and so easy to bend to his will. He wondered if he could turn a horse from its path. Or ten horses. With a rider aboard it would be a true battle of wills and power.

It was something the others weren't fully aware of yet. In an animal, the will and mind were inextricably linked to the energy map and lifelines. An Ascendant interrupted the lifelines to control the animal, like he had with the eagle and gorthock. The sharper the mind, the harder it was to control and the more energy he had to draw on to perform the Work. It was tiring. Or it would be until he learned a way to use the energies of nature to help him.

Jhered was walking towards him. The Gatherer was very quiet but Gorian could see his energy map; bright, vibrant and very, very tall. Its outer tendrils reached out at the air around him, linking him with the earth and the elements in a way he would never be able to sense. That's what made the Ascendants different from every other citizen. Funny, really. Animals knew they had a link and used it. They could follow the energy of the earth and the thermals in the sky or in the water. But humans were blind to it. Most humans.

'There's nothing bad out there,' said Gorian without turning.

Jhered walked on and stood at his right shoulder. 'Did it disorient you when you first had this all-round sensory vision? How did you know which way was forward if you were walking at the same time?'

Gorian suppressed his senses and looked up at Jhered, massive and imposing from down here, but still just a man who didn't understand.

'Energy gets stronger and brighter as you near it,' he replied. 'It wasn't a problem.'

'Of course not,' said Jhered. 'Are you all right to carry on?'

Gorian nodded. 'I'll take Mirron's watch. She's tired.'

'All right. If you're sure.'

'Anyway, if the Tsardon come, there's something I want to try out.'

Jhered dropped to his haunches so that their faces were level. 'You will try nothing. You will tell me and we will deal with what we face. I am your commander. I give the orders and I make the rules.'

'You don't rule me,' said Gorian. 'No one rules me.'

'Why must you bait me, boy?' Jhered's face was cold, the lines of energy dimmed. His voice was a hiss and his eyes did not blink. 'I will not repeat myself. You will do what I say and we will all stay alive. Do not cross me.'

Gorian felt his heart pounding and his body trembling. Jhered's face was so close he could make out every scar and line even in the darkness. He couldn't find the words to get back at him. The forest was chaotic behind him, Gorian unable to focus well enough to separate the maps surrounding them.

'I must practise my abilities,' he managed.

'Not tonight. Not if we are under threat. You must only use those Works of which you are absolutely certain.' Jhered's voice softened. 'I can see you're afraid. Could you perform a new Work right now if you had to? Any Work?'

'I'm not sure,' said Gorian.

'No. Fear does strange things, even to one such as you. That is why you must act under my command. I will show you what to do when the time comes.'

Jhered rose and Gorian felt a familiar anger. His sensory vision cleared, the flares and splashes of colour calming down to more familiar lines and shapes. Trees, rodents, birds. Men.

Gorian grabbed Jhered's arm and dragged him back down.

'Someone's coming,' he whispered.

Jhered nodded. 'All right,' he said, his voice low and calm, easing Gorian's anxiety. 'Tell me how many, how far away and in what direction.'

'There are six that I can see. No, seven. They are walking. Not quite towards us. They are at the top of the slope, about thirty yards away.'

'Good. Now tell me, are they walking down the slope or along it? You have time. Keep calm because you know they can't see you.'

Gorian found Jhered's voice incredibly comforting. 'They are coming down towards the river but they will pass to our right unless they change direction. They are in a line.'

'Good.'

'What do we do?'

'Nothing at all,' said Jhered. 'Just sit as quiet as you can. They aren't tracking, probably just coming down to get some water.'

'We must wake the others.'

Jhered tensed. 'Not yet. For once in your life, trust me.'

'We can't just sit here.'

'Yes, Gorian, we can. And we will.' Jhered put a hand on his arm. 'If they come close, tell me. When they are beyond your sight, tell me.'

Gorian watched the Tsardon, if that was who they were, walk carefully down the slope. They had no light with them, no energy flare bleeding into the darkness. They made no sound that Gorian could hear with the river at his back. It was hard to concentrate and only Jhered's presence by him lent him the courage to keep the figures distinct from the rest of the energies of the forest. It should have been easy. They were awake, their lifelines bright with activity. But it wasn't. He felt undone by his fear. It was something he would have to conquer quickly.

The figures moved on. Gorian concluded they were on an animal trail or something like it. They didn't deviate at all. And it was with a growing relief that he watched them closing down to the bank of the river and away out of sight. Just as Jhered said they would.

'They've gone,' said Gorian, his breath rushing out.

'Have you been holding your breath all this time?' Jhered was smiling.

'Probably,' said Gorian, feeling light-hearted with relief. He suppressed a laugh. 'What now?'

'Well, you keep watching where they went while I wake the others.'

'What's the point? They've gone.' Jhered shook his head and Gorian's irritation grew. 'I don't like being patronised.'

'Then don't ask dim questions. You have much to learn, young man.' Jhered pointed the way the figures had gone. 'That is the direction we came from. If they are trackers they might see our path. So everyone needs to be ready, that's all.'

'Oh,' said Gorian, deflated. 'I see.'

'Anything else you want to question me about? My sword technique, perhaps?'

Gorian felt stung and shook his head. He was glad the others were asleep. He'd show Jhered one day. Show him where the power lay. But he could wait. Jhered moved back to wake the others so Gorian did as he was told. He let his anger help him focus, leaving no room for the fear that had grown again at the knowledge the figures might be back.

He could hear Jhered's low voice above the sound of the river. People rudely awakened from deep sleep and frightened at what he had to say. Menas was at Gorian's shoulder very quickly, her bow strung and nocked, her sword on the ground by her side.

'Anything?' she asked.

'No,' he said.

Though it was full night, there was a lightness in the air. The sky was full of stars and the eyes of god were in the sky as they were every change from solastro to dusas. When he suppressed the energies surrounding him and within, he could see clearly about ten yards. Beyond that, the shadows got too thick.

He didn't really believe Jhered. If whoever they were had just come down to collect water on their way somewhere, why would they be even looking at the ground? It didn't make sense at all. In a while, they'd all go back to sleep and Jhered would be embarrassed at the scare he'd given Mirron. And poor feeble Ossacer. He shouldn't do that. They weren't as strong as Gorian. He shook his head.

'There's something . . .' said Menas quietly.

She stretched her bow. Gorian froze. He let the energies cascade through him, searching through them like he should have been the whole time, checking for anything that moved. For a moment he couldn't see anything but the dull resting energies of tree and grass before the sun warms them. No men approaching.

'You'll be looking too high,' whispered Menas. She clucked her tongue softly.

Gorian stared at the ground. For a moment, his fear caused the energy trails to flare and jump in his mind. Probably only twenty yards away the figures were coming. Two were crouched low and moving straight along the line of the river. The others were crawling like lizards, almost invisible, their brighter energies hidden by long grass.

'Talk to me,' said Menas. 'Quietly.'

Gorian felt another presence behind him. Jhered.

'They are spread out,' he said. 'They are all coming this way. Crawling.'

'Good, then they don't have bows ready,' said Jhered. 'Menas, target their right flank. I don't want anyone behind us.'

They would be able to see each other soon. Gorian wanted to get up and run but it was as if Jhered sensed it. He put a hand on Gorian's shoulder.

'Go back to your friends,' he said. 'On my order, I want a barrier from the river five yards in front of you. They know it. Be ready.'

Gorian crept backwards, shuddering as he turned his back, wondering if a blade would carve through his unprotected flesh. He saw Kovan crouched behind a tree nearby. His sword was drawn and ready, his buckler on his shield arm. Their eyes met. Kovan nodded at him.

Back in the camp, the Ascendants were grouped by their kit. Mirron looked as scared as Gorian felt. Ossacer had his eyes closed and Arducius knelt between them. He beckoned Gorian over.

'Join our minds. See our focus.'

Jhered moved right of Menas and checked Kovan was ready. They needed to be quick and accurate. Seven on three and a few unarmed children. Gorian's brief description had given them an edge. He could see indistinct shapes low to the ground moving very slowly and all but silently. They were good and he'd warned Kovan and Menas so. In a few yards, they would be seen. He turned and nodded at Kovan. He in turn, nodded at Arducius just a few yards behind.

Something changed in the air. Jhered could feel it. Like warmth flowing underfoot. He shuddered. It felt alien. Wrong. The vegetation shivered ahead and towards the river bank. Bamboo groaned.

'Don't let me down,' he whispered.

He surged to his feet and charged out of the camp. He heard Menas's bow thud. Men shouted in front of him. He saw shapes come to their feet and he heard weapons drawn. To his right, roots boiled from the ground. Grass grew dense and twined around the trunks of trees. Branches speared down, new leaves sprouting. The low brush thickened and grasped. Over an area at least ten yards from the river bank, the barricade sprang up. He heard cries of fear, pain and surprise.

In front of him, the Tsardon resolved from the shadows. They were lightly armoured for speed and dark paint was on their faces. Jhered came upon two. He punched one in the face with his left fist, knocking him back. The second reacted, bringing up his blade. Jhered caught the weapon on his own and turned it aside. He brought the gladius back, raking it across the man's face and reversing it through his leather and into his gut.

He saw Kovan run by him, heard the clash of weapons and swung round to his second enemy. The man had not raised a defence. He was staring past Jhered at the growing, impassable wall of vegetation. Jhered advanced on him. He backed away.

'Fight,' said Jhered.

The Tsardon shook his head. Jhered rushed him. He backed away, stumbled on a root and fell backwards. Jhered pounced and drove his gladius through the man's chest. Blood fountained from his mouth, splashing into Jhered's face. He straightened to wipe it and was barged off the body, tumbling backwards. His right hand struck a branch, the blade springing from his hand.

The enemy was above him. Jhered rolled fast. A sword thudded into the ground behind him. He kicked out, forcing the Tsardon back and drove to his feet. Dimly, he heard the sound of a bow string followed by a scream of agony. The Tsardon circled him. Blades were still clashing down towards the river. He towered over the smaller man, watching his movements.

He feinted forward and Jhered dodged back, thumping into a tree trunk. The enemy's eyes widened and he stabbed forwards. Jhered ducked. The blade struck the tree above his head. Jhered butted the

Tsardon, knocking the wind from him. His arms encircled the man's midriff and they tumbled across the ground. Jhered ended up underneath but was quicker with his fists. He pushed the Tsardon up with one hand and crashed a right hook into his chin. The Tsardon's jaws cracked together. Teeth broke and splintered. He fell away. Jhered followed him, drew a dagger and thrust it into his throat, holding his head to one side while his life bled away into the ground.

Jhered listened. There was no more fighting but someone was speaking down towards the river bank.

'Menas!'

'Here, Exchequer,' she replied, trotting over to him. Her bow was still in her hand. 'Two down here.'

'Good. I've taken three.' Jhered cleaned his dagger on the dead man's clothes and stood. 'Kovan.'

'Sir. Over here.'

Menas followed him. Kovan was standing near one body and with his gladius to the neck of the last Tsardon scout. Kovan was cut on his upper arm but smiling. Jhered could see why. The Tsardon's arms and chest were entwined in the Ascendants' natural barrier. His eyes were wide and scared.

'Put that up, young Vasselis,' said Jhered. 'Get back to the Ascendants, see they are all right. Have Ossacer look at that cut.'

'My Lord,' said Kovan.

'Well, well, well,' said Jhered. 'A rat in a trap. Do you speak Estorean?' It was plain the Tsardon did not. 'Karku?'

'Yes. Please. Cut the plants away.'

Jhered dropped to his haunches. 'I will. And I will let you run, too. Take this message to your masters. The Conquord has a new weapon. We can see you when it is dark. We have all of God's creatures and every tree at our command. We can call storms on you. We can bring lightning from the sky. We can split the earth and the mountains. Fear us.'

Jhered and Menas cut the thick, tight roots from the Tsardon and dragged him to his feet. Menas took his weapons.

'Do not look back. We will know,' said Jhered. 'Run.'

And the Tsardon did. Jhered smiled.

'Exaggeration?' said Menas.

'I'm not so sure it is. Anyway they'll almost certainly ignore him. But the seeds will be sown.' He shrugged. 'You never know.' He pointed back to where they had been fighting. 'Look for my gladius, would you? It'll be near the last man I killed.'

'Of course.'

Jhered walked back into the camp. The Ascendants and Kovan were all very still.

'What's—?'

He heard the unmistakable sound of bows being tensed and raised his hands above his head.

Chapter 59

848th cycle of God, 35th day of Solasfall
15th year of the true Ascendancy

'I'm amazed she hung on for as long as she did,' said Willem Geste.

Hesther's tears were spoiling her message on Genna's mask. The meaning she wanted to convey was of warm light and endless love. She just couldn't form the words to make sense of it.

'Don't wipe them away,' said Willem. 'Let them soak in. More eloquent a memory than any words.'

Hesther squeezed Willem's arm and straightened from the table. 'I'll have to come back. I can't do this now.'

She walked out into the late afternoon sunshine. Poor Genna. Her heart broken by Ardol Kessian's death but her will to see the Echelon survive denying her rest. She barely ate or slept in the last days. The haunting look had never left her eyes and it crushed Hesther daily to hear her weeping in her bedroom. She refused to wallow publicly in her grief, her dignity so typical of her strength. She kept working and she kept believing.

But Ardol's call was stronger than anything here under God's blessed sky. And today, Hesther hadn't heard her footsteps whispering along the marble outside her room as dawn broke and had known she was dead. Another one of the Echelon taken prematurely. Another celebration overshadowed by uncomfortable feelings of anger and injustice.

A new gloom had settled over Westfallen. The town wore it like a cloak heavy with rain. The air stank of furnaces and rang to the sounds of hammer and anvil. They were more a forge than a port. To her left, the stockades and gates were all in place from shore, curving away over the slight rolls in the ground at the borders of the town to shore. The artillery was being put in place too. Onagers and bolt-firers had been set on platforms or drawn up on open ground behind the stockade, ready to defend the town from the Order. Or the Tsardon, whichever came first. The beacon fires still worried at the night sky and their smoke smudged every day.

Hesther sighed and rubbed her hands across her cheeks, drying them on her dress. Westfallen was a fortress. She hated what they had become in no time at all. Imprisoned by their desire to set the Conquord free. Arvan Vasselis did what he believed to be right but his determination that this defence would only be temporary didn't carry total conviction. She prayed he was right. She couldn't live like this and she wouldn't demand it of any of the citizens here. It was unnatural.

The tide was coming in. Waves reached further and further up the bay and lapped against the harbour walls on which onagers were standing. Their ugly silhouettes were monstrous reminders of where Westfallen found itself today. Everything was wrong.

Hesther drew in a breath and rejected the desire to run back into the House of Masks. There would be no answers there. She headed the Echelon now. She was its figurehead, not Ardol. But how fragile a thing that had become. Its members were riven with uncertainty about their calling. Questioning whether it should continue. Genna had been outspoken in her criticism of the introspection. But she was gone now and Hesther wasn't sure she had the strength to hold them to their purpose.

A movement by the bluff at the western turn of the inlet caught her eye. A sail, deep blue, moving gently into sight. The trireme eased into the channel, her oars dipping and rising. The beat of the drum echoed faintly across the bay. It shouldn't be sailing in here. Vasselis had told them they would never see his warships unless there was threat of invasion by sea. Or unless . . . Hesther's breath caught in her throat. She began to run down to the dockside. By the time she got there, the harbour wall was five deep with Westfallen citizens, levium and palace guard. All of them straining to see the name on the prow and the identity of those walking the deck.

Hesther was standing by Meera and Jen Shalke. They had stopped Jen from diving into the sea to swim out to meet the ship. The buzz of chatter grew in volume with every stroke of the oars. The sail was furled and the ship began to turn to nudge up against the deep water berths. The prow swung away, revealing the name agonisingly slowly. Hesther wasn't the first to see it but word was passed around the crowd.

It was the *Cirandon's Pride*. The ship that had been on station the day the Ascendants had left Westfallen. Hesther hugged Meera and Jen to her, praying for good news.

The clamour was loud in the main reception hall of the Ascendancy villa. The news that the Ascendants were alive and well had brought an outpouring of joy and relief. But now the tears were dried, that joy was being swamped under a tide of disquiet.

'Please,' said Hesther, standing and holding up her hands. 'The captain is trying to answer a question. Please don't ask another ten. One at a time. God-embrace-me but you are worse than the children.'

The Echelon quietened, embarrassed. Marshal Vasselis, sitting next to Hesther, suppressed a laugh.

'Captain Patonius, please continue.'

The powerful woman nodded. She was devoid of humour and clearly uncomfortable in this company. She had not sat down as offered and stood by a marble table, fingering the small statue of Herine Del Aglios, formally posed, that adorned it.

'I am reporting facts, not justifying decisions,' said Patonius stiffly. 'Exchequer Jhered outranks me. I could not refuse him. It is easy for you to sit here and remind me of my orders. And I resent the implication that I have somehow betrayed my Marshal. You were not in the centre of the Tirronean Sea with a Gatherer ship either side of you. And you are ignoring the fact that they are now under the protection of one of our finest swordsmen and an elite guard. If you do not believe me, you can always direct your question to my Marshal.'

'Arvan?' Meera spoke into the brief quiet.

'I can't understand your concern, I really can't,' said Vasselis. 'Paul Jhered is not just as Patonius describes, he is also one of the few outside this room who genuinely understands the Ascendants. And he is a man of unimpeachable integrity and honour. The journey is dangerous. I cannot think of a man more capable of seeing them safe.'

'Yes,' said Willem. 'But he has no intention of taking them to Sirrane, does he, Captain?'

Hesther frowned at him. 'What are you talking about?'

'Does he, Captain?' repeated Willem.

Patonius shook her head. 'He's taking them to join Roberto Del Aglios. He wants them to help him win the war.'

'He has no right to do that. They are just children.' Andreas's voice was the loudest of them, rising above the outrage that swept across the Echelon. And this time, it was not Patonius that was the target, it was Vasselis. 'He's your friend. How can he do this?'

'Enough,' said Vasselis. He stood up, imposing himself and demanding attention. There was anger on his face. This wasn't Arvan, this was Marshal Defender Vasselis, their ruler.

'You cast your accusations about but you don't have all the facts. Exchequer Jhered has considerable powers in time of threat to the Conquord. That gives him the right to second anyone he chooses to aid a defensive effort in anyway he sees fit. It does not matter if they are fresh from the womb or breathing their last. He has not exceeded his rights.'

'But his moral and ethical—'

'Andreas, I do not want to order you out of here,' said Vasselis. 'Calm yourself. Look, I know this is difficult for you to hear. And remember my son is with them. Whatever dangers they are facing, he is facing too.' He nodded ruefully. 'Yes, forgot that, didn't you?'

'I am sorry, Arvan,' said Andreas.

'No need,' said Vasselis. 'Now, Captain. Something isn't right here. The beacons tell us there is a threat to the Conquord. My messengers have relayed that our eastern front has collapsed. But there is considerable defence in the area. Why has he decided he must take them to Del Aglios?'

'Your next messenger will confirm the threat is mortal,' said Patonius. 'Atreska has rebelled. Marshal Yuran has sided with the Tsardon. Nowhere is safe.'

She paused and all Hesther could hear was the sound of nervous breathing and the buzz of the citizens gathered outside the villa, waiting for news. Vasselis motioned her to continue. His face had paled.

'Lord Jhered feels the Conquord could fall unless decisive blows are struck. And he believes the Ascendants are the key. I know you think they are a force for peace but I have seen their potential as a weapon, as has he.'

'But they are just four young children,' said Hesther. 'How can they stop whole armies?'

'It remains to be seen if they can,' said Vasselis. His voice was flat. 'With respect, I don't think any of you can really grasp the seriousness of our position. When Atreska rebelled it gave the enemy a seaboard in the north of the Tirronean. If the Tsardon armies invade Gestern too, then Caraduk is under direct threat.'

'Captain, I presume you have been signalled by Kester Isle?'

'Yes, Marshal. We will rest and resupply here tonight, with your leave, and will sail on the outgoing tide tomorrow. The colours of the Ocetanas will be flying from the mast.'

Hesther shook her head. 'Our children. Our poor, poor children. How has all this happened to them? What have we done?'

She felt Vasselis's hand on her shoulder. 'Unpalatable as it is, what you have done is give the Conquord the means to defeat the Tsardon and save Caraduk from invasion. They are in the best hands possible.' He spoke to the room. 'We all fear times like these. So what we must do is ensure we neither flinch nor falter and that our enemies do not succeed.'

He sat down and Hesther could see the strain on his face. He wiped a hand across his mouth.

'My son is out there,' he whispered. 'Please God let him be safe.'

There was an urgent rap on the door. Captain Harkov strode in.

'Marshal,' he said. 'We need you at the gates. Trouble's coming.'

Appros Harin felt sick. His shoulder wound ached terribly and the wind that blew through the basilica was icy. Marshal General Niranes stood with him but they did not stand united. They watched the Advocate walking up the steps in response to their summons. On the tactical map table in front of them, the muster and marching reports were laid out, held down by carved stone paperweights. Birds and riders had been arriving in Estorr from all over the Conquord in the previous days and what had begun as serious had become desperate.

'All the reports are in, I take it,' said the Advocate.

'Yes, my Advocate,' said Niranes. 'And I have already responded demanding more. I don't know what else we can do.'

Harin cleared his throat noisily and felt his face flush with irritation. He looked pointedly at the tactical map and its feeble number of legion markers.

'You are in every way a product of the Jhered school, Appros Harin,' said the Advocate. 'What is it that so taxes you?'

'The Conquord is complacent, my Advocate,' he said, marshalling his courage. 'And it will fall because of it. We stand here talking about demanding more support but we will get none. Even if we did it would arrive too late.'

He pushed a hand at the muster reports.

'Pick any one of them and it tells you all you need to know. Bahkir has managed a third of its expected numbers and cites western sea raiders as a reason not to send more. Morasia's muster is pathetic. Tundarra claims the Omari are threatening her borders. Similarly, Dornos. We had to have their numbers on the Atreskan border. We are short by twenty thousand soldiers and cavalry. They know the Tsardon aren't going to invade them because King Khuran wants to sack Estorr and that is as far as he will go. So when it comes to it, when war begins to extend its hand, all those countries who gloried in the wealth of the Conquord are effectively turning their backs. All they are sending us in great quantity is food.'

The Advocate stared at him long and hard. He felt himself begin to wilt under the pressure. Eventually, she gestured back towards the palace.

'I have representatives from all those countries staying on the Hill,' she said quietly. 'What do you propose I do with them?'

'With respect, my Advocate, it doesn't matter. They are all loyal Conquord people but their influence clearly doesn't spread to the palaces and villas of their home countries. Not enough are coming. We have everything we could hope for from Neratharn, Avarn, Caraduk, Easthale and Estorea. But latest reports suggest at least forty thousand rebels and Tsardon are on the march west through Atreska. We will muster twenty-five thousand at best. It will not be enough.'

'Marshal General Niranes, your thoughts?' The Advocate turned her gaze upon him. He started. Harin bit his lip to avoid laughing.

Niranes waved a hand at the map. 'We can hold them for long enough that more will come. They are the Tsardon. We are the Conquord. But if you are worried, let's take defence from the eastern coast of the Tirronean Sea and send it to Neratharn.'

'Suicide,' muttered Harin. 'Idiot. They are too far away already.'

'Appros Harin, you will mind your words,' said Niranes

Harin felt the last vestiges of his respect disperse. 'Damn you, I will not. You have not listened to me. You have not taken up my contingency plans. You have relied on every territory sending eighty per cent of the maximum numbers. The Neratharnese front is too broad to defend against such numbers. I asked you to move the coastal reserve north fifteen days ago. Now it is too late.'

'Not if we use the fleet to transport them,' hissed Niranes.

'And leave Kester Isle a helpless sentinel should the Tsardon fleet be on the way? Why didn't you listen to me?'

'Enough!' The Advocate slapped her hand on the table. Her voice echoed through the basilica. Heads turned. 'What are you telling me. That we cannot defend the Conquord? That is not acceptable.'

'We can,' said Niranes. 'Move legions from Estorr and Caraduk's coasts using the Ocetanas.'

'And I will welcome the Tsardon into Estorr's harbour myself.' Harin turned to the Advocate. 'May I speak freely?'

'You mean, you haven't been so far?' The Advocate's tone was without humour. 'Why not? I'm standing here wondering if I'll have a Conquord to rule come genastro, and I find myself listening to bickering children. And when you have spoken, I will hear the Marshal General. Also without interruption.'

Harin bowed and took a deep breath.

'It is a rule of war the Marshal ignores, that you cannot attack or defend with potential numbers of home forces, only with absolutes. Therefore, we cannot currently expect to hold the Neratharnese border. We could, just possibly, reinforce in enough time by raping the coast of its infantry defence. But the transport and supply of ten to fifteen thousand infantry on a sea journey of that length is not to be undertaken lightly. If it isn't done properly, they will be in no condition to fight when they arrive.

'The second rule the Marshal has ignored is that you must prosecute defence on your enemy's potential numbers and not on known absolutes. My Advocate, Gesteris lost at Scintarit almost eighty days ago. It is inconceivable that the Tsardon fleet has not moved to attack either the east coast of Gestern or, more likely, their Tirronean coastline directly. Make no mistake. King Khuran wants his flag on the Hill now that he has us on the run. And he will move on both fronts.

'The Atreskan navy is sizeable and we can assume widespread defection. The Tsardon navy is reportedly enormous. The Ocetanas is spread the length and breadth of the Tirronean Sea already. To move a hundred ships off station invites the Tsardon to sail in virtually unopposed. We could have moved defence by road fifteen days ago and left the Ocetanas to guard the coasts. Critically, we could have taken a couple of thousand horses. I was ignored by this civil servant and now it is too late.'

The Advocate raised a hand to silence Niranes while she thought. Harin watched her study the map. Her eyes moved to Tsard.

'Give me options. I will not cede the Conquord. We have armies in the field in Tsard. What of them?'

'We know that Atarkis is pledged to defend the Gosland front. He will hold but he will not break through either, in my opinion. We have no word from Jorganesh. We can assume that he is heading for Gestern but we cannot rely on it. And your son is marching south. The number of Tsardon pressing the Gesternan border is too great for Marshal Mardov to counter for long and then the western coast of Gestern is open to the enemy.

'General Del Aglios is your most capable commander but even he has been damaged by plague. Both he and Atarkis have moved away from Atreska because they had to hope we could stay the advance. Your son will be angling to protect Estorr from invasion and I have no doubt he will succeed.'

'But he will be too far from Neratharn to help us when he does,' said the Advocate.

'Yes, my Lady.'

'There has been a disastrous error of judgement,' she said.

'Yes,' said Harin. 'But we can still buy a little time and hope for a miracle.'

'Is that all we have to hope for?' asked the Advocate.

Harin shrugged. 'If your son is victorious sooner than we could dream of and marches faster than we can imagine, he might reach Neratharn through Atreska in time. Or we can pray that Exchequer Jhered was right and the Ascendants are the weapon to win the war.'

'But you will refer me to rule one if I cling on to that,' said the Advocate.

'Indeed I will.' Harin could feel the change in the mood.

'And tell me, Appros Harin, how you will buy me some time for the miracle we must pray for from now on.'

'Release me from my duties here. The levium are mustered at the Solastro Palace. I know they should ride to secure Estorr but that is no use to us now. Let me lead them to Neratharn. Over three thousand horse. We'll be late to the battle but we'll get there before the end.'

The Advocate considered for a moment. 'But where will I find another Harin to advise on tactics?'

'Appros Derizan is in Estorr,' said Harin. 'She is more than capable. I can brief her before I leave.'

'Good. Then go, Harin, and take my blessing, my good wishes and the hope of the Conquord with you.'

'One more thing, if I may,' said Harin. The Advocate nodded. 'I'm going to break rule one. Lord Jhered will come through. Look for him at the time you need him most. He has an uncanny knack of being at your side.'

The Advocate smiled. 'I pray to the Omniscient that you are right.'

Harin thumped his right fist onto his chest and marched from the table. He heard the Advocate speak to Niranes, a smile cracking his face.

'I have a new title for myself,' she said. 'Marshal General of the Conquord.'

'I—'

'You, Niranes, might have cost me the Conquord with your pig-headed arrogance. Go home and implore God that the next person to knock on your door is me, not King Khuran. Get out of my sight.'

Chapter 60

848th cycle of God, 35th day of Solasfall
15th year of the true Ascendancy

Roberto broke away from the embrace, but still couldn't quite believe it. The absurdity made him laugh and it was a moment before he could speak.

'Of all the people for my scouts to bring back, absolutely the last in my thoughts was you.'

'I'm just glad to be here. There were some with distinctly twitchy fingers on those strings.'

'They were just irritable you got the quarry first,' said Roberto. 'What madness has brought you into the wilds? Actually, stow that, because I know more than you think. I just didn't believe it.'

'So, in reality, you've been expecting me,' said Jhered.

He was in need of a shave but had lost none of his presence. The quiet that had swept the army when he passed by on his way to Roberto's tent was proof enough.

'Technically.'

'I'm impressed messengers have reached you. Which way did they come?'

'I've had three,' said Roberto. 'Two from the south via Gestern and one from the west through Atreska. They've been slow so the news is old but I expect the picture is accurate enough.'

'I have far more recent information about Gestern.'

'Good,' said Roberto. He pointed the way to the tilted desk on which his maps were pinned. 'We'll deal with your cargo in a moment. But let me tell you where we are right now.'

He indicated a map that covered Atreska, Gosland, eastern Tsard, Gestern and the Tirronean Sea to its western coasts.

'The war has not yet reached the Neratharnese border but it is imminent. We do not have forces capable of holding the enemy for long. Gestern, I understand, will be embattled at much the same time. At least Gosland appears relatively secure. The Tsardon have organised very well. I only hope that what we have seen represents their entire strength.'

'What news of resistance in Atreska?' asked Jhered.

'Fractured and insignificant. The scale of Yuran's betrayal is immense and it is clear most of his people love him enough to believe in him still. Any loyal legions we have are either destroyed or fleeing north or west where they may be of more use. Some awoke with the blades of those they thought friends at their throats.' Roberto shook his head. 'Atreska is a mess. One day its people will see the folly they have sanctioned. The Tsardon spill lies about a liberation. But they will not leave unless the Conquord forces them out. Only the most naïve would believe otherwise.'

'And what is left should the Tsardon break through our defences in Neratharn?'

'Precious little. Coastal defence. The 1st legion. Not enough.' Roberto wiped a hand across his face and felt the despair growing again. 'Paul, I think I have made a mistake that might cost us the Conquord.'

'What? No. No. To march south was the best decision of your life. Believe me.'

'How can that be? Jorganesh will be in Gestern by now. The Tsardon cannot get through, they do not have the numbers. I should have fought through Atreska and relieved Neratharn. Dammit but I've lost seven hundred of my Atreskan alae because of it. I all but called them cowards and traitors. But it's me who is the coward. Running from battle.'

'Never speak like that,' snapped Jhered, grabbing Roberto's chin in one huge hand. 'Never. It does you disservice. And it is not true. You know why you decided to march south. And I thank the Omniscient that you did.'

He paused and slackened his grip, dropped his hand with an apology. He was biting his lip.

'What's wrong, Paul?'

'Jorganesh isn't in Gestern,' he said quietly. 'And he never will make it.'

'What are you saying?' asked Roberto.

'He was ambushed in Lubjek's Defile. His army was slaughtered. There is no one stopping the Tsardon southern front reaching Gestern.'

Roberto couldn't get his thoughts into order. He stared down at the map. In his mind's eye, he could see the spread of the Tsardon across his beloved Conquord like a rising tide. Unstoppable. Inevitable. And one by one, all those he knew and trusted were being drowned. Gesteris, and now Jorganesh.

'Are you sure?'

'I saw it for myself.' Jhered cleared his throat. 'There's something else. You've been marching unmolested, haven't you?'

Roberto nodded. 'It's been a blessing. Confusing but a blessing. We are being tracked though. They know we're coming. But we aren't gaining ground on them fast enough.'

'That's because they aren't ahead of you. Your scouts aren't going to find their path. And they aren't attacking you because you're going in the wrong direction. They plan to attack and take the Gesternan coast, travel as far south down it as they can to take ship to Estorr. I'm certain of it.'

Roberto focused on the map once more. 'Dusas will beat them,' he said. 'The Atreskan rebel navy is not large enough to take an invasion force and the Ocetanas will wipe them out. They cannot build enough ships in Gestern, even assuming they have the skill and the resources before dusas renders a crossing too risky.'

'They won't need to,' said Jhered. 'Their armada has already sailed from the Bay of Harryn. Hundreds of sails, the Karku say. Enough, certainly.'

'Then I am already too late.' Roberto's despair threatened to clog his throat.

'No,' said Jhered. 'Not if you change your direction now and chase them by the fastest route. The Tsardon are mustering but they have not yet attacked.'

'What difference will it really make? If Jorganesh is gone, then my eleven thousand face at least three times that number. Even with the Gesternan defence, these are poor odds.'

'Trust me. I have just delivered you the most powerful weapon of this war. One that can stop whole armies at a stroke without you having to prime one scorpion.'

'The Ascendants?' said Roberto, shaking his head. 'I have

conflicting stories concerning them. None in which I place the remotest faith. And accusations concerning your loyalty to my mother and the Omniscient. I also have a message from my mother asking me to scout for you. It's playing out like a bad piece of drama. Perhaps you'd better give me your side. I could do with having my mood lightened by more exaggeration.'

Mirron sat with Menas, away from the others, in the tent that had been cleared for them. They had come in under the scrutiny of the whole army so it seemed. Mirron had found it quite overwhelming while the others had seemed excited at it all. So much noise. So many people in endless rows of tents. Her ears were full of the sounds of hammer on metal or sword on sword where soldiers sparred. There was a barrage of conversation, too. And the pandemonium that came with hundreds of horses corralled together.

On their heads-bowed walk in she had endured wolf whistles and countless invitations. Some of them she hadn't even understood. Menas had thrown a protective arm around her and made her Gatherer cloak public knowledge. That had silenced some of them. Kovan had been at her side too but had since run off to see if he could find any of his friends in the Estorean hastati.

That left Ossacer and Arducius practising the capture of energies from the still air, along with Gorian. Ossacer thought that if they could make it efficient, it could be a source of power, greater than fire, earth, sea or tree. He'd been saying it for years. Only Arducius really believed him and that was only because he was a Wind Harker and wanted to call hurricanes from nothing. She hadn't felt like helping out. She was tired and her stomach ached. Only Menas seemed sensitive to her mood.

'Feeling a little alone?' asked the Gatherer.

'I don't know why it should be. There are so many people about.'

Menas smoothed hair from her brow. 'Oh, Mirron, you really have been kept from the real world, haven't you?'

'I'm only fourteen, Erith,' said Mirron sharply. 'Anyway, I haven't been kept from it. Westfallen is the real world. Was.'

'But it's so different from this, isn't it? There are more than ten thousand people in this camp. You've never been in such a large gathering before, have you? Never been to Port Roulent, let alone Cirandon or Estorr, I doubt.'

Mirron went to the door of the tent. They weren't under arrest but there were guards either side. She looked out over the canvas city just beginning to fade at its extremities as the sun dipped away west. Earlier and earlier now that dusas was just around the corner. The noise had not abated. Clashing, shouting, barking, running, singing. Kovan said it wouldn't die away until the dead of night and even then, some would choose not to sleep.

'So why do I feel alone?' she asked. 'And why do I feel . . . I don't know.'

'Threatened?'

'Yes.' She walked back to Menas and sat down, a little shudder across her shoulders. 'This is our army, isn't it? I should feel safe.'

'It's not to do with enemies and friends. This just isn't a place for young people like you and your brothers. You most particularly. These are battle-hardened men and women that used to be farmers and potters like those in your home town. Most of them remember their past lives only as dreams. They still desire to return to their old lives but in the middle of a desperate situation it is dangerous to think of it. So they make this army all of their existence. Do you understand?'

'Sort of.'

'And you don't belong in it. You can feel the aggression but you can't hope to understand it. They desperately need routine and discipline and our arrival with the Exchequer is like throwing a stone into a mill pond. They will be suspicious until they understand your presence here. Even if the Exchequer does convince General Del Aglios of your worth, many of his army will never accept you. Remember what you told me about the reaction on the ship? It will be the same here, only there are ten thousand, not two hundred.'

Mirron slumped. She looked at the others, deep in concentration and could feel only hopelessness for them all.

'People shouldn't hate us,' she said. 'Why can't they see we are here to help them win and get back to their stupid lives? That's what Jhered wants us to do. Why can't he make them see?'

'I'm sorry, Mirron. But that's the real world, too. You've grown up with what you have. But nearly everyone else has no idea of your abilities. An army believes in the strength of its arms and artillery. Nothing else.'

'So why am I worse off than the others?'

Menas sighed. 'Oh, Mirron, have you never looked at yourself?'

'What do you mean?'

'Why do you think Kovan and Gorian fight over your attention?'

'Well, I'm not that stupid.' Mirron was aware that she was blushing. 'I know boys will chase me.'

Menas smiled. 'Well that's a good start. But you need to realise that you are a beautiful young woman and not a little girl. Not out here in the midst of an army of many men and few women. You've taken the blood of fertility, haven't you? And it's coming on again, isn't it? In a day or so. Captain Patonius spoke to you about this, didn't she?

'Men will desire you. And the women in the army will not get in their way. Why do you think there are so many women camp-followers?'

'Oh.' Mirron shrank back against Menas, finding herself very afraid. 'But you won't let them touch me, will you?'

Menas's face hardened. 'I am here to protect you, Mirron. No one will hurt you while I am with you. I promise.'

Mirron smiled. She felt admiration mixed with her relief. 'I'm glad you're here.'

'Me, too.'

Menas put an arm round her and pulled her close.

'Maybe I can join the Gatherers,' said Mirron. 'Be the first Ascendant to take the cloak and travel with you forever.'

'Maybe,' said Menas. 'Maybe.'

Roberto put down his watered wine and stood up. He walked to the door of his tent and checked again that his guard was standing away as he had ordered; forming a perimeter out of earshot. When he turned, he could see the belief in Jhered's face but he just couldn't share it.

'The heights of Kark must have starved your brain,' he said. 'Can't you see that this isn't just a desperate last throw, it is complete madness. How can you expect me to believe it?'

'I'm asking you to trust me,' said Jhered.

'On what grounds?' Roberto fought to keep his voice down. He pointed out of his tent. 'I am just about keeping body and will together out there. Since my first and only victory this year, I have had plague, desertion, forced march, rebellion and every scrap of news that has come my way has been bad. And now you expect me to walk out there and tell my army that four children are going to win the war for us? If I do that, I will lose them all. They would laugh in my face and I would not blame them. I would have mutiny and this stitched-together force would disintegrate.'

'It is nevertheless true,' said Jhered.

'But you have no proof,' he shouted before he could calm himself. 'Dammit, Paul, it sounds like pure invention. Tales to tell babies. And it is heresy against the Omniscient. I will not countenance it.'

'And you think I haven't struggled with it, too?' Jhered stood and marched across the tent to stand toe to toe with him. The Gatherer was a full foot taller than him and his glare could melt stone. Roberto didn't flinch. 'Do you really think that I have travelled all the way here with them on a whim? The levium will have mustered at the Solastro Palace and I should be with them. They will ride without their commander. I am staking everything on the Ascendants because I believe that whatever their heretic status, they can save the Conquord.'

Roberto nodded and waved one of the pieces of paper in his hand. 'And my mother trusts you so far that she believes you. For now. But she isn't here. She does not know the morale of my army.'

'But still—'

'Paul, you base their war-winning abilities on nothing. So they make the wind fill sails. So they can force roots to grow into a little barrier. If I choose to believe it, which I don't. But you extrapolate to the conclusion that they can bring down mountains, call hurricanes and lightning and tear the earth apart beneath our enemies' feet. It is nonsense and I do not understand why you of all people would have anything to do with it.'

'Please, Roberto. See them. See their eyes. Let them show you what they can do.'

'No!' Roberto turned from Jhered; he had to. This was like Shakarov all over again. A man he thought he knew and admired turning out to be a stranger. 'Have you not listened to a word I've said? If they can do what you say, what do you think a demonstration in this camp would do to my army? I don't care whose side they are on. Dear God-embrace-me, Exchequer, how can you expect this of me?'

'Because you know you can trust me. Because you know I do

nothing unless I believe it will benefit the Conquord and my friends. People like you, Roberto. And your mother.'

Roberto shook his head. 'I'm sorry, Paul, but no. I will change the direction of my march because I believe your intelligence about the enemy. And I also believe I can win this war for the Conquord without assistance from any Ascendant witchcraft. I can fall on the Tsardon lines and, with Gestern, we will crush them. Then we will turn and take back Atreska.'

'This from the man who earlier today thought the war all but lost,' said Jhered, and Roberto heard a contempt in his voice that pained him. 'You have found confidence from some source I would love to tap.'

'I think you've said enough,' said Roberto. 'Because you are still my friend, I will afford you protection. Your Ascendants too. But they are not to act or I will have them executed for treason and heresy, do I make myself clear? I am the general of this army and I will not have that authority undermined by anyone. Not even you.'

Jhered nodded. 'I respect all that you have said, just as I respect you as the finest general in the Conquord. I'm not here to undermine your authority. I'm here to help.' He moved towards the tent entrance but paused and turned on his way. 'And perhaps you can win the war exactly as you describe. But I think you should add up the days it will take you to beat Tsard's thirty thousand at Gestern with your eleven thousand and then march to relieve the Neratharn border.

'You do not have the time, Roberto, before the Tsardon break through up there. You know it and I know it. What is the point of scoring victory in Gestern if the Conquord is lost to the north? I can give you that time. Think on it, general. Let us help you.'

Roberto dropped into the chair in front of his maps when Jhered had gone. He snatched up his wine and drained it. He called for more. Ten days to the Gesternan border. Another ten north to Byscar chasing the Tsardon, should he win. And six at least to the Neratharnese border through hostile territory. And that last into the teeth of dusasrise.

He was in the middle of nowhere and any direction he took would let the Tsardon through in another place. He put his head in his hands and didn't even notice Herides come in with his fresh wine. The Conquord was failing.

Chapter 61

848th cycle of God, 35th day of Solasfall
15th year of the true Ascendancy

'It's like some demonic procession of Caraducian trades and skills,' muttered Marshal Defender Vasselis.

He stood with Harkov and Hesther on the left-hand gate-turret of Westfallen. Two days since Harkov had given him the news of the approach and the disorganised but sizeable rabble were within sight of the town.

He passed his magnifier to Hesther. He didn't need it; the images would be etched forever in his mind. The determined, angry, frightened faces of his citizens. Some carried placards and banners. Others, in bitter irony, the Caraducian flag. It flew from Westfallen's gate-turrets too.

Just ordinary trades people and farmers. Men, women and children. His people. Whipped into action by the words of the Readers and Speakers that walked with them. And kept moving by the few soldiers of the Armour of God riding by them. He even recognised one or two. They must have travelled from all over the south. From Cirandon, Port Roulent and every town they passed through on the way. All in one-eyed ignorance. There were several hundred of them. He wondered if any of them had the first clue what they hoped to achieve.

'Such is the power of the Chancellor's will,' said Hesther, a tremble in her voice. 'Fear and hate. So easy to create, so hard to dispel.'

'We will do what we must,' said Harkov, turning to them both.

'You won't fight them, surely?' said Hesther.

'I have orders from the Advocate,' said Harkov. 'I am a Captain of the Palace Guard. We will do what we must.'

'Talk to them, Arvan,' said Hesther. 'Make them understand.'

Vasselis couldn't look at Hesther. Nothing about this situation made sense. The Conquord was battling for its life across the Tirronean Sea and yet here its people fought over issues they did not and could not understand. Yet, at the same time, this coming fight could be the most important in Conquord history. It was a fight for progress and evolution.

'I will say what I can,' said Vasselis. 'But you aren't naïve, Mother Naravny. Nor are any of the Echelon. Westfallen's secrets have always been maintained at a price. Its survival may come at a higher cost still.'

Hesther stared at the side of his head until he turned to her. He could see the conflict within her.

'You would fire on your own citizens?'

'If my hand is forced I will not hesitate,' he said. He saw Hesther shudder. 'I'm sorry. None of us wished this.'

'Perhaps it won't come to that,' said Harkov. 'They are poorly armed and they have no artillery. Only a fool would attack us.'

Vasselis breathed deep. 'Perhaps not yet. But they may merely be the vanguard.'

He looked to his left and right. Levium lined the stockade. Bows were leant against the timbers, gladiuses in scabbards. The sight of the hundred cloaks should be enough to keep them out of bowshot. But if not, his men manned catapults and scorpions. And a hundred further Caraducian guard were billeted throughout the town. He hadn't bothered to summon any to the gates. What was coming at them today would never force a breach.

When the first of the crowd were within a hundred yards they began to slow; bunching up and pausing at the edge of bow range. Vasselis took up his magnifier again. Uncertainty had replaced much of the determination. The reality of the new face of Westfallen and its defenders took much of the energy from the march. Vasselis shook his head.

'Now what will you do?' he whispered.

The answer was quickly forthcoming. Ten people broke from the front of the crowd which spread across the open space in front of the gates. A few shouts came over the sound of the wind rippling flag and banners. Four riders of the Armour of God shadowed six Readers and Speakers. They advanced under the banner of the Omniscient.

He felt a keen disappointment on recognising Speaker Lotheris from Port Roulent. The Prime Speaker of Caraduk was not with them, he noted. It was to be hoped that he continued to display a greater wisdom.

It was Lotheris who spoke from a position only ten yards from the gates.

'Marshal Defender Arvan Vasselis—'

'Here we go, charges and demands,' muttered Vasselis.

'—you are accused of heresy against the Omniscient; of the harbouring and protection of named heretics; of the perversion of the scriptures and the murder of soldiers from the Armour of God. We few here represent but a tiny minority of those saddened by the truth and must reluctantly demand justice. We have served you and Caraduk unflinchingly and unfailingly. But now you must stand to account before us.'

Lotheris gestured behind her.

'These are your people. They demand you answer to them. They demand your surrender for trial before them. It is as the law allows and you may not refuse.'

'Your command of the laws of the Conquord is commendable,' said Vasselis, pitching his voice for the ten below him only. 'And I look forward to standing before my people to prove my case. But not like this. This is a mob and no ruler will bow to a mob. Moreover, it is a mob whipped to action by half-truths, supposition and the testimony of a discredited Chancellor who herself faces trial for murder in Estorr.'

Vasselis paused at Lotheris's reaction. Sweat was on her brow and her puffed cheeks were red.

'Omitted that small detail, did she? I am surprised. Her mind is normally so sharp where crime against the Conquord and the Omniscient is concerned.' Vasselis shook his head. 'But there's something else you've missed, isn't there? I am also aware of the laws of the Conquord. And naturally, I will walk from these gates as you require.'

He laid a hand on Hesther's arm in response to her gasp.

'But first, I wish to read the countersigned warrant from the Advocate. She is the only person capable of agreeing to your demand for my arrest. A formality, I'm sure. Which of you has it?'

Vasselis felt a cold contempt in the pit of his stomach. He waited for the silence to grow.

'What did you hope to achieve by this pitiful display, Lotheris? Did you think my remorse would be so great that I would rush gratefully into your care to plead for mercy and confess my wrongs? The Chancellor has spread her rumours and lies expertly, I can see. So well that they have removed reason from otherwise intelligent individuals.'

He raised his head and filled his lungs to shout to his citizens.

'Go home, all of you. You are victims of deception. There is no heresy here. There are no criminals to be tried. And these beneath the gates have no authority on which to act. Go back to your businesses. Pull together for the true cause, for the war against the Tsardon. Dusas is coming. Your home fires are warm. The land you stand on now will freeze beneath you.'

Some of them heard him. He saw the ripple of conversation through the crowd. He returned his attention to Lotheris.

'You are a misguided fool. I do not believe myself in breach of any law or Omniscient scripture. Why would I submit to you? Look around me. I am here to defend this town and the innocents within it from the excesses ordered by your Chancellor. I have artillery, I have levium, I have Caraducian guard. All here by order. All trained professionals. I have everything I need for a comfortable dusas. And I will use it to its fullest capacity.

'Go away. The citizens of Port Roulent need their Speaker with them as the Tsardon threat grows. Don't let the Chancellor deflect you from your appointed tasks under God.'

Lotheris spat on the ground and rubbed the saliva in with her heel.

'The air has a bitter taste here, Marshal,' she said. 'I have tried to reason with you. We don't want more bloodshed over this heresy. All we desire is justice. But you can have a struggle if that is what you want.

'I can see your defences and they are strong indeed. But the Armour of God is stronger. And they are coming. Your time is short and the pain of your followers will be deep.'

She turned and stalked away back to the crowd which fell silent to watch her come.

'How long do you think we have?' asked Hesther.

'They're bluffing,' said Harkov.

'No,' said Vasselis. 'I know the Chancellor. She will not stand the humiliation without seeking redress. But how many will she send? As to how long we have, I have no idea. All we can do is be ready for whatever Felice Koroyan decides to throw at us. Damn her but the Armour should be in Neratharn or defending the coast. How can the Advocate not know about this?'

The weather was cooling rapidly and the first rain of the changing season had struck them the day before. Despite them moving south, the chilling of solas towards dusas was undeniable. Roberto allowed no slackening of pace. The ground was flat, hard and good for walking, helping them achieve thirty miles a day.

Jhered, Menas and Kovan had been given horses and they rode these beside the wagon in which the Ascendants were travelling. Roberto had forbidden them to be seen outside of tent or wagon and Jhered had endured them reverting to type as a consequence. They had moaned about their conditions, about getting up early, about travelling so far every day, about army rations, about his mood. Anything.

Roberto had refused to speak to Jhered on any matters other than tactics and military intelligence since their first discussion. He had also taken his command team into his confidence about the Ascendants. And despite his determination to keep the circle of knowledge limited, rumours had run through the army, some far too close to the truth for comfort.

It meant that Jhered rarely strayed from them day or night, such was the interest in them from the ordinary soldier. He had even suggested that they travel with the followers rather than the engineers at the rear of the column. Roberto had disputed the wisdom, saying that would leave them too open. Jhered was only half-worried about that and Roberto knew it.

The exchange with Roberto had left Jhered frustrated and irritable. He was aware his temper was short and it was now that he needed the Ascendants to be with him more than ever. But yet another bickering dispute had seen him tie his horse to the wagon and climb in the back to quieten them down.

'Has someone stolen your biscuit, Ossacer?' he said. 'Or is it something far more serious, like whose turn it is to sit on the cushion versus the straw?'

A babble of protest rose from all four in the darkened, stuffy wagon. He stared back at them until they realised he was not going to respond.

'You really are all very stupid,' he said. He raised a hand. 'No, you had your say. Your problem was you decided you would all have it at once. Now it's my turn.'

He waited for them to be ready to listen.

'Why must you constantly disappoint me? You want me to treat you like adults but the moment I think you've earned that respect, you demonstrate once again how immature you really are. You know the position we are in. General Del Aglios is only protecting us because he doesn't want his army finding out what you are and because, at heart, he is a very good man. If he wasn't, we would be abandoned in the wilds right now. I don't want to give him cause to change his mind. For you that means obeying the rules of the army without complaint. For me it means trying to alter his perception of you. But to do that, you have to back me up and this endless whingeing does not help me.

'You think he doesn't hear us up at the head of the column because it is two miles away? Think again. He has his ears everywhere. In the wagon behind us is Rovan Neristus. He's the chief engineer and one of the general's closest friends. They talk every night. He's the man who is charged with improving artillery and transport. It takes a lot of thought. But what do you suppose he is telling the general at the moment? He's telling him that he cannot think because four wailing children are distracting his mind.'

Jhered sighed and spread his hands.

'Help me out, here. This can't go on. Yes, Arducius, speak.'

'We don't mean to complain. But this is worse than Marshal Vasselis's ship. We never get to see the sun. It's like being in prison. We're bored and all around us there are people we could help. Last night, they spent hours digging wells because the Tsardon have dammed the river. Any of us could have told them where to dig and how deep. Instead, we all went thirsty. And so many have blisters, cuts and bad feet. Ossacer could help. Instead, they are made to walk in pain.'

'I hear you,' said Jhered.

'No, you don't,' said Mirron. 'You just say you do. If we were allowed to show what we can do, the army would accept us.'

'I'd love to say you were right but I'm afraid the opposite is true. Did you know that Roberto has had to practically gag his own Order Speaker to stop him giving you away and stirring up hatred? It would be so easy. If you heal wounds and divine water, it will stoke suspicion and fear, not earn you slaps on the back.'

'So how long will we be cooped up like this?' asked Arducius.

'When we reach Gestern, we can leave the army,' said Jhered. 'Perhaps take ship to Neratharn and do some work there. I don't know. I'm as frustrated as you.'

'That's five more days,' said Ossacer plaintively.

'For me, too,' said Jhered.

'Yes but you can ride in the fresh air. We have to put up with Gorian farting smellier than a horse.' Ossacer waved a hand under his nose.

'Those aren't mine, those are Ardu's,' said Gorian.

'Strange that they come from your side of the wagon,' said Ossacer.

'They do not. How can you tell?'

'Because I can trace the trails in the air, that's how.'

'No you can't, no one can.'

'Just because you can't doesn't mean no one can. I can.'

'There's nothing you can do that I can't.'

'You're still no good at healing people. Only useless animals.'

'Like the one pulling this wagon. If it drops dead, you'll have to wear the yoke.'

'And if the driver dies, who will steer it?'

'Perhaps you can do it with the power of your mind, if you're so bloody clever.'

'Well actually, I could. Perhaps it's you that can't.'

'Oh, like I couldn't control that eagle, you mean? Don't be pathetic.'

'An ox is bigger than an eagle.'

'It's about will, not size, Ossacer. As I *keep* having to tell you because you are so thick.'

'Dear-God-around-me, will you shut up!' roared Jhered.

The silence spread further than the wagon but was broken by a ragged cheer and the odd smattering of applause. The backcloth twitched and Menas's head poked in.

'Everything all right in here?' she asked.

'Don't you start,' said Jhered. 'Yes. It's fine. We were just having a talk about maturity.'

Menas withdrew and Jhered turned back to the Ascendants, who were staring at him with a wary expectancy. A thought struck him and despite the risk to order, he couldn't resist voicing it.

'Ossacer, if you are so troubled by the smells emitting from whoever's arse, why do you not just identify the energy lines that give rise to the chemicals making the sour odours and manipulate them into something more agreeable?' He shrugged. 'You could do that, couldn't you?'

'I don't see why not,' said Ossacer. 'Though it seems a shame to waste energy on something so trivial.'

'You said it,' growled Jhered. 'So perhaps if you would spend more time considering solutions to problems rather than bitching about them, we might all be a little happier, yes?'

There was a reluctant series of nods and mutterings of assent. Jhered grunted his satisfaction and sat down, stretching his legs across the width of the wagon.

'Look, there will come a time when there is nothing left but for you to show others the full range of your power. I might have got it wrong. It might not be to stop the war. It might be something else. But there will come a time. And you have to be ready. Now we've discussed all sorts of scenarios for wartime. I still think that is the likely avenue for your emergence into full public attention. And while we are travelling with this army, it is even more likely since they are marching to battle at the earliest opportunity.

'All I ask is this. That you bend all your efforts into being ready on the instant because you may not get much warning. And to divert yourselves from baiting each other and irritating the good citizens who have to travel near you. And most importantly of all, if Roberto Del Aglios deigns to come and see you, which one day he will, I want you ready to be polite, deferential and respectful. He is the son of the Advocate. To have him on your side would be so very valuable to you. What do you think?

'Except you, Gorian. I know what you're thinking without asking. It's not as simple as that. A random demonstration of your power is not the answer. Trust me.'

Any questions they might have had were forgotten. An order was shouted and trumpeted down the column. From without, they could hear the thundering of thousands of feet and hoofs. A large number of cavalry galloped past. Wagons followed them. Their own wagon draw to a halt. It was barely past mid-morning.

'Why have we stopped?' asked Mirron.

Jhered dragged himself to a crouch.

'I don't know. I'll find out. Remember what I've just said and act on it. Please. It's important.'

He left the wagon. There was no need to find out why they had stopped. He already knew.

Roberto had been concerned but not surprised at the amount of scouting activity from the Tsardon. Jhered had been right in one thing; while they had marched south, the Tsardon hadn't been worried by them. Now they were worried, and the speed with which they responded was frightening.

He had been leading the Conquord forces across deserted farmland, much of it stripped by his enemies. Vision was clear for miles all around and the single column he had been able to adopt had moved at an excellent pace. Four days of fast marching had bought them some time, and on this fifth day the land was changing.

They were moving into an area that had been over-logged and had led to a rising of the water table. Huge areas of sodden marshland spread from river to river, drying out only on the higher southern plateaus for which Atreska was rightly famous. These flat, forested lands were home to the best hunting grounds in the Conquord and before the war, the sport had been burgeoning, making rich men of local landowners.

Roberto had moved onto the grounds as soon as he was able, leaving the marshes to his north but limiting his options for new changes of direction in the pursuit of greater speed. Now his scouts reported a previously unseen force on the march. How it had remained hidden was a matter for debate. Presumably it had been stationed beyond the marshlands, west, in reserve. It hardly mattered. They were closing fast and threatened to cut off Roberto's preferred route to the Gesternan west coast.

The decision to halt and form the army into marching battle order had been a simple one to make. He ordered Davarov and Kastenas to his side.

'How many and how fast?' he asked his scouting team, still red from the gallop.

'Perhaps seven thousand, General. Light infantry and cavalry, very little artillery. Moving faster than we are.'

Roberto, Davarov and Kastenas had ridden the short distance away from his army to speak with the scouts. Atreska's beauty and her vulnerabilities were laid out below them. South-west, the plateau continued on for a two-day march before sloping back to sea level. It was slower because it kept them from the Conquord highway to Kirriev Harbour for longer.

Roberto had drawn up at the western edge of the plateau and looked down a gentle slope onto a small plain through which ran a narrow, shallow river.

'What's the ground like down there?' asked Davarov.

'Better than the marshland,' said the scout. She looked back down the slope up which she had ridden. 'It's damp for about half a mile either side but the river flow is fast and the seepage doesn't seem too bad. You could fight on it easily and bring up the artillery.'

'Good,' said Roberto. 'What else do I need to know?'

'The plain is less than two miles across to where you can see the two plateaus rising either side of the valley down which the Tsardon are coming. There are no Tsardon on top of either plateau and as you can see, they're both steep-sided and hopeless to attack up or down. There's a lake on the left-hand plateau but the right-hand is just forested. North, where the river comes in, the ground reverts to deeper marshland, and south, it's covered in rock down the river course. No one will attack from either direction.'

Roberto nodded. 'Elise, what does the enemy commander want?'

'He wants to hold us up,' she said. 'The Tsardon know they block the quicker route. I think he'll fight a running battle if he can because it'll delay our progress. He'll know we have better numbers and plenty of artillery so he won't want pitched fighting.'

'And will they head us off if we continue south-west?'

'They could,' said Davarov. 'But if they commit to battle here in the bowl, to backtrack would cost them a day. I can't believe they'll follow us because we can take them apart on the slopes here. Our problem is that they know we'd rather take them on now, to stop them joining their army at Gestern.'

'So the choice is largely made,' said Roberto. 'They'll be here in, what, four hours?' The scout nodded. 'So we can deploy in advance and take the better ground in the bowl and across the river.'

'And if we find we're chasing them up the plain?'

'Then we do,' said Roberto. 'We can place cavalry on the higher ground to counter threat from above. And if the going remains dry we can match them if we need to.'

'You don't have the time,' said a new voice from behind.

Roberto turned in his saddle. 'I don't recall inviting you to this discussion, Exchequer Jhered.' He looked at the scout team. 'Go.'

'You must trust me. Let them come. But fake your move. Be prepared to carry on south-west. Let me deal with these Tsardon.'

Roberto laughed. 'Of course, no problem. I'll happily put the lives of every citizen in my army in the hands of your little children. A command decision for which I will gain understandably huge respect.'

Jhered remained impassive. 'When have I ever advised you to make a poor decision?' Roberto refused to answer him. 'Think about it, General. Quickly.'

He turned and rode away in a hurry.

'Do you think there's anything in this Ascendants story?' asked Davarov. 'This is Jhered we're talking about here, not some in-bred from Gosland's northern marches.'

'I know,' said Roberto. 'That's what makes it all so strange. But how can I trust it? If he's wrong, Gestern and I face forty thousand rather than thirty thousand. If he's right, I don't know how many of my army will still be in camp tomorrow morning. I can't afford to believe it.' He frowned and looked at Kastenas and Davarov. 'I am right, aren't I?'

Kastenas nodded. 'There is no weapon powerful enough to defeat whole armies. If there was, the Advocate would have ordered us to use it, not just look out for him and take him in.'

'I agree,' said Davarov. 'And frankly the whole thing is so pre-posterous, not even my Goslander in-bred would have invented it. It's deranged, Roberto and if you trust what he says, you'll lose the army.'

Roberto felt relieved. Something about Jhered was so compelling, made it so very hard to say no. The same thing that made him such a good Exchequer.

'Right,' he said. 'Give the order. We're deploying. The camp will be on this plateau tonight. Get to it.'

*

It might have been cooling off outside but in the wagon it was plenty hot enough. Arducius was trying his best to keep Ossacer and Gorian from yet more argument. Mirron wasn't helping. She was siding with Gorian today and it was infuriating. But then again, what did he expect? After all, Kovan wasn't in the wagon with them at the moment so she could fawn all over Gorian without any guilt whatever. Jhered's appearance at the tail of the wagon was an unusually blessed relief.

'You lot, can you ride?' he asked.

'We aren't bad,' said Arducius. 'Horses listen to us so we don't get thrown or anything but we aren't cavalry.'

'Good. What does Ossacer do?'

'He rides behind me,' said Arducius.

'Excellent. Then four horses will do it.'

'Do what?' asked Gorian.

'Time to prove yourselves, my young Ascendants,' said Jhered. 'So, if you've been lying to me about the extent of your powers, start praying I drop dead in the next hour.'

Arducius watched the smile broaden on Gorian's face.

'What do you want us to do?' he asked.

'There's a piece of the Atreskan landscape that needs rearranging.'

Chapter 62

848th cycle of God, 40th day of Solasfall
15th year of the true Ascendancy

With the army in the midst of its deployment, they were ignored for just long enough. Their wagon was drawn up near to the crest of the plateau and they could all see what it was Jhered had described to them. Down on the plain, the Conquord army was singing as it marched. They had reached the far side of the river.

Coming towards them along the valley, the Tsardon travelled under a cloud of dust that was hemmed in by the sides of the plateaus. It seemed to Jhered, through his magnifier, that they were approaching in line order. Cavalry flanked a wide front of infantry. They were moving quickly. Jhered chewed his lip. If they got within a half mile of the legions they would be too close to Roberto and beyond what Gorian had rather chillingly called the 'raw materials' for the Work.

'Any questions?'

Jhered looked along the line of Ascendants and felt a powerful sense of guilt pass through him. They looked so young. In this army of veteran infantry and cavalry, they were tiny dots. Vulnerable and alone. God-surround-them but they didn't even have any armour. Just tunics, furs and boots. No weapons on their belts, no bows across their backs. Nothing.

What am I doing? He almost laughed at the absurdity of it all. At least, standing here, he understood Roberto's reaction. The noise and spectacle of the marching Conquord army brought him back to himself. The song rolled across the bowl, underpinned by the rhythm of thousands of feet tramping in unison. Whatever Roberto's problems, however shaved his army was of its bulk, he operated a discipline that was the envy of every Conquord general. It gave him an advantage over anyone he faced. This time, though, it wasn't going to be enough. He could spend days chasing the Tsardon down. The Conquord simply didn't have that luxury.

'Well?'

The Ascendants were staring down at the army open-mouthed. A vast swathe of humanity moving across the ground like a cloud shadow.

'I take it you are all happy with what you need to do?'

Finally, they looked at him. Ossacer with his hand on Arducius's arm, thoughtful and determined. Arducius himself, pensive. Mirron, scared and fretful standing very close to Gorian, who stood tall, proud and confident.

'We're ready,' said Arducius.

'I will not kill anyone,' said Ossacer.

'It won't come to that,' said Jhered. 'All you need to do is block their path and scare them away. Come on.'

He nodded at Menas and the two of them walked the short distance back to the wagon where their driver and mounted guard were waiting for them.

'I'm sorry,' said Jhered to the guard.

'Why?' he asked.

Jhered drew his gladius and placed it to the guard's neck. 'I need your horse and your shield. Right now.'

Menas was covering the driver, who already had his hands in the air. She took his rectangular shield from the seat beside him.

'In the back,' she said.

'The general will have you executed for this,' said the guard.

'I doubt it,' said Jhered. 'But even should he do so, I will die knowing I did my duty by the Conquord. Come on, get down. I am not your enemy.'

The guard dismounted. 'My friends do not hold swords to my throat.'

'Nor do they let your comrades die needlessly,' said Jhered. 'I'm sorry you don't understand. Watch and learn. But get in the back of the wagon until we are gone.'

The guard moved away reluctantly and Jhered took the reins of his horse. An oval shield was lashed to the back of the saddle. She was a placid mare, not a cavalry horse. So much the better. She did not resist as he trotted back to the Ascendants.

'Mount up. Kovan, take Mirron. Gorian, you're behind me. Menas, I need your hands free to fire if you have to. Arducius, this one is for you and Ossacer. Quickly now.'

Jhered heard a shout behind him. Guards on the supply wagons, the mobile forge and the engineers were moving towards them. He cursed and turned to help first Arducius and then Ossacer on to their horse.

'Be ready,' he said.

Gorian had the reins of his mount. He swung up quickly into the saddle and felt Gorian mount behind him.

'Let's go!'

Jhered kicked his heels and his horse moved forwards and down the slope. It was an easy descent and he urged the animal to a fast canter. He looked behind him. The others were with him. Menas had held back against any pursuit but the guards were on foot and easily outpaced.

'You ready for this?' he asked Gorian.

'It was what I was born for,' replied the Ascendant.

'Good lad.' He turned to shout over his shoulder. 'In line behind me. Don't deviate.'

He moved to a gallop and headed for the right-hand side of the lines. They were deployed and ready. Hastati to the front, principes stepped behind them and the triarii forming the third rank of the triplex acies classic battle formation. Jhered was relying on their discipline and order. He couldn't afford to ride around the cavalry. Too much risk of them being stopped.

The commotion of the left-hand end of the column completing its march covered his advance perfectly. He could see Roberto dead centre behind his triarii and in conversation with Neristus, his engineer. He rode past the slower-moving artillery pieces, knowing that suspicious eyes would track them and that the shouts would follow.

He put his head down and urged more speed from his horse. He tore past Roberto, past standing ranks of archers and down between two lines of triarii. The thumping sound of his horse's hooves filled his ears but he could sense the outrage spreading quickly through the army. By the time he had cleared the triarii and slowed to turn right and then left to drive between two maniples of principes, heads were turning their way from all corners.

He dared a quick glance behind him. The Ascendants and Menas were still with him. The angry faces of triarii and principes were a backdrop to everything and he could see flags beginning to wave. Archers were on the move.

He ploughed on. On an order, hastati were turning. Jhered cleared the principes and dragged the reins hard left. The horse slewed around. Gorian gripped his waist tight and went with the turn. Ahead the maniples were closing and sarissas were swinging from front to back.

'Clear!' he roared. 'Clear!'

They could see he had no intention of stopping. He had to trust that his horse would not pull up at the wall of hastati. Had to trust a gap would open for it to see. He turned right. There was a space. He hurried down it. In front of him, hastati dived left and right out of his way. He felt fists on his legs and heard the abuse rain down on him.

He burst clear of the army. Gorian shouted in triumph. On the open ground, his horse picked up speed and galloped towards the neck of the valley.

'They're all with us. They've made it.'

Gorian's voice in his ear was welcome relief. He nodded.

'Tell me how near you need to get. Don't leave it too long.' The first arrows fell around him. 'Stop this, Roberto. Let me be.'

He looked to the flanks of the army. Detachments of cavalry were riding parallel to him but not closing. Not yet. He prayed that none of the arrows would find a mark and pushed on, desperate to be out of range. In his ears, howls of derision from the army rolled over them. Ahead the Tsardon jogged on, keen to reach their stand before the advance of the Conquord army. They were little more than a mile away now. This was going to be awfully close.

'Gorian?'

'Keep going. We must be almost beneath the walls of the plateaus.'

Jhered breathed deep. They were closing on the enemy so quickly. Already, he could see Tsardon riders moving ahead of the line. They were cautious, having seen the advance Conquord cavalry. For that, Roberto had to be thanked though it surely wasn't his intent.

'Pull up,' said Gorian.

Jhered reined in. Gorian dismounted and ran back a little way to see to the others. Jhered slid off the horse and patted it away. The arrows had long since stopped but the taunts of the army came on unabated. He could hear laughter mixed with the abuse. They were perhaps half a mile ahead of the Conquord lines. Far too far away for any defence should they need it. The cavalry detachments monitored them but did not move in.

'Come on,' said Jhered. 'Hurry.'

The Tsardon saw only a handful of enemies ahead. No threat, just easy targets. Their horsemen had returned to the lines. Archers were moving ahead. They would be in range before the Work was done.

'Kovan, Menas. Shields ahead. Get down behind them. Ascendants, get inside the shields as far as you can. Get working. We are short on time.'

Out here, their vulnerability was acutely plain. Mirron was shaking, Arducius bit his lip and Ossacer could obviously sense the advancing army. Fear had creased his face. Gorian seemed unfazed. No doubt he was quaking inside but here, on the grass between opposing armies, the Ascendants would have to deliver.

Roberto shook his head and signalled the archers to stop wasting their arrows. He hadn't wanted to hit them, just stop them running. He sent an order to the cavalry to stand down and denied his light infantry the opportunity to take them into custody before the Tsardon got within bow range.

'Let the Tsardon take them,' he said. 'Why should I care if they die?'

'Because Jhered is with them,' said Neristus.

'Is he?' Roberto looked down at Neristus. 'I don't recognise him. The man out there is not the man I know and love.'

He looked out over the heads of his citizens. Eleven thousand standing to watch a few fools throw their lives away.

'I'm sorry, Paul. You are beyond my help now.'

Arducius had a sick feeling in his stomach. He knew it was fear but he had to try and ignore it for the benefit of Mirron and Ossacer. They could sense each other's state through the lifelines and energy trails. His sampling told him that neither of them could focus properly at the moment. Only Gorian appeared unflustered.

'Just concentrate,' said Gorian. 'You have to ignore where we are.'

'How can I do that?' said Ossacer. 'There are thousands of

Tsardon coming and if we get this wrong we could kill some of them.'

'And the longer you delay, the more chance there is,' said Gorian.

'We're all scared,' said Arducius. 'We know this is the first time we've been under this pressure. But we also know we can do this. Gorian is right, we must try and ignore everything but the targets.'

'It's so hard.' He could see Mirron's shivering in her energy map. 'We can't do this wrong. They'll kill us.'

'The Exchequer won't let that happen,' said Arducius. 'He'll get us away before we are in real danger.'

'Concentrate,' said Gorian again. 'Feel out through the earth, see where the trails are strongest. And feel where the life surrounds us. The river is behind, there is a breeze in the air and there is growth all around. See where the energy maps of men and beasts are standing. Their circuits are closed to us for this Work.'

'That's it, Ossacer,' said Arducius. 'Breathe slowly. Let your mind open your body. That's it. Good.'

That was more like it. They stabilised. The flaring was lessening now they were concentrating hard enough to push aside the reality of the enemy closing on them. The thundering of hooves and the roar of so many thousands of voices began to fade.

'None of us is a natural Land Warden,' said Arducius, his words dancing in the air for them all to see and absorb. 'So we will link together and use the energies around us. We are each other's strength and guide. We will draw on all that we can. We will use our bodies to amplify the elements surrounding us; and we will project them at our targets along the strongest energy trails beneath the earth. Are we of one understanding?'

One by one, they affirmed that they were. The trembling was gone from Ossacer's voice as the beauty of the energies revealed themselves to him and he lost himself in the science of their planned creation. Mirron still harboured fear but the comforting strength of Gorian enveloped her and kept her focused. And Arducius knew for the first time that they really could perform the Exchequer's wishes. Excitement surged in him.

He opened his body and accepted the power that coursed through him. It made his lifelines blaze in his mind's eye. The others were there too. He could feel his body vibrate. The link they shared drove the power through them all, spiralling up in intensity within the closed circuit of their bodies. He breathed out. With his mind, he searched for the paths through the earth that led to the plateaus to their left and right. The paths where trickles of water ran down from the lake into the river. Or where the roots of countless blades of grass, flowers, shrubs and the trees that dotted the landscape found their purchase.

'Keep strong,' he said, aware this was more energy than they had ever dared contain and amplify before. 'Remember how far the targets still are. We cannot let the energy dissipate on its journey.'

'It's wonderful,' said Mirron. 'Look what we can harbour. Look how easy it is.'

'I told you,' said Gorian. 'I always told you. And now it's time to show them what the Ascendants have brought to their world. Arducius?'

'We have the understanding,' he intoned as Father Kessian had taught them, to nail down their concentration. 'We have the energy within us and we have the vision of our Work. Under God, let us act.'

The Ascendants opened the circuit and ploughed the augmented energy along the trails, feeling it boil life into the earth and everything it found there. They pushed hard, seeking the edge of the plateaus and the targets they knew they would find: the roots of the trees that clung to their slopes and that reached through to the bedrock beneath.

Roberto felt it as much as saw it where he sat on his horse, waiting for the Tsardon to engulf Jhered and his charges. The slightest ripple through the earth that moved through his army like wind over a field of corn. The air stilled. It was charged like the moments before a thunderstorm broke. He frowned.

It was all Jhered could do not to turn and run. He clamped his hands hard on Kovan and Menas's shoulders and crouched lower behind the shields. The enemy were still three hundred yards away but coming on fast. In half that distance they would be trying out their range.

But arrows were the least of his worries. He had listened to the words of the Ascendants and felt the energy wash away from them like a wave. Their horses had bolted away back towards the Conquord army, touched by something they could not understand. And now beneath the Ascendants, the grass grew dense and tall while beyond their circle, the life deserted the plants which withered, blackened and rotted before his eyes. And the death was spreading. Small yet but growing as life energy was channelled towards the plateaus. He swallowed, frightened by what he had sanctioned.

'Look,' breathed Kovan. 'Out there.'

Jhered looked over the edges of the shields. Multiple lines of growth fled away from the Ascendants, spreading out towards the plateaus. Grass, flower, root and stem burst from the ground, grew and withered. The energy lines drove them to brief life and stole all they had to keep moving on. And so fast, so straight. He imagined the power boiling through the ground beneath, coiling and spurting, gathering speed and density. Boring towards the latent, deep strength of the trees.

Still the Tsardon came on. They wouldn't yet see what was racing towards them. Archers were at a sprint. The first of them stopped, jabbed arrows into the ground and bent their bows. Others ran on.

'Down,' said Jhered. He heard the whisper and the thud. All fell short. 'Come on, you lot. Don't let me down.'

The Ascendants would not hear him. They were lost in their world of energy trails, lifelines and the manipulation of God's earth. And all around him, the effects of that manipulation were becoming more obvious and more corrupt. The dead circle around them was expanding faster now. The earth was drying and cracking. But still it was less than ten yards in diameter.

More arrows fell. Above the tumult of the approaching army, he could make out the shouts of the Tsardon archers closing on them. He ducked down lower. A shaft flew past his head and struck the dead ground behind. Two more rattled into the shield. Kovan winced at the impact. Menas shifted.

'It'll be all right lad. Trust your friends.'

He looked once more to the Ascendants, mouthing his desire for speed. Time was almost up. They had their range. Soon, they would have their direction too and a pair of shields would not be enough.

'More,' whispered Gorian, his voice curiously altered as if from the mouth of an older man.

Mirron moaned and Arducius said something Jhered couldn't make out. He could see their arms trembling with the effort. And their hands were buried in the ground. He looked again. The grass, the earth, the roots were growing up across and inside their hands. Their flesh looked like it was tattooed with the patterns of green and brown. They were fused with it. He shuddered, nausea sweeping through him.

There was a single loud crack that reported across the valley ahead. The voices of the Tsardon archers died in their throats. Jhered dragged his head round reluctantly and looked over the shields. He saw a trickle of rubble run down the side of the plateau to their left. A hundred yards away, the branches of a tree moved in a single violent motion.

And that was it. Jhered stared at the tiny cloud of dust that rose into the sky. There surely had to be more. The Tsardon archers ignored the lines of dead vegetation at their feet and nocked more arrows.

'More,' said Gorian. 'Push. The door is open.'

The circle of blackened grass fled away faster than Jhered could follow. He felt a bass rumble. The ground shook once, gently.

'Now,' said Arducius.

The energy flooded away again. The steep sides of the plateaus burgeoned with abrupt, vibrant life. Trees speared up to the sky. Buds formed on new branches, leaves clogged twig and bough. And roots, glorious roots, delved deep and unstoppable, searching for new purchase and sustenance.

Both sides of the valley along which the Tsardon marched burst with the deep colours of genasrise growth. The growth drove on and on, far out of Jhered's sight and a smile crossed his face. Root systems invaded every tiny crevice and crack, every weakness in the rock, quicker than a lightning strike.

A series of new, louder cracks ricocheted across the plain. The earth rumbled faintly. Jhered thought he saw the whole southern plateau shudder. More cracks, deeper and sharper. Shards of rock sprang away from the plateau sides and showered the ground in between. The Tsardon army faltered. All eyes were fixed on the unearthly sights surrounding them.

Still the trees grew. Tall and strong, their trunks thickening, their branches clawing further to the sky. This time Jhered knew he had seen the shudder in the land. He made an involuntary backward move.

'Dear God-around-us-all,' he breathed. 'It's gone so deep.'

Tangles of roots twined and pulled at the rock faces. Earth began to slide down the slopes. More and more roots burst from the top of the plateau, catapulting stone into the air. A tortured screaming, as of great metal plates torn and twisted, split the air. The northern plateau edge sucked in and crashed outwards. Thousands of tons of rock from the shivered side slid downwards into the plain. Trees, earth and stone tumbling uncontrolled and uncontrollable on a length of a mile, two miles. Far farther back than they had planned or could control. Dust clogged the air.

A heartbeat later, the southern plateau cracked and fell. A line tore in its eastern edge, roots burst through it, forcing it wider and wider until it split. Eighty yards and more collapsed out and began to fall. And behind it, the lake bed was fractured and the water burst outwards, shorn of its rock shackles.

A wall of blue and green and grey exploded into the plain. Jhered saw slabs of stone tossed hundreds of feet into the sky as the pressure of ages was released. Mud, trees and stone all poured down in a wave that engulfed the plain and the Tsardon army within. They had nowhere to go.

He saw horses rear and men began to run away from the colossal volume of water thundering down towards them, directed along the valley by the Ascendants at his feet.

They could not know what it was they did. The density of bedrock and hard wood crashing down on to the helpless enemy. And as fast as they ran, the water gushed after them, catching them and grabbing them in its drowning embrace. Or the sides of the plateaus rushed down to catch them in great stone pincers. Battering, threshing, crushing.

The sound of the earth tearing itself apart smashed around his ears. The screams of the Tsardon were lost in the roar of water. The drumming of hooves silenced under the hail of rock.

'Stop!' he yelled into Gorian's ear. 'Stop. The Work is done.'

Water charged against the opposite side of the valley in a wave and fell back. The wash came towards them. Calmer now, rolling stone a few yards before depositing it and rippling on. It was the wetness over their hands and legs that brought the Ascendants round.

They slumped back on to the ground, faces lined with age, hair lank and fingers wrinkled. They gasped great lungfuls of air and lay helpless and exhausted. Mirron was the first to try and rise but Menas was to her feet very quickly, pushing her back down.

'Don't look, honey. Best you don't look.'

Jhered stood and turned his back on the devastation. On the countless bodies broken by water, rock and wood; on the screams of the wounded and the fleeing; on the few Tsardon who by some miracle had survived; and on the lucky ones far enough back along the march to escape. On the rout of seven thousand.

He looked away to the Conquord legions and the banners and standards still held high and proud. To the faces of legionary and cavalryman. Of centurion and general, surgeon and engineer.

And the silence rolled over him.

Chapter 63

Eventually Roberto ordered the army back to the plateau to make camp. He had waited for them to break and run towards the plain. To overrun Jhered and his witches and tear them limb from limb for the atrocity they had caused under God's sky. But they hadn't. After all, if they could do that to a hillside, what could they do to a man?

He had sat on his horse and let the noise surge around him. He had listened to the prayers and exhortations for deliverance. He had heard them try and explain it all away. A natural phenomenon. A visitation from the Omniscient on the evil Tsardon. The prayers for mercy had even turned in some quarters to those of thanks. But in all their hearts, they knew. They had all seen the dark spread from the kneeling children in a perfect circle. They didn't know what it was but it had heralded the sloughing of the rock onto the plain and the destruction of the enemy.

He had ridden across the back and front of the infantry lines. Their discipline was first-rate and he was gladdened by it. But he could see the confusion and fear in every face. It was in the set of their bodies where they stood in strict maniple order. And the centurions who kept them steady had fared no better. Eyes gazed up at him from under plumed helmets and he nodded his thanks to them.

He had kept back a hundred cavalry under Elise Kastenas's personal guidance to defend their retreat. She had taken her detachment to the edge of the valley. It was covered in bodies and boulders and the shattered trunks and branches of trees. It was as if God had grabbed a fistful of the earth and thrown it down, not caring who He killed.

Finally, Roberto had calmed himself enough to ride alone across the half mile from his front lines to where Jhered, Appros Menas, the misguided Kovan Vasselis and the Ascendants remained. The boy had found two of their horses and held the reins of the skittish animals in one hand.

Two of the Ascendants appeared distressed as he approached. He could find no sympathy for them. Indeed, this was the closest he had been to any of them and he found the proximity distasteful. He dismounted a few yards from them and let his horse wander away to find some grass on which to graze. He nodded curtly at young Vasselis.

'You should know better. Why did you let him get you into this?'

Jhered stood from where he and Menas had been tending to the youngsters and walked towards him, stopping Kovan's response with a hand.

One of the Ascendants, a strong-looking lad, well-muscled though with an age-lined face, caught his eye. Roberto flinched. The orbs he met were unnatural. Colours chased across their surface; orange clearing to a slate grey.

'Look at what we did,' he said, his voice dry and cracked. 'We helped you. Won a victory for you.'

'Is that right?' said Roberto. He fixed his gaze on Jhered. 'What have you done here?'

'Exactly what Gorian said,' replied Jhered. There was the lightness of satisfaction in his tone and his expression. 'We have used the trees to break the hillside. We've saved you days. And you haven't sustained a single casualty.'

'No?' Roberto kept his hands firmly by his sides. 'Every man and woman in my army is damaged, Exchequer. Every one of them will relive what they have seen in their nightmares. Some of them may never be able to keep the quiver from their sword arms. I lined up almost eleven thousand citizens and you gave them a freak show.'

'You wouldn't listen, Roberto,' said Jhered. 'I told you we could do this. I had to prove it to you. You had the option to keep every citizen in your legions out of sight.'

'You gave me no option,' snapped Roberto. 'We needed this battle. We needed to feel enemy flesh beneath our swords to give us belief. We have had nothing but plague, desertion and betrayal since genas-fall. And you denied us even that. This . . .' Roberto waved his hand around him. 'This demonstration does not help my cause. It is self-serving, it is against my orders and it leaves me with an army uncertain whether the next mountain they walk beneath will fall on their heads.'

'We are on your side.' Jhered's voice rose in volume. 'The Ascendants will never harm a Conquord soldier.'

'And you think I can ride up and tell them that so they believe me? I know what I saw and it scares me to my very heart. You are a maverick, Jhered. You're dangerous.'

'Damn you, do not disrespect me, General Del Aglios.' Jhered's eyes flashed. 'Everything I do is for the Conquord and for your mother. And I will not stand by while you call that into question.'

'Then go, Exchequer Jhered. I will not stand in your way. But neither will I have you with my army or even with the camp-followers. You really have no idea what you have done, do you?'

'I have destroyed or scattered an army of seven thousand today, General. What have you done?'

Roberto raised a gauntleted finger and pressed it to Jhered's chest. 'Be very careful, Exchequer. You might hold great sway in Estorr and in the provinces you terrify into paying your taxes. But out here, it is me who rules.'

'One day, Roberto, you will see your error. And on that day, I will be proud to embrace you as my friend. I only hope that when that day comes, we still have a Conquord to serve.'

Roberto dropped his hand. 'I do not see that day,' he said quietly.

'Do not hate us.'

One of the Ascendants had spoken. Roberto glared down at him, sprawled on the ground, exhausted.

'What?' he asked.

'Speak up, Arducius,' said Jhered.

'Do not hate us, General Del Aglios. All we want is to be back with our families and those we love. Just like you and your army. We are not evil. No one should fear us.'

Roberto shook his head. 'You are unnatural. No one should have the power to break mountains. No one.'

He turned and rode away without a backward glance.

'Even the lion-hearted are prey to fear.'

'Hmm?' Jhered turned from staring at Roberto's receding back. Kovan was walking across to him.

'It's something Father Kessian used to say. He knew in his heart that the acceptance of the Ascendancy would be fraught. He always tried to put a smiling face on it but he knew.'

Jhered pushed a hand through his hair. It was covered in dust and damp. 'He knew a lot of things we could use right now.'

'What do we do now?' asked Kovan.

Jhered felt all their eyes on him. He'd been so sure that Roberto would see beyond the confines of their faith for the purposes of winning the war. The demonstration should have been all the proof he needed. The last thing in his mind was to be stranded here beneath the Atreskan plateaus. Far from safety, far from the next conflict. And without enough horses to take them all.

He forced his disappointment aside and shrugged off the crushing feeling that he had failed. He crouched by the Ascendants, between Arducius and Gorian. Mirron was lying in Menas's arms and her tear-stained face pained his heart. Ossacer could not take his sightless eyes from the jumbled plain, his mouth moving soundlessly. They were problems to be tackled just a little later.

Jhered placed what he hoped would be a fatherly, encouraging hand each on Gorian and Arducius's shoulders.

'What we don't do is give up,' he said. 'General Del Aglios might be frightened of your power. He and his army might hate you. But we know what we are doing is right and the only choice if we are to save our homes, our families and our Conquord. I am proud of you. All of you. I asked a huge task of you and you did not let me down. More, you won a great victory and there will come a day when it is written into the legends of the Conquord.

'It is easy to despair at the reactions of those we are endeavouring to help but we must not. I believe in you. The Karku believe in you and that cannot be underestimated. And soon enough, the Conquord will accept and believe in you too. You are the future of this world.'

He felt both Arducius and Gorian respond under his hands. They straightened where they sat and, despite the exhaustion they must have felt, managed to look at him with the belief he wanted from them. But Mirron had not responded at all and Ossacer's aged face was crumpled with grief.

'You made us kill,' he whispered, his voice broken. Arducius dragged him into an embrace and he began to sob again. 'We aren't here to kill. And thousands are dead. I can sense nothing out there but grey and dark. You've made us into murderers.'

'Shhh, Ossie,' said Arducius. 'It wasn't anyone's fault. We couldn't know that the roots would find so many weak points in the rock. We couldn't know it would travel so far. You can't blame yourself.'

'Thousands are still dead. And we made it happen.'

'Yes,' said Jhered. 'You did. But you were doing my bidding. And as your commander, the blood is on my hands and not yours. It is my responsibility.'

He knew his words must sound hollow to Ossacer. He was so young. Too young to be faced with what he had done.

'Look,' he said. 'We need to get away from here. The sun will go down and it will get cold. We need a fire and hot food. So let's get up to the plateau you broke, because one thing we do know is that there won't be any Tsardon on it. All right?'

'But where are we going to go?' asked Ossacer, wiping the tears from his eyes.

'Right now, south to Gestern. Because whatever Roberto Del Aglios thinks, we can help stop the Tsardon fleet reaching Estorea and Caraduk. And if he still does not want you, then we will go to the one corner of the Conquord that does. The one place where you are accepted for what you are and can protect those you love. We will go to Westfallen.'

'You cannot let them go free, General,' said Ellas Lennart, the army's Prime Speaker. 'They are heretic. They are against the scriptures and they act above God. For the sake of your army, you must arrest them.'

'And do what, Ellas?' Roberto rounded on him.

It was late, he was tired and still shaken from what he had seen. He had endured a procession of senior soldiers through his tent demanding anything from their immediate burning to their use as the greatest weapon the Conquord possessed. He was only surprised the Speaker had left it so long to visit.

'Your duty as an officer of the Conquord legions and a believer in the Omniscient.'

'Don't speak to me of duty, Ellas. There is not one here who understands his duty more keenly than I do.' He turned from the door of his tent and the single fire on the shattered southern plateau.

'And if I bring them here, what then? I stir fear among my legions because at our centre are the very children responsible for the annihilation of an entire Tsardon army. If I want mutiny, then I can think of no quicker way to provoke it.'

'Then you must see them tried and executed.'

'You are so sure of their guilt?' asked Roberto. 'Why bother with a trial, eh?'

'Why indeed.'

Roberto raised his eyebrows. Ellas, normally so mild-mannered, had a face that burned with zealous fury.

'Because, Ellas, the Advocate has forbidden us to harm them. For whatever reason, Paul Jhered has persuaded her of their worth for now at least. And I will not defy her word. But not to harm them does not necessarily include bringing them to my bosom and it certainly does not include bringing their evil to the heart of my army.'

'But if you believe them evil then surely—'

'Enough, enough,' said Roberto. 'The decision is made, Ellas. And now I am tired and we are marching in just a few hours. Give a man the chance to rest, please.'

Ellas stiffened. 'It is not a chance you are giving me. I will find no rest while those things are out there mocking my God. Our God.'

'That is something I will just have to live with, isn't it?'

Roberto waved the Speaker out. He walked over to his cot and sat down heavily. The Conquord might have won the day but he felt robbed of victory. His army was as unsettled and frightened as if the day had been taken by the Tsardon.

'Damn you, Paul, what have you done?'

He lay down and stretched out tired legs. He forced himself to find a clear path through the confusion that had encased his mind since the unbelievable events of the day. There were positives. They had been spared days of chase and skirmish and they had suffered no physical casualties. Their marching path was clear; seven thousand Tsardon were out of the game and they could join the battle for Gestern at the earliest opportunity.

In the morning, he would send messengers to try and break through to the Neratharnese border. Right now, they would have no hope. And without hope, they would not hold the line against the Tsardon and rebel Atreskan armies. He had to give them that hope. That if they could hold until mid-dusasrise, then they would be relieved. That he, Roberto Del Aglios, would come and bring his legions with him.

In the morning.

He awoke fully dressed on top of his cot, feeling disoriented. The camp was quiet and a chill wind was ruffling the canvas of his tent. He rubbed at his bare arms and sat up, meaning to remove his boots and pull up his blanket but not sure that it was the cold that had awoken him. He blinked into the darkness.

'It's customary to announce yourself before entering the tent of the General,' he said. 'And I always wanted to know who it was that had come to kill me.'

'I have not come to kill you.'

The shadow Roberto had made out came closer, resolving itself into a filthy Atreskan swordsman. He was holding a dagger.

'Goran?'

'I'm sorry to have to disturb you, Roberto,' said Shakarov.

Roberto's eyes had adjusted to the dark a little more. Shakarov was dressed in the clothes that he had walked away in, though he was furnished again with weapons and Conquord armour.

'There are a lot of dead legionaries in Atreska,' he said, noticing Roberto's gaze. 'That's why I'm here.'

'How did you get in here?' Roberto's shock was subsiding to anger.

'Not everyone who remained with you agrees with you. You're not naïve enough to believe otherwise. I had need to get access.'

'Davarov?'

'No,' said Shakarov. 'He would kill me if he knew I was in here.'

'He's not the only one. Where's Herides? Where are my guards?'

'Temporarily diverted,' said Shakarov. 'None are to blame. You are under no threat from me.'

'No?' Roberto stared at Shakarov. He sighed. 'Well you're here now. God's sake, put that dagger away and sit, sit.' He indicated the chair at his map desk. 'Come to beg for a return?'

'No, General,' said Shakarov. He sat down and laid the dagger in his lap. 'But to divert you from your disastrous course.'

'Fantastic,' said Roberto, finding himself irritated beyond belief. 'Someone else I don't want to see turns up unannounced and tells me how to run my army. Go away, Goran. Go back to your deserters.'

Shakarov bristled. 'Deserters run and hide. We have been fighting Tsardon in my country. Doing the Conquord's work.'

'You should have stayed here. Done your work where it was best directed. I have nothing to say to you.'

'Roberto, you must listen to me. The battle for the Conquord is not going to take place on the Gesternan border. It is taking place now, throughout Atreska and all the way to the Neratharn border. I've travelled my lands for twenty days. I've seen what is going on.'

'But not what is going on in Gestern and the Tirronean Sea,' said Roberto. 'Make your point. This camp comes to order in a couple of hours and it would be best if you were gone.'

'Gestern has a defence numbering four legions, dug in all along their borders. They have Jorganesh coming to their aid. Atreska needs you. It needs us fighting side by side.'

Roberto propelled himself off his bed and loomed over Shakarov.

'Let me tell you how it really is. Gestern's four legions, should they all have mustered, face a force in excess of thirty thousand strong descending on the westernmost point of their border with Atreska. Jorganesh is not coming to their aid because he and his whole army are gone. And the Tsardon fleet is heading up the Tirronean Sea to transport their army direct to Estorr. Unless I stop them, they will take our capital almost before the first drop of blood is spilled on Neratharn's soil.'

'They have already taken my capital,' shouted Shakarov, pushing out of his chair. 'And I have seen your new weapon. You could break your army in two and win on both fronts.'

'It is not my weapon,' grated Roberto. 'What you saw was evil given expression. And calm your voice or the guards you have not diverted will hear you.'

'And so they should hear me. The Tsardon have washed over my country with the blessing of the traitor Yuran.' Always short-tempered, Shakarov was abandoned to rage now. 'And they will wash through Neratharn too. Gestern has the Ocetanas to sink the enemy. We have nothing!'

'I will not be shouted at by a man not brave enough to stand with me.'

'You must help us, General. You must turn around. Atreska is—'

'Atreska is already lost,' snapped Roberto. 'Go back to your fight. Leave me to make sure Gestern does not join her.'

'No, Roberto, no.'

Shakarov gripped Roberto's shoulder with his left hand. Roberto reacted, slapping it away and pushing the Atreskan from him. Shakarov's riposte was pure instinct. He lashed out with his right hand. The dagger thudded into Roberto's chest up to its hilt.

Roberto gasped and staggered back, tasting blood in his mouth. He stared at Shakarov who had stumbled back against the desk, his mouth open, his eyes wide with shock.

'Roberto, I did not mean . . .'

But Roberto didn't really hear him. He frowned and stared down at the dagger which had caught between his lower two ribs. Blood was pouring down his tunic and filling his mouth. He started to phrase the question but his vision wasn't right. The strength left his legs and he thumped to his knees, one hand gripping at the side of his cot.

'Oh dear God, have mercy,' muttered Goran.

Roberto heard feet and he heard shouting. A steepling pain seared through his body followed by a cool numbness. He closed his eyes and welcomed it in.

Dahnishev stepped away from the cot and wiped bloody hands down his apron. They had moved Shakarov's body from the tent and tried to minimise the leaking of the news but the whole camp was already awake and the rumours had begun.

He had lain Roberto on his side so he wouldn't choke on his own blood. And he had stitched the wound in his chest as best he could and bound him up. His breathing was shallow and pained. Shakarov's eight-inch blade still lay on the map table. Dahnishev had removed it with growing despair. He wiped the back of one hand across his forehead and turned to face Davarov, Kastenas and Neristus.

'Well?' asked Kastenas. The tears on her cheeks mirrored his own. 'He's alive, isn't he? You have saved him?'

Dahnishev nodded and felt like a fraud. 'But he is dying.'

Davarov gasped. Kastenas had a hand to her mouth. Neristus dropped his head to his chest.

'It can't be,' said Davarov. 'You're the miracle-worker. He's Roberto. He survived the plague. He can't die.'

'He's bleeding to death. The dagger has torn into his lung and sliced more veins than I can guess at. So much internal bleeding. I can't stop it.'

'How long?' asked Kastenas.

'What does it matter?' Davarov's tone was angry. 'Even if it's ten days, we don't move until he goes. I will not disrespect him.'

'I don't mean that. This is nothing about marching,' said Kastenas. 'How can you think that of me? Dahnishev?'

'Well it certainly won't be ten days,' he said. 'Less than ten hours I would say. As-God-looks-down, I don't know. He could be dead by dawn.'

'You know what we must do,' said Neristus. 'We cannot delay the appointment.'

'We will not replace him while he still breathes,' hissed Davarov.

'Perhaps it won't be necessary,' said Kastenas.

'Don't be ridiculous,' said Davarov.

But Kastenas was already pulling on gloves. She pointed at Dahnishev.

'Don't let him die before I get back.'

'Where are you going?' asked Dahnishev.

'Just don't let him die.'

Kastenas ran from the tent. Dahnishev looked back to Roberto and knelt by his head.

'You heard her,' he said. 'Don't you dare slip away from me yet, old friend.'

Chapter 64

The Ascendants were sleeping. It was the deep, still sleep of the exhausted body. Jhered had seen it countless times before. Already, there were signs that they were regenerating. Arducius looked much more himself facially though his hands were still dry and wrinkled. He was the best of them. Ossacer was unchanged from the time he had closed his eyes. His had been a disturbed rest.

Jhered had propped himself up by a tree to watch over them the whole night. Kovan had tried to do the same but the day had proved too much and he was sprawled asleep across his scabbard. The fire was still going, welcome warmth on what had become a clear and cold night. Dusas was in what . . . five days. It felt like it had arrived early.

He reached out a hand and stroked Ossacer's hair.

'Getting soft in your old age?'

'Appros Menas, you are supposed to be on lookout.'

'And I am, my Lord Exchequer. And I see my commander's mask begin to slip.'

Menas walked into the firelight and warmed her hands. Her breastplate shone, her fur cloak hung straight at her back. Jhered chuckled.

'They really did it today,' he said. 'And I am proud of them. I won't see harm come to them.'

'And not just because they are a valuable weapon?'

'What do you want me to say? That I care about them? Then yes, I care about them. They've made it bloody difficult but they're all right. Under all the moaning.'

Menas laughed. 'Such graceful acquiescence.'

'Menas . . . Erith.' He cleared his throat. 'Thank you.'

'For what?'

'For everything you sacrificed to come with me. And for being a friend to Mirron. I'm not sure she'd have made it without you.'

Menas was blushing beneath her plumed helmet. 'You are the Exchequer. And I am a Gatherer. I'd go anywhere you ordered, my Lord Jhered.'

'Paul. Out here, I think Paul is fine,' he said gruffly.

'Are you sure? What about them?' She indicated the sleeping Ascendants. 'We agreed to keep a discipline.'

'I know,' said Jhered. 'And it was the right thing to do. But we've moved to a different plane now. They've done something that will live with them forever. They will feel guilt and regret. They need more than a barking sergeant. They can call me Paul, too.'

'Are you sure you're cut out for the fatherly role?' asked Menas, another smile brightening her face.

'I'm absolutely certain I'm not,' said Jhered. 'So you'll have to help me. Perhaps I'll start at distant Uncle and work my way up. Anyway, what was it you came to report?'

'That horse you can no doubt hear. There's no risk.'

'Sure?'

'Sure.'

They waited. The lone rider cantered into the camp and dismounted in a rush. The helmet was dragged off and the rider thumped her hand into her chest.

'Master Kastenas,' said Jhered, standing up. 'You're bringing your general's sincerest apologies for abandoning us out here, I trust.'

Kastenas's eyes filled with tears that spilled down her face before she could stop them.

'Please,' she said. 'You must help. It's Roberto. He's been stabbed. He's dying.'

Jhered made up his mind in a heartbeat. He roused the camp and looked into every tired eye and irritable face, settling on the only one who could help.

'Ossacer, come on lad. This is what you were born to do so you keep on telling me.'

'You lied to us,' he said, his nightmares still fresh. 'You made us kill.'

'And I take all the responsibility and all the guilt on my shoulders.

But now here's the chance to do what you love. Save my friend. Save the Advocate's son.'

'I'm so tired,' he said. 'I can't do it. Not yet. Not for another day.'

'He won't last another day,' said Kastenas. 'You have to help him.'

Ossacer shook his head but Arducius gripped his arm.

'You can, Ossie. I'll come too. You can use me to make the circuit and channel the energies. All you have to do is direct them. I'll be the feed for you.'

Ossacer put his hands on Arducius's chest. He frowned and bit at his bottom lip.

'You have so little in you,' he said. 'I can't take more. I could really hurt you.'

Jhered made to speak. Arducius got there first. 'We must take the risk. I'm the only one you can use. Please, Ossie. You're the best Pain Teller there ever was. Show them what else we can do.'

Ossacer nodded and dragged himself wearily to his feet. Jhered smiled.

'Thank you, Ossacer,' he said. 'I won't forget this. Nor will the Conquord.'

'All right, all right,' said Ossacer. 'I'm going, aren't I?'

'Right. Good. Ossacer, you'll ride behind me. Arducius, behind Kovan. Menas, keep the camp secure. If you need to move, head south-west. I'll find you.'

'Yes, sir.'

'What about me?' said Gorian. 'We should all come.'

'Gorian, count the spare horses. Shouldn't take you long. I don't have time to argue.'

'You need the rest,' said Mirron. 'We both do.'

'We all do,' said Gorian. 'What about Ossacer?'

'Please,' said Jhered sharply, desperately. 'Not now. A man is dying.'

Silence about the camp. The Ascendants were staring at him. Gorian nodded and sat back down, dragging Mirron with him.

'Save him, Ossacer,' he said. 'Don't risk yourself, either of you.'

Jhered raised his eyebrows. 'Thank you.'

Menas rode next to him on the way out of the camp before they opened up to the gallop.

'Well done, Uncle Paul,' she said.

*

Mirron woke early. The sun was rising above the mountains of Kark, sending a beautiful golden light across Atreska. It lit the camp through the scattering of trees and played shadows across Gorian's sleeping form. He was looking much better. Most of the lines were gone from his face. The last wrinkles around his eyes still clung on but that didn't stop her stomach turning over at his beauty.

He looked so peaceful lying there by the smouldering embers of the fire. She let his energy map flood her senses, seeing the calm green and gentle red lines intertwining around his form. A gentle pulsing from the ground around him and a slight shimmering in the air above him indicated his drawing on the elemental energies to replenish his body. She imagined it filling out his smooth muscles and bringing new sheen to his gorgeous hair.

She looked away from him, feeling a warmth through her body that was both delightful and a little scary. Away at the army camp, Ossacer and Arducius might still be working to save the general. A man whom the Exchequer was desperate to save despite his obvious hatred of them. She didn't really understand it. She didn't think that saving him would make any difference. After all, that rigger had despised them even more when his sight was returned.

Menas would know what it was all about. The two men had been friends and perhaps it was as simple as that. She would be about somewhere, probably close, watching over them or looking out for danger. Mirron got up and wandered a few yards, trying to see her. It had been dark when they arrived at the camp site and in the light of day, she could see it was a lovely spot.

They'd slept on a patch of flat ground in a glade of trees. Above her, a tumble of rocks was covered in moss and heather and somewhere to the right, she could hear running water. She walked that way, feeling thirsty and dusty.

Life surrounded her. She left her senses open and felt the presence of birds in the air following her. Looking up she could see them land in the trees, fluttering their wings and twittering their songs. She smiled. They were singing to her. She hugged herself as she walked, feeling the strong resonance of the trees like great arms around her. Ahead, the brook gargled over rocks. She could see the ripples in the air above the water, scattering energies that settled or were blown away by the breeze. Ossacer said they could harvest those tiny motes. She wasn't so sure.

Reaching the little stream which was no more than three feet wide, she followed its course. It descended, out of the trees, away over the edge of the plateau and into the plain where . . . Her world darkened with the memories of yesterday. The screams still echoed in her mind. The thundering of rock and water, battering men and horses to mangled death. She had done it.

The beauty of the stream, the grass and the flowers still blooming at its edge was tainted. She imagined the water running red. She knelt at its edge and saw her wavering reflection in it, bordered by trees and cloudy blue sky. She looked a bit of a mess. Her long, dark hair was tangled and sat in clumps on top of her head. Her face was covered in dust.

The water was cold. She could see that in the deep slow colours of its energy lines. She took a breath and plunged her face into the gentle flow, feeling the thrill of the cold flood her body. She dipped her hands in and scooped water over her head and down her back, then lifted her head out and flicked it back, feeling it slap on to her tunic dress.

She sat down by the stream and her heart lurched.

'You scared me,' she said.

'Sorry,' said Gorian. 'I didn't mean to.'

He came over and sat by her, trailing his hand in the water, flinching at the cold.

'It's lovely,' she said. 'You should do what I did.'

Gorian reached up and smoothed her hair all the way over her head and down her back. She tensed and arched at his touch, breathing deeply. He moved his hand to her cheek, brushing away a trickle of water. She smiled.

'Menas sent me to find you,' he said.

'Oh,' she said, feeling a little disappointed. 'Well, now you have.'

'Yes, I have,' he said.

His body was warm next to her and she nestled in a little, cold where the water had soaked her dress. His arm was around her shoulders and she laid her head on his chest.

'Doesn't it make you sad, the people we killed?' she asked. 'I can't get them out of my head.'

'We only meant to stop them attacking our citizens,' said Gorian.

'I know it went further than we thought it would but it isn't our fault what happened.'

'How can you say that? We made the roots weaken the stone. We made the lake burst. It makes me feel so sick remembering what they sounded like.'

'They were invaders,' said Gorian. 'They shouldn't have been there. They forced our action and felt the consequences.'

'But they had no chance to retreat. They had no warning.'

Gorian leaned around with a gentle hand on her cheek and moved her face towards him. 'They are the enemy. They would kill Hesther and Andreas and Jen and everyone in Westfallen if they could. They would kill Ossacer, Ardu, me and you. Don't grieve for them. They had it coming.'

She dropped her gaze but he lifted her chin and they were kissing. The heat spread from low in her stomach and suffused her entire body. She felt the smoothness of his lips and his tongue darting into her mouth. She responded, putting a hand behind his head and drawing him closer, pressing their mouths together. Her heart pounded in her chest. His fingers running up and down her back sent shivers through her, tingling and wonderful.

He pushed against her and she let herself lie back against the soft grass. His face was close to hers, his eyes closed and his caress on her mouth so gentle she never wanted it to stop. She touched her tongue to his and they fell deeper together. He shifted so that his legs were astride her and his hand moved from under her to run up and down her side, snagging on her dress, dragging it up a little with every stroke.

She rubbed his arm, feeling his muscles bunched, and moved up to his shoulder, so broad and powerful. She felt his breath over her face. He drew away and their eyes met. His smile was so full and warm she almost burst into tears.

'I've dreamed of this for so long,' he whispered, smoothing her hair from her face and kissing her forehead.

'No you haven't,' she said, giggling.

'Oh, yes I have,' he said. 'You are so beautiful and this is so right. It was meant to be this way.'

His hand moved across her belly and up to her breast.

'Stop it,' she said, jerking back a little but getting nowhere under his weight.

He moved his hand away and leaned in to kiss her again. She met his mouth and their tongues twined. The energy flooded over them, joining them and she relaxed. His hand was on her breast again, feeling, kneading her dress. The sensation was wonderful, terrible. She shifted, turned her head away.

'Gorian, no.'

'Why not?'

'Because I don't want you to.'

'Yes you do,' he said.

He let all his weight press against her and she felt hardness at his waist. She gasped. His hand moved down her side and rubbed hard at her thigh, moving her dress up and up.

'Gorian, stop.'

He raised his head and she flinched at the anger she saw there. Her stomach flipped with a sudden fear. He knelt up and she sagged in relief.

'I don't want all this,' she said. 'It's too much. I'm not ready.'

She reached up a hand to stroke his face but he grabbed her wrist and forced her arm back behind her head. He took her other hand and did likewise.

'No,' he said, his face ablaze with energy, almost blinding her as her senses were overwhelmed. 'But I am. Don't you feel it, Mirron?'

'Gorian, what are you talking about? Calm down. Let me go.'

'It's all around us. Everyone and everything feels us. And yesterday everything we have learned came true. We cannot wait to build the next generation. I could be dead tomorrow. Now is the right time.'

Mirron kicked out at him but he laid his body on her and her struggles were futile.

'Let me go,' she said, raising her voice. 'Have you gone mad? Please. Don't.'

His eyes narrowed. She felt a tickling over her wrists. He put a hand over her mouth.

'Shh,' he said. 'Don't shout out. You know this is right.'

She felt tears running down her face. There were tree roots bursting from the ground, tying her wrists. She tugged and tugged but they were so strong. And she couldn't focus her own mind to break them. Her whole body was shaking and she sobbed deep in her throat.

Gorian's other hand was on the neck of her dress and with one pull he had ripped it open all the way down. The cold of the air rushed across her.

'Please.' She mumbled through his hand. 'I love you, Gorian, please.'

But she could see in his eyes that he was gone. His free hand was fumbling at his waist. He lay down on her again. She felt him feeling between her legs, forcing them apart with his own. There was a sharp, stabbing pain. She felt wet on her thigh and he was inside her. His hand pressed hard on her mouth, keeping her screams and cries muted. Every thrust jolted through her. She pulled and pulled at the roots but she could not break their hold.

He grunted and heaved on her. His eyes bored into hers. They were devoid of anything she remembered about him and more terrifying than anything she had ever seen. She froze, unable to turn her head away. Pleading silently with him to stop. He shuddered along the length of his body. He tensed, gasping in breath, his face red with his exertion. He dragged himself from her. The pain was horrible. He rolled away and she found her voice.

Her screams put the birds to flight.

'Shut up,' said Gorian. 'Shut up. It's too late now anyway.'

'Get away from me!' she howled, wrenching at the roots, slippery with her blood. The ache between her legs grew and grew and she couldn't make it stop. 'Get these things off me.'

He stood over her, smoothing his tunic down over himself. 'Not until you stop wailing.'

'Gorian! Step aside. Now.'

Menas's voice rang out like blessed mercy and Mirron burst into fresh tears. The Gatherer walked towards them, her gladius in her hand. Gorian turned to her.

'Why?' he said.

'Do it.' Her voice was cool and threatening. 'Don't make me force you.'

'You can't force me to do anything.'

He sauntered towards her. His back was to Mirron but she could feel the waves of energy rolling from him, empowering him.

'Be careful, Erith,' she said.

'Yes, be careful Erith,' mocked Gorian.

Menas glanced over at Mirron and her face crumpled with

sadness. She mouthed comfort to Mirron before turning back to Gorian, her expression bleak with fury.

'You pathetic bully. Want to try me? No?'

Gorian stepped back away from her but she followed him, her sword ahead of her.

'I don't want you,' he sneered. 'You are no Ascendant. Just a soldier. Weak.'

'Don't try me, boy. Get those roots off her wrists right now.'

'Or what?' Gorian laughed in her face. 'What will you do, stab me? Me? I am an Ascendant. You cannot hurt me.'

Menas dropped to her haunches and swept a leg out, taking Gorian's feet from him. He fell flat on his back and she was kneeling on his chest, her sword at his throat before he could move.

'I do not have to cut you to hurt you,' she said.

'Nor I you.' Gorian's hand grabbed her chin and she stiffened. 'You really have no idea, do you?'

Menas gasped and her sword fell from her hand and bounced on the grass. She clutched at his wrist. Mirron felt sickness sweep through her. Their energy maps were one, flowing over and around each other. But Menas's was blazing far too brightly as her life was forced through her while Gorian's pulsed slow and so strong.

'Gorian,' she whispered. 'No.'

It was a curious sensation. Fascinating. Menas weakened so quickly. It was so easy. He drove her energy through her veins and arteries and into every muscle, cell and bone like forcing life into the roots of a blade of grass or a tree. He observed them flare with forced life while he tired with the effort. He wondered why he couldn't use her energy to replenish himself but it didn't work. That circuit wouldn't open.

But he could drive her whole life through her in moments just as he could any plant. Her efforts to break his grip ceased and her hands dropped away. He looked at her face. Her hair was long, thin and white. Her face was lined and brown-spotted, her eyes milked over.

Dimly, he could hear Mirron screeching again but she was easy enough to ignore. Menas's mouth dropped open and she gasped for his mercy. Her teeth were rotten. The flesh fled from her chin, her cheeks sank and her eyes receded into her head. One last time, a wrinkled, long-nailed hand clawed at his. Her head fell to one side and her lifelines guttered and became dark.

He pushed her away and she fell on top of her blade. He lifted a trembling hand in front of his face and saw the deep lines that covered it. It was like looking at Father Kessian's. He felt exhausted, barely able to stand. He felt so old. Worse than ever before. He turned his head and found Mirron staring at him. The moment their eyes met she began to scream again.

'Don't,' he said, trying to shout her down, but his voice was tired and broken.

He dragged himself over to her on his hands and knees. She quietened. There was blood between her legs and her eyes were red from crying, her face wet. Grief washed over him, threatened to overwhelm him. She was hurt. In pain. And she hated him.

'What have I done?' he whispered.

He moved to her head and touched her face. She flinched and glared at him with such venom that his eyes filled with tears.

'Please, Mirron,' he said. 'I'm sorry. I'm sorry.'

'Sorry?' She spat in his face, the spittle running down his cheek. 'Murderer. Murderer!'

There were voices down below and getting louder, closer. Mirron was yelling the word over and over. Gorian felt a deep terror and had to gasp for breath. Menas was dead. Mirron was hurt. He had to run. He had to hide. He was spent and scared. He looked around. Across the stream there were more trees. If he could dredge up one more effort he could get away. Until the problems had gone and they forgave him. In his mind, he saw Father Kessian beckoning him towards them, showing him the way to salvation.

He dragged himself through the water and half ran, half stumbled away, Mirron's voice in his ears.

Chapter 65

848th cycle of God, 41st day of Solasfall
15th year of the true Ascendancy

There was a smattering of snow on the frozen ground. Flakes were swirling in the air and the day was darkening to late afternoon gloom. Very fitting. Westfallen was silent. There was no chattering in the forum. The wind mourned around the stockade and whistled though slat and onager arm. The Caraducian flag snapped at its mast.

Arvan Vasselis stared out over the fields before the town and stood a little straighter. The Armour of God was approaching. A full legion of five thousand infantry and cavalry. Oxen pulled wagons, catapults and bolt-firers. The standards and pennants of the Omniscient fluttered from a hundred staffs.

And at their head, Horst Vennegoor, Prime Sword of the Omniscient. He had come to finish the job he had started back when genastro still warmed the earth and Ardol Kessian still lived. Caraducian guard and levium warrior watched the assembly. Their expressions were impassive beneath their helmets though their hands gripped spear shafts tight.

Vasselis watched the legion come to a halt and the tented encampment begin to go up. Like Lotheris before him, Vennegoor came forward with a few guards to speak. But unlike Lotheris, he had the strength to destroy Westfallen in a few hours. And he knew it.

'It's late, my warriors are tired and I have no wish to enter into discourse with you, Vasselis,' said Vennegoor without preamble. 'The situation is simple. At dawn tomorrow, you will hand yourself into my custody along with all surviving members of the Ascendancy Echelon. I have no fight with your levium or your guard. They are free to ride away. If you do not hand yourself over, I will destroy this pretty little town you have ruined with this ugly and feeble defence. And I will kill every man, woman and child within it. I will slaughter every sheep, cow, dog and cat.'

He turned his horse and rode away.

'Can he do it?' asked Hesther, standing next to Vasselis. 'Can we defend against that many?'

'No,' replied Harkov. 'This is overwhelming. Beyond our worst expectations. All we can do is make a stand and pray for a miracle.'

Vasselis stared at the Armour of God. 'What is heroism, do you think?' he asked.

He felt an uncomfortable clash of emotions and thoughts run through him. He turned from the enemy and looked over Westfallen. The jewel of Caraduk reduced to a miserable sham existence. Its people walking with the hunched bearing of the condemned. Still, at times, disbelieving of the chasm of change in their circumstances. Vasselis shook his head. If he let it, the anger and injustice would consume him.

'It is never turning your back on your beliefs. It is about dying for the things you believe in if that is what you must do. It is about standing tall in the face of evil.'

'Or is that a romantic view of an ideal, Captain Harkov?' Vasselis said. 'This is wrong, you know.'

He looked at Hesther and saw in her eyes the fear that had gripped the town. And it would get worse. Most of them hadn't even seen what it was that was ranged against them.

'What is wrong, Arvan?' she asked.

'How long have you got?' he said.

'Come on, Arvan, that's not like you. We're here because we have no choice. If you're about to take responsibility for what will happen I am going to get very angry. You are not to blame. The Order, the Chancellor, are.'

Vasselis's mind cleared. 'Let me tell you what heroism is, and what it isn't. It isn't about presiding over a massacre because you are too stubborn to turn from your path. It isn't about letting your citizens die because you are confused into thinking that all they are is the place in which they live. Heroism is recognising that the right way to save all those you love, to remain true to your beliefs, isn't necessarily by your skill with a sword. It is in understanding that the stone on which you stand does not define you or those you love. And that you can protect them all without spilling a drop of blood.'

Hesther was shaking her head. 'No, Arvan, no. You are not riding out there to be murdered by that bastard. I won't let you. Westfallen won't let you. We might all be scared but we will all stand with you until the end.'

'I know,' said Vasselis. 'But that wouldn't make me a hero either. I don't believe in heroic failure as this will surely be. I don't believe failure to be heroic. This is about survival of work and ideas. Achieve that and we are all heroes. And who said anything about riding out there anyway? You misunderstand me, Mother Naravny. I have no desire to die tomorrow.'

He looked out over the bay and his ships bobbing at anchor.

Horst Vennegoor stood on the dockside gazing out over the empty, silent bay. He had dreamed of planting his feet right here while the flames of Westfallen's burning buildings and its heretics warmed his back. And while the blood of Arvan Vasselis dried on his hands.

'My Lord Prime?'

Vennegoor turned to his centurion. 'And?'

'No one, my Prime. The shelves are empty, too. They've left nothing.'

Vennegoor nodded and looked back down at the letter that Vasselis had left him. Sailed for the heart of the Conquord, it said. To where the Order cannot touch those it seeks to persecute.

'How wrong you are, Vasselis,' said Vennegoor. 'Not even the Advocate can keep you from the judgement of the Omniscient.'

'And now it's time for you to go, all of you. I still have work to do here.'

'But for the Advocate's order paper, you would be complicit in helping these heretics escape, Captain Harkov,' said Vennegoor. 'Consider yourself marked and watched.'

'As you wish,' said Harkov.

'This isn't over,' said Vennegoor. 'It will never be over. When they return, so will we. And not you nor the Advocate will be able to save them.'

Roberto opened his eyes. Dahnishev was sitting in front of him.

'How do you feel?' whispered the surgeon as if not daring to speak aloud.

'I feel—'

Roberto clamped a hand to his chest and sat bolt upright. There was no pain. He could feel no wound beneath his shirt.

'I dreamt about Shakarov.'

'It was no dream,' said another voice.

'What's he doing here,' said Roberto refusing to acknowledge Jhered.

'I will not give you the glib answer,' said Dahnishev. 'Look at me, Roberto.'

'What's going on?' Roberto felt lost and confused, the two things he hated most.

'Shakarov was here. He tried to kill you. He should have succeeded.'

Roberto shook his head. 'That wasn't his intent. He came to talk. It got out of hand.'

'I'll say it did.' Dahnishev laid a hand on Roberto's. 'You should be dead. He stabbed you at the base of a lung. He ripped veins and arteries. If you didn't choke on your own blood you should have bled to death.'

Roberto tensed and leaned away from Dahnishev, feeling a cool fear seep into him.

'What have you done to me?'

'It was the single most incredible thing I have ever seen,' said Dahnishev. 'That boy put you back together just by placing his hands on you and using his mind. He stitched you back to life from the inside out. Roberto. There isn't even a *scar*.'

There were other people in the tent. Davarov, Neristus, Herides. Roberto looked inside his shirt and touched where he knew the blade had driven into him. There was the smallest tender spot but otherwise not a mark.

'Is this true?' he said.

'You were dying,' said Davarov. 'We couldn't let that happen.'

'If it was my time to return to the embrace of God, you had no right to change that,' said Roberto. 'It's not natural.'

'It is,' said Jhered quietly. 'It is as natural as the morning sun.'

'How can you stand here and say that? You. The Exchequer.'

'Because I have opened my eyes. Like Surgeon Dahnishev has. You assume the Ascendants to be an affront to God and I understand that. It is exactly what I thought. But they are not an affront to God, they are a gift *from* God. And you are blessed because the ability to save your life was at hand.'

Roberto frowned and looked round the assembled senior team. That they were with Jhered was obvious.

'What else can it be?' asked Dahnishev. 'It was not your time to return to God because it was He who made these Ascendants available. As saviours. Can you think of the effect your death would have had on the army? Can you think of the effect it will have that you still live and are ready to ride right now?'

'They will think me invincible,' said Roberto and he couldn't deny the excitement beginning to course through him.

'You survived the plague and a dagger to the heart,' said Jhered. 'You are God's most blessed, most loved. Think what this does for the Advocate's rule when word spreads. Surely she is as the scriptures say, the embodiment of God on this earth.'

'And God has released these Ascendants, this gift, into your care,' said Davarov. 'Not to Gesteris, who is missing. Not to Jorganesh, who is dead. But to you. You who still maraud as a free army and are the best chance of beating the Tsardon. Give them up for trial when you get to Estorr if you must but as-God-surrounds-us Roberto, you must use them to win the war first.'

'And you think I can persuade the army of this?' said Roberto.

'They are already talking about it. The rumours of your survival are rife. Show your face and the job is as good as done,' said Davarov.

'But they are mavericks, a weapon beyond the scriptures. The Order condemns them as heretic.'

'With all respect due to Ellas Lennart, this is war.' said Neristus. 'Who cares?'

Roberto eyed Jhered and a smile crawled on to his lips despite the misgivings he felt. 'Who indeed?'

Mirron's screams had brought them to her. Kastenas had rushed from her horse to cover her with her cloak. Kovan had hacked away the roots holding her arms and she'd sat up and buried herself in his arms, sobbing without end.

Kovan had called for Gorian, dared him to come and face his death but there had been only the answering silence. It was a while before he had seen Menas, lying still on the ground. Kastenas had touched her, rolled her over on to her back and recoiled. She looked again and vomited, having to kneel to compose herself.

Kovan had demanded Jhered be brought back here. Kastenas had left at a gallop and Kovan had held Mirron the whole time until the Exchequer had arrived. Others were with him. Cavalry from the army. Jhered had studied Menas and seen Mirron on to a horse and away back to the camp. And then he had stalked around the stream and the trees either side, roaring for Gorian to show himself.

So certain was he that Gorian was there, that he had hidden close by, that he stayed until night touched the sky. He even offered him mercy and help with what he had done. That was when his anger had burned out.

For a brief time, Gorian thought he might do as Jhered ordered. But the whole time the cavalry searched and found nothing he stayed hidden far beyond their capacity to see. And though he wanted so much to show himself and run to Jhered, be forgiven and be embraced back into the Ascendants, there was a stronger part of his mind that told him it would be otherwise. That this time no promise he could make would be enough. He knew what he had done and for all that his guilt threatened to swamp him, they would not see his remorse. He would be cast out.

By the time Jhered had left and the sound of his horse had thumped away to echoes and nothing, Gorian knew what he must do. He broke the circuit with the broad beech tree to which he had joined and fell to the ground from its lower branches, unable to move for a moment.

He still found time to be satisfied with his Work. He had hidden in full sight of the scene of his crimes. At one stage, Jhered had even stood beneath him to demand he approach. Father Kessian had always said that they would find answers in their times of greatest need and so it had proved again.

The thought had occurred to him that it should be simple to develop the effect of their skin taking on the appearance of the energy with which they worked across their whole bodies. And it was. He'd hidden his clothes in the bole of the same tree, covered them with leaves and then hauled himself into its boughs. He opened its life map circuit and set himself within it, letting the tree's energy flow over his, disguising him more surely than shadow ever could. And it took so little effort, even replenished him a little. His earlier work had left him seriously fatigued, though, and being forced to remain still for so long had been difficult. That and dealing with the pain in his bladder and through his groin.

He started to uncover his clothes. He was cold and the air was chilling fast. A tear fell down his face and soon he was crying hard. He'd lost everything. His brothers, Mirron, poor Mirron, and everything he belonged to. All gone. Alone here on a plateau in an invaded country he had nothing to call his own and nowhere to go.

Gorian belted on his tunic and pulled his boots over his feet. He rubbed at his arms. The tree had kept him warm during the day but his fur cloak was back in the campsite. He doubted it was still there but he had nothing to lose by checking. He let his senses probe ahead. There was no one hidden in the trees and no one waiting by the camp site. His pack and furs were where he had left them but everything else was gone.

He bent to pick them up but straightened and turned instead. Kovan walked into the half-light, an arrow nocked in a tensed bow.

'Paul said you'd make the same mistake but not even I thought you were that stupid. He said you'd come back to this camp and I would have stayed here all night to make good on my bet. Now that's twenty denarius you owe me as well.'

'As well as what?'

'Shut up, Gorian. Shut up and sit down.'

'Or what?' he smiled.

Kovan marched in until he was only two yards away. He held the bow rock steady and there was a determination in his eyes that made Gorian wary.

'Menas is dead because she wouldn't strike you. Don't make the mistake of thinking I have any such problem. In fact, the only reason you are not already lying with this arrow in your neck is that the others begged Jhered for your life.'

'Did they?' Gorian felt a rush of love and hope. He would be forgiven after all.

'And I listen to what my friends want. And I listen to what my commander says. And I act upon it. I hate it but I act upon it.'

'So you are here to bring me back?'

'*Back*?' Kovan gaped. 'You are surely as cracked as Mirron says you are. As I always knew you to be. Back. Don't make me laugh. You are alive and that is more than you deserve. You have your pack and your cloak and that is more than you deserve too. You are a murderer and you are a rapist. They don't want you dead but they never want to see or hear of you ever again. Roberto has ordered any of his army to kill you on sight. Paul Jhered will set the levium on your tail. There is no place in Caraduk or the Conquord where you will ever be welcome. You are nothing. Outcast. Banished. You'll die out here.'

Gorian studied Kovan for a moment, wondering if he could get to him like he did Menas but concluding he could not. He did not have the strength. He knew Vasselis was lying anyway. They would not hate him for long.

'Finished?' he asked.

'Why did you do it?' asked Kovan. 'What possessed you?'

'You never really understood, did you, soldier-boy? The Ascendancy is more important than me or Mirron alone. It must grow to achieve its destiny. It will be the dominant force in this world and I have a responsibility to ensure the seed is sown in the most fertile place for that to happen.' He spread his hands. 'I'm sorry I hurt Mirron but she will understand one day. She's very young in mind. I am older, wiser.'

'No, Gorian, you are insane. Your talent does not put you above honour, decency and the law.'

Gorian laughed. 'Listen to you, Vasselis. You speak from an age long dead.'

'Maybe I do,' said Kovan, walking towards him once more, the bow still aimed at his throat. 'But it is only honour that is keeping you alive right now. And let me assure you of one thing. If you ever come close to Mirron again. If you try to harm her, threaten her or even speak to her ever again, I will kill you.'

'You don't have the balls,' said Gorian.

Kovan whipped his bow up. The arrowhead raked across Gorian's cheek and nose, just missing his left eye. Gorian staggered back clutching his face. The pain was extraordinary. And there was blood. He balled his fists.

'Uh-uh,' said Kovan, his bow trained and steady once again. 'Don't test me.'

'I'll kill you for that, Vasselis,' said Gorian, already imagining his face ageing crumpling in his hands. 'One day.'

'Really?' Kovan dropped his bow and strode forwards. 'Try now, Gorian. Try now.'

Gorian flinched backwards. Kovan beckoned him on.

'Not so big now, eh? Not so clever, little Ascendant.'

Kovan thumped his right fist into Gorian's mouth, splitting his lip. Gorian cried out and stumbled backwards. He raised his hands, suddenly scared. There was blood in his mouth. Blood everywhere. Kovan came on and drove his right fist into the side of Gorian's head. There was a roaring in his ear. His legs gave way and he fell to his hands and knees. Kovan's foot caught him in the gut, spinning him onto his back.

Gorian grunted in pain. 'Stop it. Stop it.'

Kovan loomed over him. Gorian's whole body ached. There was a sharp pain in the side of his head. He felt tears in his eyes.

'That's what Mirron said, isn't it? But you wouldn't listen, would you?' Kovan's foot came in again, right below his ribs. Gorian wailed. 'This is what it feels like.'

Kovan dropped on to his body and rained blow after blow into his face with both hands. Gorian didn't have the strength to stop him. Kovan's punches struck his eyes, nose, mouth and cheeks. Every blow brought new pain until he went numb with it all. He was crying now, unable to control himself. Eventually, Kovan relented and stood up.

'Hurts, doesn't it?' he said, flexing his reddening hands. 'I'm going back to the camp now. I have a horse and I'm looking forward to hot food and a warm comfortable cot inside a roomy tent. Got any plans, Gorian? Perhaps you should see to your face. It's an awful mess. Going to swell up and be painful. Still, at least it will go away. What you did to Mirron, that lasts forever.'

Gorian said nothing, just watched him, hating.

'This isn't going to go away, Gorian. They are never going to let you back in. This is your life now. Get used to it.'

He turned and walked from the camp.

'Right,' said Gorian, nodding to himself. 'Right.'

The camp was breaking up to march. It was three hours before dawn. The noise of the striking was everywhere. Horses snorted, hammers fell, stockade sections slapped together on flat bed wagons. They would be ready for the advance cavalry and light infantry to leave shortly. The first maniples would march within the hour.

Jhered and Roberto were standing with Dahnishev in the surgeon's operating tent. None of them had slept a wink. The doctor had first examined Arducius and Ossacer under orders from Roberto, then Mirron under those of Jhered. Both for entirely different reasons. Finally, there had been the grim task of examining Menas's body. The surgeon pulled a blood-stained cloth over her corpse. Jhered bit his lip as her head disappeared beneath it.

'So, any conclusions?' asked Roberto.

Dahnishev blew out his cheeks. 'For the second time in a day, I have never seen anything like it. You tell me she was how old?'

'Thirty-four,' said Jhered. 'Young, fit and very quick.'

'Extraordinary.' Dahnishev frowned. 'If I had to guess, I'd say this body was a hundred years old and more. She died of old age. I've examined her organs, I've looked at her skin and eyes, her hair. Nothing is damaged other than by the ravages of the years. This isn't possible.'

'It shouldn't be,' said Roberto quietly and Jhered felt the general's eyes on him. 'Want to tell me how this can happen?'

'You'll get a better answer from Arducius but in essence, their talent lies in the ability to use small amounts of energy from within themselves or from nearby sources and use it, amplify it in other directions to make things grow.'

'Grow?' Roberto gestured at the body.

'Ah,' said Dahnishev, getting it immediately. 'And in making things grow, they age as a consequence.'

'Precisely,' said Jhered.

'Dear God-around-us,' breathed Roberto.

'But it will have taken everything from him, left him exhausted,' said Jhered.

'Well, thank the Omniscient that he can only kill one every now and again,' said Roberto.

'Look, I know this is all very hard to take in.'

'You have a gift for understatement, Lord Exchequer,' said Roberto.

'Whatever Work they perform, it leaves them tired. The greater the effort, the worse the effects.'

'Yes,' said Dahnishev. 'I saw the signs of ageing in your other Ascendants. They age in fractional proportion to their Work, don't they?'

'Yes. Gorian will have been in a very poor state. Kovan mentioned as much.'

'Though not as poor as his victim, Paul,' said Roberto. 'We shouldn't let him run free. That was not a good decision.' He shook his head. 'The moment I begin to see the possibilities, even accept them, you present me with a murderer. An assassin who needs no weapon, no poison, no training. Just his touch and his mind.'

'And a bed next to his victim so he can rest afterwards,' said Jhered. 'Roberto, you're overreacting.'

'He's a murderer,' said Roberto.

Jhered sighed and couldn't help but look back at Menas. 'I know. Look, I don't like it either. But the others don't want him dead by our hands.'

'You're the Exchequer. You are not beholden to three minors, no matter how important they might be. And neither am I. If my people find him, they will kill him.'

'Just go with me on this one. Deep down somewhere, the Ascendants want to feel he will achieve redemption. This grants him that possibility.'

'Dusas is coming and he's not even fifteen,' said Dahnishev. 'How much chance do you really think he has?'

'After what he did, freezing to death if he doesn't starve first is better than he deserves. He should burn.' Jhered shut Gorian from his mind. 'Tell me about Mirron.'

'Nothing you don't already know,' said Dahnishev. 'I can confirm the rape. She has lost her virginity, she is bruised and bleeding and there was dried semen on her thigh. It's her head you need to worry about. Not only because of the violation. She witnessed the murder too.'

Jhered nodded. 'I'll deal with it. Try to, anyway.'

'They need to be ready to go in two hours,' said Roberto.

'We will be.' Jhered turned to go.

'And Paul?'

'Yes?'

'They are your responsibility. And they are under probation. No transgressions. I won't have indiscipline in my army.'

Jhered walked through the dismantling of the camp and to the wagon in which the Ascendants had bedded down when their tent was struck. He nodded to the members of Roberto's extraordinarii surrounding it and looked in the back. The two boys and Kovan were asleep but Mirron was sitting up. In the lantern-light, he could see the tear stains on her cheeks.

'You don't have to do it quietly,' he said.

She turned her head to him. 'I don't want them to hear me, Exchequer. They need to sleep.'

'Paul. I told you, call me Paul.'

In the next moment she was across the wagon and flinging her arms around his neck. She buried her head in his shoulder and cried hard. He held her to him awkwardly, one hand on the base of her head, the other stroking her back.

'It's all right,' he said. 'No one can hurt you now.'

'Why did he have to kill her? She was protecting us all.'

'I know, Mirron, I know. She was a great Gatherer and will be a greater loss. I'm so sorry you had to see it.'

Mirron sniffed and drew back, wiping at her eyes. 'Where will he go?'

'Gorian? I don't know,' said Jhered.

'Will he be alright?'

'I—' Jhered stopped, at a loss.

'He will be alright, won't he? He'll find somewhere safe.'

Jhered looked into her eyes and saw the yearning there. The desire for reassurance. It was something he could not give her.

'I don't know, Mirron. Worry about yourself, not him.'

'You can't change her,' said Ossacer from the depths of the wagon. 'It's always been like this.'

'What are you talking about?'

'What Gorian did will make no difference,' said Ossacer. 'Not in the end.'

'I don't—'

'She loves him. She always has.'

Chapter 66

848th cycle of God, 1st day of Dusasrise
15th year of the true Ascendancy

The days cooled, the march was unremitting, hard and south-west all the way. The scale of the victory the Ascendants had wrought became more and more apparent with every step. Scouts and cavalry worked up to two days ahead, destroying enemy intelligence-gathering, interrupting supply and harassing Tsardon raiding parties.

But there was no serious force turned to oppose them. Roberto sent armoured foragers into every settlement to flush out enemies and take supplies where he could find them, though there was precious little the Tsardon had not already taken. The army marched close to the Gesternan border, looking for the right place to cross and chase the enemy.

He crossed the Haroq City highway, his scouts reporting no action along the frontier. Gesternan flags flew at the forts. Defences were intact and undamaged. Every pace, every piece of information, brought Jhered's initial guess closer to the truth. And if the Tsardon had chosen to mass their attack on the coastal side, they had done it with everything at their disposal.

It was with grim satisfaction that it became obvious that the task of the seven thousand had been to delay them a significant time. Their arrival now was unexpected and unheralded. Roberto found himself hoping that some of them had escaped the devastation and had taken the news to their masters in the southern armies. An invading army looking fearfully over its shoulder would be absolutely ideal.

Two days from the road linking Kirriev Harbour to Byscar, the most likely focus of attack, Roberto saw the first signs of battle. He was marching the army down the Herolodus Vale. The Karku mountains were at his back, the slopes of the Atreskan southern plains were on his right-hand side and the deep, wide, slow-moving force that was the River Herol was on his left.

A cold rain had been falling for three days, exactly as Arducius had predicted, and his spirits were high. The rainfall had deadened the dusty earth, masking his army's passage along the border. Half of his cavalry was broken up into raiding parties of thirty on the southern plains, keeping him safe from ambush. And his scouts had reported back from the highway.

That evening, he spread maps out over the dining table set up in his tent and along with his command team welcomed Jhered and Arducius to drink, dine and plan. Ossacer was helping Dahnishev in the surgery. Mirron was with the blacksmiths. The inclusion policy had been recommended by Jhered and seemed to be working. Despite considerable anxiety among citizens, attitudes were softening. And they were charming children, though smiles were rare.

'These aren't the absolute best but key terrain is indicated,' said Roberto.

He looked across to Arducius, just an excited child, completely awed by his surroundings and barely able to keep himself in check. It was so hard to believe he was possessed of such power.

'The Tsardon have moved into Gestern, immediately south of our position. They don't have significant supply from Atreska and we've already taken out some of what they do have. Best reports suggest they are heading south beyond Kirriev Harbour. Presumably they are marching directly for Portbrial. They'll be harassed all the way but if the estimates of their strength, around twelve thousand, are right, they won't be stopped.'

'So they didn't mass as expected,' said Davarov.

'No, it's worse. They have a greater force than previously indicated. Now, the good news is that the border around the highway to Kirriev Harbour is still holding. It's fortified and Marshal Mardov has clearly made her play there. They have the mountains west and a secure line all the way to the port.'

'Have we had contact with the defence?' asked Jhered.

'No,' said Roberto. 'I haven't risked a scout. We have upwards of thirty thousand Tsardon battering away down there and if they don't know we're coming, I don't want to give them any hint by handing them a scout.'

'Can that be possible?' asked Neristus. 'Our marching column is almost three miles of chattering infantry, snorting horses and rattling wagons. I find it hard to believe.'

'There is no one so blind as the man who does not expect to see.'

'A pearl of Atreskan wisdom, Davarov?' asked Roberto.

Davarov smiled. 'We have many. But actually, I agree with Rovan. I find it impossible to believe that one Tsardon scout has not escaped the net.'

'I don't know,' said Elise Kastenas. 'Don't discount it. We've seen little activity. The supply trains we've attacked have been poorly defended and hastily put together. It shows little tactical awareness, little planning.'

'Well—' Arducius put a hand to his mouth. 'Sorry.'

Roberto gestured at the map. 'Not at all, young man. You are here to talk with the rest of us. What do you have to say?'

Arducius blushed scarlet and looked over at Jhered, who encouraged him to speak.

'It's just that they didn't expect to be here, did they? Not when the fighting started in Tsard.'

Roberto leaned back in his chair with a hand over his mouth, hiding his smile.

'How long have we all been in the legions?' he asked.

There was a brief silence.

'A combination of something like ninety years,' said Neristus.

'Most of them yours, Rovan,' said Davarov.

Laughter bounced around the tent.

Roberto hushed them. 'Thank you, young man, for opening our eyes. A hundred days ago, the Kingdom of Tsard was fighting for its life. They were losing ground in the north and the south and on the verge of having their whole underbelly opened up. They were fighting guerrilla actions in Atreska with no real belief in success.

'And now they are threatening the heart of the Conquord. Of course they aren't ready, of course they aren't organised. Most of their commanders have never prosecuted an invasion. Dear God-who-looks-over-us, it took us four years to gather ourselves for the Tsardon campaign and there are some around this table who felt, correctly as it turns out, that this was not long enough.

'The Tsardon have taken their chance, following the rout at Scintarit, and everything has gone their way so far. Atreska folded,

Yuran defected, Jorganesh was taken out of the game. They have a fleet on the move. Now it's our turn. We can chase those that have already invaded Gestern or we can fall on those attacking the Kirriev Highway border.' He opened his palms. 'Which is it to be?'

'There's no choice,' said Jhered. 'We have to secure one of the major western ports in Gestern. It's unpalatable, the thought of Tsardon running unchecked through Gestern but it's temporary. Defeating the Kirriev Harbour invaders releases Mardov's defence to tackle them. And it lets you turn around to chase the remnants of the defeated Tsardon north and move to the relief of the Neratharn border.'

'My legions are already looking forward to the forced march,' said Roberto.

'But he's right, isn't he?' said Davarov. 'Unless there are enough ships in Kirriev to transport us, which there will never be.'

'Time remains short,' said Roberto. 'How long can Neratharn hold?'

'They have to hold long enough to see you there,' said Jhered. 'So you have to give them hope. There won't be enough ships at Kirriev to take eleven thousand to Neratharn but you can commandeer one and send a messenger.'

Roberto looked around the table. There were no dissenters.

'Done,' he said. 'So now the question is, can we reach them unseen?'

'A little early snow wouldn't go amiss the day after tomorrow,' said Kastenas.

'I'll start praying,' said Davarov.

'No need,' said Jhered.

'I'd forgotten you'd abandoned God, my Lord Exchequer,' said Roberto, unable to stop himself. Jhered didn't react.

'Arducius, think you can bring on a little snowstorm?'

All eyes fixed on the young Ascendant. He shrugged.

'Of course. I can bring the clouds from Kark.'

There was a disbelieving silence around the table. The statement, so matter of fact, so extraordinary, hung in the air.

'Can it really be done?' Davarov's expression was troubled.

'Reality bites, doesn't it?' said Jhered. 'If Arducius says he can do it, he can do it.'

'What will happen, Arducius?' asked Roberto.

'There are two weather fronts affecting our route at the moment,' he said, Roberto watching him grow in confidence. 'The winds over Kark are very strong and driving cloud over us. It will continue as rain because the temperature is still too high down on the plains.

'But the air is much cooler offshore. With Ossie and Mirron, I can maintain cloud cohesion and bring cold air to land. When I tear the cloud it will snow.'

They were all staring at him. Roberto knew how they felt.

'Can we really rely on this?' asked Elise. 'I just can't conceive it.'

'Absolutely you can,' said Jhered. 'You saw what they did on the plains. This, so Arducius says, is easier.'

'And you can localise this storm, can you?' asked Roberto. He suppressed the urge to laugh at the ludicrous nature of his own question.

'I don't have the ability to do anything else. I will need to be able to see the target area, which might be a problem. How wide do you think it will need to be?'

'We can get you to a viewpoint easily,' said Kastenas. 'The enemy army is spread over a front around four hundred yards wide and about a mile deep if you include the reserve. You don't have to cover it all, just the eastern edge if that's all you can do.'

Another shrug from the boy. 'No problem. For you, it'll be like looking at the storm from behind a window.'

'Tell me something, Arducius. How hard will the wind be blowing that you bring from the coast?' asked Roberto.

'As hard as you like. We can make it a blizzard or a gale for a while if you want.'

'I want very much,' said Roberto, the thrill already growing inside him and the amazement at the potential undimmed. 'Do this right and not only will they not see us, they won't hear us coming either.'

Prosentor Kreysun had moved his onagers up overnight and left his Tsardon army in the field to make camp and sing. The fires had been bright and the celebrations loud and long. Eight days of battle on the border. Attack after attack repelled by defenders he had grown to respect but who were ready to fall. He outnumbered them three to one now and if he could knock over the walls, he would have Gestern and the road to Kirriev at his mercy.

It had been a fierce battle. He'd spent days trying to break their flanks but his steppe cavalry had met withering arrow fire from deep positions across the river, or been hampered by woodland in which the Conquord legions could break up their charges. Every feint he made was matched by a reserve force he guessed numbered four thousand. Now it was time to push straight through the centre.

The border itself was marked by a wide bridge over which sat a menacing concrete-and-stone structure. A flat roof housed thirty heavy onagers in three ranks. Turrets held bolt-firers. So far, he'd kept out of their way. Not any more.

The day had dawned cold and the rain had continued to fall as it had for three days. Today, though, it had been made colder by a high wind that had blown up overnight from the Tirronean Sea. He had wanted the enemy to see what was ranged against them as dawn broke. Let them fear him before he launched the assault. And when the first Conquord onager had fired at his front line, he had charged with everything he had. Four thousand cavalry backed by light infantry had swept across the shallows and engaged the archers and infantry in the woodland.

His warriors flooded towards the fortifications, the pike blocks and shield walls. The enemy could see what he planned and their onagers were directed at the ground between his infantry lines and artillery, trying to keep them back. He ordered them forward anyway. Seventy catapults, most of them taken from the Conquord and refitted for travel to the south, dragged by pairs of oxen and pushed by crews of twelve.

Conflict at the front was savage. The Conquord legions were skilled and desperate to fight for every inch he took. Tsardon blood was thick on the ground, bodies dragged away by the hundred. Enemy sarissas were a forest in front of his warriors. The damned legion discipline was embedded and unbreakable. Triarii were mixed with the hastati in front of his warriors, he was certain.

Kreysun ran along the back of his lines and in front of the reserve that roared and chanted them on. He was an old-fashioned commander, not given to the ways of the legions he faced whose commanders hid on their horses, far from blade and arrow.

'Keep them moving backwards. I need the room behind.'

His sentors acknowledged him. More troops were fed in from the standing reserve. Noise redoubled. The clattering of weaponry and the roar of opposing forces colliding anew slapped in his ears.

The prosentor watched for a time, seeing the defenders standing firm. The sarissas of the phalanx dripped with the blood of the Tsardon yet still shone in the weak sunlight. Onager arms thudded. Stones flew overhead. Kreysun followed their progress, watched them tear up the ground less than twenty yards in front of his catapults and well behind the standing reserve.

His artillery was still out of range. He had to get inside the enemy arc of fire. There was time to cover the ground while they reloaded. He sprinted away from the fighting line, his bodyguard with him. He reached the artillery just before the next stones ploughed troughs in the earth and threw mud forty yards back, spattering hard into his back.

'Faster.' He beckoned them on. 'Put your damn shoulders in harder. The less time you spend in the kill zone the less of you will die! Move.'

He ran through them, shouting encouragement, demanding effort and speed. In truth, he knew they were giving him all they could but it seemed so tortuously slow. And up on the fortifications, the defenders knew they were coming. The thirty onager arms cranked back once more but this time they waited.

Kreysun had no choice. He watched while his crews walked on. The moment they passed the first stone half-buried in the earth, the catapults fired again. Two- and three-talent stones rolled lazily in their arcs. There was a whistling in the air. The balls struck. Most of them short but two found their targets.

The first grounded between the ox pair, gouging the inside flanks of both to the bone as it shattered the yoke and frame. The animals died instantly. The second crashed full into the front of its target, splintering the arm and blasting through the base of the wagon and down through the rear axle. The whole structure bounced and split from the impact, men thrown aside, tumbling away. Splinters of wood filled the air, slashing and whispering through flesh.

'Move, move. Twenty yards more.'

Kreysun walked with them. Their courage had to hold. Victory would be today and these men held the key. He watched the Conquord onager arms winding back. He could see the activity on the roof of the fort. It was ordered and calm. The carefully rounded balls flew straight, true and far. Their height advantage gave them increased range.

The multiple thud sounded again. The air was filled with the whining and whistling. Behind the catapults, his crews hunched reflexively against impact and prayed for fortune. The stones approached. The impact shook the ground, hurling earth high into the air. Screams filled his ears, along with the crunching of wood crushed by rock.

Prosentor Kreysun did not look round. He was staring into the sky beyond the falling stones. The wind blew to a gale across him, right to left, and was getting stronger by the moment. At the same time, the temperature was falling though the day was on the rise. But this was not what sent the fear through him. There were clouds moving swiftly across the sky. Heavy and laden with snow.

The words of the cowards he had executed for desertion came back to him. They had spoken of a Conquord magic that could bring down mountains and break solid rock. One that diverted water and caused roots to spring from the earth. He had ignored them as the pleas of men desperate to avoid the slicing blade. Laughed in their faces as they were bled into the fire.

Perhaps he should not have laughed. The clouds banked and built above his army, darkening the sky with unnatural speed. Clouds that moved against the wind. The first flakes of snow stung his face, whipped by a gale that stank of evil.

Chapter 67

848th cycle of God, 2nd day of Dusasrise
15th year of the true Ascendancy

'A few days ago, you were robbed of your chance to revenge your-selves on the Tsardon. And I know how many of you were scared by what you saw.'

Roberto rode slowly up and down the front of his army, ranged three hundred yards either side of him and four hundred yards away from him. Just a hundred yards behind him, a curtain of snow was falling under the direction of the Ascendants. They could hear the howl of the gale that drove it. But here, the light rain still fell under a stiff breeze. It was bizarre and it was unnatural and the army had approached it warily.

'I know because I was scared along with you. Well, today it's your turn.'

The roar washed over Roberto, building as his words were passed back over the army. He prayed Arducius was right about the noise of the gale behind the snow curtain. He held up his hands.

'Most of you have met these children now. They are different from us but they are not evil. They are a gift from God. The fact that I sit here before you bears witness to this.'

Another wave of noise. Roberto punched the air.

'When I give the signal, the horns will sound and you will charge. You all have your orders. The curtain will fall and the snow and wind will cease. Do not falter. Do not take prisoners. Today, we fight to save our Conquord. Today, the blow we strike will drag the heart from our enemies. You are my army, my pride. Show them what that means.'

Roberto unsheathed his sword and held it high. The tip caught the sun. He swept it down and the sky filled with the sound of battle horns.

The battle raged on but the attention of both armies had wavered. The blizzard was so thick a man could barely see the enemy in front of him, and casualties from friendly strikes were rising. Onager stones still whistled across the sky but now Prosentor Kreysun's artillery was answering. And they were finding their targets.

Kreysun ran back through his onager wagons and towards the front line. Soldiers loomed out of the blizzard in front of him. A flight of stones screamed overhead. Death would come to people unseen. He heard impacts on the fortifications in front of him.

Ragged cheers reached him on the gale that washed across the battle front. He found the back of the lines and a sentor straining to see anything other than vague shapes and shadows five yards ahead.

'You must keep them pressing in the centre,' he shouted. 'Get word to the flanks to hold steady.'

'Yes, Prosentor.'

The battle was not controllable. He couldn't disengage. The damage from enemy onager on withdrawal would be too great. He had to push for victory. Beneath his feet, as he advanced further forward into the waiting lines, the trampled snow was smeared with blood.

The stench of fighting and dying filled his nose. The heat from thousands of men packed together reached him. The cries of triumph, rage and agony mingled together with the extraordinary din of weapons. He wanted to see the fort. He needed to know it was damaged.

He elbowed his way into the press. In front of him, and above the roiling greyed-out mass of the battlefront, a dark shape loomed out of the blizzard. It was too far away to see anything but a suggestion of its form.

'Damn this storm,' he said.

He looked up. The sky was dense with flakes scattering in the gale. The Conquord catapults thudded into their rests. More death to fall from the sky. A new sound came from the left. A whining half-lost in the din that filled his world. A scorpion bolt slewed through his men, spearing two and slicing the arm from another. Soldiers spilled away from it. He ran to the wounded.

'Get me stretchers, get me help,' he roared

A hand clutched at his. He looked down on one soldier. The bolt had taken his left leg off below the hip. Blood was gorging into the snow.

'Don't waste them on me, Commander,' he said.

'Nothing is wasted,' said Kreysun. 'Die a hero of the kingdom.'

His own catapults answered. Stones screamed close by as if mourning the newest losses. He heard them impact the fort and he stood up, straining to see. A rumbling sound echoed back to him. He began to move forwards again. Undeniably, he saw large shapes tumbling against the backdrop of the fort. The building was starting to fall.

'Yes.'

The cheer met him next and he felt the energy surge through his men. He ran for the battlefront to oversee the push to victory. The sky whined again. He frowned. It was too soon to be Gestern's answering fire. Stones and bolts smashed into the reserve and the rear of his forward infantry, gouging left to right along the field. The damage was high and frightening. His warriors rippled and bunched forwards. Ahead, new anxiety fed into the line.

'Keep fighting. You have them.'

The Prosentor looked left. The blizzard was obscuring everything. The missiles had to have come from that way. He blinked. His eyes were playing tricks on him. There were shapes in the mist. Thousands of shapes. And the snow was beginning to abate.

'Oh, no,' he breathed. He turned and bellowed for defence.

Roberto led the charge with his extraordinarii, plunging through the curtain of snow in the wake of the first artillery rounds. He found himself in another place. Snow lay thick on the ground, blown into drifts around the edge of the Work. A wind strong enough to pluck him from his saddle howled around his ears. Visibility was almost nothing.

His horse tensed and stopped, paced backwards and threatened to rear. He fought to keep it calm. Behind him, the army was coming. He must have cut quite a figure with his horse stamping and snorting but it wasn't quite what he had in mind.

'Come on, Arducius. You must have heard the horns.'

His horse took a pace forwards. The snow was thinning rapidly, the battleground ahead of him lightened. The wind fell away to nothing. Sun bored through the weakening cloudbank.

'Well done, lad.'

His army saw their quarry, roared the Conquord war cry and ran into battle. Roberto rode swiftly along the front of his light infantry.

'Javelins!' he shouted.

Hundreds of short spears flew out over his head, dropping into a Tsardon army turning in disorder and disbelief at the enemy racing into its flanks. Roberto kept on riding left. The first of his light infantry was past him, oval shields held out in front, second spears at the ready. At the centurion's command they released.

This time, the quicker Tsardon had shields to bear but still the missiles reaped great reward in the undefended. In the next few strides, the light infantry were engaged. Simultaneously, half of Elise's cavalry swept south across the river to counter the threat of the steppe riders already grouping for riposte.

Roberto watched it begin to unfold. His army tramped onto snow covered ground. The formation was as solid as it was beautiful. The front was twenty maniples wide, presenting a line of two hundred shields. Flanking cavalry rode at both ends. The Conquord anthem was shouted from every mouth. Behind the hastati, his archers jogged forwards. Principes and triarii were in their wake and the magnificent Rovan Neristus and his crews hurled stones ahead of them.

Roberto watched the next volley drop. Tsardon scattered from the impacts. Men were hurled into the air or ploughed into the ground, broken and twisted. Two enemy catapults were struck, sending smashed timbers cart-wheeling across the snow. And amidst it all, the Tsardon commanders toiled for order, attacked now on two fronts. Their army was large, far larger than Roberto's and Gestern's defence combined but the advantage was with the defenders.

The light infantry disengaged and ran back through the hastati. Enemy archers had turned to fire after them.

'Wall!' he ordered.

The command rippled through the maniples. Shields snapped into place above heads, the legionaries answering their centurions' calls. The hastati struck, bursting through the fragmented Tsardon flank defence and in their midst, an unmistakeable figure.

'Davarov,' said Roberto. 'Big Atreskan bastard, what are you doing?'

*

Jhered helped the Ascendants to their feet and waved away the offered help from their cavalry guard. The ten of them had stood with the horses a respectful distance away during the Work. Arducius looked very tired. His black hair was limp and dull and the backs of his hands were wrinkled. The crowsfeet were deep when he smiled. Mirron and Ossacer who had been amplifiers of the energies Arducius directed had not used so much of themselves. Both were able to stand unaided while their brother leaned hard on the Exchequer.

They were gathered on a bluff above the battlefield and no more than three hundred yards from the northern edge of the Conquord lines. The guard post had been cleared by scouts the night before and Jhered had moved the Ascendants up under cover of darkness. They had been able to work carefully and efficiently over the course of the hours before dawn to create the parameters and scale of the Work. It had paid off handsomely.

Jhered could not keep the smile from his face. He hugged all three of them to him while the din of pitched battle rolled up the sides of the rise towards them.

'Well done, well done.' He rubbed Ossacer's head. 'And you killed no one.'

Ossacer pulled away a little.

'Yes, but people are dying as a result.'

'Ossacer, please,' said Arducius. 'People would have died anyway. This is a battle. What we did was give our people, our citizens, the best chance. If the Tsardon do not choose to run, that is their fault and not ours.'

Jhered could see Ossacer didn't believe what he said. He turned to Mirron.

'Are you all right?'

She looked up at him and shrugged. The nod came later.

'Didn't think so,' he said. 'Come on, let's get you back behind the lines. I expect Dahnishev could use you, young Ossacer.'

'An Ascendant's work is never done,' said Ossacer.

Jhered ushered them towards the waiting cavalry and horses and looked down on the battle below them. The Conquord legions had gained huge ground in the first moments of the attack. Down towards the river and the fort, he could see the Tsardon in all sorts of trouble. Kastenas was fighting across the river on the borders of the woodland and he could see Roberto pacing up and down behind the hastati.

Up towards Jhered's position, the hastati and principes had crashed over the first of the enemy onagers like a wave. The bodies of crews were lying in puddles and smears of blood on the snow. Ahead, the reserve further along the original battlefront were organising fast and moving back to counter the threat. Neristus and the Gesternan defenders were throwing heavy stones into the bulk of the Tsardon army, causing awful damage.

And way back to the Tsardon camp, those few who had been left on guard could just be seen standing and watching. Fearful and uncertain. Yet, for all the Conquord's advantage of surprise, the Tsardon had the greater numbers by far. Tens of thousands of men fighting or ready to fight. The Conquord a moving wall of shield and steel. The Tsardon desperately trying to drag themselves to cohesion. It came down to whether the enemy could recompose and bring fresh soldiers to bear quickly enough. The day was not yet won.

Davarov ran in with the front rank of the hastati and could feel the confidence they drew from his presence. With his shield a blazing red against the deep Conquord green of his legionaries and his plumed helmet standing higher than the plain crests of his citizens, he was surely a target for every Tsardon. That was just the way he liked it.

Without a pause he led them into the barely prepared enemy defence. Soldiers who, scant moments ago, couldn't see through the blizzard to their foe a hundred yards away now found themselves surrounded. Davarov ordered shields high and braced himself against the impact, half-crouching and leaning forward.

He felt the Tsardon give and heard the surge of noise. He took another pace, drove his shield out and left and stabbed ahead with his gladius. The blade pierced leather armour and plunged deep. Davarov growled pleasure at the blood that burst over his hilt and across his glove. The Tsardon buckled and fell forwards. Davarov deflected his body to the left with his shield.

'This is my country,' he muttered and then raised his voice in a scream that carried clear over his maniple. 'This is my country!'

He let the fury settle on him and launched himself into the Tsardon infantry. He beat aside a shield with his own and chopped down with his sword into an enemy neck. He kicked the dying man aside and blocked a strike at his open flank. He ducked a flailing blade and jabbed his shield upwards into the sword arm. He followed it with a sweep his gladius wasn't designed for and he felt the satisfying vibration of edge carving into scale armour, grinding and tearing.

It was so long since he had been in the thick of battle. Roberto would have his balls for it but he didn't care. He called over his left shoulder to the hastati a pace behind him in the stunning morass of sound, men, steel and blood.

'For Atreska. For the Conquord.'

His shout was taken up and he saw the surge ripple along the line of the army as far as he could see. He stared into the eyes of a Tsardon warrior. The man was scared. He butted the boss of his shield into his gut and punched over the top of it. Fist and gladius pommel crushed his nose. Davarov's shield thudded up under his jaw and knocked him flat.

Beside him, young hastati were crowding to force their way deep into the heart of the Tsardon ranks.

'Keep it solid,' he shouted. 'Never more than a pace. Discipline.'

The shout came too late for one. He moved into a gap that wasn't really there. Tsardon blades came around from both sides. He took one on his shield but the other evaded his blade and chopped into his cheek. His skull split and he collapsed. Davarov cursed.

'Discipline, order, victory!' he bellowed. 'With me, hastati.'

He set his shield square in front of him and stepped back a pace, seeing the line order reform to his right. The Tsardon were only too glad of the moment's respite and mirrored the move.

'Again.'

Davarov led them back across the yard's space, cracking his sword into an enemy shield. A volley of arrows flashed overhead, falling among the gathering Tsardon defence behind their wavering line. The air stank suddenly of tar smoke. From the fort, flaming stones blazed across the sky and thumped down in the middle of the press created by the dual Conquord assault. He felt the ground shake under him and heard metal twist and tear. Spears of flame grabbed at the sky and steam rose in clouds from the snow-covered earth.

He looked over the top of his shield at his next enemy. The man was confused, scared and running out of support. Behind him, the line was thinning and the reserve was being scattered by the onager stones. Neristus sent over another volley. Whistling death biting into the ground.

'Run,' said Davarov. 'Get out of my country.'

'No.'

The big Atreskan smiled. 'So be it.'

He launched himself into the attack, slashing round the edge of his shield, forcing his enemy into a desperate block. The Tsardon sword came at him but too low. He batted it aside easily. His enemy was unbalanced and brought his shield in front of his body. But Davarov wasn't striking there. He stabbed straight forwards over it and buried his gladius in the Tsardon's mouth.

'Sing to me now, bastard.'

The Conquord line was moving inexorably forward. Davarov heard running feet. Javelins flew overhead, hundreds of them. Again the Tsardon wavered but again they held firm. Davarov moved up again, bringing his maniple with him. He felt the pulse around him.

In the stress at the heart of battle, young hastati fought in the heat and noise like veterans. There was a rhythm to the assault that sang of inevitable victory. Rectangular shields pushed forwards, opened to allow strike, closed in defence. Gladiuses stabbed forwards or slashed overhead. In the tight spaces, Tsardon blades still fell, searching for any gap in the Conquord defence. The price for a slip in concentration was the very highest.

'Keep it tight,' said Davarov, his shield vibrating under two strikes, his gladius diverted from its path. 'They'll come back at us.'

Davarov squared his shield again and picked his next victim.

Elise had them on the run. She'd brought a thousand riders across the river and burst on the steppe cavalry and their archer support with almost complete surprise. There was hand-to-hand fighting along a stretch of a hundred yards at the edge of the woodland as she had approached and she'd signalled the break at a distance of less than twenty yards.

The cavalry split into units of six to give them some form amongst the sparse trees. The sixes had driven in, cutting down riders and infantry like corn in the first wave, turning and galloping back to open ground to allow the next wave in. The Gesternan defenders had responded magnificently, dropping bows and turning to their blades to close the pincer.

Scattered in skirmishes, the steppe cavalry was in no position to reform and become the fighting force it was in the open. They had dispersed left and right, riding hard back towards the river, only to find Elise's archers one side and Conquord infantry on the other.

Elise ran down another Tsardon, leaning from her saddle to sweep her blade through his back and send him tumbling to the earth. She broke clear of the trees and could see the pressure Davarov's soldiers were exerting on the main force of Tsardon. In front of the ruined fort, Gesternan defence had become determined attack. It wouldn't take much to push the enemy into a rout.

She signalled her hornsmen to sound the regroup and trotted up to the edge of the river. Behind her, the cavalry emerged from the trees or swung round to join her while the Gesternans surged into the remaining Tsardon, chasing them away or cutting them apart.

She waited, watching. There was a crisis point at the angle of the two fighting lines. The Gesternans were spread across the highway and in front of the fort while her own people had come in perhaps twenty yards north. And though cavalry kept the Tsardon from a flanking movement, it was becoming a focal point for them. They had not given up and a breach in either Conquord line would prove disastrous with the weight of numbers heavily on the Tsardon side.

'Close column,' she called. 'Ride for the axis. Sound the charge and keep sounding. I need those riders out of our way.'

She raised her sword and swept it down, put her heels to her horse's flanks and charged. The cavalry thundered through the ankle-deep water near the bridge, thumped onto solid ground and careered towards the enemy. In front, her cavalry flank defence heard the horns, turned from the Tsardon and rode away behind friendly lines. Sensing a breakthrough, the enemy began to pour towards the gap, only to see a thousand horses bearing down on them. The fledgling Tsardon advance stuttered and faltered. Gaps began to appear.

Elise smiled and plunged into them, carving her sword out and down, taking the arm from an enemy swordsman. Her horse reared, looked for open ground, stamped down and set off again. Her pace had slowed dramatically but there was barely a Tsardon looking her way. She urged the horse on, sweeping back down with her blade, leaving her left side defended by her cavalry while she hacked again and again. Other riders came past her on the right, driving hard and deep. She heard a roar from the infantry. It was close now. A Tsardon blade came at her. It was blocked by her hornsman. She nodded thanks and thrust her blade through the enemy's chest.

Arrows came thick from the right, taking down horse and rider together. In response, her own archers let go a volley and the charge turned as a whole, trying to drive a wedge up behind the Tsardon lines. But the enemy had regrouped and were ready to come back. She signalled the wheel and darted back to safety, the arrows of her citizens covering her withdrawal.

'One more,' she shouted. 'Let's have them.'

She executed a tight right-hand turn, let her cavalry form around her and they hammered in again.

'What's happening there?'

Mirron had stopped her horse to look out over the battle to the far edge of the Tsardon artillery. She could see fires around the catapults. The army hadn't managed to get that far yet and to her eyes, there was little movement except that more and more enemy seemed to be appearing from further down the river. Jhered came to her side. They were halfway down the slope and standing right above Neristus and his artillery.

'They're turning their catapults round,' he said. 'They're going to use flaming stones to try and break up our lines.'

Mirron looked up at him and saw the worry in his face.

'Well, can't our soldiers stop them?'

'Not yet.' He pointed down to the right. 'We've got them on the retreat there but they are holding firm enough. We didn't get the quick breakthrough so they still have plenty of onagers to use on us.'

Mirron turned back to the fighting. The noise was indescribable, the violence hideous. As she watched, burning stones flew out from the fort over the bridge. She watched the flight and saw men running in all directions trying to escape them. Down they came. She winced. And when the smoke and spray had cleared, she saw the dark stains of blood and so many bodies where the stones had fallen. There was a man running away. He was on fire. And others just moving, crawling and hobbling. It was disgusting.

'I can stop that,' she said.

Jhered shook his head. 'You've done enough. You need rest.'

'But a shield can't stop a stone. It's not fair.'

The others were continuing down the slope. Jhered waved them on.

'It's why people fear the onager. We'll take them soon enough.'

Mirron shook her head and dismounted. 'Not soon enough for some people.'

'Mirron.'

She looked up at him. 'Let me do something. Let me try.'

He held up his hands and dismounted too. 'All right. I'll watch over you. Just be careful with yourself.'

Mirron felt safe and secure. She knelt on the grass at the edge of the slopes and looked across the battle lines to the Tsardon catapults and fires. The distance was quite extreme and she had to push out with all the energy at her disposal, opening her body to the earth beneath her feet and feeling the grass begin to nudge up around her ankles and knees.

The Tsardon fires stood out against the mass of energies Mirron could see. They spoke to her and even at this distance, she could feel the chaos into which she would enforce her order. Blank shades near the fires represented onagers. Their crews were flares of life, stressed and packed with adrenaline. Mirron pushed out through the earth and the sky, seeking the path that would take her to them.

She drew on the energy in the grass beneath her feet, and the underground stream Arducius had found and used for the storm Work. A loneliness and vulnerability descended on her quite without warning. Out here so close to battle with the noise surrounding her. The fear rolled over her. She couldn't shut it out, not without Arducius and Ossacer with her. Not without G—

Mirron shook her head and dragged in a breath.

'Mirron?' It was the Exchequer.

'I'm all right,' she said, fighting her shudders down. 'I can do it, I can do it.'

'Mirron?'

'Nothing.'

I can do it. She forced images of Gorian from her mind and calmed her heart. Instead, she brought Father Kessian to her mind and remembered that time long ago in the villa gardens when she had first broken through. All she had to do was take the flames and bring them where she wanted them. And surrounding her was the energy to amplify all that she wrought.

*

Ossacer squeezed Kovan's waist. Kovan half-turned in his saddle. They were approaching the reserve and camp lines, the cavalry detachment still surrounding them. Kovan had seen suspicion and disbelief in their expressions during the Work; and on the ride back, the distance between them and their protectors was no coincidence.

'What is it, Ossie?'

'Mirron's not with us.'

Kovan tensed and felt his heart miss a beat. He turned and ducked both left and right to get a view past Ossacer.

'Neither is the Exchequer,' he said.

'We have to go back,' said Ossacer.

Next to them, Arducius turned his head from where he'd been resting it against the back of the stiff cavalryman who escorted him. He looked dreadfully tired and old. It was all he could do to keep in the saddle.

'No,' he said, voice cracked and dry. 'I have to rest and you have to help Dahnishev if you can.'

'But Ardu, you said that we shouldn't leave each other ever. We should always be near each other. Especially out here.'

Arducius's grey brows pinched in a frown. 'Gorian has changed all that, hasn't he? Perhaps it's time we all learned to live without each other.'

'What are you talking about?' Ossacer's voice held a slight tremble. 'When the war is done we'll be going home. All three of us.'

'Do you think so?' asked Arducius. 'Do you really think so?'

'What's the matter with you?'

'Everyone knows about us now. We can never go back to how it was before.'

Kovan heard Ossacer's sharply indrawn breath.

'He's just tired, Ossie,' he whispered. 'Listen, you go back with him. I'll trot back up and make sure Mirron's all right.'

Ossacer slipped from behind him. 'Thanks, Kovan.'

'It's why I'm here,' he said and turned in the path.

Jhered stood near Mirron and felt the familiar but unsettling change in the air. The young Ascendant was deep in her Work now. Out on the field, Roberto's infantry were still on the drive but behind the front line of the Tsardon, more were racing up to steady them. Jhered saw Kastenas's cavalry charge in again behind volleys of arrows and javelins.

The Gesternan defence was holding against a renewed push. He could sense the Tsardon just beginning to stem the tide. Soon, confidence would flow in the wake of the flaming onager stones unless Mirron stopped them flying. He remained confident Roberto would win the day, the question would be at what cost.

He spun half about at a sound to his right. There was movement ahead of him. He dragged his gladius from his scabbard and placed his shield in front of him. He'd have pulled Mirron away but there was no time and his horse had moved off when she had begun. Perhaps she'd have time to do what she had to do before they were both killed. Not even he thought he could hold off six by himself.

Chapter 68

848th cycle of God, 2nd day of Dusasrise
15th year of the true Ascendancy

'Davarov, I need a breakthrough at their artillery,' shouted Roberto.

The Atreskan Master of Sword had just emerged bloodied and grinning from the front line to find his general waiting for him. He did his best to appear embarrassed but the joy coursing through him could not be hidden.

'We have them, Roberto, I can feel it,' said Davarov.

'Very probably. We'll speak about why you felt you had to assess from quite such close range later.' Roberto paused. Onager stones roared overhead, trailing smoke and flame. He watched them detonate behind his front lines and too close to his own artillery for comfort. 'But they are getting their range and I don't want more damage than I have to bear.'

Davarov nodded. 'What do you need me to do.'

'Take triarii from the northern reserve. Four maniples from the Haroq's Blades. Back it up with principes of the Hawks. You need to break through around their flank. Cavalry will protect you. Get into the artillery then get out.'

Davarov smiled and began to move off.

'And Davarov,' said Roberto. 'If you must go with them, try not to die, all right?'

'Today isn't my day to die,' said Davarov.

He ran along the back of the line. It was solid and confident. Neristus's stolen onagers fired in response, their own burning stones making smoke trails in the air. He prayed each one crushed a dozen Tsardon. Approaching the northern end, he could hear the ferocity of the fighting. Cavalry were running the flanks, keeping each other from engaging the infantry. Both sides desired the breakthrough. Only one had real belief.

Davarov barked his favoured Atreskan centurions to him. 'Maniples to me. Bring your support principes maniples for reserve and flank defence. Move, move.'

He moved on up the line, searching out the flank cavalry commander. Another Atreskan, nominally of the Haroq's Blades. He was studying the ragged edge of the battle where the two horseborne forces fenced with each other, looking for a gap, any small advantage they could exploit. Onager rounds dragged scratches in the cloudy sky, plunging down ten yards ahead of the Conquord artillery. Too close.

'Captain Cartoganev.'

'Master Davarov.' Cartoganev looked down the nose flute of his helmet. 'What is it? I'm a busy man.'

'And about to get busier,' growled Davarov. 'We're going after the artillery. I need you to keep the steppe away from my infantry.'

'It's what I was created to do,' said Cartoganev.

'Funny.'

'Not at all. I am stretched here, Master Davarov.'

'Then let's see them broken. If we can move up our weapons, we can do that.' Davarov shrugged and smiled. He could hear the maniples moving to order behind him. 'It's Roberto's order. What can you do, eh?'

Cartoganev stared over his head and grumbled in his throat. 'Leave it with me. Do what you have to but make it quick or we'll lose this flank.'

Davarov bowed. 'Just a little opening is all I need.'

Cartoganev turned and bellowed orders.

Mirron could feel it coming together inside her body. She could taste the warmth of the pitch fires and the energies of the earth filled her. She created the energy map of fire in her mind, huge and amplified. Now she must project that map onto the wood and rope of the Tsardon artillery. Onto the new fuel. It was so much easier when it was right ahead of her but this time, she must channel it along the natural lines of the air. It was going to be tiring. She took a deep breath and pushed out. Heat washed over her face.

She concentrated harder, aware that she was smouldering. She moved her left hand out towards the pitch fires. Their chaotic lines danced for her. So beautiful. She teased open a break in the first firelines and with her body holding it open, she pushed out harder. The created fire map fled away across the sky, smoke trailing from clear air. All she needed was one link and for the rest, it would be like knocking over a line of dominoes.

Somewhere near her, Jhered was speaking but it wasn't to her.

'This way,' said Jhered to the Tsardon running at him. 'Your chance to make every tax-evader happy.'

He moved left slightly, covering Mirron from their sight for as long as he could. How they had seen him he had no idea, but they must have been circling for hours to dodge the cavalry. Chances are, they were the relief for the guard post come to see if their comrades had escaped. It was an error not to have seen the possibility.

'I need help here!' he shouted over his shoulder, where only dust hung in the air. Pointless. The noise of the battle below was too great. The Tsardon spread out around him. Two had bows strung, four held their slightly curved swords and oval shields. 'Oh, shit.'

The bowmen fired. Jhered ducked. Both shafts missed high, sailing over the bluff and lost. He stood again. The Tsardon had stopped. Hardly a surprise. The bowmen bent their weapons again. This time one of the shafts slammed into his shield, the other into the ground. He glanced behind him. Mirron was lost in her Work. Jhered really only had one choice. He ran straight at them.

Keeping his head and body inside his shield he roared determination, covering the thirty-yard gap at speed. The bowmen flexed and released, flexed and released. One arrow parted his plume. Another bounced from his shield. A third bit into the earth at his feet. He made for the middle of the six. He wanted them all around him, concentrating on him, giving Mirron the maximum time to work and escape.

The Tsardon stood their ground, expecting him to pull up to strike. He had no such intention. He barrelled straight into the central pair, battering them down. He fell, half-twisted and rolled on to his back, scrambling to his feet even as they turned to face him. He was up fast. By his feet was a groggy Tsardon. Jhered stamped on his neck and launched himself back at the four standing. His shield clattered into an enemy's. His gladius thumped into another. He ducked a flailing blow, feeling it shear across his defence, splintering the finish.

He backed off a pace. The bowmen had swords now. Behind him, the surviving Tsardon was getting to his feet. He butted his shield forward again. His target dodged aside, striking out with his blade. Its tip scored across the Conquord emblem. Sparks flew. Jhered backed off again, moving left this time, bringing the fifth enemy into view. All of them had their backs to Mirron now. He took a glance behind him. The edge of the bluff was at his heels. The Tsardon spread into an arc.

'Which one of you is good enough to take me, eh?' He hefted his gladius. 'Well?'

They rushed him.

Prosentor Kreysun could feel the wheel turning in his favour. Never mind that the other Conquord force had managed to approach without him seeing. Never mind the evil gale that had blinded his men. He had so many warriors. And now he was pushing back on the border defence; the new front was steadying though still just on the retreat, and his onagers were finding their targets.

Conquord rounds from the fort exploded into the ground around him, obliterating men and splashing their fire across the little snow that still remained. He turned to his crews, forty at least.

'Faster. Let's give it back to them. I want these bastards running back into the hinterland.'

He marched to the lines of onagers. All of them were turned to the east now and moving forward in steps, trying to get the range of the Conquord's pieces. Pitch fires glowed hot and his engineers worked feverishly to get stones covered and lit while the arms of the catapults cranked back.

Heat came from nowhere, like a hot gust across the steppes when solastro was at its height. He frowned. Perhaps the fires were hotter than he thought though he wasn't standing that close. Kreysun saw it all happen but he still didn't believe it. Engineers backed away from a pitch fire glowing far too hot. Flame was spilling over the iron barrel, gouts of orange shooting into the air, coiling and jabbing down at clothing and shield. He saw men begin to smoulder. He saw hair singe and shield blacken.

'Korl spare us,' he whispered.

A wide tongue of fire lashed out from the barrel and engulfed the onager. The crew turned and ran. The heat was immense, stopping him in his tracks, leaving him able only to stare. The fires burned through rope, enveloped the arm and wheels, took the support frame and weakened the hinges. It would be so much ash in no time. He took a pace backwards. One after another, his pitch fires blossomed to bring the onager into their destructive embrace.

'Put them out!' He began to run amongst them. 'Put them out.'

But his crews barely heeded him. Most of them were running, their backs already indistinct in the choking smoke of dozens of fires.

Kovan jumped from his horse and ran past Mirron's crouched form. Ahead, Lord Jhered took a battering blow on his shield and his legs half-buckled. His gladius stabbed out but missed its target. The sword blows rained in again. Four men stood around him, two bodies lay on the ground. Jhered blocked one, took another two on his shield and the fourth missed his left leg by a whisker.

Jhered surged upright again, forcing the enemies back. But they were strong and there was only going to be one outcome to the fight. They spread just a little and he couldn't hope to defend against them all this time. Kovan wouldn't make it. He shouted but they didn't hear him. Ten yards away and it might as well have been ten miles.

There was only one thing he could do to distract them. He threw his gladius and prayed. The blade tipped end over end. Ahead a Tsardon raised his sword for a fatal blow. Kovan's gladius speared into his back knocking him forward off his feet. The others paused a fraction of a heartbeat. It was enough. Jhered thumped his shield into an open body and rammed his gladius into the throat of another.

Two left, one of them winded. Kovan snatched a curved blade from the first body he passed, feeling its unfamiliar weight and balance. He took it in both hands and swept it through the legs of one of the enemy. The man pitched back, screaming. Jhered punched his shield again and again into the last man, driving him to the ground where he finished him through the heart. Kovan stabbed the Tsardon blade through the stomach of the other, leaving the sword quivering.

He straightened and wiped a trembling hand across his mouth. Jhered was in front of him, handing him his own sword back and smiling.

'Just in time, young Vasselis, thank you.' He clapped a hand on Kovan's shoulder. 'It's a good job you're in love with Mirron, isn't it?'

Kovan felt himself blush. 'I don't—'

'No one comes back to save the taxman, boy.'

Jhered laughed and led the way to Mirron. She was lying on her side now, breathing heavily. Kovan knelt by her and stroked her lank hair.

'It's all right, Mirron, I'm here.'

She clutched at his arms. 'I did it. I stopped the fire stones.'

'And so much more,' said Jhered.

Kovan followed Jhered's gaze down on to the battle. The enemy onagers were burning. All of them. Black smoke clouded the sky and Tsardon were running in all directions. Behind, there was a great roar from the Conquord lines as word was passed. The legions surged. Down below them, cavalry galloped hard into their counterparts, forcing a slight hole. And into it poured Conquord troops, led by a man with a red shield.

'That's—'

'Davarov,' said Jhered. 'Come on. Kovan, get her up. Time we were leaving.'

Roberto signalled the artillery to advance and he galloped across the back of the line, spreading the word of the destruction of the Tsardon weapons. They had done it. The Ascendants. He didn't know how, and right now he didn't much care. This was the moment and with Davarov probably aware his targets were already gone, the Atreskan master would be able to put his maniples to different use.

'Commit to the lines,' ordered Roberto as he passed. 'Principes to the front. Let's break them.'

He urged his horse to the north end. A critical break here and the Tsardon were lost. He watched Cartoganev's cataphract break up a charge by the steppe cavalry. Horse archers thundered along in their wake, filling the air. A sword detachment rode into the skirmish, forcing the enemy to turn to regroup.

He looked behind him. 'Come on Rovan, let's have those arms swinging.'

He needed the stones to fall without reply. From the fort they still fell trailing smoke and flame but there were not enough of them to shiver the Tsardon morale. Roberto reached the right flank perimeter. Principes were adding to the weight. Down amongst them,

Davarov led his maniples into the gap the cavalry had forged. Tsardon were turning to cut them off.

'Archers, shoot behind the front line. Do it.'

The order was passed. Arrows flew in high arcs, falling out of sight. The right edge rippled and moved forward again. Just a yard but a big advance.

'They're turning,' he yelled at his centurions, to anyone who could hear him. 'They're turning.'

Rovan Neristus's stones scoured the grey sky. Roberto watched them go. He saw them plunge into the centre of the Tsardon reserve where it was grouping to defend. Where they thought they were safe.

'Not any more,' said Roberto. 'Not any more.'

The Conquord legions closed their shields under command of their centurions. Flags dropped, horns sounded afresh. They rushed the weakening line. Discipline. Order. Victory.

Somewhere out there, he could have sworn he heard Davarov shouting the self same words. Roberto smiled. Perhaps, just perhaps, they could save the Conquord after all.

Admiral Gaius Kortonius, Prime Sea Lord of the Ocetanas, breathed the cold sea air that blew across the Kester Isle plateau from the north west, bringing with it the first ice of dusas. The signs of the season were everywhere. From the sleet that had been falling on and off for five days; to the roar of the Ocetanas Palace hypocausts; and the sea mist that clung to the rocks and obscured the sea beyond two hundred yards.

Normally, it was a time of year Kortonius loved. Born on the shores of the Tirronean Sea in a tiny fishing village north of Port Roulent, he was a proud Caraducian sailor. He had watched the mists roll in and out ever since he was a small child. It was a fascination that had never left him.

There was a calm about the Isle and the sea when dusas called. The Quietening, the Ocetanas called it. When the bulk of the fleet was docked in the great caverns that arched beneath the plateau and the crews could rest in the city, spend time with their families and give thanks to sea Gods that would cause the Chancellor to boil over in pious rage.

But not this dusas. The timing of the invasion, if such it really was, could not be worse. The normal duties of the navy were stretching and tiring enough. They were based on the capacity to stand down in stages over dusas. Kortonius had done what he could. Much of the Ocenii squadron was in the Isle, as were over half of his battleships.

The scout ships and fast-attack triremes, though, were still out there. Forced to patrol the north of the Tirronean against the threat of the renegade Atreskan navy; required to patrol the entire eastern and western seas boards, particularly Estorr; and with a rolling blockade across the south of the Isle. Never mind the trouble in Gorneon's Bay and the Tundarran coast.

Too many ships at sea for too long a time. Yet, if the Gesternan reports were accurate, the Tsardon had sailed from the Bay of Harryn. A brave move with the storms that assaulted the southern tip of Gestern at the turn of the season. He would match them. No one seriously believed the reports of the fleet's size.

Kortonius turned away from his balcony and drained the last of his sweet herb tea. His breakfast was settling well in his prodigious gut and it was time for the constitutional the damn surgeon demanded to relieve his arteries. He laced up leather boots over his bare legs and hung a fur cloak about his shoulders. He smoothed down the front of his toga, slashed blue and gold in the colours of the Ocetanas. Finally, he pulled his pointless plumed helmet over his head. At least it would keep the sleet off his white hair, what little of it was left.

He walked out of his rooms and along the arched and colonnaded passageway that bordered the great hall, the floor of which was three storeys below. At the end of the passageway, he opened the doors to the western ramparts and let the freezing air flood his lungs. The sleet was falling hard and the mist had closed in more than ever. The Isle wasn't quiet. Too many guards, too many lookouts and too much readiness among the artillery crews covering the rock.

War. God-around-him but he used to love it. Now it was an irritation to the routine of his middle-age.

He strode outside. Below him to the right, the south courtyards and gardens of the palace, were full of busts, columns, fountains and flags. And to the left, the Tirronean Sea and the shrouded coast of Gestern. He looked down over rock and terrace. At the edge of his vision, he could see the water spray against the base of the Isle, but the view was dominated by the mist, deepened by the steady fall of sleet on this still day.

Today, he would do what the surgeon said he must every day and walk all the way to the watch tower at the far end of the ramparts. On his way he took salutes, nodded at senior civilian staff and stopped for the odd conversation with others taking the air. There was a certain sort that actively enjoyed the weather on the Isle and he could respect them for it. A life on the coast meant a love of it and an awe of the sea and the elements that never quite faded.

Halfway up the stairs, he regretted his earlier determination to do the surgeon's bidding. He felt hot, his face flushed. He paused regularly on the long, spiral climb of three hundred steps, emerging barely in a state to take the surprised salutes of the watch crew. One of them pulled a chair up for him and he sank into it gratefully.

'Thank you,' he said. 'A brave move and a welcome one.'

'Health does not recognise rank, Admiral. We all ail from time to time.'

Kortonius chuckled through his wheezing, his heart just beginning to calm. 'You are a born diplomat, young woman. I am merely overweight.'

The three lookouts all found their magnifiers requiring close attention. Kortonius couldn't see over the edge of the wall from his seat. The watchtower was narrow up here. Only room for eight or so people. It held a small iron stove under a fluted cover on its landward side as well as a pair of chairs. A bell and a flag pole marked its centre.

Kortonius stood and moved to the seaward edge. 'A thankless task on a day like today.'

The legionary woman opened her mouth to speak but a bell sounded away towards the southern end of the isle. Its urgent tone was picked up by others, the sound getting louder. Whatever it was that had been seen by the remote towers, it was coming closer.

Kortonius's heart thrashed anew in his chest. He moved to a spare magnifier, set on a pole at head height and put his eye to it. The mist obscured everything down at sea level and away to the south.

'Flags are going up,' said one of the watchers.

Kortonius swung the magnifier to the nearest tower to the south. The red flag was flying, the watchers pointing south. He could see a rider galloping along the cliff path towards the palace. He moved the magnifier back out to sea. There were shapes in the mist, and every passing heartbeat chilled him more and more.

The water was crowded with masts, hulls and oars. Looming out of the mist, moving serenely into view. Biremes, triremes, warships and finally, huge artillery galleys. Rumoured to have over as many as two thousand oarsmen, over ten times the crew of an attack trireme. Great, ponderous vessels. Siege ships.

'Where's my blockade? What happened to my blockade.'

Evaded or sunk without a trace. The major part of the southern defence was already gone. The din of the bell sounded over his head. The red flag unfurled.

'Ocetarus save us,' he muttered. 'How did they get this close without us knowing.'

'Admiral?'

He shook his head to clear it. 'Order the exodus, method one. I want every ship crewed and out on the water. Get the sea gates open. Get the Ocenii among them. Signal the fleet north. Messages to Gestern and Estorr. Go, go.'

Two of them left, one had to stay to ring the bell. Kortonius stared at the Tsardon fleet rowing towards them, ships fading and growing from the roiling mist. He couldn't take his eyes from the siege galleys. Two of them now, lumbering up the sound. They couldn't take the Isle. Could they?

Perhaps they could. Already, they were too near the sea gates for comfort. And if they could blockade the harbours before his ships were at sea in enough numbers, the battle would be over before it had begun.

He yelled down the steps for the watch team to run faster.

Chapter 69

848th cycle of God, 2nd day of Dusasrise
15th year of the true Ascendancy

In the end, led by Davarov and the Atreskans, it had descended in to massacre. It had been as distasteful as it had been necessary. Roberto nor the Gesternans wanted thousands of Tsardon prisoners. And he was not prepared to chase more than he had to through Atreska.

He still had much of his cavalry and light infantry in the field despite the fact that the light was beginning to fade. They were herding the fleeing remnants of the Tsardon army to the east, hoping they took the only option Roberto would leave open and returned to their home country. A few survivors taking stories of witchcraft and devils back to Tsard could do considerable good besides removing them from the war.

The rest of his army was celebrating victory, clearing the battlefield or working with the Order ministry to return the Estorean dead to the earth. Tsardon dead would be burned this time. Roberto would not allow their collection this far into Conquord lands and the risk of disease was too great.

Jhered rode with him to the Gesternan encampment a couple of miles behind the border fort, leaving the Ascendants with his army. Roberto chuckled, feeling his exhaustion lift. Jhered turned to him, a cut he had sustained protecting Mirron livid on his cheek in the light of lanterns carried by his extraordinarii.

'What is it?' asked the Exchequer.

'Just musing on the change of the army mind,' said Roberto. 'Five days ago, any of them would have killed Ossacer for laying hands on them. Just before we left, I heard someone complaining that they weren't getting the right treatment because the lad is tired and resting. And the lascivious glance at Mirron has become the fatherly arm. There's hardly one amongst them that would see her harmed. Her work on the Tsardon onagers will live long in the memory.'

Jhered nodded. 'And what about Ellas and the rest of the Order ministry?'

Roberto blew out his cheeks. 'That is a longer road. But even he cannot deny the number of his flock saved by the intervention of the Ascendants today. But he still fears them.'

'And what about your mind, General?'

'I have to be honest with you, Paul, I still struggle with it. And when they pause to think, the army will struggle with it too.' Roberto fought for the right words. 'I can see the force for good in them. For now. But their power is only going to grow. And when they reach full adulthood, who is going to control them then? Look at Gorian. I fear what he might do. Perhaps they will all go his way and believe that no one should guide them. They are only fourteen and they can crack hillsides and bring gales at their command. Sorry, I'm babbling but you know what I'm trying to say.'

'I understand more than anyone. We don't have a frame of reference for them, for what they are and where they might go. And the conflict with the scriptures and the beliefs of the Omniscient are there for all to see. All we can do is guide them and pray they only ever use their abilities for the good of us all. And remember, however powerful they are, they are just flesh and blood. Don't mistake their power for immortality.'

'It's a comforting thought, I suppose,' said Roberto. 'But I still don't understand your decision to let Gorian go. You said yourself he should burn. Instead he's not even been punished. It's like he's been forgiven.'

'You're wrong there,' said Jhered. 'The four of them have a bond closer than mere love. They have barely spent an hour apart from each other since they were born. Go and talk to Arducius. He'll tell you what it is they've really done.'

Roberto wasn't sure it would make any difference. The boy might still be alive and so remained a danger. They rode the rest of the way to the Gesternan border headquarters in silence. The road was littered with the injured and displaced. Exhausted and frightened soldiers and citizens watched them pass. Dirt and despair were everywhere despite the victory and songs that echoed into the night sky. Roberto's intervention had been a stroke of true fortune and the shock of their escape from defeat was settling on them.

The headquarters was set in a small village that was submerged in a city of tents, paddocks and temporary wooden structures. They were met by guards and shown to the tiny basilica that headed the likewise small forum. Inside, the wind-blown structure was warmed by open fires and lit by lantern and brazier. And there stood a welcome surprise.

'Marshal Mardov,' said Roberto. He embraced her and kissed her forehead but his smile died on his lips. 'Your presence is not to join the victory celebrations, is it?'

Mardov shook her head and looked across at Jhered. 'Well, well, Paul. Seems you were right after all.'

'I have my moments,' said Jhered. 'What's wrong?'

Mardov looked as tired as any of them. She ushered them to a table on which was pinned a map of Gestern, its borders and the Tirronean Sea. On it were marked arrows and figures. Roberto didn't like the concentrations along the west coast and near Kester Isle.

'We've had a stunning victory here,' said Mardov. 'But it only delays the inevitable.'

Roberto felt like he had been slapped around the face. 'Not true, Katrin. This victory has given us real hope for the first time since early solasfall. We've taken thirty thousand out of the game. And you can feel the morale in my army.'

'And we have the Ascendants,' said Jhered. 'Don't discount their influence. Not now they're proven.'

'If they are, it hardly matters. Neither they nor you, Roberto, can be in two places at once.' Katrin pointed to the map. 'The Tsardon over-ran border defences to the east eight days ago. We couldn't reinforce from here and we couldn't release anyone from the defence to chase them. We've been able to track them and they are moving fast, using the highways. There's no one to stop them, Roberto. Ten thousand of them and more, the same that destroyed Jorganesh, I think.'

'They're heading for the coast?' asked Jhered.

'Portbrial,' said Mardov. 'They'll be there in ten days, no more.'

Roberto looked at Jhered, who shrugged.

'Then you have to chase them now. Hope the Portbrial and Skiona defences can hold them up,' said Roberto. He stopped and felt a chill pass through him. He looked again at the marks on the Tirronean Sea. 'Where's the Tsardon fleet?'

'We had a flagged message from the on-station ships all the way from Kester Isle. The Tsardon are already there,' she whispered, glancing about her to make sure none overheard who shouldn't. 'Five hundred sails.'

'Five hu—' Roberto's mind reeled.

'The Ocetanas can't stop them all. The crossed flag has been flying, they are blockaded. By the time the Tsardon army reaches the coast, their fleet will be waiting to take them to Estorr. We're already too late.'

'We can't think like that,' said Jhered. 'Roberto, I warned you this might happen. We can counter them.'

Roberto looked round at him, thoughts clamouring through his head, images of Estorr in flames livid before his eyes.

'Even if they weren't blockaded, Kortonius has three hundred sails at best under the Isle.' Jhered stared down at the map. 'We have to get men across the sea, beat them to Estorr if we can't stop them in Gestern.'

'What with?' asked Katrin. 'We don't have the ships to make a difference.'

'And you must turn north, Roberto,' said Jhered. 'Neratharn must have relief.'

'Why, so we can retake the ruins of Estorr from the Tsardon?' spat Roberto, the hated despair gripping him. 'So we can pick up my mother's body and return it to the earth?'

'Yes, if that's all we can do,' said Jhered. The Exchequer's eyes were wide. 'We can only do what the Omniscient grants us. The Conquord can survive without Estorr. It can survive—'

'—without its current Advocate,' finished Roberto.

Jhered let his head drop slightly. 'Yes,' he said quietly. 'Should it come to that.'

The silence around the table was painful. Roberto searched the map for answers. He felt sick.

'Does she know what's happening?' he asked.

'The signal will have reached Estorr as it has reached us. And we will send word on the Tsardon army heading for the coast.'

'It hardly matters,' said Roberto. 'She won't leave anyway.' He smiled while the tears built up behind his eyes. 'Stubborn, my mother. I used to believe it was one of her great strengths.'

'And so it remains,' said Jhered.

Roberto held up his hand, stopping Jhered's next words. 'I never thought I'd hear myself say this, Paul. Never thought I'd be putting my faith in three fourteen-year-olds and a taxman, even a senior taxman. One sail against hundreds.' He gripped Jhered's shoulders. 'Save Estorr, save my mother.'

The Quietening had been shattered by the desperate, savage sounds of war. Multiple impacts rumbled and echoed through the caverns of Kester Isle. Oarsmen, sailors and marines thronged the passageways from the underground crew barracks, heading for the docks.

Karl Iliev, Trierarch of Ocenii squad VII and overall Squadron Commander thumped the gunwale of his spiked corsair in frustration and stepped back on to the wall. The sea gates were closed against the assault. To row out into the harbour now would be suicide, even for the Ocetanas elite.

Through the grilles he saw the end of the few Conquord vessels that had managed to put to sea before the Tsardon fleet forced the closure of the sea gates. Curse the mist. Curse Ocetarus for his capricious will. And curse them all for their complacency.

Iliev gripped the bars on the gate and prayed for the cycles of those about to be lost. Eight sails against ten times that number crowded around the outer harbour walls. He shuddered to guess how many more were hidden by the mist.

One bireme had not even made it to open water. Struck amidships by a stone aimed at the harbour defences and fallen short. Splintered timbers and corpses floating on the surface were all that remained.

Iliev's frustration was shot through with enormous pride. How hard the few fought. No thought of attempting escape. He could see hand-to-hand fighting on three enemy galleys. A Conquord bireme thundered its ramming spike into the rear quarter of a Tsardon trireme to the roars of the helpless watchers. Enemy oars splintered, marines swarmed over the bow and on to the stricken ship. But more, many more enemies were coming to the fight. And elsewhere, the navy was being overwhelmed.

In an area of open water, three corsairs of the Ocenii squadron powered across the ocean. Iliev prayed. It was not enough. The arc of target ships fired. Massive twin-hulled siege galleys standing well offshore launched three-talent stones. Triremes and biremes, fired bolts and smaller stones.

Stripped for maximum speed, the low, open corsairs had no defence. The leading squad took a stone at the bow. The impact catapulted the stern into the sky, flinging men into the water. The wrecked hull slapped down, keel up, after them, sinking fast. The others took hits from multiple projectiles, battering oar, man and craft.

Immediately, the siege galley began to move in. The next volley of stones from those already on station rattled into the gate and the emplacements surrounding it. The impacts reverberated through the cavernous dock. Iliev heard the answering fire and the screams of the injured and dying. There was a rending of metal. A heavy onager crashed into the water before the gates in a hail of rock. Freezing water washed through the grilles, soaking him from head to foot.

He spun on his heel and roared his impotence at the waiting crews. There were more than forty vessels trapped inside. Triremes, assault galleys, corsairs. It would be the same in all four docks.

'We're like rats!' He searched the faces staring back at him for a spark of inspiration. 'The tenth, twelfth and twentieth squads are gone. The *Brial's Dawn* is sinking. Her sister ships are swamped. Our marines are dying. Will we let these land slaves show us our business? Will we?'

'No!' The answering call echoed across rock and still water.

'Will we let our fallen Ocetanas go unavenged?'

'No!'

'Captains of the fleet, Trierarchs of the Ocenii to me. And someone get me Admiral Kortonius. We're getting out of here.'

Kortonius had returned to the palace and ordered his aides to bring messages to him at the western hall. Designed to view the glory of the Ocetanas during solastro festivals, the western hall was an opulent reminder of times now under mortal threat.

Paintings of great victories adorned the walls. Statues and sculptures on plinths depicted famous generals, the ships that had helped forge the reputation of the Ocetanas, and the god of all sailors. Kortonius bowed to Ocetarus. The powerful body, carved with fish scales and carrying the classically stylised head of flowing hair, large eyes and crown of starfish loomed over him. How they needed his blessing right now.

Out on the viewing stage, Kortonius gazed down at the unthinkable. He rested heavily on the ornate balustrade. His hands gripped hard to the carved motifs of interwoven seaweed and eels. Through the mist, part burned away by the endless flaming rounds from his defensive artillery, he saw the immensity of the western flank of the Tsardon fleet. Onager arms thudded. Rocks hurtled into the blank walls of Kester Isle. He felt the distant rumble of the impacts. Splinters and shards of stone whipped away to fall on the shore.

Directly below him, some five hundred feet down, a catapult position took a direct hit. Wood and metal was smashed and bent. Braces snapped. The entire turret swung outwards, hanging for a moment before shearing from its last stays and plummeting down towards one of his blockaded harbours.

The Ocetanas artillery answered, without risk now the last of his vessels was burning and sinking in the midst of the enemy. Burning stones were loaded onto every cup. The missiles arced out from sixty platforms set high and low in the western cliff face. He watched them streaking the sky with their smoke and falling away down almost out of sight in the remaining mist to the ocean below. Trails crisscrossed and flame blazed or guttered. He strained to see.

Plumes of water leaped up to snatch at the air before falling back. Too many missed their targets. It was so difficult. The Tsardon were moving in a long circle taking them fast across the face of the Isle and then away out of range. They were well spaced and understood the angles and spread of fire they faced.

Even so, they suffered. Three stones ploughed into the deck of one of the massive siege galleys. He saw fire drag from bow to stern and the forward mast shudder and fracture. It fell across the deck, destroying rail and weapon. A fourth stone thundered into the vessel amidships, smashing a hole the size of his body and plunging through the massed ranks of oarsmen. The ship began to list and he heard the shouts of triumph waft up to him on air that was thick with the scent of pitch.

It still wasn't enough. The Tsardon knew they could maintain the barrage for as long as their rounds held out. They didn't want to take the Isle but to render it helpless for long enough that those ships continuing north were well out of the Ocetanas' ability to catch them. In a day or so, they would have achieved their goal.

More Tsardon stone rattled against the Isle. Kortonius turned away, a pain in his side that reached up to his chest. A pity his surgeon couldn't prescribe him something as simple as a walk to take the cause away. A messenger was running along the colonnaded central mosaic to where he stood. He was out of breath, no doubt sent from the docks.

'Admiral,' he said, bowing.

'What is it?'

'Commander Iliev requests audience at the north-west dock at your earliest convenience. He says to tell you that he has had an idea for you to approve. He wants you to speak to the navy.'

Kortonius smiled. A fine sailor, Iliev. And a man whose ideas were always worth hearing. To the haunting echoes of onagers cranking and firing, he made his way to the lift platforms that would take him down to the dock.

Chapter 70

848th cycle of God, 3rd day of Dusasrise
15th year of the true Ascendancy

'I wonder what's happened to Gorian?' asked Mirron. Arducius squeezed Ossacer's hand to stop him saying something stupid. She looked round at them where they waited in the general's tent. 'Well, don't you?'

Arducius nodded. Try as he might, he couldn't keep Gorian out of his mind and his heart. The guilt was growing. It was worst when they were left alone to think.

'What are we doing here anyway?' asked Ossacer.

'Waiting for orders,' said Kovan from the map table.

'Can't he just give them to the Exchequer?'

'Perhaps he wants us to hear it first hand, Ossie,' said Kovan. 'He's in charge. He can do what he wants.'

Ossacer shrugged. 'We're wasting time. We should be going back to Kirriev Harbour if it's all so urgent and desperate.'

'Doing it wrong is worse than not doing it at all,' said Kovan.

Arducius smiled. 'I think you've spent too much time with Paul Jhered. You're beginning to sound like him.'

Kovan just returned to his study of the map, after a glance at Mirron. Arducius thought he understood. He felt the same way, sort of.

'Are any of you going to answer me?' asked Mirron. 'He's our brother. He—'

'Yes, I'll answer you,' said Kovan, he turned and walked towards her. 'I wonder what's happened. And whenever I do, I hope that he's dying slowly. That the cuts I gave him are infected and are killing him. That the stench of his slowly rotting body is his last memory. That the Tsardon have found him and are using him like he used you. He's a rapist and he's a murderer. He's no one's brother.'

The slap reported around the tent. Arducius winced and Kovan put his hand to his stinging cheek.

'And you still can't get him from your mind. After all he did to you. What's wrong with you?' Kovan's eyes were full of tears. 'He's gone. I'm here.'

The tent flap moved and Jhered came in with General Del Aglios.

'We all right in here?' asked Jhered.

'Ask her,' said Kovan.

Jhered sighed. 'Later. When we're underway.'

He looked to the general who strode into the middle of the tent.

'Right, gather where I can see you.' Del Aglios clicked his fingers. 'Quickly, quickly.'

Arducius stood in front of him and the others either side of him. The general looked them over. He was a daunting figure this close. Uniform perfect and armour shining even after so many days in the field. His green plumed helmet was proud on his head and his cloak was trimmed with the colours of his family. Arducius saw him as if for the first time, feeling his authority. They were in the presence of greatness and fame. Two of the most powerful men in the Conquord talking to them almost as equals.

'You'd be dead already if it was not for the belief of this man,' said Del Aglios, indicating Jhered. 'Remember that and remember to do exactly as he says. Sounds like an old story, does it? Well, that's because it works. Discipline, order, victory. I don't know who you really are or what it is that you possess. You may be a gift, you may not. All I know is that it worries me, my army and every right-minded person walking God's earth. But right now, I also understand that we have our Conquord to save and that we must use every weapon we possess. We do not have the luxury of consideration or moral debate. Not just yet.

'We are pressed on two fronts and do not have the forces in place on land or sea to defend either of them successfully. We, my army and you, have to make the difference. It's best you know this now because for all the work you think you have done, it is for nothing if we falter now.

'I go to relieve the Neratharn border, marching my army through the dusas snows to keep the northern approaches safe. And to you, I entrust the survival of our capital city and our Advocate. There is no job of greater importance. You cannot, you will not, fail. Signal your victory with the golden sun banners from the beacon masts. Give us reason to fight on. And when I am victorious, I will respond.'

He nodded and a grudging smile spread across his face.

'Any questions?'

Kovan came to attention and slapped his right fist into his chest. Arducius dug an elbow into Ossacer's ribs as the blind boy read the salute in the trails and threatened to laugh. Kovan managed to ignore him.

'General Del Aglios, I hope you will excuse me but the Exchequer bade me ask you what it is that you do after battle?'

Del Aglios laughed and looked round at Jhered. 'Did he, indeed? He was giving his talk about facing and recognising fear, no doubt. Yes . . . you were by no means the first one to hear it. Well I'll tell you. The lives of thousands hang on the accuracy and wit of my orders and tactics. It is a fact to strike even the bravest with nerves. And when I return to my tent and look back on what might have gone wrong, those nerves get the better of me and I vomit my stomach dry.

'Now let me ask a question of one of you. Arducius. Tell me why you freed Gorian rather than burning him. I consider it forgiveness.'

'Forgiveness?' said Arducius. 'No. We have punished him in the worst way we can. We have left him alone.'

There was nothing to hear but the lapping of water on hull in any of the four docks. There were no lanterns, barring the tiny lights that lit the walkways. Karl Illiev wanted the Ocetanas as adjusted to the night as they could be. He walked among them. Every one was smeared in charcoal-based paint as were the decks, mast, oars and hulls of every ship. It would wash away soon enough but by then it wouldn't matter. Deck-mounted scorpions had been covered with black canvas but all were primed and ready. The sea-gate mechanisms had been oiled.

Outside, the Tsardon fleet was standing out of onager range. Lights blazed from a hundred points in a wide arc around the dock. The barrage of the first day had wrought significant damage on both sides, but in the end the Tsardon had been forced to relent. Kester Isle had an inexhaustible supply of ammunition and despite losing many emplacements was still more than capable of destroying the fleet should they move too close for long.

Instead, the Tsardon had decided to sit it out, knowing they outnumbered the Conquord vessels trapped in the four docks. Signals from the fleet at distance and from the observation decks topside whenever the mist slackened indicated the enemy's intentions. At least a quarter of their fleet, now known to be in excess of seven hundred sails, had continued sailing north. Ocetanas followed them but, outnumbered, were not engaging. Others would move south to intercept but the bald fact was that the Conquord did not have enough ships at sea to counter them. Not yet, anyway.

'The fate of every Ocetanas out there in the Tirronean Sea is in our hands. The vengeance for every Ocetanas taken by the Tsardon these past two days is ours to dispense. The sanctity of the Isle and the harbour at Estorr are ours to protect.'

Every eye was on Iliev. His torso was covered with blackened light leather, leaving his long powerful limbs bare and free to row, climb and fight. His shaved head bore the dark blue skullcap of the Ocenii but even its emblem was covered tonight. His gladius was at his hip, its scabbard and hilt wrapped in dark cloth.

'You all know your roles. Do not deviate. The sea at night is unforgiving, the enemy are numerous. Ocenii, be ready. Ours is the task of the battering ram. Those of you tempted to turn back to help, do not. The fleet must break out to muster.' He glanced down at the hourglass that sat on the dock master's stone table by the sea gates. The last grains were bunched to drain away. 'For Ocetarus, for our dead, for the Conquord.'

The hourglass emptied. Iliev nodded at the Ocetanas. 'The gates,' he said and ran for his corsair, his sandals whispering over the stone.

The corsair sat low in the water, its heavy spike balanced by the Ocenii marines at its stern. They were the ballast and the balance. A team of six that ran the gangway between the thirty oarsmen that powered the assault craft across the water. It was the marines that set the ramming angle and cruising attitude, using their weight to maximise sea conditions beneath the hull. One mistake and the spike could ram too high, or dip below the waves and swamp the deck. Only the best were drafted to the corsairs.

Iliev took the tiller and looked along his ship. Ocenii squad VII. All ready to die for him. 'Take us into the channel,' he said.

The corsair slid away from the dockside, joining the other of the front rank pair. Eight squads were in his dock, lined up while the sea gates opened. The ponderous movement was mesmerising. The reinforced steel grids made tiny eddies on the surface of the water while the crews wound the oiled mechanisms, ratchets unlatched.

Iliev commended his body to the sea and his heart to Ocetarus. Around him, the marines leaned against the aft rail, keeping the spike raised. With the slightest of clangs, the gates nestled into their open positions. There was no need for more words. Iliev pointed one gloved finger to the open sea and the Ocenii moved.

The corsairs were hidden from casual view by the outer harbour walls. Iliev indicated quiet running while they negotiated the wreckage of ships and artillery that still floated on the surface. In the deeps below, the eyes of the Ocetanas gone to their rest would be on them. It was nothing to trouble a trireme but a corsair's bow could dip if snagged.

Iliev looked along the coast and growled in his throat. The damage to the Isle's defences was more severe than he had thought. Smashed artillery littered the rocks at its base. Metal hinges glimmered in the faint starlight while broken timbers and frayed rope nudged the shoreline, flotsam from the barrage.

He glanced back. The eight corsairs were all out of the gate and the first of the attack biremes was ready. Clustered in the gloom behind, the rest would be ordered for action. Now the Tsardon would know the fury of the Ocetanas.

'Go,' he said.

It was four hundred yards, no more, to the first Tsardon vessel. Their arc stretched away out of sight, north and south, where the lights on their decks were lost to distance, darkness and mist. The Ocenii turned north-west, gathering just beyond the harbour walls, a line of spikes aimed at vulnerable wooden hulls. Out came the first bireme into the harbour. Iliev's hand rose and fell. The Ocenii dipped their oars.

Acceleration was smooth and quick. The thirty blades moved as one. Stroke, lift, return, dip, stroke. Iliev could feel the wind begin to caress his skin. He narrowed his eyes and focused on their target. A pair of triremes, lashed together to hold heavy onagers and defending a siege galley.

The marines began to move forward as the prow rose, keeping the maximum hull area against the water and the oars at the perfect angle. The Tsardon in their ships had made a grave mistake. Whatever guards they had would not be able to see beyond the pools of light cast by their lanterns and torches. If their ears were as blunted as their eyes, they would not know the Ocenii were on them until the first spikes were five strokes from their hulls.

Below him the sea ran a slight swell. His oarsmen drove their blades through the water at a forty rate. With a following wind, they could achieve speeds in excess of twenty knots over a short sprint. That was what he asked for now. To his starboard, squad IX rowed for the bow of the target. Two hundred yards to go.

'Not one arrow on this deck. Not one marine down before Tsardon blood is spilled. Stroke up. Forty-five.'

Oars strained against the water. Wood creaked, sounding like explosions to his ears across the silence of the water. How long before a lookout heard them, he wondered. How long before the bells started to ring. He could see the Tsardon trireme clearly now. Lanterns were hung in six places along its length, casting light fifteen yards across the water. Guards stood by each one, other men walked the length of the vessel. It was ferociously painted, as they all were. Homages to gods, beasts and the sea's elements adorned the hull. They were bright reds, greens and blues. At the prow, the spike was decorated as a ram's head. Soon to see nothing but the pit of the ocean.

'Unlatch the ladders,' he said. 'Ready the grapples.'

Marines knelt to the quick-release ties that held the ladders in place along the gangway. Others held the ends of grapples designed to keep the corsair fast against the enemy.

'Sixty and closing,' said Iliev. 'Prepare for impact. Stroke steady.'

The sudden strain of impact was enormous but expecting it was half the battle. Conquord scientists had struggled for years to construct a bracket that dispersed the recoil forces through the hull without shattering it.

The corsair hummed across the wavecaps. His oarsmen didn't falter and didn't slow. The speed energised every nerve and muscle in Iliev's body. He'd seen action off Tundarra, Dornos and Bahkir and he never tired of the fight. He was born to this. Born to the sea and the sword.

The first Tsardon shout was away to port and by the time the alarm had begun to spread in earnest, he was inside his target's arc of light. He saw guards running to the rail. He heard shouts and the bell rang out the attack. Ten yards. He crouched and grabbed the stern rail.

'Oars!' he shouted.

They were raised off the water and shipped. Oarsmen spun to face forwards, gripping the leather stays that would stop them tumbling forwards.

'Brace and use it. Now.'

The corsair's spike skewered the trireme's hull just above the waterline, driving into its haft and boring a jagged, splintered hole bigger than a man's skull through its planking. The impact shuddered back through the ship. Timbers screeched and protested. The Tsardon vessel was shunted sideways across the water.

Iliev strained hard against the rail, a growl dragging itself from his mouth. He felt his muscles bunch and tense. And at the moment of release, the entire squad was up. The ladders thumped against the side of the ship. Marines swarmed up followed by the oarsmen. Another shudder through the trireme signified squad IX at the bow. Iliev barked at his men to move faster. Up on the deck, fighting had begun. Arrows struck the corsair from another enemy ship close by.

'Move, move,' Iliev yelled as he scrambled up, last as protocol demanded.

He raced up the ladder, leaving behind his grapple, men who had turned to their bows to return fire. The Ocenii were spreading out along the deck. Already, Tsardon were dead by their hand. The confusion was spreading through the ship. Sleepy crewmen would be woken into chaos. He needed them kept where they were.

'Secure the hatches! Let's use their fires. I want this ship on the ocean floor.'

The second squad were scaling the bow. He saw the anchor rope chopped away. He turned away, heading for the aft hatch. He glanced across to the second ship, to which this one was lashed. It was coming to order quickly. They would have to work fast. Up on the aft deck, a marine thrust his gladius through the defence of the steersman before turning his attention to wrecking the tiller.

Iliev reached the hatch. 'Keep seven topside against the sister-ship defence. Twenty with me. The rest of you, back to the corsair. We're going to need a quick escape.'

Fire flared in the night sky. Iliev looked left. A sheet of flame was licking up the mast of a Tsardon trireme. He bared his teeth. Now the whole Tsardon fleet would know they were attacked. Here was where it began. He led twenty down the hatch into the confused gloom of the Tsardon oar deck. The odd lantern was still alight. Running footsteps behind him.

Iliev jumped down the bottom two steps and ducked. A sword flashed over his head and embedded itself in the steps. He spun on his back heel and stabbed upwards. His gladius found flesh. He dragged the blade down, twisting it out of the man's groin. Blood flushed on to the deck. A second blade jabbed above Iliev's head, finishing the man through his throat. His squad was thumping to the deck around him, going forward.

Iliev came to his feet. 'Wrecking team, get to work. Leave me an escape. Let's move.'

He swung around the stairs and headed for the curtained-off quarters aft. Arrows sang through a gap in the cloth, taking one of his men in the chest. Iliev swore and moved faster, two marines right behind him. He grabbed a knife from his belt, tore the rough woollen curtain aside and flung the weapon down the exposed way, hearing a shout of warning.

'Go, go.'

The Ocenii made it a hail of knives flashing past his ears, keeping the enemy heads down. They ran in after the volley. Left and right of a split piece of decking, bed rolls were scattered. Tsardon were still coming to their feet, groggy from sleep and drink. Iliev took dead centre, giving his men the room to spread into the space either side of him. It was cramped and low. He ran at a crouch, gladius and a second knife held in front of him.

Tsardon came at them. He blocked a blow and punched the enemy in the face with the hilt of his sword. Iliev moved up. The quarters were filled with the sounds of clashing blades and the shouts of men. More arrows came from the gloom ahead, one striking a Tsardon in the back of the head. Iliev punched out with his knife, feeling the blade slice into his enemy's arm. Others of the squad moved up on his left. Behind, the wrecking team was already at work. He could smell smoke.

'Pushing back,' ordered Iliev.

He spun a kick into the side of wounded man's head and watched him rock back. Iliev planted the foot and thrust forwards. His gladius drove in under the Tsardon's ribs, dropping him where he stood. The enemy crew were beginning to panic. Flame flared garish light on their faces and cast the Ocenii into yet deeper shadow. Iliev dropped to his haunches and swept his foot through the ankles of his next foe. He tripped sideways.

The heat began to rise. The trapped were ready to break. Smoke was filling the enclosed space. The line of Ocenii made an initial rush forwards, forcing the Tsardon oarsmen into a reflexive move back. He had no idea how many of them were back there. Thirty or forty, at least. They were shouting and bunching ahead, scared by the fires they could see taking firm hold.

'Back and up,' he ordered.

The Ocenii withdrew fast. Iliev backed past the last of the wreckers sprinkling light oil on the central decking, feeding the flames and obscuring their retreat. The smoke was choking and clogging. Arrows flitted through the smoke. Iliev lost another man.

'Go, up.'

The Tsardon broke. Iliev flew up the ladder, arms hauling him to the deck. A ring of Ocenii stood around the hatch, gladius and flask in hand. The last of his people was dragged up, a deep cut in his ankle. Oil and a torch were thrown down on the enemy crew first to the ladder. The hatch was slammed shut. Two Ocenii bent to nail it down.

Iliev scanned the ship. The mast was alight, the sail consumed by thick black smoke and harsh yellow flame. Men from VII and IX were firing across to the sister ship, keeping the crew from the platform that bound them together and on which three catapults sat. To the bow, the forward hatch belched smoke and flame. And along the length of the deck, the Ocenii held sway. The bodies of the Tsardon outnumbered those of his fallen, five to one. Below his feet, the screaming was starting and smoke edged up through the planks.

'Back to the corsair!' he yelled.

He ran to the ladders, waving his squad to him. One after the other, they slid forwards down the rungs, thumping into their oar and balance positions. His grapple men had been at work widening the ramming spike hole, deepening it to below the water line. Arrows began to fly from the sister ship and from another portside that was moving into position. Iliev ducked down below the rail. Three men to go.

Across the platform, he could see Tsardon working feverishly at the bolts that held their ship to the stricken vessel which was beginning to list. It had been a textbook assault. The change of angle would make the bolts harder to shift, pinning them into soft wood. Soon, the only way would be to hack them clear.

The last man reached the ladders. He slid down one and rocked it back to place in position between the oarsmen.

'Ready for release,' said Iliev.

'Ready, sir.'

'Clear.'

Iliev took a step back and jumped at the ladder, riding it down to slap into the gangway.

'Let go grapples. Oarsmen backwater. This ship is coming down on top of us.'

And indeed it was. Sea water was sluicing through the holes forward and aft and settling quickly in the base of the hull. The counterbalancing of the sister ship wasn't enough and the list was growing by the moment. Iliev held the tiller steady. The oarsmen pushed, forcing the spike out of the trireme. Marines stood at the bow keeping it down to ease the exit.

'Clear water.'

Iliev leant hard on the tiller. Marines ran astern to lift the spike. Arrows flicked into the water around them. The corsair moved up the flank of the ship, chasing squad IX to open sea. The Trierarch looked back. Flame and smoke gouted from every oar hole. The deck was one sheet of fire, reaching high into the night sky and burning away the mist. It was unstable, falling quickly on its starboard side. Catapults slid from the platform across the burning deck and smashed through the rail on their way to the ocean floor.

'Stroke forty at first opportunity,' ordered Iliev. 'Let's clear this bastard. Target two at four hundred yards north. Good job, Ocenii. Ocetarus smiles on us.'

Rounding the bow, he could see that the enemy couldn't release the platform from the sister ship. He saw men chopping with axes, hacking with swords, desperate to free themselves. The target trireme began to go down. Steam scorched into the sky. The platform ripped free at last, shearing down through the hull of the sister ship, tearing a massive hole that exposed oar deck and keel timbers. Helpless to do anything else, the crew jumped into the frothing waters.

'Two for one,' said Iliev and his men cheered.

But behind them, the Tsardon had seen the heavy Conquord warships rowing from dock. The gargantuan siege galleys were moving into range. Their smaller sisters were already firing. Iliev saw a bireme of the Ocetanas hit with three consecutive stones. Its hull and mast were smashed, one stone shearing through the oar deck.

He commended the bodies of the dead to Ocetarus and turned for the looming new target. There was much work still to do.

Chapter 71

Herine Del Aglios looked down over Estorr, across its harbour and out into the mists that hid the sea from her. The Omniscient brought the dusas mists every year. This year, though, there was a malice in their coming. She stared at the flags flying from both harbour forts, wanting them to be lowered but knowing that would not be the case. Kester Isle was compromised. The Tsardon were sailing almost unhindered along her coasts.

She doubted they would bother landing until they were within sight of their prize. Perhaps they would be yet more confident than that and beat her harbour defences and take on the legions in the heart of the Conquord. And practically the first they would know of it would be when the artillery began to fire.

Herine chewed her bottom lip. She had put in place all that she could. The Tirronean Sea north of Estorr was still hers. Reports had the rebel Atreskan fleet scattered or sunk. Every available legionary was on or nearing the Neratharnese border. The Caraducian and Estorean coastlines were alive with her soldiers, who would move with the Tsardon fleet.

But still she was blind. Communication was slow, even by bird or ship. The beacon flags did not provide for update, only absolutes of victory or defeat. And across the sea, there lay her most troublesome unknowable. Gestern. She did not know if Katrin Mardov held the Tsardon at her borders or if Roberto had come to her aid. God-embrace-her but she had no certainty that he was still alive. Nor whether Jhered had found him and whether the Ascendants were still in the Exchequer's care.

'Oh Roberto,' she whispered. 'What will you do?'

It was in times like these when, despite all her confidence in her favourite son, she found it hard to have real faith. When all those on whom she relied so easily in peaceful days became feeble mortals in the dark dreams and visions that plagued her day and night.

'It is the waiting that saps the will most, is it not?'

Herine turned from the balcony and looked back through the grand gallery, past the paintings, tapestries and statues from around the Conquord to see the speaker. She forced a smile onto her face.

'Chancellor Koroyan,' she said. 'Come to minister to my troubled mind?'

'How else could I serve the Conquord better?' asked the Chancellor, walking forward gracefully.

She wore a formal toga, slashed Conquord green and covered with the rich, leaf-work embroidery of her office. Her sandals hissed over the bare stone and her eyes sparkled like the jewels in her tiara. Despite the breeze pushing into the open front of the gallery, she wore no stola or cloak over her bare arms. An impressive sight as always. Herine reminded herself to be on her guard.

'The city is quiet,' said Herine, turning back to her view.

The dusas sun was breaking through grey cloud as the morning chill began to lift. The bustle of Estorr was subdued. It was an uncomfortable atmosphere and added to the disquiet that had gripped every quarter. The unshakeable belief in the strength of the legions had been seriously eroded. Uncertainty had replaced complacency and overconfidence.

'But you are not surprised, surely?' asked the Chancellor, coming to her side.

'Naturally not. Even I will admit to having misgivings from time to time, Felice.'

'That's not unnatural. The Omniscient is angry. His head is turned from us and the mists are shrouding our enemies from us.'

Herine snorted. 'Oh, Felice. I could respect you so much more if you weren't so pompous.'

The Chancellor's expression was as cold as the day outside.

'Don't look like that,' said Herine. 'Listen to yourself. You're creating fear where there should be none.'

'Surely, my Advocate, you would agree that were the Omniscient behind us in our fight against the Tsardon, He would have forbidden the mists to fall. Instead, He aids their progress towards us. Hastens our doom.'

Herine shook her head. 'No, I would not agree. The dusas mists are a yearly meteorological phenomenon that our scientists explained a long time ago. The timing of the war is unfortunate and the Tsardon have been quick to capitalise on their advantages. But it will turn. The Ocetanas will break out. Neratharn will hold until Roberto arrives. We will win.'

'God is punishing us for your harbouring of the Ascendant abomination,' said the Chancellor. 'Only if you denounce them will the Conquord be saved.'

Herine felt anger building inside her twinned with a frustration that threatened to overcome her.

'And instead of preaching belief and calm, you peddle these fears and drive anxiety through the citizens of Estorr and god knows how far into the outlands. Why must you act so divisively?'

'Because faith in the Omniscient is not a thing to be called upon at our convenience. We either believe, or we do not. Perhaps you should ask yourself on which side you stand, my Advocate. Though it is not a question one would normally have to direct at the living embodiment of God on earth, is it?'

'You are treading a very, very fine line, Felice. Look down before you fall.' Herine gestured out at the city and its splendour. 'I am on the side of saving the lives of as many of my citizens as I can. We have been down this road before. If I can stop the Tsardon destroying all that we have built over so many centuries, I will. If the Ascendants are part of that, I am happy to employ them.'

'And in saving their bodies, you will lose their hearts.' The Chancellor moved away a pace. 'I hear what they say because I move among them.'

'You stoke their fears for your own ends,' said Herine. 'And believe me, it will be to your detriment when the war is done and the reckoning comes. Don't push me, Felice. Religion is evolutionary. I think it's time you went back to the Principal House and considered where your future lies. Thank you for easing my troubles, by the way.'

The Chancellor's glance radiated hate. She made to turn but the sound of horns in the harbour stopped her. She rejoined Herine at the balcony. They waited for the tones that would indicate attack but none came. Instead, the horns sounded the stand-down and three ships moved sedately into the calm waters inside the harbour walls. Two sailed in while the third was clearly in trouble and under oar. Her mast was gone, snapped about halfway up and there was damage to the deck and gunwale.

Even at their distance, Herine could make out the large deep blue flag that fluttered from mast and stern of the lead boat to indicate who was aboard. Beside her, Koroyan froze. Herine saw her face harden to a vicious contempt.

'Your accuser is paying a call,' said Herine. 'Surprised to see him, are you?'

'The movements of Arvan Vasselis are no longer my concern,' said the Chancellor. 'You made that abundantly clear.'

'I thought I had,' said Herine. 'But remind me. The legion of the Armour of God under Horst Vennegoor. Their orders were to secure the coast north of the Karals, am I right?'

The Chancellor inclined her head warily.

'I thought so. Presumably he lost his map or is unsure of north and south.'

'My Advocate?'

'It's just that my last reports had him marching south at upwards of twenty-five miles a day, heading deep into Caraduk. Towards Westfallen, perhaps.'

'Herine, I can assure you that—'

'And he would have reached there, let's guess, about twelve to fourteen days ago, I'd say. Just about the amount of time it would take to sail from Westfallen to Estorr, if you were forced to run.'

'My Advocate, if you are accusing me of—'

'Oh, do be quiet. Your protestations are so tiresome. You might hear what the citizens of Estorr say, Chancellor Koroyan. And I am sure they reinforce everything you wish them to. But I see and hear *everything*. And I never forget disobedience or betrayal. I will go and welcome Marshal Defender Vasselis and whoever it is he has brought with him to my capital. And if I see just one of your Readers or legionaries on the dockside, if I hear just one comment about his faith, I will have you arrested.' She waved a hand at Felice. 'Enjoy your afternoon.'

*

'Back port oars, starboard forty stroke.'

Iliev dragged the tiller towards him and the corsair slewed hard to port. The Tsardon trireme emerged from the smoke of a blazing Conquord bireme heading straight for them. Enemy arrows peppered the water and thudded into the gunwales.

'Back starboard oars. Port thirty stroke.'

Their discipline made him proud. The enemy thought they had his squad. They weren't even going to get close. He pushed the tiller away hard, turning starboard and driving away from the trireme at a steep angle. His crew were tired, pushed beyond any notion of normal limits. And still they responded to him.

Dawn was breaking, casting a cool luminescence through the mist that swirled at sea level and climbed high into the sky. There were fires and smoke in every direction. Burning wreckage was strewn across the ocean. His marines stood in the stern, keeping the damaged, bent spike above the water. In three engagements he had lost seven oarsmen and two marines. Not critical yet but he needed to find another squad before he made a final assault.

It was so difficult to gauge the success of the breakout. His squad were several miles north of the dock, shadowing a flotilla of twenty tri- and biremes trying to clear the siege and make way towards Estorr harbour. Their goal was ten days away under regular sail and oar. Ten days was three too many in Iliev's opinion. The Ocetanas would have to find new strength from somewhere. As for his squad, they would hitch a ride with whoever they could.

The battle had raged throughout the night. The early skirmishes had been easy. Surprise had been complete. The Tsardon had never seen the Ocenii squadron before but they knew all about them now. Thirty corsairs had ranged to the northern fringes of the Isle to devastating effect until the Tsardon, some of them, had begun to learn. Then, stones were heaved onto vessels spiked to their prey. Barrels of flaming oil were poured down ladders. And every enemy crewman had bow and sword in hand by the time the squads reached deck.

To a large extent, though, the damage had been done in the first hour. Now it was a case of securing the flotillas and making headway up the Tirronean, there to find what they would. Iliev was with the western ships, heading directly to Estorr. Others travelled with the eastern ships, rowing the coast of Gestern, where it was rumoured a Tsardon army waited to board.

Behind him, the enemy trireme was coming about. They were a fresh crew, moved in from the north of the siege arc. They moved quickly and surely across the easy swell. Iliev cursed under his breath. They would catch the flotilla easily. He couldn't afford that. These crews needed rest and clear water.

He looked down at his crew, stroking at twenty to keep pace with the rearmost Conquord trireme. The mist was thinning a little, giving him a view of most of the twenty. To the east of his position, more of the Ocenii squadron could just be seen, presumably shadowing other vessels of the Ocetanas. West, the sight he had hoped for edged out of the haze, angling towards him. Squad IX, whom he had feared sunk and lost.

'Seven, we're going around one more time. Nine will be with us. Will you pull for me?'

'Never doubt it, Trierarch,' said the stroke oarsman.

Iliev nodded. 'Thank you, Gunnarsson. Stroke at thirty, let's build some speed.'

He backed the tiller, taking them into a long sweeping turn and close enough to signal his intentions to squad IX. He wanted damage enough to slow the enemy, that was all.

'We are not boarding, marines. Stow weapons, this is about balance and pace. Keep the spike from dragging.'

'Sir.'

The Tsardon trireme saw them coming. Archers appeared on deck. The scorpion crews readied. Iliev saw groups of men bow and stern, ready for the anticipated ram. This was going to be interesting. Iliev could see the strain on the faces of his squad, the stress in their muscles and the many small cuts opening to spill fresh blood down their arms and legs.

'Easy thirty,' said Iliev. 'Coming about.'

The two corsairs crossed in front of the enemy, pulling at fifteen knots now. Iliev's squad cruised down their port side just out of arrow range. The scorpions fired. He watched the bolt in its shallow arc. Distance was good, direction not so. The shaft fell into the sea well adrift of them. They stroked on to fifty yards distance behind the trireme. Squad IX would have turned earlier, losing themselves in the mist, executing a move that would bring them in towards the enemy bow.

He pushed the tiller away, bringing the corsair about. The Tsardon increased their stroke rate. He could hear the dull thud of drums. They were at twenty, perhaps twenty-two. Closing in on the stern of the target, Iliev saw for the first time the flaw in the Tsardon ship design.

The outrigger for the top row of oarsmen was just a little too wide. The sweeping arc of the stern from the waterline to the tiller just a little too broad. He pushed the tiller out, adjusting their heading.

'Trust me,' he said. 'And just be ready to back the moment we strike. Forty stroke. A quick sprint, seven, it'll be all over soon.'

The corsair picked up speed. Two of the marines moved down the gangway, settling the bow. Iliev saw squad IX move back across the enemy and make a tight turn towards the trireme's port bow. Iliev was shielded from stone and bolt. Tsardon were clustering at the narrow stern and away down the port deck, trying to get angles on him to fire. They began a turn to port. The drum beats increased.

'Too late for that,' said Iliev. He adjusted their heading. 'Prepare for impact. We're going to be riding up.'

He smiled down at his oarsmen. They had their backs to the target. Not one tried to turn. Discipline, order, victory. Arrows began to fall. Iliev gritted his teeth. Two marines answered back. A shaft took one of his oarsmen clean through the back, sending him slumping forwards. A marine dived to his position, bringing the oar up and dragging the body back. Not quickly enough to prevent a clash of blades along the starboard rank. Iliev pushed the tiller out, counter-ing the sudden slowing and turn. In the next stroke, the corsair struck.

'Brace!'

Marines charged back along the gangway. The momentum of the corsair drove it part way up the Tsardon tiller. It was a stout, strong pole but not designed to withstand such an angle of pressure. Iliev felt it crack and break beneath his hull. The corsair slapped back to the waves, the spike dragging through the stern planking.

'Back,' shouted Iliev.

The trireme shuddered and moved to starboard. Squad IX had struck. Iliev's corsair retreated.

'Clear water.'

More arrows. Shafts struck oar and arm. Iliev swung them about.

'Stroke forty at first opportunity. Let's go, seven. Job done.'

The corsair hastened away from the trireme. Iliev could see

Tsardons leaning out, trying to assess the damage. They'd have another tiller but fitting it would take a day.

More enemies were coming from the south. Sails clogged the horizon where the mist gave way. In amongst them, Conquord sails indicated the scale of the breakout. For them, it was down to individual skill and their orders to slow and break up the enemy fleet. For Iliev and Ocenii squad VII, the long night's work was over.

He took them beyond the reach of enemy missiles and back to the flotilla. The *Cirandon's Pride* was with them. He made for the Caraducian flagship, already thinking of laying out flat on her deck while her crew winched his corsair up to hang beneath her stern, between tiller and hull.

'Stroke twenty-five,' he said. 'Stand down marines. Let's get some rest and commend our dead.'

Thomal Yuran, the erstwhile Marshal Defender of Atreska, was now its de facto king. It was the only thought that could still bring anything approaching a smile to his face. He refused to sit on the throne; it was like committing a fraud against what remained of his loyal populace. And most of them seemed to be resident in Haroq City. It was the only place that had seen no combat, barring the altercation with the Gatherers. Barely thirty-five days ago now and it seemed like ancient history.

Days in which he had struggled with his decision, and his country had become exactly the battleground he had feared. And even that had seemed unlikely in the immediate aftermath of the repatriation. So much joy in Haroq that fed out to the countryside. People chanting his name and imploring him to rule them as king of a new nation. The flags of old Atreska flew proudly. Even the beacons had been extinguished inside his borders.

There had been a full five days of celebration when everything Sentor Rensaark, now Prosentor Rensaark, had promised him came true. Then the Tsardon army, bolstered by legions of their new Atreskan allies, had marched west. So complete had been the transformation that the Tsardon commanders had been able to divert greater numbers south to Gestern. It had been a time when Yuran could see the end of the Conquord and a new power-base grow, with him as its fulcrum.

A time now as dim a memory as his last sight of Paul Jhered. The man still haunted him. He was still out there and the reports of his actions, or rather the actions of those in his care, were terrifying if they were to be believed. Yuran was a superstitious man. He was also one able to read the truth in a man's eyes and found himself unable to dismiss all the stories he had been told.

Atreska was in flames. West, south and north, palls of smoke caught the eye in dozens of places. And whether it was Tsardon raiding and retribution for supposed misdemeanours or the actions of the resistance that had so slowed the main advance, was a moot point. The result was that there would be precious little of his country left when the war was over; and he was left hoping rather than assuming that the Tsardon would prevail. Certainties were fast becoming mere possibilities to his mind. Practically his only solace was that he had sent Megan away. At least she would be safe, whoever won the war. A Conquord loyalist the Tsardon dare not touch.

'You worry too much,' said Rensaark, still seated at the dining table.

'Do I?' Yuran turned from the balcony windows, catching his reflection in a mirror. He had aged. Grey hair, sunken lustreless eyes and sagging skin were hardly attractions for Megan should they ever see one another again.

'In every war there are reverses,' said Rensaark.

'My country is in ashes. All but one of my neighbours is now my enemy. And it is not certain that our joint forces will breach the defences at Neratharn. God-surround-me but look how long it has taken us to beat a path through our own territory.'

'And that is why we are allied,' said Rensaark. He was dressed in fine clothes. A tunic of spun Tundarran weave, a jerkin of Karku furs, and gold-threaded sandals. The riches of the Conquord might have been fading for the ordinary citizen but they were not lost on Tsard's senior military. 'We knew there would be resistance. It may have taken longer than we wished but it has been overcome.'

Yuran moved back to the table and picked up his wine. It was cold outside and the fires around the hall struggled to keep the chill from the air. There had been the first solid snowfalls of dusas these past two days and conditions out in the field were only going to get worse.

'This is a bad country in which to battle in the ice and frost,' said Yuran. 'The plains channel howling winds across the fields, the snow drifts so deep it could cover this castle and the temperature can drop enough to freeze the blood in a man's body. Your men and mine lodge in tents near Neratharn. The enemy has superior structures. They have the supply of the Conquord behind them. We have barely enough to feed ourselves, meal to meal. We have taken too much time to marshal ourselves. If they hold out for ten days, they can beat us.'

'The battle will not last ten days,' said Rensaark. 'They are outnumbered three to one at least. They will barely last a day against us.'

Yuran shook his head. 'They have heart and hope still. And they will know by now some of what has been happening to the south. They will soon know that bastard Del Aglios is marching to help them. Marching through my country with nothing to slow him bar the weather.'

'He will have nothing but the bodies of his citizens to bury,' said Rensaark. 'And he will have no choice but to chase us all the way to Estorr. A city that will be ours already. They have lost and they know it.'

'And this new weapon. These children who can bring down mountains? You don't deny they are a threat.'

'Indeed not. But unless they can fly, they cannot help the Conquord at Neratharn either. Relax, Thomal. Take a bath or something. Soon, the threat of the Conquord will be gone forever and we can forge a new peace with independent states. Just as it used to be. And you will be the hub of it all. King Yuran, backed by the might of King Khuran, need never fear invasion again.'

Yuran took his leave of Rensaark and walked back to his private rooms in the castle. As always, what he said was so plausible. But there was a flaw if only he knew where to uncover it. And the nagging doubt remained that Rensaark was playing him for an imbecile, using him to expand Tsard.

Yuran ordered water to be brought in for a bath before sinking into his favourite leather chair to soak up the warmth of the grand open fire in his hearth. Presently, he heard his servant arrive and he moved though to the baths to prepare. He frowned on seeing the kitchen lad who had pushed in the heavy, wheeled urn to mix his bath. He was older than most of them for a start, but thin and rather bedraggled. Like someone had starved him and rolled him in mud before letting him attend his king-in-waiting.

'A bit old for this task, aren't you?' he said. 'And a mess, too. Am I running out of kitchen boys?'

'No, my Lord,' said the lad. He turned, his head bowed. 'I am sorry if I give you offence. None was intended.'

Yuran waved his hand. He had more important matters to consider. 'Just mix my bath. The rosemary essence tonight, I think.'

'I had to speak with you,' blurted the youngster suddenly.

Yuran sighed. 'If you are petitioning for food, I have none. If you want to join the legions, report to the master-at-arms at the basilica. Now, finish your job and go before I have the guards drag you out.'

'No,' he said, and Yuran was so surprised he let him speak on. 'Because I need a place to hide and you need a defence against the rise of the Conquord, whether the Tsardon defeat them or not. You are alone and adrift. So am I. And there is a power coming to this world that you cannot deflect with mere swords.'

'And I suppose you can, is that right?' Yuran's hand had strayed to the hilt of his gladius. 'I have enjoyed our talk but you are out of time, whoever you are.'

'Who am I?'

The boy raised his head and Yuran moved backwards, transfixed. Under his dirty blond hair, the boy smiled and a sweep of warm green flowed across his eyes, settling to a neutral grey. Yuran's gaze dropped to the column of water the boy supported on one outstretched palm with no vessel to contain it. He pointed vaguely but no words would come.

'Don't be afraid,' said the boy. 'Let them fight. Let dusas pass. Bide your time and hide me. And one day it will be you and I who rule this world. Not today. Not this year. Perhaps not in ten years. But one day. All you have to do is trust me.'

Yuran felt as if he were choking. There was a thumping in his head and a tremor in his limbs. He groped for a wall and leaned heavily against it. The Tsardon with the dread in their eyes had all spoken the truth. And here stood one of them now. A boy who could make a mountain fall.

'Who are you?' he managed.

The boy smiled again. 'I am the one who sees the truth. I am Gorian Westfallen and I am humbly at your service, Marshal Yuran.'

Chapter 72

848th cycle of God, 16th day of Dusasrise
15th year of the true Ascendancy

Under his eye-patch the itch had begun again. The scar was infuriating, ever more so as the weather got colder. The discharge, he wouldn't think of it as tears, froze and pushed at the sides of the wound. He let his hand trail down the length of it, all the way around his right cheek and to the hinge of his jaws.

The surgeon had called it luck. The Tsardon blade, filthy with Scintarit mud, had glanced rather than hit him full force. If it had, he would have been dead rather than standing here, one of the few survivors of the rout. Yet, as he looked out over the defences to the sea of enemies assembled in front of him, he wondered whether it wouldn't have been better to have died. To preside over one defeat was hard enough to bear. Two was reason enough for suicide. And defeat it would surely be.

The bird from Gestern had cheered the senior team and given great heart to the legions massed to defend but the reality was out there for all to see. Roberto was four days away and that was two days too many. They had so nearly done it. The legions adrift in Atreska picking away at the advancing Tsardon and rebel forces. They had bought the defenders time to reinforce and build. To bring up every piece of artillery they could find and repair, arm every citizen strong enough to stand and drill the legions to new heights of discipline. They had even built a highway-class road running north to south along the back of the permanent defensive structures, to hasten movement. Everything was in place except the force of arms he knew he would need.

From the southernmost shore of Lake Iyre to the sheer faces of the Gaws, the Neratharnese border with Atreska was just nineteen miles long. The highway crossing point was heavily fortified and much of the land south impassable to an army. Some great geological event of the ancient past had showered fields of rock down from the Gaws to lie as silent traps for wheel, hoof and ankle. Lookout posts and forts punctuated the length of the border and he would staff them all, though the likelihood of major incursion on this ground was unlikely.

But it still left him an area of friendly ground, almost two miles long, to defend. He had an armoured gate across the highway, with artillery platforms, oil and rock runs, archer positions and secure staging for cavalry or infantry. He had two other forts a mile apart and he had the Atreskan civil strife of the last decade to thank for the fact they still stood and were maintained. None of it, though, had been built to counter what he faced this cold, crisp dawn.

He gazed south along the line of his defence. He was proud of what had been built in the short time they had been afforded, much of it before he had arrived and assumed control. The open spaces between the two forts and the highway gate had been blocked by a wall of stone and wood. The whole had been sealed with concrete. It had a rampart for archers and was lined with artillery platforms. But it would not stand up to a concerted barrage.

Immediately behind the wall stood every other onager he had at his disposal, a hundred pieces grouped in tens. And behind them would stand the lines of artillery and cavalry currently housed in the stockade, corrals and tented encampments a few hundred yards away.

None of it would be enough. He had twenty-five thousand regular legion infantry and cavalry at his disposal. Three thousand levium would maraud around the north of Lake Iyre and undertake flanking actions. And he had two or three thousand farmers and potters from the Neratharn hinterland. Brave but doomed.

He looked to the east from his position atop the highway gate. It was hard to believe. He had been surprised by the sheer weight of numbers at Scintarit. Here, it was the level of the betrayal. He had clung to the hope, despite all the fragmented reports coming out of Atreska, that the Conquord alae would remain true. This morning was the final evidence that Yuran and his bastard traitors held complete sway among the Atreskan people.

Throughout the vast army ranged in front of him were dense

pockets of men wearing Conquord armour and weapons. Enough of the artillery he'd seen through his magnifier was Conquord-made to give him a sick feeling in his stomach. But it was the faces of men and women he recognised and that had fought for him that lodged like cancer in his gut. His loyals were going to die under the sweep of weapons forged in the Conquord. It fed his brooding rage.

He opened his eyepatch to let the cold air wash over the wound for a moment. The cold was stunning on the raw flesh that was smeared with balms against infection and irritation. He blew out his cheeks, enjoying the sensation as it worked through his face down the crack of his cheek and into the stiffness of his jaw.

'General Gesteris?'

He turned, letting the eyepatch fall. In front of him stood a messenger dressed in furs and, by the sweat on his face and the smell that surrounded him, fresh off a horse.

'Yes,' said Gesteris.

He adjusted the strap on his new green-plumed helmet and smoothed his fur-trimmed cloak down with his gloved hands. His armour was his own, beaten back into shape and polished to a sparkle. He needed everyone to see the remaining scars in the shine and know that it represented the rebirth of a hope that he didn't share.

'Appros Harin reports enemy staging complete, sir. He advises they will attack imminently.'

Gesteris managed a smile. 'He is a diligent soldier but he is not asking you to deliver me surprising news, is he?'

The messenger looked at the ground. Gesteris found that a lot these days. He had never been a man to draw envious glances. Now he drew none at all but for morbid fascination and sympathy. He had no time for either.

'Did he give you a renewed estimate of numbers?'

'His estimate now stands at fifty thousand, General.'

Gesteris nodded. 'In line with my assumptions. You can get back to him safely?'

'Yes, sir.'

'He is to act independently but not to attack until the enemy are committed against our walls. Go quickly.'

The messenger slapped his right fist into his chest and ran back through the gate guards and away. Gesteris watched him go. He turned back to the enemy. They were drawn up much as he was. Archers and artillery to the fore, infantry in attendance to build on any breach. And cavalry nowhere to be seen. No doubt what they had was patrolling their flanks and supply lines.

There were men and catapults as far as he could see to the south and all the way to the lake's edge north. Through his magnifier he had counted five distinct ranks of infantry. No doubt there was a mobile reserve too. Once again, Gesteris thought about sending out riders to try and take down some of the artillery and again he dismissed it. The weight of archers would overwhelm any force he could muster. It was the worst of all worlds. Their doom was standing less than half a mile away and all they could do was watch it come.

Gesteris frowned, becoming aware of a sound floating to him on the still, cold air. They were singing. It was something he hadn't heard before. Not harsh anthems of imminent victory, the ones that stirred the blood and energised the body, but something altogether more melodious. The bass rumble of tens of thousands of voices rolled across the open space. It raised the hairs on the back of Gesteris's neck and swam through him like the ambling power of an ocean.

It was a song of melancholy and of loss. He could understand none of the words but the emotion was as plain as a written script before his eyes. It came to him then why they sang, and why every man and woman in his defence listened without thought of raising a song of their own in response.

'They think they're going to lose,' said one of the gate guards, against the haunting, beautiful dirge.

'No,' said Gesteris. 'They know they are going to win but they know the cost too. Like so many of us, so many of them won't be going home.'

Roberto was in no mood for a pause to dispense succour though he felt the pressure of his Atreskan friends to do so. Their country had been destroyed. The level of devastation had taken them all by surprise. On their march south to Gestern, they had travelled routes ignored by the Tsardon. On the way to Neratharn along the highway all they saw was ruin.

Burned-out towns and villages; evidence of crops and livestock taken by force; the bodies of men, women and children littering the roadside and anywhere his scouts and foragers travelled. Some had died under the blades of one or other opposing force. Others had frozen. Some of the youngest had plainly starved, left nothing by an army desperate to fill its stomach.

The highway was intermittently clogged with refugees travelling to Byscar. Everyone of them was as desperate an innocent as the next. And Roberto knew that he could not take in a single one of them. The army had replenished supplies at Gestern but there would be no more until the battle was done. It had reopened the tensions between Atreskans and Estoreans.

Roberto was walking his horse at the head of the column to show solidarity with his infantry, who were being marched at a murderous pace. On the highway, he wanted thirty-five miles in a day. Only just possible with the snow and ice beginning to build. He would have made promises about demobilisation and sending his people home but for too many in his army, there would be no home to go to. Morale among the Atreskans was understandably low.

'Just a gesture,' said Davarov. 'Make my people understand you care.'

'If they don't know it by now, they never will,' said Roberto. 'And I hardly think that scooping a hungry child into my arms is a cure for our ills. I can't afford the deflection in our focus and I certainly can't afford the loss to our stores. And, Davarov, I have already had to issue warnings about giving food and blankets to people begging at the stockade at night. I need you to enforce those warnings among your people. I am tired of having to post so many guards at the walls. There is a bigger world in trouble out there.'

'Don't lecture me about the greater good, Roberto,' said Davarov. The big Atreskan master's face was turned away. Roberto knew how hard he fought to contain his frustration. 'These are the people we are supposed to be saving.'

'Do you think that the look on every orphan's face doesn't cut me to the bone? Do you not think that I crave to help these people? Grant me some respect. But stop to help one and we are morally bound to help them all. It is not in our gift to choose. What is in our control is whether to continue the pace of our march and carry out the Advocate's orders.

'We are going to be hungry, cold and tired enough when we get

there, without giving up the things that keep us alive. And when we
do get there, I pray that there is a battle still left to fight. More than
that, I pray that we are in a condition to fight it. I cannot let anything
get in the way of that chance.'

'You are condemning people to death.'

Roberto nodded. 'That's right, I am. And when you're general you
can live with the shit decisions instead of me.'

Davarov turned away but Roberto called him back.

'General,' he said.

'Yes,' said Roberto. 'I am. And since we are being formal, let me
remind you that I didn't dismiss you. Neither did I ask for your
opinion. I understand your concerns but like it or not, there is a
greater good to serve. I need you, Davarov. More than ever. Don't
turn from me now. Tell your people what must be done and remind
them that should anyone choose to break my rules, they will find
themselves joining the refugees and their ration shared among those
able to follow my orders. I trust I make myself clear.'

The two men stared at each other, Davarov unwilling to back
down, Roberto refusing to let the man reach his heart.

'Dismissed,' said the General.

In the open sea the mist was a barely remembered dream. Above
them, the sky was an angry grey. Snow was coming and the wind
whipping up under the clouds was going to make it an uncomfortable
day's passage. Already the swell was six feet and was set to worsen.

Iliev checked the condition of his injured squadmen before heading
up on deck to join the others who, with no room below, had all been
forced to sleep topside. Patonius had rigged up a makeshift shelter
from sail canvas but the nights were very cold and the barrel fires had
been put out when the ship began to pitch and yaw. But the Ocenii
squadron was bred tough and he heard not a whimper of complaint
from any of his men.

'At least it'll slow the enemy down too,' said Patonius, coming to
his side on the starboard rail where he was looking out at the
assembled Ocetanas fleet.

'Let's hope it hit them two days ago or we'll not catch them.'

'Don't be so sure, Karl,' said Patonius.

'We've been clearing barely seven knots without sail.'

Iliev put his back to the rail and looked at the red-faced skipper.

Like him, she was bare-armed, defying the cold in a plain woollen tunic and sandals. Her hair had been freshly cropped and her face still alive with the memories of the run from the Isle.

'We're chasing, what, a hundred sails at least,' he said. 'Fresh crews, fit from the journey out of the Bay of Harryn and undamaged by battle. I'm surprised you want to catch them.'

'Well, I suppose we could come about and try and dodge the two hundred or so that are chasing us. Any preferences?'

Iliev chuckled. 'They'd be surprised to see us looming up on the horizon. But I don't think the Advocate would thank us for it.'

'Probably not.' Patonius stared past Iliev at the fleet. 'Any more news on stragglers?'

'We're a credible size. Seven Ocenii corsairs, ninety triremes, forty assault galleys. I'd love to see more sailing up behind us. I'd love to hear the songs rolling across the ocean but we can't rely on it.'

'We aren't enough, are we? Not with the numbers coming from the east,' said Patonius. 'And we can't stop them getting into Estorr harbour before us. They're looking to you for a solution, you know that.'

'I'm no Admiral,' said Iliev quietly. 'I'm a glorified marine.'

'None of the fleet flagships made it,' said Patonius. 'You're the highest ranking officer of the Ocetanas able to walk a deck.'

'I know,' said Iliev. 'And you wonder why I feel uncomfortable.'

'I've heard crews and other skippers. You're the man they're looking to. You masterminded the breakout.'

'And we lost almost half of our ships.'

'We gave ourselves a chance,' said Patonius. 'It's all any us want.'

'And that's what you call this, is it? We're a day behind at best. Estorr is only five away if the weather holds. You've done the sums like I have. You know me, Patonius, I live for bad odds. But this . . .' He shrugged. 'We aren't going to catch them.'

'But if the weather really broke . . . We're far better sailors than them in bad weather. Far better.'

'We'll pray to Ocetarus but . . .' He smiled and spread his hands. 'We can't rely on a miracle. And we all know the typical weather patterns in the mid-Tirronean. What is it?'

'Nothing.' Patonius had a rueful look on her face. 'Just been struck by an unfortunate irony, that's all.'

'Care to elaborate?'

'Maybe another day.'

'Any time in the next five days is good,' said Iliev. 'After that, I might be busy.'

He listened to the drums. The heartbeat of the ship. He felt the draw of the oars. The prow dipped into a wave . Water showered the deck. He stared at the horizon, wondering if the smudges he could see there were really enemy sails or just dust shadows on his eyes. So distant.

'Ocetarus's heart, Patonius, can't this ship go any faster?'

Ossacer sat in his darkness and waited for an end to his confusion. It was the first time for ages he'd had the space and peace to contemplate, the way he liked to. He hadn't said much to anyone in the days since they'd set sail from Kirriev Harbour. Kovan and Arducius were so excited at the prospect of reaching Estorr they'd forgotten what it was really all about. All they saw were palaces, aqueducts and grand colonnades. Ossacer thought they might be too late to see all that.

He sat and wondered why he felt apart from them like Mirron did. He heard her crying in the quiet of her cabin every night when she was alone. When the bravado of sunlight was gone and the memories of Gorian ran unhindered through her mind. And he still couldn't work out whether she hated him or missed him.

When he reached out with his mind to see her body map it was jumbled and confused. Not like Jhered's, full of purpose and clear like a lantern in the night. He supposed he was seeing the emotions in Mirron but whatever they were, they undermined her strength of being.

It was then that his mind cleared. Strength came from understanding and belief in oneself. It had nothing to do with the needs of others. Only when you had inner calm could you truly be of service the way the Omniscient demanded.

Ossacer levered himself off his bed and let his mind guide him. The faint, loose energies in the air showed him his path to the blank slab set in even darker shadow that was the cabin door. Beyond it, the open hatch up the aft stairs was a blaze of clashing life and power. The rolling dense cloud he could sense held huge potential and Ardu would be loving how it felt. He was the one who could really mould it into something destructive. But he shouldn't want to. That was the problem.

He climbed the ladder and felt the cold on his face. It was invigorating, laced with life. His senses read it and passed the information to the map in his mind. In the lazily shifting trails that everything from a bird to a ship through the water left for him when it moved, he traced the maps of his friends. Kovan, Arducius and Jhered were standing together halfway down to his left. Port, so the skipper kept on telling them.

Arducius flowed towards him as soon as he sensed him coming. His aura was bright and confident. Ossacer was so jealous of him sometimes. Despite his brittle bones, he was so certain and assured.

'Ossie, why didn't you say? I'd have come and helped you.'

'I am quite capable of helping myself,' said Ossacer, immediately irritated by the assumption of helplessness. 'Anyway, what am I supposed to do, send you a message?'

'I know but it's tiring for you to tune into the trails all the time.'

'One day, Ardu, as you are so fond of saying, you won't be there. I've always been able to help myself anyway.'

'All right,' he said, his head flushing with the calm browns that meant he was backing off an argument. 'I just . . . you know.'

'Yes, I know,' said Ossacer. 'I'm sorry too.'

'I didn't say I was . . .'

Ossacer raised his eyebrows. 'I need to talk to the Exchequer.'

'I'm all ears for you, Ossacer,' said Jhered, helping him to a firm grip on the rail. 'What do you need?'

Ossacer looked down and saw the dark lines of the oars in the livid coloured life of the ocean. He felt anxious. His heart began to thud and the words he had been forming deserted him.

'I can't.' He gripped the rail harder. 'It isn't right. I don't. I can't do it any more. I won't.'

Jhered knelt in front of him and Ossacer saw the concern in the lines that made up his face. 'Calm down, young man. Take your time. Tell me what's wrong.'

Ossacer nodded. 'We have to be true to ourselves. We can only do the Work we were put here to do. What you expect us to do next, I can't. I won't. The Omniscient gave life to me to help and heal people. Not to kill them.'

Jhered leant back a little. 'We've been through this. What happened on the plateau was a mistake, an accident. No one wanted it to go that far. And now, what I ask you to do doesn't kill.'

'Mirron killed with her fire. And the gale and the snow . . . the Work with the sea and the sky you want us to do next, it helps one lot of people to kill another. I won't do it any more. I can't.'

He could see Jhered battling with anger. His whole outline tautened, its colours at once a dense purple that cleared to a calmer blue-hued brown a moment later.

'Ossacer, I hope you aren't saying what I think you're saying. Everything you love is under threat. You three Ascendants have the unique opportunity of saving the Conquord and at the same time proving your right to exist to the doubters and those who would brand you heretic. What more justification can there be for the actions I ask you to take?'

Ossacer felt his face flush red and the tears threaten. 'People will always hate us if all we do is demonstrate how easily we can kill or call storms and violence in the elements. Who will ever truly trust us? I can't live knowing there are so many people unsure if we should live or die.'

'And can you live knowing that because you refused to act, that the Echelon, your parents, everyone in Westfallen was killed?'

'That's unfair,' said Kovan. His support was unexpected but welcome. 'You cannot make him responsible for that. The Tsardon invasion was caused by an overstretch of our armies and the defeat at Scintarit. Blame the Advocate if you must blame anyone.'

Jhered growled in his throat. 'God-surround-us but you are your father's son. We are not talking about blame. The invasion has happened. What we must do is use every weapon available to us. I'm sorry, Ossacer, but that includes you.'

Ossacer shook his head. 'I will not,' he said quietly, biting back his fear. 'Father Kessian always told us only to use our abilities for peace. We all forgot that for a time. Well I've remembered now. I've woken up again. And there's no one in Westfallen who would curse me if they died because I did what the Father always wanted.'

Jhered stood sharply and turned away. Ossacer could see the bloom in his lifelines and the pulsing in his chest when he gripped the rail.

'We are already in desperate trouble,' he hissed, not to Ossacer.

'We have to work together. Arducius, you must tell him. Make him understand.'

'He will do what he must,' said Arducius, and Ossacer's heart warmed. 'And I will stand by his decision. If it comes to it, I will work alone and it'll have to be enough.'

'Very principled,' snapped Jhered. 'Very strong and very impressive. I'm sure Father Kessian is proud where he rots. But unless you want to join him, I suggest you change your minds. You've got about three days to wise up.'

Chapter 73

848th cycle of God, 17th day of Dusasrise
15th year of the true Ascendancy

Gesteris ran along the rampart. Tsardon onager stones tumbled towards the battered defensive wall. They had barely touched them the day before. It had been mere sighting for their catapult and exercise for their archers. But as dawn had broken, a cold, grey and snow-blown morning, the singing had stopped for the last time and they had begun in earnest.

'Hold your positions. Don't you dare back off one pace. You have nowhere to go.'

Gesteris watched the stones fall. Along a four-hundred-yard section of wall and gate tower, the Tsardon concentrated their artillery fire. Stones of one and two talents slammed into the walls his legions had built while over their heads came the flaming rounds. Their direction and range was erratic but behind him on the ground, they were causing significant damage.

'I want faces on the walls. I want them to know that one pace forward means an arrow in the eye. Stand. Stand with me.'

His legionaries steadied themselves under the shuddering impacts. On the platforms, his crews wound the windlasses, dragging the onager arms backwards. He was still only firing the catapults his enemy could see. Those on the ground behind were out of range and he wanted something in reserve to break up the charge when it came.

The Tsardon were massed behind their catapults, waiting for the first breach. And for an hour, the fortifications had withstood everything the enemy had thrown at them. But now the sheer density and weight of impacts was beginning to tell. While the southern end of the defensive line was relatively untroubled, the northern point was under increasingly fierce bombardment. More weapons had been brought to bear on perceived weak points and Gesteris had his reserve primed and ready for the inevitable.

From his left and right, his remaining catapults and heavy scorpions fired. He'd lost a third of them but he could still trace the paths of twenty. Stones ploughed the ground in front of the enemy or dug furrows between the standing artillery. Bolts bounced from the ground. Just one stone found its mark. It struck an onager square on, dashing it to fragments and scattering its crew. Men cheered.

'Get your angles right,' he roared. 'Crank harder. All you're doing is giving them rounds to fire back at us. Work Conquord, work!'

He looked back to the enemy. Across the churned mud and burned ground his citizens had cleared, the Tsardon were shifting. Every second catapult was being pushed forwards. Meanwhile, those standing were cranking back to fire again. Gesteris snapped his fingers and an aide passed him his magnifier. He put it to his eye. Behind the catapults, infantry were checking weapons. On the ground at their feet, ladders, grapples and ropes. The standing catapults were being angled for a higher trajectory, those on the move were being turned in to focus their target area.

'Seems they're in a hurry,' he said. 'Get a message out along the line. They're going for the weak spots. Others will fire at the ramparts. The infantry will be on us the moment there is a breach. I want every archer on standby. Flag the reserve artillery to be ready.'

'Yes, General.'

He looked around at those standing near him. 'They are going to attack the gate fort hard. That is where I will be standing. Don't you flinch. Don't let those left and right of you flinch. Stand. We are the Conquord.'

Gesteris made the flat roof of the fort just as the enemy fired their first rounds. The air whistled and the silence spread along his ranks of citizens. Dozens of incoming rocks rolling through the sky. The roof of the fort was without turrets but had a high rampart for archers. Eight onagers were primed to fire on the approaching artillery. Gesteris could see south, along the impressively straight line of his defences until they dipped away out of sight.

Like every member of the Neratharn legions, he prayed to be spared. On a low trajectory, the first stones drove into the gates over the highway. The multiple impacts shuddered the stone under his feet. He heard the reinforced timbers rattle in their hinges and chains. The crack of wood echoed loud.

Moments later, the higher arc stones fell. He heard the whine of dozens passing directly over the walls. A stone of over a talent struck the rampart where he had so recently been standing. The rough fixings shattered and wood disintegrated. The missile swept through man and catapult, dragging broken bones and machinery after it to fall on the open ground behind the walls. The sound of the impact, like an explosion, cracked over them. Men and women were screaming. There was a five-foot break in the rampart pathway.

Other stones had fallen into the midst of the catapults gathered below. Two more were smashed and his stretcher and surgeon teams shouted orders and tried to calm citizens whose limbs were torn away and whose lives flowed into the frozen mud. Heartbeats later a net of smaller stones split against the side of the fort. Razor-sharp shards burst outwards.

Yelling a warning, Gesteris dropped to the ground. He heard some of them fizzing above his head and the dull contacts of stone on stone and the thud into wood. He pushed himself to his feet, turning to the onager crews. Right in front of him, a man stood. He was staring down at his chest, his hands smeared in blood. A knife of rock jutted from his breastplate. He mouthed words to Gesteris and fell backwards.

'Stretchers to the roof.'

The air was full of emerging alarm. He rounded on those still standing. 'Return fire! Full spread. Get that pathway boarded up. I need engineers ready on the gates.'

Again, the Conquord onagers and scorpions cast their missiles out towards the enemy. He heard the satisfying crump of stone crushing wood. His crews worked feverishly to crank the windlasses. The arms and bows bent back again. The Tsardon fired first. Gesteris watched them come in. Rounds thumped against the blank strong wall above the gate. More thundered into the wood. The gates bowed in. He heard wood fracturing as one stone battered straight through. Missiles plunged into the walls south. The noise was painful, the vibrations through his feet all but constant.

'Stand!' His order was flagged again and again. 'Stand!'

He ran to the front of the fort. Onager rounds whipped away either side of him but he paid them no heed. He leaned over as far as he dared. Rubble covered the ground on the road and was scattered either side. He could see the gates leaning crooked on their great hinges. Timbers were broken and split. Iron bindings hung out, bent and twisted. He could hear the gate captain screaming for more wood.

A third concentrated volley of Tsardon rounds flew in. Gesteris stepped away from the edge. Behind him, crews dragged their catapult arms back. He watched the cluster of missiles approach, hypnotic and lethal.

'Brace!'

Every stone struck the doors. The blows knocked Gesteris from his feet and juddered onagers out of aim. He heard stones bouncing away down the highway behind the gate and the sound of iron work striking paving. From the Tsardon lines came a mighty roar.

He dragged himself to his feet. In that same moment, more Tsardon missiles cruised into the defenders three hundred yards from him. Legionaries were thrown in to the air. He saw a section of the wall bow inwards, sag and collapse in a cloud of dust and debris. In front of the gates, a similar cloud was clearing. Through it, he saw the Tsardon running.

On the entire length of their line, they moved, surging into the open space and around their catapults even as they were being primed for another volley. The wave of sound rolled across the walls and a thundering, getting louder by the moment, could be felt through their feet.

'Ready the reserve. Archers to the walls. Let's have you, Conquord. Discipline. Order. Victory.'

Gesteris moved back to the open rampart to the right of the fort. Behind him, stones were loaded into baskets and set afire. Archers thronged the defences. His forward artillery fired again. He turned to face the enemy and prayed for the strength to last out the day.

Three thousand cloaks were at Harin's back, riding south along the shores of Lake Iyre. The expected bombardment had come and he had scouts on a rise ahead, looking down over the battlefield. He knew Gesteris would send him messengers but he could not afford to wait for them. If a decisive blow was struck by the enemy, he would have to be ready.

They had already encountered and slaughtered two detachments of

Tsardon steppe cavalry but survivors would still relay his position. More enemy riders were approaching from the east. For Harin, it was all in the timing. He needed to get in and out of the Tsardon infantry before he was caught.

Every one of the levium heard the pulsating cry of the Tsardon that preceded an all-out attack. Up on the rise, he saw three levium approaching at a gallop, spears raised to display flying pennants. He called the halt and turned his horse around.

'Levium. We ride for the Conquord and for the Exchequer. We ride to break the Tsardon advance. Fight hard, fight quickly. Fight for the cloak you bear and the citizens that flank you. Levium! To battle.'

They would advance as trained. Not a word from their lips. No cries to raise the blood, no warning for the mass of the enemy. They trotted on up the rise and towards the clouds of war that hung across the fields ahead. They were arranged in detachments of five hundred. They knew their orders, their signals and muster points.

The tumult grew stride by stride. Away to their right the Tsardon were charging. Harin brought the levium up the last few yards of the slope and began to travel down, trying not to let the shock of what he saw affect him. This was his first mass battlefield, and surely the first time any of the levium had seen such a number of enemies ranged against the Conquord.

On the crest of the rise, they were a quarter mile from the first infantry. A few riders were with them but insignificant compared to the number of levium. But away east, the steppe was coming. Harin upped the pace and angled them towards the gate fort. Stones clattered into the shaking defences. He could see the gates were hanging crooked but still stood. As far south as he could see there were Tsardon approaching the border. Tens of thousands acting with a single purpose.

The Conquord artillery fired. Stones flamed into the sky from behind the walls, crashing down on helpless infantry, smearing scorching paths. There was the briefest faltering. In front of him, the enemy was becoming aware of the new threat. Catapults were turning in their direction. Sword and pikemen were being drawn off the rear of the advance to face them. Harin raised his spear high. Ahead, less than a hundred yards of open ground.

'Levium! Charge.'

He swept his spear down to his side and kicked his heels into his horse's flanks. The animal sprang forwards. He gave the mare rein, let her run free. The enemy came up so quickly. He hefted his spear and threw it, seeing the shaft bury itself in a Tsardon chest. He dragged his sword from his scabbard, nudged his horse a little left and brought the levium beating into their foe.

Now the Exchequer's citizens gave voice to their anger. The levium hit the Tsardon infantry, half turned and unprepared, like a wall. He blazed deep into their ranks, dozens more cloaks around him, hacking down and sweeping up with his blade. He felt it cutting into flesh, rebounding from helmet and breastplate and clashing with steel.

The Tsardon scattered in front of them but even as they cleared, he could see the defence forming. Along a line a hundred yards long, pikes and spears were levelled to protect the onagers that were his target.

Next to Harin, a rider took an arrow through the throat and plunged left from his horse. The air clouded with shafts, crossing in the air and falling on infantry and rider alike. Harin blocked a sword thrust and kicked out, knocking the man from his feet. His horse half-reared, striking a Tsardon with her hoofs, splitting his skull.

The first artillery fired. Stones and bolts flashed over his head. He glanced back to see man and horse obliterated, ploughed into the ground over which they had run. Others reared. Riders were thrown to be trampled under the hoofs of their friends. Some slowed, their mounts unwilling to move on towards the threat.

They were through the first ranks. The toll on the levium was high but they galloped on. He pushed hard towards the spear line. A levium volley whipped into the enemy, taking down three in front of him. The spears held firm. He closed. Thirty yards, twenty. They weren't going to break. Like a Conquord pike block, they knelt in front and stood behind with metal tips bristling forwards. At ten yards he dragged his horse left before she took the decision to slow herself and throw him on to the enemy weapons. He rode down the front of them, looking for the end of the line and a way through to the catapults.

On the horizon ahead, he saw horsemen gathering. Steppe cavalry. The nearer detachments of levium had already seen them and were breaking off to regroup. Down by the gates, two detachments were deep in the fighting and had a little more time. Harin cursed and swung his sword at a spear tip, seeing it spin away. He wasn't going to break them. Not this time.

'Regroup!' he yelled, raising his sword above his head. 'To the muster point. Ride levium.'

He swung his mount away from the jeering enemy. His archers fired volley after volley to cover their retreat. His horse picked her way over so many dead and dying bodies of friend and enemy. Too many cloaks covered the ground. Too many horses cantered riderless or lay screaming in the frozen mud. Praying to the Omniscient to spare him from an arrow in the back, he galloped back for the rise and brief safety.

Gesteris saw the levium turn from their attack on the onagers without a single piece being damaged. He muttered grudging respect for the order of their spear line. No horse would cross it and the levium would have been fools not to shear away. As if in contempt, the enemy catapults thumped their barrage at his walls. Men were plucked like ears of corn and dashed to the ground. More of his timbers cracked, more of his wall gave way and tumbled. Three breaches now.

His own catapults swung their arms. Seventy flaming stones arced out above his head and plunged into the advancing Tsardon. The carnage was terrible. The flames splashed in a wide radius, the stones bounced and rolled, gathering flesh and crushing bone. It barely halted the charge. They were within fifty yards of the walls now.

Gesteris watched his archers peppering them. It was harder to miss than to hit, though the Tsardon made a passable attempt at a shield wall in places. The force coming at them could simply overwhelm them. He saw fear in the eyes of every citizen. He knew where he had to be.

Two large detachments of Harin's levium crashed into the right flank and rear of the Tsardon approaching the gates. Gesteris snatched up his shield, drew his gladius and ran down the steps to ground level.

'Keep firing,' he told his rampart centurion. 'Keep the onagers going. I'm going to secure the breach south.'

In the time afforded them by the levium, his engineers were trying to salvage the gates. Rock was being piled at their base and new planks secured at every level they could reach. Anything to hamper the advance.

'Are you strong?' he asked his chief engineer.

The man indicated the maniples of hastati drawn up behind the gate and the ranks of archers waiting at the flanks.

'We have support, General. We'll hold.'

'Good. Three hours of light left. Even they won't fight on after dark.'

Gesteris called his standard bearer and extraordinarii to him and ran south beneath the rampart. Enemy artillery rounds soared overhead or struck the walls as he passed. There was a constant running of pebble and small rock from the backs of the walls. Behind them, the tracks of two-talent missiles through mud and bloodied snow told stories of lives snuffed out. But despite the barrage, the legions were standing and determined. He was running beside maniples of principes heading to bolster the wall breaches. Riders communicated the latest position to the ground commanders.

Thousands of legionaries waited to be fed into battle. They couldn't see what was beyond the walls. All they had were their imaginations, fired by the deafening noise and the scenes of death around them. Soon enough, they'd see it all. He could see Order Readers and Speakers moving among the citizens, offering prayer and comfort, giving strength. Never would they be more important.

Gesteris assessed the breach as he approached it. The hole was twenty feet of clear ground with ragged edges surrounding it. The space had been cleared for a pike block. Dozens of archers stood ready, supported by infantry hastati and the arriving principes.

'Wait!' the centurion in charge ordered. 'Wait.'

Gesteris could see the Tsardon through the gap. At ten yards distance, a tide of hate and rage was coming to smash the will of the Conquord.

'Now.'

Archers fired at will. Tsardon boiled through the gap to attack the pikes. They were impaled, stabbed and forced back. More arrows. Conquord men fell. Others moved to take their place. The principes shouted encouragement. The Tsardon came in again. More of them this time, flooding left and right too. Right behind Gesteris, an enemy volley battered a hole in the wall. It collapsed along a length of ten yards. He spun around, seeing the Tsardon almost on the new gap.

'Conquord!' he roared. 'For Estorea and for me!'

He ran at the enemy. Reserve maniples surged with him. Spears and arrows fogged his sight momentarily. Tsardon breached the walls. He was first at them, cracking his shield into the body of one, thrusting his sword through the gut of another.

The Conquord surrounded him. Two centurions barked for a spear and pike line. It formed to the front and moved forwards. On the flanks, the Tsardon began to make headway. Gesteris was with them to the right. He caught an arrow in his shield, blocked a sword-thrust with his gladius and moved forwards.

Again and again, he hacked down and stabbed forwards, like in his old days with the hastati. The fear left him. His citizens fought with him under his standard. Gesteris felt his blade shear ribs. He grunted his satisfaction and heard the song of the Conquord in his head.

He gave it voice and the legions sang with him.

'The fighting is more intense north near the gate house. They've breached up there, they must have.'

He took the magnifier from his eye. It was hard to see in the chaos and dirt exactly what was going on but it was clear that near them, the defences were holding relatively comfortably.

'Then let's bring ourselves there,' she said, shrugging. 'It's our best chance of getting through to the other side anyway. They've blocked the gates in the other forts with stone and cement.'

They had reached the Gaws, the mountains south of the battlefield, moving quickly behind the enemy advance. Whether they had been seen or tracked was open to debate but they were currently being ignored by the mass of the attacking army.

The Tsardon had committed more than half of their number to the attack, leaving the rest well behind the catapults. Through his magnifier he had seen levium moving to attack and being forced off.

There was a space of a few hundred yards between the Tsardon ranks. The onagers looked invitingly vulnerable.

'Can we take some artillery down too?' he asked.

'We can,' she replied. 'And we can run the flanks for you too. For a time.'

'Don't get yourself killed over this,' he said. 'We're so close.'

'Let's just get on with it.'

They returned to their people and issued the orders. There was risk and there was death out there. But whatever the outcome, one thing was certain. The Revenge was coming.

Chapter 74

848th cycle of God, 17th day of Dusasrise
15th year of the true Ascendancy

'Push. Keep Pushing.'

The centurion marshalled his pikes with classic discipline. Slowly, they were driving the Tsardon back. Gesteris launched himself at the Tsardon still coming through the gap. He was bleeding freely from a cut on his sword arm but he couldn't feel the pain. He stabbed his blade forward, feeling it connect with armour. His shield was before him, defending his body. It held three arrows now and he took pleasure in pushing the flights into the faces of his enemies. He punched the boss into a Tsardon stomach. The man staggered. Gesteris dropped him with a hack through his shoulder. No one came to take his place.

Behind the pike men, his archers were gathering in greater numbers. They fired with withering density into the Tsardon. The push-back gathered momentum. The pike men closed the gap.

'Wall!' bellowed the centurion.

Shields formed the barrier. Tsardon arrows still came in thick and fast but now they found less flesh. Sarissas came to join the pikes at the forward line. A small phalanx grew. Gesteris nodded his pleasure. It was the same behind him at the first breach. The Tsardon catapults were silent for now, with their own army as much at risk as their intended targets. Up on the rampart, his archers exacted a heavy toll on those clustering at the breach. It was the enemy's move. Gesteris expected retreat.

'General!' He turned. A messenger ran down a flight of wooden steps from the rampart. 'Up here. You need to see this, sir.'

Gesteris nodded and followed him up between the two sections of ruined rampart. A surgeon followed him, brandishing a bandage.

Halfway up, Tsardon horns sounded across the field. He frowned. It wasn't retreat, the flat fast tones were warning of an attack. He looked out over the field.

'Who under the Omniscient's sky is that?'

They'd covered half the distance before the Tsardon and rebel army had so much as challenged them. Nunan marched them calmly onto the battlefield, knowing their stitched-together appearance and lack of standard would mark them as no different to any rebel force fighting with Tsard. To any eye they appeared to be moving to support the attacks on the gate fort and dual breaches just south of it.

But their luck couldn't hold forever and a single challenge from a Tsardon prosentor had blown their cover. His body hitting the ground had triggered the sounding of attack horns and Nunan had ordered the dead run. He couldn't swear to prime legion discipline but he made sure his legion did not fragment.

Kell took her two hundred cavalry away towards the reserve and the artillery. Her archers shot helpless crews and her swordsmen slashed rope and hacked into hinge and windlass. Even if they did not destroy many outright, repairs would be long and difficult.

Nunan sprinted at the head of the Revenge, angling towards the nearest breach in the walls. The Tsardon were pushing hard, trying to establish a critical foothold. They were encountering stiff resistance and paid no heed to those approaching from behind.

The same could not be said of the rest of the Tsardon. They broke from the attack and the standing reserve and closed in, their discipline lost in their chase to head off the new Conquord force. With the gap being closed both sides, Kell turned from the enemy artillery and rode her horses round to cover the flanks of the infantry.

She swept up and down the column, which ran in maniple order, her cavalry split into two to provide some security to both flanks. When they were two hundred yards from the rear of the enemy attacking the breach, the arrows began to fall. Nunan was also becoming aware of cheers and encouragement reaching him from the walls.

'With me, Revenge. Let's give them more to shout for!'

Cavalry rode back past him. He heard weapons clash and the whinny of horses. He felt the stamping of their hoofs and the rumble of the approaching Tsardon under the swell of their voices. They were almost going to make it, but not quite. He hoped that their hastily practised defence would not fail them.

Nunan dropped back into the front rank of the first hastati maniple. He held his shield in front of him and made up the ground as fast as he could. Tsardon were turning from the breach. Conquord arrows were still falling among them. More enemy appeared on his right.

'Contact!' he shouted.

He swung his blade at the first Tsardon, seeing it batter a huge dent in his helmet and knock him senseless. His shield he swung out to the left, connecting with another enemy, pushing him back. The hastati in the front line waded in beside him, while all down the column, the defence was developing. He daren't glance back. He had to keep his focus ahead. It was critical he and these hastati kept on moving. They'd driven a wedge into the Tsardon who, deflected from the battle in front of them, were starting to fall more rapidly under the Conquord's arrows.

Behind him, his spearmen would be facing outwards in two ranks left, two right, and walking crablike when headway was made. They held shields ahead and above their heads. Inside the maniples, reserve swords stood ready while his archers fired between the gaps, trying to keep the Tsardon back. It was Kell who took the greatest risk, dropping to guard the rear.

Nunan let his desire to see her safe drive his tired body to greater effort. He ignored the pain in his legs and the heaving in his chest from the sprint. He forced himself to take another pace, slipping in Tsardon blood. He crouched to regain his balance. A blade nicked the top of his shield and he thrust up again, its edge catching the enemy's chin. The Tsardon's head flicked back and Nunan stabbed his gladius up and into the open throat.

'Keep moving. We are the Revenge!'

Men were dying around him. The Tsardon were gathering in great numbers, pressurising the flanks. He was only a few yards from the opening. The Conquord infantry behind the walls dropped their phalanx stance and came at the remaining Tsardon with gladius and dagger.

Nunan felt hot blood on his arm. He looked left. His hastati was sliced across the face and falling. Nunan waited for him to drop, then lashed his sword across the space, catching the Tsardon on the top of the head and biting into his skull. He withdrew behind his shield and punched it out again, flattening an enemy. He stamped on the man's chest on the way over his body, feeling his ribs give way.

Arrows flew in from both sides from Tsardon crouched in the lee of the wall. He felt searing pain low in his leg and two more of his line fell.

'Shields to flanks. Hold. We're nearly there.'

Nunan put his foot down and his leg buckled under the arrow wound. Immediately, a hand grabbed his sword arm and hauled him up. Other hands dragged him forward through the breach. He batted them away and turned.

'Entrance,' he roared. 'Entrance.'

The shout was relayed down the column. He could see his citizens stretching out. He made to move back out but was stopped by his own hastati. The Revenge began to pour through the breach and into relative safety. Cavalry ran up the flanks one last time, forcing enemy infantry back. Arrows and spears poured down from the broken ramparts.

In and in they came, and on and on fought the Tsardon. He watched the left flank collapse inwards and a rush of Tsardon spill into the midst of the column. The fighting became instantly desperate. No one could get back out for fear of blocking the entrance for those racing to safety. And in the end it was a headlong charge by his legionaries. At the very rear, one centurion rallied enough to provide a brief defence.

'Come on,' he urged. 'Don't fall now.'

The casualties were mounting. Blood smeared the ground at the breach. Citizens in sight of sanctuary stared at their goal with dead eyes. Tsardon fell, pierced by arrow after arrow. Legionaries were cut down as they ran, or lost their lives trying to defend their friends. Still they boiled through the breach until the last was dead or inside and the Tsardon threatened to forge in after them.

Horns sounded. It was a retreat.

Nunan sagged to the ground, ignoring the ache in his calf. They might have killed hundreds but it had cost him hundreds too. The Revenge roared their song of victory nonetheless while the jeers of the defence chased the Tsardon back to their camps. He felt a hand on his shoulder. It was Kell.

'Was it worth it, do you think?' he asked.

She helped him up and away from the breach. 'Come on. They've only retreated so they can start another bombardment. You don't want to be here and you need that leg seen to.'

She had a long deep cut down the side of her face and on to her neck.

'You don't look so great yourself.'

'Well, thank you, Pavel. That's the last time you share my tent.'

Kell directed them towards one of the surgeon's tents. It was packed with the wounded and dying. Blood covered the floor, and everywhere bodies lay with left hand to chest and eyes closed. Honoured before commendment by the Order.

'What a mess,' said Nunan.

In front of them, a broad-backed man straightened from leaning over a surgeon's table on hearing his voice. Nunan's heart missed a beat. It had to be. The man turned and a smile split his features, creasing the patch that covered his eye and moving the long ugly scar on his face. He had brand new stitches in a wound on his hand.

'General,' breathed Kell. Nunan could only nod.

'Come here,' said Gesteris.

All pretence at protocol disappeared and the three of them came together in a gasping hug. Around them, people were laughing and cheering.

'We thought you dead,' said Nunan. 'Only rumour and our hearts kept you alive.'

'Do I look like a rumour?' growled Gesteris. He let them go. 'It appears we have won the day. Thank you. I like the name of your new legion, too.' He shook his head. 'I never thought to see you two again. The Omniscient smiles on us today but it's only a pause. The barrage will begin again soon and we must work on how to keep them beyond us. Roberto is coming and we must try and hold.'

'How far is he away?' asked Nunan, his mood lightened further by the news. 'Last we saw him, he was headed south to Gestern.'

'And he won there but so much more is happening. Estorr is under threat from sea and land now. Out there, the Tsardon still have an overwhelming advantage. Still, get a little rest and repair, you two. We'll talk later. Tomorrow will be much harder than today.'

'You're feeling helpless so you come to talk to your prisoner, the one person more helpless than you, is that it?'

Herine was surprised at the bitterness. Megan's chambers were luxuriously appointed. She had private baths, three servants and a personal cook assigned to her. She had books, magnificent views and even a consort if she would only look at him.

'You are not a prisoner,' she said, moving into the main chamber and settling herself on a recliner.

The windows were open on the cold late evening and through them, she could see Estorr's northern beacon burning fiercely into the light fall of snow. Inside, the room was warm. Fires burned in three grates around which decorative columns stood, bedecked with winter blooms. The yellows of the room were calming. Herine was almost jealous. A servant poured her some wine and withdrew at her gesture.

'You understand, though, that you are the emissary of a traitor and to give you full run of the city would be politically difficult.'

'I pose no risk,' said Megan. 'Compare me to a hundred Tsardon sails and ten thousand Tsardon cavalry.'

She turned from a fireplace and walked over to the opposite recliner. She perched on its edge. She wore a toga not dissimilar to Herine's, cream wool and slashed Conquord green. Her hair was sculpted in a bun and held by a golden circlet. She looked stunning and Herine questioned why she always chose male escorts for herself. Perhaps, when she was beyond child-bearing age, she should reconsider.

'I know,' said Herine. 'But I must occasionally assuage the fears of my council, mustn't I? Besides, all of my prisoners would die to be held in such conditions as you.'

'So why have you come here if not to gloat on my poor choices?'

Herine shook her head. 'You have a lot to learn, Megan. You had no knowledge of Yuran's betrayal and are hence blameless. More, you are a capable stateswoman, though you bury it in impetuous outbursts. I have come to leave you with a thought. When we are victorious and the Tsardon are turned away, we will bend our efforts to reclaiming Atreska. Your proud country will need a strong and effective ruler. You should consider your own qualities.'

She saw Megan tense and the colour drain from behind the blusher she wore. 'I couldn't . . .'

'Why not? Who was Yuran before his promotion but a senior soldier and adjutant to the king?'

'But I love him. I cannot succeed him.'

'It is difficult, I know. And I loved my father too. But continuity is critical and surely you would provide that.'

'I was just an aide.'

'You are currently an ambassador,' said Herine.

'What will become of him, when he is brought before the Conquord?'

Herine smiled sadly. The girl knew the answer. Traitors never prospered.

'It will be the earliest test of your strength. I want you on my side, Megan but for that you must prove yourself. They say the earliest decisions a ruler makes are the most difficult and anxious. I would agree, and for you it will be no different. When he is brought to trial, his successor will sign his execution order as is demanded by protocol and law.'

Herine rose. 'Perhaps you are wondering why I come to you with this when the Conquord is so threatened. It is because I understand only victory and when that victory inevitably comes, I must be ready to advance. I will know your reply come the morning. Sweet dreams, Megan.'

Prosentor Rensaark, now commander of the eastern Atreskan forces, frowned up at the throne on which Yuran sat. Gorian was at his right hand.

'I do not understand,' he said. 'The battle is far from won. We accepted we could not stop Del Aglios and so we agreed to send legions to reinforce the Neratharn border. You cannot change your mind at this stage. We are so close.'

'Prosentor, your promotion is long overdue and my respect for your thoughts is not in question. But I must look to the future. I am, after all, still the ruler of Atreska. I cannot sanction the removal of the remainder of Haroq's standing legions. What if Del Aglios chooses to come here rather than go to Neratharn? It would be an intelligent tactic to take the seat of power. So I am recalling them. They didn't ever reach the lines so they will not be missed.'

Rensaark shook his head. 'This is a poor military decision. We have all studied the numbers and we all know where Del Aglios is leading his army.'

Yuran waved a hand. 'Call it what you will. It remains my

decision. Relax. Our victory is assured, as is your place in the history of the Kingdom of Tsard.'

'What has happened to you? You barely even sound like yourself any more. This boy has poisoned your mind. His appearance and your dimming wit are no coincidence.'

'Don't be ridiculous. Has he not supplied you with information? Has he not been useful to both of us?'

Rensaark pointed a finger at Gorian. 'I have my eye on you. Remember that.'

Gorian merely smiled and his eyes flooded with deep orange clearing to grey. 'Whatever makes you feel comfortable.'

Rensaark stalked out of the room. Yuran turned to Gorian, all pretence at bravado gone. He began shaking again.

'It's all right,' said the boy. 'You've done the right thing. You do trust me, don't you?'

Yuran's voice clogged in his throat. It wasn't trust he felt, it was terror. Gorian moved the hand from the back of his neck and the cold began to ebb away.

'Don't be frightened,' he said. 'I have no desire to kill you. We need each other. You'll see.'

Yuran looked into the future but all he could envision was darkness.

Chapter 75

Even with the extraordinary arrival of Nunan and Kell the afternoon before, Gesteris was still operating with over two thousand fewer in his defence than had started the battle. Casualties on the walls had been high and though only three breaches had been forced, the Tsardon assault all along the walls had shorn him of so many archers and swordsmen.

He had no doubt that the Tsardon had suffered even more greatly but this was a war of attrition he could not hope to win, not at the current ratio. He had walked up to the gate fort before dawn, after a long and largely sleepless night. There had been so much work to do.

Out in the field, the Tsardon were shifting their artillery. They knew a good number of pieces were effectively out of the fight for the day but others were being repositioned. It was maddening not to know exactly where. He had sent out some scouts but they had not returned. People he could not afford to lose.

His engineers and craftsmen had worked without a break. They'd patched up breaches and gates as best they could. Brave citizens had been lowered outside to cement stonework back together and replace smashed timbers. They had suffered attacks from cavalry throughout the night, leaving the atmosphere tense and dangerous. And though their efforts were magnificent, they all knew it would not delay the Tsardon for too long. At their roots, the walls were weak. Gesteris did not expect them to last.

And now the light was growing and, with Nunan and Kell patched up and standing with him, the enemy's plan was laid out before them.

'Yesterday was just to soften us up,' he said. 'And the legions are already drained and scared. It makes you wonder if they were really trying before.'

'Oh, they were,' said Kell. 'But you've forced their hand. Take it as a compliment. They must know Roberto is coming or they wouldn't resort to this.'

'Something has certainly happened to alter their tactics,' said Nunan.

'You call this a compliment, do you?'

Gesteris gestured at the field as it was slowly revealed to them. His matching order had already been communicated and the din of activity was loud below them. They might be ready in time if they were lucky. The Tsardon song was echoing across the empty space once more. Long might it continue.

Every piece of artillery was drawn up in one of four places, all of them at the northern end of the defences. Gesteris estimated that thirty catapults were grouped in each area. The bolt-firers had gone, no doubt cannibalised for parts to repair damaged onagers. Wagons flanked each group, piled with stones.

And behind these four groups stood the bulk of the army. There were forces ranged further south, just enough to stop him clearing his walls. He hoped Harin was watching. But even he and the levium could surely do no more than deflect one of the attacks. Eight to ten thousand men at each stress point at best guess. He could muster half that at best unless he denuded every other piece of wall and dragged every injured citizen to stand. Even so, he had no reserve.

'What are they singing about?' asked Kell. 'It sounds so sad.'

'It's a war dirge. I had an Atreskan loyal translate some of it for me yesterday. It speaks of the dream of returning home and of death in battle. There's no glory in it.

> *Ever dawn does rise on me and you do seek my breath*
> *I reach out with my steel in hand to seek of your caress*
> *One step from me your warmth remains, my strength runs into*
> * sand*
> *I cannot grasp, I cannot feel through the blood upon my hand*
> *Through my long fall your arms do seek to soften where I lie*
> *Your tears they set upon your cheeks not knowing here I die.*

'And then they take up swords and try to batter our skulls to fragments.' Gesteris raised his eyebrows and turned to the mustering below. The song mourned over him while he spoke.

'Listen to me. Hear me. Listen to them too. They know they are far from those they love and they expect to die. And in that knowledge they are secure in their destinies. It takes the fear from them, channels it to hate. They hate being out here on the battlefield and they hate us because of it.

'I want you to remember that, too. None of us should be out here. Every enemy you face has betrayed you. None of them deserve your mercy. They deserve your sword through their hearts. When this day is done, they can sing their dirge as they clear away their dead. But we are the Conquord. We will sing victory, we will sing honour and we will sing strength.

'Just one more day. Just one more time to make the sacrifice you swore you would. And we will be relieved.' He held up one finger. 'Just one day. Stand with me Conquord. Live with me. Do I have you?'

The roar and thundering of weapons on shields shook the fort under his feet. The Tsardon song ceased. Silence swept the battlefield, broken by the squeak and rattle of wheel and axle. Gesteris turned to Kell and Nunan.

'Here they come again.'

Jhered walked along the port rail to the bow where Mirron was standing alone, her fur cloak wrapped tight about her. It was a cold and windy day. Both sails were up and the oars were shipped, giving the crew a welcome rest from the punishing pace he'd demanded. The cloud above was broken and rushing across the sky.

With every day that passed, he worried more about what lay in wait at their destination. Not the Tsardon. Beyond them and beyond the harbour. Up on the hill. Even should they beat the Conquord's enemies, the Ascendants would be walking right into the heart of the Chancellor's power. Who knew what she had been whispering to the Advocate in his absence.

Arducius and Ossacer were both below decks while Kovan stood with the skipper at the stern. He was pretending to learn a little about seamanship but in reality he was staring at Mirron, trying to think of a way to get through to her. Jhered knew what she needed, but Menas was dead and Gorian's memory was crushing her.

'Not thinking of jumping, I hope,' he said, standing by her and putting an arm around her shoulders.

She almost laughed but the face she turned to him had tears running through the cold salt spray. 'Even if I did, I wouldn't drown.'

'Life must be truly awful when it's so difficult to kill yourself.'

This time she did laugh but the sobs came too and she buried her face in his cloak. He held her while she cried.

'We've always been together and now we barely even talk,' she said eventually, freeing her head from his chest but not breaking the embrace.

'It's part of growing up,' said Jhered, knowing his words were little comfort. 'You will eventually all lead separate lives.'

'Not if we hadn't left Westfallen,' she said.

'Well, at least we're on our way home now.'

'Hardly. We don't even know what we'll find do we? You said so yourself.'

'I know. But you have to have hope.'

'You said war would crush our hope.'

Jhered smiled. 'That little speech went in, did it? Well, it's true, but from the ashes, you build new hope. Just think. When you left Westfallen, you didn't ever think you would return. On the plains of Atreska, the armies either side of you both hated you. But look now. Roberto hopes you can save Estorr. You can hope you are going to see Westfallen again.'

Mirron nodded. 'It sounds so simple when you say it like that but I can't help thinking of what is coming and it scares me so much.'

Jhered dropped to his haunches and clutched Mirron's shoulders. She looked so vulnerable in her distress. All he wanted to do was hold her until the pain went away, promise her everything would be all right. But he'd never been a good liar.

'Look, I know I can't take away what has happened to you and I can't even help you with the loneliness you're feeling. But I can promise you that I won't let anyone hurt you again. You have my undying admiration, all of you on this ship, and I will protect you from now until the day I die. Have faith in me. Have faith in yourself.'

'It's so hard to carry on believing.'

'Tell me why you think that.'

'Ossacer is so troubled by what he has done and he is so worried about how angry he has made you. And I wonder if I can do what must be done, knowing what it did to Gorian.'

Jhered blew out his cheeks. 'You know what Erith would have told you about Gorian? That he was always this way. It wasn't the Work you did on the plains that turned him into something else. It was always inside him. He always believed himself stronger and above us all. I saw it when I first met you. He's different from you. There was nothing you could have done to make him act another way. Only Father Kessian had him under control and when he died, the shackles dropped away.'

Mirron nodded. 'I suppose so.'

'Think about it, Mirron. I need you. Arducius needs you for what is to come. God-embrace-us-all, the Conquord needs you. Let us help you find your faith.'

'But quickly, eh?' she said in mimicry of him. 'We might see the enemy tomorrow.'

'I expect we'll see them today. And as for Ossacer, I'm not angry with him. I respect what he has said and how he feels, just as I do with you all. He must follow his own path, as all strong men do. And women.'

'It's strange, isn't it? Gorian always thought him the weak one. But it was never like that. He just feels more deeply. I think he's the strongest of us all.'

'I think you might be right. Tell him I'm not hurt or angry. Tell him how proud I am of him. No, better still, I'll tell him myself.' Jhered stood. 'Promise me you won't jump in while I'm gone?'

Mirron smiled and wiped a gloved hand under her eyes. 'I promise.'

Jhered kissed her forehead and walked back to find Ossacer, unsure if he had done any good at all. He looked away to the horizon. All too soon, they would see the mass of sails converging on Estorr's harbour. That was when he would know.

'Oh-dear-God-protect-us,' breathed Gesteris. 'Clear!'

The archers at the front of the wall were already scattering. Thirty stones whistled towards them. After an hour of poor targeting, this time they'd got it right. Gesteris ran towards the gate fort, where the damage was already severe, but his catapults were still firing. The impact behind him threw him from his feet. He clutched to the sides of the wooden rampart to stop himself falling over the edge. The booming of collapsing stone hurt his ears. Beneath him, the rampart swayed out and began to fall, catching itself at a thirty-degree angle to the ground.

He let himself slide to the edge and drop to the ground, grunting as he hit. He turned and stared into the clearing dust cloud. Twenty yards of the wall were gone. Just gone. Onager platforms had been obliterated. Cemented timbers and slabs were shattered and cast over fifty yards into the ground behind.

The trailing enemy stones had fallen straight through the new gap and smashed into the reserve and catapults immediately behind. He saw infantry and archers lying broken in the rubble. Chaos was taking hold and the Tsardon army were coming. He could hear them chanting as they charged.

'Sarissas to the gap,' he yelled into the mess. 'Phalanx centurions, I need you now. Archers back to the walls. Stand with me.'

Behind him, panicked shouts filled the air. He spun around in time to see dozens of missiles crashing on to the roof of the fort. Bodies, splintered planks and pieces of carved stone were hurled into the sky in all directions. The entire back of the fort bulged under the pressure. More stones struck and it buckled out and collapsed. The noise was of an avalanche. Shorn of its support, more of the fort went with the first slide, taking a bite of the wall and rampart next to it.

Citizens were running away from the tumbling of stone. Dust, dirt and smoke billowed into the air. Debris struck reserve onager, pitch fire and forward tenting, sweeping it aside. The whole of the roof was gone, taking its catapults with it, and every brave man and woman who had stood to the end. But the gates still held. The fort was nothing more than a cracked and weakened wall now, but to the Tsardon it represented a barrier. And every moment was precious to Gesteris.

Already, order was being restored. Stretcher parties ran among the wounded and dying while the phalanx formed up just short of the great rent in the wall, only two hundred yards from the broken fort. Archers clustered at the gap and the stones in his remaining onagers were set with pitch fire.

'At will,' shouted Gesteris, running to the gap. 'Let's burn those bastards before they reach us.'

The artillery engineer nodded. Thirty arms thudded into their stays and the stones flashed away. Through the gap, Gesteris saw them fall. Tsardon shields were raised instinctively but the stones destroyed them and the men who held them. Burning rocks scattered men and drove deep into their ranks, bouncing just enough from the packed and frozen ground to keep rolling and killing. He heard the engineer bark for the winding of windlasses.

On came the enemy. Archers began to fire through the gap. More came from the right of the breach. Answering shafts whipped through. Men fell. Arrows slammed into shields. The phalanx was ordered forwards, swordsmen came to the flanks. Archers backed away to take up new firing positions. The first Tsardon came through the gap and died on the ends of the sarissas standing three deep.

More screams. Gesteris saw his people dashed from the ramparts a further hundred or so yards south. The rough crenellations disintegrated. Two men were struck square on by a stone. It picked them up and drove them down, smearing them on to a catapult. The weapon collapsed in a spray of blood and gore, its structure crumpling and splitting.

Back at the gate, the Revenge were gathering. Rubble was being cleared as far as possible. He saw Kell astride her horse and Nunan talking to her. The breach by him would hold for now but the Tsardon would be moving their weapons to strike at another area of wall. Nunan and Kell knew it too.

'You're sure about this?' asked Gesteris when he reached them.

More burning missiles crossed the wall to land among the Tsardon infantry. More enemy rounds answered. They were aiming for the gate now. It took three or four impacts, shuddering and shaking. The walls of the fort wobbled.

'Now or never, General,' said Kell. 'It's the best time. They've committed men forward of their artillery. If we don't get out there, we'll lose the gates.'

'Don't let our catapults stop. We'll be out of range,' said Nunan

'This is suicide,' said Gesteris.

'So you said last night. But it's no better staying here. We must give you a chance to hold,' said Nunan.

'The Omniscient protect you.'

'He'd better,' said Kell.

Gesteris nodded. They waited for the next stones to fall. The

Omniscient looked their way just for a moment. Just two struck the gate, the rest falling short or striking the base of the walls.

'Open the gates!' he ordered. He clasped each of their hands. 'For the Conquord and for me.'

Kell spurred her horse and led the Revenge away to death.

This time there would be no stopping. To turn away would be to usher in defeat and Harin would not entertain the thought. A thousand levium were riding north to distract as much of the steppe cavalry as they could. He led the rest back onto the battlefield from the north-east. Yesterday, he had lost five hundred. Today, they would fight to the last cloak.

Already, the Tsardon had made great strides. One section of wall was just so much rubble while further south, cracks and sags were evident in two other places. They couldn't afford another breach.

Tsardon horns sounded warning of their approach. Heads and spears turned towards them. The block formed quickly. Two hundred yards from the rear of the lines waiting to attack the gates, Harin raised his sword and swept it down. The levium broke into three sections of almost five hundred each.

The centre drove headlong into the mass of the enemy, hoping to occupy the bulk of the spears. The left flank turned to ride along the back of them and drive into the gap vacated by the infantry already assailing the walls. Harin had the right flank. He angled down the side of the enemy at a full gallop. His archers turned in their saddles, loosing shaft after shaft into the body of the army, forcing them to raise shields. Tsardon bowmen replied. Harin hunched in his saddle.

Ahead of him, the enemy onager arms swung up. Stones soared away. He followed their trajectory, seeing them crack into gate and wall base. Some fell short, rolling harmlessly to a stop. He blinked. The gate was opening. A smile cracked his face.

'That is some timing,' he said.

Riders galloped from the opening followed by infantry in strict maniple order. They moved immediately right, heading out into the field and up towards the second catapult group. The Tsardon reaction was instant. Infantry broke away. Some thousands running to their left in lines that lacked a certain discipline.

'Levium!' he shouted, his sword up once more. They cleared the front of the standing Tsardon army, the front of which was breaking to defend its artillery. 'Sweep!'

He circled his sword and dropped it back to his side. His reins in his left hand, he steered his horse across the front of the enemy and galloped away to the ranks of onagers. Behind him, his detachment spread wide. Riders moved in an arc to his right to come to the front of the onagers. To his left, they charged across the front of the infantry and drove in amongst them. The sound of ten thousand voices tore through the air.

Harin kept his head low. Those to his left and right did the same. The artillery crews were turning. Some had bows in hand, others swords while a handful still worked at the windlasses. Arrows flicked by Harin's head. He came up on the first crewman, carving his sword up in an arc as he pulled his horse left. The blade chopped through the man's arm, broke his bow and dragged up his face.

Harin's horse kept him moving left. He bore down on a helmet, blocked aside a thrust and stabbed a third man through the chest. Levium clattered by all around him, galloping through the artillery. He swung his horse about, barging an enemy from his feet. In the moment's space, he slashed at the bindings holding the cup in place and hacked through the heavy rope spring at the base of the arm.

Not pausing, he moved on, seeing the Conquord legion spreading from the gate to tackle the enemy at the breach and take down more Tsardon weapons. But the enemy were rushing them with a huge force and the thousands at the breach would quickly prove too many in the open space.

Harin glanced back. Tsardon had broken through his levium defence and were coming to the aid of their stricken crews. Away north and east he could see the levium deep in fighting but the way back to them was blocked. He urged his horse forwards to a fresh target. He couldn't go back so he had to go on. Everywhere, Tsardon were flooding the field now they all knew their enemy was in their midst.

He needed to make open ground in front of the walls and he had to bring as many cloaks with him as he could. They were running out of time.

Roberto could see the evidence of battle at the Neratharn border and, critically, so could the whole of his army. The days had been long and brutal. The camp followers had long since turned back to Gestern. There was to be no booty here, just mud, cold and death.

He didn't have the time to worry that every man, woman and probably horse, hated him. His blisters were as bad as anyone's. His body ached from endless hours on the march. His knees were swollen, his armour weighed him down and his hands were frozen and useless half the time. Their boots were all hanging off by now and the rags so many had to tie to their feet were no real protection against the frostbite that stabbed at their extremities.

Despite the urgings of Dahnishev, he refused to ride. Only those incapable of walking sat on a horse all day. His cavalry too had been ordered to stride by the infantry. Solidarity, he had said, was the key to this march. They had suffered broken wagons, broken bones and desertions. The former had been abandoned where they stopped, the latter he couldn't afford the time to worry about. And as for the human breakages, they too were left unless a friend volunteered to support them.

Roberto knew he only held them together by a thread. He had driven them harder than even he thought possible. They were exhausted and hungry. They were angry too. But they would reach the battle a day early. It might make all the difference. His scouts said the border was still holding. He prayed it would do so through today. The distant sounds carried to them on the breeze from time to time.

He walked the length of his army, demanding their allegiance and stoking their anger. Some snarled at him. Most were too tired to react. A few still had the strength to laugh and joke. He could kiss Davarov for that. Whatever his personal feelings, the man was a mountain of loyalty. And where he marched, the morale improved. He had even heard singing.

Today, the snow fell hard and the wind was in their faces. Today, the march was at its worst and he could not afford for them to falter.

'Feeling angry today?' he asked as he strode down the column, trying hard not to limp or let the pain of his blisters show on his face. 'Good. Keep it in your heart and let it burn. Hate me today? Good. Remember that hate and when we are done you can swing for me. But that is tomorrow. That is the day that we meet the Tsardon and all our hate and anger can fall on them.

'By nightfall we will be able to smell the stink of their fear because they know we are coming. And the Conquord we save will sing of us forever. Your sleep this night will be blessed, for tomorrow when dawn comes, you will feel the blood of your enemies on your faces. And they will know what defeat tastes like.

'March on. For when tomorrow is done, we can all dream of home.'

Chapter 76

848th cycle of God, 18th day of Dusasrise
15th year of the true Ascendancy

Many of the cavalry had armed themselves with axes. As Kell led them on a charge across open ground into which the Tsardon were pouring to head her off, she hefted the uncomfortable weapon in one hand and dug her heels into her horse for greater speed. Ahead of her, the artillery crews had stopped turning their weapons and were lining up to meet the threat.

Kell had left Nunan and the infantry well behind in her wake. For them the task was not dissimilar to that of the day before. They had to keep the Tsardon back and maintain a secure corridor if at all possible. Further south, catapults sang on freely. Stones spat into the walls. Every volley brought more damage. She feared the effects of another breach on the already stretched defence.

Away towards Byscar along the coast, the cloud of dust that signified Roberto Del Aglios was plain for all to see. But they had no idea how close he was and neither did the Tsardon. They were gambling everything on victory today and had turned no one to face him. He could be thirty miles distant, he could be seventy, it was impossible to tell.

Just before she surged into the onager crew in front of her, Kell looked to the north and east. Tsardon were breaking away in line order from the side of the force gathered to attack the gates. Thousands of them. Kell's heart missed a beat. This was going to have to be a quick in and out or they would be swamped. In amongst them and attacking the catapults, she saw the levium. Proud skilled riders hopelessly outnumbered but moving her way.

Kell ran her horse straight through the flimsy barrier created by the enemy crew, her cavalry barrelling in after her. They scattered through the thirty heavy weapons. Kell slid off her horse and thumped her axe two-handed into the rope spring of the first catapult. She levered it out to strike again but spun at movement behind. The Tsardon's blade swept down. She took the blow on the haft of the axe. She turned the blade aside and down, then beat the back of the axe's head into the swordsman's face. He staggered back. She followed up, letting her hand slide down the haft before swinging from the waist and burying the blade in his gut.

She put her foot against the man and levered the axe clear. Her cavalry rode by to either side, keeping her way clear, striking down enemies from the saddle. Arrows flashed away right. She heard the thud of body on ground. Turning back to the catapult, she hacked into binding, rope and metal bracket. One down.

Kell raised her head. The enemy were close. In her immediate vision, all she could see were her own horses and the bodies of Tsardon crew. She ran to an undamaged catapult and set about it. An arrow thudded into the structure by her head. She jerked back. A lone archer was striding towards her. There was no one else close. She faced him. He nocked another arrow. Only one thing to do now. She ran at him, screaming.

The Tsardon stretched his bow. A thrown knife took him through the neck, knocking him sideways to the ground. Kell heaved a huge sigh of relief. Hoof beats closed on her.

'Get aboard. Time to go.'

She looked up into the face of a levium rider flanked by two others and nodded her thanks.

'Where's my horse?'

'No time. Get up behind me now.'

Kell caught his arm and hauled herself into the saddle. He spurred the horse and she leapt away in an arc to join a regrouping of Gatherer cloaks forward of the artillery. More than half the catapults were gone and the crew of all were scattered or dead but the Tsardon were upon them from ahead and left. She could see so many riderless horses galloping in the confusion while her remaining cavalry rode hard into the advancing lines, trying to buy more time.

As she watched, one of the captains signalled the retreat and they broke off to make the run back. Tsardon archers had gathered and the moment the Conquord had cleared their lines, they fired. They thickened the air and fell dense among her people. Horses and men tumbled to the earth. She closed her eyes.

'We have to protect your infantry. They're in trouble.'

Nunan. Kell looked around the rider to the walls. Stones still fell towards the gate fort and further south. The Revenge infantry was caught in a pitched battle in which all sense of order had been lost. The Tsardon had caught them from both sides and broken the maniple order in more places than she could count.

'They're being taken apart,' she muttered.

'Not for long,' said the Gatherer. He wore the badge of an appros. 'Levium! Let's make these bastards understand what a cavalry charge is all about.' He held his sword high in the air. The riders came to order around him. 'Clear the breach!'

His sword came down and the charge began. The Appros led the cavalry in a slight arc to bring them into line with the deep-laid Tsardon forces in front of the gates. They pushed to full gallop and thundered towards the enemy. Kell switched her axe to her left hand and yelled her excitement and fear. Her right hand was tucked into the belt of the Appros and she leaned out left, ready to swing.

The Tsardon saw them coming but they were woefully late. They had only half-turned before three hundred riders tore into them. Kell let her axe scythe through them, watching ahead while bodies were beaten aside by the weight of horse and rider, or taken down with sword, lance and spear. The Appros urged his mount further and further towards the wall. It slowed in the crush of men but more levium were striding up on both flanks.

The Tsardon at the edges of the charge scattered aside. Kell hacked down at one caught between two mounts, splitting his helmet with her axe. The Appros signalled the turn and executed right, bringing them into the back of those still attacking the Revenge infantry.

'Revenge to me,' shouted Kell.

Some of them heard and saw her and the fighting intensified on the ground. From above, archers were picking their targets. The Tsardon began to break.

'The other side,' she said. 'We need to clear the other side.'

'Done,' said the Appros. 'Levium!'

He turned and rode from the wall. In the confusion much of his cavalry remained deep in the fighting. They turned in ones and twos where they saw him, perhaps only seventy in all disengaging to join him. Across the field the Tsardon were coming in a wave. Overhead and south, stones fell. Four struck the wall dead centre, battering straight through it. The structure held for a moment, then collapsed forwards. Kell cursed.

'We need to get inside,' she yelled into his ear, not sure if he could hear her in the furore that surrounded them.

'You read my mind.'

Horns blared across the field. The remaining Tsardon at the breach disengaged and ran. Kell thought she heard Nunan roaring for order but it was difficult to be sure. She scanned the ground and saw him. She patted the Appros on the back and slid off his horse. He nodded at her and rode on, bringing the levium between the infantry and the enemy.

Flaming stones soared out from behind the walls, arrows described high arcs. Tsardon were scattered around the Conquord troops and were chased off or cut down. She fought her way through to Nunan, who was shouting for a retreat through the breaches. His infantry were responding.

'Come on,' she said. 'Time to go.'

'Lunchtime already?' he asked, smiling. 'Was it worth it?'

Kell looked back over the battlefield. The Tsardon advance was deliberate rather than a charge. More stones flew at gate fort and walls. Lessened considerably but still too many.

'I don't know,' she said. 'But whatever, we've brought them onto us for the final act.'

'Best we're ready for them then.'

Nunan bellowed his order once more and raced in through the twenty-yard breach with Kell and the levium hard on his heels.

The silence was difficult to bear. After hours at a volume that could draw blood from the ears, the quiet hurt, leaving them with a buzzing that would not die. The Tsardon catapults were halted and drawn back. Their army stopped out of arrow and artillery range. Remnants of the levium from the fighting further east rode around them unopposed. And now a party of three was advancing under a parley flag.

'Why didn't they just come at us?' asked Kell.

'Because they are scared we might hold out,' said the levium Appros who had introduced himself as Harin. 'We've lost two-thirds of the levium muster out there but the steppe cavalry are almost gone and the back of their lines has taken a fearful battering. We've hurt them this morning.'

'Not badly enough.'

Kell looked down from their vantage point on the walls and over the masses gathered before them. They had come with ladders, grapples and a battering ram for the gates. There would be no stopping it once it had started. Behind her, preparations were feverish. Sarissa maniples had been formed at the breaches. Archer companies were under independent control for fast deployment and every hastati maniple that remained was sprinkled with principes and triarii. This was not a time when a single citizen could afford to turn and run.

Even with the welcome addition of the levium, they were still outnumbered at least two if not three to one. Poor odds.

'If only they knew they just had to tap on the gates to bring them down,' said Gesteris, pointing at the battering ram. He was adjusting his armour and uniform, trying to hide the rips and stains.

'We won't stop them coming through for long. The surrounds are unstable.'

'Well, at least they don't know that. Come on Kell, Nunan. You too, Appros. A cloak might just give them a little more pause.'

Gesteris led them down a ladder and out through the main breach in the walls. Above them, legionaries cheered and hooted. Gesteris waved back at them. Ahead, the three Tsardon had stopped. In the centre, the commander stood with a hand on the pommel of his sword. His armour shone in the grey light of early afternoon. He was clean-shaven and approaching middle age. Either side of him, his men were proud of bearing and wore identical insignia.

'Ah, the one-eyed general,' said the commander in thickly accented Estorean.

Gesteris inclined his head. 'I'm a busy man. State your business.'

The Tsardon raised his eyebrows but his smile did not falter. 'The battle is lost. Your army fights bravely and dies in its thousands. As does mine. But we are the far greater force. There is no need for further bloodshed. The outcome is already certain.'

'Is it? How interesting. Perhaps we could discuss it for a few hours.'

'You are a busy man.'

Gesteris smiled tightly in turn. 'You and I both know the real situation. The difference is that I am not having to lie to my legions. There is an army coming to relieve us this coming dusk and you have no confidence in breaking us before they arrive. And I have no confidence in you, either. I will never surrender to you. This is Conquord territory and so it shall remain.'

'I beat you at Scintarit, I will beat you here,' said the commander.

'That remains to be seen. One thing.' Gesteris relaxed just a little. 'That song your people sing. It has touched us all. We respect you for it.'

The commander nodded, a sadness in his eyes. 'We sing it for our enemies too. War tears the heart from all of us. It is what makes your decision so tragic. When I return to my army and you to yours, thousands more will die.'

'We will defend our country to the last citizen. Your song is your way, this is ours. You will never break the Conquord.'

The commander walked away. Gesteris did the same.

'The end game,' he said.

'This evening, you say, General,' said Nunan. 'I thought we weren't lying to our people.'

Gesteris chuckled and clapped him on the back. 'That depends on your definition of lying. I prefer to call it estimation.'

'Let's hope it's one of your better ones.'

'Only one way to find out, isn't there?'

They stepped through the breach in the wall. Tsardon horns sounded.

'Exchequer!'

The call came from amidships. The weather had been clearing throughout the morning and they had caught distant glimpses of the Estorean coast through the thinning mist. The wind strength had dropped and the oars were beating time through the gentle swell once more. The sail was still deployed but the skipper was keeping an eye on it lest it start acting as a brake to their progress.

Jhered hurried forward from his position at the tiller. Lookouts were positioned at four points around the deck, scanning for the enemy. Apparently, they had been spotted.

'East-south-east, sir. Sails. Plenty of them.'

The sailor handed Jhered his magnifier and directed his gaze.

Jhered found the horizon and scanned left to right. There they were. Looming out of the mist and bearing down on the heart of the Conquord. It was difficult to gauge how many there were. Dozens he could see, and that probably equated to a force well into three figures.

'What's your assessment. Speed, direction, landfall.'

'They are heading straight for Estorr, Lord Jhered. They're under sail so presumably enjoying the back of the weather we had this morning. We're converging. I wouldn't like to say who will make the harbour first. It's that close in my estimation.'

Jhered irritated at his top lip with his teeth. 'Nothing from the south and south-east, no?'

'Not so far, sir.'

'Damn it, where are the Ocetanas?' He turned to the stern. 'Arducius! Someone get me Arducius. And any other Ascendant who needs some fresh air. And the rest of you, keep looking for our fleet. They've got to be out there somewhere.'

He waited, tapping impatiently on the rail, until the Ascendants appeared. He was particularly happy to see Ossacer. Their talk earlier in the day had given him great satisfaction.

'Can we see them yet?' asked Arducius, the excitement in his eyes.

'Indeed we can,' said Jhered. 'You can see them in the magnifier. Soon you'll be able to without it as well. They are on intercept with us for Estorr harbour. Take a look.'

Arducius did. Jhered could see him tense when he found them under the lookout's direction. He handed the magnifier to Kovan who had followed them up.

'There's a lot of them.'

'Yes,' said Jhered. 'I need them stopped. Not sunk necessarily but made to turn back.'

Arducius looked at him askance. 'I know but—'

'Now would be a good time. We have to give the Ocetanas the hours to make it up the coast, assuming they're coming at all. If they're still blockaded, we're all dead anyway.'

'They're a long way away,' said Arducius.

'Yes, and I want them to stay that way. But by dawn tomorrow, they will be practically alongside unless we do something about it.'

'No, you don't understand. I can't send a gale or a storm or whatever it is you think you want that far away. Look what happened on the plains. It was at our outer limit and that was much nearer than those ships. Even then, we couldn't control what happened to the energies and we all saw the result.'

'Absolutely, and I'm sorry, Ossacer, but you aren't talking to a man who much cares whether your storm gets out of hand. In fact, that might be a very good thing.' Jhered felt a little frustrated.

'It's complex,' said Ossacer quietly. 'It could work against us.'

Jhered sighed. 'So try me. I am not altogether stupid.'

'Well, wind and weather energies aren't like those in trees or plants, not really. With those, if we stop feeding and amplifying, the effect just ceases. But with a storm, once it is created, it must be tightly controlled and then allowed to bleed away under control. If it is just set loose, it becomes a random weather pattern.

'And that means it might simply dissipate in the face of clashing natural energies or it might feed on them and develop into something far more powerful than we first created.'

'The problem being?' asked Jhered.

'That it isn't under our control,' said Ossacer, as if that should have been the most obvious thing in the world. 'So it might turn and come for us. Weather's like that. It's random and difficult.'

'Don't patronise me, young man. And don't take me for a fool either. For one thing, Arducius can predict the weather. That's why we've made such good time on this crossing. And for another, if he detected the storm turning, you simply harness the energies as I know you can and drain it away. Is that not so?'

There was a satisfying silence. Jhered waited for a time for someone to respond.

'So, what's the real problem?'

Arducius shifted and Ossacer looked at the deck timbers, a reflex reaction from his sighted days.

'There are only three of us now,' said Arducius. 'We can't ask Ossie to channel energy for me because we all know what might happen. And if I've invested so much in creating a storm strong enough to cause them trouble so far away, I don't know if I would have the strength to diffuse it if it came back, even with Mirron. But I'll try if you want me too.'

Jhered breathed out through a smile. His frustration was borne away on a wave of fatherly pride.

'You lot,' he said. 'Don't hide such fears from me. You know me well enough now. This doesn't mean I'm going to blame any of you because you think you might fail. And I respect your knowledge of your abilities and your strength. If there's nothing we can do, then so be it. We just have to find another way to do what must be done. Let's see how close they get to us through the afternoon but if there is a Work you can do today, we can't leave it too late or you'll be in no condition to do anything tomorrow. Go on, get on with you to whatever you want to do. But do one thing for me; think about when you can act and using what, all right?'

He ruffled Ossacer's hair and watched them walk away. He turned back to the rail and put his head in his hands.

'We had to put them out of the game and we had to do it now,' he said.

'But surely the closer the enemy gets the more accurate we can be,' said Kovan.

'No, you don't understand.' Jhered lifted his head and looked at the young Vasselis. 'Only if we're very lucky will the first ships we see from the south be Conquord ships. If they aren't we have to face the fact that no help will be coming soon enough from the Ocetanas. Two fleets, two directions? I don't care how clever a Wind Harker Arducius is, he simply won't be able to stop them all.'

Chapter 77

848th cycle of God, 18th day of Dusasrise
15th year of the true Ascendancy

Still they held the gates. They'd used their shields, slabs of stone, breastplates, anything that could be leant against the shivering doors and gate frame, for that was all that was left of the fort in reality. He had archers braving the danger of the frame to shoot down enemy after enemy operating the battering ram. He had citizens lining the broken walls next to the fort to throw rock, spear and fire shaft down on the attackers.

The Tsardon had wheeled up a simple construction. Three tree trunks strengthened with steel rods, bound with steel sheeting and capped with a conical steel casing, suspended from a wheeled frame at two points, allowing it to be heaved back and swung in with significant force by a relatively small crew. Kell was standing by with a detachment of cavalry composed of the Revenge and Harin's levium to deal with a breakthrough.

The Tsardon had attacked on a wide front, expecting to overwhelm the defenders but had found them more tenacious. They had flooded forwards under their shield shell, heedless of arrow and onager, to attack the walls with ladders and grapples for climbing, and with hammer and axe to break through at the root.

Gesteris strode down the front of his reserve and behind his archers. His standard bearer was at his shoulder, horn and flagmen in his wake. He could feel the nerves picking at every citizen and he kept his bearing confident. Up on the rampart, the fighting was continuing in cycles as it had for the past two hours. Ladders hit the walls. Beside them, archers fired up, hoping to keep back defending bowmen. Lines of Conquord citizens maintained a barrage of shafts and rocks while teams chopped at ladder stays or pushed them away with long split poles.

Inevitably, the enemy would gain a foothold somewhere but it was always brief. The narrowness of the rampart worked in Gesteris's favour, and beneath it his archers could pick out targets which were framed by the sky. The death toll was rising fast on both sides. He came across Nunan, fresh from leading a push against a determined ladder attack. The Master of Sword was bloodied but energised, directing the attack in one of three designated zones.

'How are we faring?' Gesteris had to shout to make himself heard above the thundering noise of voices, weapons and the hammering at the base of the walls.

'The ramparts are all right but only just. We can't get enough fire down to the miners below. We're out of oil and we're losing too many leaning out to drop rocks. They're just being picked off.'

'Suggestions?'

Nunan's grimed face stared back at him. His eyes were bright in the mid-afternoon light. 'General, we just have to be ready for them to come through. They're attacking the wall in two dozen places at least. We'll struggle to contain them when they start making holes. Just pray the gate holds a little longer too. That's a huge area.'

Gesteris looked down to the main breach in the wall. The fighting was as intense there as it had been since this phase of the battle began. The phalanx was holding but the pressure of enemies from without was starting to tell. His citizens were exhausted. Inch by inch, they were being pushed back.

'Keep enough down there at the flanks to stop them forcing their way round. Archers to the angle as well. Start cycling your legionaries, Pavel. And pray Roberto is coming here at a run.'

There were two hours of daylight left. Gesteris wondered if the Tsardon would stop. Somehow, he didn't think so.

'Something else you need to be aware of, General. We're running short of arrows.'

Gesteris cursed. 'Then tell your people to make every one count. We cannot let them get free run up their ladders. Go.'

The general watched Nunan turn back to the battle. A fine man, a brave man. A concerted shout from the rampart took his attention. Archers were pointing out into the field. For a brief moment, Gesteris's heart leapt at the thought that Roberto had reached them.

But it wasn't that. There was brightness like lanterns in the sky. Flaming onager stones traced their arcs.

Ignoring the risk to his own men, the Tsardon commander was firing the inaccurate pitch-covered rounds. Gesteris watched them come in, hypnotised. Twenty, thirty, forty of them in three waves. Probably every piece that was available to them was back in use.

Over the wall came the first wave, dropping steeply. Panic gripped the standing reserve. Citizens scattered. Not nearly fast enough. The stones smashed down in their midst, scattering fire. The terrible crump of impact shook Gesteris. Legionaries dashed to the ground. Others broken, torn and twisted, hurled to lie dead at the feet of friends.

The second wave struck. Stones collided with the top of the wall, battering through the rough battlements, destroying Conquord and Tsardon fighter alike. With an echoing detonation, part of the wall five feet below the top burst inwards carrying with it the remnants of a ladder and those who had been climbing it. The debris fell into the cleared space behind the walls only ten yards from the breach. He saw men in the phalanx look around nervously. He started towards them.

'Face forwards,' he ordered while behind him, the screaming of the wounded filled his ears. 'Don't falter. Don't—'

The third wave pounded down. Half the stones fell among the Tsardon fighting at the breach or rattled the timbers either side. But not all. Two rounds rolled lazily down from the grey sky and all Gesteris could do was watch them bowl into the centre of the phalanx.

The shield defence so effective against arrow and spear was as paper to a two-talent stone. Hideous memories of Scintarit crowded his mind as his men were tossed aside, struck afire or simply crushed to nothing. The front and centre of the phalanx collapsed backwards. Sarissa tips were raised and the waiting Tsardon, those not slaughtered by their own artillery, surged into the gap.

'Get those damn catapults firing double time!' he yelled at his engineer, already running towards the enemy pouring inside his walls.

Arrows and spears thronged overhead the Tsardon, driving his phalanx further and further into disarray. Men and women backed over the dismembered smouldering corpses of their friends under the pressure of the enemy. Around the flanks of the breach, Nunan's people mounted a counterattack. Tsardon spilled in faster and faster.

'To me,' shouted Gesteris, his voice tiny in the tumult but his standard a beacon for order. 'To the General.'

He ran into the fight, chopping down overhead through the shoulder of a Tsardon archer. He stepped up and thrust his shield straight out into the face of another and stabbed his gladius out right, feeling it glance off a metal breastplate. Extraordinarii and legion reserve filled in around him. The centurion commanding the phalanx bellowed for order and courage. Sarissa tips began to level once again. Faces were turned back to the battle.

But the enemy was in the ascendant here at the walls. Archers clustered behind their sword line, firing overhead into those coming into bolster the defence. His bowmen responded. Tsardon and Conquord swordsman fell in their dozens. Gesteris smashed his shield up under the chin of a man wearing Conquord armour but the insignia of rebel Atreska. He spat on him and stepped back.

'I need order. I need a battle line. Discipline, Conquord.'

Temporarily, at least, that order was lost. Tsardon fought deep into the phalanx, cutting their way through the legionaries hampered by their unwieldy weapons. He had to get them out of there.

'Levium, for the Exchequer!'

Gesteris grunted his satisfaction. Harin. From the left of the breach, they came in. A line of thirty facing and at least eight deep. Infantry shields taken from the dead formed the wall and Gesteris could see the glint of sharpened blades. The Gatherers ran into the side of the Tsardon incursion.

Gesteris saw Harin's intention. The rear ranks held shields above their heads against the bows turned on them while the left-hand end of the line pivoted around the right, closing the gap pace by pace. He called his extraordinarii to him and moved back into the attack, using his shield to force a way through the determined Tsardon infantry. He stepped in front of a frightened hastati sarissa-bearer and shoved an attacker back.

'Get out of here,' he shouted over his shoulder. 'Back to the reserve and regroup. Go.'

The Tsardon came on again. Gesteris caught a blade on the top of his shield. The edge bit deep. Gesteris pulled back sharply, dragging the enemy forward. His gladius was waiting and drove clear through the man's stomach. He gurgled and collapsed, pulling his sword down with him. Gesteris moved further in, his guard around him, taking up his lead.

They fought their way into the centre of the phalanx. Gesteris punched out again and again with his shield, beating the enemy back. To his right, the levium swung inexorably towards them. Harin was at their centre, directing the move. The Tsardon backed away in front of them, unable to break through the line of cloaks. Gesteris herded more and more of the phalanx out of the way.

He caught Harin's eye. The Appros motioned him back. Levium arrows shot through their lines, felling more enemy. They began to retreat. The thud of an arrow reminded Gesteris to keep his shield in front of his body. This time, they would close the gap but the Tsardon would come on again. He feared their casual attitude towards their own and waited for the catapults to fire.

He didn't have to wait long. But this time, they destroyed the gate and the bulk of the levium were too far away to help.

The day was moving towards dark and Roberto had halted the army for a brief break. The cold inched into their bodies, sweat drying and chilling on their skin. Some had fires going quickly and a few would get a hot drink. For the rest, it was no more than a break to ease the agony in thigh, calf and heel. He had received word of Jhered's progress towards Estorr and it had cheered him. Their two conflicts would break at almost the same time.

Roberto moved through them as his command team would be doing, speaking words of encouragement and bolstering flagging energy and morale. There was little talk in the army and that worried him more than anything else. It spoke of a drain so complete, there was nothing left but to sit and stare. He saw the hollow look in their eyes and feared for those who dare not sit lest they could not rise to march. He knew how they felt.

The sound of a rider approaching from the west turned every head. Roberto thought he heard quiet before but not like this. It spread down the two-mile-long column like a blaze across oil. And over it, they could hear the distant roar of battle at the border.

Roberto stepped away from the column and beckoned the rider over. The woman half fell from the saddle and he could see the sweat on the animal's flanks, the froth under the tack and the tremble in its legs. He supported her and she clung on to him, forgetting herself for a moment.

'Sorry. I'm sorry, General.'

'No need,' said Roberto. 'Speak. What's going on?'

'They couldn't keep them away from the walls,' she said, gasping after every few words. 'I've ridden as fast as I could. We're maybe fifteen miles away still. No more. The defences are full of holes. The enemy won't stop at nightfall. They know we are coming.'

'Is anyone turned to face us?'

'Nothing significant.'

Roberto nodded. 'Report to the surgeons. Get on a cart and have a rest. You've done well.'

'Thank you, General.'

He released her into the care of some legionaries.

'This means we'll have to fight before we rest, doesn't it, General?'

Roberto pursed his lips and nodded. 'I'm afraid so, centurion. Where's Davarov, where is my Master of Sword?'

'Right here, General,' said Davarov who had been trotting up the column.

Roberto couldn't help but smile. 'Is there no end to your energy?'

Davarov drew to a halt and threw his arms around the shoulders of the two nearest legionaries. 'No. And I will carry these men to the battle if I have to.'

A ragged cheer went up and Roberto beckoned Davarov away from the line to speak to him privately.

'I need a declaration taken the length of the column.' He wiped a hand across his brow. 'This is difficult. We have to go faster. And we have to fight the moment we arrive. Neratharn's defence is on the verge of falling.'

Davarov stared at him. 'Faster? These citizens have nothing left.'

'They have to find it. Five miles an hour for three hours and then a battle. I'll be leading them in. The cavalry will form the vanguard when we get close. It has to be this way, old friend, or all our sores and blisters will have been borne for nothing. Every man and woman that has died on the march will have been a life wasted. I can't have that.'

'All right,' said Davarov. 'I'll put the word through the triarii. One last march.'

Roberto put a hand on Davarov's shoulder and nodded. 'One last march. And Davarov, earlier on in the march, I was wrong about you. I'm sorry.'

'No, General, you were right. Sometimes even old soldiers need new eyes to see the true path.'

'Very profound.'

'Let's hope I can be as profound with the legion.'

The Tsardon came through the gate on a wave of triumphant song. Underfoot were rubble, broken gates and the bodies, split and mangled, of too many Conquord soldiers. Kell calmed her horse, dragged her own eyes from the tumbling burning stones that had dashed their defence aside, and sounded the charge. Horns behind her brought the levium on behind her. A few standing archers sent arrows in ahead of her.

For a moment, it worked. The Tsardon had not formed a coherent line and the cavalry burst through them. Every strike seemed to find a target. Kell whipped her sword down, ripping through the back of an enemy helmet. She dragged the blade up and into the chest of a second. She pulled it clear and beat the pommel down on the head of a third. Her cavalry surrounded her and they scattered the Tsardon backwards.

But beyond the gate the density of enemy was so great. The brief charge slowed and even with the levium flowing easily around the flanks to drive them further backwards or be caught in a net of horse flesh and steel, it faltered. Kell wheeled to withdraw, her cavalry reading her action and trying to follow. The Tsardon poured back behind her and there were not enough Conquord infantry to stop them.

She found herself hounded by the enemy on both sides. She hacked left and then right, keeping them at weapon's length while she forced her way back through the gates to regroup for another charge. Behind her, the numbers overwhelmed the riders. Tsardon hacked at leg of man and beast alike, bringing them to ground. Kell yelled in frustration and sought a centurion.

'Get your maniple out there. I've got to have foot soldiers or we'll be swept aside. Go, I'll support you.'

The centurion nodded and ordered his nervous hastati maniple forward. Escaping horsemen flowed around them, turning to form up for another charge or switch to their bows. Kell swung her horse around. She saw a lone Revenge rider in a sea of enemies. The woman slashed wildly around her, keeping her horse turning around and around. So brave but the end was inevitable. A spear skewered into her side and cast her from her horse. The Tsardon bunched and came on through the gates once more.

Harin withdrew his levium and called for his horses. The phalanx reformed but it was just a matter of time before more catapult stones found their target. The Gatherer mounts were in a paddock just behind the reserve. Their saddles had not been taken from their backs and they waited in nervous expectancy while the tumult rolled around them.

'Quickly and up,' he ordered the two hundred with him. 'We're going to play a holding role. Where we see a breach, we ride in, give the infantry time to form up. Levium, for the Conquord and for me!'

Tsardon onager rounds were still falling and still the Conquord answered them. The damage behind the walls was terrible and the rampart was shattered in a dozen places. He rode around to the south, away from the gates which were under serious threat but where a solid concentration of soldiers was gathered and holding firm. He saw Kell among them. While she still rode, they would not break.

Gesteris was down at the major breach, his life on the line every heartbeat. Nunan was next to him, directing forces. Above, they were slowly losing control of the rampart. The available number of archers was thinning along with their supply of ammunition. And every swordsman that went up there knew they would not be coming down.

'Hold here,' he said. He rode to Gesteris. 'General.'

'Appros, how are we doing?'

'Badly,' said Harin. 'You must cede the rampart. Let them climb. Place archers and swordsmen below. We're wasting good citizens up there.'

Gesteris looked up. Fighting was continuous along the top. Soldiers fell out into the enemy and back onto their friends. The ground was covered in bodies too numerous to clear.

'Not yet. While they're up there, they don't know we are losing ground. I have to buy more time.'

'Don't leave it too long. We'll—'

A multiple shuddering impact south of them shook the ground under their feet. From without, the Tsardon roared again. Two more sections of the wall collapsed inwards. Tsardon surged in behind, running free behind the walls. Maniples set waiting engaged them hard under the direction of triarii within their ranks. Gesteris did not have enough fit centurions left.

Harin nodded at Gesteris and dragged his horse around, pushing it hard back to his levium who were waiting his call.

'Into the gap,' he shouted. 'Break their charge, isolate those inside.' He pointed at one rider. 'You, get to the rest of the cloaks. I need them mounted and mustered right here. We're going to lose the walls. Quickly now.'

It was surely hopeless. Harin galloped into the running Tsardon flank. Enemies bounced from his horse. He leant out and forwards, slicing into their faces. He kept low against the threat of arrows. Behind him, the levium carved their way through. Horses picked their way over bodies and debris. He swung round again and began to come back, angling towards the wall where they kept on coming. Hundreds of them. And thousands still waited outside.

More impacts. On the ground behind the walls a flare of fire in the fading afternoon light. Conquord artillery was shattered, crews dead in an instant. A third section of wall exploded inwards, sending rock high into the air to crash down on the few reserve not committed. Five breaches including the gate. Tsardon had broken through unopposed in two places and were heading for the few remaining artillery pieces.

Harin kicked out at a Tsardon head. Pain flooded him. He gasped. An arrow had pierced his armour at the base of his breastplate. Blood flowed. He breathed in, trembling. His sword came down on the shoulder of an Atreskan legionary running with the enemy. He kicked at the flanks of his horse, kept her moving forwards. Levium crowded him, seeing his injury.

The horns he had been fearing blared across the Conquord lines and the shout was taken up by every man and woman in the legions.

'Retreat! Retreat! Make for the stockade. Defend the camp.'

The levium moved to take him that way but he stopped them as soon as they'd cleared the immediate threat.

'No, no. To the muster point. We have to get out of here, get behind them. It's our only chance to help. Horses are no good inside a stockade.'

'You're hurt sir, we must get you to safety.'

'Safety? Show me where that is and I'll lead us all there. Levium, for the Exchequer, for the Conquord and for me. Let's get out of here but first, let's give the legion as much time as we can. Let's ride.'

Gesteris saw the levium moving and all he could do was mouth his thanks as he ran back towards the stockade. Again and again, the levium rode down and through the Tsardon advance. It bought them precious yards in their flight to the final plank of Conquord defence in the north.

Behind them, triarii held a solid triple line across the front of the enemy charge. They fell back as fast as they could, taking advantage of Harin's bravery and the sacrifice of the levium, who were cut down in number every time they broke into the enemy lines. Kell was with the triarii. What few remained of her cavalry, less than thirty, rode the flanks of the fall back.

There were dozens, hundreds of Tsardon and Atreskan rebels amongst the legions. Gesteris didn't have time to care. He needed to focus the final defence and hope Roberto was closer than he had any right to be. But the Omniscient had apparently turned away from them this day. Gesteris had wanted to hold the walls until dusk and retreat under cover of dark if he had to. But this smacked too much of Scintarit. The one difference was that he was in a position to help the stockade.

It was a four-hundred-yard sprint back to the stockade past the abandoned and sabotaged onagers. The Conquord flag snapped proudly at its gates which stood open. There were already four hundred infantry and engineers inside. They lined the ground in front of the camp and the platforms and rampart inside. Bolt-firers sat in towers. Catapults on the parade grounds inside. This stockade hadn't been built to house an army, only to provide a last refuge.

Gesteris paused to look back. In the failing light, the levium rode past one more time, turned and charged directly at the Tsardon line. Gesteris nodded and wished them luck under his breath. He signalled the horns and the fallback line turned and ran.

His people were flooding inside the stockade. Onager rounds thumped out overhead. Scorpion bolts whined by. And as Gesteris and the last of the legions came under the long shadow of the gatehouse, the archers set up a withering fire. The Tsardon slowed, forced to defend with shields high and above their heads.

How many people Gesteris had, he had no idea. He ran in, slapped the rump of Kell's horse as it thundered past him and ordered the gates shut as the final archer ran inside. Out there, the Tsardon would mass. They would bring their catapults and scorpions up with only a few hundred levium at best able to upset their progress.

Here was where it would end. Here, like in the harbour at Estorr, the Conquord's fate would truly be decided. The first of Gesteris's few fell from the rampart, an arrow in his face. The Tsardon were not even pausing for breath.

Chapter 78

848th cycle of God, 18th day of Dusasrise
15th year of the true Ascendancy

Harin ignored the scything pain in his side and hacked down with his sword. Countless times he'd made the move and his arm ached like his thighs, his arse, dammit the whole of his body. The levium chopped and slashed their way through the heart of the Tsardon. Harin brought his blade back to the ready. He moved it smartly aside to block a spear thrust and reversed it back to thud onto a helmeted head.

Levium rode seven abreast either side of him. He knew they were trying to shield him but everyone had to fight. The mass of the Tsardon flowed around them, content to let them go knowing their true goal, their true victory, lay ahead. Directly ahead, though, the defence was stout and they knew their own catapults were at risk.

The rubble and broken walls towards which they rode were a hideous backdrop. The Tsardon who ran through the gaping holes were like rats invading new carrion feeding grounds. They poured around the bodies that lay abandoned in their thousands, helpless before the Omniscient. Friend and enemy together, as would always be the way at the end of life in battle.

The sun was setting quickly behind the levium, sending stark, cold shadows across the battle ground. Birds were already flocking in the sky, waiting their chance to feast on dead flesh. Harin's anger dulled the pain away. He kicked his horse again and she sprang forwards, her front hoofs kicking out and catching a Tsardon in the chest. She found firm purchase and moved ahead. Harin beat about him with his sword, seeing Tsardon fall or scatter before him.

At his back were perhaps ten per cent of the levium who had ridden to battle just a few days before. Three hundred but with any number of others scattered to all points of the compass during the fighting. Too many, though, lay dead.

The power of the gallop saw them through the sundered gates and out into open ground. He could see the light of fires around catapults being secured for onward movement. Clustered about them were groups of archers and swordsmen. The enemy jeered, thinking they were fleeing the battle. Harin couldn't resist demonstrating their mistake.

He raised his sword and pointed at the nearest group of weapons. Levium came into a wide line, two deep, and rode in a crescent formation. The wings galloped at greater pace, closing in on the artillery crews and their defence. Harin barked his satisfaction. The encirclement was long in the training. It was gratifying to see its execution.

In front of him, the archers and swordsmen bunched together, trying to cover all the angles. Arrows came at the levium who hunched low. The target area was small, the depth of the line slight. And his archers were far better from the saddle than these Tsardon from firm ground.

Harin circled his blade and the levium cruised in. He sheared his horse left and swung his blade out and back, striking the arm from an archer. Three hundred riders choked every hint of space. Archers picked off their counterparts, swordsmen used their height advantage to drive the enemy into the ground. It was a slaughter. Unedifying but intensely satisfying.

Harin smashed his blade through the neck of a frightened boy soldier and kicked the corpse off its tip. He left the destruction of the weapons to his Gatherers and swung out to seek the next target. No one was coming back to them from the direction of the walls and the Tsardon catapults were open. Further south, artillery was already moving away into the gloom. Nearby, panic was evident and two or three archers had broken off to sprint away to call for help.

He turned his horse full circle. The low cloud was hampering his vision and in the dusk, snow began to fall again. But away north-east, a shadow was moving. It was broad and pinpoints flashed in the last light of the sun. Harin trotted his horse a few strides towards it, straining to see. The shadow resolved itself.

'Oh no,' he breathed.

Riders. Hundreds of them heading back onto the battlefield. Those pinpoints of light were reflections from the tips of blade lances. Only one force used them in such numbers and he had thought in his naivety that they had been defeated and scattered. He wondered if they had been seen. If not yet, then soon.

'Levium! We have to go. Steppe cavalry north-east.' He rode past them while they disengaged from the destruction of the artillery. One small blow for the Conquord. 'Whatever it is, leave it.'

He pushed his horse as fast as she would go. The levium tore through the outer reaches of the enemy encampment, ignoring the handful of guards. Once on the highway again they galloped away east, aiming to be lost in the foothills of the Gaws.

He heard shouts from up ahead and knew the Omniscient was not done with them. More riders were heading towards them along the highway. They must have numbered over a thousand. Harin felt like weeping. At every turn, they were thwarted. Luck never rolled in their favour. It had been so at the walls and it was so now.

Harin made the front of his levium to lead the charge to their doom. There was no point in turning back into the teeth of the others. He ordered them to drop to a trot. They would wait until the opposition was within a hundred yards and then charge afresh.

'Ready levium. Make this our glorious charge. Every rider you unseat is one less for Gesteris to face. Make your lives count.'

He raised his sword into the air. One more drop. One more charge. Harin glanced over his shoulder. Every face that stared back at him was steady. There was no fear, just determination and pride. The cloak sat well on all of them. He turned back.

'Levium!' But his sword did not drop for the charge. Instead he lowered it in front of him. Relief flooded through him and his head felt so light he thought he would faint. 'Stand down, stand down.'

He pointed at the standard flying at their head. It was the crest of the family Del Aglios.

The levium stood in their saddles and cheered. Unseen by them, pain had swamped Harin and his sword dropped from his hand. He clasped himself over the arrow wound. His armour, saddle and the flank of his horse were soaked in his blood. His faintness had nothing to do with relief. He swayed in his seat.

Ahead, the riders picked up their spear tips. At their centre, the Master of Horse raised a hand and the thundering of hooves died to a rumble as the cavalry came to a trot and finally a stop a few yards away.

'I am Appros Harin and these are my Gatherers,' he managed. There was a roaring in his head.

'Elise Kastenas, Master of Sword, the Del Aglios legions.' She trotted over. 'Are we too late?'

'Not yet,' said Harin, fighting to keep upright. 'To the north and on the battlefield, you've got a thousand steppe cavalry. Ride west along the highway. The Neratharn defences are gone. General Gesteris is under siege in the camp stockade. He's got ten thousand at best. Outside, thirty thousand Tsardon.'

'It's a siege that isn't going to take long to resolve.'

Harin nodded. Nausea swept him. 'He's good, Gesteris. He has Kell and Nunan with him but he won't last the night. I know how he feels.'

Harin knew he was falling but he didn't feel the impact. He heard noise and there were faces all around him. Someone was pressing hard at the wound in which the arrow head was still lodged. No sense in trying to take it out now. It had sliced into something more than mere flesh. He was losing sensation from all over his body.

'Get him on a pallet.' He heard Kastenas shouting. 'Get him to Dahnishev.'

'No,' he said. He grabbed her arm, made her turn towards him. 'Listen to me.'

'Rest, Appros. You've done all you can.'

'No,' he said. He shook his head to keep back the blackness sweeping over him. 'Do what I couldn't. Take the levium too. Draw off their cavalry. Destroy catapults. Buy time.'

'I won't fail.'

Harin nodded. 'How many are you?'

'About nine thousand, including what you see here. Let's hope it's enough.'

'It will be,' said Harin, seeing her fade to the distance. 'It will be.'

'Legions, are you angry!'

The answering roar spread through the army.

'Are you ready to fight!'

Roberto, finally on his horse, trotted alongside Davarov, amazed at the volume and carry of the Atreskan's voice. Harin had died but his report to Kastenas had signalled another change. The fast march was now a trot, the single column was now in battle order.

'Remember every corpse we saw on the road. And look at every loyal we pass in our last mile. That is what you are fighting for. Your people, your Conquord, your General.'

The roar was louder this time and Roberto heard his name chanted through the maniples. It carried across the army, bellowed from the mouths of eight thousand, five hundred exhausted soldiers. Roberto stood in his saddle, the horse keeping pace with the infantry. He held up his hands for quiet.

'Let them hear us. Let them know we are coming. We have fellow legions to save, great Generals to hail. And we have traitors and Tsardon to kill. Shout. Shout until your sword runs red. We are the Conquord.'

The noise was deafening and Roberto punched the air in salute of them all. He sat back down in his saddle and made for the head of the army, Davarov alongside him.

'Roberto, if I may?'

'Yes, Davarov.' He felt full of fatigue but there was something left. Enough for one last blow.

'Let me lead the chanting. Something to make the rebel bastards with the Tsardon weep for their mothers and lose their courage to fight us.'

Roberto looked down on him and saw the pride shining from him. 'You have something appropriate?'

'Oh yes, General, very much so.'

The onagers were out there, and when they arrived the battle would be almost done. Light had all but gone and still no sign of Roberto Del Aglios. When he arrived, they would be so much ash. Steppe cavalry were on the field now, standing and waiting. The stockade was completely surrounded. There was fighting on all four walls. The ramparts were soaked in the blood of his legionaries.

His archers worked tirelessly, shooting down those that sought to set light to the stockade. Fire parties stood ready. Down on the parade ground, the shield shell was complete while volley after volley rattled on it.

Gesteris felt no fear. With every moment that passed, the chance of relief came closer. And at this final juncture, the Tsardon seemed almost at a loss as to what to do. He didn't understand why they weren't either standing off and pummelling them with artillery once it was assembled or attacking them with more ladders, hooks and grapples than they could repulse. Perhaps they were not quite as ready as they should be. They hadn't even tried to hook the stockade walls and drag them down.

The general was in the gatehouse with Nunan and Kell. His catapults and scorpions still fired, forcing the Tsardon to vacate their firing arcs. Right now, they had no riposte. But as he watched the pitch fires were lit and the archers, finally, were dipping their arrows. And through the gloom, the first onager rolled into view.

It didn't fire. It had no opportunity. Cavalry stormed out of the shadows surrounding the Tsardon fires and engulfed it and the back of the lines. Gesteris's mouth hung open. Sudden anxiety fed through the enemy below. The press of attack on the stockade faltered for a moment as thousand upon thousand of heads turned.

Flying the crest of Del Aglios, they carried out the perfect hit and run. Riding in at a shallow angle, they released arrows by the hundred, chopped down on head, body and catapult spring before turning back out. Tsardon horns sounded and the steppe cavalry took off in pursuit. Gesteris hardly believed it had happened but for the cheering of his citizens. The sound of hoof beats faded but the nervousness of the Tsardon remained. The reason soon became evident.

The sound of singing growing quickly louder echoed from the Gaws and across the expanse of Lake Iyre. Not like the war dirge of the Tsardon but a song of pride that swelled the heart and pounded through the veins. It was a song all here had heard before, and many of those facing them as enemies. Gesteris knew every word.

The first time he had heard it, at Marshal Defender Yuran's investiture, it had brought tears to his eyes after long years of bitter struggle on Atreskan soil. It threatened to do so again. He lifted his voice to join those approaching, while below the Tsardon command tried to turn their army to face a new threat.

'The dawn does rise on Atreska's might
The heart of Conquord pride!
The light does warm our righteous fight
At Estorr's right hand side!

The enemy may descend on us
But we are one and I
Will swear my oath to Atreska's land
Til my turn comes to die.

Atreska! Atreska!
O land that God has blessed
Atreska! Atreska!
O land that God has blessed.

For the first time, there was fear among the invaders. Fighting had all but ceased. Every voice in the stockade had lent itself to Gesteris's and he felt a thrill course up his body. It was magnificent, and whether they won or lost when all was done, none who survived would forget the moment.

The first sight of Del Aglios's army was the lanterns carried behind the front line and through the triplex acies that came through the ruins of the walls and gates. They emerged, singing, into the firelit night, three hundred yards across and bristling with belief. Pike block central, hastati in perfect form, left and right. Principes and triarii way back in the shadows. And behind them all, the unmistakeable rattle of cart pulled by oxen. Artillery.

At a signal he didn't see, the singing ceased. His stockade sang the final verse one more time and he too ordered quiet. Silence rebounded across the open space with only the distant sound of horse and weapon to break it. Del Aglios stood his army a hundred and fifty yards away from the enemy, daring them to continue their attack.

Gesteris said nothing, letting the order and power of the new army do its work on the Tsardon, now caught between two forces. They were coming from all sides of the stockade to bolster their defence front and back. No arrow flew now. No sword thrust came and no ladder was climbed. He smiled and spat on the ground between his feet.

'Not so sure about it now, are you, Tsardon bastards?' he growled.

He looked over at Kell and Nunan. 'Looks like we're going to last the night after all.'

Behind them, high up in the Gaws, the beacon fire still burned. It was a backdrop to Roberto Del Aglios whose exhausted legions marched into the attack.

Chapter 79

848th cycle of God, 19th day of Dusasrise
15th year of the true Ascendancy

'Neristus, I need our onagers angled across the enemy. Faster. They are at the stockade gates with the ram. I need a path and I need it now.' Roberto bellowed orders on the gallop. His extraordinarii peeled off to see them done. 'Cartoganev, take your cavalry to our left. I want a wall exposed. Gesteris's legionaries cannot help us from underneath their shield shell. Davarov will bring Atreskan triarii to help you. When you have secured it, bring the walls down. Levium, I want every spare Tsardon catapult destroyed before it reaches us. Guard against cavalry attack, we do not know where Elise has led the steppe.'

Roberto rode back between his hastati and principes, braving the arrows that fell from behind the Tsardon front lines. They needed to know he was nearby. The battle scene was cast in garish light from the three forces but there in the midst of the front, it was dark and hot and hideous. His legions were tired. Too tired to fight though they had to. Exertion and fatigue was on every face that turned to him and in the shake of every limb. He needed a quick victory or the Tsardon could break them.

The first advance had seen good ground made. The infantry had driven the Tsardon back hard. But they had steadied and recovered to fight effectively on both fronts. The stockade was still surrounded on all sides but Roberto's intervention had drawn off reserve from everywhere, leaving the Tsardon a little thin to his left. If Davarov and Cartoganev could usher them away, the battle would turn.

Before that he wanted to hear his onagers and scorpions sing. Neristus was taking too much time organising fire angles to miss the stockade. It was the dark that did it. God-surround-him but he hated fighting at night. His legionaries were already exhausted and the Tsardon were beginning to stretch them. A few well-placed stones could change all that. Gesteris and his defenders still had catapults at their disposal, though the loss of the gates would see them down. The Tsardon had few pieces left and what they had they'd turned on Roberto. Back in the reserve he was suffering too much damage.

He galloped back around the edge of his infantry and away to the engineers.

'Rovan, I need you now. Can you get to any of their heavy pieces? I've reserve hastati being taken apart here. Dahnishev cannot cope.'

The little engineer hunched reflexively as a dozen Tsardon stones fell from the night sky and well in front of their position. Roberto winced at the impacts and screams that followed. Fire flared briefly into the night.

'I doubt it. I need to be further forward but then I don't get the angle with the scorpions over our own heads. The levium need to get to work.'

'How long before you're ready?'

'We're about done.'

'Too slow.'

'Well, at least we won't be killing our own men.'

Roberto leaned down a little closer. 'No, Rovan, we are letting the Tsardon do that. Get firing.'

He rode away towards the left flank. Davarov had drawn his four favoured maniples aside as he had done at Gestern.

'Earning your wage tonight, General?' he shouted over the frenzy behind him. Davarov's eyes were bright, as if he'd just woken from a refreshing sleep.

'You could say. Right now I make up the entirety of our right flank cavalry defence. If Elise falters, we are in big trouble.'

'Take Cartoganev, then. We can handle this on our own.'

'Big words, blind eyes,' said Roberto, smiling. 'Just get that side taken. I need Gesteris's legions out here. Then we might just win this.'

'Has that engineer of ours—?'

Catapult arms and scorpion bows thumped. Flame launched into the sky. Roberto watched the trails disappear into the belly of the Tsardon army. His hastati there pushed forwards again. Every pace was pained. Every blow was tired.

'Yes, he has. And time you went in too.'

'Keep a drink in the victory cup for me,' said Davarov.

'Just remember the mantra. We win when the banner flies from the beacon. Keep your people believing.'

'Think Jhered'll make it in time?'

'How can you doubt it? He's a taxman. They always show up when they aren't wanted.'

Davarov's booming laugh turned heads. Cartoganev's horns sounded and his cavalry drove out towards the stockade. Roberto rode back to his principal front. Neristus's catapult and scorpion rounds had caused significant damage in the Tsardon ranks and confusion in the centre of the army. His hastati had gained more ground in the immediate aftermath but, once again, their enemy had stabilised. Phalanxes were secure and sword infantry ebbed and flowed around them.

Away at the stockade gates, the Tsardon ram was working hard. It wouldn't be long before they were through. Gesteris was directing arrow-fire down at it but there was an inevitability in the booming crunches that echoed over the battlefield. He needed Davarov to be successful and quickly. And he needed the Gatherers, enraged by the death of their leader, to take out the damned artillery falling on the heads of his reserve. It was going to be a long night.

'Let's give them some support!' yelled Gesteris, racing from the gatehouse and onto the left-hand rampart, his shield held high and to his right.

He had seen the light of a hundred and more torches racing down the army's right flank and had known immediately what was being attempted. The remaining Tsardon artillery had been dragged away to his left and out of the firing arcs of his few pieces when Roberto had appeared. They had been firing diagonally across the battlefield ever since. But they were exposed to a charge, defended neither by the bulk of the army, nor by those assaulting the stockade. Roberto had seen it too.

Smoke billowed up the stockade walls from the fires set by the Tsardon below. His people threw everything at them. Knives, spears, rocks, arrows. Almost anything the came to hand. Behind the fire-starters, Tsardon archers kept up a dense barrage. He was losing too many people.

On the opposite side of the stockade, Kell and Nunan supported a move by Roberto's infantry and cavalry to drive the Tsardon from the walls. He had his engineers ready to drag the stockade in should they succeed.

'Divert your fire towards the catapults and the Tsardon flank defence. Forget the fires. Do it.'

Archers crouched to reload, stood to fire. Every time, an answering volley would come and every time, someone was struck and killed. This could not go on.

'Come on, Roberto, I need you to break them in front,' he muttered.

Out of the night sky, Conquord stones battered into the Tsardon centre. Gesteris could see anxiety there. They had no defence and the answering artillery was only a third that of the Conquord's. If that was silenced too . . .

Gesteris watched the riders approach at full gallop. They crossed the fighting lines travelling four abreast and out of the reach of enemy pikes. Arrows and spears dropped on them from the dark. He saw people pitch from saddles or slump aside and be trodden under the hoofs of their own. Thirty were down before they had travelled a hundred yards.

Behind the defence, the enemy was moving to cover their artillery. Archers and swordsmen turned from the walls to tackle them. Immediately, his own bowmen saw their chance. They emptied their quivers into the backs of the enemy, forced infantry to put up a shield wall to defend them. For a moment, the pressure on the wall eased.

'Come on,' said Gesteris. 'Make it count.'

The attrition rate on the riders was so high. Gesteris saw the flash of a cloak as a man took an arrow in the throat. Levium. So often a name to curse, now one to raise in chant and cheer. The leading riders thundered past the artillery. They swerved in close to the thin pike line defending it. In the half-light, Gesteris saw the glitter of glass and watched the hypnotic sight of torches turning end over end.

The Tsardon were unprepared for it. Sheets of flame spread across ground and wood. They ate into rope and weakened stay, bracket and cup. Six or seven artillery pieces were engulfed. Tsardon ran to try and beat out the flames. His archers turned their attention on them, those with any shafts left.

Every moment the fires were alight was a moment the battle turned just ever so slightly. Gesteris saw an onager arm twist and fall to the side, its rope spring burned through. On the rampart his infantry cheered. The levium, what few remained, galloped away west and were lost to sight. The enemy was going to lose more than half of its remaining artillery to the fires.

But the Tsardon weren't done. The battering ram struck its decisive blow and the gates splintered. Above it, the gatehouse rocked. Tsardon flooded into the compound. At the rear of the stockade, flame rose hot. Legionaries stumbled away while outside, dragging poles were pulling at the weakening wood. Gesteris needed to get some of his people out to counter them before he was attacked back and front. He looked up into the sky. Dawn was still hours away. When it came, he wondered if it would be the last for the Conquord.

They were all up before dawn broke, crowding the bow of the *Hark's Arrow*. All night, there had been lights from the south and south-east, growing brighter. When the sun finally cast its light on the home waters of Estorea and the western limits of the Tirronean Sea, Jhered saw much more than he had feared.

At best guess, two hundred sails chased them from the south-east. The *Hark's Arrow* was a mile ahead and would reach the harbour mouth before them but not by much. South, the first sails he saw were not of the Ocetanas. They were some distance behind and would not catch the Tsardon before they entered Estorr less than five miles away. The invasion would see the Omniscient-blessed city crumble to dust.

The light was picking out her most glorious towers and playing off the aqueducts. He could see the palace, glittering as it always did in the dawn. The city rose as if in welcome to the sun, white, red and beautiful.

'Take a good look, children,' he said. 'This is a sight all should be given the chance to see. And you're going to be among the last. Are you listening to me?'

It was plain enough that they weren't. Arducius and Mirron were deep in conversation. Ossacer stood by them, sullen, his eyes closed. Only Kovan was staring as he should be and he'd seen it all before.

'You'll regret this when it's all so much smoke and ash,' said Jhered. 'This is the best sight in the Conquord. In the world.'

'How wide is the harbour?' asked Arducius.

'I, well, I don't know.' Jhered didn't know whether to be irritated or confused by the question.

'Three hundred yards, fort to fort,' said the skipper who had been standing with them scanning the situation with his own magnifier.

The Ascendants disappeared into another brief conversation. Arducius spoke up again. 'We need to get in close.'

'Close? I'm going all the way to the dockside and then running into the hills,' said the skipper. 'What was it you had in mind?'

'No, we have to stop outside the harbour,' said Mirron.

'Why?' asked Jhered.

'Because,' said Arducius. 'We have to use the sea outside the harbour because it has greater energy about it and if we don't, the wave won't be wide enough.'

Jhered looked over at the harbour. 'You mean to block the entrance.'

'But if I'm not close enough, I won't be able to control the energies, not even with Mirron to help me.'

Jhered turned to the skipper. 'Let's get that sail down. I want double time all the way home. This is not over.'

Iliev pounded the forward rail, the only outlet for his impotence and frustration. They were closing on the enemy all the time but still two miles behind. Two miles that meant the difference between invasion and sanctuary. They had seen the fleets to the east. The Tsardon rowing strongly, one ship well ahead of the rest of the fleet but being caught slowly. Patonius had said she thought it a Conquord vessel but Iliev wasn't so sure. If it was, he wished them luck and the grace of Ocetarus. Far too distant, other ships from the eastern docks of Kester Isle followed. By the time they reached the harbour, it would all be over.

The sky was a pearl white today. A thin covering of cloud and a bright sun just without the strength to break through. The winds of the last days that had risen again this morning had blown away the early dusasrise mist and Iliev reflected that at least the good folk of Estorr would see the end of the Conquord approaching.

There was no way to bring more speed to the fleet. No wind that would carry them fast enough to take the enemy by surprise. Despite all their prayers to Ocetarus, the weather had remained doggedly reasonable, allowing the Tsardon to keep far enough ahead that even the Ocenii could not hope to catch them.

'We were a day too long in the docks,' he muttered. 'Just a day and look what it has cost us.'

'Don't blame yourself, Karl,' said Patonius, leaning on the rail next to him with a magnifier to her eye. 'If we'd left a day earlier we would not have been disguised, they would have seen us, sunk us and we would not even have got this far.'

'Then we should have had better warning,' he said. 'We should have been alerted from the southern watchtowers on the Isle.'

'Why are you doing this? Is this some sort of bizarre cathartic ritual, preparing your mind for failure? You know why you weren't alerted. The Tsardon didn't sail into the Isle until they were ready to attack. They used the mists like the Ocetanas have done for generations.'

Iliev saw her stiffen and take her eye from the magnifier briefly. She wiped the end with a cloth and looked again.

'Karl, look to the harbour.'

Iliev did. There was a shadow growing near it. It must be a trick of the light. Frankly, he wasn't too worried about that. It was what was happening closer that brought new hope to his heart. The pair of them stared at each other for a moment.

'Oars, maximum stroke!' yelled Patonius. 'Ready the corsair. Signal the fleet for battle. The Tsardon are turning.'

Arducius knelt at the stern of the vessel with Mirron by him to help channel and amplify. The ship had been turned away from the harbour. The crew were nervous. They'd been told what to expect and he'd seen them all clutching keepsakes and praying to their god of the sea. Now it was down to him, and every spare man was watching him.

In Estorr, warning gongs, bells and horns had sounded at sight of the Tsardon fleet. Across the water, he could hear the thud of drumbeats and the cries of crews straining every muscle. They would be on top of the *Hark's Arrow* before the hourglass was a quarter through.

'Feel the power of the tide,' said Arducius. 'Feel the swell beneath the keel and the slumbering energies. Open your mind to the circle it creates. Bring it to you.'

'I feel it, I see it,' said Mirron.

Arducius could see the immense resonant power of the water, the mesh of lines that ran through it, dark red and thick as his body, pushing, pulling. Or so it seemed. Their energy maps were joined, bright and glorious with the life that flooded into them, held in check by the closure of their lifelines. Slowly, slowly, Arducius reached out with his mind and his right hand. Combined, they could exert the right sort of control. Arducius gasped as he opened his life circuit and joined it with the ocean.

Such unbelievable force. He would not have to amplify it at all but it would take all his strength merely to hold it. Water climbed the side of the ship in response. It swept around his knees, up his body and away over the stern to complete the circuit.

'Steady, Mirron. Can you feel it trying to wash you away.'

'Yes.'

That was how it felt. Like they were part of the wave motion and of the swell that formed the ocean. Arducius knew what he had to do. When the swell came in, he let it flow until it almost reached the blank dark that represented the harbour forts. And there he stopped it going in or out. He let the next wave roll into his static one and push the whole mass higher.

Each time he did, he felt the drag on his energy, the drain on his life to hold that of the ocean still. More and more he built. The boat moved towards the growing wall of water that was climbing straight from the ocean around it. He heard the skipper bark an order and the oars begin to dip, taking them away from the base.

'Enough, Arducius, enough,' said Mirron.

'Hold on,' he said. 'Paul wants fear. We can give him that.'

Wave after wave fed into the towering barrier. He could see it grow. Twenty feet, forty, sixty. He wanted a mountain. A living, vibrant mountain shimmering in the morning sun. Its outline wavered. Wind picked off the cap, turning it into a fine spray. He could hear a gentle bass roar too, as the water rolled around itself in the wall, churning gently.

He felt himself shiver and had to stop building. He admired what he had done. It stood a hundred feet high, maybe more, and sixty across its base. It rose from the ocean like a giant's palm; the flickering cap was its fingers, tattering and reforming in the wind. It reached from fort to fort. It was magnificent.

'Get through that,' he muttered.

But he wondered how long he and Mirron could keep it that way. He wondered if he really could buy enough time for the Ocetanas to get here.

In a corner of the palace of Estorr, Hesther clung to Arvan Vasselis while the rest of the Echelon stared down at the barrier in front of the harbour forts. Crowds were gathering on the dockside. The Order were out in force very quickly, to denounce the force as a punishment of the Omniscient.

One moment, they had been watching the large Tsardon fleet approach. The next, the water had massed and climbed into the air faster than a man could walk. The crowd had begun to panic. People were running away from the dock or kneeling to pray. Others stood and gaped at the wall that could sweep the dockside clean away. The sound of the citizens was ugly, angry and terribly frightened.

Hesther was crying but she didn't know if it was in happiness, relief or fear.

'They're out there,' she managed. 'Dear God, Arvan, our children are out there.'

The battle was going against them. Dawn was beginning to banish the shadows and as inevitably as the sun's rise, the Tsardon were winning. The levium had taken out as much of the enemy artillery as they could. Elise Kastenas had destroyed the steppe cavalry. But the former was lost somewhere behind the enemy and the latter in charge of horses too exhausted to take another step.

The Tsardon had taken the gatehouse and the artillery up there was destroyed, sabotaged by its own crews. There was fighting deep into the compound. The rear wall was torn away along a fifty-yard length. Gesteris was trapped. Davarov and Cartoganev hadn't managed to force their way to the stockade's wall. Even the artillery was stuttering. Ammunition was in short supply and they'd suffered breakdown after breakdown as the temperature plummeted through the night and ropes snapped or wood cracked under the strain.

The Conquord was losing heart. Roberto could feel it. His legionaries were utterly spent, the effects of the march claiming them at last. The Tsardon had known that to hold them would be to beat them and it was going to happen unless he could think of a way to break them. What he needed most was the white and gold banner to fly from the beacon in the Gaws.

Down to the left, that was where the key to the battle lay. He couldn't commit any more infantry from his stretched and fatigued main line. Davarov would fight all day but even he needed some encouragement. Roberto chewed his lip and gauged the distance to the walls he was desperate to free. It would be a risk but he felt he had to try it. He kicked his heels to his horse and rode for Neristus and the artillery. All the way, he had his eyes on the beacon fire, willing the banner to be raised.

'Come on, Paul, don't let me down.'

The skipper of the *Hark's Arrow* dragged his tiller round hard and drove the ship back across the front of the wave. Jhered saw the disbelief in his eyes and knew his own were mirrors of it. He hardly dare look at it, teetering above them, its great crest gnawing at it, desperate to fall and swamp them all.

And it had worked so well for a time. Every ship in sight had turned to flee and the taunts of the crew had hidden their own fear. He could imagine the confusion and consternation. Thousands of superstitious sailors would have seen a gate of water rise up from the ocean and slam shut the way into Estorr harbour right in their faces. Dear-God-embrace-him but he had wanted to run, too.

Further south, the Ocetanas had come on and were engaging the vessels that had turned more or less straight into their path. But plenty remained free of attack and the braver amongst them had decided to come for a closer look. It had been five at first, realising that the *Hark's Arrow* was the key to it all. To sink her would remove the problem.

The skipper had enough manoeuvres in him to outwit them but now another twenty were coming and more were turning to do the same. The Ocetanas did not have enough ships to come to their rescue.

'We have to go further out,' said the skipper. 'I'm going to get stuck against this damned wall.'

'No.' Jhered looked to the aft hatch. Ossacer had put his head out. 'You can't move away. Look at him. He's already struggling. Mirron is shaking, I can see it in her life map. Try to imagine him holding two ropes together while teams try and pull them apart. If you move away, you are pulling harder. Eventually he will lose his grip. And if he does that, the wave will just subside.'

'Down!' yelled the skipper.

Jhered ducked reflexively. A scorpion bolt slammed through the port rail, crossed the deck and tore out through the starboard. He jerked back to his feet. A Tsardon trireme was heading directly at their aft section. It had appeared from behind a decoy travelling across their path.

'Stroke thirty,' called the skipper.

He leaned hard on the tiller. The trireme missed them to stern. Arrows whistled across the deck. Jhered threw himself across Ossacer.

'What do you suggest we do?' he said, rolling away.

Ossacer looked up at him. Jhered felt uncomfortable every time he did that. Those were eyes that saw nothing and everything.

'How many ships are chasing us and how many are heading in from the east and how near are they?'

Jhered peered above the gunwale. Tsardon ships were everywhere, converging on their position. He counted twenty in an inner circle, another ten outside and away east, another thirty or forty making their way back in. He relayed the information.

Ossacer nodded and helped himself to his feet. His gaze never left Jhered's and an expression of abiding sadness and regret crossed it that stole Jhered's heart for a moment.

'We have to use the energy in the wall,' he said. 'Reverse it.'

Jhered frowned. 'I beg your pardon?'

'We have make it fall straight down. Cause a whirlpool and suck them all down.'

The wall of water loomed massive and lethal right above them. It had a sound of its own, a sucking, roiling noise that spoke of dreadful power.

'It'll kill us, too. Drag us to the bottom.'

'We're dead already. And this way, more of the enemy come with us and more of the Ocetanas escape it because they are far enough away. Arducius has to use the energy he's stored up before the Tsardon get him.'

'I thought you only sought to help, not harm,' said Jhered.

'I don't want my brother to die thinking he failed.'

'And what about you, Ossie?'

Ossacer smiled. 'I will die knowing he didn't fail too.'

Jhered had to look away. He caught the skipper's eye and the big man nodded that he'd heard and accepted. The Tsardon were closing the net. Any hope they had of escaping was being blocked off. Jhered shook his head. He hadn't expected to die on the ocean.

'Go talk to your brother. Just do it quickly. I'll be right behind you.' Ossacer moved away. 'Ossacer.'

'Yes?'

'Proud of you, young man. Really proud.'

Iliev landed on the deck and ducked a wild sword thrust. He came up quickly and stabbed the sailor up through his chin and into the roof of his mouth. He dragged the blade clear, swung left and knocked a blow aside with his dagger. He kicked out straight, taking the man in the stomach. He staggered back. Iliev jumped and planted a foot in his chest, sending him slithering across the deck. He made to rise but another of the Ocenii put a blade through his throat. The deck was clear.

'Ocenii, let's get this ship turned. It is going in the wrong direction.'

The battle was going with them. The Tsardon ships fleeing the wall had met a dense and concerted ramming charge from every Conquord vessel. The Ocenii squads were amongst them, taking on the ships at the back of the enemy fleet, hitting them as they tried to turn back east. He was proud of the Ocetanas. They felt the same fear as their opponents but they had overcome it. And now the tide of the fight was with them.

His men were below already, subduing oarsmen. Two ran to the tiller and began to move it to port. Slowly, the trireme turned away from the water cliff and again, Iliev caught himself staring at it. He murmured thanks to Ocetarus for it was surely his work. Yet it terrified him. Nothing could create that in nature. Some force was at work. He had to believe it was the hand of God. It was the only thing that kept him and his squad from running.

The ship wasn't turning fast enough. Hardly an oar was dipping. The sluggish turn was exacerbated by the drag of the corsair. The spike was buried in its side, high up because the Ocetanas needed to capture triremes, not sink them. He ran to the hatch amidships.

'I told you to arrest them, not stop them. Get those bastard oars moving.'

He sniffed the air and straightened, eyes back to the north-west. Something was changing. He could feel it in the air and smell it on the wind. It was a faint odour but fetid somehow. It was the wall across the harbour. It hadn't smelled wrong before but it did now. And he hadn't spent his life at sea to ignore his instincts this time.

It wobbled at its upper edge, spilling water in great swathes. Below them, the sea was being dragged towards it faster than any incoming tide. That was enough.

'Ocenii. Get out of there. Get off this ship now! Move.'

One last glance and he sprinted to the aft quarter and the ladders. Ocetarus was about to wreak his vengeance on the Tsardon.

Chapter 80

Jhered and Kovan stood over them. Ossacer was talking to them and Mirron was crying. He made an embracing movement with his hands and the others nodded. Above them, the barrier was beginning to falter. The skipper had made another audacious move and, once again, had found a little open water. But it was all he could do. Ships closed in from every quarter. Two were heading straight at them and he couldn't dodge them both.

'We aren't going to survive this, are we?' said Kovan.

Jhered shook his head. 'But we die knowing we helped save the Conquord for those we loved.'

'Or died with them,' said Kovan. His face was white and scared.

Jhered nodded. 'And that's a comforting thought.'

'I should have killed him. Gorian.'

'Don't regret your decision. It was what they wanted. He's dead somewhere anyway.'

'I don't share your confidence.' Kovan nodded at the Ascendants. 'They'd know if he was. They'd feel something. And now he'll be the only one left.'

Jhered looked forward. Men lined the rails carrying bows or spears and shields. How small a number they looked.

'Your Ascendants had better be quick,' said the skipper.

'We have to give them the time they need,' said Jhered.

'Understood. Guard your port flank.'

Jhered nodded. He hefted his gladius and set his shield on his arm. Below, the beat of the drum sounded over the splash of oars and the rumble of the unstable wall of water to his right. Ahead, the Tsardon triremes closed. They would both strike the port bow. Jhered set himself against the imminent impacts and took one last glance at the Ascendants. Ossacer was still talking. He stroked Mirron's head and had his other hand on Arducius's shoulder.

'Goodbye,' he whispered. 'May the Omniscient welcome you to his embrace.'

The noise gained in intensity. Every sound was amplified. The shouts of the Tsardon. The answering taunts of the crew. The straining of oarsmen and the beating of time. And something else, a shuddering that he could feel beneath his feet as well as in his head. The ship shifted sideways slightly.

'Kovan.'

'Yes, Exchequer.'

'Your father will be proud of you. You are a hero of the Conquord.'

'And you.'

'No, boy. They pay me to be here. You do it for love.'

'Brace!' roared the skipper.

Conquord and Tsardon ship collided in a splintering and groaning of timber. The sick sound of destruction. Men stumbled and steadied. Arrows and spears flew. Bodies slumped to the deck. Grapples crossed the divide. Moments later, the second vessel struck. Tsardon soldiers poured on to the ship. Weapons clashed.

'Stand firm,' said Jhered. 'Keep your shield up. Here they come.'

Arducius felt the energy flowing into him from Ossacer. His words had been like sunlight through cloud. What he asked should have scared him but the thought of his death was tempered by the knowledge that he would achieve his destiny.

The lumbering power of the ocean flowed through him and around him. He strained every muscle to maintain the cohesion of the wall. With every heartbeat, his control slipped a little more. It was as if the water had a will of its own that was set against him. He had not realised how quickly it would drain him. When Ossacer had touched him, he was on the point of losing the circuit he had formed with the ocean.

Now, he had fresh direction and a fresh reservoir of energy. The map of the water wall was serene, almost unmoving. Deep blues flowed across its surface. Using Ossacer and Mirron to amplify his actions, Arducius reached out to it. As the energies rolled through him, he focused them, dragged them close together and twined them around each other again and again.

In his mind, the new energy map formed and he imposed it on the mass of the ocean that towered above him. The image was that of a tornado, narrow at its base, wide at its head and turning faster and faster. Applied to water it created a vortex, a sucking power that would drag everything within its compass down to its deep, dark heart.

The energy lines flared with the power he fed them from Ossacer and Mirron, no longer blue but a resonant, pulsing orange shot with white, raw and violent. He fought to contain what he created.

'Place it,' said Ossacer. 'Place it before you lose it.'

'I can't,' gasped Arducius. 'I have to anchor it or it'll disperse too quickly.'

'Make it as tight as you can. Then we'll go.'

Jhered blocked a thrust to his midriff and cracked his gladius into a Tsardon helmet. He staggered back, dazed. The deck was covered in skirmishes. Oarsmen had rushed up fore and aft to join the fighting. The three ships drifted ever nearer the water wall which had begun to ripple alarmingly along its length.

Next to Jhered, Kovan fought well. His fear had gone and his training had taken over. He blocked and parried like a veteran, with Jhered offering him encouragement and a rock-solid flank on which the enemy broke.

The dazed man came back at Jhered. He raised his sword. Jhered blocked it aside and finished him, jamming his gladius up under the rib cage. The man collapsed to the deck. Two more were coming at him. Kovan was engaged with a third. At their backs, the Ascendants still worked on, unmoving.

Jhered brought his shield in front of him. The first enemy ran at him, the second hanging back. Light leather armour covered their torsos, small round shields were worn on their forearms. Leather skull caps kept the hair and sweat from their eyes and their faces were covered in lurid colours, like living masks.

Jhered let him strike, fielding the blow on his shield. He jabbed straight out. The strike glanced off a buckle. He drew back inside his defence. The Tsardon stepped up. A mistake. Jhered rammed his shield full into the man's body and as he began to fall backwards, came around with his sword and felt it bite deep into flesh.

Straightening, Jhered saw the second man take a pace. He was hefting a spear. He cocked his arm but didn't make the throw. An arrow pierced his neck. Jhered glanced behind him and nodded his thanks at the skipper who had left the tiller and was reloading his bow.

'I'm doing no good th—'

He gasped and dropped to his knees, a Tsardon arrow shaft jutting from his neck. Jhered turned round. Another trireme was bearing down on them fast, ramming spike glinting in the sun.

'Kovan, your left. Defend your left!'

The Ascendants were standing. It was poor timing. They hadn't seen the threat aimed directly at them. Jhered started to move but knew he wasn't going to make it in time. They were between him and the port rail. Twenty yards away, Tsardon primed bows. Others held javelins.

Kovan split the skull of his enemy and swung left. Jhered saw him tense. Ossacer and Arducius were moving towards the stern rail. Water was coiling around them, covering them in a liquid sheath, obscuring them from view. A wind was building fast. The ship dragged more quickly towards the wall which had begun to split as if some great blade was slashing at it. Mirron was moving towards Jhered.

'No!' yelled Jhered into the rising tumult. 'Mirron, get down.'

A javelin flew straight and fast. Jhered leapt at Mirron, knowing it was futile. A shape crossed his vision. He heard a dreadful thud. Jhered caught Mirron and hauled her down to the deck. Kovan crashed down right next to them. All three of them stared at the javelin buried in his chest.

Mirron screamed. Kovan reached out a hand and pressed it against her. Blood was pouring from his wound and trickling from his mouth.

'Don't cry, Mirron. It doesn't hurt.' He smiled and his eyes fluttered and closed.

Jhered blinked away a tear and saw Arducius and Ossacer jump from the ship.

Freezing cold water closed over their heads. Arducius swam with Ossacer holding on to his waist. The weight of the water bore them down so quickly he hardly needed to kick his feet. In his tiring mind, he clung on to the base of the energy map he had created. It hammered at him, trying to shake him off. It was an unnatural shape, even more so than the wall he had made.

But he would not let go. Back on the surface, Jhered and Kovan had fought and would die to give him the time to succeed. And on the shore the Echelon and Marshal Vasselis were waiting for an invasion. He would not let that invasion happen. He would not let them down.

So down he went, Ossacer with him, keeping the energy flowing through him and the circuit complete. Already, the surface of the ocean would be chaos. And the deeper he went, the further that chaos would spread. The only thing Arducius regretted was that he would never see what he had created.

The wall of water had fallen with such suddenness it took the breath away. Air rushed into the void it had left and for a heartbeat there was no sign, no ripple, to signify it had ever been there. The fighting stopped in the same instant, every eye taken by the appearance of Estorr from behind its shroud.

A beat of silence was punctuated only by the distant sound of drums on Tsardon triremes. And then the ocean began to pour in on itself.

'Omniscient bless him,' said Jhered, scrabbling to his feet. 'He's done it.'

Astern of the *Hark's Arrow*, an eddy had become a spiral and the spiral had accelerated, becoming a drain, sucking down the sea and everything that sat upon it. It expanded at an extraordinary rate. Its outer edge plucked at the ship and dragged it backwards and around. Behind him, men had started to scream but he ignored them, staring down into the maw of this monster, hypnotised by the swirling that gathered in pace moment by moment.

Jhered looked down. Mirron was lying across Kovan's stomach, crying and stroking his hair. He bent down and picked her up.

'Leave him now, Mirron. He's at peace. Come and see what your brother has done. Let's watch together how he beat the Tsardon.'

He set her on her feet and she hugged him. With panic exploding on the deck around them and in every ship near them, they alone stood still to greet their deaths. Already, the whirlpool had caught other ships. Men were diving from decks trying to escape only to be sucked into the deeps. Jhered breathed in, enjoying his final lung-fuls of air. The *Hark's Arrow* was spinning around the edge of destruction, moving towards the point where the spiral steepened.

The noise of the water grew. A rushing and roaring combined with wind whistling in his ears. The sight and sound battered at Jhered's senses and set every nerve tingling. The ship was being tugged faster now. They were below the horizon, surrounded by the sides of the whirlpool. Through his fear, Jhered experienced a moment of clarity in which he admired the awesome power Arducius had created.

'Don't let me go,' said Mirron. 'Whatever happens.'

And then the *Hark's Arrow* pitched suddenly and drove straight into heart of the swirling, battering mouth of the ocean.

Iliev took his hand from the tiller and just stared open-mouthed. His crew all stood too. They'd rowed far enough and fast enough to escape but the bireme had been sucked into the clutches of the vortex and snatched from view.

Ocetarus had reached out his hand and dragged ship after ship into his embrace. Over the wind, he thought he had heard the screams of men and the frenzied beating of drums. But so many had not escaped, clawed backwards out of sight. Tens, dozens. Gone in moments. And any that had survived were scattering away. Rowing so hard as if expecting Ocetarus to reach out and slap them to the ocean floor.

The whirlpool had quickly lost intensity and the wind had slackened. Iliev knew it was done when waves reached them, washed gently under them. Iliev steadied the tiller. He gazed out at an empty ocean. At silence. The jaws of Ocetarus had snapped shut.

'Ocenii.' Iliev's voice was a croak. 'Ocenii. We give thanks to Ocetarus for sparing us this day. We give thanks that He took our enemies from us but we mourn those of our own lost on this day of victory.'

And it was victory, no doubt about it. But it didn't feel right. Like he had been robbed of the chance to prove himself and be the first ship into the harbour, bearing the scars of war but flying the victory flag. Around them, the battle had ceased. Tsardon and Conquord crews stood and stared. Below decks, oarsmen had stopped rowing, sensing the passing of a force too powerful to oppose.

Iliev's crew sat back down and took up their oars. Iliev pulled the tiller in and the corsair came about, heading towards the harbour.

Signals were being flagged throughout the Conquord fleet. Trireme and assault galley began to row for the harbour to seal it from the Tsardon. But those Tsardon who had seen the vortex had no appetite to fight on, and those who followed up would either be turned by their fleeing comrades or be met by an overwhelming Ocetanas force.

A few hundred yards away, a barrel broke surface and bobbed on the calm surface of the sea. Iliev nodded.

'Remember we are sailors and marines and we still have honour. Let's look for survivors. Ocenii, twenty stroke, easy.'

Jhered felt a serenity over his mind. He could still see the light dancing on the water but it was distant and dull. The whirlpool had dissipated and no longer was he being dragged down. He'd managed to unclasp his cloak and lose his breastplate when that last breath had gone but it was too far back up. He had accepted that he would drown and had ceased to kick, letting the embrace of the sea take him. His eyes had closed and his mouth had fallen open.

Death played with him. There was a warm sensation in his lungs and his face felt as if it were being stroked. His lips bubbled and the brush against them sensuous, like love.

He snapped open his eyes.

Mirron was before him. Her mouth was over his and she breathed life into him in a kiss that lingered and held. He put his hands up to the side of her face. This close, she was blurred and the water moving past them was still thick with bubbles from the debris being taken to the deeps. But he was free, and unless this was his dream of death, he was alive.

They were rising. Slow and steady. He felt light, able to swim. He made a move but she stilled him with a shake of the head. So they kicked their feet in unison and rose gently together, her lips back on his and their bodies locked in embrace.

For Jhered, it could have gone on forever. There was a magic to the world below the sea and he felt a freedom he had never felt before. She was breathing for him and she was kissing him. He banished the thoughts that crowded his mind unbidden. This was a wonder to be enjoyed, not sullied.

They broke surface and Jhered breathed in a huge gasp of cold fresh air. He gagged and coughed, his body in spasm. Mirron had let him go and was swimming round him protectively. He tried to thank her but only coughed up more water. All he could do was lie on his back, exhausted.

'I couldn't hold on to you,' he said. 'You came back for me.'

'I couldn't let you die down there. I couldn't let you go.'

He must have faded out of consciousness because the next thing he knew was a sensation of warmth. He heard wood creak and the sound of oars in the water. He opened his eyes again, wondering if everything below the water had been a dream. But it wasn't. Mirron was stroking his hair. She looked like she'd been crying. There was a man's tunic about her shoulders.

He was lying in the bottom of an open boat. Against his back, he felt harsh slats and he pushed himself up on to his elbows. It was an Ocenii corsair. The man at the tiller stared directly ahead, a scowl on his face.

Jhered let Mirron help him into a seated position. They weren't the only pieces of flotsam to have been dragged from the water. Up towards the bow, Arducius was lying out flat with Ossacer near him. Jhered could barely contain his delight. Ossacer had his hands on Ardu's legs. His face was lined and grey from his Work. But he was alive.

'My but it's difficult to kill you lot,' said Jhered. 'How is he?'

'He'll live,' said Ossacer. He breathed in hard. 'He's exhausted and something broke one of his legs. It was lucky I kept hold of him.'

He turned and threw his arms around Jhered's neck. 'We thought we'd lost you, Paul.'

'I did too, Ossie. I did too.'

He held Ossacer for a long time before letting him go and nodding his head back to the tiller.

'Thank you,' he said.

'Can't have you freezing to death, Exchequer Jhered,' he said.

'You have me at a disadvantage.'

'Karl Iliev. Ocenii squad seven. We found all of you in the same area. Can't understand why any of you are still alive.'

Jhered's stomach lurched and his delight was gone. 'But we lost so many. Poor Kovan. I should have taken that javelin. Too old, too slow.'

Mirron put a hand to his face. 'If he hadn't died then, he would have drowned. There was no one down there to save him.'

Jhered nodded. 'But he saved you. I always knew his courage would show.'

Mirron's head dropped. She didn't fight against the tears.

'Who was he?' asked Iliev.

'The son of Arvan Vasselis, Marshal Defender of Caraduk. A lad who has great potential. Had.'

Iliev nodded. 'This display of your doing, was it?'

Jhered shrugged. 'In a manner of speaking. Arducius is the architect though.'

'I suppose we should thank you but . . .'

'It's all right,' said Ossacer. 'We understand.'

Jhered pulled him close once more.

'Come on, Neristus, make this your best shot.'

Roberto rode hard down towards the left flank where Davarov still fought hard among his exhausted infantry but they were all flagging. The cavalry had wheeled for yet another tired pass and that was the signal the engineer had been awaiting. Ten stones whistled by overhead. Roberto heard his tutor speaking to him as if it was yesterday. *Never fire on your own people. Never demonstrate that you care nothing for them. No matter how desperate, never be tempted.*

He saw people running from the ramparts. 'The Omniscient spare them. And God help me if this goes wrong.'

The stones fell, plunging into the back of the Tsardon attack on the wall and battering into the stockade wood at its centre point. Roberto punched the air.

'Again, Rovan!' he shouted though Neristus wouldn't hear him.

Ahead, Davarov had seen the stones fall. The triarii surged into one last desperate assault, taking the Tsardon by surprise. Confusion fed through them and into the mess came Cartoganev. He broke through on the far left and an infantry maniple drove in after him. Roberto prayed for the breach to hold. There were great dents in the stockade wall. The rampart was clear. Behind, Neristus would be adjusting some of his trajectories. He fired again. This time every shot fell on the heads of the Tsardon.

Cartoganev continued his attack. Davarov took the triarii further in. A maniple turned to block enemy support from the right. Three more battered their way to the wall. In front of them, the Tsardon were falling back in disarray. The Conquord had broken them. The onager rounds had savaged Tsardon defender and attacker alike and they weren't going to stand and wait for more.

Already, Roberto could see more enemy running around from the back of the stockade to block the breach. In turn his hastati, his weary but extraordinary hastati, pushed harder. He heard horns sounding from behind the stockade. Not Tsardon, Conquord. The remaining levium clattered into the back of the enemy ahead of Davarov. The battle began to turn again. The stockade was smothered in smoke and flame but inside enough would be standing rested and ready to fight.

One panel of the stockade behind Davarov came down, folding outwards to slap on to mud and bodies. Gesteris's legions surged out, spreading round to bolster Cartoganev and to provide flank for Davarov. Roberto felt his heart warm. The enemy were rippling, unsure.

'Harder, Conquord,' he bellowed, galloping down behind the lines. 'We have them on the turn.'

Horns. Horns from every quarter. From the engineers, the principes, the triarii and God-surround-them, from the surgeons. Roberto knew what it must mean. He swung in his saddle and stared up at the Gaws. The great gold and white banner snapped at the mast, reflecting the firelight and shining out.

Estorr was secure.

Every Conquord throat howled celebration and took up Davarov's song. Energy flowed through aching muscles. Swords fell faster and harder. Bewildered, the enemy had no response. Neristus dropped more stones and bolts in their midst. From the gates, Tsardon spilled out backwards. There was fighting again in the gatehouse.

'We're going to do it,' said Roberto, listening to the song roll over him. Tears stood in his eyes. 'We've won. I don't believe it, we've won.'

Jhered directed the corsair to the Gatherer berths. The dockside was thronged with Estoreans come to welcome the victorious fleet into port. The Advocate was there in the centre of it all, taking cheers and waving at her citizens. She applauded every ship that was announced by the horns at the harbour entrance.

It meant Jhered could dock at the extremity of the harbour almost unnoticed. Almost. There were people running down the dockside.

People who should know better than to be so undignified. How they were there he didn't know but the Echelon were in Estorr, there to greet their loved ones. The children who had saved the Conquord from destruction.

Jhered had Arducius in his arms. The boy was barely conscious, his pain dulled by Ossacer who had a hand on his body and was flooding him with anaesthetising energy. Mirron stood ready, tired but unable to contain her excitement at those she saw approaching. The corsair nudged home and marines leaped out to tie her off.

'Thank you, Commander,' Jhered said. 'You have done a service greater than you know.'

Iliev only nodded and the eyes of the crew followed the Ascendants while they left the boat. Jhered heard prayers.

The Echelon enveloped them. Tears, laughter and unrestrained joy exploded all around him. He kept them away from Arducius, refusing to let him go. He would walk the boy all the way to the palace if he had to. He'd seen enough, he needed rest. God-surround-him, they all did.

Too quickly, the excitement subsided. The two missing boys were a void that stole laughter and stilled celebration. In all the wild commotion consuming the harbour, Jhered felt alone in the middle of a chasm of silence. Vasselis was marching down the path towards them, guards surrounding him. The Echelon opened to let him pass. Mirron was talking to Meera. Gorian's mother. She was too stunned even to cry. Jhered wondered what Mirron was telling her.

But most of their questions had been aimed at him. He had answered as best he could, keeping from them the worst, saying only what he must. To Arvan Vasselis, though, he had to say not a word. Vasselis knew. The expression on Jhered's face told him everything. Vasselis swallowed hard and took in the three Ascendants.

'You got three of them back, then,' he said. 'Well done, Paul. It was more than any of us dared hope.'

'Arvan, I'm so sorry. Kovan died a hero of the Conquord. He took a javelin meant for Mirron. He saved her.'

Vasselis even managed a smile. 'If he had to die, then that is the most fitting reason.' He clamped his lips together against their quivering. It was a time before he could continue. 'I'm glad you were there. I'm glad he didn't die alone.'

Jhered would have embraced him but for Arducius in his arms. Here, amid the cheers, Vasselis's heart was broken. He made no attempt to hide the tears that dripped from his cheeks.

'Come on,' said Jhered. 'It's time we got these children somewhere warm.'

They walked from the dockside, happy to let the incoming Ocetanas deflect the attention of the city away from its true saviours.

'What's this,' said a voice thick with hate. 'Evil entering the heart of the Conquord?'

Jhered raised his head from Arducius's pale and sick features. The Chancellor had emerged from the crowd, bodyguards either side of her. The Echelon stopped moving. Vasselis tensed and drew himself upright.

'Back off, Felice,' said Jhered. 'This is not the time or the circumstance for your poison. You will leave these Ascendants alone.'

'They will never be left alone,' said the Chancellor. 'Every breath they take is an affront to the Omniscient. But only three, I see. At least that is one less to plague us. And Vasselis, why is your son not with them? I told you God would extract a heavy price. His blood is on your hands.'

Vasselis started to go for his sword. The Chancellor's bodyguards moved a pace forwards. But none of them saw Hesther. Jhered could feel all the pent-up rage, frustration and injustice behind that slap. The Chancellor's head snapped back and right, a deep red mark growing on her cheek. Her lip was split.

'You stupid, stupid woman,' spat Hesther. 'How dare you? How *dare* you speak of our children like that? But for them you would have a Tsardon dagger in your heart. And I would have cheered it as it plunged in.' The Chancellor balled a fist at her side. 'What are you going to do, strike me like you did Father Kessian. Coward.'

'Enough,' barked Jhered. 'Felice, get out of my way. If I have to put this child down to make you, I will not stop at a slap across your cheek.'

'Come on,' said Vasselis, his voice lifeless. 'Too much breath has been wasted already. And none of us knows when one more will be our last.'

The Tsardon horns had sounded the retreat within an hour of the critical breakthrough. The enemy commander had done well to stop them routing but he knew his situation was fast becoming hopeless. There was nothing better than new belief to turn a battle. The two sides had parted and resorted to jeering at each other across a distance of a couple of hundred yards while Roberto met his opposite number in the centre of the no-man's-land, along with General Gesteris. All that remained was to give the Tsardon a chance to withdraw.

'You fought a brave battle,' said the Tsardon. 'You will make a fine ruler of your Conquord one day.'

'We have one already.'

The commander shook his head. 'She has made a grave mistake. She invaded Tsard. We will not be taken. It's a shame so many had to die to prove it.'

'It is the way of great empires to seek to expand. It has been the making of the Conquord and your Kingdom.' Roberto managed a smile. 'But I doubt we will be setting foot on your territory again for quite sometime.'

'A wise choice. And Atreska?'

'Atreska, we will take back. Atreska is ours. I would advise your king not to maintain a force there. You will be attacked. Just as I advise you to withdraw now. Leave your weapons and my territory. I do not wish to order more death on you.'

The Tsardon commander eyed him for a time. 'And the rebel Atreskans?'

'Can sit inside their borders and live in fear of the day we return.'

He surprised Roberto by laughing. 'You have courage and you have fire. We should be allies, the Conquord and the Kingdom. Not enemies. Perhaps one day we can sit at a table as friends, General Del Aglios.'

'Don't look to my arrival any day soon,' he said. 'You will withdraw?'

The commander inclined his head. 'The season is cold. Only a fool steps across his threshold when the snows come.'

'There at least, we can agree.' Roberto offered his hand and the commander took it. 'By nightfall. My cavalry will shadow you into Atreska. Don't turn back.'

Roberto inclined his head and turned away. Gesteris walked with him back to his lines.

'I'm getting too old for this,' he said.

'Nonsense,' said Roberto. 'You've just saved the Conquord, General. My mother needs men like you.'

'Behind a desk, I hope.'

'There'll be a job for you anywhere you choose.'

Davarov had bustled his way to the front and stood square in front of Roberto, not quite managing to look fierce.

'Well?'

'Tend your blisters and secure your gear. War's over.'

Davarov enveloped him in a bear hug, overbalanced and the both of them fell to the floor. The cheers of the army couldn't cover their laughter.

The three days of joy and reunion had been tainted by the loss of Kovan and Gorian. Mirron hadn't the heart to tell Meera all that had happened and they had agreed to let it lie for now that he had run off and become lost after one too many arguments. It was close enough to the truth.

Those three days had passed in a fog for Mirron. Everywhere she went, the people of Westfallen were waiting to welcome her. The Marshal had brought them all to the safety of the palace complex. Mirron had never lived in such luxury before. Her own private baths, a servant her own age to whom she chatted to and never ordered to do a thing, and a bed so comfortable she had slept in it for a whole day before the sound of celebration reached her once again.

And now they were in the presence of the Advocate. The *Advocate*. Herine Del Aglios herself was sitting on an uncomfortable-looking throne. Mirron sat with Ossacer and Arducius on chairs in front of her, with the Echelon behind them. Arducius was still drawn. Ossacer had been too tired to help him at first and one of his legs was still splinted. None of them smiled, though. The memory of Kovan being snatched from their grasp was too fresh.

Jhered stood nearby, unwilling to be far from them even now they were in the bosom of safety. Only one other person was missing. How Father Kessian would have been proud to see this moment. Acceptance, if that was what it was to be, of all he had striven for his long life.

'The Conquord owes you a great debt,' said the Advocate. 'And it owes you an apology too. I owe you an apology. People fear what they cannot comprehend and I was victim to that, too. You were hounded from your homes and hated by everyone you tried to help. Yet here you are, saviours of our great empire. And that is something I will never forget.

'But with what you have comes a great responsibility, which falls upon my shoulders as it does yours. To imagine you will be accepted by all is naïve. You have powerful enemies and so you will have my protection so long as you remain loyal.

'But we cannot let that cloud the great deeds you three have done. The countless lives you have saved and the maturity you have shown. The Exchequer was right to believe in you.'

The two of them shared a glance and Mirron failed to hide her smile from him. He winked back at her though his expression was stern and neutral.

'And I will never be far from you,' he said. 'I owe you my life. You will always have my arm and my heart. All of you.'

He thumped his right hand into his chest. Mirron's heart swelled.

'All that remains is to decide what to do with you,' said the Advocate. 'After all, abilities such as yours cannot be allowed to fall into the wrong hands or be abused.'

Mirron froze. Beside her, Arducius and Ossacer's life maps flared with their anxiety.

'I have here a report signed by senior members of the Conquord, including the Exchequer, recommending your being housed here in Estorr while you are investigated. I have accusations laid by the Chancellor. I have complaints by the dozen about sightings and troubles all attributed to you. And I will soon have the Order knocking on my door, demanding I arrest you for assuming the place of God by meddling with His ocean. These will be dangerous times for young Ascendants in Estorr. And, I as the appointed representative of God on this earth, have a duty to serve the Omniscient, do I not?'

Mirron found herself nodding.

'I cannot have you running around my streets. Not when there is somewhere far more appropriate and secure for you to go.'

'Prison?' managed Ossacer.

The Advocate's peal of laughter echoed around the room. 'Oh my child, what kind of monster do you take me for? I have only told you all this because you, and all those who stand here, must understand the burden as well as the joy you carry. It is a burden which you can never shirk and that is why you must be in the best care possible. Mother Naravny, please.'

They turned to look at Hesther who stood up and held out a hand.

'Come on, you lot. Time to go back to Westfallen. Time to go home.'

Mirron screamed with delight, hugged her brothers and burst into tears.

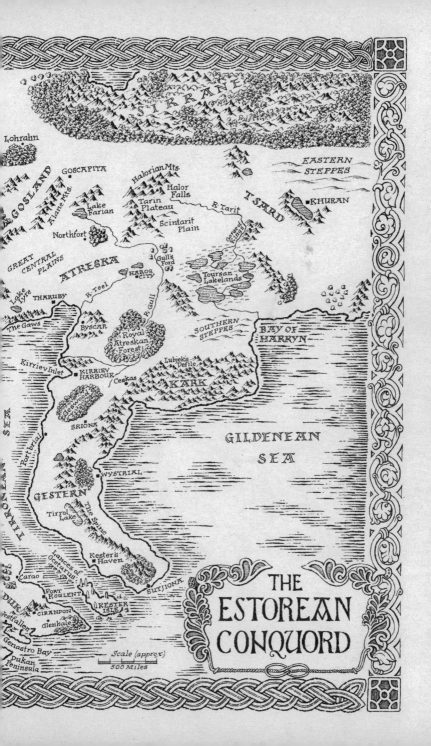

THE
ESTOREAN
CONQUORD